P9-CQO-695

Dawn is the
deadliest hour...

DEAD BY MORNING

"Do you think you can put together a profile with what little information we have?" Maleah asked.

"I'm going to try," Derek said. "The Copycat Carver has gone to a great deal of trouble to copy Jerome Browning's MO and yet he deliberately sent the pieces of flesh he removed from the victims' bodies to you instead of hiding them away somewhere the way Browning did. Why?"

"The reason he didn't stick to Browning's MO was because he wanted to send me a message."

"Very good reasoning. We've agreed that for some reason, it's important to the copycat for you to be personally involved in this case. That's why he chose Browning to emulate."

"Because Browning killed Noah Laborde, my former boyfriend. But the question is why me? If Nic or Griff is the real target, then . . ." She paused for a full minute. "Could it really be that simple? Is he making me jump through hoops simply because he can and he wants Nic to know he can control her best friend?"

"It's definitely what Griff thinks and it does make a crazy kind of sense. If tormenting Nic and Griff is his objective, then he's punishing them for some reason. He's going to strike again and again, possibly getting closer and closer to his ultimate target with each kill, eventually discarding the Carver's MO."

"If that's the case, then what are the odds that he'll try to kill me before he moves on to Nic and Griff . . ."

Books by Beverly Barton

AFTER DARK
EVERY MOVE SHE MAKES
WHAT SHE DOESN'T KNOW
THE FIFTH VICTIM
THE LAST TO DIE
AS GOOD AS DEAD
KILLING HER SOFTLY
CLOSE ENOUGH TO KILL
MOST LIKELY TO DIE
THE DYING GAME
THE MURDER GAME
COLD HEARTED
SILENT KILLER
DEAD BY MIDNIGHT
DON'T CRY
DEAD BY MORNING

Published by Zebra Books

DEAD By MORNING

BEVERLY BARTON

ZEBRA BOOKS
KENSINGTON PUBLISHING CORP.
http://www.kensingtonbooks.com

ZEBRA BOOKS are published by

Kensington Publishing Corp.
119 West 40th Street
New York, NY 10018

Copyright © 2011 by Beverly Beaver

All Kensington titles, imprints, and distributed lines are available at a special quantity discounts for bulk purchases for sale promotion, premiums, fund-raising, educational, or institutional use.

Special book excerpts or customized printings can also be created to fit specific needs. For details, write or phone the office of the Kensington Special Sales Manager: Attn. Special Sales Department. Kensington Publishing Corp., 119 West 40th Street, New York, NY 10018. Phone: 1-800-221-2647.

Zebra and the Z logo Reg. U.S. Pat. & TM Off.

ISBN-13: 978-1-4201-1035-7
ISBN-10: 1-4201-1035-7

First Printing: May 2011
10 9 8 7 6 5 4 3 2 1

Printed in the United States of America

To Beth Bange Bynon,
in memory of her husband Colby

"I love thee with the breath, smiles, tears of all my life."
—Elizabeth Barrett Browning

Prologue

With the patience and precision of a surgeon, he sliced into his victim's upper arm and carefully lifted the triangular piece of flesh. After placing the small chunk in a cubbyhole of the sectioned plastic cooler he had brought with him, he returned to the job at hand. One by one, he cut out more triangles from the dead man's arms and legs and then carefully stored them in the container.

"I always used a new scalpel and then tossed it afterward."

He had purchased disposable scalpels online. They came ten to a pack, with plastic handles and individually wrapped and sterilized high carbon steel blades. Cost didn't matter. He always spent whatever necessary to accomplish the job. But the scalpels were one of the least expensive tools he had ever used—less than a dollar each. And the little blades did double duty, first to slit the neck and then to make the intricate carvings.

He hummed as he worked, a mundane little ditty that he had heard somewhere years ago.

He took pride in his kills. He never did less than his best.

"I wanted the kill to be clean, quick, and relatively painless. The sweetest pleasure is in those few seconds of initial horror they experience. I prefer psychological torture to physical torture."

Whether or not the death was quick and painless didn't matter to him one way or the other. He was not opposed to making a victim suffer and had on occasion used both physical and psychological torture, but not with these particular people.

"It's such a quiet way to kill a person. With their trachea severed, they can't scream."

His preference was not the up-close-and-personal. He preferred killing from a distance. A quick, clean shot to the head, if death was the only agenda. However, he always did whatever was necessary to accomplish his goals. That's why this kill, like the three before it and the ones that would come after it, required him to get his hands dirty.

With his task completed and the four triangles carved from each arm and each leg now stored neatly in the cooler, he lifted the old man by his broad shoulders and dragged him along the bank of the river.

"I never left them where I killed them. I would move the body, usually near a river or lake or stream. I even dragged a woman from her bedroom outside to her pool. There is something peaceful about water, don't you think?"

He had been forced to leave the first body in her apartment, but he had taken her into the bathroom and filled the tub. Not exactly a river or even a pool, but under the circumstances, it had been as close as he could get her to water. As luck would have it, he had been able to drag the second victim from the back porch, where he had slit her throat, to the river nearby. He had dumped the third victim in a shallow streambed located on the man's property.

"I always struck after midnight. Never before. I wanted the body to be found in the morning. There is something beautiful about the morning sunlight caressing a corpse."

In his opinion, there was nothing beautiful about a corpse, neither in the dark nor in the full light of day. As a general rule, the time of day—or night—was inconsequential, unless there was a reason for specific timing. But he was following a sequence of events with these murders, somewhat like following a road map to reach a specific destination. Each step in the procedure was a necessity. The exact time of death was not important—as long as the person was dead by morning.

"I had a special upright freezer where I kept my carvings."

He never kept trophies. He didn't want or need any.

The souvenirs from these kills were not for him. They were for someone else. Someone who would appreciate their significance.

Chapter 1

Maleah hated weddings and wedding receptions.

So why am I here?

She was at the Dunmore Country Club out of a sense of obligation. After all, the bride, Lorie Hammonds, was her sister-in-law's best friend and the groom, Mike Birkett, was her brother's best friend. Lorie and Mike had gone through hell to earn their second chance at love. Their reunion was like something out of a fairy tale, albeit an adult fairy tale. Against all odds, they had fallen in love again, nearly twenty years after their teenage love affair had left them both broken hearted. Maleah certainly would have bet against their ever making it to the altar.

Okay, so maybe happy endings were possible. For other people. Not for her.

"Come on." Her sister-in-law Cathy motioned to her. "They're leaving. Did you get your little bag of bird-seed?"

Groaning inside, Maleah forced a smile and held up the tiny net bag tied with a narrow yellow ribbon. Following the other wedding guests, she went outside and took her place in the crowd awaiting the bride and groom's departure. The groomsmen had attached tin cans to long streamers that they had tied to the bumper of the groom's restored antique Mustang. A hand-painted sign announcing JUST MARRIED hung precariously from the same streamers.

A roar of excitement heralded the couple's exit through the double doors that opened to the front lawn of the country club. Lorie wore a pale peach tailored suit with matching heels. Mike had changed from his tux into a sport coat and dress slacks. Arm-in-arm, huge smiles lighting their faces, they hurried along the pathway. They laughed as handfuls of birdseed sailed through the air and rained down on them.

Maleah glanced across the brick sidewalk at her brother Jackson, who stood behind his wife, his arm draped around her and one big hand resting possessively over her belly. Cathy was three and half months pregnant.

When the bride and groom drove away, the crowd dispersed, many returning to the ballroom where the band still played. Maleah felt someone beside her and knew exactly who it was, even before she saw his face.

Derek Lawrence!

She turned, glanced at him, and did her best to maintain a pleasant expression. Despite his devastating good looks and undeniable charm, Derek Lawrence was pure poison as far as Maleah was concerned. From the moment they met several years ago, she had intensely disliked him. But she had to admit that after working with him on the Midnight Killer case for the Powell Agency earlier this year, she now disliked him less. And much to her dismay, she couldn't deny that she found him attractive.

What woman wouldn't?

He was tall, dark and dangerously handsome. And he possessed the kind of striking looks attributed to matinee idols of her grandmother's generation. If Derek had one flaw, it was his physical perfection. He was too damn good looking.

Being attracted to Derek—the last man on earth she should be attracted to—was why she thought of him as pure poison.

"Nice wedding," he said.

"Yes, it was a very nice wedding," Maleah replied. "Lorie and Mike seem happy, don't they?"

"They say that marriage agrees with some people."

"I've heard that."

"But you don't believe it?"

She shrugged.

"Jack and Cathy seem blissfully happy," Derek said.

"Okay, I concede that a small percentage of couples somehow manage to get their happily-ever-after, but most don't."

"Not willing to risk it yourself, are you?"

She looked at him, slightly puzzled by his question. "It's a moot point. I'm not even dating anyone right now."

"I wasn't aware that you ever dated. I've known you for quite a while and—"

"I date," she told him emphatically. Too emphatically. "I'm simply selective about whom I date." She gave him a condescending glance. "Unlike you, my tastes are more discriminating."

His oh-so-perfect lips lifted at the corners in an amused smile. "Are you implying that I'm some sort of Romeo who romances every woman I meet?"

"Oh, I'm not *implying* anything. I simply stated a fact."

Before Derek could respond, Jack and Cathy joined

Beverly Barton

them. He still wore his best man tux and she wore her matron of honor gown, a floor-length creation in light aqua silk.

"You two aren't arguing again, are you?" Cathy looked pleadingly from Maleah to Derek.

"No, of course not," Maleah assured her sister-in-law. "We were just discussing dating."

Lifting his brow inquisitively, Jack grinned. "So, who finally asked who?"

"Huh?" Maleah said.

"What?" Derek asked.

Cathy draped her arm around Jack's. "I don't think they were discussing dating each other."

"God, no!" Maleah said.

Derek chuckled. "You thought I asked Maleah for a date or that she asked me? Where would you have gotten such a far-fetched idea?"

"Oh, I don't know," Jack said. "Maybe the fact that—"

When Cathy gently punched him in the ribs, Jack grunted and instantly shut up.

"We're heading out," Cathy said. "I'm exhausted. It's been a wonderful day, but a very long one."

"I'll see y'all at home in a little while," Maleah said.

"Stay as long as you'd like," Cathy told her. "The band will be here until midnight and there's still a ton of food."

Maleah felt Derek's body heat as he moved in closer. When he slipped his arm around her waist, she tried not to gasp at the unexpectedness of his touch.

"Come on, Ms. Perdue, let's dance the night away." Derek's black eyes sparkled with a definite challenge. "Since neither of us brought a date tonight . . ."

"You two have fun," Jack told them as he led Cathy away and herded her toward their car.

As soon as Jack and Cathy were out of earshot, Maleah jerked away from Derek. "It's late. I'm tired. I have to get up early and drive back to Knoxville in the morning."

"Excuses, excuses." His grin widened. "What are you afraid of, Maleah?"

He's goading you. Don't let him get to you.

"I'm certainly not afraid of you, if that's what you're implying. You should know by now that I'm immune to your charm."

He held out his hand. "I don't doubt that you are. So . . . ?"

From the first moment they met several years ago, Derek had seen Maleah Perdue as a challenge. She had disliked him on sight, a reaction he was unaccustomed to getting from women. In the beginning, he had tried to charm her, and when that hadn't worked, he had ignored her. They had managed to steer clear of each other for the most part, more or less ships passing in the night, although they were both employed by the Powell Private Security and Investigation Agency. Maleah was a Powell agent. He was a consultant. His background as a former FBI profiler had proved to be a valuable asset to the agency. Three months ago when they had been assigned to work together on the Midnight Killer case, they had entered into the partnership reluctantly. Oddly enough, they had made a great team.

When she slid her small, soft hand into his large hand, he felt as if he had won a prize. The lady was not an easy conquest and because of that fact, he found her all the more appealing. Common sense cautioned him to keep their relationship strictly professional and not dip a toe into personal waters. But Derek had never been able to walk away from a challenge—or from a beautiful woman.

As he led her into the country club and straight into the ballroom where dozens of wedding guests remained, he subtly scanned her, out of the corner of his eye, from blond head to pale pink toes. Maleah had the type of wholesome blond beauty that once would have won her the title of All-American Girl. Five-four. Trim, nicely rounded figure. Peaches and cream complexion that tanned to a golden hue. Sun-streaked, shoulder-length blond hair. And topaz brown eyes that changed color depending on the color she wore and on her mood, alternating from a smoky yellowish hazel to a fine, golden bourbon.

When he put his arm around her waist and pulled her toward him, he felt her stiffen. "It's just a dance," he reminded her. "You're not committing yourself to spend the night with me."

"God forbid." Her gaze lifted and clashed with his.

He drew her closer, allowing their bodies to touch intimately. "Relax, honey. You're stiff as a poker."

"Don't hold me so tight." She wiggled her shoulders. "And do not call me honey."

He loosened his hold, giving her a little breathing room. "Better, Blondie?"

"Yes, thank you." She frowned. "Blondie?"

He grinned. "It suits you."

She huffed. "I suppose it's better than honey. Not quite as generic. But you could just call me Maleah, you know."

"I could." His grin widened. "Would it help to know that I've never called another woman Blondie?"

"You're determined to aggravate the crap out of me, aren't you?"

He laughed. "It's what I live for . . . Blondie."

As they danced to the smooth, romantic jazz tune, Derek tried to think of some innocent subject, something that wouldn't lead them into another verbal confrontation.

"Lorie was a beautiful bride," he finally said.

"Yes, she was."

Silence.

"It's great about Cathy being pregnant," he said. "Jack's over the moon about it."

"Yes, he is. He's really excited about being with her through the entire nine months since he missed out on doing that the first time around."

"Some men are cut out to be fathers. Jack's one of them. So is Mike."

Maleah nodded. "Cathy's a great mom. And I think Lorie will be, too. She's great with Mike's two kids."

"Do you ever think about having children?"

She paused mid-step. "I wouldn't bring a child into this world without having a husband first and since I don't intend to ever marry—"

"You're really an old fashioned girl, aren't you?"

"Only about some things."

"I agree, you know, about not ever getting married and having kids."

"Why am I not surprised? Why settle down with one woman when you can have your choice of women to sample, a different flavor every week?"

"Why indeed." Yeah, he could pretty much have his pick, had seldom been turned down, and had successfully avoided committed relationships. He had never allowed himself to care enough about any woman who could tempt him to willingly give up his freedom. He had learned, at his mother's knee, how a woman could use love to manipulate a man, turn him inside out and eventually destroy him.

Just as one tune ended and another began, Maleah pulled away, but Derek grabbed her hand and refused to relinquish his hold.

"One more dance," he said.

While she debated his request, his cell phone vibrated in the inside pocket of his tuxedo jacket. Reluctantly, he released her hand, reached inside his jacket, and removed his phone. Derek noted the caller ID. Griffin Powell, his employer.

"Yeah, Griff, what's up?" Derek's gaze connected with Maleah's, both of them aware that it was highly unlikely that Griff would be calling if it wasn't important business.

Maleah waited until he had answered the call and then walked with him off the dance floor.

"He's struck again," Griff told Derek. "I don't have all the details, but we're relatively sure it's the same person who killed Kristi and Shelley and Holt's brother."

Absolute dread tightly coiled Derek's stomach muscles as he asked, "Who's the victim?" Was it another Powell employee, as the first two kills had been, or was it a Powell employee family member, as the third murder victim had been?

"Ben Corbett's seventy-year-old father," Griff said. "Ben's the one who called me. A couple of fishermen found the body this morning, but there was no ID on the guy. Apparently he didn't have his wallet on him. They ran his fingerprints and didn't get a hit."

"How did they finally ID him?"

"It seems Mr. Corbett has a breakfast date with a lady friend every Saturday morning and when he didn't show up, she went to his home. When she couldn't find him, she started searching for him. One thing led to an-

other and she finally went to the police earlier this
evening."

"Ben's on assignment, isn't he?"

"He was in California. He chartered a plane and is
flying into Birmingham and renting a car. His dad lived
outside Cullman, which is about an hour drive from
Dunmore. I want you and Maleah to head down that
way as soon as possible. You two can get there before
Ben can. When he arrives, he doesn't need to handle
this alone."

"We're leaving now," Derek said. "I'll pick up my laptop at the hotel. You can send me any other info that
we'll need."

As soon as Derek slipped the phone back into his
jacket pocket, he faced Maleah. "The boss wants us to
drive to Cullman tonight. Ben Corbett's father has been
murdered."

"Damn. Griff thinks that it's the same person who
murdered Kristi and Shelley and Holt's brother, doesn't
he?"

"Yeah, he does."

"Why didn't you tell Derek everything that we know
and about what we've decided?" Nicole Powell asked
her husband moments after he ended his conversation.

"We'll explain it to him and Maleah together," Griff
said. "I'll have Barbara Jean compile all the information
the agency has accumulated. Maleah and Derek can
read over everything and digest it all before I tell them
that I expect them to take over as lead investigators on
the case."

"We might be closer to solving this mystery, if it hadn't
taken us more than two months to connect the dots."

Griff draped his arm around Nic's shoulders as they

stood on the patio overlooking Douglas Lake. "When Kristi was murdered, there was no way we could have known that her killer would target another agent. Until he killed Kristi and then Shelley, their murders identical in almost every way, we couldn't have known he had a specific MO. And even after Holt's brother was murdered and Barbara Jean discovered there had been three killers in the past with a similar MO—the Savannah Slasher, the Carver, and the Triangle Man—it took time to study each killer and figure out if our guy was copying one of them."

"After what we just found out, do you think Maleah is the key to everything that's happening?" Nic asked.

Griff squeezed her shoulders. "Possibly. But we can't rule out any of our other scenarios, especially since we don't know why anyone would be out to punish Maleah by killing people connected to the agency."

"Unlike you and me. We both have enemies from the past who could be targeting us."

He nodded. "Yeah, unlike you and me. The logical assumption is that whoever is behind these murders is doing it either to punish me or to get my attention."

"But it's possible that the rumors floating around Europe about Malcolm York being alive have nothing whatsoever to do with these murders. You can't assume you're the target simply because someone, thousands of miles away, may be pretending to be the man who kidnapped you twenty years ago. It could just as easily be someone from my past, someone connected to one of my cases when I worked for the Bureau."

"You're right, of course, " Griff agreed. "That's why we cannot rule out any possibility."

"You don't think there's even the slightest chance that the real Malcolm York is alive, do you?"

Griff's square jaw tightened. "York is dead. I have no doubts. Yvette, Sanders, and I killed him sixteen years ago. Unless he's found a way to rise from the dead, whoever the hell is calling himself Malcolm York is an imposter."

"This man is in Europe somewhere, not here in the U.S. To date, all the murders related to the Powell Agency have occurred here in America. We have no evidence to indicate a connection between him and these murders."

"Yes, I know. And the only apparent connection between the agency and the murders is Maleah."

"She is going to freak out when we tell her that our research shows the three previous murders almost identically mimic the murders committed by the Carver and that one of his first victims was Noah Laborde."

"It's no coincidence that the original Carver murdered Maleah's college boyfriend. What it means, we can't be sure, not at this point. But sooner or later—"

"Maleah has become my best friend." Nic rested her head on Griff's shoulder. "What better way to get to me than by using my dearest friend?"

"And what better way to send me a warning than to use my wife and her best friend to send that message?"

"Maleah will want to follow through and see this out to the end. You know she will. She'll feel that it's personal because the original Carver killed Noah Laborde."

"Yes, I know, she will. I also know that we need Derek's expertise. We need a professional profile of our killer. And Derek has a keen sixth sense about these things. I can't give him and Maleah the choice of not working together, despite their personal animosity," Griff said. "I'm putting the entire staff—office employees and agents in the field—on high alert. This case takes precedence over every other case. Until we find and stop this killer, no one connected to the Powell Agency is safe."

Nic turned into Griff's arms. He cocooned her within his embrace.

She might have doubts about why this was happening and about who was responsible, but Griff didn't. Not really. She knew her husband. No matter what she said to him or how many scenarios she presented to him, he laid the blame squarely on his own shoulders. He truly believed that innocent people were now paying for his past sins.

Chapter 2

Maleah and Derek arrived in Cullman shortly after midnight, checked into the Holiday Inn Express, dumped their bags, and drove straight to the sheriff's office. As they had expected, someone from the Powell Agency had called ahead so the sheriff himself was there to meet them. Griffin Powell and his agency had become legendary, their success rate far exceeding that of regular law enforcement. Only occasionally did the agency come up against police chiefs or sheriffs who resented Powell involvement. Thankfully, Sheriff Devin Gray welcomed them with a cautious smile and a firm handshake. Looking the man in the eye, Maleah instantly felt at ease.

Gray was about five-ten, slender and young, probably not a day over thirty-five. Clean shaven, his sandy hair styled short and neat, he projected a squeaky-clean appearance.

"Come on into my office." Sheriff Gray backed up his verbal invitation by opening the door and waiting for Maleah and Derek to enter.

The moment she crossed the threshold, she saw the

heavyset, middle-aged man sitting in the corner, his gaze directed on her. He rose to his feet and waited until the sheriff closed the door, affectively isolating the four of them from the activity outside the office.

"This is Freddy Rose, the Cullman County coroner," Sheriff Gray said. "Freddy, these are the Powell agents we've been expecting."

Freddy's round face, rosy cheeks, and pot belly made her think of Santa Claus, but his bald head and smooth face brought up an image of a short, rotund Mr. Clean.

Offering his meaty hand to Maleah, Freddy said, "Ma'am." And once they shook hands, he turned to Derek.

"Derek Lawrence." He exchanged handshakes with the coroner, and then nodded toward Maleah. "And this is Ms. Perdue."

"Ordinarily, we wouldn't share any of this information with outsiders," Sheriff Gray explained. "But when the governor calls me personally . . . Well, that's a horse of a different color, if you know what I mean."

Maleah knew exactly what he meant. Griffin Powell's sphere of influence reached far and wide, not only to the office of state governors, but to the powers that be in Washington, D.C. Griff's connections were strictly behind the scenes, of course, but she suspected he wielded far more power than anyone knew.

"We appreciate your both being here this late," Derek said. "Mr. Corbett's son Ben is one of our people. Ben is on his way here now and Ms. Perdue and I would like to get the preliminaries out of the way before he arrives. He will have enough on his plate as it is coming to terms with his father's murder."

"Absolutely," the sheriff agreed. "That's why Freddy's here. He hasn't performed an autopsy, of course, since the state boys will be here in the morning to claim the body, but he's certain about the cause of death."

"Sure am," Freddy said. "No doubt about it. Mr. Corbett's throat was slit, pretty much from ear to ear. Sliced through the carotid arteries on both sides and the trachea as well. Death occurred within a couple of minutes."

"Any idea about the blade the killer used?" Derek asked.

"The cut was smooth and straight," Freddy said. "No jagged edges. I swear it looked so damn precise, I'd swear a surgeon did it using a scalpel."

Maleah's gut reacted instantly to that bit of information. The medical examiners in each of the previous cases believed that Kristi, Shelley, and Norris Keinan had been killed with a scalpel, their necks cut with the expertise of a surgeon.

"Does that fit other murders?" the sheriff asked. "I was told you'd want to compare this case to some previous murders."

"Yes, so far, it does fit," Derek said, and then turned to Freddy. "What else can you tell us about the body?"

Freddy's gray eyes widened. "Damnedest thing I've ever seen. The killer cut out these little triangle-shaped pieces from Mr. Corbett's upper arms and thighs." Freddy shook his bald head. "Did it postmortem, thank the Good Lord."

"Does that match what was done to the other victims?" Sheriff Gray looked at Maleah. "Are we dealing with a serial killer? Is that what's going on?"

"Yes, the other victims also had triangular pieces of flesh removed from their limbs," Maleah replied. "And yes, with three murders, now four, it appears to be the work of a serial killer, but—"

"But that's all we know at this point," Derek finished for her. "We're working under the assumption that a serial killer has murdered four people now. Unfortunately the latest victim was the father of one of our agents."

Why had Derek cut her off mid-sentence like that? What had he thought she was going to say? My God, did he actually think she'd been about to reveal the fact that all four victims were in some way related to the Powell Agency? Did he think she was that stupid? Up to this point, the press had made a connection only between Kristi Arians and Shelley Gilbert. But since no "guilty knowledge" details of either murder were ever released, it was assumed that Shelley died in the line of duty on assignment in Alabama and that Kristi's murder in her Knoxville, Tennessee, apartment had been the work of another killer. The fact that they were both Powell Agency employees was believed to be simply a coincidence. Norris Keinan, a corporate lawyer, had lived in Denver, Colorado, and the fact that his younger brother was a Powell agent had not been an issue, either with the Denver PD or the local Denver media.

"I didn't know Mr. Corbett personally," the sheriff said. "But he and the mayor's dad played golf together. I understand he was a fine man, well thought of in the community. We're sure sorry something like this happened in Cullman."

"Would it be possible for us to get copies of the reports, once they're filed, and also copies of the photos taken at the scene?" Maleah asked.

"Yes, ma'am, I can see to it that you get copies of whatever you need."

"Then I can't think of any reason we should keep y'all up any later than we already have." Maleah glanced from the handsome young sheriff to the fifty-something coroner. "Mr. Lawrence and I are at the Holiday Inn Express." She pulled a business card from her pocket and handed it to Devin Gray. "We'd like to stay here and wait on Ben Corbett, if that's all right with you?"

"Certainly," Sheriff Gray said. "Feel free to use my office."

When Sheriff Gray and Freddy said their good-byes and started to leave, Derek called to them. "By any chance, was Mr. Corbett found in or near a body of water?"

Both men froze to the spot. Freddy cleared his throat before glancing over his shoulder and saying, "He was found on the riverbank, face down, his feet in the river."

"Were the others found in water?" Sheriff Gray asked, his gaze sliding slowly from Maleah to Derek.

"Yes, they were," Derek replied quickly.

"Just another similarity, huh?" Freddy said. "Guess it's looking more and more like the same person who killed those other people killed Mr. Corbett."

"Apparently so." Derek glanced at Maleah.

She knew what he was thinking.

Four innocent victims, their only connection the Powell Agency. But who had killed them? And why?

Maleah and Derek waited for Ben Corbett. When he arrived at the sheriff's office at a little after three that Sunday morning, they shared with him all the information the sheriff and coroner had given them.

Ben had been with the agency for several years, coming straight from the army after his retirement. Three-fourths of the Powell agents had either law enforcement or military backgrounds. A few, such as Maleah, had been chosen because of their high IQs and willingness to learn on the job.

Although Ben had managed to control his emotions, Maleah hadn't missed the subtle signs of anger and hurt. While they had explained what had happened and how they suspected his father's death was related to the other three murders, his gaze wandered aimlessly, often focusing on the wall. Once or twice he had mumbled incoherently under his breath, then quieted suddenly and clenched his jaw, as if it was all he could to maintain his composure.

"Dad was a ladies' man," Ben told them. "He loved to flirt. Never bothered Mom. She'd just laugh about it. He never cheated on her, loved her to the day she died." He swallowed hard. "I suspect he loved her till the day he died."

"We've been authorized to help you in any way you need us," Maleah said. "If you'd like us to make the arrangements or help you make them—"

"Thanks. That won't be necessary. Dad made all the arrangements right after Mom died. Paid for everything. Chose his casket, picked out the suit he wanted to be buried in. Made his will. Told the minister what songs he wanted at the funeral. He said he didn't want me to have to worry with any of it when the time came."

For several minutes, the three of them remained silent. Then Ben asked the inevitable question. "Who the hell is doing this and why?"

"We don't know," Derek said. "The only thing the victims have in common is their connection to the Powell Agency. The killer's MO is identical in all four cases, so we're relatively certain we are dealing with one killer. But we have no idea what motivates him or how he chooses his victims."

"At random, maybe," Ben said. "Anybody associated with the agency is a target, right? And for whatever reason, the killer picked my dad." Ben's dark eyes misted. He turned his head.

Derek clamped his hand down on Ben's shoulder. "We're going to catch him and stop him."

Ben nodded.

"Is there anything, anything at all, we can do for you?" Maleah asked.

Ben cleared his throat a couple of times. "No, thanks. I can't think of anything. I'm going over to Dad's place and try to get a few hours of sleep. When are y'all heading up to Griffin's Rest?"

"If you don't need us here, we probably won't stay longer than mid-day tomorrow," Derek told him. "Copies of the reports and the crime scene photos can be sent directly to the office as soon as they're available. I expect Nic and Griff will be moving forward with their plans to form their own task force and since I'm the agency's profiler—"

"Count me in on the task force," Ben said. "After Dad's funeral."

Neither Derek nor Maleah responded, knowing it would be up to Griff and Nic to choose the agents who would lead the investigation and those who would assist. If Ben had been a police officer, he wouldn't have been allowed near the case because his dad had been one of the victims. But Griff's rules and regulations differed from regular law enforcement. On occasion, the Powell Agency came damn close to doling out vigilante justice, a fact that often created tension between Griff and Nic.

* * *

He could go days without sleep and could easily get by with four hours per night on a regular basis. He was no ordinary human being. Years of training, self-sacrifice, and stern discipline had honed both his mind and body into a superior being. He had no weaknesses, wasn't vulnerable in any way, and therefore was practically invincible.

The espresso at the airport coffee bar was barely acceptable, but it served the purpose of giving him a caffeine boost. To pass the time while he waited for his flight to Miami, he flipped open his laptop and scanned the information about Errol Patterson.

Patterson was a former member of the Atlanta PD SWAT team, a crack shot and a decorated officer. He had loved his job, but when his fiancée had insisted he find a less dangerous profession, he had chosen love over duty and signed on with the Powell Agency.

He smiled.

You made a life-altering decision. Too bad for you that it was a deadly mistake.

How could he or his fiancée have known that choosing to work for the Powell Agency would cost him his life?

Patterson had been chosen for two reasons—he was associated with the Powell Agency and he was male.

I chose two women and then two men for the first four kills . . . But after that, I altered my choices, just to throw them off. I kept them guessing. That's how I stayed one step ahead of them.

He did more than stay one step ahead of the authorities. He outsmarted them, never leaving behind even the vaguest clue to his identity. Over the years, he had gone by many names, so many that it was easy to forget who he really was. His true identity was a guarded secret, known by only a handful of individuals. In certain circles, he was known as the Phantom. Nameless. Faceless. An illusion. Unseen. Unheard. A dark angel of death.

Maleah woke to the sound of incessant pounding. Inside her head? No, outside her hotel room. Some idiot was knocking on her door and calling her name.

Go away. Leave me alone.

She shot straight up in bed where she lay atop the wrinkled floral spread. Groggy and only semi-alert, she slid off the side of the bed and stood unsteadily on her bare feet for a few seconds.

"Maleah," Derek called to her through the closed door.

Damn it! What time was it? She glanced at the digital bedside clock. 8:30 A.M.

She groaned. Three and a half hours was not nearly enough sleep.

"I'm coming," she told him as she padded across the carpet. When she reached the door, she cracked it open, glared at Derek, who looked fresh as a daisy, and asked him, "Where's the fire?"

He shoved open the door and breezed past her. She closed the door and turned to face him. Obviously he had shaved, showered, and pressed his slacks and shirt. His stylish, neck-length hair glistened with blue-black highlights. His deep brown eyes focused on her with amusement.

"I forgot how grumpy you are in the morning," he said.

"You'd better have a good reason for beating down my door."

"Duty calls."

"What?"

He looked her over, taking in her sleep-tousled hair,

her wrinkled clothes and her makeup-free face. "Griff called. He wants us at Griffin's Rest ASAP."

Maleah groaned, and then when Derek's smile vanished, she asked, "What's happened?"

"What makes you think—?"

"Damn it, Derek, it's too early in the morning to play games, so let's not do twenty questions."

He clasped her shoulders, turned her around and urged her toward the bathroom. "Toss your clothes out to me and I'll press them while you grab a quick shower. We'll pick up coffee and biscuits on the way to Griffin's Rest."

She curled her toes into the carpet and dug in her heels. "I'm not moving another inch until you tell me what's going on."

"Why do you have to be so stubborn?"

"Why do you have to be such a macho jerk?"

Derek frowned. "Griff and Nic are organizing the task force today." He paused, studied her expression and then said, "I'm pretty sure they plan to put the two of us in charge."

She groaned. "Why us? Why not you and Shaughnessy or you and Angie or you and Michelle or you and Luke or—?"

"I get it. You don't want us to be partners on another case. But I don't think it really matters what we want. It's what Griff and Nic want."

"I can't believe Nic would pair us up again, not when she knows . . . well, she knows that we mix like oil and water."

"I thought we made a pretty good team on the Midnight Killer case."

Maleah huffed, hating to admit that he was right. "Yeah, yeah, I suppose we did."

"Besides, Shaughnessy is more muscle than strategist. His expertise lends itself to the physical. And now that she's pregnant, Angie isn't working in the field. Michelle is on a much-needed vacation after that last two-month case in South America. As for Luke, you know Griff reserves him for special duty."

Accepting his explanation, she nodded her acquiescence and said, "Give me five minutes." She turned and went into the bathroom.

She closed the door, stripped hurriedly, and then eased the door open enough to toss her clothes toward Derek. Smiling at the thought of him ironing her slacks and blouse, she adjusted the hot and cold faucets on the shower and stepped under the spray of warm water.

The FedEx truck had been stopped at the front gate by the guards on duty. Shaughnessy Hood had been dispatched from the main house to drive down and pick up the package addressed to Maleah Perdue in care of the Powell Private Security and Investigation Agency at Griffin's Rest.

Barbara Jean Hughes, Griff's right-hand man Sanders's assistant, best friend and lover, took the sealed, insulated shipping box from Shaughnessy, placed it in her lap and carried it with her down the hall to Griff's private study. The door stood open so that she could see Griff behind his desk, a cup of coffee in his hand. Sanders stood nearby, his gaze fixed on the box she held.

She cleared her throat.

Griff glanced up, saw her, and motioned for her to enter.

Without hesitation, Barbara Jean maneuvered her

wheelchair into the study. Sanders reached down, took the box from her and placed it on the desk directly in front of Griff.

He studied the insulated container for several silent minutes. "Did you notice the sender's name and address?"

"Yes," Sanders replied. "Winston Corbett, Cullman, Alabama."

Griff scrutinized the shipping label. "What time frame did the Cullman County coroner give for Winston Corbett's death?"

"Between midnight and five A.M., yesterday," Barbara Jean replied.

"Then I'm curious as to how Ben's father managed to send Maleah a package after he died."

Chapter 3

Cyrene Patterson stretched languidly on the beach towel, her bikini-clad, five-eight body soaking in the morning sunshine by their pool directly outside the bedroom's French doors. The deluxe honeymoon package at the Grand Resort there in the Bahamas included not only a luxury villa suite, but butler service. She and Errol had enjoyed breakfast in bed, and then made love as if they hadn't already spent half the night screwing like crazy. She had left him asleep, slipped into her bathing suit and taken a dip in the pool. Life was good. Just couldn't get much better. She had waited a lifetime for Mr. Right—thirty years. But he had been well worth the wait.

Neither she nor Errol had been naïve youngsters, with stars in their eyes, when they said their I-dos. Both had been married before when they were too young and too stupid to know what they were doing. She had married the first time to get away from home, an alcoholic mother, a father who showed up once in a blue moon, and younger siblings who were more than her grandmother could handle. Her two-year marriage to

Polo had proven the old adage about jumping out of the frying pan and into the fire. Thank God she'd been smart enough to leave the abusive son of a bitch before she got pregnant. Errol, on the other hand, had married at nineteen the first time because his girlfriend told him she was pregnant. She had lied to him, but by the time he had found out the truth, she actually was pregnant. He had lived in hell for three years. But before little Tasha's second birthday, Errol had known he needed to end the marriage and had sued his wife for full custody. Two weeks before their divorce was finalized, Errol's wife, who had been granted visitation privileges, had taken their child for a joy ride and both had been killed in a head-on collision with an eighteen wheeler. Witnesses had said that it appeared she had deliberately caused the "accident."

Cyrene lathered SPF 15 sunblock on her arms and legs to protect her golden skin from UV damage. The popular belief that darker skin didn't need protection from the harmful rays was false. Even the darkest skin could burn.

She intended to do everything possible to take care of her skin and her overall health. That's why she'd never taken drugs. Sometimes, Errol accused her of being a health nut. If following an exercise routine, being a vegetarian, not smoking, doing drugs or drinking to excess made her a health nut, she would gladly don the label and wear it proudly.

"Any place you can't reach?" Errol asked her, his voice husky with innuendo.

The moment Cyrene heard his voice, she smiled, but she didn't look at him. Instead, she held the sunblock bottle up over her head. Once he grasped the bottle in his hand, she untied her bikini top and dropped it to the patio floor. With her breasts bare, she tilted her head and gave him an enticing come-here-big-boy glance.

"Start wherever you'd like." She loved to tease him. "But don't miss a spot."

He came around the back of the lounge chair, knelt beside her, upended the open sunblock bottle and squirted a large dollop of the scented cream into the center of his open palm. After setting aside the bottle, he started at the base of her neck, lathering the lotion onto her skin. He moved steadily from shoulder to shoulder in downward swipes until his big hands hovered over her naked breasts. Her nipples tightened in anticipation. The moment his fingers caressed the hard tips, she moaned with pleasure.

Errol slid his hands beneath her, lifted her into his arms and carried her off the patio and through the open French doors. She laughed with pure delight as he tossed her into the center of the unmade bed, stripped off his bathing suit and came down over her.

Cyrene reached for him, her arms and her heart open wide for the man she loved.

Maleah and Derek arrived at Griffin's Rest that evening well before sunset. They would have arrived sooner, but they had backtracked to Dunmore to pick up Maleah's vehicle, a new Chevy Equinox. Although they had lost sight of each other during the trip from Alabama to northeastern Tennessee, he caught a glimpse of her in his rearview mirror just before the I-40 Bridge crossing Douglas Lake. The moment he saw her, he couldn't help wondering if she was pissed because he was ahead of her in the home stretch. Not that he had consciously been trying to arrive at Griffin's Rest before she did or that he saw everything in life as a competition. But during their working partnership on the Midnight Killer case, he had come to realize several things about Maleah. She hated to come in second to anyone, but especially to any man. The fact he had reached the gates outside the Powells' Douglas Lake retreat moments before she had seemed completely insignificant to him, but probably not to Maleah. Sometimes her competitive spirit drove him nuts.

"You've never had to struggle for anything in your entire spoiled rotten rich life," she had once accused him. "You're an arrogant son of a bitch because you have an inflated ego. You overestimate your self-worth."

"And I believe you underestimate yours," he'd told her.

His comment had ended that conversation once and for all. Didn't she realize that he could see past all the pseudo-confidence she tried so hard to project? He suspected that deep inside Maleah Perdue a small, helpless, vulnerable child warned her not to give up a single ounce of the hard-won control she had over her life.

Derek stopped his silver Corvette at the enormous iron gates flanked by two massive stone arches decorated with large bronze griffins. After he used the voice-activated entry code, the gates opened and he drove onto the long, tree-lined lane leading to the house overlooking the lake. Maleah followed at least twenty feet behind him. He parked in front of the house, got out, and waited for her as she pulled in behind him.

The Powell home was large, approximately ten thousand square feet, but actually rather modest for a man worth billions. Despite the mansion's size, there was nothing ostentatious about either the house itself or the décor. It had been built and decorated to accommodate the man who owned the property. Since his marriage to Nicole Baxter a few years ago, Griff had allowed his wife to make any changes she wanted. But almost as if she didn't quite think of Griffin's Rest as her home, Nic had made few alterations.

Derek snorted. Good God, why did he always do that? Why did his brain instantly delve into other people's psyche and try to figure out what made them tick? Instinct, pure and simple. His instinct dictated that he profile everyone.

Maleah emerged from her white SUV, slung the straps of her small leather bag over her shoulder and approached him. If she took more time with her appearance, she could be strikingly beautiful. She had all the ingredients, from pretty face to shapely body. Shapely? *Get real, Lawrence. The woman is built like a brick shithouse and you know it.*

"Waiting on me?" she asked.

"Yeah. What took you so long?"

She glared at him, giving him an eat-dirt-and-die look. "I'm tired, I'm hungry and I'm totally pissed at you."

"What did I do now?"

"You drove like a bat out of hell, that's what you did."

He stared at her, totally puzzled by her comment. "You lost me somewhere there, Blondie. I have no idea—"

"I got a speeding ticket, thanks to you."

He grinned. "How is it my fault that you got a ticket?"

Glowering angrily at him, she clenched her jaw and huffed. "Never mind. Forget I mentioned it. Let's go inside and—"

Before she could finish her sentence, the front door opened. Sanders glanced from Maleah to Derek. "Please, come in. Griffin and Nicole are waiting for you."

Sanders had been Griffin Powell's right-hand man

for as long as Derek had known either of them. Griff
and Sanders's association went back a good twenty
years. Rumor had it that they had met during the ten
missing years of Griff's life, when he had disappeared
off the face of the earth shortly after graduating from
the University of Tennessee nearly two decades ago.

A couple of inches short of six feet, the bald, dark-
eyed, brown-skinned Sanders possessed the bearing of a
much larger man. His stance, his attitude, and his appearance practically screamed military background.
His slightly accented English suggested a foreign birth
and upbringing.

Ever the gentleman his mother had raised him to be,
Derek waited for Maleah to enter first. Sanders led
them past the large living room with the floor-to-ceiling
rock fireplace and down the hall to Griffin Powell's private study. The door stood open and inside Griff sat behind his antique desk placed in the corner by the
windows overlooking the lake. The moment he saw
them, he lifted his two hundred and forty pound muscular body from his desk and stood at his impressive six-
four height. Griff was a big man, his mere physical
presence intimidating. Include his wealth and power
and that added up to a man only a fool would ever
cross.

But out there somewhere was a fool who was killing
people connected to the Powell Agency.

Nicole Powell stood with her back to them in front of
the massive rock fireplace, one of several in the house.
When Griff rose from his desk, she instantly turned to
face them, her soft tan eyes focusing on her friend
Maleah. Physically, the two women were opposites. Nic
was a tall brunette; Maleah a petite blond. Whenever he
saw Nic, the first thought that came to mind was Ama-

zon Warrior. Standing five-ten in her bare feet, with an hourglass figure reminiscent of Hollywood sex symbols of the 1950s, the lady's size was every bit as impressive as her husband's. Derek genuinely liked both Mr. and Mrs. Powell, but it had been easier to like Nic immediately because of her outgoing personality. Griff was more reserved, a man who made others earn his approval.

"Please, come in," Griff said, then he looked at Sanders and told him, "Close the door."

Once the five of them were closeted in Griff's private study, everyone except Sanders seated, Griff spread his big hands out over the folders lying atop his desk.

"These contain all the information we have on the four murders. The info on Winston Corbett came in mid-afternoon, so we've had a chance to go over it."

"As you already know, Ben's dad's murder fit the same pattern as the previous three," Nic said. "We don't need to wait on the autopsy report to know that."

"Our killer, for whatever reason, has targeted Powell employees and members of their families." Griff reiterated an undisputable fact.

Studying the big man's somber expression, Derek noted suppressed anger combined with grief and frustration.

Sanders said, "Protecting the Powell Agency employees and their families is of paramount importance." He stood, as he so often did, at Griff's side, his body stationed slightly behind his boss.

"Everyone is vulnerable because there is no way to predict who will be chosen as the next to die."

"I've given orders for the security here at Griffin's Rest to be expanded. As of tomorrow morning, we're doubling the guards and bringing in more agents to the estate," Griff explained. "There will be guards here at our home, twenty-four/seven, as well as at Yvette's retreat."

Most people would not have noticed the slight tensing in Nic's body, but being an observer of human nature, Derek noticed. Whenever Griff mentioned Dr. Yvette Meng, Nic reacted in a subtle, barely discernable way. He suspected Nic's friendship with Yvette hinged precariously on Nic believing that her husband had never shared a sexual relationship with the exotic Eurasian beauty. Derek also suspected that there was far more to Griff's apparent symbiotic relationship with both Sanders and Dr. Meng than anyone, including Nic, knew.

"Obviously, the problem is that we have no idea who the killer has chosen as his next victim," Nic said. "We've read and re-read the reports." She glanced at Griff's desktop. "The only thing the four victims had in common was their link to the Powell Agency. They were different ages, different sexes, were murdered in different states. One was a Powell secretary, one an agent, one a lawyer who was the brother of an agent. And now, Ben's father, a retired businessman, has been killed."

"If we could figure out how he chooses his victims—" Nic said.

Derek cut her off. "To date, he's chosen two women and then two men. If he follows this pattern then the next two victims will be female."

Griffin grunted, the growling sound coming from deep in his chest. "If that's the case, then every female Powell agent as well as every agent's wife, mother, sister, daughter, and niece could be at risk. How the hell can we narrow down the choices when we have no idea what criteria he's using to make his decisions?"

"We can't," Derek said. "My educated guess is that he

is following a specific plan and that he probably won't deviate from it. He's too methodical, too precise, as if he has a blueprint that leads him step by step."

"The way a copycat killer would mimic the original killer's MO," Griff said.

Derek's gaze met Griff's and he understood that Griff and the others knew something that he and Maleah did not.

"Are you saying you think we're dealing with a copy-cat killer?" Maleah asked.

"I believe it is a good possibility." Griff picked up two file folders and handed them to Sanders. "Later, I want you both to read over this information." He motioned to Sanders to distribute the folders, which he quickly did.

Derek glanced at the typed heading on the folder. *Jerome Browning.*

The name sounded vaguely familiar.

"Who's Jerome Browning?" Maleah asked.

"He is a convicted serial killer serving half a dozen consecutive life terms at the Georgia State Prison." Griff made direct eye contact with Maleah before he continued. "Browning became known as the Carver when he viciously murdered nine people by slitting their throats and carving triangular pieces of flesh from their upper arms and thighs. His first kill was twelve years ago and his killing spree lasted less than three years before he was caught, tried and convicted."

The way everyone else in the room seemed focused on Maleah piqued Derek's curiosity. He sensed that Griff was on the verge of revealing information that would in some way personally affect her. His protective instincts kicked in automatically, urging him to place himself between Maleah and whatever might harm her.

"I'm getting the distinct impression that I'm not

going to like whatever else you have to say." Maleah glanced around the room, taking note of how everyone was staring directly at her.

"Maleah, I'm so sorry . . ." Nic's voice trailed off.

"Jerome Browning's third victim was a young man living and working in the Atlanta area," Griff said. "His name was Noah Laborde."

Maleah gasped, the sound sharp and highly exaggerated in the hushed stillness. "He killed Noah?" She spoke the man's name softly . . . sadly.

"Who was Noah Laborde?" Derek asked.

Nic walked over to Maleah and draped a comforting arm around her shoulders. Maleah looked at Derek. "Noah was my college boyfriend. We . . . we were almost engaged. We broke up right after graduation. His sister called me a year later to tell me that Noah had been killed, but I . . . Oh, God, I never knew the details. I never asked."

Of all the killers this person could have chosen to imitate, why had he picked the man who had murdered Maleah's former boyfriend?

The answer was obvious, of course—because of the Powell Agency connection.

"So what do you think, Derek?" Griff asked.

"I don't think it's a coincidence." Derek knew exactly what Griff was asking. "Our killer chose this man Browning because he had killed Noah Laborde, Maleah's former boyfriend. Maleah is a Powell agent and therefore connected to the agency. He handpicked the Carver as the killer he would imitate for the same reason he has chosen his victims."

"Because they are all, in one way or another, connected to the Powell Agency." Griff pummeled the desktop with his huge fist. "God damn son of a bitch."

"I can only surmise that his real target is the Powell

Agency." When Derek's gaze met Griff's, he saw the pain in his employer's eyes. "I would assume that means his target is either you, Griff, or you, Nicole." He glanced at Nic. "Or possibly both of you."

"It's not Nic. I'm his real target," Griff said. "He's striking out at me through my people."

"That's one possible scenario," Derek agreed.

"I could be his target," Nic said. "He could be someone from my past, someone connected to one of my cases when I was a federal agent. After all, he has chosen to copy a killer who has a direct connection to my best friend."

"We can debate this all day and still won't know for sure," Maleah told them. "Once we find out who the killer is, we'll have the answers to all the whys, won't we? That has to be our first order of business—identifying our killer."

"Maleah's right," Derek said. "Since it seems obvious that the new Carver murders are copycat killings, that means we need to start with some basic questions. Is our guy someone who has been in contact with Jerome Browning, maybe visited him in prison? Is he an admirer? A student of the Carver's methods? Is he perhaps even a protégé of Browning's?"

"There is one person, other than the killer himself, who may be able to answer those questions," Maleah said.

"Jerome Browning." Derek's voice filled the quiet room. All eyes turned to him.

"Browning is the reason y'all decided to pair me with Derek on this case." Maleah stared right at Nic.

Nic simply stared back at Maleah.

"I think it's obvious that our killer wants you involved," Griff said.

Maleah gave Griff her undivided attention. "You

think because of my connection to Noah, Browning's third victim, the copycat is sending me an invitation to become personally involved."

Griff nodded. "Don't you agree, Derek?"

Reluctantly, Derek replied, "Yes, I agree. And it could be that by singling out Maleah this way, it's the copycat killer's way of getting as close to Nic as he possibly can without actually involving her. At least not yet."

"See, I told you that this could be all about me and not you." Nic glared at her husband.

Griff frowned, but didn't verbally acknowledge Nic's comment. Instead he spoke directly to Maleah. "Someone will have to interview Browning. Since the killer chose a specific connection between you and the killer he is imitating, it would seem logical that you should be the agent I send to Georgia to talk to Browning."

"I'll accompany her, of course." No way in hell was Derek going to let Maleah confront Browning alone. She might project a tough as nails image, but he knew just how vulnerable she really was.

"Of course," Griff agreed. "We'll want you to study Browning while Maleah interviews him."

"She needs to know the rest." Nic glared at her husband. "No secrets. If Maleah is going into this, she needs to go into it armed with all the facts."

Derek's gut tightened.

Griff nodded. He stood, reached down behind his desk and lifted a small thermal cooler from the floor.

"We received a package sent via FedEx this morning," Griff said. "There was a small plastic case inside an Arctic foil insulated package, the type used to ship perishables such as food and medical supplies."

Griff flipped back the lid on the cooler, reached down inside and lifted out the plastic case. "The package was addressed to you, Maleah, in care of the Powell

Agency. The sender was, supposedly, Winston Corbett."

Derek sensed that Maleah was holding her breath as Griff removed the top from the plastic case. He inched in closer, placing himself directly behind her. Looking over her shoulder, he had a perfect view of the sectioned interior of the case and the first layer of its contents.

"Are those . . . ?" Maleah swallowed hard. "Are those what I think they are?"

"We've had our lab verify that those small triangular objects are human flesh," Griff said. "I think we can be relatively certain that the pieces in the top section were cut from Winston Corbett's body and those in the other three sections belong to the other victims."

"And he sent them to me." Maleah balled her hands into fists and pressed her fists against her upper thighs.

Derek reached out and clamped his hand over Maleah's tense shoulder, conveying his support. "We're in this together, Blondie. You and me. From here to the bitter end."

Chapter 4

Despite her earlier claims to Derek about being hungry, Maleah skipped dinner that evening. The information that Nic and Griff had shared with her had not only taken her appetite, but it had given her the mother of all headaches. *Why me?* was the one question that replayed itself over and over again in her mind. Could it really be he had chosen her only because she and Nic were close friends? Or was it possible that she was simply the only Powell agent with a connection to a serial killer? She'd have to remember in the morning to ask Nic.

Lying there staring up at the ceiling, she positioned her index fingers on either side of her head and rubbed her temples in a circular motion. She had been prone to having tension headaches all her life. Usually a couple of aspirin or Aleve gave her relief within an hour or less. But this headache was hanging on.

"Maleah?" Nic asked after rapping on the bedroom door.

"Yes, what is it?"

"May I come in?"

Maleah sighed heavily, lifted herself into a sitting position and replied, "Sure, come on in." After all, she was a guest in her friend's home. And Nic was probably worried about her.

No sooner had Maleah's bare feet hit the floor than Nic entered, a serving tray balanced in one hand. "I brought you something to eat."

Maleah rushed toward her friend and took the tray from her. "Thanks, but you didn't have to do that. I don't think I can eat a bite."

"It's Barbara Jean's mac and cheese, with her Mexican cornbread. If that doesn't tempt you, nothing will." Nic closed the door and then followed Maleah into the small sitting area of the bedroom. A couple of sky blue upholstered arm chairs flanked a small, low mahogany table set between the chairs and love seat covered with yellow and blue floral material. Maleah lowered the tray to the table, removed the cloth covering and eyed the plate of food. Her stomach growled.

Maleah and Nic smiled at each other.

"See," Nic said. "Your stomach knows you're hungry, even if you think you're not."

Realizing it was useless to argue with Nic, especially when she was right, Maleah sat down on the loveseat and picked up a fork from the tray. "I've read through the folder Griff gave me, but I'm afraid I didn't retain much of the info. I have a splitting headache. I'll read the files again later."

"Did you take something for your headache?"

Maleah lifted the plate from the tray. "A couple of aspirin. They helped a little."

"Eat something. It could be a hunger headache." She scanned Maleah from head to toe. "You look like you've lost weight."

Maleah groaned. "Don't I wish."

They both laughed.

"Why don't you wait until in the morning to re-read the files on the Carver," Nic said. "It could be days before you can interview him. Griff is still working on pulling some strings to get you and Derek permission to visit him. There is a lot of red tape involved in being granted visitation privileges. If we were a government agency, it would be a lot easier. Under normal circumstances, since we're an independent firm, it would be highly unlikely one of our agents would be allowed to see Browning. Unless of course, he asked to see one of us."

Maleah lifted a forkful of macaroni and cheese to her mouth, ate the delicious casserole and dived back into the plate for more. "This is delicious." She ate several more bites before asking, "I don't suppose y'all have checked to see if any of the other agents have any connection to a serial killer, have you?"

Nic's eyes widened as her expression changed from puzzlement to understanding. "No, we haven't. Narrowing down the copycat killer's MO to perfectly match a former serial killer took some time, so we only recently came to the conclusion that our Powell Agency killer was mimicking the Carver. But I see what you're getting at. Did he choose the Carver because he's the only serial killer with any connection to one of our agents?"

Maleah munched on the Mexican cornbread and washed it down with iced tea. "I realize that with nearly two hundred people now employed by the agency, it could take forever to make any kind of connection. So, how did our killer unearth the connection between Jerome Browning and me when I didn't even know about it myself?" Maleah tightened her hold on the cool, damp glass. "God, I should have asked more questions about Noah's murder when his sister Jacque called me. But I hadn't seen him or spoken to him in over a year when it happened." Quick jabs of pain shot through Maleah's right temple. She pressed the side of the iced tea glass against the throbbing pain.

"Are you okay?" Nic studied Maleah closely. "Maybe you need something stronger than aspirin."

"No, I'll be fine. I'm just feeling a little guilty remembering how unaffected I was by Noah's death." She set the glass on the tray. "He was such a nice guy. Any woman in her right mind would have snapped him up in a New York minute. But not me. I think I broke his heart when I turned down his proposal."

"Why did you turn him down?"

"I didn't want to get married." Maleah slid her left hand beneath her hair at the nape of her neck and massaged her scalp. "I feel as if my entire head is being squeezed in a vise. I know it's just tension, but . . ."

"You don't need to tell me tonight. Maybe you should lie down and rest."

"I want you to know, to understand why I rejected him. At the time, I told myself that I didn't marry Noah because I didn't want to get married, that I intended to never marry anybody. But looking back, I realize that was only half of the reason."

"And the other half was because . . . ?"

"I don't think I was in love with Noah. I loved him, yes. But something was missing. I wanted to be in love, told myself that I was, needed to be, at least in my own mind, enough to justify the fact that he was my first."

Nic smiled. "No one ever forgets their first, do they? But we all know that most of the time, the first one is not The One, not for a lot of woman and certainly not for most men. Of course, there are exceptions, especially for our parents' generation."

"It breaks my heart to think about the way Noah died. He deserved to live a full life, with a wife and kids and . . ." Maleah exhaled a huffing breath. "Dear God, how am I going to face the man who killed Noah? How am I going to interview him without wanting to strangle him with my bare hands for what he did?"

"You'll be able to do it because you're a professional. If Griff or I had any doubts about your ability or your competence, we would never pair you with Derek again and put the two of you in charge of a case that is highly personal for us."

"Griff really does believe that these murders are somehow connected to his past, doesn't he?" Maleah looked squarely at Nic.

"Yes. And he could be right. But it's also possible that the killer wants us to believe that. He may want us to think that Griff is the ultimate target, when actually it may be me."

"Have you ever considered the possibility that neither of you are?"

"No, not really," Nic said. "The killer has murdered agents and members of their families, which means he's targeting the agency. Griff and I own the agency. It stands to reason that this killer wants to harm the agency, wants to hurt Griff and me."

"Then why involve me?" Maleah asked. "Both you and Griff have been personally involved with serial killer cases in the past. Why not copy one of them? Why go back into my past and choose someone who had killed my college boyfriend?"

"I don't have a conclusive answer for you because I simply don't know. It could be what we said earlier, that he's getting to me through you, my best friend."

"Maybe. If you're the one he wants to hurt. But if his

real target is Griff, then maybe I'm simply phase one in his plan."

"Which would make me phase two, right?"

Maleah shook her head and waved her hand in the air. "It's all conjecture at this point. I'm probably talking nonsense. I shouldn't come up with conspiracy theories when I'm tired and sleepy and can't shake a bad headache."

"Look, I'm going to leave you alone so you can finish eating, grab a shower, and then go to bed." Nic rose to her feet. "We'll both have clearer heads in the morning and be able to get a fresh perspective on things."

Maleah stood and walked Nic to the door. They exchanged hugs and pecks on their cheeks. Once Nic walked down the hall, Maleah closed the door, leaned back against it, and closed her eyes.

"I'm so sorry, Noah. Sorry that you were so brutally murdered. Sorry that I didn't ask for details about your death when your sister called me. Sorry that I didn't love you enough to marry you."

Griff poured Macallan single malt Scotch whisky into two glasses, handed one to Derek and lifted the other to his lips. After taking a sip, he motioned for Derek to take the left of two leather chairs flanking the seven-foot-high rock fireplace in his private study. As Griff sat in the opposite chair, Derek studied the man briefly, noting the weariness in his expression. The four recent Powell Agency–related deaths had begun to take a toll on the seemingly invincible billionaire.

"I had Sanders put a call in to the Georgia governor," Griff said. "I saw no point in wasting my time going through the normal channels to acquire visitation privileges for you and Maleah at the Georgia State Prison."

Derek nodded. Why indeed? There would be no point in Griff calling the prison's warden when he was on a first name basis with the governor.

Born into a wealthy, old Southern family, Derek had taken for granted all the things most people struggle for on a daily basis. His mother hobnobbed with other society matrons, his sister married a suitable young man from a proper family, and Derek's grandparents had left him a trust fund worth more millions than he'd ever spend in one lifetime. Griffin Powell had been born dirt poor, but was now one of the wealthiest men in the world. No one knew how the former UT football hero had earned his billions during the ten years after he had mysteriously disappeared.

"I'd rather not send Maleah to do the initial interview even if she is one of our best agents. But under the circumstances, I feel she's the only choice. The killer didn't choose to copy the Carver's murders without a reason."

"You're assuming Maleah is the reason, right?"

"In a roundabout way," Griff said. "He wanted a connection between the killer he copied and one of our agents. It could be a coincidence that Maleah is that agent. Or it is possible that Maleah's friendship with my wife is the reason. What hurts Maleah hurts Nic and what hurts Nic hurts me."

"That's the way love and friendship works."

Griff took a hefty swallow of the aged whisky. Holding the drink in one hand, he absently stroked the side of the glass with his other hand, tapping his fingers rhythmically on the smooth surface.

"Do you think Browning personally knows our killer?" Derek asked. His gut instincts told him that the Powell Agency killer and Browning were at the very least acquainted. Possibly friends. Or more likely, student and teacher.

"Probably. What do you think?"

"Probably."

"Browning could well be the key to unlocking our killer's identity."

Derek took his first sip of the premium Scotch whisky. He wasn't a drinking man himself, but he did enjoy an occasional sip of the good stuff. Not that he was a teetotaler by any means. But seeing what alcohol addiction had done to his father and older brother made Derek conscientious about his drinking habits. After the smooth liquor made its way down his throat and warmed his belly, he glanced at Griff, who was staring into the cold fireplace.

"We both know that Browning isn't going to willingly offer us any information," Derek said.

"No, he'll sense from the get-go that he has the upper hand. And he'll use it to his advantage. He'll want something in return for anything he gives us."

"For anything he gives Maleah."

Griff nodded. "She's strong and smart and I'd trust her with even the most difficult assignment. But this is different. From what I've read about Jerome Browning, he's going to play hardball and I don't know if Maleah is a tough enough opponent."

"She's not going into this alone," Derek reminded his boss.

"That's true." Griff stared at Derek, as if he was judging his worth as a warrior. "She's going to need you. She won't like it and may even resist your advice and assistance. You know what a stubborn little mule she can be."

Derek chuckled. "That's an understatement. She is

without a doubt the most stubborn woman I've ever known."

"Nic is worried about her. She understands why Maleah is the one who should interview Browning, but they're close, almost like sisters, and know each other's weaknesses. Nic's concerned that Browning may use any weakness he senses in Maleah against her."

"If Browning picks up on any weakness in her, I have no doubt that he'll use it. But I'll be there to advise her." Derek took a second sip of whisky and then set the glass down on the floor beside his chair. "Before we leave for Georgia, I'll go over all the files we have on Browning and do an in-depth study on the guy. After we meet him, I'll work up my own profile and compare it to the old FBI profile the agency put together."

Griff nodded. "I want the copycat killer found and stopped before anyone else dies." He downed another gulp of the Macallan, huffed out a deep breath, and took another swig.

It was Derek's opinion that recently Griff had been drinking too much. The man had a high tolerance for alcohol, was able to drink enough to knock another man on his ass, and usually knew his limit. But for the past couple of months, Derek had noticed a distinct change in his boss, and not only in his drinking habits.

"You do know that these murders are not your fault," Derek said.

Griff's grumbling growl came from his chest, a combination of anger and pain. "He is sending me a message. No matter what anyone thinks, I know that I'm the ultimate target. He wants me to suffer, to know that he's killing these people because they are in some way associated with me."

"I know that's what you believe, but there is no way you can be sure."

"I'm sure."

"Look, Griff, I've never asked for specific details about your past, about those missing ten years," Derek said. "I figured everything that happened to you and how you earned your billions was nobody's business. Certainly not mine. What I know, you've told me yourself, and I appreciate your trusting me with the information. But if there's something specific that I need to know, something that could help me—"

"Go with Maleah to see Browning. Size up the guy. Get all the info you can out of him and then we'll talk." Griff finished off his glass of whisky.

Derek didn't need to say more. He understood that Griff had dismissed him. He stood, said good night and closed the door behind him when he left.

As if he were standing guard, Sanders waited across the hall from Griff's study, his muscular arms crossed over his broad chest. With a stocky, fireplug build, every muscle toned, a sharp mind always in observation mode, the man appeared to be battle ready at all times.

"He's drinking too much." Derek paused long enough to make direct eye contact with his boss's right-hand man.

Sanders nodded.

"He thinks the murders are his fault."

"Griffin carries the weight of the world on his shoulders," Sanders said.

"Someone who knows him far better than I do needs to convince him that he's not to blame, no matter what the killer's motives might be."

"Griffin is a man who accepts responsibility."

Derek stared at Sanders, not quite understanding his comment. Did he believe that Griff was in some way responsible for the actions of a psychopath?

"No one person can right all the wrongs in the world, no matter how rich and powerful they might be," Derek said.

"One person can try."

"My God, what grievous sin did he commit that he feels compelled to atone for by wearing a hair shirt the rest of his life?"

"I advise you not to profile Griffin Powell with that analytical mind of yours, Mr. Lawrence."

Derek nodded. He now knew that he had hit too close to home to suit Sanders. Griff lived with his past sins haunting him and they were no doubt the driving force behind his need to rid the world of evil. He had founded the Powell Private Security and Investigation Agency as a means to bring to justice those whom regular law enforcement had difficulty apprehending and punishing. His clients paid according to their ability to do so and many cases were worked pro bono.

Without replying to Sanders, Derek walked away, his thoughts centered on Griffin Powell's mysterious past. Why was Griff so certain that the copycat killer was sending him a message?

Errol watched Cyrene while she slept. He had never thought it possible to love a woman the way he loved her. He couldn't look at her enough, couldn't touch her enough, couldn't make love to her enough. After his disastrous first marriage and the death of his little girl, he had thought he was destined to be miserable the rest of his life.

And then he had met Cyrene. In a coffee shop of all places. He'd stopped by to meet his sister for breakfast on his way to work and had accidentally bumped into the most gorgeous woman in the world while waiting in line. The moment she smiled at him, the whole world lit up, bright and warm and joyous. Yeah, sure, he hadn't missed the fact that she had a great body. And yeah, right after her thousand-watt smile, her big boobs had been the first thing he'd noticed. But her body was icing on the cake. The woman inside was as beautiful as the sexy wrapping.

They had dated for six months before they slept together. She was a cautious lady, determined that no man would ever take advantage of her. By the time they made love for the first time, he was already in love. And so was she.

When he asked her to marry him a few weeks later, she had only one request—that he change jobs.

"I want a husband who doesn't put his life in danger every day the way you do being an Atlanta police officer. I don't want to have to worry if the father of my children may not come home one night because he got killed on the job."

Errol reached down from where he lay beside her, his body propped up on his folded arm, and tenderly caressed her cheek. As much as he had loved being a police officer, he loved Cyrene more. Then and now.

He'd been lucky to find another job that he truly liked, one that actually paid better and afforded him and his new bride a more affluent lifestyle. He'd been with the Powell Agency for four months, having hired on a few weeks after his engagement. They had just bought a new house in Farragut a month before their wedding. And his new boss—Griffin Powell—had given them an all-expenses-paid two-week honeymoon at the Grand Resort in the Bahamas.

He laid his head on his pillow, stretched out his

naked body beneath the cool, slightly wrinkled sheet, and closed his eyes.

Life was good. At long last.

Errol knew he was one damn lucky SOB.

Wearing tan cargo shorts and a hideous floral shirt, he sat at the end of the bar nursing some elaborate rum concoction, doing his best to look like a typical tourist. Most of the visitors at the resort were couples, many newlyweds or second honeymooners. In order to fit in, he had made a point of flirting with several single ladies who were obviously there man-hunting. He had already decided that tomorrow night he'd take one of those ladies to his room and ease some of the pre-kill tension he always experienced. A night of rough sex would do wonders for him.

He was in no rush. The most important thing was timing. Errol and Cyrene Patterson were on their honeymoon and spent a great deal of time in their room. The couple had been inseparable since their arrival at the resort last week. He didn't want to kill both of them, but if necessary, he would. But only one was his target, only one was destined to become the Copycat Carver's fifth victim.

Just as he took another sip of the syrupy sweet rum drink, his mobile phone vibrated in his shirt pocket. He lifted the phone from the pocket and glanced at the caller ID.

No information. Unknown number and name.

He tapped the answer key and put the phone to his ear. "I'm enjoying my vacation in the Bahamas. I've met some lovely ladies. Unfortunately some of the prettiest women are married and here on their honeymoon. There's one woman . . ."

"I don't need to know the details tonight. I prefer to allow my imagination to paint a mental picture of all the gruesome details."

"Whatever you want."

"Did you send Ms. Perdue her gift?"

"She should have received it today."

"You sent it in care of her employer?"

"I did."

"Then it's only a matter of time before he arranges for her to visit the Georgia State Prison."

Chapter 5

Maleah wasn't surprised that Griff had managed to arrange for visitation privileges for Derek and her at the prison in Reidsville so quickly. He had placed a call to the governor over the weekend and by noon Monday, she and Derek were packing their bags. Barbara Jean, who handled a lot of the mundane details for the agency, booked them two rooms at the Hampton Inn in Vidalia, a twenty-minute drive from Reidsville. They had checked into the hotel before six and then had driven over to the county seat of Tattnall County where the state prison was located. Before they had left Griffin's Rest yesterday, Sanders, who had confiscated their laptops earlier that morning, had informed them that all pertinent files on Jerome Browning had been loaded into a file folder. One file contained info on the penitentiary, the oldest state prison in Georgia. Constructed of marble in 1937 and opened in that same year, it remained the largest contributor to the city's economy.

Numerous buildings containing four two-tiered cell blocks with single cells, the newer buildings spanning from the original structure, housed the convicts. The cell blocks were divided by population into two categories: general population units and one special management unit. As a convicted serial killer serving multi-life sentences, Jerome Browning was housed in a maximum security area.

Maleah hadn't slept worth a damn. She would never admit it to Derek, but she was more than just a little nervous about meeting Browning. In all honesty, she was borderline terrified—terrified by the thought of how she might react when she actually came face-to-face with Noah's killer. While she had tossed and turned for hours, longing for sleep that wouldn't come, her mind had wandered back more than a dozen years, to the day she had met Noah Laborde, sophomore class president. It hadn't been love at first sight. She didn't believe in such a thing, not then and certainly not now. But it had been interest at first sight. They had dated for nearly a year before she had finally agreed to have sex with him.

Remembering the past in such vivid detail, recalling moments with Noah that she had thought long forgotten didn't help Maleah's already frayed nerves that morning. After grabbing a quick shower and brushing her hair up into a loose bun, she dressed in her professional garb—navy slacks, white shirt, lightweight tan jacket, and a pair of sensible low-heel navy shoes. After applying a minimum of makeup, she put on her wristwatch and small gold hoop earrings. She took all of half a minute to inspect herself in the mirror before slipping her small leather bag over her shoulder and leaving the room.

She didn't bother stopping to knock on Derek's door as she headed for the elevator. During the entire time they had worked together on the Midnight Killer case, she couldn't recall a single morning that he hadn't gotten up early, always before she did. The Hampton Inn provided a full breakfast, which meant they wouldn't have to search for a place to eat this morning. Just as she had figured, he was waiting for her in the dining area adjacent to the lobby. Sitting alone at a table for two, a cup of coffee in front of him, a folded newspaper in one hand, and a soft-grip mechanical pencil in the other, he glanced up from the crossword puzzle and motioned for her to join him. As she approached, he laid down the paper and pencil and rose to greet her with a smile.

"Morning, sunshine."

God, she hated that he could be so chipper at six-thirty in the morning. And she hated even more that she had noticed how damn good he looked. Derek was nothing more to her than her partner on this case, just as he had been on the Midnight Killer case. Their personal relationship went no farther than that. They certainly weren't friends, not by any stretch of the imagination. On good days, they worked well together. On bad days, they tolerated each other.

"Have you eaten?" she asked.

"Nope." He glanced at the half empty cup on the table. "However, this is my second cup of coffee."

"Coffee sounds good. I think I'll grab some cereal and a cup of yogurt."

"You do know that breakfast is the most important meal of the day," he told her. "You should fill up on protein—bacon and eggs. And of course, a couple of biscuits smothered in butter and jelly."

"If I ate like that every morning, I'd soon be waddling when I walk."

When she headed toward the self-serve breakfast set-up, she felt Derek's gaze on her and knew he was looking at her butt. Okay, so she had a bit of a hang-up about her wide hips and ample rear-end. Nic had told her guys didn't like flat asses, that her JLo butt was a definite asset. If that was true, then why was it that Derek seemed to prefer the long, lean, borderline skinny model types?

Damn it, why do you care what type of woman Derek prefers?

Maleah hurried through the line, grabbed a carton of non-fat strawberry yogurt and, deciding against eating cereal, headed toward the coffeemaker. Not fully concentrating on what she was doing, she bumped into Derek and quickly apologized before she even looked at him.

Their gazes met and locked for a full thirty seconds before Maleah broke eye contact.

"It's okay to be nervous about meeting Browning," he told her.

Ignoring his comment, she grabbed a cup, filled it with hot coffee, and picked up a packet of Splenda and a stir stick.

By the time Derek joined her at their table, she had drunk half her coffee. As he set down a plate filled with bacon, eggs, and biscuits, he glanced at her unopened yogurt carton. After he sat across from her, they ate in relative silence for several minutes.

"You aren't nervous, are you?" Maleah asked.

"Unsettled would be a better word to describe how I feel about meeting Jerome Browning this morning," Derek told her. "Unsettled, curious, and wary. You need to be wary of him, too. He's cunning. If he senses any weakness in you, he'll use it against you."

"And you and Griff think I'm weak, don't you? You think I'll fall apart just because Browning murdered my college boyfriend."

"Neither Griff nor I think you're weak. But you will

be vulnerable because of your connection to Noah Laborde."

She heaved a heavy, labored huff. Derek was right. There was no use denying the obvious.

He reached over and laid his open palm across her tightly fisted hand. The moment he touched her, she jerked her hand away and lifted it off the table.

Ignoring her reaction, he said, "The way I see this interview with Browning is you and I act as a tag team, both of us questioning him. If at any time you become uncomfortable and want to terminate the interview, then don't hesitate to let me know."

"And you'll whisk me up in your big strong arms and carry me off on your gallant white charger." The moment the silly comment left her lips, Maleah regretted it. She had a problem about speaking before thinking things through, and this was especially true with Derek.

He didn't respond.

She groaned. "Sorry."

He laughed. "I didn't know you thought of me as a knight in shining armor."

She rolled her eyes, but couldn't help smiling. "Most of the time, I think of you as a royal pain in the butt."

"Likewise, Blondie." He lifted his coffee cup and saluted her with it.

Barbara Jean had lived at Griffin's Rest for several years, ever since Griff had placed her under the agency's protection during the hunt for her younger sister's killer. Within a few days, he had put her to work, there in his home, under Damar Sanders's guidance. Her attraction to Sanders had not been love at first sight, but rather a recognition of two lonely, wounded souls in need. Despite the fact that they were lovers and sometimes in their intimate moments she called him Damar, she thought of her friend and lover as Sanders. No one used his first name, not even Griff and Yvette, his closest friends.

She admired and respected Griffin Powell as she did Sanders and shared a deep affection with Nicole. She considered Yvette Meng a friend, but they were not close, not the way she and Nic were. The beautiful Eurasian psychiatrist possessed a quiet, gentle personality. Almost shy. Her unique empathic abilities that allowed her to gain insight into a person's thoughts and feelings by a mere touch separated her from others. Until recently, Yvette had lived in London, half a world away. But then, three years ago, Griff had begun construction at Griffin's Rest on a retreat for Yvette and a small group of her protégés, young men and women with special psychic talents.

Barbara Jean knew less about the missing years of her employer's life, from age twenty-two to thirty-two, than Nic knew. And even though Sanders had told her that he and Yvette had shared those years with Griff, he had not divulged very many details. Sanders had been married long ago and had lost his wife and child. He had never told her the specifics and she had never asked. He, Yvette, and Griff had been held captive on an uncharted Pacific island by an insane billionaire named Malcolm York. They had eventually escaped, after they killed York. The horrors they had endured together had united them as comrades and bound them to one another forever.

Nic and Yvette shared a precarious friendship, somewhat one-sided since Nic couldn't quite manage to overcome her concerns about Griff's love for the other woman. Where Nic needed to know more about her husband's past and allowed the secrets he couldn't share with her to come between them, Barbara Jean accepted Sanders for who and what he was. His past was just that—his past. It had made him the man he was today, but other than that, it had nothing to do with her.

If only Nic could see things as she did.

Barbara Jean maneuvered her wheelchair out onto the patio where Nic sat in a chaise lounge, her computer resting in her lap.

"I've put on the kettle for tea," Barbara Jean said. "Would you care for a cup?"

"No, thanks." Nic glanced over her shoulder and smiled. "I've been going over the information on Jerome Browning again and some things don't add up."

"Such as?" Barbara Jean asked as she wheeled herself out into the morning sunshine.

"The original Carver didn't mail the pieces of flesh he removed from his victims to anyone. Those triangular pieces were never found." Nic paused for a moment, closed the lid on her laptop and faced Barbara Jean.

"So, the copycat killer is not following every detail of the Carver's MO, is he?" Barbara Jean said.

"No, which makes me ask why he isn't. And if he's differing in one aspect, then he's possibly going to differ in other areas."

"I haven't actually studied copycat cases in general, but it stands to reason that there might be differences between the original and the copy."

"In most cases, the copycat closely mimics the original, but often deviates in small details," Nic said as she closed her laptop and set it on the glass and metal side table to her right. "Our killer sending Maleah the triangles of flesh from the first four victims, coupled with the fact that he's copying the killer who murdered Maleah's college sweetheart, tells me that he wants her involved."

"Does that mean that neither you nor Griff is his ultimate target?"

"I don't know. My gut tells me that it's one of us, but what if this new Carver has been killing Powell Agency people in order to set things up to lure Maleah into some sort of vicious game he's playing?"

"Have you talked to Griff about your theory?" Barbara Jean asked.

"I'm afraid Griff is concentrating so much on a possible connection between the Powell Agency murders and the rumor in Europe about Malcolm York being alive that he isn't giving consideration to any other possibility."

"Sanders says there is no way York can still be alive." She lowered her voice. "When they left the island, York was dead. They were certain of it." Barbara Jean preferred not to think about the fact that Sanders was more than capable of cold-blooded murder, as were Griff and Yvette. She understood why they had killed York and knew in her heart that under the same circumstances, she would have done what they did. They had destroyed the monster who had tortured them with such great pleasure.

"Griff says the same thing." Nic stood to her full five-ten height, her feet bare, her long, tan legs clad in white walking shorts. An oversized orange and white UT T-shirt hung loosely to her hips. "He's convinced that someone in Europe is using York's name, but he has no idea who or why."

"I know very little about the years Sanders spent on Amara, only that he blames York for the death of his wife and child, and that York forced him to do some terrible things."

"I've grown to hate Malcolm York with every fiber of my being." Nic walked to the edge of the patio and gazed out over Douglas Lake. "Even after all these years, he still haunts Griff."

"As he does Sanders and Yvette."

At the mention of Yvette's name, Nic glanced over her shoulder at Barbara Jean. "They both love her, you know. My Griffin and your Sanders."

"Yes, I know. And she loves them. But . . ." Barbara Jean paused, hoping to find the right words. "Griff worships the ground you walk on. You are the love of his life. Never doubt that for a moment."

Nic offered Barbara Jean a forced smile, then looked back out over the lake. "I don't doubt his love for me. But as long as he doesn't trust me with the complete truth about his past, that past will stand between us."

Maleah was in the driver's seat. Derek had learned early on during their partnership on the Midnight Killer case that she preferred being the driver. Since he couldn't care less, he hadn't put up a fuss about it. No doubt it had something to do with her personal control issues. The lady most definitely had a problem with any man—but him in particular—being in charge of her.

He kicked back and relaxed as she headed her Chevy Equinox southeast on GA-30 E/US-280 E. If they weren't delayed by roadwork or accidents blocking the highway, they should be at the prison in about twenty minutes. Even though their scheduled visitation with Browning was at ten, Maleah had insisted on leaving the hotel at nine.

"I'd rather get there early and have to wait than run the risk of our being late," she'd told him.

He had learned the hard way not to argue with her over insignificant matters. He chose his battles. Otherwise, they would be at each other's throats all the time.

In the beginning of their professional association, they had disagreed on everything. If he said the sky was blue, she'd say it was gray. If he said the sun was shining, she'd say it was partly cloudy. If he voiced an opinion she didn't like, she'd call him an arrogant jerk.

"Do you want to go over anything again before we get there?" he asked.

"No. I think we've talked the subject of Jerome Browning to death, don't you?"

"Probably. Just remember—don't underestimate him. And don't expect him to give us anything without wanting something in return."

"I'm not an idiot, you know." She kept her gaze fixed on the road ahead.

He wanted to reply that no one had said she was an idiot or even thought it. A prickly pear, yes. High-strung and confrontational, yes. But instead, he asked, "Mind if I find some music on the radio?"

"Be my guest. But please make it something soothing."

He found a "lite sounds" station, the first tune, a relaxing piano concerto. "Does that meet with your approval?" he asked.

"It's fine." When she glanced his way, he smiled and winked at her. She frowned and hurriedly looked away, returning her gaze to the view through the windshield.

Ignoring her completely, he closed his eyes. His mind immediately focused on Jerome Browning.

Derek hated the deals law enforcement made with criminals, plea-agreements that allowed lesser sentences in exchange for information. The DA who had prosecuted Jerome Browning had been forced into one of those god-awful deals. Browning, who should be on death row, was instead locked away in the maximum security division of the penitentiary. He had brutally murdered nine people, five women and four men. But not long after his arrest the authorities learned that he had killed before, when he had been a teenager. Twenty years before Browning had been arrested and charged with the Carver murders, a series of six missing teen girls in Browning's old neighborhood had been presumed murdered. Their bodies had never been found. And all six cases had remained unsolved. Browning had bargained for his life—and won! He had agreed to confess to the murders of the six teen girls and tell the police where they could find the bodies. In exchange for the information that could bring closure to six families, Browning had been granted life imprisonment instead of the death penalty he deserved.

Browning would spend the rest of his life behind bars, but he was alive. Like the families of the people he had murdered, Derek believed that Browning should have been executed.

Everything Derek knew about Browning forewarned him that Maleah would be facing a deviously clever psychopath, one who would not hesitate to use her for his own amusement.

But Maleah was no featherweight in any battle of wills. She was strong, tough, and smart; and God help her, she never gave up on anything or anyone she believed in with her whole heart. He didn't know what demons she had fought and won in her past, but he saw beyond the exterior beauty to the deep scars inside her. Maleah Perdue was a survivor.

Derek suspected she just might be a worthy opponent for Browning.

But at what cost to her?

Griffin Powell had entrusted Maleah to Derek, expecting him to keep her safe and protect her from emotional trauma. Griff had a protective attitude toward all of his employees, but Maleah was special to him because she was his wife's best friend. And the big man possessed an exaggerated sense of responsibility when it came to the people in his life, especially the women. Apparently, on a subconscious level, Griff thought of women as the weaker sex. He was, in so many ways, an old-fashioned gentleman. A good old Southern boy, raised the right way by his mama.

Derek might have been born with a silver spoon in his mouth and Griff a poor boy, but Griff was far more of a gentleman than Derek ever had been or would be. Derek had spent most of his life rebelling against his mother, his family, and the inherent snobbery and self-indulgent lifestyle that inherited wealth so often imposed on the heirs to multi-million-dollar fortunes. From his early teens, he had deliberately done the unexpected, anything and everything to piss off his mother and grandparents, and to snub his nose at the society in which they existed. Military boarding school had been their solution. His response had been to skip college after high school graduation and bum around the world like a penniless vagrant. He had certainly seen the world through the eyes of a man who had to earn his keep wherever he went.

At twenty, flat broke and determined not to touch his trust fund, he had joined a group of unsavory characters, a sort of ragtag group of wannabe mercenaries, bluffing his way into their fold. He had learned later on that he hadn't fooled them and they hadn't expected him to survive his first mission. He'd been nothing more to them than an expendable foot solider.

At twenty-four, he had returned to the States, world-weary and old beyond his years. Then he had taken just enough money from his trust fund to attend Vanderbilt and had graduated summa cum laude. He came from a long line of highly intelligent savvy businessmen and his family had expected the prodigal son to take his place in the business world alongside his uncles and cousins. He had shocked them all when he had joined the FBI.

"Are you asleep?" Maleah asked Derek.

"Nope."

"We're almost there."

He opened his eyes and sat up straight. "Have you ever been inside a maximum security prison before today?"

"No, I haven't." She paused just long enough to inhale and exhale. "I suppose you have."

"Yes, I have."

"I don't need another lecture, so whatever you were going to say, keep it to yourself."

"I wasn't going to give you a lecture," he told her.

"Good. Just remember that I will be conducting the interview, okay?"

"Sure thing. As long as you understand that I may want to occasionally make a comment or ask a question."

"Keep your comments and questions to a minimum, will you? You're here as an observer. That is your area of expertise, isn't it, observing and forming an opinion?"

"Yes, ma'am, it is."

He had to bite his tongue to keep from telling her that he had been observing her for quite some time and had formed a definite opinion. She was, without a doubt, the most irritating, aggravating, combative woman he'd ever known.

They followed normal procedure, up to a point. They had parked in the facility's designated visitor parking lot. They had presented positive ID prior to their admission and then undergone a preliminary search by electronic surveillance instruments. But after that, they were escorted to the warden's office. Slender, gray-haired Claude Holland greeted them with quiet reserve, his facial expression giving away nothing and his handshake firm and quick. He scanned Maleah, his gaze simply sizing her up. She suspected that her appearance surprised him as it did so many people who expected a female private security agent to be big and burly, not blond and petite.

"I've arranged for you to meet with Mr. Browning in our visitation area, but there should be no physical contact with the prisoner at any time," Warden Holland said. "I mention this simply because you might normally expect to shake hands."

Maleah nodded. "I understand."

"This is not a scheduled visitation day, so there will be no other inmates seeing visitors. You'll have one hour with Browning, but if at any time before the end of that hour, you wish to leave, then simply tell one of the guards."

"Yes, thank you."

"I assume that if we need to visit Mr. Browning again, that could be arranged," Derek said.

"My instructions from the governor's office are that your visitation privileges are open-ended," Warden Holland replied. "All I ask is that you give us twenty-four hours' notice."

"Yes, of course," Derek said.

"And I should warn you, Ms. Perdue," Warden Holland said, "Browning will be in restraints during your interview."

"I assumed that was common practice for convicted murders, especially serial killers, but I have to admit that my knowledge of the penal system is limited."

"No, it's not common practice for inmates to be in shackles during visitation periods. But Browning is no ordinary inmate. His charm is deceiving," Warden Holland said. "We learned that early on. He can go from calm and cooperative one minute to aggressive and dangerous the next. He has attacked the guards and other inmates on numerous occasions."

"Thank you for telling us," Maleah said.

Claude Holland nodded and then motioned to the two uniformed guards standing at the back of the room. "Please escort Ms. Perdue and Mr. Lawrence to the visitation area. I'll call now and have Browning brought there to meet you."

Doing her best to concentrate not on where she was but on what she needed to do, Maleah walked quietly alongside Derek. Neither of them commented on their surroundings. The moment they entered the visitation area, her heartbeat accelerated, the sound drumming in her ears. There was no reason to be afraid, no reason whatsoever. She and Derek were perfectly safe.

Derek stood at her side, her shoulder brushing his arm. The two guards remained in the room, each stationed on either side of the door through which they had entered. She took a deep breath, held it, and then gradually released it, beginning with her belly and working upward to her throat. A yoga relaxation technique.

Two more guards entered the area, one on either side of the prisoner as they escorted him into the visitation area. Maleah stared directly at a handcuffed and shackled Jerome Browning. He looked older than the photos included in the Powell Agency files she and Derek had been given; but he was still tall, slender, and intriguingly handsome. Even dressed in prison garb of white shirt and pants and confined with restraints, he managed to exude an aura of worldly sophistication that totally surprised Maleah.

The moment he saw her, he smiled. A hard knot formed in the pit of her stomach. The smile was neither warm nor friendly. It was the type of smile she imagined would be on a cat's face when he had just spotted a delectable little mouse, one he looked forward to tormenting before devouring.

Chapter 6

Derek studied Browning closely, mentally comparing the information he had on the man with the man himself standing there before him. Browning was forty-nine and although he looked his age, he had the kind of features that aged well. In his youth, he would have been referred to as a pretty boy. No doubt, he had used his good looks and his charm to lure his victims, especially the female ones, to their deaths. Behind that handsome façade lay the mind of a cunning and diabolical killer.

One of the guards who had escorted their prisoner into the room indicated for Browning to take a seat. Without a moment's hesitation, he sat. His gaze never left Maleah.

Derek's gut tightened as his instincts flashed a warning—danger!

"I don't get many visitors," Browning said in a heavy Southern accent, his voice as smooth as glass. "Certainly none as pretty as you, Ms. Perdue."

Although Derek sensed Maleah tense, the action wasn't visible. He had to give her credit for not even flinching.

"And I'm unaccustomed to visiting murderers in prison," Maleah replied. "Especially ones as reprehensible as you are, Mr. Browning."

His chuckled softly. "Touché, my dear."

Maleah took the chair facing Browning, almost close enough to touch him, but not quite. She looked him square in the eye. They sat there staring at each other.

Derek barely controlled the urge to move in behind Maleah and stand at her back. His protective male instincts urged him to issue the man a warning. If you mess with this woman, you'll have to deal with me.

"Do you know why I'm here?" Maleah asked.

Browning's smile widened, showcasing a set of amazingly white, straight teeth. Apparently the state of Georgia provided great dental care for their inmates.

"I assume that you . . . or rather whatever agency you work for wants something they think only I can give them."

Derek was sure that Maleah wouldn't buy the man's I-don't-know-anything act.

"You know who I work for," Maleah said. "You were informed that Mr. Lawrence—" she inclined her head slightly backward toward Derek "—and I work for the Powell Private Security and Investigation Agency before you agreed to meet with us."

"Knowing who you work for and why you're here is not the same thing."

Maleah fixed her gaze on Browning. "I'll ask you again, do you know why I'm here?"

"We are allowed newspapers and magazines and television in here. And I occasionally have a visitor. People talk. I listen."

"What have you been listening to?"

"This and that. Whatever interests me."

"What interests you, Mr. Browning?"

That's it, Maleah, Derek thought. *Stay calm, keep things easy, remain completely in control. Don't let his evasiveness get to you.*

"Why don't you call me Jerome?" Browning's blue-eyed gaze traveled over Maleah, pausing on her breasts, which were modestly concealed by her lightweight blazer. "I'm more inclined to share confidences with people I'm on a first name basis with."

"All right, Jerome, what have you heard recently that interests you?"

He leaned back in the chair, spread his legs apart as far as the shackles allowed, and dropped his hand-cuffed hands between his thighs. "Well, Maleah . . . I can call you Maleah, can't I?"

She nodded.

Derek knew that Maleah hated the way Browning was ogling her, but she acted as if she didn't care, as if she wasn't even aware of what he was doing.

Smiling, he lifted his gaze back to her face.

"It's a pretty name for a pretty woman," Browning said. "Family name? Were you named after your grand-mother?"

He's trying your patience. Derek wished he could tell her, but suspected she knew what Browning was doing. The man wanted to get a reaction out of her, wanted her to become impatient and lose her temper.

"We've just met, Jerome," Maleah told him. "We aren't at a stage in our relationship where we exchange personal information. Right now, today, our conversation is about business."

His smile disappeared as he cocked one brow and lowered his lids until his eyes narrowed to mere slits. "Whose business, mine or yours?"

"That's what I want you to tell me. I'd like to know if your business and Powell Agency business are related."

Forced and all the more deceptive, his smile returned. "What business could I possibly conduct in here? I'm considered a maximum security inmate. My privileges are limited. No way to get my hands on a scalpel. And as I'm sure you know, without the proper tools, I can't work."

"But you could teach, couldn't you, Jerome?"

Bull's-eye! Derek wanted to pat her on the back or high-five her. She was not only holding her own with Browning, but she was scoring points.

Browning couldn't manage to maintain his phony smile. The pulse in his neck throbbed. He clenched his perfect white teeth.

Silence lingered for a couple of minutes.

Then Browning recovered quickly and grinned. "Hmm . . . yes, I see your point. Those who can, do. Those who can't, teach." He sighed dramatically. "It's a sad state of affairs, don't you think, my dear Maleah, when a master must live vicariously through the accomplishments of an apprentice."

"And is that what you're doing?"

"What do you think?"

"I think you're enjoying our visit," she replied. "I think you like playing games. I think you will eventually tell me what I want to know. But not today."

"Smart and intuitive as well as beautiful." He straightened in the chair, deliberately rattling his manacles and gaining a guard's attention. Before the guard reached him, he settled quietly, his shoulders squared and his back straight.

"I don't believe there is any point in my prolonging this visit." Maleah rose to her feet and looked down at Browning. "My time is valuable, unlike yours. If you decide you want to be more informative, send word to the warden and Mr. Lawrence and I will come back for a second visit. Otherwise . . ."

"I'd be inclined to be more cooperative if you came alone." He glanced at Derek.

Son of a bitch! He sees me as a threat. He thinks that without my presence, Maleah will be more vulnerable.

"You cooperate with me and I'll cooperate with you," she told Browning.

"Give and take. I like that. You give me something I want and I'll give you something you want."

"Agreed."

"Come back tomorrow," he told her. "Alone."

Once Maleah drove away from the penitentiary, she glanced at Derek, who hadn't said a word since they had left the warden's office where she had arranged a second meeting with Jerome Browning. At ten o'clock tomorrow. Wednesday morning.

"Well, what are you waiting for?" she asked Derek. "I know you're dying to critique the initial interview. Tell me what I did wrong, how I screwed up, what I should have done differently."

"You didn't do anything wrong. I can't think of anything you should have handled differently. You were calm, cool, and in control every minute of the interview. You even managed to surprise Browning a couple of times."

"I can't believe it. Are you actually complimenting me?"

"I'm stating facts. You did a good job. Browning now knows that he's dealing with a worthy opponent. And never doubt that's how he sees you. For him, the game has begun. You may be ahead by a couple of points, but he learned a great deal about you today, far more than you learned about him."

Maleah gripped the steering wheel, breathed deeply

and told herself not to overreact to Derek's comments. "Are you saying that you think I revealed too much about—?"

"What I said was in no way a criticism. We had a file folder filled with info about Browning. We already knew a great deal about him. He knew next to nothing about us . . . about you."

"He'll be looking for my Achilles' heel, won't he?"

"Oh yeah, without a doubt. And if he discovers it, he'll use it like a sledgehammer to beat you into the ground. But only if you let him."

"Do you think he knows that Noah Laborde was my boyfriend?"

"Our copycat killer knows," Derek said. "It's possible that, if he and Browning have communicated, as we suspect they have, Browning is well aware of the fact that you were practically engaged to Laborde."

An overwhelming sense of doom threatened Maleah. She couldn't allow the foreboding thoughts and feelings to deter her from what she had to do.

They continued along Reidsville Road until they reached GA-30W, the highway that would take them back to Vidalia.

"How about an early lunch?" Derek asked.

"I'm not hungry."

"I am and you should be. You didn't eat much breakfast."

"I ate enough."

"Think of yourself as a warrior preparing to go into battle tomorrow. You need to be in tiptop shape mentally and physically. You're going to eat a decent lunch and dinner. And in the morning, you're filling up on protein—bacon and eggs."

Maleah groaned silently, but didn't reply. She knew that Derek meant well, that he wasn't trying to take control, that he really was thinking about helping her become battle ready for tomorrow morning's confrontation with Browning.

When she didn't say anything for several minutes, he asked, "Giving me the silent treatment?"

"Huh?"

"You're pissed that I dared to suggest—"

"You don't suggest, Derek, you command."

"Yeah, I suppose I do. Sorry about that. It's just that taking care of you is part of my job."

She practically stopped the SUV in the middle of the highway, slowing down so much that vehicles doing forty-five miles an hour flew past her.

"I shouldn't have said that," he told her. "I shouldn't have put it in those precise words. Let me rephrase—"

"Don't bother."

Suddenly realizing that doing twenty-miles an hour on a major highway could be hazardous, Maleah returned the Chevy to the allowed speed limit.

"I do not need you or anyone to take care of me." She kept her gaze focused straight ahead. If she looked at Derek, she might be overcome by the urge to slap him. "I'm an adult, not a child. I don't need or want anyone to fight my battles and take the hits meant for me. And I certainly don't need anyone overseeing my meals to make sure I eat properly."

"I realize that. What I should have said is that we're partners and partners depend on each other, right? I've got your back and you've got mine. Nobody's the boss. We're two equals doing a job and looking out for each other."

"Griff told you to take care of me, didn't he?"

Derek shrugged. "You know Griff."

"Yes, I do. He thinks I can't take care of myself."

"That's not it. He's concerned. After all, you're Nic's best friend and—"

"I'm going back to the prison alone tomorrow morning to see Browning." *Don't you dare tell me that I can't go without you!*

"All right."

"That was too easy. You agreed too quickly."

"You can see Browning without me. I'll wait in the warden's office."

"What's the catch?"

"The only catch is that we make a bargain."

"Uh-oh, I don't like the sound of that."

"You can see Browning alone, but you'll allow me to coach you before every visit."

"You mean you want to tell me what to do and what to say and—"

"I want to coach you, advise you, work with you."

"I'll think about it."

"It's not negotiable," he told her. "We strike a bargain or you don't see Browning alone."

Michelle Allen watched her seven-year-old niece Jaelyn as she swung across the monkey bars on her backyard swing set. Her brother's only child reminded her of herself in so many ways, and not just physically, although the resemblance was striking. But then she and Keith looked enough alike to be twins. She had always been a bit of a tomboy and enjoyed playing sports. She had excelled at basketball in high school and won a basketball scholarship to college. She'd been good, but not quite good enough for the WNBA.

"Watch me, Aunt Chelle," Jaelyn called to her. "I'm going to do a somersault in mid-air."

Michelle jumped to her feet. "Be careful. Don't fall." She raced toward the swing set positioned over an enormous bed of mulch, put there to protect Jaelyn if she fell. Keith and Shannon were conscientious parents and tried not to be overprotective. But it wasn't easy for them, walking that fine line, especially not with an only child, a child they knew would be their only biological offspring. And since at thirty-nine, Michelle doubted she would ever have children of her own, she felt a strong maternal protectiveness toward her niece.

Since Keith and Shannon didn't entrust their daughter to just anybody, they seldom had any alone time for just the two of them. When she was given a week off from work after her last assignment for the Powell Agency, Michelle offered to babysit her niece so that her brother and his wife could get away for a long weekend alone. They had left early Saturday morning and were due to return sometime tonight. A part of her was eager to return to work, to become involved with a new case, but another part of her hated to leave Paducah and the genuine pleasure she found in playing doting aunt to a child she loved as if she were her own.

Jaelyn performed a perfect mid-air somersault, caught hold of the overhead bars and lifted herself atop the swing set. Beaming with pride about her accomplishment, she tossed back her head and laughed. Michelle released the anxious breath she'd been holding and smiled adoringly up at her niece.

Michelle applauded. "Great job, sweetie. Now, come on down and let's go clean up for supper. Your mom and dad are due home later, so we'll want you fed and bathed and in bed before they get here. We don't want them to think I've been spoiling you."

"But you do spoil me, Aunt Chelle."

"That should be our little secret."

Jaelyn climbed down the side steps, taking her own sweet time. When her feet hit the ground, she raced straight to Michelle and threw her arms up and around her aunt's waist.

"I love you to pieces," Jaelyn said. "I wish you didn't have to leave when Mommy and Daddy come home. I wish you could live with us all the time."

Michelle leaned down, hugged Jaelyn and then lifted her off her feet for a forehead kiss. "I love you to pieces, too, angel pie."

As Michelle eased her niece back on her feet and grasped her little hand, Jaelyn giggled. "That's such a silly thing to call me—angel pie. Why do you call me that?"

"That's what my daddy used to call me," Michelle said. "You don't remember Papa Allen. He went to heaven before you were born."

"He was my daddy's daddy, too, wasn't he?"

"That's right. Your Papa Allen called me angel pie and he called your father pudding head."

"My daddy's a pudding head. That's so funny, but sometimes my daddy is funny. Mommy tells him he's being silly."

"Oh, he's silly all right."

Hand-in-hand, sharing aunt-and-niece conversation, they walked across the yard, onto the back porch and into the kitchen, both of them smiling happily. Tomorrow morning, she would return to Knoxville and return to work. But tonight, she would eat hot dogs and potato chips, oversee a seven-year-old's bath, watch the Disney Channel until eight o'clock, and listen to Jaelyn read aloud another chapter of *Could You? Would You?* before they exchanged good night hugs and kisses.

* * *

Tonight was the night. In a few hours he would slip the scalpel into his pocket, leave his room, and follow through with his plan for the fifth Copycat Carver murder. The closer it came to the actual moment when he would jab the scalpel into the side of the victim's neck and then slice across his throat, the more excited he would become. It had always been that way for him, even that first time, so many years ago. To say that he had been born to kill might be inaccurate. Surely no one was born to be a killer. But even as a child, he had derived a thrilling pleasure from capturing and killing animals. Birds and rabbits and squirrels. And then later on, neighborhood household pets. Cats and dogs.

He had been fourteen when he'd graduated from animals to human beings. He clearly remembered that day as if it were yesterday and not thirty years ago. They say you never forget your first. And that was certainly true for him. Renee Billaud had been a promiscuous sixteen-year-old with enticing tits the size of ripe cantaloupes. He had followed her into the woods where she had met a local man, a married man whose wife had been a friend of his grandmother's. He had watched them fucking, his penis growing steadily harder with each passing minute. As soon as the man had finished with her, he had zipped up his pants and walked off, leaving Renee lying on a bed of leaves beneath an enormous old oak tree. While her blouse was still unbuttoned, revealing her luscious breasts, and her skirt was still hiked up around her waist, he had come out from behind the bushes and stared her.

"What were you doing, you nasty boy, spying on me?"

He hadn't answered her. Instead, he had pounced on her. At first she had fought him like a wildcat, but once he'd managed to unzip his pants and free his penis, she had settled down and begun laughing when she realized he didn't know what he was doing.

"You've never done this before, have you?"

She had reached down, circled his penis with her hot little hand and guided him into her. He had pumped up and down only a couple of times before ejaculating. Renee had seemed to think his premature climax was amusing and proceeded to joke about what a poor lover he had been.

He would never forget the look in her eyes when he had tightened his hands around her neck and squeezed. And squeezed. Until she was gasping for air and struggling to loosen the death grip he had on her throat.

He had never known such pure pleasure as he did the moment she stopped breathing. A sexual orgasm paled in comparison.

Lost in a haze of sweet memories, he barely heard the tapping on his bedroom door. Already aroused and ready for action, he walked across the room, opened the door and smiled at the woman standing in the hallway. He had met her in the hotel bar last night and had struck up a casual conversation. She'd been one of the women he had noticed Sunday night. A woman on the prowl.

"Are you going to invite me in or do you want to do me out here and shock the other guests?"

He grabbed her arm, pulled her into his room, and kicked the door closed behind them.

Chapter 7

Maleah had needed time away from Derek. Time to clear her head. Time to think. Common sense told her that Derek was not her enemy, that she didn't need to do battle with him again and again just to prove a point.

And that point would be?

He could not control her. She would never allow anyone to have that kind of power over her, not ever again. Just when she thought she had finally come to terms with the terrors of her childhood and teen years, something or someone forced her to face those old demons.

Admit it, you're tempted to lean on Derek.

The thought of being even partially dependent on someone else for any reason terrified Maleah. And that irrational fear demanded she never relinquish the control she vigorously maintained over her life.

She had tried talking to her brother Jackson about their childhoods, about their stepfather, about the years they had lived under his tyrannical rule. But revisiting the past had proved painful for both of them.

"There's not a damn thing we can do to change what happened," Jackson had told her. "There's no need to dredge up the past. It's better left there, dead and buried with Nolan."

Her brother was right, of course. But sometimes she felt as if Nolan Reeves was reaching out from beyond the grave to influence her decisions. Deep inside her, the little girl who had lived in terror of her stepfather still existed. The little girl who had not known that her older brother had made a bargain with the devil in order to protect her. Nolan had punished Jack for every perceived misdeed by taking him to the old carriage shed and whipping him unmercifully. He had whipped the blood out of Maleah's legs and bottom only once. After that, although she lived in constant fear, he had never touched her again. What she hadn't realized at the time was that Jack had taken all her beatings for her.

She owed Jack more than she could ever repay. He had protected her as best he could and she would always be grateful. Jack's bargain with Nolan had saved her from more physical abuse, but not from Nolan's iron-fisted control over her life or his incessant verbal abuse.

Maleah had undergone therapy, paid for by Jack, when she'd been in college. The months of in-depth counseling had helped her immensely, enabling her to live a reasonably normal life. *Whatever normal is.* But nothing short of a lobotomy could erase the memories that still plagued her, often on a subconscious level.

"Damn you, Nolan Reeves. Damn your mean, black-hearted soul to hell."

Maleah's hands trembled. Her stomach lurched as emotions from her long-ago childhood resurfaced.

Don't do this to yourself.

Don't let your fears and uncertainties weaken you.

You have only one battle to fight, one enemy, one combatant that you have to outsmart and outmaneuver—Jerome Browning, not Derek Lawrence.

Checking her wristwatch, Maleah noted it was nearly eight o'clock. She had turned down Derek's invitation to join him for dinner that evening, but she couldn't avoid seeing him again tonight. They had made a deal—he would coach her on how to handle Browning and he wouldn't insist on accompanying her to the visitor's area at the prison.

She needed to freshen up and get her head on straight before Derek showed up at her door. He tended to be punctual, which meant she had less than ten minutes to throw cold water in her face, smear on a little lipstick and add some blush to her pale cheeks before he arrived.

Jerome usually spent the hours after dinner working on his handbook, a sort of *How to Get Away with Murder* manual. The idea had come to him nearly a year ago after he'd had a dream about the night he had been captured. In retrospect, he could see quite clearly the mistakes he had made. If he had it to do over again . . .

But there would be no second chances to get it right, only the opportunity to train others. He had no doubt that once he completed his work on the informative handbook, publishers would beat a path to his door. His book could make him even more famous than he already was. And how opportune that Maleah Perdue had come into his life today, just when he had begun plotting the chapter on manipulation.

The chapter heading would be: How to Use Others to Get What You Want.

And just what did he want from Maleah?

Jerome smiled.

Maleah was a delectable little morsel. She looked like nothing more than a sweet piece of blonde fluff. But looks could be deceiving. He knew that fact better than anyone. Hadn't he used his handsome face to his advantage all of his life? How many people had trusted him without question because of the way he looked? Poor fools. They never suspected that behind the pleasing façade, the mind of a genius existed, a mind capable of executing brilliantly complicated plans.

After being apprehended and charged with nine murders, hadn't he used his superior intelligence to avoid the death penalty? He had been in possession of a valuable commodity, one that both law enforcement and the families of six missing girls had been willing to bargain for on his terms. The whereabouts of those six teenage girls had been his ace in the hole. Not quite a get-out-of-jail-free card, but the next best thing.

He had been barely sixteen when he had killed Mary Jane Ivy, a meek little mouse of a girl who had lived down the street from him. He had never killed a person before that, although he had fantasized about it for years. During the next four years, he had killed five other girls. And he had gotten away with all six murders. No one suspected the good-looking high school jock, the boy voted most likely to succeed by his senior class. Not being found out had been almost as exhilarating as the kills themselves. Almost.

He had been locked up in this godforsaken hellhole for nine years now, with only occasional opportunities to participate in conversations that he found intellectually stimulating. A rare visitor from time to time. An intelligent, young minister certain he could save Jerome's soul. His former lawyer, who hadn't been in touch since his final appeal had been denied.

But tomorrow, Maleah would return for a second

visit, this time without her watchdog. He did not like the man with the dark eyes who had studied him as if he were a specimen under a microscope.

If he played this just right, he should be able to gain hours of pleasure from holding out a carrot stick in front of Maleah, letting her see it, smell it, lick it, even nibble a tiny bite.

Jerome laid his journal aside, fell back onto his cot and rested his hands behind his head. Closing his eyes, he visualized the way she would look tomorrow morning, all blond and golden and sweet. So very sweet.

"Ah, Maleah . . . Maleah . . ." He whispered her name. "Sweet Maleah."

The moment he tapped for the second time, Maleah swung open the door and much to his surprise actually smiled at him.

"Come on in." She waved her arm through the air, inviting him to enter.

He held out the plastic bag he had brought with him. She eyed the offering.

"Thin sliced turkey on wheat," he said. "Lettuce, tomato, and mustard only. No mayo. No onion." When she accepted his gift, he added, "A small bag of baked chips and an unsweetened tea, with several packets of Splenda."

He watched the play of emotions on her face and knew a part of her hated the fact that he remembered her likes and dislikes, that he knew she never used mayonnaise and ate only cooked onions. And she always preferred tea over cola, if tea was available.

She grabbed the sack. "Thanks. I appreciate your thinking of me, but I'm really not—"

"You've been skipping too many meals," he reminded her. "You need to eat."

He closed and locked the door behind him, then waited for her to blast him for daring to tell her what she should do.

But she surprised him again by taking the bag over to the desk, emptying the contents and saying, "You're right. I need to eat. And actually, I am hungry."

He eyed her suspiciously. It was on the tip of his tongue to ask her who she was and what she had done with the real Maleah Perdue.

"Sit," he told her. "Eat."

She pulled out a chair and sat; then she removed the paper wrapping from her sandwich and took a bite.

"I'll put on a pot of decaf coffee," Derek said. "Coffee will be good with our dessert."

She looked at the two small Styrofoam containers she had removed from the sack. "I usually don't eat dessert."

"It's Italian Cream cake."

Maleah moaned. "My favorite." She set aside the cake containers, tore the paper from the straw and inserted the straw through the hole in the lid of the iced tea cup.

Derek had observed Maleah on a daily basis while they had worked as partners on the Midnight Killer case and knew she struggled to maintain control over every aspect of her life. Being short and curvy, maintaining an ideal weight was a challenge for her. Under ordinary circumstances, he would never tempt her with a fattening dessert, but in an odd sort of way, tonight's meal paralleled the last meal served a person before they were executed the next day. In the morning, she would be walking into an arena to do battle against an opponent who would go for the jugular. He would do it subtly, hoping to take her unaware.

Derek rinsed out the coffeepot, poured in fresh bottled water, filled the reserve tank, and added the decaf provided by housekeeping. Once he set the machine to brew, he glanced at Maleah, who had a mouthful of the turkey sandwich in her mouth. He grinned.

"I spoke to Sanders this afternoon," Derek told her. "He wanted us to know that, by sometime tomorrow, they should have the names of everyone who has visited Browning and the dates of the visits."

Maleah swallowed, wiped her mouth on a paper napkin and said, "It's possible that our copycat killer and Browning exchanged letters and that Browning may have called him, but both the letters and the phone calls were probably monitored since he's a high-risk prisoner. Browning would have had to be very careful about what he said over the phone."

"Yes, he would have," Derek agreed. "My guess would be that if there has been any contact between the copycat and Browning, it started with a visit."

"I understand that my meeting with Browning in the hopes of bargaining with him for information is my top priority, but I don't want to be excluded from the investigation. I want to be part of every aspect of—"

"No one is going to exclude you."

"But if I'm at the prison every day—"

"Who said you'd be visiting Browning every day?"

"I just assumed—"

"You assumed wrong." Derek strode across the room, his gaze linked with hers as he approached. "You'll see him tomorrow, but after that, we will take it slow and easy. We want him playing this game by our rules, not the other way around."

"I understand." She nibbled on the sandwich.

Derek reached over, grasped the back of a chair by the windows and dragged it over to the table. After he sat, he picked up the bag of chips, opened it and offered it to her. She shook her head. He pulled out several chips and popped them into his mouth.

"When the time comes, I want to be the one who questions each of Browning's recent visitors," Maleah said.

"If we can locate them, and that's a big if, we will question them together, as partners. If the copycat visited Browning, I don't think he would have used his real name or given his current address, do you?"

"No, of course not, but the Powell Agency has a high success rate of tracking down people who do not want to be found."

"We're overlooking one other possibility—our copycat may not have visited Browning. He may not have ever been in contact with him."

"Then how could he possibly know so many details about Browning's murders, details that were never released to the press?"

"He could be in law enforcement."

Maleah frowned.

"Or he could have hired a PI or be a PI himself and found a way to dig up the info."

She shook her head. "I think Browning knows something."

"Browning wants you to believe he knows something."

After finishing off one half of her sandwich, she washed it down with the tea and dumped the rest in the wastebasket by the desk. She wiped her hands off on the napkin and tossed it, too.

"You're practically psychic when it comes to reading people." Maleah might not be Derek's biggest fan, but she respected his ability as a profiler and more recently as a detective. "Paint me a picture. In your opinion, does Browning have any personal connection to the copycat?"

"I'm intuitive, yes. Psychic, no. I leave all that paranormal stuff to Dr. Meng and her protégés."

"I'm surprised Griff didn't enlist Yvette or one of her protégés to interview Browning." Maleah eyed the cake container.

"I doubt Browning would have agreed to see anyone other than you. Griff knew the right person to send. Neither Griff nor I think it was a coincidence that the copycat chose to mimic the killer who murdered your former boyfriend. It's as if he chose you for a specific reason."

"Yeah, but the only problem is that we have no idea what that reason is."

"We can make some educated guesses."

"Such as?" she asked.

"Such as you're the copycat's ultimate target." When her face paled, Derek quickly added, "Or you were chosen because you're Nicole Powell's best friend. Or because the copycat is using your connection to Browning as a red herring to send us off on a wild goose chase."

"What's your intuition telling you?"

"The copycat and Browning have, at the very least, met and talked. I don't know if Browning is pulling the strings and the copycat is a disciple or if the copycat used Browning's knowledge for his own purposes."

"Neither Griff nor Nic were involved in Browning's capture and arrest, nor was I. Why would he be targeting the Powell Agency?"

"Excellent question. Griff has a theory, as does Nic. And I have several scenarios in mind, too, but we have absolutely nothing conclusive at this point."

"We need information from that son of bitch and he knows it." Maleah grabbed the cake container, flipped open the lid and eyed the cake hungrily. "He's going to want to bargain with me, to see what he can get out of me in exchange for what he knows."

Derek slid the other cake container over in front of him, then removed the cellophane wrap from two plastic forks and handed one fork to Maleah. She eyed the fork as if it were a snake and then grunted and snatched the fork out of his hand. He sliced his fork through the moist cake, balanced a bite on the fork and lifted it into the air, saluting her with the delicious morsel. She watched while he put the bite into his mouth.

"Just one piece of cake won't hurt you," he told her. "Think of the pleasure it'll give you. There's nothing quite like a sugar high to perk a girl up when she's down."

"I don't need a crutch of any kind. Not alcohol or drugs or gambling or shopping . . . or sugar!"

Without a moment's hesitation, she jabbed the fork into the cake and then shoved her piece of cake, container and all, across the table and into the wastebasket.

Stunned for half a second, Derek stared at her, then burst out laughing. My God, she had no idea that her biggest weakness, the crutch she relied on every day of her life, was being a major control freak.

When they returned from a moonlight stroll on the beach, they found a gift basket waiting for them outside their suite. Errol lifted the basket while Cyrene opened the attached card.

"It just says Happy Honeymoon." Eyeing the bottle of wine, the box of gourmet Swiss chocolates, the luscious in-season fruit and a sampling of imported cheeses,

Cyrene moaned with anticipation. "I can't think of anything better than a glass of wine before bedtime."

Hoisting the gift basket so that he could hold it with one hand, Errol reached out and unlocked the door to their suite. As his bride slipped past him, he whispered, "I can think of something better than wine."

Understanding the implication of his comment, she giggled and began undressing the moment he closed the door behind them and dumped the basket on the table in the entryway. Taking his cue from Cyrene, he unbuttoned his shirt and tossed it on the floor. By the time he loosened his belt, she had already stripped down to her panties.

He couldn't get out of his slacks and briefs quickly enough, but for a full sixty seconds, he stood and watched—totally spellbound—as his wife slowly, provocatively slid her bikini panties down, down, down, and off. His heart beat wildly. His penis hardened.

When he reached for Cyrene, she evaded his grasp. Instead, she raced over to the bed, the covers already turned down by maid service, and placed herself in the center. She arched her back, the action thrusting her breasts up and inviting him to touch and taste and enjoy. Errol kicked his briefs aside and moved toward the bed, never taking his eyes off the long, slender naked body of the woman he loved.

He straddled her hips and positioned himself over her. She lifted her arms up and around his neck, pulling him down until it was flesh against flesh. His penis probed for entry. She opened her thighs, lifted her hips and took him inside her body.

"Oh God, baby, you feel so good," he told her, his voice a husky moan.

"I love having you inside me," she said and then kissed him.

They made love for the fourth time that day and yet were as hungry for each other as they had been that morning. Errol wondered if he would ever get enough of Cyrene. Probably not. Even when they were old and gray, he would still want her, still love her, still be grateful that she had agreed to be his wife.

An hour later, shortly after midnight, they emerged from the bathroom where they had showered together. Errol belted his white robe and walked over to the entryway table while Cyrene slipped into a red lace teddy and sat on the edge of the bed to towel dry her curly hair.

He picked up the gift basket. "Want some wine now, Mrs. Patterson?"

"Wine would be lovely, Mr. Patterson." She glanced at the bedside clock. "We can toast to another glorious day of married life. It's after midnight, so if it's already tomorrow that means I've been Mrs. Errol Patterson for eleven days."

Errol removed the huge red bow and the clear cellophane wrapping from the gift basket, lifted the wine bottle and inspected it. "Hey, this is some of the good stuff. There's no twist-off cap." He chuckled.

"Only the best for us," she teased.

"I've got the best." He winked at her.

"Want me to get the glasses?"

"No need," he told her as he transferred the bottle to his left hand and retrieved the two long-stemmed wine glasses from the basket. "Want some chocolate or cheese or—?"

"I want it all," she admitted, "but I'll be a good girl and limit myself to one glass of wine."

He brought the bottle and glasses over to the bed. She took the glasses from him and held them while he rummaged in the nightstand drawer for the corkscrew that he had left there after opening the bottle of champagne the hotel had included in their "Welcome" package the day they arrived. After uncorking the wine, he poured each glass half full before placing the bottle on the nightstand.

He took one of the glasses from Cyrene. "Here's to our being this deliriously happy for the rest of our lives."

She clicked her glass to his, said, "Amen to that," and lifted the glass to her lips.

After he dimmed the lights, leaving the room bathed in moonlight, they sat in bed together, talking, laughing, sipping the wine, and making plans for their return to Tennessee. He knew that Cyrene was eager to decorate their new house in Farragut, a small town not far from Powell Agency headquarters in Knoxville. They discussed how lucky she was that there had been a teaching position open at a local elementary school. With school starting in early August, she would have about five weeks to put their new house in order.

Errol yawned. "Man, I'm getting sleepy. Must be the mixture of great sex and good wine." He removed the white terrycloth robe and flung it to the foot of the bed.

Cyrene sighed and nodded. "Must be. I can barely keep my eyes open."

Errol switched off the bedside lamp and then leaned over, kissed her, ran his hand from her shoulder to her hip and stilled instantly. The last thing Cyrene remembered was the sound of her husband snoring.

He had waited patiently. The lights in the luxury villa suite had dimmed over an hour ago, but he hadn't rushed in immediately. The odds were that Mr. and Mrs. Patterson had been sound asleep for most if not all of that hour, while he had been waiting and watching. But it was better to be certain.

Errol Patterson never left his wife's side. The two had been inseparable since they arrived in the Bahamas. He really didn't want to kill them both. Doing so would have meant deviating from the plan. The Carver had never murdered a couple.

His solution to that problem had been to send them a gift basket that included a bottle of expensive "doctored" wine.

He approached the French doors that opened onto the villa's private patio and pool. He stopped, listened, and peered through the doors into the darkened bedroom. Moonlight cast a glimmering path across the floor to the bed. After removing the small, carbide steel-bladed glass cutter from his inside pocket, he worked several minutes to make a precise round incision near the door handle. Once that was done, he pushed gently on the circle until it fell inward and hit the tile floor with a tinkling crash. He returned the cutter to his pocket. Without hesitation, he reached through the opening and unlocked the door from the inside.

He eased open the door, slipped into the room and managed to avoid stepping on the broken glass. Pausing to allow his eyesight to adjust to the darkness, he heard a mixture of sounds. Snoring. Deep breathing. The ocean waves hitting the nearby beach. The hum of distant music, no doubt coming from the resort's patio lounge that stayed open until 2:00 AM.

He walked over to the bed. Two bodies. One male. One female. Both deep in sleep. Sufficiently drugged.

He smiled.

The sheet rested at the woman's waist. Her breasts

strained against the sheer lace material of her teddy. He was tempted to touch her, but he didn't.

The kill would take only seconds, the death less than two minutes. But moving the body would require more time.

He reached inside his jacket pocket and removed the new scalpel, the fifth in a package of ten. Drawing closer to the edge of the bed, he studied the man's head and neck before choosing the exact spot—the jugular vein. With one quick, precise move, he jabbed the scalpel blade through the flesh and into the vein beneath. Blood gushed. He slid the blade down and across, slicing through the carotid arteries on both sides. He watched the life drain out of Errol Patterson's body.

I'm sorry to make you a widow while you're still on your honeymoon, lovely Cyrene. And I'm sorry that you'll awaken to a bloody bed and a dead husband.

Errol Patterson was a rather large man, probably six feet tall and weighing in at around one-ninety. But he could handle Patterson. He had maneuvered larger bodies.

He flipped back the bloody sheet, took hold of Patterson's ankles and dragged him off the bed and onto the floor. As his body hit the hard tile, it made a loud thud. He glanced up at the sleeping woman. She hadn't moved. Good.

He pulled Patterson's blood-splattered, lifeless body from the bedroom and into the bathroom. Then he turned on the tub faucets.

I never left them where I killed them. I moved the body, usually near a river or lake or stream. I even dragged a woman from her bedroom outside to her pool. There is something peaceful about water, don't you think?

Near the bathtub overrunning with water would have to do. He saw no point in dragging the body outside to the pool and certainly not all the way to the beach. No need to risk being seen.

Chapter 8

Cyrene woke with the worst headache of her life. She came to slowly, painfully, her eyelids flicking. Moaning as she stretched her neck, she tried to focus on the mundane task of keeping her eyes open. When she parted her lips, she realized that her tongue was stuck to the roof of her mouth and her throat felt parched. She remembered drinking a glass of wine with Errol last night after they had made love and showered together. Surely, she hadn't gotten drunk on a single glass. Had she drunk more than she thought she had?

"Errol . . ." She forced her eyes wide open, stared up at the unmoving ceiling fan and spread her arm across the bed, searching for her husband.

Dim early morning sunlight reflecting off the patio pool danced in waving patterns on the ceiling.

Ah, another day in paradise.

She ran her fingertips across the sheet and found that she was alone in the bed. Apparently Errol was already awake and had gotten up. He was probably in the bathroom. She could hear running water, but it didn't sound like the shower. Flipping over toward the side of the bed, she stretched her arms over her head, extended her legs and curved her feet backwards. When she rose from the bed, her bare feet encountered the cool tile floor.

Where are my house slippers?

Cyrene rounded the foot of the bed, intending to surprise Errol in the bathroom, but as she passed by his side of the bed, she caught a glimpse of something red on the sheets.

What in the world?

They hadn't spilled any wine in the bed, had they?

She moved closer, getting a better look at the dark red stains on the snowy white sheets.

How odd. It looks like blood.

Instinct kicked in, a primeval sixth sense that warned of danger.

"Errol?" She backed away from the bed. "Errol . . . Errol . . ."

Flooded with a barrage of frightening thoughts, Cyrene shook her head in denial, refusing to believe, trying to convince herself that nothing was wrong.

"Errol, where are you?" Silence. "Please, honey, answer me."

Silence.

As if her limbs were activated by some sort of remote control, her legs and feet moved, carrying her toward the bathroom. Gazing down as she walked, she noticed a smear of dried red liquid stretching from the bed to the bathroom.

Suddenly she went numb, unable to feel her hands and feet. The thunderous roar of her heartbeat threatened to deafen her. This wasn't real. It wasn't happening.

Standing in the bathroom door, she stared at the body lying on the floor beside the bathtub overflowing with water.

Errol? Oh my God, Errol.

His eyes were closed.

A thin red line marred the perfection of his smooth, clean-shaven neck and rivulets of dried blood descended from that red line like trinkets on a charm bracelet.

Cyrene stood perfectly still, her mind unable to process what she saw.

And then, in the quiet stillness of her honeymoon suite, Mrs. Errol Patterson screamed. And screamed. And screamed.

Maleah squared her shoulders and took a deep breath before entering the prison's visitation area. She didn't look back at Derek nor did she glance at the guard escorting her. After showering and dressing— khaki slacks and dark green tailored blouse—she had met Derek downstairs for breakfast. She had managed to down a cup of coffee and eat a few bites of blueberry muffin, hoping to quiet the tempest in her belly. Although she had done her best to assure her partner that she was not nervous and was ready for today's meeting with Jerome Browning, she sensed that he knew she was simply putting up a good front. And that she was doing it as much for herself as for him.

If you can act as if you are self-assured and confident, then you've already won half the battle.

She remained standing as she waited for the guards to bring Browning from his cell. Thinking about what she was going to say and wondering how he would respond, she heard rather than saw Browning enter the visitation area. When she looked directly at him, he stared back at her, that weirdly pleasant and completely unnerving smile growing wider and wider as he drew closer.

The guards instructed him to sit. He sat.

"Good morning, Maleah. I hope you had a pleasant night. I certainly did." He licked his lips. "I dreamed about you and woke this morning eager to see you again."

Is that the best you've got? she wanted to say. *A little sexual innuendo isn't going to unnerve me in the least. Not when you're in shackles and there are three armed guards in the room with us.*

"I slept quite well, thank you," she lied to him. "A restful, dreamless sleep."

"I assume Mr. Lawrence also slept well. Any man sharing your bed would sleep well after . . ." He didn't finish the sentence, but the implication was obvious.

Was he fishing to find out if she and Derek were lovers? Or was he merely hoping the comment would insult her? Either way, she had no intention of responding.

"We have an hour," Maleah said as she sat across from Browning. "I think we've wasted enough time on meaningless, uninteresting chit-chat."

"Is your love life meaningless and uninteresting?" His smile never wavered.

"Do you know why I'm here, Jerome? Why I'm wasting my valuable time even talking to someone like you?"

"Someone like me?" He laughed. "Someone handsome and brilliant and gifted. And if I may be so immodest, someone who has been told that he is a superlative lover."

Egotistical, maniacal, psychopathic monster! "You are someone who has murdered fifteen people." She

paused before adding, "That we know of. You are someone who will spend the rest of his life slowly rotting
away in prison."

He lifted his bound hands, gesturing toward his
heart. "You wound me with such harsh words." His
smile turned quickly to a frown, his expression one of
mock sadness.

"Do you know why I'm here?" She repeated her initial question.

"All work and no play makes Maleah a dull girl."

"You know why I'm here and what I want."

He stretched as languidly as his restrained body
could and glanced from the guard on his right to the
guard on his left, both men standing several feet behind him. "What am I going to do with such a dull, dull
visitor, gentlemen? All she wants to do is talk business."

Maleah eased back from the edge of the seat and
crossed her arms. "The warden has granted us an hour
today, Jerome. But if you're not in the mood to talk
about what I want to talk about . . ." She uncrossed her
arms, glanced at her wristwatch, tapped the glass face
and said, "Five minutes. That's as long as I'll wait for
you to tell me something that interests me."

Browning remained silent for four minutes. The silence in the large, nearly empty room echoed with the
sound of their quiet breathing. One guard cleared his
throat. Another coughed a couple of times.

"You're here because you think I might know who
has mimicked my unique modus operandi almost perfectly and has recently killed four people."

Finally.

"And do you know who he is?" she asked.

As if believing he now had the upper hand for the
time being, he smiled and shrugged.

"All right," she said. "You tell me what you want in exchange for answering my question."

"Ah, Maleah, my sweet beauty, you're very bright. You catch on quickly. Games are so much fun, don't you think?"

"You're wasting time," she told him.

"All right. I'll cut straight to the chase." He chuckled. "I want to know what color panties you're wearing."

Good God! Without blinking an eye, she said, "Beige. With lace trim."

He closed his eyes, licked his lips as if savoring a delicious morsel and sighed with a sickening sound of satisfaction.

"I assume the copycat killer is an admirer," Jerome said. "I assume he has studied my work. Perhaps, he's even communicated with me."

"Has he?"

"That's another question that requires payment."

Damn you, Browning.

"You haven't answered the first question yet. Not to my satisfaction." She looked him in the eye.

"I don't know who the copycat killer is," he said, and then hurriedly added, "Not exactly, but . . ."

"But what?"

"There are things I do know. Things that can help you find him."

"Why should I believe you?"

He grinned.

"Even if you answer every question I ask, how would I know whether or not you were lying to me?" she asked.

"You'd have to take me on faith. But if you do that, I can promise you that in time, you'll discover everything I tell you is true."

"Okay, let's say I take you on faith. But first, you'll

have to give me something right now, something to prove to me that I can believe you."

"He's going to kill again soon, if he hasn't already."

She snorted. "That's it? Sorry, Jerome, but you're going to have to do better than that."

"I'll tell you something about the next person he's going to kill, if you'll tell me something I'd love to know."

"My bra matches my panties," she said glibly.

"That information paints such an erotic picture in my mind," he told her. "But that wasn't my question."

"Then what is it?"

As nonchalantly as if he were asking her about her favorite flavor of ice cream, he asked, "Was he your first?"

She stared at him, puzzled by his question.

"Noah Laborde," Browning said. "Was he your first lover?"

She should have been prepared for this, but she wasn't. Damn it. She wasn't.

"You do remember Noah, don't you? Good-looking young man, fresh out of college. Quite an up-and-comer in the Atlanta business world about twelve years ago."

Get hold of yourself, Maleah. He's trying to rattle you. Don't let him get away with it. Show him what you're made of.

"Yes," she said.

"Yes, what?"

"Yes, I remember Noah Laborde. And yes, he was my first lover."

Browning smiled as if he thought he had won a great victory. He hadn't. But she had. He just didn't know it yet.

"He's going to begin varying the sex of his victims.

You won't know from one kill to the next if he will choose a man or a woman."

"We learned that from your files, so we assumed if he followed your lead, he wouldn't stick with two female kills followed by two males."

"Looks like you're a step ahead of me."

"Tell me something else, something I don't already know."

"Why should I? It's not my fault that I told you something you already knew."

"Ah, come on, Jerome. Fair's fair."

"You surprise me."

"Do I?"

"I believe I may have underestimated you, sweet Maleah."

"If you have, you wouldn't be the first." She stood up and glared down at him. "Pay your debt. Give me some information that I can use. If not, when I walk out of here today, I won't be back."

"You could be bluffing."

"Only one way to find out—call my bluff."

She turned around and walked toward the exit door, her escort following. Just as he unlocked the door and opened it, Browning called out to her.

"You'll be back. You won't be able to stay away."

She paused for half a second and then started through the door.

"The next victim won't be brown-eyed," he told her.

She kept walking without responding in any way. Keeping in step with her guard escort, she followed him back to the warden's office where Derek was waiting.

Derek took one look at her and knew the session with Browning had rattled her. But he also knew that she was okay. He could see the steely determination in her eyes and the stiffness in her spine. Whatever had transpired between her and Jerome, she had come through the battle with nothing more than a minor flesh wound.

She acknowledged his presence with a glance, then marched straight to the warden. "I won't be back tomorrow."

"Then you're finished with——?" the warden said.

"No, I'm not finished with Mr. Browning. Not by a long shot. But he needs to think that I am."

Warden Holland nodded. "I will need twenty-four hours' notice before your next visit."

She shook his hand, said thanks, and motioned to Derek that she was ready to leave. He tried to talk to her, but she told him flat out that she was in no mood for conversation.

"Not now. We can talk on the way back to Vidalia."

And so he waited, giving her the time she needed to decompress after game playing with a cunning madman.

When they reached the designated parking area, she said, "You drive." And then she tossed him her keys. He grabbed the keys mid-air, remotely unlocked the SUV and, gentleman that he was, opened the passenger door for her.

And then he waited until they were several miles from the penitentiary before he said, "The warden is going to have a list of all of Browning's visitors for the past year, along with the names and addresses of the people who have written to him and the names and phone numbers of the people he's called compiled and sent to me and to Powell headquarters as an e-mail attachment. He's promised we'll have the information by the end of the day."

"Great. We've finally got something to work with, don't we?"

"Yep." When she didn't continue their conversation, he asked, "Are you all right?"

"Yes, why wouldn't I be?"

"We'll have to talk about your interview with Browning. I'll need to know what he said, everything you can remember."

Maleah adjusted her seat so that she could lean further back. She rested her head on the cushioned leather and folded her hands together in her lap.

"He asked what color my panties were and I told him beige with lace trim and that I was wearing a matching bra."

"Son of a bitch." Derek growled the comment under his breath.

"He still didn't give me the copycat killer's name or a description of him. But he did say that he knew things about this guy that could help us find him."

"Did you believe him?"

"I didn't disbelieve him."

"He's playing you. He may not know a damn thing."

"He said if the copycat follows the Carver's MO, he'll alter the sex of his victims pretty much willy-nilly."

"Something we already knew."

"We didn't know that his next victim wouldn't have brown eyes."

"What?"

"He called out to me just as I was leaving. He said the next victim wouldn't be brown-eyed."

"How could he possibly know that?" Derek suspected that Browning wouldn't say something like that off the top of his head. If he wanted Maleah to come back to see him, he would try to impress her with his knowledge.

"I have no idea, but maybe we should check and see what color the first four victims' eyes were. Maybe there's a pattern."

"We'll contact the agency—"

Derek's phone rang. No music. Just a strong, routine ring tone.

With one hand on the wheel and his eyes fixed on the road ahead, he pulled the phone from his pocket, hit the On button and said, "Derek Lawrence speaking," without checking caller ID.

"I want you and Maleah at the Vidalia Municipal Airport as soon as you can get there," Griff Powell said. "There's a charter plane waiting to fly y'all to Atlanta. Nic and I will be taking off in the Powell jet within the next thirty minutes. We'll pick y'all up in Atlanta. We're flying from there straight to Nassau. The copycat struck again last night. He killed Errol Patterson. Errol's wife found his body in the bathroom of their hotel suite. She's under a doctor's care at the moment and heavily sedated. She's going to need all the help we can give her."

"We'll pick up our bags at the hotel and drive straight to the airport."

Succinct and to the point. Conversation ended.

"What's happened?" Maleah asked.

"The copycat killed Errol Patterson last night and his wife . . . his new bride . . . found his body this morning."

Chapter 9

Derek and Maleah boarded the Powell private jet in Atlanta. Nic met them the moment they arrived, but Griff was nowhere to be seen.

"He's in the bedroom making phone calls," Nic explained. "He's double checking with Barbara Jean about the arrangements for Cyrene's sister to fly in to Nassau as soon as possible. From what we understand, Cyrene is in no condition to return home alone and we felt it best for a family member to be with her."

Maleah had known Errol for several years, but only in a professional capacity. They had never worked a case together and she had probably seen him, at most, a dozen times. And she had never met his wife. With more than fifty agents employed by Powell's, some had never met and many knew one another only in passing. Agents were chosen for cases by their specific qualifications for the job and by their availability. Only when partnered with another agent or when pulling duty at Griffin's Rest together did the agents get a chance to form friendships.

It was not a surprise that when Nic introduced them

to Brendan Richter, the agent who had accompanied Griff and Nic, Maleah drew a blank. She had no memory of ever meeting the somber, auburn-haired Powell agent.

"Good to see you again, Richter," Derek said as he shook hands with the spit-and-polished man who looked as if he should be in uniform.

Maleah wondered if he had come straight out of the military.

"Likewise, Mr. Lawrence," Richter replied with a slight, almost indiscernible accent.

To Maleah's ear, the accent sounded German.

"That's right, you two know each other," Nic said. "Brendan is accompanying us to Nassau. He will be staying and overseeing Powell Agency concerns connected to Errol's murder."

"How long have you worked for our agency, Mr. Richter?" Maleah asked. She also wanted to ask how he and Derek knew each other, but she didn't.

When Richter looked at Maleah, his cold blue eyes inspected her with aloof detachment. "Six months."

He had answered her question without giving her any other information. "Are you retired military?"

"No, Ms. Perdue, I am not."

Seeing no point in continuing this line of conversation, she turned to Nic. "How much information do we have about Errol Patterson's murder?"

"Nothing really, except that he's dead and that his wife found him in the bathroom of their hotel suite. So far, Griff hasn't been able to find out anything else, no details."

"Then we don't know for sure that his throat was slit or that his body was mutilated?" Maleah asked.

"No, we don't know for sure, but Griff is convinced

that the Copycat Carver has struck again." Nic glanced at Derek. "What do you think?"

"I think Griff is probably right."

Maleah's mind whirled with various thoughts, combining information and mixing it until an idea hit. Suddenly, she said, "I know this is going to sound like a really stupid thing to say, but—Errol was African American, but he had green eyes, didn't he?"

Everyone stared at her. Her comment didn't make sense to anyone except Derek.

"Is there some significance to the fact that Errol was green-eyed?" Nic asked.

"Jerome Browning told me that the copycat's next victim would not be brown-eyed."

"Perhaps it was only a lucky guess," Richter said. "Or perhaps Mr. Browning chose his victims by eye color, eliminating those who had brown eyes, and he assumes the copycat killer will follow his lead. Do we know the eye color for the first four victims?"

"Shelley had blue eyes," Maleah said. "And so did Kristi."

"I don't know about Holt's brother or Ben's father," Nic said. "But I can find out."

"How would the copycat have acquired such a seemingly unimportant piece of information about the original Carver's victims?" Richter asked.

"Two ways," Derek told them. "Either he has access to police records or Jerome Browning told him."

"Neither Norris Keinan nor Winston Corbett were brown-eyed," Griff said from where he stood in the open doorway to the bedroom suite. "I had met both men in the past."

Everyone stared straight at Griffin Powell, his huge frame filling the doorway.

"My guess is that none of Jerome Browning's victims were brown-eyed." Griff came over, sat down beside Nic, and looked at Maleah.

"So the information he gave me is useless." Maleah wanted to hit something or someone, preferably Jerome Browning.

"Not entirely useless," Griff said. "If the copycat follows suit in this one area, then no brown-eyed Powell agents or brown-eyed family members are at risk. That means Nic is not in danger, nor are you and Derek." He glanced at Richter. "On the other hand, you and I, Brendan, are possible victims."

Before the conversation could continue, the pilot informed Griff that they were ready for take-off. Richter immediately moved toward the front of the cabin and isolated himself from the others. Maleah watched him pick up a leather briefcase beside the plush seat and place it in his lap before buckling his seatbelt.

While Nic and Griff put their heads together in a private conversation during take-off, Derek took the seat next to Maleah, but didn't say anything until they were airborne.

"Some of the information you'll get out of Browning will be useless, some only marginally helpful and some could even be misleading. But you never know when he'll let something slip and actually give us a diamond mixed in with all the rocks and pebbles he'll be tossing out."

"You're assuming that I'll actually go back to see him."

"You'll go back and you'll play his game."

"Think so, do you?"

"Know so."

"And if you were a betting man, who would you lay odds on to win, Browning or me?"

She held her breath, waiting for Derek's response. He looked at her and grinned. "I'd put my money on you, Blondie."

Maleah exhaled. She didn't know if she should believe him. He could have told her what he knew she wanted to hear, what she needed to hear in order to work up the courage to face Browning again.

"He mentioned Noah Laborde," Maleah said.

"Bastard." Derek murmured the word under his breath. "He didn't waste any time, did he? He was testing you. You know that, don't you?"

"Yes, of course, I know."

"How did you react when he asked about Laborde and how quickly did you recover?"

"You assume that I—"

"I know you. If he took you off guard, and I assume he did, then you reacted, even if only for a second."

"Okay, so I reacted," she admitted. "He might have seen me flinch, but that's all."

"He'll try to use Laborde again. I wouldn't put it past him to share the gory details of the kill. If he does, can you take it?"

Could she? Would she be able to listen to Browning describe how he had killed Noah without running from the room in tears or physically attacking the SOB?

"I don't know."

"You'd better know," Derek said. "You'd better be prepared. Once he's done his worst with it, he'll move on, so all you have to do is hold your own against him and survive the attack."

"I'm wondering if it's worthwhile to play his sick little game. Do you honestly think that Browning is going to help us?"

"Not willingly. Not without getting something out of it and since there are no more deals to be made through legal channels, we both know that what he wants is the pleasure of tormenting you."

"Lucky me."

Derek laid his hand over hers where she clutched the padded armrest. Her first impulse was to pull away, but she didn't. If she intended to continue interviewing Browning and survive the assignment, she would need Derek Lawrence.

There, she had admitted it. She couldn't do this alone.

Maleah flipped her hand over, grasped Derek's hand and squeezed. "Just don't go all macho-protective on me. I'm not some helpless female who—"

Derek chuckled. "Blondie, you are the least helpless female I know." He released her hand.

"And don't you forget it. And don't think that this changes anything between us or that we're going to wind up being friends. We're co-workers and partners on this case. That's all."

"Ah, shucks, Miss Maleah, I thought for sure that you and me would wind up getting hitched."

How he kept a straight face, she'd never know. But he did. She stared at him. Then, unable to stop herself, she smiled. "All right. I get your point. I made a big to-do over nothing."

He nodded.

Feeling somewhat relaxed, in large part to Derek, she glanced around the cabin. Griff draped his arm around Nic as she rested her head on his shoulder. Were they thinking about Errol and Cyrene Patterson and how less than twenty-four hours ago, the newlyweds were enjoying their honeymoon? Were they thinking about how life can turn on a dime, that you can be blissfully happy one moment and dragged down into the misery of hell the next?

Brendan Richter seemed totally absorbed in whatever he was doing on the laptop he had removed from the leather case.

Noting her interest in the new Powell agent, Derek said in a low, quiet voice, "Richter was with the Criminal Investigative Division of Interpol. We worked together when I was with the Bureau."

What an interesting coincidence that he should be leaving the Grand Resort just as the Powell entourage arrived. Although he had never met the famous Griffin Powell, he knew a great deal about him. Others might see him as strong and powerful, practically invincible. But they were wrong. Powell allowed his conscience to weaken him. He was a man on a mission to do good. He was loyal to his friends and benevolent to his employees. And he loved his wife. Loyalty was a weakness, as was kindness. But love was the greatest weakness of all.

They didn't notice him as they passed him in the lobby, Powell and his beautiful wife Nicole, along with Derek Lawrence, Maleah Perdue, and Brendan Richter. But then there was no reason for any of them to recognize him. He appeared to be nothing more than another tourist, an invisible man no one was likely to remember.

Richter and Lawrence were former law enforcement heavy hitters, but oddly enough, out of the three agents, Ms. Perdue possessed the most power at the moment. Ordinarily, she was a lightweight, a political science major with a desire to right wrongs, defend the underdog, and help the helpless. Using her connection to the Carver had been a stroke of genius, even though he couldn't take credit for the idea himself.

Without a backward glance, he waited outside for

the bellboy to load his suitcase into the hotel's van. He had a nonstop 3:00 P.M. flight to Atlanta.

Once seated inside the air-conditioned luxury van, he avoided direct eye contact with the other occupants.

"I can't get away from this place fast enough," the skinny, gray-haired woman sitting across from him said.

If she was talking to him, he would ignore her.

"I heard that the poor man was butchered like a pig," another woman replied. "They say there was blood everywhere."

"His wife probably killed him," someone else said. "It's usually the spouse."

"One of the maids told me that the wife had to be sedated and is under a doctor's care."

"She's probably crazy. Anyone who could cut a man to pieces that way . . ."

He settled into his seat, closed his eyes and mentally escaped from the chattering magpies. Since he had gotten no sleep last night, he would probably sleep on the plane. Once he arrived in Atlanta, he would make one phone call from the airport.

In the morning, he would rent a car and drive to Savannah, where the Copycat Carver's next victim lived.

Griff had called Derek's room and asked that he and Maleah join them for dinner in his suite that evening.

"Nic needs Maleah," Griff had said. "You know, another woman to talk to about things. Seeing Errol's wife . . . his widow . . . was difficult for Nic."

"When are you expecting her sister to arrive?"

"Tonight. I've arranged for a doctor to fly in with her and to accompany Cyrene back to the States."

When they arrived at the Powell suite, Derek could tell that Nic was still visibly shaken after seeing Cyrene

Patterson. Even though she had freshened up and changed clothes, she still looked shell-shocked.

Nicole Baxter Powell was a strong woman who had excelled in her position as a special agent for the FBI. She was definitely all woman, but she didn't have a silly, frivolous, or clinging bone in her body, like so many women he knew. But Nic had a kind heart. She genuinely cared about other people.

Derek lingered in the foyer with Griff, while Maleah and Nic went into the living room and exchanged hugs before sitting down on the sofa.

"I've arranged for you and Maleah to go with Richter in the morning for a meeting with the Chief Inspector and the inspector assigned to the Patterson case," Griff said. "I don't think you'll have a problem getting whatever information you want."

Derek nodded. "That's good. Once we know the particulars of Errol's murder, we'll be able to compare them to the details of the other four murders."

"I'm taking Nic home tomorrow. I didn't want her to accompany me on this trip, but she insisted. Why she has to be so damn stubborn . . ." Griff cleared his throat. "She thinks she has to be in the thick of things, getting emotionally involved and putting herself out there in harm's way."

"You know you wouldn't change her if you could."

"Damn right, I wouldn't." Griff glanced into the living room at the two women sitting side by side, deep in conversation. "Like I said, I'm taking Nic home tomorrow. But I want you and Maleah to stay here a couple of days and find out everything you can."

"Sure thing."

"Richter will be staying on for at least another week or two, keeping tabs on the police investigation and doing some independent investigating. Holt volunteered to go to Cullman to follow up on things there with Winston Corbett's murder. I think he, of all people, can persuade Ben not to try to do any investigating on his own."

"Agreed. And I think once Maleah and I finish up here, we should return to Georgia," Derek said.

"You think Browning really knows something about these copycat murders?"

"He knows something, but my gut tells me he doesn't know as much as he's pretending he does. Maleah's willing to play his cat and mouse game on the off chance he actually does know something and will willingly or inadvertently share it with us."

Griff moved closer to Derek and lowered his voice. " plan to send Luke Sentell to London. He'll be traveling wherever the rumors take him, on to France and Switzerland and Italy."

"You haven't told Nic, have you?"

"No, not yet. She thinks I'm obsessed with the notion that I'm the killer's real target and this killing spree i somehow connected to my past . . . to Malcolm York."

"Is she right?"

Griff didn't respond immediately and then before he could reply, Nic called to them. "What are you two talking about in there?"

"I was filling Griff in on Jerome Browning," Derek lied as he entered the living room area of the suite.

"What a coincidence," Maleah said. "I was doing the same thing—filling Nic in on my visit with Browning."

"I ordered dinner half an hour ago," Nic said. " should be here in the next few minutes."

"Anyone care for a drink?" Griff asked as he heade toward the bar area.

The room telephone rang. Griff paused and stare at the phone. Nic and Maleah stopped talking.

"It's probably room service calling about our dinner order," Maleah said.

When she stood, obviously intending to answer the phone, Griff told her he'd get it. He picked up the receiver and said, "Yes, this is Mr. Powell."

Whatever the person on the other end of the line said, Griff did not reply. Without uttering a word, he replaced the receiver.

"Who was it?" Nic asked.

Griff looked at her.

Derek suspected bad news of some sort.

"Griff?" Nic prompted.

"I don't know who it was, but the voice sounded male."

"What did he say?" Nic rushed to Griff's side.

Reluctantly, as if he considered lying to his wife, Griff finally replied, "He said 'If I don't decide to kill her first, your wife will make a lovely widow.'"

Chapter 10

The Assistant Superintendent, the Chief Inspector and Inspector Yates Thompson, who was in charge of the Patterson murder case, met with Derek, Maleah and Brendan Richter. Derek seriously doubted that even the inspector would have agreed to this meeting if not for Griffin Powell's considerable influence. How Griff went about getting what he wanted, Derek never asked, but he had a pretty good idea that his boss used whatever means necessary to achieve his desired goal.

After personally assuring them that everything humanly possible would be done to find the person who had killed Errol, the Assistant Superintendent shook their hands again, as did the Chief Inspector. Pretty much as he had thought, these two men had been commanded to put in an appearance, an order no doubt issued by the Commissioner of Police himself. But it was unlikely that they were expected to do more than that—show up, talk the talk, make assurances and appease the Powell agents.

"Inspector Thompson will answer any questions you have," the Chief Inspector said. "He will cooperate with" you in any way possible and will keep you updated on the investigation."

Once his superiors departed, the tall, rawboned, ebony-skinned Thompson invited them to sit, which they did. But he remained standing.

"My orders are to cooperate with you," Thompson said. "And naturally, I will follow the Chief Inspector's orders, although I am unaccustomed to civilians involving themselves in police business."

"We understand," Richter said. "But Errol Patterson's murder is no ordinary murder case."

"So I have been told." Thompson glanced from Richter to Derek and then his gaze settled on Maleah. "You were Mr. Patterson's friends, yes?"

"Errol Patterson worked as an agent for the Powell Security and Investigation Agency, just as we do," Maleah replied.

Thompson nodded. "I understand other Powell agents have also been murdered in the past few months."

"Before Mr. Patterson was killed, yes, there were four others connected to our agency. We suspect all four deaths were the work of a serial killer," Derek said.

"One victim was an agent, one a secretary, one the brother of an agent, and the fourth the father of an agent," Richter told the inspector.

Thompson nodded again. "And these four people were murdered in a similar manner and you suspect the same killer in all three?"

"That's right," Richter replied, a note of aggravation in his voice.

Thompson tapped a file folder lying on his desk. "Mr. Patterson died almost instantly. His jugular was punctured, his trachea severed and his carotid arteries slashed." He paused, as if waiting for one of them to say something. When they didn't, he continued. "His wife found his body in the bathroom next to the tub which was filled to overflowing."

Derek and Maleah looked at each other, but said nothing.

"Were the others killed in a similar fashion?" Thompson asked.

"They were," Richter said. "Was there anything else, anything unusual about the body?"

Thompson's lips curved downward in a contemplative frown. "I assume you are referring to the triangular pieces of flesh cut from the victim's upper arms and thighs."

Yes, that was exactly what Richter had been referring to, that final piece of information that irrefutably linked Patterson's murder to the other four.

"Yes," Derek and Richter answered simultaneously.

"An autopsy will be performed," the inspector said. "And a toxicology screening has been ordered. Mr. Patterson was a large man in his prime, a security agent trained to protect himself and others, so how was it possible for someone to overpower him? And why did his wife sleep soundly while her husband was being murdered?"

"They were both drugged." Richter stated the obvious.

"We suspect so, yes."

Derek's opinion of Inspector Thompson as an investigator rose by several degrees.

"In the other four murders, the killer left behind no evidence that could help identify him or enable the police to track him," Derek said. "Is that true in this case?"

Thompson grunted. "Unfortunately, yes." He looked directly at Derek. "That is the sign of a true professional, is it not, Mr. Lawrence."

Thompson had done his homework, no doubt running a check on the three of them, which meant he knew that Derek was a former FBI profiler.

"Professional in the sense that he was no amateur," Derek said. "He is a skilled killer, which tells us that he's killed before, perhaps numerous times."

The thought that the copycat could be a gun-for-hire had crossed his mind, but that possibility was only one of several scenarios that he had considered. Until he had more evidence to back up any one theory, he had no intention of suggesting to Griff that the man they were hunting could be a professional assassin.

As if understanding Derek's assessment of the situation, Thompson simply nodded before inquiring, "Is there anything else you would like to know?"

"I think Ms. Perdue and I have what we need," Derek said.

"And you, Mr. Richter?"

"I would like to speak to the first responders on the scene," Richter said. "As well as any witnesses your people interviewed. I'll need copies of all the reports, photographs, and preliminary findings."

"Yes, of course."

"Mr. Lawrence and Ms. Perdue will be leaving Nassau tomorrow, but I will be staying on for several weeks, as the Powell Agency representative."

Inspector Thompson barely managed to hide his negative reaction. He quickly turned his frown into a forced smile as he shook hands with each of them.

"I wish you both a safe flight tomorrow." And then his dark gaze settled on Richter, each man sizing up the other. "I have the greatest respect for you, as a former ICPO agent, Mr. Richter. I suspect I may be able to learn a great deal from you."

Yes, Inspector Thompson had done his homework. Derek didn't doubt that the man probably knew what he, Richter, and Maleah had each eaten for breakfast that morning.

Nic knew her husband well enough to understand that he was not concerned about his own life, but was greatly concerned about her welfare as well as the lives of everyone associated with the Powell Agency. He was a man who took his responsibilities seriously. His primitive protective instincts made him a dangerous opponent when those he cared about were in danger, but those same instincts were his personal Achilles' heel, his only weakness. Griffin Powell's ability to love equaled if not surpassed the passion with which he hated. She admired his ability to stay calm under pressure, a trait she tried to emulate. But beneath that cool, controlled exterior, a violent rage smoldered just below the surface.

And it was that rage inside Griff that worried her.

They had calmly discussed the untraceable phone call he had received at the Nassau resort. She had struggled to match his restrained composure when faced with a threat against both of them.

If I don't decide to kill her first, your wife will make a lovely widow.

"He's taunting me," Griff had said. "He wants me to know that all roads lead to Rome, that every murder is leading him closer to me."

"Maybe he just wants you to think that. Maybe he's trying to steer us in the wrong direction."

"Maybe, but unlikely."

Nic still wasn't totally convinced that Griff was the ultimate target, that the copycat killings were connected to his past, to a dead man named York. Admittedly, that possibility frightened her far more than any other. Was that why she clung so doggedly to other theories?

At his request, she joined Griff in the agency's home office, an area inside their house that had been designed to allow Griff to oversee his vast empire without ever leaving Griffin's Rest. The Powell Building, located in downtown Knoxville, housed the inner workings of the agency, as well as the staff for the numerous Powell philanthropic endeavors. Each year, the Powell Empire required more and more employees, which meant that at the present time, approximately two hundred people and their families were at risk. Of course, those directly employed by the Powell Agency comprised only the tip of the iceberg. Indirectly, Griffin Powell employed countless thousands.

When she entered the state-of-the-art office suite, Nic paused in the doorway, allowing her gaze to travel around the room and pause on each occupant. Her initial thought—"round up the usual suspects"—would have made her smile if not for the seriousness of the situation.

Dr. Yvette Meng, the epitome of exotic elegance, stood away from the others, alone and infallibly serene. If her goal had been to be as inconspicuous as possible, she had failed. There was no way the dark-eyed beauty, whose very presence in any room commanded attention, could be overlooked.

Sanders stood behind Griff, who sat at the head of the conference table. She respected her husband's guard dog, which was the way she thought of the quiet, reserved man with the perpetual hint of sadness in his dark eyes.

Barbara Jean, her friend and confidant, glanced up from where she sat in her wheelchair at the far end of the table. She offered Nic an encouraging smile. One of the many things Nic loved about Barbara Jean was her optimistic outlook on life, which considering the tragedies she had endured was in and of itself a miracle.

Powell agents filled five of the ten chairs at the table, leaving the end chair—her chair—unoccupied. As she entered the office, she quickly noted which agents had been called in for duty at Griffin's Rest. Shaughnessy Hood, who had been with the agency since its infancy, a bear of a man at six-six and three hundred pounds; Luke Sentell, a former Black Ops commando, the most mysterious and most deadly member of the team; Saxon Chappelle, a Harvard graduate, who like Derek Lawrence possessed a borderline genius IQ. And then there were the two female agents: Feisty, petite Angie Sterling Moss, five months pregnant and presently on restricted duty. And Michelle Allen, an expert in martial arts, recruited after the death of her fiancé with whom she had owned a franchise of martial art studios throughout the state of Tennessee.

As Nic approached the conference table, Griff looked at her. The moment she took her seat, Griff broke eye contact with her and surveyed the others in the room.

"Starting today, from now until the Copycat Carver is apprehended, security at Griffin's Rest will be tripled and access both in and out of the estate will be limited. Those living here should be safer than any of the Powell employees living and working on the outside. Unfortunately, we have no way to predict who the copycat has chosen as his next victim."

An unnatural silence fell over the room.

"Luke will be leaving tomorrow for an assignment in London," Griff said.

Nic tensed. Griff had deliberately not discussed Luke's new assignment with her. She knew he had been trying to protect her, trying to postpone the inevitability that his actions would upset her, and trying to avoid yet another argument. But what she couldn't get through his stubborn head was how that type of protective maneuver only made matters worse in the end.

"Angie, you may choose whether you want to stay here at Griffin's Rest or if you prefer to take a temporary leave of absence. Talk it over with your husband and let him know that he's welcome to stay here with you."

"Yes, sir," Angie replied. "Thank you."

"I'm bringing in Cully Redmond," Griff said. "He will join you three—Michelle, Shaughnessy, and Saxon—who will rotate between the house here and Dr. Meng's retreat. You will be on duty twelve hours and off twelve, but you will not leave the estate."

Griff had made his decisions without including her in the process. Oh, she could call him on it and he would tell her that they *had* discussed the situation. They had, to some degree, but talking about something and making definite decisions on how to handle the problem were not the same thing.

She knew he was doing what had to be done, and she agreed with his decisions, even the one to send Luke Sentell to London. She also knew that he would move heaven and earth to protect those he loved. And in her heart of hearts, she knew that he loved her more than anyone or anything and that he would die to protect her.

Poppy Chappelle loved her grandmother, loved the big old house in Ardsley Park, Savannah's first suburb, a mere ten-minute drive from downtown, and loved her summers here with her father's family. She had been barely two years old when her parents divorced, so she couldn't actually remember a time when the three of them had been together. Her memories of her dad were sketchy, but she had a picture in her mind of a big, sandy-haired man who had laughed a lot and had called her "my little sugarplum." He and his latest lady friend had died when his single-engine Cessna had crashed on their flight back from Vegas five years ago.

"Miss Poppy," Heloise, her grandmother's housekeeper and companion for the past forty years called to her just as she reached the front door. "Your grandmother wanted me to remind you that she is expecting guests for dinner. You need to be home no later than five-thirty."

"I've already promised her that I won't be late. She knows that I'm going sailing with Court and Anne Lee this afternoon."

Heloise snorted. "Mr. Court and Miss Anne Lee are totally irresponsible. Your grandmother is sorely disappointed in those two."

"It's hardly their fault if they're spoiled brats," Poppy said. "Grandmother should blame their parents for their behavior, but she won't criticize Aunt Mary Lee the way she does my mother because she's her daughter."

"I have no intention of getting into a conversation with you about the dynamics of the Chappelle family. It's not my place to agree or disagree with you. I shouldn't have said anything about your cousins. I simply meant to remind you not to be late this evening."

Poppy rushed over to Heloise and hugged her. The dour-faced old maid who seldom smiled cleared her throat and patted Poppy's back.

"You're a good one, Miss Poppy. You and your uncle Saxon. You two are the best of the lot, if you ask me." She shoved Poppy away and gave her a push toward the front door. "You behave yourself with those hooligan cousins of yours and don't let them get you into any trouble."

"I won't. I promise."

A car horn announced her cousins' arrival. Poppy opened the door and stepped out onto the porch. She paused, glanced over her shoulder and waved at Heloise, then bounded down the brick steps and hopped into Court Dandridge's black BMW M6 convertible.

Maleah and Derek ordered dinner in her suite, the same luxury suite that Nic and Griff had occupied before their departure from Nassau that morning. Nic had insisted she use the suite since it was paid for through the end of the week. The butler, included with the suite, cleared away the table, stacked the dishes on a serving cart and wheeled it away.

"Will there be anything else, ma'am?" the prim and proper butler asked.

"Uh . . . no, thank you."

"Very well."

As soon as he pushed the cart out into the hallway and closed the door behind him, Maleah laughed.

"What's funny?" Derek asked.

"I'm glad I'm not rich. I don't think I'd ever get used to hot and cold running servants."

Derek stared at her, an odd expression in his black eyes. "You have to be the only woman I know who wouldn't love having servants to do her bidding."

"You need to get to know a better class of women."

He chuckled. "Yeah, maybe I do."

She eyed their twin laptops, provided by the agency, lying side by side where they had placed them on the coffee table when the butler had set the table for their dinner. "We should check to see if Sanders has any new info for us before we go over the list Warden Holland gave you."

"You check your e-mail and I'll pull up the file containing the list of Browning's visitors, telephone calls, and correspondence."

Maleah picked up her computer and took it with her over to the sofa. She kicked off her low-heel sandals, wriggled her toes, and settled at the end of the sofa. After flipping open her laptop, with an attached USB-Connect device, she logged on to her Powell Agency e-mail account.

"Nothing from Sanders," Maleah said.

After removing his sports coat, neatly folding it and laying it across the back of one of the chairs at the dining table, he got his laptop and joined Maleah on the sofa. They sat at opposite ends, leaving a wide space between them. Derek pulled up the file that Warden Holland had sent him about an hour ago. This was his first chance to take a look at the lists.

"Want me to read it to you or would you rather we take a look at this together?" he asked.

She shrugged. She wanted to read the info herself, but that meant close contact with Derek, something she usually avoided.

Grow up, will you, Maleah, she told herself. *He may have a Don Juan reputation, but it's not as if he's going to try anything with you. The guy is no more interested in you—in that way—than you are him. You're not his type. And God knows he's not your type.*

Who was she kidding? Derek Lawrence was every woman's type.

She scooted across the sofa until she sat beside him, only inches separating their bodies. He grinned. She faked a pleasant smile. He lifted his laptop and rested it between them, one edge on her left knee and the other edge on his right knee.

Look at the damn computer and stop thinking about Derek's knee pressed against yours.

"The first list has the names of all of Browning's visitors for the past year," Derek said.

They looked over the list, which turned out to be extremely brief.

"There are only three names," Maleah said.

"Albert Durham, Cindy Di Blasi, and Wyman Scudder," Derek read. "Scudder is listed as his lawyer. He visited him twice."

"The other two are listed as friends."

"Did the warden send Sanders a copy of this?"

"I don't know, but I forwarded it to him before lunch, just in case."

"Then it's too soon for us to expect Sanders to have found out anything about these people."

Derek grunted. "Let's move on to telephone calls."

"Same three names," Maleah said. "His lawyer and his two friends. One call to the lawyer, one call to Durham and one call every week to Ms. Di Blasi."

"Curious. I'm surprised Browning hasn't asked for conjugal visits."

"Don't make me sick. What woman in her right mind would willingly have sex with a psycho like Browning?"

"Different strokes for different folks," Derek told her.

Maleah groaned. "Don't remind me about how many screwed-up women there are in this world, women who willingly demean themselves. They make me ashamed of my own sex."

"Women don't hold a monopoly on stupidity. The world is full of pussy-whipped men being led around by the nose by heartless bitches who get their kicks out of emasculating the idiots."

Maleah snapped her head up and stared at Derek.
Their gazes joined instantly, fusing together like two
pieces of hot metal. Good God Almighty! She and
Derek were two sides of the same coin. Why had she
never realized that fact until two seconds ago?

"Uh . . . did we just say the same thing, sort of?" she
asked, still partially puzzled by the revelation.

"Sort of," he agreed. "You have no respect for weak,
spineless women who let men use them. I have no respect for weak, spineless men who let women walk all
over them."

*If you know what's good for you, you'll break eye contact
with him. Do it now before something happens between the two
of you that you will regret.*

"We should look at the third list," she said, her voice
softened by emotion.

"Right." He looked straight at the computer as he
brought the next list up on the screen.

"Hmm . . . two names," Maleah said. "Albert Durham
and Cindy Di Blasi. He received two letters from
Durham and sent two replies to the man."

"Cindy has written to him every week for the past
four months and he has replied to every letter." Derek
went back to the first list. "Check out the dates. Durham
visited for the first time five months ago, and then four
months ago, Di Blasi visited for the first time. Why did
they both start visiting Browning all of a sudden?"

"What about the phone calls?" Maleah asked.

They scanned the list of Browning's telephone calls
again, checking the dates. "He called Durham two days
after Durham's first visit."

"And he called Di Blasi two days after her first visit."
Maleah pointed to the date. "Do you think there's a
connection between Durham and Di Blasi?"

"There could be," Derek said. "It depends on exactly

who Cindy Di Blasi is and what her relationship with Browning is and how long they've known each other. She could be just one of those women who is fascinated by hardened criminals."

"And if she's not some wacko who's fallen in love with Browning?"

"We don't need to get ahead of ourselves and put the cart before the horse. Until Sanders does a background check and we know who these people are, we're wasting our time trying to figure how they're connected to Browning."

"Call Sanders and ask him to do a rush job on those background checks," Maleah told him. "And I'm going to get in touch with Warden Holland."

"Dare I ask why you're calling the warden?"

"He told me that he needed twenty-four hours' notice for me to see Browning again. I plan to talk to Browning again tomorrow afternoon."

When Derek didn't respond, she said, "Don't try to talk me out of it."

"I wouldn't dream of it."

"Good. I'm glad we're in agreement."

"We're not in agreement," he told her. "But I choose my battles wisely."

Ignoring his remark, she said, "The copycat killer is going to strike again. We all know it's only a matter of time. If there's one chance in a million that Browning knows something about the copycat, I'm willing to do whatever it takes to get him to tell me what he knows."

"And I'll do whatever it takes to keep you safe."

Their glazes clashed, but neither said anything, each knowing the other would not give an inch in a confrontation.

Chapter 11

Derek had misgivings about Maleah seeing Browning again, but had kept his concerns to himself. Although he hadn't tried to talk her out of coming to the penitentiary today, he had insisted on accompanying her. She tried not to think about how protective Derek was, chalking it up to just a generic masculine trait that all men possessed. It was nothing personal.

She had to admit that in some ways Derek reminded her of her brother Jackson. She suspected that as Jack had once done, Derek would volunteer to be her stand-in and take any beatings intended for her. And that, too, wasn't personal. The guy probably saw himself as hero material. After all, it was no secret that Derek Lawrence had a reputation with the ladies. Women tended to take one look at the guy and swoon at his feet.

She could not deny she understood why women swooned. He was incredibly handsome.

Good God, Maleah, is that ever an understatement.

Derek was drop-dead, eat-him-with-a-spoon gorgeous. And he was highly intelligent and rich and charming. And he made her laugh. But on the other hand, he could be an arrogant know-it-all. And his way-with-the-ladies was just a nicer way of saying he was a womanizer.

Maleah didn't want Derek or anyone else protecting her from the big, bad world. She no longer needed a big brother to run interference for her. She was fully capable of taking care of herself in every way. She was an excellent marksman, adept with both a handgun and a rifle. She had earned a black belt in karate, thanks to Michelle Allen's excellent tutelage. She earned a six-figure yearly salary as a Powell agent, so she certainly didn't need to depend on anyone else financially. And after several years of intensive counseling, she was in a reasonably healthy place mentally and emotionally.

Okay, so she still had some control issues.

The creak of an opening door followed by the clinking of chains against the floor brought Maleah from her thoughts and into the present moment.

Standing with her back rigid, her hands gripping and releasing repeatedly, she took several deep breaths and did her best to relax. Browning would instantly sense her nervousness and use it against her. He was the type of animal who would pick up the scent of fear and gladly use it against his opponent, quickly seeing them as easy prey.

Maleah was once again slightly disoriented by the man's good looks and air of sophistication, even in his simple prison attire. And once again she wondered how many people had been fooled by this man's physical appearance.

"How delightful to see you again, Maleah," Browning said as the guard indicated for him to sit. "You're looking quite lovely. That shade of teal brings out the green in your eyes."

She ignored his compliment. Odd that the salesclerk who had sold her the blouse had said exactly the same thing about the teal bringing out the green in her hazel brown eyes.

"Your copycat has killed again," Maleah said. Succinct and to the point.

"Has he? Male or female?"

"Male."

"Not brown-eyed."

"No, not brown-eyed. But then none of your victims were brown-eyed, were they?"

"My mother was brown-eyed. I loved my mother. She died when I was six, you know."

"Yes, I know. You were an only child. Your father married a woman with two daughters and a son. You tried to strangle one of the daughters. You were ten years old. Your father sent you to live with your mother's uncle."

His sickening sweet smile never faltered, but she noted the momentary flash of anger in his eyes. "Did you find my life story fascinating?"

"I found it instructive. Tracing your life from birth to the present allowed me to see the slow, steady progression of a psychopath from a boy who tried to kill his stepsister, to a teenager who killed six young women, to an adult serial killer who got his kicks from slitting his victim's throats and slicing pieces of their flesh from their arms and legs."

"Souvenirs. Little trophies that I could take out and look at from time to time."

"In order to relive each kill?"

"Something like that." He looked up at her. "Why don't you sit down, Maleah, or do you think standing over me gives you some type of psychological advantage? I assure you, it doesn't."

"Then what difference does it make to you whether I sit or stand?"

He shrugged. "I simply thought you might be more comfortable sitting. And it might be more pleasant for both of us if we're facing each other, eye to eye."

Maleah made an instant decision. She walked over and sat down in the chair facing Browning, the protection of two guards securely between her and any physical danger. But she and Browning were now at the same eye level. She squared her shoulders and calmly rested her loosely clasped hands in her lap.

"Now, isn't that better?" Browning asked.

"I have a question."

"Let me guess . . . hmm . . . You want to know what I did with my souvenirs. The police never found them, you know."

"I'm not interested in your souvenirs. It doesn't really matter where you stored them. Not to the police. Not to me. Not to anyone."

"He's not keeping them the way I did, is he?"

How the hell did he know that? "No, he isn't."

"Aren't you going to ask me how I knew?"

"If I did, would you tell me?"

Browning laughed, the sound as smooth as his silky voice. It was a practiced laugh, nothing about it genuine. "I find it curious that you have no interest in my trophies, considering the fact that I took eight little triangular souvenirs from Noah Laborde's body. I could tell you about that night, every detail, from the moment I punctured his jugular until I left him on the banks of the Chattahoochee River."

Noah's smiling face—young, handsome, sweet—flashed through her mind. "I want the answer to a question."

"Then ask your question." He seemed only slightly perturbed that she remained unfazed by his reminder that he had killed Noah.

"Who's Cindy Di Blasi?"

Browning stared at Maleah as if trying to see inside her head, wondering how much she already knew and what price she was willing to pay for his answer.

"Cindy is a lady friend."

"How did you meet her?"

"We have friends in common."

"How long have you known her?"

"For a while."

"How long is a while?" Maleah asked.

"That's four questions," he reminded her.

"And only three answers."

"A mutual friend on the outside hooked me up with Cindy. A guy gets lonesome for a little female companionship in a place like this."

"I'll bet."

"You could say that Cindy is my girlfriend." Browning winked at Maleah. "If Cindy finds out about you, she's going to be jealous."

"I won't tell if you don't."

Browning laughed again, just a hint of sincerity in the sound.

Maleah didn't buy any of it. Not the part about Cindy being a friend of an old friend. Or that she visited Browning, wrote him letters, and took his phone calls because she was now his girlfriend. Maleah didn't know who Cindy di Blasi was or what her real relationship was with Browning, but she intended to find out.

"Is Albert Durham a friend, too?" she asked.

Browning smiled. "An acquaintance. And before you ask, Wyman Scudder is my lawyer." He leaned forward, his piercing gaze unnerving and intimidating.

Maleah didn't flinch, didn't even blink. *Good try, you cunning son of a bitch, but no cigar. Not this time. That crazy, I'm-dangerous glare doesn't scare me.*

"Interesting," Browning said. "Nerves of steel, huh, Maleah? Makes me wonder just what it would take to unnerve you, just how hot the pressure would have to be to melt that steel."

He knew that she knew what this game was all about, that his ultimate goal was to see her fall apart completely. He would keep chipping away at her armor, searching for the weak spots.

"Sticks and stones, Jerome," she told him. "I'm not afraid of you."

He studied her for several minutes. She examined him just as thoroughly. Whatever he dished out, she could take, and then dish it right back to him.

"I'm glad that you're not afraid of me," he finally said. "Makes things all the more interesting, doesn't it? I'll be thinking about you during the time between your visits. Thinking about curling your long blond hair around my finger." He held up his right index finger. "Thinking about running my hands down your throat. Thinking about what I could do to make you afraid of me . . . very afraid."

"If you don't tell me something I consider useful in my investigation about Cindy Di Blasi or Albert Durham or the copycat killer, I won't be coming back for another visit."

"Oh, Maleah, you disappoint me. Resorting to idle threats?"

"Not a threat. Just stating a fact. I have no intention of wasting my time pursuing a dead end. And that's what you're becoming, Jerome—a dead end."

He tensed his jaw and narrowed his gaze. One hand curled into a tight fist. She had pushed the right buttons. Mentally patting herself on the back, Maleah rose to her feet.

"Leaving already?" he asked.

"Unless you want to answer my questions."

"Another time, perhaps."

"Perhaps."

"You'll come to see me again," he told her.

"Only if I get what I want before I leave today. And I'm on my way out right now, so you'd better hurry."

Silence.

She turned her back on him and walked toward the door where her escort waited. "I'm ready to go now," she told the uniformed guard.

The guard opened the door.

"Wait," Browning called to her.

She paused.

"Albert Durham is writing my biography," Browning said.

Maleah's breath caught in her throat. Durham was a writer? If so, then he had come to the prison to interview Jerome, to pick his brain for information. Was it possible that Durham was the copycat killer?

"Thank you, Jerome."

"You'll come back tomorrow?"

"Not tomorrow," she told him. "But soon."

Derek didn't immediately question Maleah about the interview. Outwardly, she seemed completely unaffected by today's encounter with Browning. She shook hands with Warden Holland, thanked him and requested a third interview for next Monday.

Why wait until next Monday? *Don't ask. She'll explain later.*

On the way to the parking area, Derek glanced at the overcast sky and commented about the weather. "Looks like rain."

Her gaze followed his. "Hmm . . ."

"I was thinking we could have a nice lunch at the Steeplechase Grill when we get back to Vidalia," Derek said. "I checked the place out online after the clerk at the hotel mentioned it was a great place to eat."

"Sure. Whatever." Maleah unlocked her SUV. "Have you heard anything from Sanders this morning?"

Derek opened the passenger side door. "As a matter of fact, he sent us the info we requested about Browning's recent visitors while you were chit-chatting with the guy."

Maleah shot him a screw-you glare before opening the door and sliding in behind the wheel. She waited until he got in before asking, "Do we have addresses? Phone numbers?"

"We have an address for Wyman Scudder. He isn't Browning's original attorney nor is he even with the same law firm or in the same city. Someone hired him six months ago to represent Browning's interests."

"Why would a man who confessed to murder, struck a deal with the DA, and exhausted all of his appeals need a new lawyer? It's not as if Browning has been screaming 'I'm innocent' for the past ten years."

"Scudder isn't exactly the best money can buy. According to Sanders's report, the guy's reputation as a lawyer isn't all that great. He's in debt up to his eyeballs, has an ex-wife who's still bleeding him dry after their divorce two years ago, and he was living in his office up until six months ago."

"Who retained Scudder for Browning and why? Sanders needs to get the Powell team to dig deeper and get us the answers."

"He's already on it."

Maleah started the engine and pulled out of the parking slot. "Is that all you've got on Scudder?"

"For now."

"What about Cindy Di Blasi?"

"Cindy Di Blasi is a mystery woman. Seems the Georgia driver's license that she used as ID for her visits to Browning is a fake. The street address on the license is for a church in Augusta. The phone number Browning called when he talked to Cindy was for a pre-paid cell phone. No way to track it."

"Interesting."

"Confusing."

"Do you think Cindy Di Blasi is an alias?"

"Could be," Derek said. "Using the description of the woman we got from the guards who remember her, the Powell team will compare her description, along with approximate age, to see if there's a woman by that name anywhere in the state of Georgia."

"Browning told me that Cindy is a lady friend and that a mutual friend hooked them up."

"And that mutual friend could be Wyman Scudder or—"

"Or Albert Durham."

"Albert Durham is a real person, not an alias. Sanders is checking out the info on the driver's license ID he used when he visited Browning. The man's a writer. He writes biographies about historical figures, presidents and generals, world leaders in various areas."

"This is becoming more and more curious, isn't it?" Maleah glanced at Derek. "Do you have a theory?" She refocused on the road immediately.

"I think we have three possible scenarios," Derek told her. "The Copycat Carver hired Scudder, Durham and Cindy and has used them as go-betweens to contact Browning. Or the Copycat Carver is actually one of them—Scudder or Durham or Cindy."

"Cindy? I thought everyone was in agreement that the copycat is a man."

"Who said Cindy was a woman?"

Maleah snorted. "I say Cindy is a woman. Either a woman or a very small man. The guards said she was about five-two and maybe weighed a hundred pounds soaking wet."

"Yeah, Cindy is probably female. But that still leaves Scudder and Durham."

"Agreed. So, what's your third scenario?"

"Ah yes, my third scenario."

"Stop being so dramatic and just tell me."

Derek grinned. "Someone hired Scudder, Durham, and Cindy, as well as a professional killer to copy Browning's murders."

"This is the Griffin Powell theory, isn't it? Some mystery man over in Europe who is using the name Malcolm York is striking out at Griff by killing Powell agents and members of their families."

"It's one of three theories. At this point, I don't have a favorite. I don't know enough to make a judgment call. I don't even have a gut instinct pick."

Maleah remained silent for several miles, but Derek knew she was thinking, mulling things over, and deciding what she wanted to say.

"Browning was careful not to tell me anything I couldn't easily find out on my own," Maleah said. "That Scudder was his lawyer and that Cindy was his lady friend. But he did share something about Durham that seems odd to me."

Derek waited, allowing her to progress at her own speed.

"Just as I was leaving, Browning told me that Albert Durham was writing his biography."

"Why would a renowned biographer of historical figures choose to write the bio of a condemned serial killer?"

"What if he's not the real Albert Durham?"

"If he is or isn't the real Durham, you do realize that Browning probably believes he is," Derek said. "And Browning would have been inclined to share numerous details about the murders with his biographer."

"Which means Durham would have the info he needed to duplicate those murders."

"If we can find Albert Durham, we just might find the Copycat Carver."

Chapter 12

Wyman Scudder, you're a fool.

How many times had his ex-wife said those exact words?

She'd been right. Sheila had been right about a lot of things.

You're a fool. You're a drunk. You're a sorry excuse for a husband. You've ruined your life and tried to ruin mine, but I'm getting out while the gettin' is good.

Wyman lifted the open bottle of Wild Turkey 101 proof bourbon whiskey and poured his glass three-fourths full. The damn stuff had cost him sixty bucks, but he had the money, didn't he? It was nobody's business what he paid for his pleasures and a good bottle of bourbon headed his list of carnal delights. He lifted the glass to salute his ex-wife, his ex-associates, and his ex-life. He might have been on his way down six months ago, but not now.

"Here's to Wyman Scudder. Long may he live the good life."

He downed one long, glorious gulp, shivered, coughed, and then laughed. When he left his office today—a right nice office, if he did say so himself—he'd be going home to a Mill Creek Run apartment. After living in his old office for nearly a year, he had every right to celebrate his good fortune, didn't he? A new office on Third Street, a first-rate apartment, a good bottle of bourbon, and a new suit. He ran his hand over the quality material of his thousand-dollar pin-striped suit. It might be off the rack, but it was a damn expensive rack.

Wyman took a sip of the smooth whiskey and then another before placing the glass on a fancy soapstone coaster atop his desk.

He had a chance now to put his life back together and that's just what he intended to do. Screw Sheila. Screw his old law firm. Two years ago, both his wife and his firm had thrown him out as if he were yesterday's trash.

He'd show 'em just what he was made of.

You're a fool.

"Shut the fuck up," he hollered into the emptiness of his new office.

You've gotten yourself mixed up in something really nasty.

If anybody asked him who had hired him to represent Jerome Browning, he'd tell them the truth. He hadn't done anything illegal. He'd seen Browning only a couple of times, did what he'd been paid to do—consult with his client—and that was all there was to it.

If someone connects all the dots, what then?

Then you're screwed.

He could be considered an accomplice, couldn't he? An accomplice to murder? No, not just one murder. Five murders now.

But I didn't know. I swear to God, I didn't know what they were planning. If I had . . .

It was too late for ifs. He had taken the job, taken the money, and unless somebody put the puzzle pieces to-

gether, he'd get away scot-free, just as the others would.
They would all get away with murder.

The Steeplechase Grill and Tavern was located in
downtown Vidalia. Atop the signpost outside the restaurant, a wooden cutout of a comic laughing horse's head
welcomed customers, setting the tone for the casual atmosphere inside the trendy establishment. Upon entering, the tantalizing aroma instantly whetted Derek's
appetite.

"Nice place," he said as the hostess showed them to
their table.

"Nice enough." Maleah climbed up and sat on one
of the bar stools that graced a row of dark wooden tables.

They had arrived at 12:30 P.M., prime lunchtime in
downtown Vidalia, so the restaurant was packed. He
glanced around at the dark paneled walls, lined with
metal signs, and then looked up at the whirling ceiling
fans and down at the floral/leaf design in the dark carpet.

Maleah scanned the menu hurriedly, laid it on the
table and tapped her fingers absently. Turning her
head right and then left, she searched for a waitress.
"We should have just picked up fast food and gone
straight on to Macon."

"Settle down and relax," Derek told her. "It'll take us
less than two hours to drive to Macon. It's not as if
Wyman Scudder is going anywhere. In the grand
scheme of things, taking an hour for a decent meal isn't
going to matter."

She heaved a labored sigh. "You're probably right."

"Are you okay?"

"Yeah, sure, why wouldn't I be?"

"Half an hour with Jerome Browning, playing his sick little cat and mouse game, would have an adverse effect on anyone."

She stared at him, her eyes speaking for her, telling him that even though she hadn't walked away from the second interview with Browning without a few minor wounds, she had won today's game.

"You bested him, didn't you?" Derek grinned.

"I held my own. And yes, in the end, I won."

"He'll be all the more determined to draw blood next time."

She nodded. "I'm well aware of that fact."

The waitress appeared, all white teeth, freckled nose, and friendly attitude. "What can I get you folks to drink?"

"Sweet tea," Derek replied.

"Unsweet iced tea, please," Maleah said.

"Y'all know what you want or do you need a few minutes?"

Derek quickly looked over the extensive menu. One item caught his eye.

"I'd like the Charleston Chicken Salad," Maleah said.

"Yes, ma'am. And you, sir?" the waitress asked.

"A rack of baby back ribs, baked potato, fully loaded and onion rings."

As soon as the waitress walked away to place their order, Maleah made a disapproving tsk-tsk sound with her tongue.

"You disapprove of my lunch choices?" he asked.

"It's your health and your arteries that you're clogging, not mine."

Derek grinned. He had learned months ago when not to argue with Maleah's reasoning, especially when she was right.

Despite the crowd, the service was good—fast and ac-

rate. The waitress returned quickly with their drinks
d a loaf of delicious brown bread coated with a hint
 sea salt.

After their meals arrived, they ate in relative silence.
pparently Maleah thought that would save time and
low them to get off to Macon all the sooner. Halfway
rough eating the delectable ribs, Derek's phone rang.
sing the wipes provided with his meal, he cleaned the
rbecue sauce from his fingertips, retrieved his phone
d noted the caller ID. The Powell Agency's number
 Griffin's Rest.

"This is Derek Lawrence."

"Hi, Derek. It's Barbara Jean. Sanders received some
dated info on Wyman Scudder he thought y'all
ould have immediately. I'll send a complete report
 e-mail attachment later, and I'll text the new ad-
ess, too, but I thought you needed to know that the
dress we had is incorrect."

"Okay, give me the correct address."

She called off the new address on Third Street in
wntown Macon. "It seems that Mr. Scudder just
ned a lease on a new office and a new apartment a
w days ago."

"You don't say."

"What?" Maleah asked.

He waved her off, his actions requesting that she
it.

"Scudder has been making monthly deposits to his
count," Barbara Jean said. "A thousand a month up
til the first of June, when he deposited fifty thou-
d."

Derek whistled softly. "Now, why would anyone think
uy like Scudder was worth that kind of money."

"Sanders suggested that you and Maleah might want
ask him."

"Tell Sanders that he can count on our doing ju
that."

"We're still working on tracking down Cindy D
Blasi," Barbara Jean said. "And after you texted us wit
the info that Browning told Maleah Durham is writin
his bio, which implies this guy really could be the rea
Albert Durham, we had some luck finding him. Or a
least more info about him."

"No address or phone number?"

"It seems Albert Durham is a recluse and guards h
privacy. He owns several homes, but keeps on the mov
a lot, travels abroad, works on extended vacations, tha
sort of thing. As soon as we come up with any informa
tion about where you can find him now, I'll be in touch
Until then, we're working under the assumption tha
the man who visited Browning is the real Durham. Th
info on the ID he used to enter the prison matches tha
of the real Durham, at least his physical description an
date of birth. And the address is for one of Durham
homes."

"Thanks, BJ."

Barbara Jean laughed when he used the nicknam
he had given her—BJ. She was a good woman. A kin
and caring woman. Sanders was a lucky man.

As soon as he slipped his phone back in his jacke
pocket, Maleah snapped her fingers in front of his fac
"Damn it, Derek, tell me."

"Scudder has a new office, a new apartment, and fif
grand in the bank."

Maleah's mouth dropped open, and then she smile
"You can tell me the rest on the way to Macon." She la
her fork on the table, removed her napkin from h
lap, tossed it alongside her half-eaten salad, and slippe
off the wooden stool and onto her feet.

Derek eyed the remainder of the delicious ribs, gulpe

own a swig of iced tea, and knowing better than to sug-
est they finish their lunch, he motioned to the wait-
ess. When she was within earshot, he said, "We need
ur check, please."

Wyman Scudder had served his purpose and had
een paid well for his services. Unfortunately, Scudder
as a liability now, a loose end that needed to be tied
p.

Scudder first; then Cindy Di Blasi.

Albert Durham wasn't a problem. Even if the Powell
gency could find the reclusive author, there wasn't a
amn thing the man could tell them.

He had known the Powell Agency would eventually
et around to interviewing Browning, which would
rompt them to check out his recent visitors. However,
ey had moved a bit faster than he had anticipated.
oo bad Scudder wouldn't get to enjoy his big payoff.

The walk from the Travelodge Suites on Broadway
treet took only a few minutes and would have been
ather pleasant if not for the rain. When he had left his
otel, the sky had been overcast. He had gone to his car
 drop off his jacket and had picked up an umbrella.
y the time he reached the corner of Walnut and
hird, heavy droplets had begun falling. Now that he
ad reached the building that housed Wyman Scud-
er's new law office, a steady drizzle had set in.

After entering the lobby, he closed his black um-
rella and headed straight for the elevators. While he
aited for the Up elevator, the Down elevator opened
d a man and woman emerged. The couple was so ab-
rbed in their conversation with each other that they
arely noticed him. Later on, if asked, they would say
ey had seen a black-haired man with a neat mustache

and Van Dyke, wearing jeans and a short-sleeved plaid shirt. And perhaps one of them would remember that he had a large skull tattoo on his left arm.

He had learned long ago that a disguise should be simple and the effect subtle. Sometimes little more than a cap and a pair of glasses were needed to alter his appearance.

Scudder's office was on the third floor, a corner office that faced the street. The outer door was closed.

He knocked.

No response.

He tried the handle and the door opened to an empty outer office. No furniture. No secretary. Scudder hadn't had time to acquire either.

"Hello, anybody here?" he called out, wondering if perhaps Scudder had gone home early.

The door leading into the private office opened. A bleary-eyed, middle-aged man with a receding hairline and a slight paunch hanging over his belt stood in the doorway and stared at him.

"Who are you?" Wyman asked, his speech slightly slurred.

The idiot was drunk.

"A potential client, Mr. Scudder," he said using his best good old boy accent.

"Well, come right on in, Mr.—" Wyman squinched his eyes and studied his visitor. "Have we met before?"

"Might have, if you've ever been down to Perry. I got a motorcycle repair shop." He moved toward Wyman, who backed up into his office as his guest approached. "You got a motorcycle, Mr. Scudder?"

A perplexed look crossed Wyman's face. "No, I don't have a motorcycle."

He closed the door behind him. Wyman staggered toward his desk.

"Just how can I be of assistance, Mr.—?"

"Just call me Harold." He reached inside his pants pocket and pulled out the strong thin strip of nylon cord.

Wyman lost his balance and fell toward his desk, but he managed to steady himself by grabbing onto the edge of the only piece of furniture in the room other than a leather swivel chair.

"Yes, sir, Harold. Tell me why you need a lawyer."

"I don't need just any lawyer. I need you."

Before Scudder had a chance to turn and face him, he moved in for the kill. Quickly. Adeptly.

With the expert ease gained from years of experience, he walked up behind an inebriated Wyman Scudder and brought the cord over his head and across his neck before the unsuspecting fool realized what was happening. He struggled, but he was no match for a stronger, more agile, and sober man.

Halfway between Vidalia and Macon, the bottom fell out, and within minutes, Maleah could barely see the road. The rain came down in thick, heavy sheets, all but obliterating her view through the windshield. With little choice, for safety's sake, Maleah slowed the SUV to a crawl—twenty-five miles an hour.

"Maybe we should find a place to stop," Derek said. "At least until the worst passes."

"I'm okay," she assured him. "If it gets worse, I'll exit the interstate."

When he didn't respond, Maleah knew what he was thinking. Derek wished he was driving. Being the superior male, he could probably use his x-ray vision to see through the heavy downpour and his innate masculine abilities to maneuver the SUV through floodwaters.

After several minutes, Derek ended the awkward silence. "Do you know what puzzles me?"

"What? That I have managed not to wreck us?"

"Huh?" He laughed. "No. You're doing a great job. Better than I could do. I hate driving in heavy rain. Makes me nervous."

Maleah almost took her eyes off the road to glance at Derek, to see if he was mocking her. But she didn't. He sounded sincere, so she'd take him at his word.

"Okay, tell me what puzzles you."

"Why would someone hire Wyman Scudder, or any lawyer for that matter, to represent Jerome Browning, a man who confessed to murder and is serving consecutive life sentences?"

"I have no idea. You tell me."

"Let's say Albert Durham is our copycat killer. He wanted Browning to reveal all his little secrets so that he, Durham, could duplicate Browning's MO. Maybe simply telling Browning that he wanted to write the story of his life wasn't enough incentive for Browning to open up and share all."

Derek was right. Damn, he was always right! "I see what you're getting at. Durham promised Browning a new lawyer, maybe made him think Scudder could find grounds to reopen his case, as far fetched as that idea is. And he promised Browning a lady friend."

"Cindy Di Blasi. What are the odds that Cindy, or whatever her name is, gets paid by the hour?"

"A prostitute? Makes sense."

"Another thing that puzzles me is, if Durham isn't the copycat killer, why a writer with Durham's reputation would get involved with Browning. He's never chosen a convicted criminal as the subject of one of his biographies. If someone hired him to do it, why would he agree?"

"Maybe he needs the money."

"Possibly. But he'd have to know he was getting himself mixed up with something illegal."

"What if he's being blackmailed," Maleah said. "Or maybe Durham really is our copycat."

"Maybe he is. But if he is, why would he leave us a trail leading straight to him?"

"He wouldn't."

"We have too many unanswered questions."

"You're right. We need answers, so we start with Scudder. We know where to find him. He may be able to tell us something."

"I figure Scudder will talk for the right amount of money," Derek told her. "But I'm not sure how much he actually knows."

"Hopefully the agency will dig up more info on Cindy and Durham and once we've questioned Scudder and gotten some answers, we'll be able to move on pretty quickly to Cindy and Durham."

"It could take time to track them down, especially if they don't want to be found."

Maleah and Derek continued discussing the case, their conversation gradually dwindling down to an occasional comment by the time Maleah exited the interstate. The rain had slacked up to little more than a drizzle, but the pavement was slick and mucky with roadway residue. Muddy water filled the potholes and gushed across low-lying areas in the highway.

Following GPS directions, they watched for Mulberry Street, which crisscrossed with Third Street where Wyman Scudder's new law office was located.

Maleah noted the congestion ahead, but neither she nor Derek immediately realized that the next street was partially blocked by emergency vehicles, including a fire truck, an ambulance, and several patrol cars. As they drew nearer, she noticed a uniformed officer directing traffic. He stood in front of their destination.

"What the hell's going on?" Derek studied the situation while Maleah slowed the Equinox to a crawl. "Shit! It looks like something has happened in Scudder's building."

"Obviously I can't park here," she told him.

"I'm getting a bad feeling about this."

"Yeah, me, too."

"Let me out at the next corner," Derek told her. "You find a place to park while I see what's going on."

She hesitated, her competitive instinct interfering with her logical thought process. *You and Derek are partners,* she reminded herself. *You're playing on the same team.* "Yeah, sure."

Since traffic was pretty much bumper-to-bumper, it took Maleah a few minutes to maneuver the SUV into a position where she could come to a full stop. Without hesitation, Derek opened the door and jumped out and onto the street. Once the door slammed, Maleah moved forward and began her search for a parking place.

Five minutes later, out of sorts and perspiring enough to dampen her underwear, Maleah made it back to the cordoned-off area swarming with law enforcement and emergency personnel. She searched the crowd of curious onlookers for any sign of Derek, but didn't see him. Just as she stood on tiptoe and strained her neck in the hopes of gaining a better view, Derek came up alongside her.

"Looking for me?"

She released a startled gasp, but quickly recovered. "Damn it, I'm going to put a cow bell around your neck."

"Sorry."

She might have believed him if he hadn't chuckled softly.

"Well, what did you find out about all the hullabaloo going on?" she asked.

"A body was found on the third floor of that building." Derek pointed to the four-story office building in front of them.

"Don't tell me—"

The news crews in the crowd rushed forward as the ME's staff came out of the building carrying a body bag laid out on a stretcher. Questions zipped through the air like mosquitoes on a hot, humid summertime night as the reporters questioned officials on the scene. Their questions went unanswered as the officials ignored them.

"From what I've been able to find out, a young woman who had an afternoon interview for a position as a secretary for a lawyer in the building got quite a shock when she showed up for her appointment," Derek said. "She found her potential employer's body."

"It's Scudder, isn't it?"

"I couldn't get anybody to verify the victim's name, but when I asked if the dead man was Wyman Scudder, nobody said it wasn't. So, yes, I'm ninety-five percent sure it's Scudder."

Chapter 13

Derek had known that they wouldn't get any information by going through legal channels there in Macon. At least, not yet. The detectives in charge of the case had remained tight-lipped, as had the emergency personnel involved. He and Maleah had separated and moved through the crowd as discreetly as possible, both showing a casual interest in what was happening. Downtown Macon on a Friday afternoon buzzed with activity, and the entire block swarmed with curiosity seekers. The police had sealed off the building and rounded up all the occupants for questioning. The one person Derek would love to talk to—the secretary interviewee— would be detained, questioned, and cautioned not to speak to the press.

Thirty minutes after they had parted company and circulated through the on-lookers, Derek and Maleah reconnected at the end of the block.

"Anything?" Maleah asked.

Derek shook his head. "Not much. I heard the name Wyman Scudder more than once. It seems to be the consensus that the victim was the newest renter in the building, a lawyer named Scudder."

"I tried speaking to the policemen in charge of crowd control, but that got me nowhere."

"They won't bring the secretary out the front way," Derek said. "Which means they'll take her out a back exit and possibly escort her to the police station or at the very least walk her to wherever she parked her car."

"Even if we knew the location of that exit, we have no idea when they'll bring her out. And it's not as if they're going to let us get anywhere near her."

"You're right, but we could get a good look at her and I could snap her photo with my phone."

"I don't think we should go the let's-play-secret-agent route," Maleah told him. "But I assume you weren't serious. I think our best course of action is to call Sanders and let the agency contact the Macon Police Department and see what information they're willing to share."

Derek grinned. "Ah, gee whiz, Mom, you won't let me have any fun."

She rolled her eyes. "Come on. Let's get out of here. You can call Sanders while I drive."

"Why don't we find a downtown hotel, check in and then go out for dinner while Sanders is working Powell Agency magic to get us the info we need about Scudder's death?"

Why not? She knew her easy acquiesce to his suggestion would surprise Derek, but in this instance she agreed with him.

"I'm okay with going out to dinner and possibly staying overnight." Zigzagging through the slow-moving traffic, they crossed the street together, Maleah a few steps ahead of Derek. "When you talk to Sanders, be

sure to ask him about any updates on Cindy Di Blas
and Albert Durham."

"Yes, ma'am. Glad you thought of it."

"Bite me." Maleah snapped out the words.

Not slowing her pace as they left the bedlam behind
them and walked up the block, she cut him a sideway
glance. "We need to know for sure that Scudder wa
murdered, that he didn't have a heart attack or any
thing."

"Your gut instinct has to be telling you that he wa
murdered. I'd say what we really need to know is how
he was murdered and if the police have any suspects."

Maleah led Derek to her SUV. "You think the Copy
cat Carver killed him?"

"Don't you?" Derek asked as he sat down in the pas
senger seat.

Maleah slid into the driver's seat, inserted the key
into the ignition and started the SUV. "Probably. Ap
parently Scudder knew too much and could ID the
copycat, so he had become a liability."

"Of course being murdered eliminates Scudder as a
suspect. So, at least for the time being, that leaves Cindy
and Durham as our only leads."

"I think there's a good chance that Durham is ou
copycat."

"I think you could be right," Derek said.

As she eased the Equinox into traffic, Maleah cast a
quick glance in Derek's direction. "If we're right, then
he'll go after Cindy next, won't he?"

"More than likely. And if Durham isn't our guy, then
he and Cindy probably know who he is and that put
them both in danger."

"What we should be concentrating on is finding
Cindy and Durham. If Sanders has any leads on either

of them, I say we head out tonight. There's no point in our staying on here in Macon, is there?"

"Nothing except a decent meal and a good night's sleep."

"Call Sanders now," Maleah said. "There's no point in checking into a hotel until we know for sure whether we'll be staying or moving on tonight. I'll drive around for a few minutes while you call him."

Derek put a call through to Sanders's private number, used only by Powell agents. It was no surprise when Barbara Jean answered.

"We're in Macon," Derek said. "We just left a crime scene on Third Street. We're relatively certain that Wyman Scudder has been murdered. We need the agency to find out the particulars ASAP."

"I'll let Sanders know immediately and we'll get back to you with that info once we have it," Barbara Jean said.

"Anything on Cindy or Durham? If the copycat killed Scudder—"

"We believe we located Cindy. Her real name is Cindy Dobbins. She worked as a stripper for a while when she was younger. That's when she started using the name Di Blasi. She's been arrested half a dozen times in the past few years. Solicitation. Drug possession. Public intoxication," Barbara Jean said. "Check your e-mail. I sent you a complete report about half an hour ago, along with several arrest photos. Cindy's thirty-five. She looks fifty."

"Do you have a last known address?"

"We do, but she's not there. Hasn't been there in three weeks. We sent a local Atlanta contact to check it out."

"Do we know where Cindy was from originally?"

"Sure do. She was born and raised in a little wide-place-in-the-road town just over the Georgia state line, outside of Augusta. A placed called Apple Orchard, South Carolina. She's got a sister who still lives there."

"Maybe our little bird went home to roost," Derek said.

"The sister lives on Lancaster Road, number fourteen twenty. Her name is Jeri Paulk."

"Thanks, Barbara Jean. I'll fill Maleah in." He was pretty sure they would be heading straight to Apple Orchard, South Carolina. "By the way, anything else on Durham?"

"Durham owns three homes, a house in Tennessee, a condo in Aspen, and an apartment in New York City. But according to our investigation, he rents out all three. From what his agent told us, apparently he travels a great deal. The last time he checked in with her, he was in Virginia doing some Civil War research, but they haven't been in contact for nearly two weeks. It seems Durham doesn't own a cell phone."

"Doesn't this guy have any family or close friends?"

"He's a widower. No children. We're digging deeper to see if we can come up with relatives. According to his agent, the guy is a loner. He has dozens of acquaintances, but no bosom buddies."

"Got any recent photos of him?"

"Book jacket photo," Barbara Jean said. "I can send you a copy of that."

"What about his age? His background? Any military service?"

"Durham is sixty-three. No military background. The guy is an academic. He's got half a dozen degrees. Actually, he's Dr. Albert Durham."

"Doesn't sound like the type who'd get involved with a serial killer."

"Or become a copycat killer," Barbara Jean said.

After his conversation with Barbara Jean, Derek relayed all the information to Maleah. And just as he'd thought, she didn't hesitate to tell them they were going straight to Apple Orchard this evening. Checking online, Derek quickly found out that the small South Carolina town was a two-hour-and-forty-minute drive from downtown Macon.

"Let's at least stop for fast food on the way," Derek suggested.

She groaned. "You'd think you could skip a meal every once in a while."

"Drive-through will be fine."

She didn't reply.

Maleah headed the SUV north and continued in that direction on the interstate.

Poppy Chappelle had no idea she was being watched. Otherwise, he doubted the teenager would have removed her bikini top while she sunbathed in what she believed to be the privacy of her grandmother's backyard. No doubt, she and her cousins had spent the afternoon frolicking in the pool, but Court and Anne Lee Dandridge had left over an hour ago, only moments after he arrived. Poppy was now enjoying the late afternoon sunshine all alone while she stretched languidly on a padded chaise lounge.

It would be so easy to kill her. The grandmother probably hadn't come outside all day. He suspected the old woman took afternoon naps and avoided the June heat by staying indoors. The housekeeper had backed the late-model Mercedes from the garage fifteen minutes ago and headed toward downtown Savannah.

A brick fence flanked the back courtyard on either

side and connected to an eight-foot-high iron fence that ran across the back of the property. Towering crape myrtles heavy-laden with buds just beginning to burst open lined the fencerow. Although neatly maintained, an assortment of trees, shrubs, and flowers grew in profusion and partially obscured the view. He stood less than thirty feet from Saxon Chappelle's young niece, just beyond the unlocked back gate. He had parked his rental car blocks away, wore a ball cap and dark sunglasses, and had tossed his hand up and spoken to neighbors down the street as he passed by. If they remembered him, it was doubtful they could give anyone an even halfway accurate description of him. After all, he was just an average-looking white guy. His ability to appear quite generic had always given him an advantage.

He didn't especially like the idea of killing a sixteen-year-old, but she wouldn't be the first. In order to get the message across, he needed for the victim's death to matter. He supposed he could have chosen Saxon Chappelle's mother or his sister or the nephew or even the other niece, but his employer had seen Poppy's unusual given name as a sign, like a beacon glowing in the dark. She was the one.

Standing at the gate, he watched the rise and fall of Poppy's small, perky breasts. Her tiny rosebud pink nipples puckered as a warm breeze swept over her naked skin. He reached out and quietly lifted the latch. His pulse raced as the pre-kill adrenaline rush swept through his body, but it was only the first stage of the incredible high yet to come at the moment of the actual kill.

The urge to kill her now almost overwhelmed him.

But years of experience had taught him how to control his urges.

Wait. Now is not the right time. This is only a preliminary scouting trip.

"Poppy, what the devil are you doing?" a female voice demanded.

He dropped his hand away from the gate and took several careful steps backward while he searched for the source of the voice. An old woman, straight and tall, her white hair gleaming in the sunlight, came through the French doors that led into a back room of the two-story house.

Poppy reached down and grabbed her bikini top off the patio floor and hurriedly slipped it on before she got up and faced her grandmother. "I was sunbathing."

"In the nude?" the old woman asked.

"I wasn't nude. Besides, I'm all alone out here."

"In my day, a proper young lady—"

"Please, don't preach to me," Poppy said as she walked toward her grandmother. "I get enough of that from Mom."

Mrs. Chappelle sighed and shook her head, but when Poppy approached her, she opened her arms to give the girl a hug. "Your father was always testing my patience. He had a mind of his own and so do you. I can't tell you how much you remind me of him." She grasped Poppy's chin. "You're a Chappelle through and through. You'd do well to remember that."

"Yes ma'am."

"Well, come on inside and have a glass of the fresh lemonade Heloise made before she left to go shopping." Mrs. Chappelle took hold of her granddaughter's hand. "I do so love these weeks you spend with me every summer."

"So do I, Grandmother."

He waited until Poppy disappeared inside the house

before he latched the gate and turned to leave. As he
walked away, the excitement coursing through his body
began to fade ever so gradually, allowing his heartbeat
to return to normal by the time he reached his car. He
had checked out of the hotel in downtown Macon several hours ago and driven straight to Savannah without
stopping. Two hours and fifty minutes. He had been
careful to drive at the speed limit. The last thing he
needed was to be stopped by the highway patrol.

Despite the desire to kill Poppy right then and there,
he had not acted on impulse. He hadn't planned to kill
Poppy today. In keeping to the Carver's timeline, he knew
that the body should never be found before morning.
There was no hurry, of course. He could come back
tonight or tomorrow night or even the night after that,
and kill her before dawn. When the moment was right,
he would act. He would slit her throat, remove the small
triangular pieces of flesh, and leave her body floating in
her grandmother's pool.

You don't have to be satisfied with only one kill today, he
told himself as he slid behind the wheel of his rental
car. Humming softly, a favorite tune from childhood,
he drove down the street and within minutes left Ardsley Park.

They traveled east on I-20, went through Augusta
and exited off US 25 North going toward Newberry, but
they left the main highway after less than fifteen miles.
Derek had spent most of the trip reading aloud the reports that Barbara Jean had sent via e-mail attachments
and they had discussed the information. A strong wind
had blown in from the south, rocking the SUV and fore-
casting an oncoming storm. Keeping control of the
Equinox, Maleah followed the road signs that led them

straight to Apple Orchard, an unincorporated town in Edgefield County. Maleah had traveled around the U.S. and definitely throughout the South enough to recognize the signs of a dying small town. Apparently, the only remaining business was the mini-mart / gas station up ahead. To her left, the rusted hull of an old cotton gin near the railroad tracks rose into the eerily golden twilight sky like the giant carcass of an ancient beast. On the opposite side of the road, a centuries-old clapboard church stood vacant. Half the windows were broken and one of the double front doors, hanging precariously by a single hinge, thumped rhythmically in the wind.

They hadn't met a single vehicle in the past five minutes and she didn't see even one human being anywhere.

Derek hummed the theme from the old *Twilight Zone* TV show.

"Will you shut up," Maleah snapped at him as she slowed the SUV and turned off into the mini-mart parking lot. "Apparently there are very few street signs around here. We'll probably have to go in and ask directions."

"Actually, there are very few streets around here." Derek grinned.

Did he always have to have a smartass comeback? Okay, she knew that wasn't true. She was tired, frustrated, and hungry, but she shouldn't take it out on Derek. And yes, if she had driven through a fast-food place on the way here from Macon, as he had suggested, she wouldn't be hungry.

Talk about cutting off your nose to spite your face.

Why was she having so much difficulty accepting the fact that she didn't have to fight Derek for control? He was her partner, a co-worker she had learned to respect, and a man she was beginning to actually like. He deserved better from her.

Derek cleared his throat. "Want me to go in and ask directions or would you prefer to do it?"

"Why don't we both go in," Maleah replied. "I need to use the bathroom and I wouldn't mind picking up something to eat. Maybe a pack of crackers and a Dr Pepper."

She halfway expected him to mention his earlier suggestion about fast food, but he didn't. Instead, he got out, came around to her side of the SUV and walked alongside her toward the mini-mart. In the early days of their working relationship, he had acted like a real gentleman, but after she'd bitten his head off a few times, he had backed off. Occasionally, he still did little things like opening a door for her, and she had stopped reprimanding him for his good manners. She appreciated that a lot of men still treated a lady like a lady, but with Derek, she had seen it as condescension. But she had been wrong. So wrong. Derek didn't look down on her for being female or consider her a member of the weaker sex.

When they entered the Apple Orchard mini-mart, Maleah noted that the place was all but deserted. Odd, considering this was a Friday night. But then, the population might top out at less than a hundred people. Maleah spotted the bathroom and made a beeline in that direction while Derek meandered along at the back of the store where the giant coolers were located.

A few minutes later when Maleah and Derek approached the checkout, the young, bubble gum smacking clerk eyed them suspiciously. "Can I help you folks?"

"We're from out of town." Derek grinned at the girl, whose chin-length, dark brown hair was streaked with purple highlights. "We're looking for someone. We have her address and were hoping you could help us out with directions."

The plump, pug-faced clerk sported a shiny gold nose ring and a band of script tattoos circled each bicep revealed by her skimpy yellow tank top. A row of belly fat protruded between the end of the top and the waistband of her low-riding jeans. "Who you folks looking for?"

Derek smiled. Few women could resist his charm. "We're looking for my girlfriend's cousin." He glanced at Maleah to indicate she was the girlfriend. "Blondie hasn't seen her cousin since they were kids, but since we were on our way up to Columbia, another cousin suggested we look her up."

The girl smiled when Derek leaned over the counter and looked right at her. "You know a woman named Jeri Paulk? That's my girlfriend's cousin." Not taking his eyes off the clerk, he called to Maleah, who had gone in search of a canned cola. "Honey, what's that address your cousin Barbara Jean gave you for Jeri?"

"I know where Jeri lives," the girl said. "It ain't half a mile from here." She practically drooled while licking her lips, all the while looking as if she could swallow Derek whole.

Maleah scanned the refrigerated coolers across the back of the store, searching for a Dr Pepper while listening to the girl.

"Y'all remember passing an old church right before you got here?"

"Yes," Derek replied.

"Just go back and turn off on the road by the church. Jeri lives down the road a piece. You can't miss it. She painted the place bright blue last year. I told her that I'd bet the astronauts could see her place from outer space."

"Sure do thank you for your help," Derek said. "Honey, you got our colas and crackers?"

Maleah removed two canned Dr Peppers from the giant coolers and then grabbed a couple of packs of peanut butter and crackers off the shelves on her way back to the checkout counter.

After laying her items down, she said, "Yeah, thanks for helping us out. I sure am looking forward to seeing Jeri again after all these years."

"Sure, no problem." The girl rang up their order.

Maleah waited for Derek to pay for the items, then picked them up and headed out of the store. Halfway to the SUV, she handed him one of the colas and a pack of crackers.

"Thanks."

"Thank you," she replied. "That was a lot easier than I thought it would be. You practically had that girl eating out of your hand."

Derek chuckled. "What can I say, the ladies like me."

She punched him in the arm playfully and they both laughed.

They sat in the mini-mart parking lot long enough to devour the crackers and finish off part of their canned colas. Maleah started the SUV and went back the way they had come into Apple Orchard. She turned at the old church and headed down the narrow paved road that twisted and turned, carrying them farther and farther away from civilization. It was past sunset and darkness was fast approaching. Without lights along the road, Maleah had to rely totally on the Equinox's headlights to guide them. Just as Miss Purple-streaked-hair had told them, the bright blue house came into view less than half a mile from the mini-mart. Even in the encroaching gloom of nightfall, the small wooden house was visible. An older model Chevy truck and a late model Ford Mustang were parked in the gravel drive. Maleah pulled in behind the Mustang.

"So, what do we say to Jeri Paulk? Do we tell her why we're looking for her sister Cindy or do we make up some lie like we did back at the mini-mart?" Maleah asked.

"I suggest we play it by ear," Derek told her. "Let's see what kind of reception we get. If you're agreeable, let me take the lead and you just follow along with whatever I say. Can you do that?"

"Of course, I can."

They got out of the SUV and walked toward the porch. As they drew closer Maleah noticed the broken recliner, the vinyl ripped and the padding showing through, sitting beside two metal lawn chairs on the right side of the porch. Suddenly a dog reared his head up off the floor on the other side of the porch and barked. Maleah jumped. Derek cursed.

The dog kept barking, but didn't move toward them. The porch light came on and the front door flew open. A bear of a man wearing overalls and no shirt and carrying a shotgun in his meaty hand stood in the doorway. Behind his massive frame, a TV screen flashed and the sound of recorded laughter drifted outside.

"Get the hell off my property," the man yelled. "I know why you're here and you ain't welcome."

Maleah opened her mouth to respond, but before she could utter the first word, the man aimed the shotgun and pulled the trigger, sending a blast of buckshot in their direction.

Derek shoved Maleah out of the line of fire, tossed her onto the ground and came down over her. Eye to eye with her, his heavy weight a protective shield, Derek said, "Maybe we should have called first."

Chapter 14

Maleah didn't know whether to laugh, cry or just slap Derek in the mouth. During the process of rolling off her, he managed to unsnap her holster and remove her Glock pistol before she could. He aimed and fired. The bullet hit the tin sign hanging over the front door of the Paulk house. The pinging sound rang out over the dog's incessant barking.

"Unless you want the next one aimed directly at you, then don't fire that damn shotgun again," Derek hollered at the shooter.

"When did you damn bill collectors start carrying guns?" the man called out to Derek, then shouted at his barking mixed-breed dog. "Shut up, damn it, Pork Chop."

"We aren't bill collectors," Maleah said, as she grabbed for her gun still in Derek's clutch.

"We're from the Powell Private Security and Investigation Agency." Derek handed Maleah the Glock and whispered, "Don't holster that thing yet. You never know what Jethro there might do."

Jethro? If they hadn't been in such a deadly serious situation, she would laugh. Derek undoubtedly meant

Jethro Bodine, the big dumb character from the *Beverly Hillbillies* TV series of long ago.

"Are you folks lost?" the shooter asked.

"We're looking for Jeri Paulk," Maleah said as she rose to her feet, pistol in hand.

"That's my wife." The man lowered his shotgun, the muzzle pointed toward the porch floor. "I'm Lonny Paulk. What y'all want with Jeri?"

Derek stood, brushed the dirt and grass from his slacks and took a stand at Maleah's side. "We're looking for her sister, Cindy Dobbins. We think she might be in danger."

Lonny stepped out farther onto the porch and came over to the edge of the steps, shotgun still pointing down, and motioned to them. "Y'all come on up closer." He twisted his head and yelled over his shoulder, "Jeri, get your fat ass out here. There's some folks here who want to talk to you about that fuck-up sister of yours. Seems she's gotten herself into more trouble."

As they approached Lonny, Maleah noted several things all at once. He was as hairy as a grizzly, his greasy brown hair was pulled back in a ponytail and he emitted an unpleasant body odor. The man definitely needed, at the very least, a haircut and a bath.

Maleah paused when she reached the foot of the steps. Derek halted directly behind her.

"Who the hell's looking for Cindy?" A short, obese woman who was almost as broad as she was wide—about five feet—came out onto the porch. The first thing Maleah noticed was the woman's hair. It looked like bright yellow straw. She wore an oversized moo-moo in some hideous floral design of purple, hot pink, and turquoise that on a taller person would have hit them mid-calf. But on Jeri, the hem reached her ankles and floated over her small, broad feet and bright orange toenails.

"Are you Jeri Paulk?" Derek asked. "And is Cindy Dobbins, also known as Cindy Di Blasi, your sister?"

"Yeah, I'm Jeri and I got a sister named Cindy. What's this all about?" Jeri waddled across the porch to her husband's side.

"We're from the Powell Private Security and Investigation Agency," Maleah told them. "We're investigating a series of murders and we have reason to believe your sister Cindy is in danger. We're trying to locate her to warn her. We want to offer her our agency's protection."

"Who is it that you two are working for?" Jeri sized up Derek and apparently liked what she saw because she licked her lips and smiled at him.

Once again, if not for the gravity of the situation, Maleah would have laughed. "We're agents for the Powell Private—"

"I heard that part," Jeri said. "But who hired you?"

"Several murder victims were connected to our agency," Derek explained. "Our employer assigned us to investigate."

"How's my sister involved?"

"The killer that we're tracking is a copycat killer." Maleah watched for a reaction and when Jeri looked as if she understood, Maleah continued. "He's copying the style of a murderer known as the Carver. Your sister Cindy has been visiting the Carver, who is incarcerated in the Georgia State Prison. We want to question her."

"You said she might be in danger," Lonny said. "How?"

Derek leaned over and whispered to Maleah, "Cindy's here."

Maleah didn't know how Derek knew or why he was so sure, but she had learned not to question his instincts which for the most part had proven to be infallible.

"Jerome Browning, aka the Carver, has had three visitors in the past year, one was a writer interviewing him for a book about his life, the other was his lawyer and the third person was Cindy." Maleah paused, giving Jeri and Lonny time to digest the info. "Browning's lawyer was murdered earlier today. We have reason to believe that Cindy could be next."

Silence.

Lonny turned to his wife. "I told you not to let her stay here. That woman is nothing but bad news. Every goddamn time she's around, trouble follows her."

Jeri planted her fat little hands on her ample hips. "She's my sister. What did you want me to do, tell her she can't come to me when she needs family? Lord knows I've put up with enough shit from that bunch of heathens you come from."

"Are you saying that Cindy is here?" Maleah asked.

A petite figure appeared in the doorway and stood behind the screen door.

"Cindy?" Maleah asked. "Are you Cindy Dobbins?"

The woman pushed open the door, came outside and moved past her sister and brother-in-law. "I'm Cindy Dobbins." She turned to Jeri. "You and Lonny go on back inside. I want to talk to these people alone."

"Are you sure?" Jeri asked Cindy.

Cindy nodded.

Jeri and Lonny went inside, but left the front door open.

"Y'all come on up here and take a seat." Cindy motioned for them to join her on the porch.

Maleah holstered her Glock and then walked up the steps, Derek directly behind her. Cindy sat in the dilapidated recliner. Maleah's first instinct was to wipe off the metal chair before sitting, but she didn't. When she sat, Derek came over and stood behind her. The yellow

bug light shining down from the bare bulb in the ceiling cast a blaring amber glow across the porch

"Is Wyman Scudder really dead?" Cindy asked.

Maleah studied the slender, petite woman, who certainly looked older than thirty-five. But she wasn't a bad-
looking woman, just old before her time. Hard living
could do that to a person. Her short, curly hair had
been dyed a dark burgundy red which made her pale
face seem colorless. Without makeup and wearing jeans
and a Harley-Davidson T-shirt, she didn't look like a
prostitute, just a rode-hard-and-put-away-wet middle-
aged country gal.

"Yes, Wyman Scudder is dead," Maleah said. "We're
pretty sure he was murdered."

"How did you meet Mr. Scudder?" Derek asked.

"Look, before I answer any of your questions, I need
to know that I'm not going to get in any trouble with
the law." Cindy glanced from Maleah to Derek. "I got
myself involved in something I wish I hadn't. But I didn't
have no idea . . . I just needed the money. I've been out
of the business for a while, you know. I've tried waitress-
ing and working in the chicken plant and all sorts of
odd jobs. I got a kid, see, and it ain't right that she's in
foster care. The only way I can get her back is . . ." Cindy
swallowed her tears.

"You have a daughter?" Maleah leaned forward toward Cindy. "What's her name?"

"Patsy Lynn. I named her after my mama."

"How old is Patsy Lynn?"

"She'll be eleven this October."

Maleah looked Cindy square in the eye. "Cindy, my
name is Maleah Perdue, and I promise you that
Derek—" she glanced at him "—this is Derek Lawrence.
I promise you that we will do whatever we can to protect
you and that includes protection from the police."

Cindy took a deep breath. "He paid me five thousand dollars. All I had to do was visit Jerome Browning at the Georgia State Prison and exchange a few letters and a few phone calls."

"Who paid you?" Derek asked. "Who hired you?"

"Wyman Scudder. I thought you knew."

"Are you saying that Wyman Scudder hired you and he's the one who paid you five thousand dollars?" Maleah asked. "You never met anyone else, were never contacted by anyone else?"

Cindy shook her head. "Nobody else. Just Mr. Scudder."

"Then you never met a man named Albert Durham?" Derek asked.

Cindy didn't respond immediately. Maleah sensed that the woman was giving her reply a great deal of thought.

"Cindy?" Maleah prompted.

"I never met him. But . . . Jerome talked about him. You know, when I'd go visit him. The first time I went for a visit, he said a man named Albert Durham was going to write a book about him and make him even more famous than he already was. Jerome liked the idea of the whole world knowing who he was and what he'd done."

"But you never met Durham?" Derek said.

Cindy shook her head.

"Can you tell us exactly why Wyman Scudder hired you?" Derek asked.

"Wyman was my lawyer, a few years back. We . . . uh . . . sort of had a thing. You know. For a while. I hired him to help me try to keep my daughter out of foster care. I couldn't afford to pay him." Cindy hung her head.

"When did Scudder first contact you about visiting Jerome Browning?" Maleah asked.

"About five months ago. He said he had a client who needed a friend, a female friend, to visit him every once in a while. I thought why not? I mean for five thousand, I'll do just about anything."

"What did you and Jerome talk about?" Derek asked.

"Everything. Nothing. Mostly about him. He liked to brag. And sometimes, he'd give me messages for Wyman."

"What sort of messages?" Maleah asked.

"Nothing really. Just things like, 'tell Wyman to come see me' or 'ask Wyman to tell Mr. Durham that we need to talk.' Stuff like that."

"You exchanged letters with Browning and spoke to him on the phone," Maleah said. "Do you still have those letters?"

"No, I ain't got them." She shook her head. "I turned each one over to Wyman as soon as I got it. They weren't really for me no how. That's what Wyman told me."

Maleah and Derek glanced at each other.

"What about the letters you wrote Jerome?" Maleah asked.

"I didn't write them letters. Wyman gave them to me, all typed out real neat like, and told me to write them out in my own handwriting and then mail them off to Jerome."

"Do you remember anything about what was said in those letters?" Derek asked.

"Not really. I didn't care. Weren't nothing to me one way or the other."

"I understand," Maleah told her. "But if you could remember something, anything, about the content of those letters, it might help us."

"Would it help you find the man who killed Wyman?"

"Yes," she replied. "And the person who has already

killed five innocent people, using the same method that Jerome Browning used in his Carver murders. If you would come with us, let the Powell Agency give you around-the-clock protection, you could work with us to prevent this person from killing again."

"But how can I help you? I really don't know nothing."

"You probably know a lot more than you realize," Derek said. "The more you think about your visits with Browning and about the telephone conversations and the letters you exchanged with him, the more you might remember."

"You think so?"

Derek smiled. Cindy responded the way all women did to Derek's charm.

"You help us and we'll help you. Tell us what you want and we'll do our best to see that you get it."

Cindy studied Derek as if trying to decide whether or not she could trust him. She nodded. "Okay. You've got a deal, but I need to talk things over with my sister first and then pack a bag." Cindy got up and headed for the front door, then paused and asked, "I can let my sister know where I'll be and I'll be able to talk to her whenever I want, right?"

"Absolutely," Derek assured her.

As soon as Cindy disappeared inside the house, Derek and Maleah got up and walked out into the yard.

"Do you think she really can't remember anything or she's playing us to see what she can get out of us?" Maleah nodded toward the house.

"A little of both. I'm sure it didn't escape your notice that Cindy isn't the sharpest knife in the drawer."

Maleah grunted. "I noticed, and apparently it runs in the family."

"I figure if Griff can find a way to get Cindy's daugh-

ter out of foster care and if we can promise to return
her daughter to her, she'll tell us everything she knows.
And I can guarantee you that she knows more than
she's told us."

When he had left Ardsley Park, he had fully intended to check into a downtown Savannah hotel and
get a good night's sleep. He had planned to kill Saxon
Chappelle's cute little sixteen-year-old niece tomorrow
evening. But as fate would have it, he had decided to
stop for a bite to eat and had carried his Netbook into
the coffee shop café. While drinking an after-dinner
cappuccino, he had removed a keychain flash-drive
from his pocket, hoping it contained some useful information. After killing Wyman Scudder, he had downloaded
the files from the man's computer before wiping Scudder's computer clean. It would take an expert a good
while to restore those files, if it was even possible.

Just as he had hoped, Scudder had kept a current address and phone number for Cindy "Di Blasi" Dobbins.
Never put off until tomorrow what you can do today.

He laughed. He had put off killing Poppy Chappelle
but not without a good reason. He wanted her alone
when he killed her. No witnesses. No collateral damage.
Following in the Carver's footsteps as closely as possible
didn't allow him much leeway.

He wasn't sure exactly how much Cindy knew, but if
she knew anything at all that might help the police or
the Powell Agency, she was a liability, just as Wyman
Scudder had been. He no longer needed either of
them, just as he no longer needed Jerome Browning.
But Browning didn't pose a threat. He had used the
convicted killer for his own purposes. And as smart as
Browning was, his ego had prevented him from realiz-

g the complete truth. However, by now, the Carver
new that Albert Durham would never write Jerome
rowning's life story.

He could have waited until tomorrow to hunt down
indy. Maybe he should have. But the moment he read
e info from Scudder's file on Cindy, he realized that
e was probably hiding out at her sister's place in
pple Orchard, South Carolina, and he had gotten an
erwhelming urge to get the job done as soon as possi-
e. And that's why he had driven straight from Savan-
ah, a nearly three-hour trip. That's why he had set up
out 250 yards into the woods, just far enough in so
at he couldn't be seen from across the road at Jeri
d Lonny Paulk's house. He had parked his car at a
fe distance, but close enough to make a quick get-
/ay. Hitting a small target, the size of a human head,
between 200 and 300 yards required the type of skill
at he had acquired years ago and had used numerous
nes. He never became attached to a specific weapon,
ither pistols nor rifles nor knives; instead he used
natever he considered perfect for the individual job.
night he had brought along a recent purchase—an
24 SWS.

One clean shot was all he needed. One shot directly
to the kill zone where the bullet would sever the
ainstem and cause instantaneous death.

He hadn't been there more than six or seven min-
es now, watching and waiting for the right moment to
ike. How long had the Powell agents been talking to
ndy? Lifting his Bushnell binoculars, he zeroed in on
e Paulks' front porch. Cindy had gone back into the
use and the Powell agents were standing in the front
d talking. Just what had Cindy told them? She couldn't
ve told them something of any real importance be-
ise her knowledge was limited. And with her out of

the way, the agents would have no way to verify what,
anything, she'd told them.

Minutes ticked by, four, six, ten. The Powell agent
hadn't left, which meant they were waiting for som
thing or someone. During the wait, he had gone ov
his plan, preparing for several different scenarios, on
that included having to kill the Powell agents as well
Cindy's sister and brother-in-law. Having to kill th
many people would complicate the situation, make
messy. He preferred neat loose ends, all tied up, no u
able evidence left behind. He always wore thin leath
gloves that had been handmade in Italy, thus leaving r
fingerprints. Whenever there was a possibility of leavir
footprints, he made sure he wore inexpensive sho
that could be picked up at Wal-Mart. He prided himse
on not making mistakes. Mistakes could be deadly. Ar
he intended to live to a ripe old age.

When the front door opened, it was Lonny Pau
who came out onto the porch, not Cindy Dobbins. Th
time he wasn't carrying a shotgun.

"Cindy'll be out soon," Lonny told Maleah and Dere
"The wife ain't too happy about her going off with y
two. She says we don't know y'all, don't know if we c
trust either of you. But Cindy says she trusts you, so
reckon that ought to be good enough."

"We'll make sure Cindy is kept safe," Maleah assur
Lonny. "She can call her sister every day if she'd lil
We're not taking her prisoner."

"She says that the lawyer she hooked up with a wh
back got himself whacked and that the guy who kill
him just might come after her next," Lonny said. "A
chance that me and the Mrs. might be in any danger

"I don't think you and Jeri have to worry. The kil

as no reason to harm either of you, especially once
Cindy is no longer staying here with y'all."

Lonny turned halfway around and hollered into the
house, "You two women stop your yakking and get out
here. You're keeping these folks waiting."

When she glanced his way, Maleah noted the smile in
Derek's eyes although he hadn't changed his expression in any way.

"Hold your horses," Jeri told her husband as she
held the screen door open for her sister. "I needed
time to say my good-byes to Cindy."

"I'm ready," Cindy said as she followed Jeri onto the
porch.

Derek moved forward, reached up and took Cindy's
small, seen-better-days suitcase while Jeri and Cindy walked
down the steps and into the yard, the two women arm-
in-arm. Maleah opened the SUV's driver's side door,
slid behind the wheel and impatiently strummed her
fingertips on the steering wheel. After placing the suitcase in the back of the Equinox, Derek stood outside
the SUV. The sisters hugged each other and shed a few
tears. Cindy released Jeri and walked toward Derek,
who had opened the door for her and waited to help
her up and into the vehicle.

Suddenly, halfway to the SUV, Cindy dropped like a
stone falling through water and instantly hit the
ground. The crack of rifle fire pierced the bucolic stillness just as the bullet entered Cindy's head. The sound
was familiar in a rural area where hunting was a major
pastime. But Maleah quickly realized that this nighttime shooter's prey had been human and that Cindy
Robbins had been killed by a skilled rifleman.

Jeri screamed at the top of her lungs.

Lonny mumbled, "What the hell?"

After reaching inside the SUV to grab the Beretta

Maleah kept under the seat as a backup weapon, Derek
got to Cindy first and checked for a pulse. He looked
up at Maleah, who rushed in behind him, and shook his
head, then rose to his feet.

"Call nine-one-one," Maleah yelled as she flipped
open her holster, pulled out her Glock, and headed
across the country road.

Derek caught up with her just as she entered the
woods. "Hold up," he told her. "We don't know where
this guy is. It could take us a while to find him, if we can
find him. Slow down and think this thing through."

"Damn it, Derek, while we're thinking, he could be
getting away."

As if on cue, a car started somewhere nearby.

Without hesitation, they both rushed from the edge
of the wooded area and ran up the road toward the
sound of the vehicle's screeching departure. The red
taillights winked mockingly at them as the car sped off
in the opposite direction.

Maleah cursed under her breath as she turned and
raced back up the road toward her SUV still parked in
the Paulks' driveway.

"She's dead," Jeri wailed. "My sister's dead."

"Shot clean through the head," Lonny said, a look of
shock in his eyes.

"Call 911, damn it," Maleah told them. "Get the sheriff out here." She jumped in the Equinox and revved
the motor.

Derek barely got the passenger's side door open before Maleah started backing up the SUV. By the time he
managed to jump inside the Equinox, she had the vehicle headed up the road, back toward the main highway.

Chapter 15

Derek noted that Maleah hadn't secured her seatbelt.

"I'm going to reach across and grab your seatbelt," he told her.

"Yeah, go ahead."

Once he buckled her in, he did the same for himself.

"I doubt the Paulks contacted 911," Maleah told him as she pressed her foot down on the gas pedal. "Call 911 and tell them what's happened and let them know that we are in pursuit of the shooter."

Knowing a reply was unnecessary, Derek hurriedly placed the call, gave them his name and then explained that there had been a shooting, the victim was dead, and her sister and brother-in-law were with the body. He rattled off the address and then explained that he and his partner, both Powell Agency employees, were pursuing what they believed to be the shooter's vehicle.

The 911 operator kept him on the line, asking questions as she began the process of contacting the proper agencies.

The scenery flashed by in a dark blur as they chased

the red taillights all the way back to the main highway.
Maleah made the turn at eighty miles an hour. The
SUV swerved and tilted as they rounded the curve and
sailed into the oncoming traffic lane. Luckily, there wasn't
another vehicle anywhere in sight, except for the get-
away car.

Derek couldn't help being impressed with Maleah's
driving skills. The Equinox had just hit ninety and was
beginning to close in on the car ahead of them by no
more than a hundred yards.

"Can you make out anything about the car?" Maleah
asked. "Make? Model? Color? Car tag?"

"Not yet," he told her.

Staying on the line with the 911 operator by placing
his phone between his ear and shoulder, he undid his
seatbelt and climbed into the back of the SUV. Maleah
didn't react. Remaining focused straight ahead, she kept
driving in hot pursuit of the shooter. Derek plopped
down in the backseat, spread his legs, reached into the
floorboard and unzipped the black vinyl equipment
bag. He rummaged around in the bag until he found
what he'd been searching for—binoculars.

"I've given you all the info I can," he told the operator. "I'm going to hang up now."

He crawled over the console and back into the front
passenger seat. After adjusting the Yukon night vision
binoculars, he aimed them straight ahead.

"God damn it," Derek cursed.

"What is it? What's wrong?"

"He's playing with us, letting us get closer. There's
no way in hell you're going to catch that bad boy."

"Bad boy?"

"Our shooter is driving a Dodge Charger. We're talking a Hemi V-8 standard on that car."

"Shit!"

Derek directed the binoculars toward the license plate. "It's a Georgia tag." He rattled off the number. "Bibb County."

"It's a rental, right? Otherwise he'd never let us get close enough to catch a glimpse of the tag. You can rent a Charger, can't you?"

"Sure can."

"Bibb County," Maleah said. "That's Macon. He rented a car in Macon, either before or after he killed Wyman Scudder."

"He wants us to know. Son of a bitch, he's telling us that he's tied up loose ends and—" Maleah mumbled a few choice curse words under her breath. "Damn, he's speeding up again."

"I'll call 911 back and give them the numbers I saw on the tag," Derek said. "I can't believe he's stupid enough to hand us that tag number on a silver platter."

"He's going to switch cars somewhere or he's got an accomplice waiting with another vehicle somewhere up the—"

"Watch out!" Derek yelled the moment he saw the pickup truck pulling onto the highway from a side road.

Maleah swerved to avoid hitting the truck, taking the Equinox all the way across the highway and onto the shoulder of the two-lane roadway. Derek's binoculars flew out of his hand and landed in the floorboard beneath Maleah's feet. Keeping her hands on the wheel and her wits about her, she managed to take charge of the quickly careening-out-of-control vehicle.

By the time she got the SUV leveled off and back on track, a couple of flashing blue lights coming from the opposite direction dove directly in front of her, effectively blocking her pursuit. She had no choice but to slow down and stop. Either that or deliberately ram into two patrol cars.

"Take a deep breath," Derek advised. "We have a lot of explaining to do. They don't know we're the good guys."

"I know. I know," Maleah said, aggravation in her voice. "These local guys just ruined any chance we had to catch the killer."

"No, they didn't. They're just the reason we ended our pursuit sooner rather than later." Once she cooled off a bit and could see reason, she would realize he was right.

In the meantime, they had to deal with local law enforcement and hope these guys would let them explain the situation before hauling them off to jail.

"Get out of the vehicle," a deputy called to them. "Slow and easy. And put your hands on your head."

Derek saw two deputies, pistols drawn and aimed, standing on either side of the Equinox, and one deputy directly in front, which mean the fourth was no doubt stationed at the rear.

"On the count of three, open your door and get out nice and slow," Derek told her. "And for once, would you please let me do the talking?"

Twenty minutes after he lost his pursuers, he drove into downtown Augusta. Once he realized they were no longer following him, he had slowed the Charger from a hundred to eighty and gradually down to the allowed limit. In retrospect, he knew he should have refrained from showing off by deliberately thumbing his nose at the Powell agents. But on occasion, he could not resist the urge to show lesser mortals that they were dealing with a smarter, superior, and more deadly opponent. There was no way they could ever best him.

He needed to ditch the rental car as soon as possible, but not before he was within walking distance of transportation. By now, it was likely that the Powell agents had given the Edgefield County sheriff's boys the license plate number and make, model and color of the vehicle. Using the GPS system, he'd gotten directions to the Greyhound bus station, which, as luck would have it, was now only five minutes away. When he reached the twelve hundred block, he pulled off the street and into the parking area for the Greene Street Presbyterian Church. After getting out, he popped open the trunk and removed a carrying case and a large suitcase. Then, working quickly, he disassembled the sniper rifle, carefully arranged the parts inside the carrying case, and placed the case inside the suitcase beneath his clothes and toiletries.

Before closing the suitcase, he removed his thin leather gloves and tossed them inside; then he closed and locked the bag. Whistling softly, the old familiar tune from his childhood, he clutched the suitcase handle and headed toward the bus station. Glancing at his lighted digital watch, he smiled. He had plenty of time to get there before the ticket counter closed at 11:59 P.M. He would go to Atlanta, take a day off to revise his plans, and then return to Savannah for the Copycat Carver's next kill.

By the time they were allowed to leave the Edgefield County sheriff's office, Maleah knew more about the sheriff and his department than she'd ever wanted to know. And she had gained a new appreciation for just how far Griffin Powell's sphere of influence reached, apparently all the way to Edgefield County, South Carolina. Otherwise, she and Derek would probably be behind bars.

Sheriff Gene Lockhart had taken charge of the murder case, the first murder in his county since he'd been elected. All three of the county's criminal investigators had been called in and two had been dispatched to the scene of the crime at the Paulk residence, along with the Chief Investigator and the forensic investigator. The third criminal investigator, Lieutenant Nelson Saucier, a middle-aged black man, with a wide smile and an intimidating stare, had been assigned to interrogate Maleah and Derek.

She had to give the man credit—he had assumed they were innocent of any wrong doing and had actually listened to what they had to say. And as soon as Derek had given him the license plate number and info about the Dodge Charger, he had issued an all points bulletin.

As difficult as it had been for her to keep her mouth shut, Maleah had done as Derek requested and allowed him to do most of the talking. There was no point in the two of them giving the lieutenant the same information. They were Powell agents working a case involving a suspected serial killer, a copycat murderer who was targeting their agency. Their investigation had led them to Apple Orchard in their search for a woman named Cindy Dobbins.

After patiently listening to Derek explain why they were on the scene when Ms. Dobbins was shot and why they were chasing the person they believed to be the shooter, Lt. Saucier interrogated them further, asking them question after question in rapid-fire succession. He expected answers from both of them and that's what he got, similar answers to each question, but not word for word identical responses.

The inspector had excused himself a couple of times, leaving them alone, but they had sat quietly and waited without indulging in conversation. The second time he had come back into the room, he'd handed each their driver's license and Powell Agency ID.

"Well, at least we know you're both who you say you are, but until I get the okay from Sheriff Lockhart, I'm afraid I'm going to have to hold y'all."

And so they had waited for what seemed like an eternity—well past dawn—before the sheriff, looking as if he, too, had been up all night—arrived at headquarters. He came in, introduced himself to Maleah and Derek and told them that they were free to go.

Maleah opened her mouth to speak, but didn't get out the first word before Derek grabbed her arm and said, "Yes, sir, thank you."

"Don't thank me," the sheriff replied. "Thank the attorney general. I've never gotten a direct order from the man, never even spoke to him before tonight."

"We'll be sure to let him know how grateful we are," Maleah said as Derek all but dragged her out of the sheriff's office and straight to where her SUV was parked.

"Give me your keys," Derek told her. "I'll drive."

She hesitated momentarily, then pulled her keys out of her jacket and tossed them to him. Before getting in on the passenger side, she stretched, tossed back her head, and stared up at the early morning sky. She ached all over, from head to toes. She was also sleepy and hungry and ill as a hornet. Despite the surprising competence of the sheriff's department, Maleah felt that too much time had been wasted on grilling her and Derek when that time could have been utilized in a better way. But then again, how could she fault local law enforcement, with their limited resources, for not catching their killer when the entire Powell Agency, with unlimited resources, had been unable to apprehend the Copycat Carver?

"Jump in," Derek said. "Let's get the hell out of Dodge while the getting is good."

Offering him a weak smile and a weary nod, she opened the SUV passenger door and hopped up and into the seat. While she adjusted her seatbelt, Derek started the vehicle, hurriedly checked his mobile phone and within two minutes, they were headed south. Struggling to keep her eyes open, Maleah began concentrating on the road signs and soon realized they were not headed back to Augusta.

"Where are we going?"

"Aiken," Derek replied.

"What's in Aiken?"

"A decent hotel that's not too far away."

"Is that what you were doing with your phone, checking for a hotel?"

"Aiken's closer than Augusta and I don't know about you, but the sooner I get something to eat and a few hours of sleep, the better."

"You won't get any argument from me."

"Will wonders never cease." He chuckled.

Although the trip from Apple Orchard to Aiken had been relatively short, Maleah had fallen asleep. She woke suddenly when Derek pulled the SUV under the entrance portico at the Holiday Inn Express in downtown Aiken.

"Get out and book us a couple of rooms," he told her. "I'll park, grab our bags, and meet you inside."

She shook her head to dislodge the cobwebs and without saying a word, got out and walked into the hotel. Before she reached the registration counter, the smell of the complimentary breakfast coming from the nearby dining area reminded her of how long it had been since she'd last eaten. *First things first,* she reminded herself, and went straight to the check-in desk. She explained to the clerk that she didn't mind paying full price for the two rooms for two nights—last night and tonight—although it was doubtful they'd still be here tonight. By the time Derek joined her, she had charged the rooms to her credit card and pocketed two room keys.

"They're still serving breakfast," she told him.

"Then what are we waiting for? I'm so hungry, I could eat a horse."

She led, he followed. After finding an empty table, he pulled over a third chair, dumped their bags into the chair and made a beeline to the coffeemaker.

As complimentary hotel breakfasts went, the food at the Aiken Holiday Inn Express wasn't half bad. Of course, Maleah was so hungry that anything edible would have tasted like a feast.

As they sat at one of the tables for two, each on their second cup of coffee, Derek reached over and flicked something off the side of Maleah's mouth. Momentarily surprised, she stared at him.

"Biscuit crumbs," he told her.

"Oh."

"Ready?" he asked.

"Huh?"

"Have you finished eating? Are you ready to go to our rooms and get a few hours of sleep?"

"Yes, I've finished eating. I'm stuffed." She had eaten far more than she should have, more than she normally did. As a general rule, she watched her diet and avoided big breakfasts, but this morning, she had indulged. Actually, she had overindulged. "And yes, I'm more than ready to go to bed."

Realizing that her comment could be misconstrued, she looked at Derek. He smiled and winked at her. Damn him. She felt a warm flush creep up her neck and color her cheeks. Crap. She wasn't the type who blushed, never had been, didn't want to be. But for some stupid reason, Derek had the ability to say or do things that caused her to feel slightly embarrassed.

"Your bed or mine?" His smile widened.

"Me in my bed and you in yours."

"Ah, shucks, Blondie, you're no fun."

"Shut up, will you? I'm too tired for your particular brand of humor."

He laid his hand over his heart. "You wound me, my darling."

Maleah groaned. "Damn it, Derek, grow up, will you?"

She scooted back her chair, gathered up her plate, cup and other items, and left him sitting there. After clearing the rest of the table and leaving a generous tip, he caught up with her at the garbage bin.

"Sorry," he said.

"No, I'm sorry," she told him. "I know you were just trying to lighten the mood a little. I shouldn't let you irritate me."

"I shouldn't kid around so much."

Maleah offered him a halfhearted smile as he picked up their bags and headed toward the elevator. She punched the Up button for the second floor and when the door immediately opened, she entered.

As the elevator ascended, she felt Derek staring at her.

"What?" she asked.

"Ever ask yourself why we seem to irritate each other so much?"

The doors opened. They got off the elevator.

"Because we're oil and water," she said. "If I say it's black, you say it's white. We're very different. And when you try to run roughshod over me, it irritates me."

"And do you think that I do that a lot, run roughshod over you?"

"Maybe." She paused outside her room, turned to him, gave him his key, and held out her hand for her bag. "This is my room. You're next door."

"I'll take your bag in for you."

She was too tired to argue, so when Derek took the key card from her, she didn't protest. He inserted the card into the lock and the instant the green light appeared, he turned the knob and opened the door for her. After entering, she flipped on the light. Derek followed her into the room and placed her bag on the floor.

"Sometimes you do run roughshod over me," Maleah said, finally admitting the truth. "I know you don't mean to and that you're usually unaware that you're doing it, but . . . Look, let's just drop it, okay?"

Derek set his bag on the floor beside hers. Instinctively, she stood her ground and watched him as he moved toward her. He came right up to her, looked down at her and grasped her chin. She struggled for half a second when he tried to lift her chin so that she had to face him, but quickly looked him right in the eye. If he thought he could intimidate her, he'd better think again.

He examined her face as if she were a bug under a microscope, studying each feature, searching for something behind her confrontational expression. The way he looked at her unnerved her.

"Well?" she said.

He reached out and caressed her cheek, his touch gentle and soothing. "Get some rest, Blondie. We can do battle another day."

She hesitated. Fraught with uncertainty, she waited. A moment passed, followed by another and then another, each one becoming tenser than the previous. Neither of them moved or spoke or even blinked.

He slipped his hand beneath her hair at the nape of her neck. Her breath caught in her throat. And then Derek broke eye contact and released her. She swayed, slightly unsteady on her feet, dazed by what had just happened.

But exactly what had happened?

She waited for Derek to say something, but he didn't. He gave her a quick nod, and as if he was slightly dazed himself, he turned and left the room. She didn't actually breathe again until she heard the door close; then she slumped down on the edge of the bed and sucked in huge gasps of air.

Luke Sentell sat at a sidewalk table in front of Le Bristrot du Peintre on avenue Ledru Rollin. The bistro, located in the heart of the 11th arrondissement between Bastille and Nation squares, was a ten-minute walk from the heart of downtown Paris. Dressed casually in jeans and a long-sleeved cotton polo shirt, he nursed a glass of Bordeaux, Cote de Bourg, as did his companion, an elderly French gentleman who called himself Henri Fortier. Luke neither knew nor cared what the man's real name was. They were not friends, not even friendly acquaintaints or business associates.

Luke's French, although not flawless, was more than adequate, but Henri's command of English was excellent. Wishing to appear as nothing more than customers wanting a good meal, they each ordered. Luke chose the rib steak in cream sauce.

"When you return to America, you will please tell my old friend, Inspector Richter, that I send him my best," Henri said.

"Yes, of course."

Henri sipped his wine, all the while studying Luke, his gaze lazily inspecting his dinner companion. "Have you ever visited St. Jakob? It's a charming little village in the state of Carinthia, Austria."

"No, I've never been there. Do you recommend I visit sometime in the near future?"

"Yes, I highly recommend that while you're traveling in Europe, you add St. Jakob to your itinerary."

Luke nodded. "Could you suggest a hotel and perhaps a tour guide while I'm there?"

"Indeed. You must stay at the Inn Steinhof."

When the waiter brought their orders, Henri smiled at the young man, thanked him, and looked at his meal, eggplant lasagna with parmesan cheese.

As soon as they were alone again, Henri tasted a bite of the delicious concoction, sighed with satisfaction and then returned his attention to Luke.

"You must ask for Jurgen Hirsch. He will know where you need to go, what you will need to see."

Luke repeated the name quietly.

He would make reservations for the first flight from Paris to Carinthia tomorrow.

"And just where can I find Jurgen Hirsch?"

"When you arrive at the Inn Steinhof, leave a message for another guest, a gentleman named Aldo Finster. Simply state in your message that you are a friend of Henri Fortier and are looking for a reliable tour guide."

Luke nodded.

Henri smiled. "I think I shall order the orange tart for dessert."

Following his informant's lead, Luke, too, ordered dessert, but he ate only a few bites before saying goodnight. He had plans to make, a flight to book, and a report to send to Powell headquarters.

Chapter 16

The ringing telephone woke Derek from a sound sleep. He rolled over, kicked back the sheet, and noted the time on the digital bedside clock as he reached for his phone. 2:15 P.M. He had slept longer than he'd intended. Instantly recognizing the caller ID, he swung his legs off the edge of the bed and sat up as he answered.

"Derek Lawrence," he said, holding the phone with one hand and rubbing the back of his neck with the other.

"We think we have found Albert Durham." Sanders's voice seldom denoted emotion of any kind, always calm and even, regardless of the circumstances.

"Alive?" Derek said the first thing that popped into his mind.

"Yes, we assume he is alive," Sanders replied. "Of course, if you find him dead, then we will know he is not the Copycat Carver."

"Right. So, where is he?"

"He owns a home in Cleveland, Tennessee, but apparently he does not live there. There are renters residing there at present. He has an apartment in New York City, but it has been subleased for the next six months. And he has a condo in Aspen that he rents when he is not in residence."

"You've told me everywhere he's not," Derek said. "Do you know where he is right now?"

"Yes, of course. Otherwise, I would not have called you."

"So where can we find the guy?"

"He has rented a house on St. Simons Island, off the coast of Brunswick, Georgia."

"I'm familiar with St. Simons Island." Derek had spent many summers of his childhood vacationing there at the beach house owned by his family for several generations. The house had been built by his great-grandmother's uncle.

"I assume you and Maleah are no longer in Apple Orchard," Sanders said.

"We're in Aiken." Derek stood up and headed for the bathroom. "We're at the Holiday Inn Express."

"Hmm . . ." Sanders remained silent for a full minute, then said, "This puts you approximately two hundred miles from St. Simons. The quickest route should get you there in four hours. If you and Maleah leave within the next fifteen minutes, you could be there no later than seven this evening."

"Doesn't the agency have anyone closer who could check things out while we're en route?" Derek asked.

"We have already sent someone up from Jacksonville to keep an eye on Mr. Durham until you arrive."

"That's great. Give me the address and—"

"Barbara Jean has sent you the information you need. Check your e-mail."

"Right. Okay. Maleah and I will be on our way in a few minutes."

He should have known that Sanders would be one
step ahead of him. The man had an uncanny sixth
sense. If he didn't know better, he'd think Sanders had
some psychic abilities of his own. In the past, Derek had
often wondered why, if Dr. Meng possessed the empathic psychic talent Griff believed she did, Griff didn't
put her gift to good use for the Powell Agency. When he
had finally posed the question to his boss, Griff had explained:

"Yvette was once forced, by a madman, to use her
special talents completely against her will. I would
never use her in that way. I have rarely asked her to help
me. How and when she uses her empathic abilities is
her choice."

Derek used the bathroom, washed his hands and
splashed cold water in his face. He had shaved and showered before lying down for a nap. His slacks and shirt
had been wrinkled, so he'd folded them and placed
them in a plastic bag. He put on a pair of jeans and a
clean cotton shirt that he'd taken from his vinyl suitcase.
Then he stuffed the bag containing his dirty clothes inside the suitcase and zipped it closed. He picked up the
holster containing his personal weapon—an 8-shot 45
Colt XSE. He seldom carried a weapon, but considering
what had happened in Apple Orchard, he had decided
to take his pistol out of his suitcase. After strapping on
his holster and lifting his jacket from the back of the
desk chair, he felt inside the coat pocket. He hadn't realized until he had removed his jacket before taking a
shower that, after he had opened Maleah's door for
her, he had slipped her key back into his pocket.

He put a tip for the maid on the bed, left his room,
vinyl carryall in hand, and walked the few feet to
Maleah's door. He knocked softly. When she didn't respond, he inserted the key and unlocked her door.

Damn it, she hadn't put on the latch or double bolte
the door. He entered, intending to remind her that sh
had neglected to take the proper safety precaution
but stopped immediately when he noticed the roon
was semidark. He set his bag on the floor, walked qu
etly over to the bed and looked down at a sleepin,
Maleah. She wore only her panties and bra, her hair wa
still partially damp, and she lay sprawled in the middl
of the bed, the sheet covering one leg and hip.

He shouldn't be standing there looking at her. If sh
knew how much he was enjoying seeing her like thi
she'd chew him out big time. But what man in his righ
mind wouldn't take advantage of the moment? Afte
all, Maleah was a gorgeous woman, even if she seeme
oblivious to the fact. Or maybe she was in denial. Mo
women wanted men to find them attractive. No
Maleah. For the most part, she wanted men to leave he
alone. He didn't suspect sexual assault in her past as th
reason. No, she wasn't afraid of men and didn't seem t
dislike men in general. But she carried a major chip o
her shoulder when it came to taking orders from
man, sometimes even Griff.

"Maleah," he called to her. "Hey, wake up, Blondie."

She stretched languidly, the movement shoving th
sheet off her completely. When she turned flat on he
back, Derek swallowed hard. Her breasts were high an
round and full, straining against the pink lace bra. An
beneath the sheer pink bikini panties, dark blond cur
created a triangular patch.

"Maleah . . ."

She opened her eyes, looked up at him and smile
"Hi."

"Hi yourself." He realized she was still half asleep.

Suddenly, as if just realizing Derek actually was stan
ing there looking down at her and that she was ha

ked, she grabbed the sheet and pulled it up to her
in. Glaring at him, she asked, "How did you get in
re?"

He held up the key card. "I accidentally put it in my
cket after I unlocked your door earlier."

"You should have knocked."

"I did. You were sleeping like the dead and didn't
ar me."

"How long have you been standing there?"

He tried not to grin, but couldn't keep his mouth
m curving into a closed-mouth smile. "Uh . . . not
ng."

"I assume you have a reason for invading my privacy
is way." She jerked the sheet off the bed as she stood
d wrapped it around her.

"Sanders called. Albert Durham is in St. Simons Is-
d, Georgia."

"Is he alive?"

Derek chuckled.

"What so funny?"

"I asked Sanders the same thing."

"And his answer?" she asked.

"As far as we know Durham's alive. Sanders sent a
well contact up from Jacksonville to keep an eye on
rham until we can get there."

"Give me ten minutes." Maleah disappeared into the
throom, clutching the sheet just above her breasts as
e dragged it with her.

Derek turned on a couple of lights, pulled a five-
llar bill from his wallet and laid it on the bed for the
id. He glanced around the room, checking for any
rsonal items, and found none. Apparently, Maleah
d left her suitcase in the bathroom after her shower.

Seven and a half minutes later, she emerged, com-
tely dressed, her hair dry and swirled up into a loose

bun, flyaway tendrils framing her face. She'd even p
on some blush and lip gloss.

"How do you do it?" Derek asked

She stared at him. "How do I do what?"

"Manage to always look so beautiful?"

At first, she glared daggers at him, but then, as if u
able to stop herself, she smiled and finally laughe
"I've learned not to take anything you say seriously. Yo
get too much pleasure out of yanking my chain, don
you?"

"If you say so."

He opened the door and held it for her. Each carr
ing their own bag, neither in a talkative mood, th
took the elevator down and quickly checked out.

By 2:40 P.M., they were headed for US-278 E.

Poppy loved her grandmother, the one constant
her life, the one person who never changed and seeme
to love Poppy unconditionally. It wasn't that her moth
didn't love her. She did. But she had other priorities.
forty, Vickie looked thirty, thanks to strict dieting, stre
uous exercise and a little Botox here and there in stra
gic spots. Why her mom hadn't handed her over
Grandmother years ago, she'd never understand. May
as revenge against her husband's family, the people wl
had never approved of her as proper wife material for
Chappelle. Poppy did know that Grandmother had tak
Vickie to court and an ugly legal battle had dragged
for nearly a year. But in the end, the court had award
custody to Vickie, with generous visitation privileges f
her grandmother. So, she had spent a couple of mont
every summer since then in Savannah, as well as eve
other Christmas, Thanksgiving, and birthday.

Sometimes, she dreamed of coming here to live p

manently, but that wouldn't happen. When she graduated from high school, she would go off to college and be in charge of her own life. It would be her choice when to visit her mother and when to visit her grandmother. Her trust fund would pay for her college education, but the bulk of that small fortune would not be hers to do with as she chose until she turned twenty-five.

"Why such a sad face?" Grandmother asked.

"Ma'am?"

"Are you worried about something?"

"Oh, no, ma'am, just thinking about when I'm older and I go off to college."

"That's a couple of years from now," Grandmother reminded her. "I much prefer to concentrate on the here and now, on today. Our guests will be arriving at seven. You should go upstairs soon. A lady should take all the time necessary to make herself presentable."

"Yes, ma'am."

"You are going to wear that lovely blue chiffon dress, aren't you? I asked Heloise to lay it out for you and . . ." Grandmother Chappelle smiled as if she had a delicious secret to share. "I took my sapphire earrings from the safe. They're in your room, on your dressing table. I would very much like for you to wear them this evening."

"Oh, Grandmother, the sapphire earrings. I couldn't. I mean they were an anniversary gift from Grandfather."

"I'm not giving them to you, Poppy. I'm only loaning them to you." Grandmother smiled. "But one day they will be yours . . . when I'm gone."

Poppy threw her arms around her grandmother and gave her a big hug. "I love you so much."

Staunch, prim and proper, stiff-upper-lip Carolyn

Chappelle hugged Poppy, then shoved her away and cleared her throat. She turned around, but not before Poppy saw the tears in her grandmother's eyes.

"I'll wear the blue chiffon," she said. She had seen the new dress Grandmother had bought for her and she hated it. It looked like something that girls wore forty years ago.

"And you'll wear the sapphire earrings."

"Of course I will."

Poppy rushed through the house and up the back stairs, taking them two at a time. She needed plenty of time to prepare for this evening, to psych herself up to "party" with the Chappelle family's friends. When in Savannah, her goal was always to make Grandmother proud of her.

For most of the four-hour trip, Maleah had concentrated on driving while Derek went over the reports from the agency, with updated information on Albert Durham, that included a recent publicity photo. The guy fit the general description of the man who had visited Browning at the Georgia State Prison. Derek shared the info with Maleah, giving her the condensed version which left her too much time to think about other things. She couldn't forget the way Derek had looked at her that morning just before he left her alone in her hotel room. For half a second, she had thought he was going to kiss her. And she kept replaying in her mind the moment that afternoon when she had awakened to find Derek staring at her almost naked body. But what bothered her the most was that she kept hearing Derek ask, "How do you do it? Manage to always look so beautiful?"

Thankfully, those introspective moments didn't last

ong. Powell Agency business kept them both occupied. arbara Jean and Sanders had also sent updates on the yman Scudder and Cindy Dobbins murder investiga- ons. The Macon PD weren't giving out any pertinent nformation, but the Powell Agency not only had been ble to discover the secretary interviewee's name, but ad already sent an agent to Macon to question her bout discovering Scudder's body. The info on Cindy's murder had come straight from Sheriff Lockhart. As ney had expected, no arrest had been made, and the iller was still at large.

So, where was the Copycat Carver right now? And ho would be his next victim?

Derek had received several text messages from the gency's contact who had driven up from Jacksonville o keep an eye on Durham.

And Griff had called Derek. After their brief conver- ation, Derek had remained silent for a good while. Fi- ally, Maleah's curiosity had gotten the better of her nd she'd asked, "What did Griff want?"

Derek hadn't answered immediately, as if he had een debating about what to tell her. "The Powell gency took a phone call from Jerome Browning a cou- le of hours ago. He left a message for you."

Maleah had braced herself. "What was his message?"

"Griff's handling it, so don't go ballistic, okay?"

"Damn it, tell me."

"Browning said to tell you that he's eager to see you gain. And . . . he sends his regards to your brother Jack nd his wife and son."

"That slimy, lowlife son of a bitch. He's threatening ck and his family. My family!"

"Griff has talked to Jack and alerted him. And he's nding around-the-clock agents to guard Jack and athy and Seth. And like Griff said, so far the copycat

hasn't warned us who he planned to kill next, so thi
probably isn't a warning from him, just part of th
game Browning is playing with you."

"God, I hope Griff is right. If anything happens to—

"It won't. They're safe. Griff is going to make sur
of it."

With the combination of daylight savings time, St. S
mons Island being in the Eastern Time Zone, and th
date being late June, nightfall didn't occur until aroun
nine o'clock. They reached the F.J. Torras Causeway i
Brunswick before seven that evening, sunset nearly tw
hours away.

Derek knew that Maleah wanted to go to Dunmor
Alabama, where her brother and his family lived, tha
she wanted to guard them day and night, wanted to b
the one to keep them safe. But he also knew that sh
would continue the investigation and allow Griff t
send in other agents to Alabama because their be
chance of finding and stopping the copycat was som
how connected to Jerome Browning. And Brownin
had chosen Maleah as the mouse in his cat and mous
game.

"Durham went fishing this afternoon." Derek relaye
the latest information from their contact watching A
bert Durham. "Since then, he hasn't left home."

"At least we know he's alive and well and we'll b
able to question him."

"Yeah, but you know something's off about that
Derek said.

"Like the fact that Durham was relatively easy
find?"

"Right. If he's the copycat killer, he wouldn't want
to find him, would he?"

"It's possible that the copycat has been using Durham, too, just as he did Wyman Scudder and Cindy Dobbins."

"If that's the case, then Durham is in danger. The copycat will be coming after him next."

Maleah turned onto Demere Road, following the GPS directions toward Beachview Drive. "He was one step ahead of us in Macon and came in right behind us in Apple Orchard. If Durham isn't the copycat, but just another pawn in his sick game, then maybe we can save Durham's life."

"If Durham isn't the killer and the copycat knew where to find Durham, then why didn't he come to St. Simons Island straight from Apple Orchard?"

"Maybe he did," Maleah said as she turned onto Ocean Boulevard. "He may be here right now, watching and waiting for the opportunity to strike. It could be that the only thing standing between Albert Durham and certain death is our Powell contact who's watching him."

Derek shook his head. "If the copycat is already here, why didn't he kill Durham when the guy left home to go fishing? Even if he knows we've got somebody watching Durham, that wouldn't necessarily stop him. We were with Cindy last night when he killed her."

"Yeah, but he took us by surprise. That's not the case today."

"My gut is telling me that there's a missing piece to our puzzle."

"Maybe Durham is that missing piece," Maleah said. "Maybe he can fill in the blanks."

"We should be able to find out pretty soon," Derek told her when he saw the Beachview Drive rental come into view.

"Is that it?" She slowed the SUV in front of a pal‹
peach stucco cottage overlooking the Atlantic Ocean.

"That's it."

She pulled into the narrow drive and parked behin‹
the late model Mercedes. "Durham's car?" she asked, a
she shut off the ignition.

Derek nodded.

"Where's our guy?"

"See the white panel van across the road?"

Maleah searched for the vehicle when she got out o
her SUV, found it, and waited for Derek to join her be
fore approaching the cottage.

Side by side, on full alert, aware of every sound
every scent, every flash of movement, Maleah an‹
Derek walked up to the front door. Maleah rang th
doorbell. Derek scanned the area from the rocky shore
line and sloping sandy beach to the wooded area be
hind the house.

They waited. No response. Maleah rang the bel
again.

Derek heard movement inside the house.

"Somebody's in there," Maleah said.

Derek nodded.

And then the front door opened. A pair of inquirin;
blue-gray eyes looked each of them over quickly an‹
then asked, "May I help you?" His voice had the rasp
quality associated with a lifetime smoker.

"We're looking for Albert Durham," Maleah said.

"You've found him. I'm Albert Durham."

He vaguely resembled the debonair gray-haired gentl‹
man in the publicity photo that had no doubt been ai
brushed. Apparently Durham had shaved and gotten
fresh haircut before the photograph had been taker
But then, the man who stood in the doorway was on v;

tion, which probably accounted for the new growth
beard and the shaggy hair.

"I'm Maleah Perdue and this is Derek Lawrence.
e're employed by the Powell Private Security and In-
stigation Agency," she explained as she and Derek
owed the man their Powell Agency identification.
Ve're here to ask you a few questions about Jerome
owning," Maleah said.

"Who?"

"Jerome Browning, the serial killer known as the
rver. The man you interviewed for the biography
u're writing."

"I have never heard of a Jerome Browning," Albert
urham said. "And I can assure you that whoever he is,
m not planning to write his biography."

"Are you saying that you have never visited Jerome
owning at the Georgia State Prison in Reidsville,
orgia?" Derek asked.

"I've never met this man Browning and I've never
en heard of Reidsville, Georgia. And I have never vis-
d anyone in prison, not in Georgia or anywhere else."

Chapter 17

Damn! Double damn!

Maleah believed Albert Durham. He didn't kno[w] Jerome Browning, had never met him, and was not wr[it]ing his biography. One glance at Derek told her that h[e], too, believed Durham. So where did that leave the[m]? Definitely with more questions than answers.

"Won't y'all come in," Durham said. "I have iced te[a,] fresh lemonade or I can stir up some cocktails, if y[ou] prefer."

"Thank you," Maleah said. "We'll forgo any refres[h]ment, but we would like to talk to you about this m[ix] up."

Derek followed her into the large living room/dini[ng] room and kitchen space. The walls were pale yellow, t[he] floor covered with beige tile, and the furnishings wer[e a] mix of new and antique, decent quality but not exp[en]sive.

"Have a seat." Durham indicated the sofa. He to[ok] the brown leather recliner.

They sat on the sofa, side by side, Maleah on t[he]

edge of the seat cushion, Derek reclining, settled and relaxed.

"I suggest y'all start by telling me why you believed I was writing a serial killer's biography," Durham said.

"I've been to the Georgia State Prison to visit Jerome Browning, who during a murder spree a dozen years ago was known as the Carver," Maleah explained. "He told me himself that Albert Durham was writing his bio and had personally interviewed him."

"The description the guards gave us of the Albert Durham who visited Browning fits your general description," Derek added.

Durham rubbed his chin, scratching his fingers across several days' growth of gray-brown beard stubble. "I have no idea about this other Albert Durham. All I know is that I've never visited anyone in prison and until you mentioned his name, I'd never heard the name Jerome Browning."

"I don't want you to take this the wrong way, but . . ." Maleah paused, waiting to observe Durham's reaction and when his expression remained neutral, she continued. "If I give you the dates when a man calling himself Albert Durham visited Jerome Browning, do you think you could tell us where you were on those dates?"

Durham smiled. Maleah thought he had a nice face. Not handsome by any means. A bit weathered, as if he spent a great deal of time outdoors. And kind eyes. A soft blue-gray. The deep-set wrinkles of a longtime smoker crisscrossed his forehead and curved alongside his mouth and into cheeks.

"You want me to provide myself with an alibi," Durham said.

"Yes, I suppose that's what I'd like for you to do," Maleah told him. "That way we can verify there's no way you can be the Albert Durham we're searching for in connection to our case."

"Certainly. I understand. And if you'll give me those dates, I'll check my calendar. Since I keep a date book, I should be able to tell you what you need to know."

Maleah reached into her pocket and pulled out a notepad filled with scribbled notes. She called off the dates. Durham pursed his thin lips as he listened.

"The dates that you mentioned are easy enough for me to remember. I spent six weeks in Japan and was there on those dates." When Maleah and Derek stared at him questioningly, he added, "I was doing research on the subject of my next biography, Emperor Hirohito, who ruled Japan during World War II."

"An interesting choice for a bio," Derek said.

"My father was a WWII veteran and I've always been fascinated by that era," Durham said. "To verify where I was, I can let you take a look at my passport, and I can probably dig up credit card statements that show my expenses while in Japan, including hotels and restaurants."

"That would be great, Mr. Durham," Maleah said. "And I apologize for having to ask you to do this."

"No apology necessary, Ms. Perdue. If someone has been using my identity for any reason, especially to commit a crime, then I want them found and stopped as much as you do."

"More than likely the man we're looking for chose your identity because you're a biographer," Derek said. "For his own reasons, he needed to be able to pass himself off to Jerome Browning as a writer interested in gathering information for a biography."

Durham rose. "I keep my passport with me when I travel, even in the U.S. I never know when I might want to take a jaunt down to the islands for a few days. I can

how you the passport, but I'm afraid I'll have to send
ou copies of my credit card bills when I return home."

"I'll leave you my business card," Maleah said. "I'll con-
act you if we need them and you can e-mail them to us."

While Durham disappeared into one of the bed-
ooms, Derek and Maleah stood and looked out the
indows at the Atlantic Ocean.

"How do we even begin to find a man with no name,
o face, and no ID of his own?" Maleah asked. "He used
urham's name and undoubtedly disguised himself to
ook like the real Durham."

"We'll start with a profile," Derek told her. "Now that
e know who this man is not, we can begin figuring out
ho he really is."

"He's smart, whoever he is. Apparently, he fooled
rowning, who may be a psychopath, but is far from stu-
id. And he's led us on a merry chase while he elimi-
ated the only two other people who might be able to
ll us something about him."

"With Wyman Scudder and Cindy Di Blasi both dead,
at leaves only Jerome Browning. If Browning really
as no idea that the Durham who interviewed him was
phony and had no intention of writing his bio, he may
e willing to give up some information once he does
now the truth."

"He won't give it up without a price," Maleah said.

"Yeah, with a guy like Browning, there's always a
rice to pay."

The real Durham cleared his throat as he returned
the living room. "Here you are." He opened his pass-
ort and handed it to Maleah.

She looked at the stamped dates for Durham's entry
d exit from Japan, which proved he was out of the
untry on the dates that Albert Durham had visited
rome.

"Thank you, Mr. Durham. We appreciate your coop
eration."

"May I ask y'all a question?" Durham asked.

"Yes, certainly," Maleah replied.

"Why do you think this man who visited a convicted
serial killer has been impersonating me?"

Maleah and Derek exchanged a how-much-do-we
tell-him glance.

Then Derek made the decision for them. "We be
lieve that this man is copying Jerome Browning's MO
and has become a copycat killer. By posing as a biogra
pher, he was able to elicit details of Browning's murder
from him, enough so that he could replicate those mur
ders as closely as possible."

Durham's eyes narrowed, furrowing his brow. His
mouth turned down in a pensive frown, deepening th
grooves around his mouth. "And this man is using m
name." He looked right at Derek. "My God, you have t
find him."

"We're doing everything we can," Derek said. "Th
entire Powell Agency is working toward that goal—find
ing the copycat killer and stopping him before he kil
again."

"How many people . . . ?" Durham swallowed. "Ho
many has he killed?"

"Five."

"Did one of the victim's families hire your agency:
Durham asked.

"In a way," Derek said. "You see, each victim was co
nected to our agency, either an employee or a relativ
of an employee."

"Then finding him is as important to you as it is
me. It's personal."

"That's right."

Durham nodded. "I wish there was more I could d

to help you, Mr. Lawrence . . ." He glanced at Maleah. "And you, Ms. Perdue."

"We appreciate your cooperation," Maleah told him.

Durham studied Derek for a minute and then said, "Derek Lawrence. Hmm . . . why does your name sound so familiar?"

Before Derek could respond, Durham snapped his fingers. "Derek Lawrence, former FBI profiler. You're a writer, too. You've written half a dozen true crime novels. I've read several of them. They're intriguing. You're quite a good writer, Mr. Lawrence."

"Thank you."

"Could I interest you two into staying and going out to dinner with me this evening?" Durham asked. "There is this marvelous seafood place—"

"I'm afraid we can't stay," Maleah said. "We appreciate the offer."

"Yes, yes, of course. I understand. Duty calls."

Durham continued talking to Derek about writing as Durham walked them to the door and followed them outside to Maleah's SUV. Then they shook hands and said their good-byes.

As soon as they were on the main road, Maleah asked, "Where to now?"

"You're actually asking for my opinion?"

"We're partners, as you keep reminding me. I'm consulting you about our next move."

"You didn't consult me before you declined Albert's offer to take us to dinner."

She shot him a quick, questioning glance. "I didn't realize we had time to waste."

"We're going to have to eat anyway," Derek reminded her. "I suggest we find a place to stay here on the island tonight and get an early start in the morning."

When she opened her mouth to protest, to suggest they travel through the night, he cut her off. "We need rest, Blondie. We're both exhausted. We've been on the road—"

"All right, all right."

"We won't waste our time. We'll order room service and work through dinner, if that will make you happy."

She shot him a menacing glare. "You don't want to know what would make me happy."

Derek laughed. "Probably not. But remind me sometime to tell you what would make me happy."

Groaning, Maleah clutched the steering wheel tightly.

Ignore him. Ignore him. Ignore him.

Derek wondered who now oversaw their family's vacation home there on St. Simons. His mother? His sister? Or perhaps one of his uncles? He hadn't been inside the oceanfront "cottage" since he was a teenager, but if he thought no one was using it right now, he'd take Maleah there tonight. Stupid thought. First of all, he didn't have a key to the place. And he doubted the same island couple who oversaw the upkeep of the house and grounds all those years ago were still alive, since they had been in their sixties when he was a kid.

Forget the family place and just check into a decent hotel.

"I need to stop at a gas station and fill up," Maleah said. "We're down to less than a quarter of a tank."

"While you're doing that, I'll find us a place to stay tonight."

"Fine."

Five minutes later, Maleah stopped at one of the Friendly Express stations on the island and Derek called to book them rooms at the King and Prince, a each and golf resort. He wouldn't mind luxury accommodations for a change and he thought Maleah could use a little pampering about now.

After swiping her credit card, Maleah placed the nozzle in the mouth of the gas tank and set the pump on automatic. She opened the door and asked, "Want something to drink? I'm getting a Coke."

"A Coke's fine. Want me to—?"

She noticed he was still on the phone. "I'll get them. You finish your call."

By the time she returned with their colas and placed them in the cup holders inside the SUV, the pump had shut off, indicating the tank was full. After hanging the pump nozzle back on the hook, she hopped into the Equinox, removed a small bottle of hand sanitizer from the console storage bin, and hurriedly cleaned her hands.

"Was your phone call to Sanders?" she asked.

"No. I haven't gotten in touch with him yet. I was getting us a room for tonight."

She started the engine. "Where to?"

He gave her the directions. When they arrived a short time later, he was surprised by her reaction. Other than giving the resort a quick once-over as they drove up, she didn't react in any way. He had thought for sure she would bitch about their staying at such a luxurious hotel.

Their side-by-side rooms were identical, both with king beds, both with oceanfront views and decorated in a cool, soothing color combo of cream, white, blue, and gold. After dumping his bag in the closet, he returned to her room. She came to the door when he knocked, but didn't invite him in.

"I thought we could go ahead and order in, eat in your room or mine, and then get down to work," he said.

"I want a nice long soak in the tub," she told him.
"Would you please order for me? Any seafood dish is
fine. Shrimp, salmon, whatever. And a salad. No dessert. Iced tea."

"I'll place the order before I hop in the shower," he
said. "Your room or mine?"

"It doesn't matter."

"I'll have them deliver to my room and I'll call you."

"Fine."

She closed the door in his face.

Smiling, he shook his head.

Maleah, Maleah.

He had never known a woman who irritated him the
way she did. Or intrigued him as much. Or made him
want to turn her over his knee and spank her. He
chuckled as he unlocked his door. She'd skin him alive
for that thought. And he had to admit to himself that if
he ever got his hands on her, spanking wouldn't be on
his Top Ten list of things he wanted to do.

No sooner had he entered his room than his phone
rang. He answered as he closed and locked the door.

"Good evening," Barbara Jean said. "I have an update for you."

"We have an update for you, too," he told her. "Ladies
first."

"Thank you." She went over some mundane basic
facts with him about both recent murders. Derek made
mental notes of anything he felt might be significant in
compiling his profile of the copycat killer. "Sanders
wanted you to know that he's discussed all the information with Griffin and Nicole. For the present, Sanders in
complete charge of the copycat case. Griff's focus on
locating the source of the rumors about Malcolm
York. He's in touch around the clock with Luke Sentell."

"I assume if there was any news on that front—"

"Yes, of course, we would inform you and Maleah. But for now, all we know is that Luke is in Austria following a lead."

"We're staying on St. Simons tonight and heading out in the morning, probably going back to Vidalia for Maleah's next scheduled visit with Jerome Browning."

"What about Albert Durham? Did y'all find him?"

"Yes, we found him," Derek said. "The only problem is that the man we talked to this evening is the real Albert Durham. The man who visited Browning at the state penitentiary is a fake. He assumed Durham's identity and posed as a biographer to get Browning to share details about his kills."

"I'll let Sanders know."

"Please do."

"Derek?"

"Yes?"

"When Maleah sees Browning again . . ." Barbara Jean paused as if wanting to choose her next words carefully.

"I'll take care of her. I promise."

"She wouldn't appreciate the fact that I asked or that you agreed. Our Miss Maleah sees herself as a tough cookie. She doesn't want to need anyone, but I learned long ago that in one way or another, at some time in our lives, we all need someone."

"So far she's held her own with Browning," Derek assured Barbara Jean.

"I have no doubt that she has, but . . . Well, let's just say that Nicole and I worry about her as if she were our little sister. And we're counting on you to rein her in if you see these interviews with Browning get out of control."

"Do you and Nic honestly think I can rein in Maleah?"

"We think you are probably the only man who can."

Before Derek had time to digest Barbara Jean's final comment, she said good-bye.

What the hell had Barbara Jean meant when she had said *we think you're the only man who can?* It wasn't as if he had any power over Maleah. He wasn't her father, brother or mentor. And he certainly wasn't her lover. They were barely friends. Maybe not even friends. Not enemies. Not exactly adversaries, because they *were* on the same side. And they were definitely more than acquaintances. Damned if he knew how to label their relationship.

Standing in the center of his room, Derek took a deep breath. Then as he walked across the carpeted floor, he tossed his phone onto the bed. He picked up the guest book that contained the menu and hurriedly scanned the items available for dinner. Noting that room service ended at 10:00 P.M., he lifted the hotel phone, dialed room service, and ordered.

Moving toward the bathroom, he began stripping out of his clothes, dropping them haphazardly on the floor as his went. Naked, his clothes strewn from bedroom to bathroom, Derek turned on the shower and then grabbed the guest soap and toiletries. As he lathered his hair and the steamy warm water pelted his body, he tried to figure out just what kind of relationship he did have with Maleah.

They were coworkers. They were partners, albeit reluctant partners.

Yeah, that was it—they were reluctant partners.

So, why would Nic and Barbara Jean think he, of all people, would be able to rein in Maleah? If he said or did anything that even hinted of trying to control a situation, she overreacted. If ever there was a woman over whom he had absolutely no control, it was Maleah Perdue.

Chapter 18

With her eyes closed, Maleah lay in the tub, bubbles
up to her chin and soothing warm water surrounding
her tired body. As hard as she tried to empty her mind,
to concentrate on her breathing so that she could relax,
her mind wouldn't slow down and allow her a few precious moments of peace. She didn't want to think about
anything or anyone. She didn't want to worry herself
sick about her brother Jackson and his family. The
thought that they could be in danger had crossed her
mind ever since Winston Corbett's murder, but she had
managed to subdue her concerns in order to do her
job. But no longer. Not now. Not after what Derek had
told her.

*Browning said to tell you that he's eager to see you again.
And . . . he sends his regards to your brother Jack and his wife
and son.*

But did Browning actually know who the copycat had
targeted as his next victim or did that evil bastard just
want them to think he knew?

Logic told her that the best way she could help her
brother, his wife, and son was to continue her visits with

Browning. For the time being, he seemed to be their only link to the killer. Pure emotion urged her to go home to Dunmore, to place herself between her brother and his family and any danger that might come their way. But Griff had already sent in other agents—one each to guard Jack, Cathy, and Seth. Knowing the danger they were in couldn't be good for Cathy or the baby she was carrying. If anything happened to that innocent little life . . .

Maleah slid down into the tub until her head hit the water, separating the thick bubbles into two big mounds on either side.

Stop thinking, damn it, stop thinking.

She sunk lower until she submerged her entire head under the water.

Jack and his family are safe. And you're going to do what you have to do—see Jerome Browning again.

Maleah rose from the watery grave, rivulets of soapy water racing down her head, across her shoulders and over her bare breasts. As she grappled around at the bottom of the tub searching for her washcloth, she shook her head sideways to dislodge any water trapped in her ears.

"Always shake your head," Jackson had told her the first time he'd given her a swimming lesson. "Like this." He had demonstrated the motion for her. "It'll help get the water out of your ears. I don't want my kid sister getting swimmer's ear."

She loved Jack more than anyone on earth. He was not only her brother. He was her hero.

"Oh, Jack, I'm sorry that my being a Powell agent has put you and your family in danger."

Tears gathered in her eyes. God, how she hated weak, weepy women. Women like her mother. She would never be like that. She would never let some man beat her into the ground and walk all over her. Even if it meant spending the rest of her life alone, she would never willingly give any man the power to hurt her.

After finally finding her washcloth, she brought it up from the bottom of the tub, wrung out the excess water and wiped her face with the damp cloth. She had no idea how long she'd been in the tub, thinking, trying not to think and fighting the almost overwhelming urge to cry. But the once hot water was now tepid and her fingertips were puckered, so she figured she had been in the tub too long.

She rose from the water, stepped out onto the bathmat and reached for a thick, fluffy towel. She draped a towel around her wet hair and then retrieved another and dried off, from face to feet. As she slipped into her clean panties, she debated about putting on a bra, but quickly dismissed the thought of going braless. After all, she didn't want Derek to think she was trying to be provocative.

If only she didn't have to see Derek again tonight. If only he wasn't her partner on this case. But he was her partner and for a very good reason—his expertise as a profiler could prove invaluable. And she did have to see him again tonight. They had work to do.

While she dressed, she reminded herself that Derek really was not a problem. He was her partner. She needed him as much as he needed her. Like it or not, they were a team.

Once she'd gotten to know him, when they had worked together on the Midnight Killer case, Maleah realized that some of her preconceived notions about Derek were wrong. But some were dead on. He was arrogant. But only occasionally. Most rich, handsome, intelligent men were. He was a womanizer who went through women as if they were Kleenex. Stupid women.

And from the first day they met when he had tried to charm her, she had begun putting up a protective barrier between them. No way was she going to fall for a guy who thought he could sweet talk any woman he wanted into his bed. But what she hated most about Derek was the way he tried to boss her around and make all the decisions for her. Or at least he had in the beginning. Now, he actually made an effort not to go all macho he-man on her, delegating her to the role of helpless female.

No, Derek was not the major problem in her life right now.

Jerome Browning was the problem.

She needed to know whatever Browning knew.

She had to find a way to make him talk.

And she would do it, no matter what the cost to her.

Alone on the patio, Nicole stared up the night sky filled with countless tiny, sparkling stars, distant light peeping through pinpricks in a heavenly black canvas. An overwhelming sense of doom settled over her, a foreboding feeling of desolation and danger. But she was safe. Everyone within the protective walls of Griffin's Rest was safe. So why did she feel as if she were dying by slow, excruciating degrees?

God, Nic, don't be overly dramatic. You're not dying. You're worried and upset and pissed at your husband.

If she didn't love Griff so damn much, she would have packed her bags and left long before now. She would have put some distance between her and Griff, for her own sanity. But she had tried that before, spending time away from him, and in the end, she always came home. Home where her heart was. Home to the man she loved more than life itself.

And the bittersweet thing about loving Griff was knowing that he loved her in the same wildly, desperately passionate way.

She didn't doubt his love or his loyalty.

And yet she didn't trust him to be totally honest with her.

In her gut, she knew he was keeping something from her, something possibly so terrible that he couldn't bear for her to know.

But Sanders knew.

And Yvette knew.

Tears lodged in her throat. She wouldn't cry. Crying was pointless. It served no purpose other than to give her a splitting headache.

Griff had left the house less than an hour ago. He had asked her to go with him. She had declined. Before leaving her, he had searched her face as if seeking her approval. He didn't need it. He did as he pleased. If she had asked him not to go, he would have gone anyway. And he would have asked her to understand.

But how could she understand?

Her husband loved another woman.

How many times had Griff told her that his love for Yvette was that of a brother for a sister, of one battle-weary comrade for another, of a friend for a friend? She believed he meant what he said.

And yet she wondered what would happen if he ever had to choose between the two women in his life, the two women he loved. The bond he shared with Yvette and Sanders, a bond he told her had been forged in hell, could not be broken and it was a bond she couldn't share. She had not lived on Amara, a captive of billionaire madman Malcolm York. She had not shared their particular torment and torture and inhuman treatment.

At best, she was a sympathetic outsider to their god-damn holy Amara trinity of wounded souls.

She had lived through her own particular hell when she had been kidnapped by a psychopathic serial killer who had hunted his victims as if they were animals. After she escaped from her captor, Griff had told her about the time he had spent on Amara. Knowing that he truly understood what she had gone through had helped her not only recover and believe she could return to a normal life, but it helped her trust Griff. Trust him with her life. Trust him with her heart.

It had taken quite some time after they married for her to realize that he had not told her everything about his experience on Amara, and that he had no intention of ever telling her.

"We made a pact, Sanders, Yvette and I," Griff had told her. "We would never tell another living soul everything we endured and that only with the other two's permission would we ever discuss any part of our experience with someone else."

Sanders and Yvette had allowed him to share a part of their story with her. To help her heal. And she knew that the threesome had agreed to bring Derek Lawrence, Luke Sentell and the Powell Agency lawyer, Camden Hendrix, into the inner circle that also included her. Their knowledge was limited, even more so than hers; but they knew that Griff, Sanders, and Yvette had killed Malcolm York, a monster who had tortured and murdered numerous people on his private Pacific Island of Amara.

Griff had not wanted her to tell Maleah, but she had finally made him understand that she badly needed to confide in her best friend. During the past few years, Maleah had become the sister she never had.

Nic rose from the chaise lounge, walked off the patio and onto the pathway that led from the house to the lake. Suddenly she sensed his presence, a gigantic form coming out of the shadows. She didn't bother to turn around and look his way. Griff had assigned Shaughnessy Hood as her personal bodyguard and she was never to leave the house without him. Ignoring her protector, she made her way down to the peacefully serene riverbank.

Damn it, Griff, why did you have to go to Yvette? Why did you feel it necessary to check on her in person? You could have called her. It's not as if Michelle Allen isn't at her side night and day, protecting her just as Shaughnessy protects me.

Room service arrived and set up their dinner on the balcony overlooking the ocean as Derek had requested. He phoned Maleah and she arrived promptly just as the waiter left. He took one look at her, hair hanging to her shoulders in soft blonde waves, a pale pink cotton sweater loosely covering her hips that were encased in white jeans, and wished she were any other woman on earth. If she wasn't Maleah Perdue, the personification of I-am-woman-hear-me-roar, he would move heaven and earth to get her into his bed tonight.

"What's the matter?" she asked.

"Huh?"

"You're looking at me funny. Do I have toothpaste on the corner of my mouth? Or did I forget to zip my jeans?"

"No toothpaste, no unzipped jeans," he said. "Come on in. We're having dinner on the balcony. I hope that meets with your approval."

"Isn't it a bit too warm to eat outside?"

"Actually, it's not." He took her hand in his. Surprisingly, she didn't jerk away from him. "It's a beautiful, balmy evening."

When they reached the door, she paused. "Dinner by candlelight? Isn't something that romantic wasted on us?"

He opened the door, held it, and quickly ushered her onto the balcony. "It's not romantic, just pleasantly civilized."

She glanced down at the candle lanterns and the covered dishes. "What am I eating tonight?"

"Madame will begin with a traditional Caesar salad, followed by Creole Florida black grouper topped with creamy Cajun crab and shrimp sauce over a bed of sautéed baby spinach."

"Oh my God, that sounds delicious."

Acting the gentleman, he helped seat her and then took his place across from her. "I know you said not to order dessert, but . . ."

"I am not eating dessert," she told him.

"It's triple chocolate cheesecake."

"You sure know how to torture a girl."

"Honey, dessert every once in a while is not going to ruin that gorgeous figure."

She snapped up her head and stared at him. He knew what was coming. She was going to tell him not to call her honey. She had chastised him repeatedly, but every once in a while, he simply forgot.

But then, to his surprise, she said, "Thank you for the compliment, even if you didn't mean it."

"You're welcome." He waited a few seconds before adding, "And I meant it."

She removed the cover from her meal and sighed. "This looks wonderful."

He followed her lead, revealed his twelve-ounce rib

eye, and lifted his knife and fork. For the next twenty minutes, they ate in relative silence, occasionally exchanging a few words.

While Derek enjoyed his slice of cheesecake, Maleah excused herself to go inside and make a phone call.

"I want to check on Jack," she said.

"Give him and Cathy my best."

"Yes, I'll do that."

After Derek finished with dessert, he blew out the candles inside the glass lanterns on the small table and waited around outside on the balcony for another five minutes, giving Maleah her privacy. He understood how concerned she was about her brother and his family. She had every right to be worried because they had no way of knowing where the copycat killer would strike next. And that was the reason he had asked Griff to assign agents to discreetly guard his mother as well as his sister and her family. There was no way the Powell Agency could provide private protection for every employee's family, but considering Derek's personal connection to Browning now, Griff had agreed that it was wise to guard Derek's family.

By the time he went inside, Maleah was ending her conversation. "Derek sends his best," she told her brother as she smiled at Derek. "Yes, I'll tell him. That works both ways, you know." She laughed. "Take care, big brother."

Maleah slid her thin phone into the front pocket of her jeans.

"What did Jack want you to tell me?" Derek asked.

"Oh, he said as my partner, he expects you to have my back."

"Ah. And you told him that it works both ways. You've got my back, too."

"Isn't that the way a partnership works, each partner takes care of the other?"

"Yes, ma'am, I believe you're right."

"Should we call down and ask them to clear away our dinner dishes?" She glanced at the remains of their delicious meal still on the balcony.

"I'll take care of it before I go to bed," he told her.

"All right then, partner, let's get to work." Maleah pulled out the swivel chair from the desk and indicated for him to sit. When he did, she plopped down on the blue and white striped sofa directly across from the desk.

He turned to face her. "Barbara Jean called earlier this evening."

"And?"

"Nothing really. She just gave me bits and pieces of information that she thought might help me work up a profile on the copycat."

"Would you mind sharing the information with me?"

He quoted Barbara Jean almost word for word and waited for Maleah to respond. When she didn't, he added, "You should know that, at least for the time being, Sanders is completely in charge of the copycat case. Griff is preoccupied with proving his theory that someone calling himself Malcolm York is behind the murders. Luke Sentell is in Austria, following a lead."

"I hope Griff is wrong," Maleah said. "Besides, don't you think it would be a truly odd coincidence if it turns out that someone impersonating Malcolm York is behind the murders, considering the fact that we now know someone is impersonating Albert Durham?"

"Stranger things have happened."

"Do you think the fake Albert Durham and the elusive risen-from-the-dead York could be the same person?'

Derek got up, walked around the white coffee table and sat down beside Maleah. She turned sideways and faced him.

"It's possible," he said. "Anything is possible."

"A lot of help you are."

He shrugged.

"Do you think you can put together a profile with what little information we have?"

"I'm going to try. We have to start somewhere and as we learn more about our copycat killer, I can revise the profile if necessary."

"Will it help to talk it out, to discuss—?"

"Absolutely. Some good back and forth discussion between the two of us could help," he told her. "We'll combine your thoughts and mine on the subject of our copycat killer."

"You talk. I'll listen and comment."

"The Copycat Carver is an odd bird." Derek leaned back against the thickly padded sofa cushions and spread out his arm, bringing his fingertips within touching distance of Maleah's neck. "He's gone to a great deal of trouble to copy Jerome Browning's MO and yet he deliberately sent the pieces of flesh he removed from the victims' bodies to you instead of hiding them away somewhere the way Browning did. Why?"

"Why did he send them to me or why did he alter Browning's MO in respect to the pieces of flesh?"

"Either. Both."

"The reason he didn't stick strictly to Browning's MO was because he wanted to send me a message and what better way of doing that than by giving me what would have been the Carver's most prized possessions."

"Very good reasoning."

"Thanks."

"We've agreed that for some reason, it's important to

the copycat for you to be personally involved in this case. That's why he chose Browning to emulate."

"Because Browning killed Noah Laborde, my former boyfriend." Maleah looked at Derek, concern in her hazel brown eyes. "But the question is why me? If Nic or Griff is the real target, then . . ." She paused for a full minute. "Could it really be that simple? Is he making me jump through hoops simply because he can and he wants Nic to know he can control her best friend? And what better way to hurt Nic than through me, right?"

"It's definitely what Griff thinks and it does make a crazy kind of sense. If tormenting Nic and Griff is his objective, then he's punishing them for some reason. He's going to strike again and again, possibly getting closer and closer to his ultimate target with each kill, eventually discarding the Carver's MO."

"If that's the case, then what are the odds that he'll try to kill me before he moves on to Nic and Griff?"

Chapter 19

"It's not as if we didn't already know that both of us r either of us could be targeted as one of the killer's ext victims," Derek said. "My guess is that he'll gradu- ly deviate more and more from the original Carver's O, so having brown eyes eventually won't protect us."

"Your putting my thoughts into words makes it seem ore real." Maleah eased back into the comfort of the fa.

He squeezed her shoulder. "I try not to think about Besides, my guess is that your being jerked around by rowning is what the copycat killer wants, not your ath. At least not yet."

"Maybe." She looked into Derek's black eyes. Her omach tightened. "What about you? What's your role all this craziness?"

"I'm the profiler. He knows my background. I'd lay lds on it. And it's just possible that he wants me to ofile him."

"Why would he—?"

"He's giving me clues to who he is and it's up to me decide which clues are true and which are false."

Absently, Derek massaged her shoulder, his touch seeming instinctive, as if he was barely aware of what he was doing. She knew she should pull away, tell him to stop. But she didn't. She leaned back against the sofa cushion and closed her eyes.

From the moment she had met Derek, she had been aware of the tension between them. And spending so much time with him these past few months had increased that live wire, just-below-the-surface unease she felt when he was anywhere near her. But on the other hand, as they had become better acquainted, her initial opinion of him had altered, at least somewhat. She had a greater respect for him, for his intelligence and his wit. She'd even gotten use to the way he kidded her.

"We're dealing with two, maybe three, separate people," Derek told her. "The copycat is playing Browning, using him, and it's possible that Browning isn't aware that he's been used. I'm not sure how much Browning knows, if anything."

"That's my job, isn't it, to find out what Browning knows." She opened her eyes and glanced at Derek.

"Yeah, that's your job and we both know he's not going to make it easy for you."

The gentle, continuous touch of his hand on her shoulder changed from soothing to arousing. She didn't know if that was his intention or just her reaction, but either way, she had to put a stop to it. Without making a big deal of it, she slowly pulled away from him.

"You said there were three separate people involved. There are Browning and the Copycat Carver. Who is the third person?"

"I said *possible* third person."

"Okay, if you want to split hairs, who is the *possible* third person?"

"Two scenarios," Derek explained. "First, the Copy-

at Carver is the man behind everything. He's working
alone targeting Powell agents and members of their
families, probably as a direct act of revenge against Griff
and / or Nicole."

Maleah nodded. "And scenario number two is?"

"Someone else is the brains of the operation and he
or she is the one controlling the copycat and Browning
while keeping his or her hands clean."

"That's Griff's theory—the Malcolm York imposter is
he Svengali puppeteer pulling all the strings."

"And Griff could be right. If he is . . ."

Maleah waited for Derek to finish his thought, but
when he didn't, she asked, "If Griff is right, then even if
we track down the copycat and stop him, this won't be
over, will it?"

"We know Browning is a psychopath and my guess is
hat the copycat is, too. Working up a profile on the
copycat is possible, but the third person—if there is a
third person—is an unknown. He could be a she. He
could be anywhere in the world, making it almost impossible for us to find him, especially if he has unlim-
ed resources."

"How likely is that scenario?" Maleah asked, hoping
Derek would dismiss it as an unlikely theory.

"I'd say between the two scenarios, it's fifty/fifty."

"Damn," Maleah mumbled. "So how do we find out
xactly who and what we're dealing with?"

"You know the answer to that question."

"We have to find the copycat."

"That's our job. Yours and mine, working as a team,
ith the power of the Powell Agency behind us," Derek
id. "And it's Luke Sentell's job to find out if the Mal-
olm York imposter is a real person or if rumors about
im are just that, rumors, and nothing more."

Maleah yawned. "Sorry."

"You're tired. Maybe you should go back to your room and get a good night's sleep."

"No, I'm okay. I thought you were going to use me as a sounding board, bounce your thoughts off me."

He grinned. Her stomach did a wicked flip-flop. As if realizing the effect he had on her, he chuckled.

Damn it! Damn him!

"If you say one thing . . ." she warned him.

"Oh, honey . . . er . . . sorry. Scratch that endearment. Not honey. Let me rephrase."

"Just skip it, will you. Stop smiling at me. Get serious."

"A little levity isn't a bad thing, not when it's easy to get sucked into the kind of darkness these evil bastards inhabit."

She stared at him. "Is that how you see them, the Carver and the copycat, as evil?"

"In a sense, yes, they are evil. Not the they're-possessed-by-the-devil kind of evil, but evil in an all too human way. Psychopaths and sociopaths have mental disorders. Some can be treated through therapy and medication, if diagnosed. Some become killers. It is believed that these people lack a conscience and feel no remorse or guilt."

"Do you agree with psychiatrists who believe that sociopaths are a result of environment and psychopaths are a result of heredity?"

"There's too much controversy in the mental health field regarding the differences between sociopaths and psychopaths for me to take sides on that issue," Derek said. "Most clinicians use the 'antisocial personality disorder' diagnosis these days to describe both."

"And yet you refer to Browning and the copycat as psychopaths."

"Browning's doctors put that label on him, not me. ut I do agree. As for the copycat, I'm going on gut in- :inct. This guy has to be highly organized. He thinks head, plans ahead, doesn't do anything erratic or un- lanned."

"Even if someone else is telling him what to do, as ould be the case in scenario number two?"

"If there is a third person who is in charge, he would ardly choose a loose cannon to do his dirty work, ould he?"

"You're right. He would choose someone capable of king orders, and someone who wouldn't draw atten- on to himself by acting in an irrational manner."

"It's not uncommon for many killers to show signs of oth the psychopath's and the sociopath's characteris- :cs, but each usually leans more in one direction than ie other."

"You believe that our guy leans more toward the psy- nopath's characteristics, right?"

"Right. So my profile starts there. The Copycat arver is organized, possibly obsessively organized. He ill be difficult to catch because he does nothing on the ur of the moment. He plans each step of his kills and akes sure he leaves behind no clues."

"And he certainly has no problem using other peo- e, without remorse or guilt, to achieve his goals."

"Our killer is probably above average in intelligence, st as Browning is. The victims are strangers to him, st as Browning's Carver victims were strangers. rowning deviated from the psychopath's norm by leav- g the bodies in plain view."

"And the copycat has done exactly the same thing."

"He is a copycat."

Maleah nodded. "I know. It's just . . . Damn it,

there's something off about this whole thing. I can't pu
my finger on it, but it's there, if only I could figure ou
what it is."

"I agree. That's why the more I think about every
thing, the more I'm beginning to wonder about th
copycat's role in these murders."

"What do you mean?"

"He's obviously intelligent, organized, mobile
skilled, has no ties to his victims, and no problem usin
murder to tie up loose ends. To date, he has mimicke
Jerome Browning's murder MO five times. He stran
gled Wyman Scudder with the skill of a trained solide
and he shot Cindy Di Blasi with the expertise of a pro
fessional."

"That's it, isn't it?" Maleah realized that the trut
had been staring them in the face all along. "The cop
cat *is* a professional."

"Yes, I think he is. He's not a typical serial killer, a
tually not even a true copycat killer. He is, most likely,
hired killer."

"A hit man."

"Yes, an assassin, bought and paid for by our *thir
person*."

"Then Griff's been right all along, hasn't he?"

"Maybe."

"What do you mean maybe?" she asked.

"Even if our guy is a professional assassin, that doesn
mean someone calling himself Malcolm York is his bos
Anyone with a grudge against Griff—or Nic for th
matter—could have hired him."

Maleah yawned again. "Sorry, I guess I am getting
little sleepy."

"Let's call it a night."

"No, not yet. I should be good for a while longer
can't stop thinking about your profile of the copycat

the fact that we agree he could be a professional killer."
Maleah kicked off her shoes, brought her bent left leg
up on the sofa and crossed her right leg over the left.
Relaxing her shoulders between the sofa back and the
padded armrest, she faced Derek. "So, tell me how you
go about profiling a professional killer?"

"One size doesn't fit all," Derek said. "Although I believe it's the consensus of law enforcement and psychiatrists that for the most part, all professional assassins
have at least one thing in common—the thrill of killing."

Maleah shivered. The thought that anyone could derive pleasure from murdering another human being
was an alien concept for her. "Are all professional killers
psychopaths?"

"No, not in the strictest sense. For some of these killers
it's a matter of showing their control because having
that kind of power—power over life and death—gives
them an unparalleled rush, an excitement they can get
no other way."

"My God, that is so sick, but you say all of them aren't
mentally ill, that they aren't crazy."

"Each of us has within us the ability to kill," Derek
said. "Given the right circumstances, you or I could and
would kill. The difference is that most of us would not
derive pleasure from the act. It would be in self-defense
or to protect someone else. Or as soldiers do every day,
we would be willing to kill or die for our country, for a
cause we believe in."

"But a soldier killing in wartime is different."

"Yes, it is. And yet . . ."

"What?"

"Nothing. Just . . ."

"Something you want to share?" She stared at him.
He shook his head. "No, not really."

When she continued staring at him, he glanced away, breaking direct eye contact. "When I was in my late teens and early twenties, I bummed around the world on my own, putting as much distance between myself and my family as I possibly could. Not long after I turned twenty, I found myself flat broke. I was damned and determined not to touch my trust fund, so I did something really stupid."

"I can't imagine your doing anything stupid. Not you." Without giving her actions a thought, she reached up on the sofa back and laid her hand over his.

He tensed the moment she touched him. She eased her hand away.

"I joined a group of guys I met up with when I was in Europe, some real badasses, and I thought I was as mean and tough as they were so I sort of bluffed my way into their circle. They were mercenaries of a sort, most of them former soldiers. They weren't all that particular about who joined them. As long as I kept my mouth shut and did what I was told, we got along fine. I spent nearly ten months with them." He looked into her eyes. "You've never killed anyone, have you, Maleah?"

"No, I haven't. But I have been in several situations where I've had to return fire. And a few years ago, I was shot and spent some time in the hospital."

"I remember. I was working strictly freelance at the time. I consulted on that case. Rick Carson was the Powell agent in charge."

"That's right."

They sat there in silence for a few moments before Derek said, "I have killed. I've killed more than just one person."

"When you were working with those mercenaries?"

"Yeah. The first time I killed a man, I was scared to death. We'd been hired by a family to rescue a kidnap victim. I thought of myself as one of the good guys and the man I killed as one of the bad guys. The second time I killed a man, I wasn't quite as scared and eventually, it got easier. And finally it became too easy. I began hating myself. That's when I got out, changed my life around and came home to the U.S."

Maleah looked at Derek Lawrence with a greater insight into the person he really was, not the man she thought he was. Why he had chosen to share with her what was obviously painful memories about his youthful walk on the wild side, she didn't know. But she was glad he had. Seeing him now, all sleek and sophisticated with his expensive haircuts, his designer clothes, his air of casual elegance, she never would have thought—not in a million years—that he had ever been a soldier of fortune when he was very young and apparently very stupid.

She would never again be able to look at him and see only an arrogant playboy.

"I really don't know you at all, do I?" She couldn't take her eyes off him because she felt that she was seeing him for the first time.

"Sure you do, hon—" He broke off mid-word. "You know me. Sometimes I feel as if you can see straight through me." He grinned, the motion forced and self-mocking. "Now, you know me a little better. I've given you more weapons in your arsenal of reasons to dislike me."

"Is that what you think, that I look for reasons to dislike you?"

"Don't you?"

"No, of course not."

"Tell me one thing you like about me," he challenged.

"I'm not playing this game with you." She sat up straight and halfway rose to her feet.

He grabbed her upper arms and forced her back down on the sofa. "Just tell me one thing you like about me and I'll let you go." He kept a tight hold on her.

She didn't fight him, didn't even squirm. "I like your silver Corvette."

His lips twitched. "That's something I own. Try again."

His tenacious hold loosened ever so slightly.

"I like . . ." Her mind went blank. He was staring at her with such intensity, as if her answer meant a great deal to him. But that wasn't possible, was it? Derek didn't really give a damn what she or anyone else thought of him.

"You like what?" he asked. "My good looks? My winning personality? My magnificent body? My keen intellect?"

"Yes." She swallowed hard.

"Yes, what? Be specific."

"Yes, I like your looks, your body, your intellect and your personality, too, except for the macho he-man part that fights me for control and tries to put me in my place."

What is the point of lying? He already knows how I feel about him.

"And what do you believe I think your place is?" He slid his left hand down her arm and slipped it around her waist, then moved his right hand up to circle the back of her neck.

Keeping her eyes focused on him to show him that he didn't intimidate her, she replied, "You think I should be a helpless, needy female who can't survive without a big strong man like you to lean on, to support me, and to make my decisions for me."

When Derek laughed, she felt as if he had thrown ice water over her head.

"What's so damn funny?"

"You are, Blondie. You have no idea how wrong you are. Would I like to see you all soft and feminine, yeah, sure I would. But you could never be helpless and needy. That's not who you are, thank goodness. You're tough, outspoken, and independent. And those are things I like about you."

She stared at him with wide-eyed disbelief.

"And FYI—I like your pretty face, your gorgeous body, and your sharp mind." With his hand at the back of her neck, he drew her closer and closer.

He's going to kiss me. God help us both! What do I do?
You resist, you idiot, that's what you do.

But she didn't resist. "What about my personality?" she asked, her voice husky with emotion.

"I like your personality, except . . ." He brought his mouth close to hers.

"Except?" she asked, her lips parting in anticipation.

"I forget," he told her.

And then he kissed her. A tender marauding that claimed her mouth.

Mercy Lord.

She kissed him back. Kissed him with equal hunger and need and passion. Not until that very moment did she realize exactly how much she had wanted Derek to kiss her.

Chapter 20

Had he lost his mind? Kissing Maleah Perdue was insanity. A huge mistake. But damn it all, he couldn't remember the last time he had wanted anything half as much. While his thoughts went wild with warnings, he deepened the kiss. As if she were a drug he had become instantly addicted to, he wanted more. But the moment his tongue touched hers, Maleah shoved against his chest, trying to push him away from her. When she managed to free her mouth from his, she gasped for air.

"We can't do this," she said breathlessly. "It's crazy. We're crazy!"

He released his hold on the back of her neck and eased his arm from around her waist. Breathing hard, he stared at her flushed cheeks, her swollen lips, and disheveled hair. Apparently, without realizing what he was doing, he had threaded his fingers through her hair.

"Do I need to apologize?" he asked, knowing full well that she was going to lay all the blame on him. And maybe she should. After all, he had started the whole thing by kissing her, hadn't he?

Maleah shook her head. "I don't know what happened." She jumped up. "But it was as much my fault as
yours." She refused to look directly at him. "I should go
back to my room."

When she turned and headed for the door, Derek
got up and followed her, catching up with her just as
she reached for the door handle.

He laid his hand on her shoulder. She tensed.

"It was bound to happen sooner or later," he said.
"There's been some sort of sexual tension between us
since the day we met. That kiss was a good thing. It defused the tension, so we don't have to deal with it anymore."

She glanced over her shoulder, right into his eyes,
and saw the truth. Who was he trying to kid? He was
lying. They both knew it. That kiss hadn't defused a
damn thing. The exact opposite was true.

"Right," she said, agreeing with his lie.

He reached around her, his arm brushing her side as
he opened the door. She offered him a weak, we're-fine
smile and walked out into the hall.

"See you in the morning," he said.

"Yeah, see you in the morning."

He stepped out into the hall and watched her until
she disappeared into her room. Then he went back into
his room and closed and double locked the door.

Cursing under his breath, calling himself every kind
of fool, he stomped across the carpeted floor and went
outside on the patio. After taking several deep gulps of
fresh nighttime sea air, he sat down in one of the
lounge chairs and looked out over the ocean.

Time for some hard truths, buddy boy.

He was attracted to Maleah. Not just her pretty blond
looks or her hourglass-shaped body. He liked that she

was smart and independent and aggressive. Hell, h
even liked the way she stood up to him, challenge
him, and wouldn't let him get away with anything.

Maleah was her own woman. She wasn't waiting fo
some man to come along and make all her dreams con
true. She didn't expect a future husband to provide h
with everything his money could buy. Not like Happ
who had married his father for his family's vast wealt
and proceeded to make the man's life a living hell. A
least that's the way he remembered his parents' ma
riage. And not like his sister Diana, who had jilted the g
she had really loved in order to marry the man Happ
had chosen for her. A man with the right pedigree, s
cial standing, and bank account.

Maleah was nothing like his mother or his sister. An
maybe that was the reason he liked her so much. To
damn much.

*You've got to let this thing go. You may want her . . . he
she may even want you . . . but it just won't work. Not for e
ther of you.*

Okay, so things would be a bit awkward in the mor
ing, but if they both just pretended it had never ha
pened . . . But could they? Could he forget what it fe
like to have her in his arms, how much he wanted fa
more than just a heated kiss? Even now, his body st
wanted her.

How would Maleah feel about having sex? No strin
attached. No deep, long-lasting emotions involved. Ju
screwing until they worked "it" out of their systems.

*It? Primitive desire. Animal hunger. Lust. Call "it" wha
ever you want.*

Maleah sure as hell wasn't the first woman he'd ev
wanted that way and she certainly wouldn't be the la
But . . .

But Maleah wasn't just any woman and that was the problem.

Derek mumbled a few self-loathing obscenities as he got up, went inside and undressed for bed.

The Inn Steinhof, located in downtown St. Jakob, possessed the old world charm one associated with rural Austria. The three-story white building provided spacious, comfortable en suite rooms. Breakfast was provided and dinner was available for an additional charge. There were tables outside for shaded summer eating and a small bar and grill was located on the main floor, just off the lobby area. Upon arrival, Luke had done as Henri Fortier had instructed and left a message for Aldo Finster, whom Luke had been told was away hiking and would return the following day.

Long ago, Luke had learned the value of patience.

And so he had waited for Finster to return to the hotel. Half an hour ago, one of the maids had delivered a note from Finster, inviting Luke to meet him in the lobby in an hour.

When Luke arrived in the lobby, he casually scanned the area, and in less than a minute, spotted the person he assumed was Finster. He was a small, plump, balding gentleman in his late forties, his blue eyes appearing quite large behind a pair of thick bifocals.

Luke approached the man. "Herr Finster?"

"Yes, I am Aldo Finster." He smiled. "And you are Mr. Sentell." He held out his hand.

Luke shook hands with Finster.

"You are enjoying your stay in St. Jakob?" Finster asked.

Luke nodded.

"Will you be here long?" he asked.

Finster's command of the English language was excellent, although his accent was quite pronounced.

"Long enough," Luke replied.

Finster nodded. "I know an excellent restaurant just down the street. A short walk. Shall we go now?"

Luke nodded again.

Once they exited the hotel, Finster said, "You know Henri Fortier, I believe."

"Yes, I know Henri."

"He suggested you ask me to put you in contact with a tour guide, yes?"

"Yes."

"I know someone who would be perfect for you, Mr Sentell. He has an excellent reputation for providing tourists with whatever they want."

"Then you can arrange for me to meet this tour guide."

"Most certainly. There will be a small fee, of course.'

"Name your price."

"Sixty-two thousand euro." Finster continued walking, his smile widening as he glanced at Luke.

"This guide must be exceptional." Luke paused.

Finster stopped and looked squarely at Luke. "I can assure you that his knowledge of Austria is priceless."

"Then by all means, make the arrangements as soon as possible."

"You understand that this will be a cash transaction," Finster said.

"I'll have your money for you in a couple of hours."

"Excellent, excellent." Finster began walking again "Perhaps we should forgo lunch today while we each attend to business."

* * *

Maleah had ordered coffee, cold cereal, and fresh fruit for breakfast and her meal was served promptly at eight. She was already dressed and ready when the waiter delivered her food. So far that morning, Derek hadn't gotten in touch with her. She suspected he was putting off the inevitable, just as she was.

Grow up, will you. It was just a kiss.

Yeah, but what a kiss.

As she sipped on her second cup of coffee—she had practically inhaled the first cup—she eyed her phone lying on top of her packed suitcase alongside her shoulder holster.

Go ahead and call him.

And say what?

Say good morning. Ask what time he wants to leave the hotel. Suggest that we should drive straight back to Vidalia, Georgia, to prepare for my next interview with Jerome Browning.

There was no reason to mention the kiss. Derek probably wouldn't say anything about it. No doubt he wanted to forget that it had happened just as much as she did. But the problem was could either of them ever forget?

You overreacted. That kiss wasn't as incredible as you thought it was.

She marched over to the bed where she had placed her suitcase.

Just pick up the phone and call him.

She reached down, grasped the phone and held it in her hand.

Aggravated with herself for hesitating, she said aloud, "Put on your big girl panties and do it."

She hit the preprogrammed number and held her breath as she waited for him to answer.

"Good morning, Blondie," Derek said.

"Good morning. I . . . uh . . . was wondering—"

"I'm ready to hit the road whenever you are," he told her. "I had my breakfast delivered half an hour ago. Have you eaten?"

She glanced at the untouched cereal and fruit on her breakfast tray. "I just now finished. I can be ready to leave in about ten minutes."

"Okay."

"I'll knock on your door when I'm ready to go."

"Sounds fine. That will give me time to check in with headquarters."

Everything was going to be all right. Derek sounded like his usual self. Apparently, she was the only one with a problem, the one who had stammered and acted all morning-after stupid.

"Derek?"

"Huh?"

"I think we should head straight back to Vidalia. I really want some prep time before I go back to the penitentiary for another interview with Browning. I'm going to need your help."

"We're thinking alike," he said. "I've already called the Hampton Inn where we stayed and reserved rooms for the next three nights. And while you're driving today, I'll start putting my thoughts down on paper and we can discuss strategy."

"Thanks, Derek."

"You're welcome, Blondie."

Poppy didn't go to church except when she stayed with Grandmother in Savannah. Her mother wasn't a religious person. Actually Vickie didn't believe in God. She said religion was for idiots and senile old fools like her grandmother. But Grandmother wasn't an idiot nor was she senile. And Poppy actually enjoyed Sunday morning services at the First Presbyterian Church. Aunt Mary Lee was Episcopal now, having converted when she married Uncle Lowell. The Dandridges had been Episcopalian for generations, just as the Chappelles had been Presbyterian.

"I thought we'd have lunch out here," Grandmother called to Poppy from the sunroom. "It's just the three of us today. I told Heloise not to worry with anything much. No sense heating up the house on such a warm day when we aren't expecting company."

"I made chicken salad before we left for services this morning." Heloise came out of the kitchen carrying a tray that held a pitcher of iced tea and three glasses. "And there are teacakes left over from yesterday. I thought they'd be good with ice cream and some fresh sliced peaches."

"What can I do to help?" Poppy asked.

"Why don't you set the table," Heloise said. "The everyday dinnerware will be fine, won't it, Miss Carolyn?"

"Certainly, certainly." Grandmother waved her hand in dismissal as she sat down in one of the big wicker chairs.

Although the Chappelles were no longer wealthy, Grandmother continued to live a comfortable lifestyle. She still played bridge with her snooty friends, still maintained a membership at the country club, still resided in the home where she had raised her family, and still kept a housekeeper, although after all these years, Heloise was as much friend as servant.

"The old bat has no idea that if it wasn't for Saxon putting money in her bank account on a regular basis, she'd be living from hand to mouth," Poppy's mother had told her. "The crazy fool thinks she's still rich."

Sometimes her mom wasn't a nice person.

Poppy often wished she could live with Grandmother all the time, not just during the summer. But when she had mentioned the idea to her mother, she'd gone ape-shit and threatened all sorts of things, including telling Grandmother the truth about her finances—that she was actually flat broke and living off her son's charity. When she turned twenty-five and had full access to her trust fund, she would help Uncle Saxon take care of Grandmother.

Sometimes Poppy hated her mother.

Luke paid Aldo Finster in cash. In exchange for the sixty-two thousand euros, Luke was escorted to a parked car outside his hotel that evening around eight o'clock. The driver got out, opened the door for Luke and waited while Luke slid into the backseat.

"Good evening, Mr. Sentell," the car's backseat occupant said.

"Jurgen Hirsch, I presume?"

"As good a name as any other and one I use on occasion."

"I understand from Herr Finster that you're the ideal tour guide for me."

In the shadowy darkness of the car's interior, Luke's eyesight adjusted, enabling him to see more clearly. Jurgen Hirsch, blond, muscular and probably no older than he, studied Luke, his gaze focused on Luke's face.

"There is someplace in particular you wish to go, someone you wish to see?"

"I'm looking for a man who calls himself Malcolm York."

Dead silence.

Luke waited, his gaze riveted to his companion's.

And then Jurgen Hirsch's lips tilted upward in a cold, calculating, unemotional smile. "I, too, have heard the rumors about a man by that name. But it is my understanding that Malcolm York is dead and has been for sixteen years."

"Then there is nothing you can tell me about him that I don't already know, but perhaps you can tell me more about these rumors."

"You are very persistent, Mr. Sentell."

"I'm fifty thousand dollars persistent, Herr Hirsch."

Hirsch laughed. A look of amused curiosity glimmered in his icy blue eyes. "Have you ever heard of Anthony Linden?"

"Who hasn't heard of Linden, the infamous former MI6 operative who went rogue. What does Linden have to do with Malcolm York, other than both men are dead?"

"Ah, but that is what makes their association so interesting," Hirsch said in his lightly accented English. "Rumors are that Anthony Linden is alive and well and has been working as a professional assassin for the past ten years."

"And?" Luke knew where this was going, a gut feeling he didn't like.

"Rumors abound, of course, but the most recent rumor circulating among my associates is that Linden is working for York."

"An interesting rumor, especially since both men are presumed dead."

"Sometimes rumors have a basis in facts. I have no proof that the billionaire Malcolm York who lived on the Pacific Island of Amara is alive, but I know for a fact that Anthony Linden is very much alive because I had drinks with him six months ago, the night before he left for America."

* * *

Griff took Luke's call at 2:30 Eastern Time that after
noon. When their brief, private conversation ended
Griff called Sanders into his study and then closed and
locked the door.

"Do you remember a man named Anthony Linden?"
Griff asked.

"A former SIS agent, I believe. He was permanently
terminated ten years ago."

"It seems that Linden may be alive and well and is re
ported to have been in the U.S. for the past six
months."

Sanders didn't react, didn't even blink. "And did
Luke ascertain what the presumed dead Mr. Linden i
doing in the U.S.?"

"It seems Linden is now a professional assassin."

Sanders's eyes widened. He clenched his jaw.

"Luke was told that Linden is working for Malcolm
York," Griff said.

Sanders's nostrils flared as he released a deeply in
haled breath. "How reliable is Luke's source?"

"As reliable as fifty thousand dollars can buy. It seems
that the source claims to have had drinks with Linden
the night before he left for America. Luke assumes that
his source and Linden are in the same business."

"If Anthony Linden is alive and if he is in the U.S
sent here in his profession as an assassin, you and
know that the man who hired him is not Malcolm York
York is dead."

"Is he?" Griff asked.

"You know he is."

"Yes, of course I know he is. He was dead when w
left him on Amara. No one could have survived what w
did to him, not even an inhuman demon like York.
Griff looked at Sanders for affirmation, needing to

ear him say the words, to vanquish the ghost that
aunted him. Malcolm York was dead and yet . . .

"What York did to us, and to many others, lives on in
ach of us, like an incurable disease," Sanders said. "But
ork is dead. He was dead long before we chopped off
is head."

Chapter 21

The trip from St. Simons Island to Vidalia took clos[e] to two and a half hours. Maleah drove straight throug[h] without making any stops. When they arrived at th[e] Hampton Inn that Sunday afternoon, they went to the[ir] separate rooms. Although they had both acted as if la[st] night's kiss had never happened, that singular even[t] stood between them, an invisible wall of uncertain[ty.] After making a concentrated effort for months to pe[r]suade Maleah to like and trust him, why had he don[e] something so monumentally stupid? Any fool woul[d] have known that by kissing her, he would alter the[ir] fragile friendship.

If he could take back the kiss, would he?

Maybe.

But when he had kissed her, she had kissed hi[m.] Crazy thing was that he suspected she had enjoyed th[e] kiss as much as he had, that it had affected her [as] strongly as it had him.

As he settled into his room, he tried to stop thinkin[g] about Maleah as anything other than his partner on [a] Powell Agency case. He unpacked his suitcase, hung u[p]

his clothes, and placed his shaving kit on the bathroom
sink counter. He picked up the ice bucket and took it
with him when he left the room in search of the re-
freshment center. He returned to his room with a full
ice bucket and four canned colas, two in his jacket
pockets and two balanced atop the bucket.

After placing three colas in the mini-fridge and the
ice bucket on the desk, he upended a glass from the
paper coaster, filled the glass with ice and popped the
tab on his Coke. Then he removed his jacket and shirt,
as well as his shoes and socks, stripping down to his
T-shirt and bare feet. After setting up his laptop, he
grabbed the glass of cola, along with a pad and pen,
and relaxed on the sofa. Kicked back, sipping on the
cold drink, he propped his feet up on the coffee table.

On the drive from St. Simons Island, he and Maleah
had avoided any mention of last night. She had focused
on driving; he had checked e-mails and text messages and
given his full attention to the copycat killer case. They
hadn't talked much and when they had, their conversation had been limited to strategic planning for tomorrow.

Maleah had a ten o'clock interview with Browning in
the morning. She understood that the first goal was to
find out if Browning knew that his visitor Albert
Durham was not the real Durham, the real biographer.
If the fake Durham had fooled Browning, then it might
be possible to coax him into betraying any confidences
the two men had shared. But he wouldn't give the info
to Maleah without equal payment in return. He would
want his pound of flesh. And he would want to strip it
off Maleah himself, inch by inch.

If Browning knew that his visitor had been a fraud,
his knowing that would change everything. That could
mean the two men were co-conspirators, working together, each getting something they wanted from their

alliance. If that were the case, then Browning wouldn'
be inclined to offer any info to Maleah. Not unless she
could up the ante and offer him something that the
fake Durham couldn't.

Derek could only imagine what price Browning
would demand.

Would Maleah be willing to pay the price?

Would he let her?

*Listen to yourself, Lawrence! Would you let her? How the
hell do you think you could stop her, short of knocking her
out and tying her up?*

While he jotted down first one thought and then an
other, anything and everything that came to mind, he
finished off the first Coke. Just as he got up, refilled his
glass with ice and reached into the fridge for a second
can, someone knocked on his door.

He set the can beside his glass on the table and
padded barefoot across the carpet. When he peered
through the peephole, he smiled. He hadn't expected
to see her again until morning.

He opened the door. "Hi."

"May I come in?" Maleah asked, her chin high, her
gaze direct.

He stepped aside to allow her room to enter. "Yeah
sure, come on in."

When she scanned him from head to toe, he realized
she was taking in his completely casual appearance. "
was settling in for the evening."

"I apologize for disturbing you." She was still dressed
just as she had been when they had arrived at the hotel
Navy slacks, tan jacket, and sensible low-heel shoes.

"You're not disturbing me," he told her as he closed
the door. "Would you like a Coke?"

She eyed the glass filled with ice and the unopened
cola can on the desk. "Do you have another?"

"Two more as a matter of fact." He moved past her toward the desk.

"Then, yes, thank you, I'd like a Coke."

"Have a seat." He busied himself preparing a second glass with ice and then split the Coke between the two glasses. He walked over to where she sat on the sofa and offered her the drink.

Before joining her on the sofa, he opened the fridge and retrieved a second cola, popped the tab and set the can on the coffee table beside Maleah's glass. When he started to sit down, Maleah reached out and picked up the notepad he had left lying on the sofa.

"Take a look," he told her. "I was just putting down some thoughts on your meeting with Browning in the morning. See if there's anything you think you can work with, anything that strikes you as doable."

She read over the page of notes, and then set the pad on the coffee table before lifting her glass and sipping on the cola.

"First and foremost, you have to find a way to figure out if Browning knows that the Albert Durham who visited him is a fake," Derek said.

"I figure a direct approach is best," she said. "I think I should lead off with the news that we spoke to the real biographer, Albert Durham, and that the man who visited him and passed himself off as a writer wanting to tell the world Browning's life story is a phony."

"I agree. Watch him closely for his initial reaction. After those first few seconds, he'll hide what he's feeling and thinking. Browning is smart. He'll figure out what you want almost immediately."

"And that's when the games begin."

"Yeah, I'm afraid so."

"What if I can't read him well enough in those first

few minutes to figure out if he already knew Durham was a phony?"

"You'll get an initial gut reaction in those first few seconds," Derek told her. "Go with your gut, let it lead you into what you'll say next. Don't listen as much to what Browning is saying as to what he isn't saying. Read between the lines. And be aware of his body language."

"I know the basics, of course, but . . . Just this once, I wish you could be there, in the room with me. You're the expert."

He reached out, instinctively planning to touch her, but stopped himself mid-reach when she scooted away from him. Ignoring his action and her reaction, he dropped his hand to his side and said, "You know enough. It's mostly common sense and an ability to read people. Browning isn't going to willingly give away anything. He's going to lie and not only with his words."

"Are you saying he'll know I'm watching his body language and will fake that, too?"

"He may try, but the more intense the conversation, the less likely he'll be concentrating on what he's doing because he'll be too involved in what he's saying."

"I wish I had time for a body language refresher course."

"How about I give you one?" Derek suggested. "Why don't I order pizza delivery for supper, get a couple more Cokes and more ice and we'll settle in for the evening?"

"Sounds like a plan." She downed half a glass of cola as she stood. "I want to get out of these clothes and into some jeans. Give me thirty minutes." She set her glass on the coffee table. "Don't get up."

He watched her walk to the door, his gaze moving from her slender neck, exposed because her hair was up in a bun, and down over her trim, toned body. When she walked through the door, he leaned back on the sofa and huffed out a get-hold-of-yourself breath. He had to concentrate on business, not his partner's shapely butt.

It was that damn kiss!

He'd always been aware of how attractive Maleah was, but now he couldn't seem to think about anything else.

Well, you'd damn well better get your mind on helping Maleah survive tomorrow's interview with Jerome Browning. She's going into battle and the more weapons and armor she has to defend herself, the better.

Maleah had tried not to think about the kiss, but the harder she tried to forget it, the more she thought about it. How many times had she replayed Derek's words: *It was bound to happen sooner or later. There's been some sort of sexual tension between us since the day we met. That kiss was a good thing. It defused the tension, so we don't have to deal with it anymore.*

Although they had both known that comment was a lie the minute he said it, they had spent the entire day pretending it was the truth. They had acted as if nothing had happened, as if the tension between them no longer existed, when in fact the exact opposite was true. She was more aware of Derek as a handsome, desirable man than she had ever been. How ridiculous was that? She had convinced herself that he was everything she disliked in a man and had denied the physical attraction that sizzled between them.

You'll hate yourself if you have sex with him.

Where the hell had that thought come from? She wasn't going to have sex with Derek. Not tonight. Not ever. She didn't have indiscriminate sex just because her hormones went into overdrive. Doing something stupid and impulsive just wasn't who she was. She chose her sexual partners with care and that was why there had been very few men in her life. For her, a sexual relationship was based on specific factors: mutual respect, a certain amount of admiration, physical attraction, and love. Not the forever-after, let's-get-married kind of love, but the friendship I-like-you-a-lot kind of love.

She and Derek were partners, working together to solve a mystery, to identify and stop a killer targeting the Powell Agency. Now was most certainly not the time for them to explore all the explosive tension they each were trying so hard to deny. Later on, when this job was over and everyone associated with the Powell Agency was safe, they would have to face whatever it was between them. The ever powerful "it" that had taken on a life of its own when Derek had kissed her.

You kissed him back! she reminded herself for the hundredth time.

Hurriedly, Maleah removed her clothes, down to her underwear, slipped on her white jeans and baggy pink cotton sweater, and then slid her feet into a pair of pink Yellow Box flip-flops. After applying fresh blush and pink lipstick, she removed the pins from her hair and ran her fingers through it.

There. I'm presentable. But I don't look as if I'm trying to impress him.

As an afterthought, she rinsed with mouthwash and rubbed some scented lotion on her arms and hands before leaving her room.

After the second knock, Derek opened the door. "I found a Pizza Inn in the Yellow Pages. It's not far from here and they'll deliver in about an hour. I thought we'd have an early dinner since we skipped lunch."

She breezed into his room, hoping her body movements expressed casual confidence. She wanted him to believe that she was completely comfortable eating dinner with him in his room, just the two of them alone. She wanted him to know that the kiss they had shared last night was the farthest thing from her mind.

"In about an hour is fine," she told him. "I am getting a little hungry."

"How does taco pizza sound? I know how you love Mexican food."

"Taco pizza sounds delicious." She picked up Derek's notepad off the coffee table and sat on the sofa.

"Don't shoot me, but I ordered dessert." He grinned. "It's cinnamon stromboli."

"You, Derek Lawrence, are a wicked, wicked man. You're trying to make me fat."

He laughed. "I like my women with a little meat on their bones."

As if suddenly realizing how what he had said might be misconstrued, he stopped laughing and searched her face. "Not that you're one of my women. Or that I think of you as one of many. Or—"

"Shut up while you're ahead," she told him.

"I really stuck my foot in my mouth that time, didn't I?" He came over and sat down beside her.

"Don't worry about it. I realize that if I hadn't overreacted so many times in the past and repeatedly bitten your head off, you wouldn't be concerned that I might take offense at every innocent remark."

His brow wrinkled as he narrowed his gaze and stared at her. "Once again, I have to ask who are you and what have you done with the real Maleah Perdue?"

She laughed. "Oh God, not another imposter. Now you're dealing with three fakes—the Malcolm York imposter, the Albert Durham imposter, and the Maleah Perdue imposter. How did you find me out so quickly? What did I do to give myself away?"

"Are you laughing at me?"

He smiled again and she noted how his whole body had relaxed. Body language. As if suddenly remembering what she was doing here in his room, all alone with him again, she said, "I'm here for my refresher course in body language, not for our mutual amusement."

"Who says we can't have a few laughs before, during, and after class?"

"We've had our before laugh, so let's get down to business." She flipped open his notepad, found the first blank page and clicked the ink pen. "If I recall correctly, some negative gestures include legs or arms crossed, more space than necessary between people, although I want as much space as possible between Jerome Browning and me."

"A general rule of thumb when you're trying to decide if someone is lying or telling the truth is to compare their gestures with what they're saying. If someone is saying yes and at the same time shaking their head, then odds are the gesture is true and the word is false."

"Okay, that makes sense."

"Unfortunately, we don't know how skilled Browning is in the art of using body language. He could use it as adeptly as a gambler who has learned how to bluff with expert ease."

"If it turns out that he's that good, I don't think a mini-brush-up course is going to help me." Maleah tapped the tip of the ink pen on the pad.

"Deciphering body language is not an exact science. Use it for what it is, an effective tool that isn't always infallible."

"I understand."

"Look for certain signs," Derek told her. "And remember to take nothing at face value, not what Browning says or what he does."

"I'm ready." She tapped the notepad with the pen again.

"People who glance to the side quite a bit are usually nervous, lying or distracted. Browning will most likely look you right in the eye, trying to intimidate you, but once you're deep into conversation, he may revert to acting in a more normal fashion."

"Got it." She scribbled down the info. "Next."

"Okay. Arms crossed over his chest means defensive. Touching or rubbing his nose could mean he's doubting you or he's lying. Rubbing his eye is a sign of doubt. Rubbing his hands together equals anticipation."

"Slow down."

"Sorry."

She scribbled hurriedly, then said, "Go on."

"You need to remember not to over-evaluate his gestures. It's easy enough to read them wrong, especially if he's playing you. Keep reminding yourself that you can't trust anything he says or any of his body language."

"Gee whiz, coach, is there any way I can win this game?"

Derek grinned. "Not if you play fair."

"Who said I intended to play fair?"

"You'd better not. If you do, he'll chew you up and spit you out in little pieces. Protect yourself at all costs."

"Yes, sir." She saluted him. They both laughed. "Now, back to Body Language one-oh-one."

For the next fifty minutes, they discussed body language, mind games, and went over techniques used to control emotions.

"If he says something that triggers a deep emotional response, there is a danger you'll lose track of the conversation. If this happens, recognize what's going on before you let it get out of control."

Maleah nodded. "I know the signs—rapid heartbeat and breathing, as well as a desire to scream. I can handle this. Some yoga deep breathing techniques usually work for me."

"If the deep breathing alone doesn't work, try refocusing for a few seconds," Derek suggested. "Just think about how you're normally in complete control."

"I can do that, too."

"And when you end the interview, you really need a debriefing. You can do that yourself or I can help you. If you can talk it out with me—"

"I will. My guess is that I'll need to vent. Besides, you'll need to know everything about the interview anyway."

A knock on the door interrupted his response. Instead he said, "That's probably the pizza delivery."

Griffin would have preferred not including Nicole in his private conversation with Sanders and Yvette. But he had allowed too many secrets to come between them and cause Nic to doubt him. The last thing he wanted was for her to feel excluded, especially when he shared confidences with Yvette. If only he had told her the complete truth in the beginning, before they married. Sanders had advised him to be completely honest with Nic; but Yvette, who had sensed Nic's jealousy, had warned him that there was one secret he should never share with his future wife. And in all honesty, he hadn't told her everything because he'd been afraid he would lose her. And losing Nic would be like losing his own life. She was his life. After knowing her, loving her, living with her, he knew that without her, he would cease to exist.

Even now, after Yvette and her protégés had been at

Griffin's Rest for nearly two years, Nic still had a problem with Yvette living nearby. He had tried in so many different ways to reassure her, to make her understand that she had no reason to be jealous of his love for Yvette. But if he were honest with himself, he would admit that it was the lies he had told Nic, the secrets that he had kept, that made her distrust him. And yet despite everything, Nic was still with him, loving him and standing by his side.

Sanders had chosen to walk over to the home that housed Yvette and seven young men and women who possessed rare psychic gifts. He had gone on ahead, half an hour before Griff asked Nic to join him. Yvette's "students" were misfits, people who didn't fit into mainstream society because they were remarkably different.

"You should talk to your wife first," Sanders had advised Griff. "She does not want to believe that the copycat murders are connected to your past. But with the information Luke has discovered, combined with what Meredith Sinclair told us that she was able to sense after Kristi's and Shelley's murders, Nicole has to accept the truth."

"Nic told me that Meredith could be wrong, even though we all know that the girl's psychic abilities are incredibly accurate."

"Nicole instinctively dislikes anything to do with your experiences on Amara. She does not know the whole story and yet on some instinctive level, she senses that there is a secret you are keeping from her, a secret that could destroy your marriage."

Griff refused to consider the possibility that Nic would ever leave him, at least not permanently.

But if she ever found out about . . .

He had to make sure that never happened.

On their walk to Yvette's home, he told Nic only that

he wanted them to all be together when he told them about Luke Sentell's most recent report. If he could spare Nic, he would. But he had alienated her too many times in the past by excluding her because he wanted to protect her.

Michelle Allen opened the door when they arrived. Griff had assigned her to live there at Yvette's sanctuary as the in-house bodyguard for Yvette and her students.

"Dr. Meng is waiting for you in her office," Michelle said. "Sanders is with her."

After exchanging pleasantries with Michelle, Nic slipped her arm through his and said, "Let's do this."

Just as they reached the entrance to Yvette's private office—adjacent to her living quarters and separate from the rooms on the opposite side of the house where her protégés lived—a young student came rushing out into the hall.

When she saw Nic and Griff, she stopped dead still and stared at them, her mouth wide and a startled expression on her face.

Yvette stepped out into the corridor and placed her hand on the girl's shoulder. "It's all right, Shiloh. We'll talk later this evening. Go back to your room now and meditate."

"Yes, ma'am." Shiloh rushed past Nic and Griff.

Yvette smiled, her gaze traveling slowly from Griff to Nic. "Shiloh did not realize that Sanders was here or that I was expecting more visitors. She simply needed to talk, which we will do later."

Griff knew how hard Nic tried to like Yvette and how hard Yvette tried to be Nic's friend. His love for both women had put each of them in an untenable position.

Once the four of them were inside Yvette's office, Griff closed the door. He looked at Nic first, and then at Yvette and finally at Sanders.

"I received a call from Luke Sentell yesterday. I shared the information with Sanders immediately. I've waited until today to tell both of you because I wanted to consider every possibility and every implication. And I've been using Sanders as a sounding board, as I so often do.'"

"We are not going to like what you have to tell us, are we?" Yvette said.

"I agree with her on that—it has to be bad news," Nic said.

"The rumors are still rumors," Griff said, "but where there is smoke there is usually fire." He paused, collecting his thoughts, considering what he had to say. "As we already know, there is supposedly a man somewhere in Europe who calls himself Malcolm York. We also know he cannot be the York that we—" he glanced quickly from Sanders to Yvette "—killed on Amara. What if any connection this Malcolm York has to the other one, we don't know.

"Luke's contact, who may or may not be a reliable source, sold Luke information concerning a man named Anthony Linden, a former MI6 agent who went rogue and was eliminated approximately ten years ago. According to official records, he chose suicide over capture. But it seems that not only has York risen from the dead, but so has Linden. And York hired Linden, a professional assassin, and sent him to America six months ago. Or so the story goes."

"Oh my God," Nic said. "This is ridiculous. The entire thing sounds like a plot invented by someone who is completely insane."

Griff's gaze met Yvette's.

They knew, he, Yvette, and Sanders, how completely insane Malcolm York had been. Diabolically insane.

"Are we to believe that this pseudo Malcolm York has

sent a hired killer to murder people connected to the Powell Agency?" Yvette asked. "And he is a professional assassin, who according to official records is dead?"

"It's all too far fetched to believe," Nic insisted, her gaze traveling the room, searching the others' faces for any signs of disbelief. "Please tell me that none of you actually believe this story."

"Far fetched or not, we can't dismiss the possibility," Griff said.

"Good God, Griff, you think it's true, don't you?" Nic glared at him. "You think somehow, someway, York is reaching out from beyond the grave to seek revenge."

"No. I don't believe that Malcolm York is reaching out from beyond the grave," Griff said. "But I do believe that a real live person is using York's name."

"But who?" Nic asked. "And why?"

"That's what we have to find out," Griff replied. "That's why I want to send Meredith to London as soon as possible to join Luke." He looked at Yvette. "He'll need her from here on out. Will you speak to her and persuade her to help us?"

Yvette didn't respond immediately. Griff could see that the idea of sending the emotionally vulnerable Meredith Sinclair to aid Luke in his dangerous investigation bothered Yvette greatly. She was extremely protective of her protégés, the way a mother would be of her children.

"The choice is hers," Yvette finally said. "But if she agrees, then I believe I should go with her."

"No, it's far too dangerous for you to leave Griffin's Rest."

"I can't let Meredith go alone."

"You can and you will, if she agrees. Luke will take care of her. He understands her special needs. He won't let anything happen to her."

Chapter 22

Maleah had barely managed to force down a piece of toast and drink a cup of coffee that morning. Her stomach was tied in knots. She had put up a brave front, but suspected that Derek knew just how nervous she was. As she waited for the guard to bring in Jerome Browning, she tried to collect her scattered thoughts. Her mind reeled with information overload. *Focus, damn it, focus. Remember what Derek told you—don't over-think anything, just go with your gut instincts.*

The moment she heard the door open, she squared her shoulders, took a deep breath and stood tall and straight. The guard escorted a handcuffed and shackled Browning into the room. As on the previous visits, Browning was neatly groomed, clean-shaven, hair trimmed. His dark complexion appeared even darker against his prison uniform of white shirt and pants.

When he saw her, he smiled. "Hello, Maleah. How nice to see you this morning. May I say how lovely you look."

"Thank you." She approached the chair facing the one in which the guard placed Browning. Using the ad-

vantage of height, she stood and looked down at him. '
told you that I would come back to see you this week."

"So you did." As he looked up at her, his smil
widened. "I appreciate a lady who keeps her word."

Enough chit-chat. She wouldn't waste another se
ond on pleasantries.

"My partner and I met Albert Durham on Saturday.

She watched Browning's face for a reaction and sa
nothing to indicate he was surprised or concerned. H
smile didn't waver. He didn't even blink.

What had Derek said about someone not blinking
Did it mean he was lying? But lying about what? H
calm reaction to her statement?

Don't over-analyze.

Assume nothing.

"And how was he? Well, I hope," Browning said.

"Quite well. And confused about why we had tracke
him down to ask about his relationship with you."

"Was he? Odd. I never found Albert to be confuse
about anything."

Browning kept his gaze focused on Maleah's face.

Unwavering eye contact. That meant Browning
thoughts about what she had said were positive. Eith
that or it meant he didn't trust her enough to take h
eyes off her.

Damn it! All this reading body language shit was dri
ing her nuts and defeating the purpose of gaugir
Browning's reactions and reading between the lines
what he said or didn't say.

Remember, gut instinct, first and foremost.

"I'm afraid the Albert Durham you know isn't th
real Albert Durham, the writer who has published mo
than a dozen biographies," Maleah told him. "Whoev
the man was who visited you under the pretense of wr
ing your life story was a phony."

Browning lifted his cuffed hands, tented them together and rubbed the tips of his index fingers across
his chin. "Was he, indeed? How utterly fascinating."

Rubbing the chin meant disbelief. Right? Didn't
Browning believe her? Who knew? Hell, maybe his chin
itched.

"Did you know he was a phony?" she asked.

"How could I have known?"

"He could have told you who he really was and what
he wanted from you."

"He wanted to write my biography because he found
me to be a fascinating subject."

"Is that really what he told you?"

Browning eyed the empty chair across from him.
"Why don't you sit down, Maleah, and make yourself
comfortable. I'm tired of straining my neck to look up
at you. And our sitting face to face is so much more intimate, don't you think."

She remained standing. She wasn't giving him what
he wanted without getting something in return. "Did
Durham really tell you he was going to write your bio?
And if he did, did you believe him?"

"He did. And I did."

She sat down then, keeping her back straight as she
crossed her arms.

Browning studied her pose and then widened his
eyes. He was observing her body language as closely as
he was his. *Got you!* she wanted to scream. She had deliberately crossed her arms, an indication that she had
put up a barrier between them, to see how he would
react. Now she knew that he would play her, not only
verbally, but with his gestures.

"Tell me about your conversations with Durham,"
Maleah said. "What did the two of you talk about during
his visits?"

"We talked about my favorite subject—me." He chuck led.

"About your favorite color, your favorite food, you favorite music—"

"About my favorite way to kill."

"He wanted to know the details, didn't he, becaus he wanted to copy the Carver's MO?"

"That's your theory."

Changing her tactics just a bit, Maleah asked, "Ai you pleased with your protégé? That is how you se him, isn't it? You taught him everything you know. Yo instructed him on how to kill."

Browning laughed.

Her gut instincts told her that the laugh was ge uine, that for some reason, her comments had amuse him.

"Do you want me to guess why you find what I said s entertaining?"

"I find you entertaining, Maleah. Oh so sure of you self. So confident and self-contained. A lady who doesn allow anyone to control her." His gaze raked over her i a sexual way, pausing first on her lips and then on h breasts. "But that wasn't always the case was it? Not whe you were a little girl . . . when you were a teenager."

What the hell did he know about her personal lif Was he simply guessing? Or did he actually know som thing?

"I'm not here to discuss me," she said. "I'm here discuss you and your association with Albert Durham.

Browning shrugged. "But, sweet Maleah, I find yo as fascinating as you find me. So, if you give me what want, I'll give you what you want. You tell me what want to know and I'll tell you what you want to know."

"What do you want to know, Jerome?"

"Oh so many things about you, my dear."

"My favorite color is pink. My favorite food is anything chocolate. My favorite song is—"

He burst out laughing; and all the while his gaze
never left her face. "And your favorite way to fuck is? Do
you like to be on top? Or do you secretly prefer for the
man to dominate you? What was Noah Laborde's favorite position? I'll bet he enjoyed your riding him like
a bucking bronco, didn't he?"

*Damn you, you son of a bitch. Damn you to hell. That's
exactly where monsters like you belong, in the hot, burning
tortures of everlasting hellfire.*

"Is that what interests you, Jerome, other people's
sex lives?" she asked in a calm voice. She was still in
complete control. "You have no sex life of your own so
you get your kicks living vicariously through hearing
about how other people fuck."

His jaw tightened. His gaze narrowed. His nostrils
flared.

Oh yes, she had pissed him off. That taunting verbal
arrow had hit its mark.

After several tense moments, he visibly relaxed. He
had suffered nothing more than a flesh wound. He was
ready for battle again.

"Noah was a handsome young man. The two of you
must have made a striking couple." Browning leaned
forward ever so slightly. "Why didn't you marry him?"

"I didn't love him enough to give up my freedom,"
Maleah answered honestly and quickly turned around
and asked for payment in kind. "Did you think of
Durham as your protégé? Is that why you agreed to
share the details of your kills with him?"

"Durham is an admirer, not a protégé. The way Elvis
Presley admired Roy Orbison's voice, Durham admired
my skills. I think of us more as colleagues than teacher
and student."

As she absorbed what she instantly knew was signif
cant information, she did her best not to act so dam
pleased. Did he realize just how much he had told her
"Then you knew, from the very beginning, that Durhar
wasn't a writer?"

"Did I say that?"

"Yes, I think you did."

"You're free to interpret what I say any way yo
please."

"You knew all along, from his first visit, that the ma
really wasn't Albert Durham and that he wasn't inte
viewing you for a biography," Maleah said. "You lied t
me."

"If you say so."

He looked at her, his gaze moving from one eye t
the other and then traveling slowly up to her forehea
his gesture indicating that he was taking an authorit
tive position. She understood that at that precise m
ment, he felt he was in charge and she was subservier
to him.

"Did you also know that the phony Durham was not
novice at killing?"

"What makes you think Durham wasn't a novice?"

"Are you saying he was?"

"Perhaps." He nodded his head. "Perhaps not." H
shook his head.

He was having fun at her expense. He knew she ha
initially been trying to read his body language and no
he was mocking her.

"Tit for tat, Maleah. You give, I give. Don't forget th
rules."

"Noah was my first lover," she said, giving him th
answer to his much-too-personal question about h
sexual relationship with Noah. "He was a gentle, co
siderate lover and not much more experienced than

as. We were young and in love. We were good to-
ether."

"Young and in love. How sweet. But you weren't in
ve enough to marry him, isn't that what you said?"

"Yes, that's what I said."

"How did you find out about his death?" Browning
bbed his hands together, anticipation evident in the
esture.

"His sister called me."

"Were you shocked?"

"Yes."

"Sad?"

"Yes."

"But not devastated. Not broken hearted."

"I was shocked and sad and angry. But no, I wasn't
vastated by Noah's death. I hadn't seen him or spo-
n to him in well over a year. We had both moved on. I
ll cared about him and wanted him to have a good
e. It did break my heart to think he would never
arry and have children and reach his full potential in
s profession."

"I took all that away from him." Browning steepled
s fingers.

She understood that he wanted her to admit that he
d possessed the power of life and death over Noah.

"Yes, you took it all away from him."

"Do you hate me, Maleah? Do you wish you could rip
t my heart? Or perhaps you wish you could slit my
roat the way I slit Noah's throat." He lunged toward
r so quickly that she barely had time to react and draw
ay from him before the brawny black guard grabbed
s shoulders and forced him back into the chair.

He sat there, his breathing accelerated, his pulse
robbing in his neck, his cheeks flushed. And then his
s lifted upward forming a self-satisfied smile.

Maleah struggled to control the unexpected fea
that surged through her, telling herself that the onl
reason she was afraid was because she hadn't antic
pated Browning's actions.

"I hate what you did to Noah and to your other vi
tims," Maleah finally managed to say. "I hate that ther
are people like you in the world. I think you shoul
have been executed for your crimes and should be ro
ting in hell right now."

Browning sighed as if her answer had given hi
some sort of deeply gratifying satisfaction. How sick w;
that!

"After his first visit, I suspected Durham was not wh
he said he was," Browning told her. "On his second visi
when I confronted him, he did not try to lie to me. H
told me he respected me too much. And that's when w
made our bargain."

"What was the bargain?"

Browning shook his head and made a clicking noi
with his tongue. "I gave you what you paid for. No fre
bies."

"Of course not. What was I thinking?" She rose
her feet.

Browning looked up at her. "You aren't leaving :
soon, are you?"

"Game playing wears me tee-totally out." She plante
her hands on her hips. If he wanted to continue the
game, she was ready, but she was damn tired of bei
jerked around. "If you want me to stay—"

"Sit back down, Maleah." Browning's voice was hars
almost angry.

She ignored him.

"Please, sit back down," he said.

"Give me a reason."

"Durham—or whoever the hell he is—wanted deta

bout my life as the Carver. In exchange, he offered to ire me a new lawyer and provide me with a female riend."

Maleah sat. "You have no idea who he really is?"

Using his clenched fists, Browning drew an X across is chest. "Cross my heart and hope to die."

He was lying, damn him. He was lying through his early white teeth.

"There had to be a reason you suspected he was not novice at killing. Was it something he said? Did he—?"

"You want an awful lot for no more than you're willng to give me."

"I do want a great deal, but I'm willing to pay for it. I ust don't want you jerking me around, giving me tid-its when I've paid for the entire meal."

"You really have no idea how expensive certain items re, do you, my lovely Maleah?"

"I have a good idea. You want me to open up a vein nd bleed all over the place."

"Yes, that, too," he admitted. "I want your blood . . . our sweat . . . and your tears. Your tears most of all. So, o we have a deal? I can give you the real Albert urham, served to you on a silver platter."

"How do I know you aren't lying? You just told me a ew minutes ago that you have no idea who he is. Re-member? Cross my heart and hope to die."

"You won't know if I'll be lying to you when I tell you bout him," he agreed. "But isn't it tempting to give me vhat I want in exchange for the possibility that I can tell ou who is killing people connected to the Powell gency and maybe even why he's doing it? Also, I could ell you why he chose to copy my kills, but I suspect you lready know that."

"Yes, I already know."

"Think about my offer. You have twenty-four hours.

If you're willing to pay the piper, I'll play you a beautiful tune." He glanced up at his guard. "We're finished here. I'm ready to leave."

The guard looked at Maleah. She nodded.

Browning stood. "See you tomorrow, sweet Maleah." He winked at her, then turned and fell into step alongside the guard.

The man once known as Anthony Linden finished a series of push-ups, lifted himself from the hotel room floor, and grabbed a bottle of water from the nearby table. He had run five miles in the warm Savannah sun this morning before returning to the hotel to exercise. His body was a well-maintained machine. With perspiration moistening his face and chest, he looked at himself in the mirror. For a man of any age, he was in remarkably good shape. For a man of forty-five, his body was in excellent condition. He picked up a towel from the edge of the bed and wiped his face and chest, and then draped the towel around his neck.

After twisting off the cap, he brought the bottle to his mouth and downed half the contents before pausing. He continued sipping from the bottle as he walked into the bathroom.

He was expecting a guest in less than an hour, just enough time to shave and shower.

He sat on the commode, removed his running shoes and damp socks, and then stood and stripped out of his jogging shorts. After turning on the shower—hot and steamy—he yanked a towel and washcloth from the rack. He laid the towel on the closed commode lid and took the washcloth into the shower with him. He had left his razor and shave cream on a ledge in the shower when he had cleaned up last night.

He took his time shaving, careful not to nick himself, and afterward washed his face, rinsed it, and then lathered his body. As he thought about his expected guest, his penis hardened. Before a kill, he liked to have sex. If he had any pre-kill rituals, they would be to eat a good meal and have a good fuck.

After drying off, he slipped on a dark blue silk robe and slid his feet into a pair of black house slippers. His profession as a death technician paid well and afforded him all of life's little luxuries, including a high-priced call girl.

Just as he poured himself a glass of whiskey, he heard a soft knock on the door. He checked the clock on the bedside table. Right on time. He appreciated punctuality.

He opened the door to an attractive brunette, long legged, slender, her breasts high and firm, obviously the result of implants.

"Mr. Hambert?"

"Yes, please come in, Ms. Smith."

He closed and locked the door behind her. When he turned around and smiled, he downed half his whiskey in one gulp, set the glass on the coffee table and then unbelted his robe.

"Do you want me to undress now?" she asked.

"No, not yet," he replied.

She nodded.

He removed his robe and tossed it on the nearby chair. His hard, erect penis projected outward.

"Come here," he instructed.

She came to him. He took her hand and brought it to his erection.

"Get down on your knees."

She did.

He clutched either side of her head. "Open your mouth."

"I really don't need instruction. I've done this before," she told him.

"I want complete control. I decide how much you take into your mouth and how far I shove my dick down your throat. Do you understand?"

She nodded. "Yes, I understand."

"After I come, clean me with your tongue."

"Yes, of course."

When she licked him from tip to shaft, he closed his eyes and savored the feel of her wet tongue on his penis. First a blow job, just to release the tension. And later, after lunch, he'd make the little whore really earn her money.

Chapter 23

While Derek had waited patiently in the warden's office, he had struggled to concentrate on the crossword puzzle in yesterday's *Savannah Daily News*. Warden Holland had picked up the copy off his desk and offered it to Derek before he'd left for an early lunch.

"Don't worry about her," the warden had said. "Ms. Perdue is just fine. There are two guards present at all times and Browning is handcuffed and shackled."

"I'm not worried about her physical safety."

"Yeah, well, something tells me that Ms. Perdue can hold her own against that wily bastard."

Derek hoped the warden was right. In a fair fight, he'd put his money on Maleah every time. But Browning wouldn't fight fair. He was a no-holds-barred kind of opponent. He'd use whatever methods necessary to get what he wanted.

And just what did he want from Maleah?

Did he want to hurt her? Humiliate her? Make her beg for mercy?

Yes, all of the above. He was the type who derived pleasure from killing, and since he couldn't kill Maleah,

he would have to settle for emotionally wounding her.
The thrill of the kill would be replaced by the thrill of
complete control.

Staring at the folded newspaper in his hand, the puzzle facing him, he turned his ink pen backward and
tapped the end against his teeth. In the past half hour
he'd filled in less than a dozen slots. Ordinarily, he
would be finished with at least a third of the puzzle by
now.

Immediately after he heard the sound of footsteps,
the door swung open and the guard escorted Maleah
into the warden's office. Derek jumped up, tossed the
newspaper into the chair and pocketed his pen.

"Thank you," Maleah told the guard, and then
turned to Derek. "Let's get the hell out of here."

"I'm ready," he said.

She went back out the door and down the hall before he caught up with her. He wanted to ask if she was
all right, but didn't. Instead, he fell into step alongside
her and kept his mouth shut. When she was ready,
she'd talk. Until then, he'd wait.

They were a good five miles away from the penitentiary before Maleah spoke again. "I stink at reading
body language."

Of all the things he thought she might say, that hadn't
been one of them. "He played you, didn't he?"

"Like a fiddle."

"But you knew enough to realize he was playing you.
Give yourself credit for that."

"He wanted to play a game of 'you show me yours
and I'll show you mine,' but he wanted to see twice as
much of mine as he was willing to show me of his."

"He thinks he can get you to pay double for everything he gives you. He's playing hardball, just as we expected he would."

"It's not even two for one. It's more like he'll give me one for every three I give him." She clutched the steering wheel so tightly that her knuckles turned white.

"What did he say about Durham?"

"At first he claimed he didn't know what I was talking about, but then he gradually changed his story. He said that he and the fake Durham made a deal. He gave Durham details about his kills and Durham provided him with a new lawyer and a lady friend to visit him. By the end of our conversation, he told me that not only had he already known the Albert Durham who visited him was a fake, but that he could tell me who he really is and why he's killing people associated with the Powell Agency. He even claimed he could tell me why the copycat chose to copy his kills."

"We know why—because of you," Derek said. "By choosing to emulate Browning's kills, he accomplished more than one goal. He deliberately connected his MO to the murder of a Powell agent's former boyfriend, but not just any Powell agent. He chose Nicole Powell's best friend. And he offered Browning more than a new lawyer and a woman to visit him. He offered Browning a special gift—someone who had loved one of his victims—you."

"So, I'm the prize, huh?" Maleah loosened her tight grip and ran her cupped hands over the steering wheel from the top to the bottom and then halfway up again.

"Offering to bring you to Browning was the copycat's ultimate bargaining chip, the one thing Browning wanted above all else—a new victim."

Maleah shivered. "Lovely thought."

"There's something else to think about," Derek said. "What if Browning has already told you everything he actually knows?"

"Are you saying that Jerome Browning is a diversion,

that the copycat is using him, that we're wasting our time concentrating on Browning?"

"Yes and no. It's all a sick game to Browning. How much he actually knows, we can't be sure. My gut's told me all along that Browning knows very little about the copycat, who he is or what his motives are. The copycat could have told Browning to string us along, to divert our attention. Then again, Browning might know something that he doesn't even know he knows."

"But if there's even a slight chance that he knows anything that can help us track down the copycat, it's worth whatever we have to pay, right?"

"What you have to pay, you mean. He wants his pound of flesh from you."

"He wants my blood, sweat, and tears," Maleah said. "Mostly my tears."

"That's what he told you?"

She nodded.

"Don't go back to see him." At that moment, Derek would have liked nothing better than ten minutes alone with Browning. Man-to-man.

"What?" Maleah cast him a quick sideways glance.

"He's stringing you along. He has no idea who the copycat is. He can't give you the fake Durham's real name because he doesn't know it. And there's no reason why the copycat would have shared anything about the reasons for his kills, especially if it turns out that he is a professional assassin, as I suspect."

"But you said Browning may know something he doesn't know he knows."

"Are you willing to put yourself through more of Browning's shit on the off chance you'll learn something useful?"

That's it, try to talk her out of it. You know Maleah, th

harder you push, the harder she'll push back. You're using the wrong tactics.

"Damn it, Derek, I'm not some fragile hothouse flower that can't withstand a little rough treatment. You've got me confused with my mother. No one controls me, tells me what to do or manipulates me. I'm not afraid of Browning."

Her mother? What is she talking about?

"Never underestimate someone who kills for the thrill of it," he told her.

Groaning, Maleah gritted her teeth.

"And as for confusing you with your mother, need I remind you that I never knew the lady," Derek said. "But if she was a fragile woman, easily controlled by others, then you learned a valuable lesson from her, didn't you?"

"I didn't mean to say that about my mother. It just slipped out. And yes, I learned from her example the type of woman I did not want to be."

"Parents can teach us all sorts of lessons, both positive and negative. You learned from your mother what kind of woman you didn't want to be and I learned from my mother and father what kind of man I didn't want to be."

Maleah glanced at him, a puzzled expression on her face. "I know it's none of my business, but—"

"Happy Lawrence is a man-eater. Apparently, she's the polar opposite of your mother. There's nothing fragile or vulnerable about Happy. She's made of carbon steel. She's a master manipulator. She wields a great deal of power and has no problem destroying anyone who stands between her and what she wants, even her own husband."

"My God! You sound as if you hate her."

"There was a time, years ago, when I hated her," Derek admitted, realizing he had already said far more than he should have. He never discussed his mother with anyone. "Now I'm apathetic toward Happy. I see her as seldom as possible, but since she is my mother, I show her the proper respect when I'm forced to be around her."

"And your father?"

"He's dead. He died when I was a kid." Derek never talked about his dad either, but for some reason he felt compelled to add, "He was a weak, spineless mama's boy who went from letting his mother run his life to letting his wife put a ring through his nose and drive him to drink and suicide."

"Oh, Derek . . ."

He forced a fake laugh. "You see, Blondie, I'm as fucked up as you are. Childhood scars and all. You've got control issues. I've got commitment issues."

"We're quite a pair, aren't we?"

"Flip sides of the same coin, huh? Maybe even soul mates."

Now where had that stupid thought come from—soul mates? Get real, Lawrence, Maleah's not the type to fall for romantic nonsense.

"I don't believe there is such a thing as soul mates," she said quite matter-of-factly. "Flip sides of the same coin, possibly. I do know one thing, the more I get to know you, the more I realize you're not who I thought you were. All I've allowed myself to see is that rich, handsome playboy image you deliberately project to the world. That's not who you are at all, is it?"

"Nope. No more than the I-am-woman-hear-me-roar image you project is all there is to you."

"That's not just an image, you know. It's actually part of who I am . . . or who I try to be."

"Yeah, I know. That rich playboy image is part of who I am, too, but only a small part. I use it as a protective shield between me and the rest of the world."

"Especially women?"

"Guilty as charged."

"You have no intention of ever being like your father and allowing a woman to put a ring through your nose, right?"

Derek chuckled. "Right. And you don't intend to ever be an easily dominated, fragile hothouse flower."

Maleah smiled. "God, you've profiled me, haven't you? And yourself, too."

"Yeah, I guess I have. But can't you see the weird two sides of the same coin analogy? Male and female. For both of us, it's all about control and commitment. We both see making a commitment to another person as giving up control."

"But it is, isn't it? At least for people who have such a strong need to be totally in control of their own lives. I know other people can make marriage work. My mother and father did. Jack and Cathy have."

"Nic and Griff," Derek suggested.

"I'm not sure about those two. I think maybe it's a constant struggle for control with them."

"But neither controls the other. They're both too strong to allow that to happen."

"I don't know. Should being in love and maintaining a healthy marriage be that much of a struggle?"

"For people such as Nic and Griff who are aggressive and independent and passionate, I can't imagine it being any other way. It would be the same for us." Now why had he said that? "I didn't mean—"

"For us?" Maleah asked, almost choking on the question.

"Not for the two of us together," he corrected. "I

meant if you or I were married to someone our equal—
also aggressive, independent, strong, and passionate—
it would take work to make a relationship work."

"Oh . . . yes, I see what you mean."

"Hey, it's past lunchtime," he said, intentionally
changing the subject. Their conversation was becoming
too much like true-confessions to suit him. "Why don't
we stop somewhere for a quick bite to eat. You barely
touched your food at breakfast."

"Is food all you ever think about?"

"Ah now, Blondie, that's a loaded question."

She groaned. "Forget I asked. You men are all alike.
Food and sex."

"Food and sex. Sex and food. Yeah, that pretty much
sums up all of us men."

Maleah laughed.

God help him, he loved the sound of her laughter.

"Please come in," Griffin said. "And close the door
behind you."

Sanders did as Griffin had requested.

His old friend stood by the windows, his gaze absently fixed on something outside, his rigid stance ex-
pressing the depth of his anxiety. Sanders knew Griffin
almost as well as he knew himself. They understood
each other in a way no one else did, not even Yvette.

"Who is he?" Griffin asked, his voice barely more
than a whisper.

"I would think he is someone who knew Malcolm
York, perhaps admired or even loved him."

"To our knowledge, York had no family, other than a
few distant cousins. His parents were dead. He had no
siblings, no nieces or nephews. And no children." Grif-

fin turned and faced Sanders. "Is it possible that someone could have actually loved a monster like York?"

"Perhaps this person was an admirer, someone who knew York quite well."

"It couldn't be anyone from Amara, could it?" Griffin settled his gaze directly on Sanders. "We didn't leave any of the guards alive and the other prisoners hated York as much as we did."

"Perhaps he is someone York encountered in his travels? Or he could even be one of the guests who visited him on Amara."

"Are there any of those special guests still alive?"

"At last count, only two," Sanders replied.

"How long has it been since Byrne contacted us?"

"More than two years. At that time, he had tracked down Sternberg."

"Then you're right, there are two of York's associates who are still alive. Otherwise, Byrne would have been in touch."

Griffin went to the portable bar, picked up a bottle of The Macallan, the twenty-five-year-old Scotch whisky his favorite, and poured the amber-red liquor into two glasses, filling each halfway. He held out a glass to Sanders.

"Of the six frequent visitors to Amara, only Bouchard and Mayorga haven't been found and eliminated," Griffin said. "Here's to Byrne finishing his life's mission sooner rather than later."

When Griffin saluted Sanders with his glass, Sanders returned the gesture. Each took a hefty sip of the full, smooth whisky that drank like a fine brandy. The combination of smokiness and oakiness gave the aged single malt its unique flavor.

Griffin sat in one of the two large leather chairs

flanking the fireplace and continued drinking. Sanders sat across from him, the two men silent for several minutes.

"Is it possible that either Bouchard or Mayorga could be passing himself off as Malcolm York?"

Sanders nodded. "Perhaps, but would either put himself in the line of fire, knowing that Byrne is hunting for him?"

"If I remember correctly, Bouchard was an arrogant son of bitch. He's the type who would think he could outsmart Byrne while taunting us."

"And I always thought Moyorga was stupid. Stupid enough to think neither we nor Byrne could find him."

"We need to find Byrne."

"He can't be found, unless he wants to be."

"Get word out to the proper channels and see what happens."

"Yes, of course." Cradling the glass of whisky in the open palm of his right hand, Sanders circled the edge with his left index finger. "There is one possibility that we haven't discussed," Sanders said.

Griffin nodded. "Are you referring to Harlan Benecroft?"

"I am."

"I thought we agreed years ago that the man is harmless. He was terrified of York. He had as much reason to want York dead as we did."

"He may have feared York and steered clear of you when you were collecting York's fortune for Yvette, but he was York's cousin and in his own pathetic way was as mentally unstable as York."

"Benecroft doesn't have the balls to pass himself off as Malcolm York."

"Luke is on his way to London," Sanders said. "Why

not have him check on Benecroft, if for no other reason than to exclude him?"

"You find Byrne. Have Richter get in touch with his Interpol contacts and while he's doing that, call in some favors with the CIA and MI6. I'll get in touch with Luke." Griffin downed the remainder of his Scotch. "Will it ever end? Will we ever be free of York?"

"The evil that men do lives after them," Sanders paraphrased Shakespeare. "The good is often interred with their bones."

"There was no good in York. He was evil personified."

Chapter 24

"I have a lead on Anthony Linden," Luke Sentell told Griffin Powell. "Someone who knows someone who can verify that Linden is alive, and this person may possibly be able to give us a description of the man."

"If only they could tell us exactly where Linden is right now."

"Have Dr. Meng or one of her underlings look into her crystal ball and see if they can locate him," Luke said sarcastically.

Even though Luke had seen Dr. Meng and Meredith Sinclair work their woo-woo magic, he still wasn't a true believer. Not the way Griff and Sanders were. He didn't quite trust anything beyond his five senses, definitely nothing in the sixth sense realm.

"You must be a little psychic yourself to have mentioned Yvette and her protégés just now."

Uh-oh. Luke got a sinking feeling in the pit of his stomach. "Why do you say that?"

"Because I'm sending Meredith Sinclair to you on my private jet first thing in the morning," Griffin told Luke. "One of our agents will accompany her. You know

Saxon Chappelle. Once they arrive, he'll turn her over to you for safe keeping."

"Damn, Griff, you know how I despise babysitting Ms. Sinclair. Once was enough for me. She's more trouble than she's worth. If you want her in Europe doing her magic act, then why not leave Chappelle here to look after her?"

"Meredith works best without distractions, which means the fewer people involved the better. You know that one-on-one is the best situation for her. And for whatever reason, her senses seemed to be fine tuned whenever you're nearby. It's as if you boost wherever signals are coming through to her. Apparently you're some sort of conduit."

"I've been called a lot of things in my life, but never a conduit."

"Hell, you know what I mean. Meredith's psychic gifts are all over the place most of the time, despite all the work that Yvette has done with her. But add you into the equation and she suddenly becomes focused and working on all cylinders."

"Yeah, lucky me. Have you ever thought maybe she's afraid of me and that's what fine tunes her sixth sense? At least when she's around me, she acts like she thinks I'm the devil himself. Maybe Dr. Meng should try a little tough love with her prize student."

"That's between Yvette and Meredith. She'll be in London by late tomorrow. I'm expecting you to work with her, regardless of your personal animosity. And it goes without saying that I know you'll take good care of her."

"I won't coddle her," Luke said. "Damn it, Griff, you know what happens, how after one of her so-called psychic episodes, she's a basket case."

"Handle her the best way you can. I don't know how

much she can help us, but at this point, I'm willing to
try anything and that includes using an emotionally
fragile psychic if there's even a slim chance she can
help us find our imposter and put a stop to these murders."

"You're the boss," Luke said reluctantly.

"Humph." Griff snorted. "I may pay your salary, but
we both know I'm not your boss. You may follow orders,
but you always do things your own way. And that's not a
criticism. It's one of the reasons I hired you. I like a
man who can think for himself."

Luke had great respect for Griff. If he didn't, he
wouldn't be working for the man. And he believed in
what Griff stood for and in the way he tried to help others. There weren't very many true champions of the
people left in the world. Griffin Powell was one of
them. It sure as hell didn't matter to Luke that the Powell Agency cut corners and circumvented the law on occasion to accomplish their goals—to do what was right.

"I don't suppose there's any chance that Dr. Meng
could come with—"

"No," Griff said. "It's too dangerous for Yvette to
leave Griffin's Rest right now."

"I work best alone. You know that. Babysitting Ms.
Sinclair is going to slow me down."

"That could be, but it's also possible that she'll be
able to help you, maybe steer you in the right direction
in your search for the pseudo York. But before she arrives in London tomorrow, I need for you to check on
Harlan Benecroft. Let's make sure he's still contained,
that he's still non-lethal."

"That pompous ass? You can't possibly believe that
Benecroft is posing as York, can you?"

"He certainly wouldn't be on my Top Ten list, but we
need to rule him out completely."

"Better to be safe than sorry, huh?"

"Yeah, something like that."

"Sure, I'll check on him, but I have a feeling that it will probably be a waste of my time. I'll put in a few calls first thing in the morning and get back to you as soon as I know anything."

"While you've got your ear to the ground, there are two other names you should listen for, discreetly of course—Mayorga and Bouchard."

"All right."

Luke didn't ask for more information. If Griff thought he needed to know more, he would tell him.

Sanders had spoken privately to Brendan Richter. As a former Interpol agent, Richter understood the necessity for discretion. Ciro Mayorga had been on Interpol's Most Wanted list for a number of years, but he had escaped capture just as he had eluded Raphael Byrne's swift and sure form of judgment. But sooner or later, Rafe would find him. Mayorga's crimes ranged from drug trafficking to money laundering. The warrant for his arrest had been issued in Spain ten years ago. Yves Bouchard had also managed to stay under the radar, steering clear of national and international law enforcement agencies that knew but could not prove his involvement in human trafficking. When Rafe Byrne eventually caught up with Bouchard, his execution would be immediate, no arrest, no trial, and no sentencing required.

Sanders had known Rafe as a beautiful, slender, wide-eyed boy of seventeen when Malcolm York had first brought him to Amara. He had been certain that the angelic teenager would not survive a week. And he wouldn't have, if Griffin Powell had not taken the boy under his wing and done his best to protect him.

The day they had killed York and fought their way through several of the ten guards he kept on duty around the clock, they had freed the four captives who were still alive, but they had been unable to find Rafe. The men they had freed had joined them in annihilating their sadistic overseers. Eventually, they had found Rafe in one of the dark dungeon cells, chained, beaten beyond recognition and starved to the point of emaciation.

Of the five men who had left Amara with them, two had committed suicide less than a year later. One had died in a car accident in Barcelona and another in a skiing accident in Aspen more than ten years ago. Only one was still alive.

Raphael Byrne.

Weeks following their escape from Amara and after Rafe had undergone several surgeries to repair his battered face, they had visited Rafe in the London hospital where he was recovering. There had been no resemblance, physically, mentally and emotionally, between the seventeen-year-old boy York had brought to Amara and the twenty-year-old man who had made a solemn vow to them that day. In a deadly calm voice, he had sworn he would hunt down and kill all six men who had visited York during the three years Rafe had been on Amara. The six men—Tanaka, Di Santis, Klausner, Sternberg, Mayorga, and Bouchard—who had hunted him by day, as if he were a wild animal, and had amused themselves with him at night, each in their own way.

Maleah was beginning to like Derek Lawrence.

And liking him wouldn't be a problem if she didn't

also find him terribly attractive. She'd been able to handle the unwanted physical attraction between them as long as she had disliked him. But now, everything between them had changed, at least for her. And to make matters worse, she felt certain that he was dealing with the same problem. He had shared a part of himself with her today, a part she suspected he seldom shared with others, just as he had told her about his youthful exploits as a solider of fortune. Why had he exposed himself to her that way? Why had he given her more than just a glimpse of the real Derek, someone as flawed and imperfect as she was, someone with battle scars from a miserable childhood, someone who, like she, was all too human?

After they had shared lunch on their return to Vidalia earlier today, she had escaped as quickly as possible. She had needed to get away from Derek and work through her unsettled feelings before facing him again. Her excuse for begging off a work session had been only a half-lie. She'd told him that she wanted to call Jack and Cathy and then take an afternoon nap. She seldom if ever took an afternoon nap unless she was sick or had been up half the night. She hadn't taken a nap, but she had called her sister-in-law.

"Seth is enjoying summer vacation," Cathy had said. "He's working part-time as a lifeguard at the community center pool and he has half a dozen girls chasing after him."

"Like father like son."

Cathy had laughed. "Oh, believe me, he's more like Jack than I ever realized."

"So how is my little niece?"

"You and Jack. You're both so sure the baby is a girl."

"She is. Just wait until you get that next ultrasound. I'm positive you'll find out the baby is a girl."

Hearing Cathy's voice, so cheerful and positive and seemingly unafraid, had gone a long way in reassuring Maleah. But she still couldn't completely shake her fear that the copycat might choose a member of her family as his next victim.

It was only a matter of time until he killed again.

After a thirty-minute conversation with Cathy, she had flipped on the television, zipped through the channels, and turned it off three minutes later.

Now, she had to find something to do. But if she went over the copycat killer files one more time, she would scream her head off. She had practically memorized everything they had on record about Jerome Browning, as well as information about Wyman Scudder, Cindy Di Blasi, and the real Albert Durham.

If only they had some information about the fake Durham. But at this point, the man was a complete mystery, except for Derek's preliminary profile. However, having so little info to work with made Derek's job more difficult.

Pacing the floor, wishing she really could take a long nap, she nearly jumped out of her skin when her phone rang.

Please don't let it be Derek. I can't deal with him right now. I need to put just a little time and space between us, between the realization that I like him—like him a lot—and seeing him again.

When she noted the caller ID, she sighed with relief. "Hello, Nic."

"Hey, are you okay? You sound odd."

"I'm fine. I was lost in thought and the phone ringing startled me."

"How are you? Really?"

"You want the truth?'

"Always," Nic told her.

"I'm thinking seriously about selling my soul to the devil in the hopes he'll give me some information that will help us find the Copycat Carver. And as if making that decision isn't enough to deal with in one day, I've just discovered that I genuinely like Derek Lawrence and . . ." She wasn't sure she could admit, even to her best friend, how she really felt about Derek.

"And what?"

"And I've got the hots for the guy." She could tell Nic anything, couldn't she? They were best friends. Nic would understand.

Nic laughed.

"Do not laugh at me. This isn't funny."

"I already knew," Nic said.

"Knew what? That I'd do whatever it takes to get information out of Jerome Browning or that I had the hots for Derek?"

"Both actually, but I was referring to your having a thing for Derek. You do know that he's got it bad for you, too, don't you?"

"Having feelings for Derek complicates my life and I don't like it. So, before you say another word, I'm telling you right now that I refuse to become another notch on his bedpost."

"You'd never be that, just as I wasn't for Griff," Nic said. "You and Derek remind me so much of Griff and me in the early stages of our relationship."

"Bite your tongue."

"Want my advice?"

"I have a feeling you're going to give it to me whether or not I want it."

"Have sex with him."

Maleah growled through her clenched teeth.

"And don't sell your soul to the devil for info from Browning," Nic told her.

"Derek said the same thing."

"Then listen to the man. Not only is he smart, but I suspect he has your best interests at heart."

"Save your breath. I'm going back to the prison tomorrow to see Browning again. It may be my last visit, but I have to try one more time."

"If I thought you'd listen to me, I'd try to talk you out of your decision, but I know you too well to even try. No one can talk me out of doing something once I've made up my mind. You and I are both as stubborn as mules." Nic paused for a moment and then said, "Griff is sending Meredith Sinclair to London tomorrow in the hopes she can help Luke."

"I bet Luke's thrilled. Is Yvette going with Meredith?"

"No, Griff believes it's too dangerous for Yvette to leave Griffin's Rest."

"He's probably right."

"Listen, Maleah, I have some rather important news for you and Derek. Griff and Sanders are both busy handling other matters, so I've been delegated to touch base with you two and give you the latest information."

"Please tell me you have good news to share, or at the very least information that can help us."

"It's information that possibly confirms Derek's tentative profile of the Copycat Carver as a professional assassin."

Maleah sucked in her breath.

"A contact in Austria sold Luke information concerning a man named Anthony Linden, a former MI6 agent who went rogue. He supposedly killed himself ten years ago instead of allowing the authorities to capture and imprison him. But apparently the rumors of his death were greatly exaggerated."

"Meaning that Anthony Linden isn't actually dead."

"So it would seem."

"And this information is important to us because?"

"Because this same contact told Luke that the man rumored to be impersonating Malcolm York hired a very-much-alive Linden, who is well-known in certain circles as a professional assassin. And York sent Linden to America six months ago."

"That's quite an interesting story, one I'm sure Griff has bought into, right?" Maleah said. "But what about you? Are you buying it?"

"It's plausible. It's possible. I don't know if it's true, but . . ." Nic's voice trailed off into complete and utter silence.

"Nic?"

"Oh God, Maleah, if the copycat continues killing, if we can't find him and stop him soon, I don't know how Griff is going to bear it. He's not sleeping. He's lost his appetite. He's drinking too much. He's preoccupied and edgy and keeps shutting himself off in his study, sometimes alone, sometimes with Sanders. I try to talk to him, try to convince him that he's not responsible for all these deaths, but it's as if he doesn't even hear me."

"I wish I knew what to tell you," Maleah said, her heart aching for her dear friend. "Griff's a strong man. He's not going to fall apart. You know that when he shuts you out, he thinks he's protecting you. Nic, you know he loves you."

"If he would only tell me everything, all the horrible things about Malcolm York and Amara, then maybe I could help him. Whatever secrets he's keeping from me are part of what's tearing him apart. He knows that the real York is dead, and yet . . . Oh, Maleah, I wish that the copycat killer would turn out to be someone seeking revenge against me because of one of my cases when I worked for the Bureau. Or if the copycat is a professional killer, then I wish someone with a grudge

against the Powell Agency and not someone from
Griff's past hired this man to exact revenge against the
agency."

"We can't rule out either of those possibilities. No
yet. That's one reason I have to go back to see Brown
ing. If only I could persuade him to tell me what he
knows."

"If he actually knows anything. And you do realize
that the odds of that are very low. Besides, all the evi
dence is beginning to stack up in favor of Griff's the
ory."

"I'm sorry, Nic. I'm so very sorry."

"There's nothing for you to be sorry about. None of
this is your fault. I'm the one who's sorry that the copy
cat deliberately involved you by choosing to emulate
the murderer who killed Noah Laborde."

"If Griff's theory is correct, then someone very badly
wants to torment Griff by whatever means necessary
even going so far as to strike out at his wife's be
friend."

"Don't go back to see Browning again. I have a ver
bad feeling about it. Please, Maleah . . ."

"I have to go. Don't worry about me. I'm tough.
Maleah faked a laugh. "Besides, I have Derek. If Brown
ing chews me up and spits me out in little pieces, Dere
will put me back together."

"Oh, Maleah."

"Hey, you take care of yourself and that husband of
yours. I'll be fine. I need to hang up now and go fi
Derek in on the news from Luke."

"Call me tomorrow, after you see Browning."

"Okay, if it'll make you feel better, I'll call."

As soon as they said their good-byes, Maleah went t
the bathroom, freshened up and changed into a pair c
faded navy sweat pants and an oversized yellow, nav

nd white striped T-shirt. After slipping into a pair of
avy Skechers, she slid her room key into her pants
ocket and left her room.

Maleah stood outside of Derek's closed door. Once
he had worked up enough courage to knock, he
pened the door in two seconds flat.

They stared at each other, neither of them saying a
vord.

He wasn't wearing a shirt. Swirls of thick black hair
ormed a perfect T across his upper chest and disap-
eared into his unsnapped jeans.

Why oh why did he have to look so good? All lean
nd muscular, handsome and sexy, he was dark, tanta-
zing temptation wrapped up in a to-die-for package.

Say something, you idiot.

Say what? I want to jump your bones?

*Tell him about Nic's phone call. Give him the latest infor-
ation from Luke Sentell. Don't keep standing here staring
t him. Just open your damn mouth and say something.*

But when she opened her mouth to speak, Derek
orcefully grabbed her shoulders, pulled her into his
rms, and kissed her.

Chapter 25

Derek drove his tongue into her mouth, deepening the kiss, taking her breath away. Capturing her neck and threading his fingers through her hair, he pulled her into his room and kicked the door shut. Without conscious thought, going strictly by instinct, she wrapped herself around him and lost herself completely in the kiss. His lips were firm and warm, his tongue moist and hot.

He walked backward, taking her with him step-by step, his hands roaming over her shoulders and back and then delving lower to cup her butt. Her femininity clenched and unclenched in an age-old preparation for mating, as her mouth worked feverishly against his.

When he toppled them over and onto the bed, she went with him willingly, as hungry for him as he was for her. Changing the dynamics of the kiss, he eased his tongue from her mouth and nibbled on her lower lip. She moaned deep in her throat as he slid his hands between them and lifted the edge of her T-shirt, exposing her naked belly and the lace bra covering her breast. The moment he lowered his head, his breath scorching

er skin, she forked her fingers through his hair and
rought his mouth to her breast. He suckled her
rough the thin material and then flicked his tongue
cross first one hard nipple and then the other.

Squirming, her body throbbing, she rubbed herself
gainst him and felt how much he wanted her.

"Oh, baby . . . so sweet . . ." He shoved his hand be-
ween her thighs and palmed her mound. "We're going
be so good together, honey, so good."

Baby? Honey?

Generic terms, endearments he had probably used
ountless times with numerous women.

He had not called her Maleah. He hadn't even called
er Blondie.

Her vow to Nic echoed inside her head, softly at first,
ut growing louder with each passing second. *I refuse to
come another notch on his bedpost.*

Gradually coming to her senses, she shoved against
s chest. His deliciously warm, hairy, muscular chest.

*Stop this right now. You are not going to have sex with
erek Lawrence.*

"Get off me," she told him, her voice a ragged whis-
er.

"What's wrong?" He lifted his head and stared at her.
Did I hurt you?"

Yes, you mortally wounded me. With words. Baby. Honey.

"No, you didn't hurt me." She shoved him up and off
er.

He rolled over onto the bed while she sat up, took
veral deep, steadying breaths and started to stand. He
ached out, grasped her wrist and held her in place on
e edge of the bed.

"Look at me, Maleah."

Now he remembers my name.

"What just happened?" he asked.

She looked everywhere but at him. "We almost made a terrible mistake."

He sat up so that they were side by side. He cupped her chin and turned her to face him. "Why did you stop what was happening between us? You were into it as much as I was, wanted me as much as I wanted you—as much as I still want you. You can't deny the truth."

"I'm not denying anything." When she looked at him, it was all she could do not to give in to her base instincts. God, how she wanted him!

"Then please tell me what just happened? What did I do wrong?"

How did she answer that question? With a lie? The truth? A half-truth? "You didn't do anything wrong. I just came to my senses before it was too late." Unable to continue direct eye contact for fear he would know she was lying, she averted her gaze.

He squeezed her chin. She glared at him, and then jerked out of his grasp and got up. "Put a shirt on, will you? You shouldn't have come to the door half naked."

"Are you afraid if I remain partially unclothed, you won't be able to keep your hands off me?" he asked jokingly as he rose to his feet.

"I'm not the one who grabbed you and kissed you," she reminded him.

He came up behind her, lowered his head and kissed the side of her neck. Shivering at his touch, she closed her eyes and stood perfectly still as he whispered in her ear, "The moment I opened the door, I knew what you wanted. You were begging me to kiss you."

Snapping around with the intention of blasting him for his accusation, she didn't realize until it was too late just how close his body was to hers. Her breasts collided with his chest as her belly encountered his erection

he sucked in her breath and shoved against him. Smil-
g at her, he stepped backward.

"I wasn't. I didn't . . ." *That's it, Maleah, lie to him
ain.* "Despite what you think, I knocked on your door
 tell you that Nic called me with information."

He looked at her questioningly. "Business first,
uh?"

"Yes. No. Damn it, you know what I mean. Business
ly."

"Ah, Blondie, do I have to keep telling you that
u're no fun?"

When she glared at him, he laughed as he walked over
 the dresser, opened a drawer and removed a white
shirt. While he slipped into the garment, Maleah
illed out the desk chair and sat. He turned around,
s gorgeous chest now covered, and grinned when he
w that she had avoided sitting on the sofa.

"You sure do blow hot and cold, don't you?" He
pped down on the sofa, propped his feet up on the
ffee table and crossed his arms over his chest. "You
nt from not being able to keep your hands off me to
t even wanting to sit by me."

"Will you please drop it? If you want me to take full
sponsibility for what happened, then I will. You're ir-
sistible. I fought my attraction to you for as long as I
uld. I took one look at your magnificent bare chest
d went wild. Pick your fantasy, Mr. Lawrence. But
at's it. I am not going to discuss what happened."

He ran his gaze over her slowly, appraisal in his eyes,
 if she were an object on the auction block and he was
nsidering a purchase. "Okay. I'll go along with how-
er you want to play this. Let's chalk it up to just one of
ose things."

"Thank you."

"You're welcome."

She couldn't tell if he was sincere or if he was makin
fun of her.

Silence hung between them for several minute
then she cleared her throat and said, "Griff received ir
formation from Luke Sentell that, if proven true, coul
substantiate your theory that the Copycat Carver is
professional assassin."

Uncrossing his arms, his eyes widening with interes
Derek leaned forward and said, "As much as I lik
being proven correct in my assessments, I know I'm nc
going to like this new information, am I?"

"Probably not." Now that they were discussing the
current case, Maleah relaxed. As long as she kept he
relationship with Derek strictly business, she'd be fin
"I have no idea how Luke made contact with this mar
but I assume it all boils down to who you know. Griff ha
contacts all over the world. And we have a former Inte
pol agent working for the agency now, as well as Luk
who is rumored to have been a Black Ops agent."

"Is there a reason why you're taking the scenic rou
with this information instead of—?"

"Sorry. I was thinking out loud." Maleah forced he
self to look at Derek. "Luke paid this person, some ma
in Austria, for the info, and as of right now, he has r
way to verify the validity of what he was told. But su
posedly there is or was a man named Anthony Linden,
former MI6 agent who went rogue and became a hire
killer. When the authorities caught up with him abo
ten years ago, he reportedly killed himself rather tha
be captured."

"Let me guess—Linden didn't kill himself. He's ali
and well and still working as a professional assassi
And for some reason Luke believes Linden may be o
copycat killer."

She marveled at how easily Derek connected t

dots. She snapped her fingers. "Just like that, you put it all together. So, how about making an educated guess as to why Luke and Griff think Linden is our guy."

"Hmm . . ." Derek stroked his chin. "The mystery man who calls himself Malcolm York and Anthony Linden are somehow connected, right?"

"Right. Supposedly Linden is working for the mysterious Mr. York, who sent him to America six months ago."

"Six months ago, shortly before Albert Durham visited Jerome Browning for the first time, and less than two months before the Copycat Carver began his murder spree by killing Kristi Arians."

"Is Griff right? Is all of this happening because of him, because the fake Malcolm York is exacting revenge for the real York?"

"Your voice is trembling," Derek told her. "That happens when you're upset and worried. Tell me what's really going on with you."

Maleah hated that he knew her so well. Damn his extraordinary powers of observation. "I'm concerned about Nic . . . and about Griff, too, because she's worried sick about him."

"If I promise I won't bite, will you come over here and sit by me?" He patted the sofa cushion. "We're friends now, aren't we? Talk to me. About your concerns for Nic and Griff and about anything else that's troubling you."

She eyed him suspiciously.

He lifted his arms in the air on either side of him. "I promise I won't touch you."

She rose from the chair in a slow, languid move and walked toward the sofa. "I have to go back to see Browning tomorrow."

"No, you don't. You do not have to see him ever again."

"I do. If he knows—"

"He doesn't know squat," Derek said. "The copycat, whoever he is, Anthony Linden or John Doe, didn't share any big secrets with Browning. Why would he?"

"But you said that maybe Browning knows something he doesn't even know he knows. Maybe he can—"

"Damn it, Maleah, he can't help us." Derek reached for her, then stopped dead still and clenched his hands into fists.

She released a relieved breath. If he had touched her, she didn't think she could have resisted the urge to throw herself into his arms.

"Nic said that Griff isn't sleeping or eating and he's pulled away from her. He blames himself for what's happened. He thinks it's somehow his fault that five people associated with the agency have been murdered."

"I don't claim to know any more about Griffin Powell than you do, but I understand him as one man understands another. Any man, especially one as powerful as Griff, hates to admit that something in his past has come back not only to haunt him, but could be the reason for five murders. And although he would never admit it, Griff's scared out of his mind that something might happen to Nic. He's the type who wouldn't want the woman he loved to see any weaknesses in him, not even if *she* was his major weakness."

"He would rather withdraw from her, even risk alienating her, than to share his fears with her and let her help him? That is so wrong."

"Yeah, I know, but we men are strange creatures."

"Would you do that?" she asked. "I mean assuming

ou loved someone the way Griff loves Nic, would you
out up barriers to prevent her from—?"

"I'm not Griff. I haven't lived his life. I don't have his
secrets. I didn't say he and I were alike. I said I understood him as one man understands another." He gazed
into her eyes. "You and Nic are best friends. You've
shared confidences and probably know each other better than anyone else does. You understand her, right?"

Maleah nodded.

"But even though you and Nic are both strong, independent women, you're also different. There are things
she has lived through that you haven't and vice versa. I
can't see you letting the man you loved keep secrets
from you. If he did, you'd walk away, wouldn't you?"

She stared at Derek, wondering if he, too, had more
deep, dark secrets, ones he had never shared with anyone. "She's tried leaving him, but she always comes
back. Love makes us weak and it certainly can make
fools of us all."

"Have you ever loved anyone like that?" he asked.

"No. Have you?"

"No."

They sat there staring at each other for several minutes and finally Derek said, "Okay, Blondie, if you're
damned and determined to visit Browning again in the
morning, then we need to talk about it. I'll take on the
role of Browning and play devil's advocate, no holds
barred, and we'll see how you react."

"You want to see just how thick my skin is, don't you?"

Derek grinned. "When it comes to sparring with
Browning, I suspect your skin is thick enough. But I happen to have firsthand knowledge as to just how really
soft and smooth your skin is."

When she reached over and socked him on the arm,

he held up his hands in a surrender gesture. "For the record, I want it to be noted that you touched me first."

She socked him again, harder the second time.

"Ouch. That hurt."

"Good. I wanted it to hurt."

"You're a hard-hearted woman, Maleah Perdue."

"Yes, I am, and you'd do well not to forget it."

Derek burst into laughter.

"Why are you laughing? Why aren't you—?"

He leaned over and without laying a finger on her, he kissed her. She mumbled and spluttered and then placed her hands on his chest to push him away. But suddenly, he lifted his head and smiled.

"Any plans for seduction that you might have for tonight will have to be postponed to another time," he told her. "We've got work to do, woman. And work always comes first."

She stared at him, completely confused for a few seconds. Then she realized his intention had been to lighten the mood. "You're the most aggravating, infuriating man I've ever known."

"And that's what you like about me, that and the fact that I'm such a good kisser."

Maleah groaned. Derek was right. He was a good kisser.

The modified Georgian-style Chappelle house in Ardsley Park had been built in the center of the lot and set back off the street. Two towering palms graced either side of the brick walkway and two overgrown holly bushes the size of small trees flanked the white brick structure. No doubt, in its day, the house had been impressive, and it was still a lovely old home. A wide variety of eclectic styles created a diversity of houses in th area, which stretched from Bull Street on the west to Waters Avenue on the east, and from Victory Drive north to Derenne Avenue south. He could leave the Chappelle home after he finished his job and be on I-16 in about ten minutes. By daylight that morning, he would be more than halfway to Atlanta.

While Poppy had attended church with her grandmother and the housekeeper on Sunday, he had broken the lock on the outside entrance to the basement at the side of the house and had slipped inside without any trouble. As luck would have it, the old woman hadn't put in a security system, so he had been able to go upstairs and take his time familiarizing himself with all the rooms. Twelve in all, not counting bathrooms and two sun porches.

Mrs. Carolyn Chappelle's room had been easy to spot. It was the largest bedroom which also included a sitting area in front of heavily draped bay windows overlooking the front lawn. The antique furniture, polished to shining perfection, overfilled the space, making the room feel cluttered. In comparison, the housekeeper's eight-by-ten room, that probably had originally been the nursery, was sparsely furnished and excessively neat. Wooden shutters covered the single window. He had checked each of the other bedrooms, searching for Poppy's room, and when he found it, he wondered if it had once belonged to her aunt Mary Lee. Two large windows overlooked the pool and enclosed patio. Feminine to the point of being frilly, the white French provincial furniture, lace adorned drapes and bedding, and floral wallpaper seemed, as did the other rooms in the house, to be trapped in a time long past.

Moonlight illuminated the predawn sky and cast shadows over the lawn. Tree branches swayed in the warm summer breeze, their tips scratching at the upstairs windows on the east end of the house. Security lights at the back of the house kept the pool area well lit, but the basement door, the lock now broken, lay hidden in darkness behind a row of red azaleas.

He had parked his rental car in the driveway. If by any chance some neighbor happened to be awake at this hour and looked out a window, he or she would see a nondescript sedan and possibly assume the Chappelles had an overnight visitor. He had no intention of returning the rental and there was no way it could be traced back to him, only to the real Albert Durham. He would leave the car at the Atlanta airport tomorrow. With the time difference between the U.S. East Coast and London, his employer would be enjoying a late breakfast when he reported in, once he was on the road. After he spoke to his employer, he would make flight arrangements. This morning's kill would be number six, the exact number he had been paid for by wire transfer to his Swiss account, which had been opened under one of his many aliases.

He was known by many names and yet he remained nameless. He was a man of a hundred disguises and yet he remained faceless, unidentifiable. In his world, he was known only as the Phantom, except by a precious few who had once known him as Anthony Linden. But he was not Anthony Linden and hadn't been in more than ten years. For all intents and purposes, Anthony Linden was dead.

Poppy woke with a start, her mouth dry and her cotton sleep shirt damp with perspiration. She kicked back the light covers and lay there, her eyes open, her heartbeat racing. She stared up at the shadows dancing on her ceiling. She'd had the most god-awful dream.

You shouldn't have watched that old Twilight show marathon on TV last night with Heloise.

Her nightmare had been a convoluted jumble of scenes, none of which had made the least bit of sense. Headless zombies creeping toward her. Pig-faced people hovering over her. Outraged men and women chasing her down the street, screaming at her, accusing her of being an alien from outer space.

Poppy shuddered.

I'm not afraid. I'm not afraid. Bad dreams can't hurt you. No, but they can sure scare the bejeezus out of you.

She wished her bedroom—Aunt Mary Lee's old room—wasn't at the opposite end of the hall from Grandmother's and Heloise's rooms. She certainly had no intention of walking up that long, dark corridor. The old house moaned and groaned enough as it was without her padding down the hall and making the wooden floors creak.

She could turn on the light, get up, and read a few chapters in the paperback romance novel on her nightstand. Or she could go downstairs to the den and watch TV or grab a snack in the kitchen.

Just close your eyes and try to go back to sleep.

The odds were if she went back to sleep, she wouldn't dream again. Not if she thought about pleasant things. *Think about going sailing with Court and Anne Lee on Wednesday afternoon. Think about Court's friend Wes Larimer.* Anne Lee had promised that Court would invite him to join them.

"I think Wes likes you," Anne Lee had told her. "If Mother wasn't best buds with his mother, I'd go after him myself. But God forbid that Wes and I hook up and make our moms happy."

"He's cute, isn't he?"

"Do Chihuahuas shiver? Girl, Wes Larimer is cream of the crop."

Think about Wes. And who knows, maybe you'll dream about him instead of weird characters out of an old TV show.

Poppy closed her eyes and imagined Wes putting his arm around her and kissing her. It would be explosive, like fireworks lighting up the sky. They were alone on Court's sailboat, just the two of them. The ocean was smooth, the sun was warm, the breeze balmy.

"Oh Court, kiss me again," she mumbled to herself and then yawned before dozing off to sleep.

He moved through the Chappelle house as quietly as smoke rising from a chimney. He turned off the slender flashlight he held, pocketed it and took the back stairs two at a time, being careful to tread lightly. Even when the old staircase creaked occasionally as his weight pressed on the carpeted runner, he didn't pause. Those living here were accustomed to the odd sounds that the nearly eighty-year-old house made in the night. When he reached the landing, he glanced down the corridor toward Mrs. Chappell's suite and across the hall to Heloise McGruger's bedroom. Both doors were closed.

He turned and went in the opposite direction, straight toward the young girl's room decorated in fancy ruffles and lace. Unlike the older ladies in the house, Poppy slept with her door partially open. A thin line of moonlight seeped through the narrow opening and painted a pale yellow-white line across the threshold and onto the floor beneath his feet. He reached out, grasped the crystal knob and slowly eased open the door all the way. His eyes had adjusted to the darkness so he could see quite well with only the moonlight brightening the bedroom just enough to reveal the furniture's silhouettes.

Poppy Chappelle lay beneath a ruffled canopy, one arm and one leg tangled in the top sheet and light-weight blanket. The upstairs central air unit kicked on, sending a rush of cool air from the ceiling vent. He stood over her bed and watched her while she slept. So very young. So pretty.

Such a pity he had to kill her.

He didn't choose the victims. His employer did.

He was simply an employee following orders, a professional doing his job.

Easing up to the edge of the bed, he rubbed his glove-encased hands together, collected his thoughts and prepared for the kill. He slipped his hand into an inside pocket, removed the disposable scalpel from the small carrying case and returned the case to his pocket.

I'm sorry, little girl.

A momentary calmness came over him, steadying his hand and clearing his mind. The rush of excitement would come later, with the act itself. The moment the knife entered her body, he would experience an unparalleled exhilaration. He always did.

He watched her for another minute, noted the rise and fall of her tender young breasts as she inhaled and exhaled.

And then he plunged the scalpel into her jugular. Blood gushed.

A mental and emotional orgasm began to build inside him. He sliced the sharp blade across her neck, from one carotid artery to the other, effectively cutting her windpipe in the process.

She died almost instantly, without a sound, never having opened her eyes.

His hands were steady, his outward demeanor calm. But a soul-deep enjoyment burst wide open inside him and sent climactic pleasure through his entire body.

Mimicking the Carver's MO, he worked quickly, cutting triangles from her upper arms and thighs and stuffing the tiny pieces of flesh into the small insulated bag he had brought with him.

He took no pleasure in the mutilation of a body, but he was under orders. This was business, a necessary part of the job assignment.

At the foot of the staircase, the grandfather clock struck four times. He would be gone well before daybreak. And it would be morning before anyone discovered Poppy's body.

Leaving his victim lying in her bloody bed, he walked across the room, opened the widow, and lifted the screen. Then he returned to the bed, picked the dead girl up into his arms and carried her to the window.

From the height of the second floor, he glanced down at the moonlight shimmering across the pool. Keeping a firm grip, he held her body out the window as far as he could reach and then released her. She sailed down, down, down, and hit the side of the pool. While her legs crashed onto the patio, her head and the upper two-thirds of her body sank into the water. Then the weight of her head and upper body submerged in the pool gradually dragged her legs into the pool and she slowly disappeared beneath the water's surface.

Chapter 26

Maleah sipped on the coffee, black with one packet of Splenda, that Derek had brought her. When she had opened the door to him a few minutes ago, her expression had been filled with questions and doubts. Knowing what she wanted and needed this morning, he had set the tone for their day. Back to business as usual. Partners working on a case, their once adversarial relationship now bordering on friendship and definitely based on mutual respect. There would be time later, tomorrow or the next day or a week or month from now, for them to explore the reasons behind the sexual tension driving them both crazy.

"Anything you want to go over with me this morning?" he asked as he sat down on the sofa, snapped open the lid flap on his insulated coffee cup and took a sip of his black coffee.

"I don't think so. I believe we pretty much took care of every possible scenario last night." She joined him on the sofa.

"More than likely, Browning is going to tell you

about how he killed Noah Laborde and the pleasure he derived from what he did. We assume he doesn't know anything else about your personal life, and if we're correct, that means he's going to use Noah. He sees your former boyfriend as your Achilles' heel."

"I'm prepared for whatever he tells me." She took several sips from the cup before placing it on the coffee table. "I'll give him what he wants. I won't try to completely control my emotions. If he wants to see me cry, I'll cry."

"I have to remind you that this may all be for nothing. You may give him exactly what he wants and get only useless information in return."

"I know. I'm willing to take that chance."

Derek nodded. "Barbara Jean contacted me about half an hour ago. Our orders are to head back to Knoxville after your visit with Browning."

"Why? Has something happened? Has the copycat—?"

"No, and since the trail is cold and we have no new leads to follow, Sanders wants us back at headquarters to sit in on a top-level powwow, the two of us, Griff, Nic, Sanders, BJ, and Dr. Meng."

"Any idea what this big powwow is about?" Maleah asked.

"BJ didn't say, but I suspect Griff wants to discuss his theory about who the copycat is, who hired him and why."

"And as Griff so often says, all roads lead to Rome."

"In this case, Rome being Malcolm York."

"Rome being Griff's obsession with the pseudo York, if he actually exists."

"I don't think any of us can dismiss the real possibility that someone who calls himself Malcolm York exists," Derek told her. "And if we accept that possibility, we also have to be prepared to accept the possibility that York hired a professional assassin to carry out some diabolical plan against Griff."

"Have you actually bought into Griff's theory?"

"I'm keeping an open mind and you should, too."

"You're right," Maleah agreed. "If all of these copycat murders are a part of some elaborate scheme to exact revenge against Griff, then we're up against far more than a single killer. Even if we find the copycat and stop him, that won't be the end of it."

"You're right. It won't end until York, whoever he really is, is found."

Miss Carolyn was an early riser, as was Heloise. They enjoyed leisurely cups of coffee each morning in the small den adjacent to the kitchen, the television tuned to WJCL, channel 22, the local ABC affiliate. Her employer, whom she thought of after all these years as a dear old friend, watched only *Good Morning America*. She had been a huge Charlie Gibson fan and bemoaned his exit from the show, but had found consolation in watching him on the evening newscast until his retirement.

"I prefer to get my evening news from a man," Miss Carolyn had said. "But I like Diane Sawyer well enough. She's a smart lady. And as long as they keep Robin Roberts on *Good Morning America*, I'll keep watching that show, too. I like her."

Miss Carolyn was nothing if not opinionated and always believed her opinion was superior to and more important than anyone else's.

Little Miss Poppy was not an early riser. She often slept until well past ten, sometimes as late as noon, much to her grandmother's displeasure.

"These young people sleep away the best part of the day," Miss Carolyn often said.

With the breakfast dishes neatly stacked in the dishwasher—she had a precise system of where to place each item—and the television turned off until the local mid-day news, Heloise began lunch preparations. Since it was only nine-thirty and lunch wouldn't be served until noon, she had more than enough time to bake a blueberry pie, using the fresh berries she had bought at the Farmer's Market. And she intended to use last night's leftover chicken to make chicken salad, which she would serve with some of the buttery croissants she had picked up at the bakery.

Wearing her wide-brimmed sunbonnet and carrying her gardening gloves, Miss Carolyn came through the kitchen and paused at the back door. "If you need me, I'll be in the garden. I want to prune the roses before it gets so hot. I can't abide these ungodly humid days. I don't remember it ever being this miserable in late June. When I was a girl summertime weather didn't hit until the Fourth of July."

Heloise didn't bother pointing out to Miss Carolyn that the Fourth was only a few days away.

After Miss Carolyn was halfway out the door, she stopped, glanced over her shoulder and said, "When Miss Lazybones gets up, please tell her that I expect her to be here for lunch today because her great-aunt Sarah will be joining us." She sighed heavily. "The woman is an absolute bore, but she is family. She was married to my dear brother Courtland for forty years."

"I'll be sure to remind her."

"Oh, is the pool boy coming today? If he is, I need to speak to him."

"Yes, ma'am, this is Tuesday and he comes every Tuesday. He should be here any time now."

"I can see the pool from the rose garden, so I'll keep an eye out for him."

Heloise smiled as she removed the blueberries from the refrigerator. Miss Carolyn had her good qualities and her bad. But being a perfectionist and expecting everyone else to live up to her high standards did not endear her to the people she referred to as "the hired help." This included the young man who cleaned the pool each week.

Heloise gently dumped the berries into a colander she had placed in the sink, turned on the water and used the sprayer to wash the berries.

A bloodcurdling scream startled Heloise. Who was screaming? The sound was coming from somewhere outside, wasn't it? *Oh mercy God, it's Miss Carolyn.* She must have fallen. Or she had come across a snake in the rose garden.

Heloise wiped her damp hands off on her apron as she headed for the back door, running as fast as her old legs would carry her. She searched the rose garden for any sign of Miss Carolyn, but quickly realized the screams were coming from the pool area.

And then she saw Miss Carolyn, soaked through and through from head to toe, on her knees, slumped over something—no not something, someone—lying at the edge of the pool.

Merciful Lord!

Heloise rushed through the open gate leading from the garden to the pool. "I'm coming, Miss Carolyn. I'm coming."

As she drew nearer, Miss Carolyn stopped screaming and looked up, her eyes glazed with shock. When she glanced down at the person Miss Carolyn was holding in her arms, Heloise barely managed not to scream herself. Apparently Miss Carolyn had jumped in the pool and pulled Little Miss Poppy's body from the water. But it was more than obvious that the child hadn't drowned. Someone had slit her throat and hacked out pieces of flesh from her arms and legs.

Salty bile rose up Heloise's esophagus. She was on the verge of vomiting. *Help me, Lord. Help me.*

"Call nine-one-one," Miss Carolyn said in a choked voice. "We have to get her to the hospital as soon as possible."

"Oh, Miss Carolyn . . ."

Heloise would call 911, but knew there was nothing anybody could do to save Poppy Chappelle.

Maleah thought she had prepared herself for the worst, and had believed she could listen to Browning describe in detail how he had murdered Noah and still remain in control of her emotions. She'd been wrong. Nothing had prepared her for Browning's self-satisfied smile or his giddy excitement as he recalled, step-by-step, the last moments of Noah's life.

While he relived what for him had been an exhilarating experience, Maleah envisioned, with sickening horror, Noah Laborde's death.

"Can you imagine it, Maleah? Noah's shock? When he woke that morning, he had no idea it would be the last day of his life. What must he have been thinking in those final few seconds before he died?"

Maleah swallowed.

I'm still in control. I'm shaky. I'm nauseated. I'm angry. But I'm not defeated.

She could give Browning a little of what he wanted—her blood, sweat, and tears—without pretending. What she felt at that precise moment was all too real.

"I—I can imagine." The tremor in her voice was not

ked. "Noah must have been shocked by what happened and so very afraid of dying."

Browning chuckled. "I'm sure he was. He knew that I
possessed all the power and he was powerless. He knew
that I had taken his life away from him."

"That's what it was all about for you, wasn't it—power
and control?"

"God, yes! You have no idea . . ." He paused, leaned
forward and glared directly into her eyes. "But then
again, maybe you do. You're a lady who prides herself
in being in control, aren't you?"

A red warning flag popped up in Maleah's mind.
How could Browning know that she had dealt with control issues most of her life?

He can't know. He's only guessing.

When she didn't reply to his question, he smiled.
God, how she hated his smile.

"What would it take to snap that tight control you
maintain?" he asked. "I would love to see that happen.
I'd enjoy breaking you, taking your power away and
controlling you."

Maleah understood that for Browning, killing another human being was far more about power and control than about their pain, but the rush he experienced
when he took a life was probably the same as a sadist
who physically tortured his victim.

"I'm not good at play-acting," she told him. "You
know how difficult it was for me to listen to you tell me
the details about Noah's murder. What more do you
want from me?"

"Ah, yes, it was difficult for you. I noticed your misty
eyes, but there were no real tears, no weeping. I heard
the tremor in your voice, but you didn't scream with un-
controlled outrage." Browning leaned back in his chair

and studied her for a moment. "It wasn't enough. No
not nearly enough. I want much more."

"So do I," she told him. "Up to this point, I've bee
doing all the giving and you've been doing all the tal
ing."

"All right, then. If you want payment for the pleasur
you gave me, I'll pay up. After all, fair's fair." He tilte
back his head, pursed his lips and hummed. Then h
lowered his head and looked at her. "I don't kno
Durham's real name. He didn't tell me and I didn't as
But he was younger than he appeared to be. Being
keen judge of human beings, I'd say that his disguis
added ten or fifteen years to his appearance. The ma
you're looking for is probably in his forties. He was a
erage height and build, but he was muscular, his boc
well-toned. Look for a man who keeps his body in ti
top shape."

Although she was slightly stunned that Brownin
had willingly given her the information, when h
stopped talking, Maleah managed to ask, "Do you reca
anything else about his physical appearance? Mole
scars or tattoos? Were his arms hairy? Did he speak wit
an accent of any kind?"

"No visible moles or tattoos," Browning said. "H
arms had a fine dusting of light brown hair, his ey
brows and lashes were the same color and his eyes wer
blue. Of course he could have been wearing contact
As for an accent . . . well, he wasn't from the South. H
had more of a Midwestern accent, as if he had practice
the way he talked, trying to make his speech pattern
nondescript as possible, you know, the way English an
Australian actors speak when they're mimicking
American accent."

"Do you think he was British?"

"Possibly."

"What about—?"

"That's all for now. If you want more, you'll have to
⸺e me more."

Maleah nodded, understanding that he was ready to
⸺t her through Act Two of *Her Torture for His Pleasure.*
⸺d she had no choice but to take on the starring role.

Derek paced back and forth in the warden's office,
⸺able to sit down, let alone relax. Everything in him
⸺nted to rush down to the interview room, barge in
⸺d rescue Maleah from Browning's evil machinations.
Not an option.

All he could do was wait. And worry.

The waiting was difficult, but the worry came all too
⸺sily. He repeatedly reminded himself that Maleah was
⸺ig girl, strong, tough, tenacious, her soft underbelly
⸺ll protected. But she would not come away un-
⸺thed. He had warned her that if she revealed even a
⸺t of weakness, Browning would go in for the kill.

Derek didn't know what the hell was wrong with him.
⸺wasn't like him to go all chest-beating, manly-man
⸺otective where a woman was concerned. Any woman.
⸺ honestly couldn't remember ever feeling like this.
⸺en they'd been kids, he'd run interference between
⸺ kid sister and his mom and even between his older
⸺other and Mommy Dearest a few times. But he'd
⸺ne that more to piss off their mother than to protect
⸺her sibling.

For the past forty-five minutes, Claude Holland had
⸺ne his best to engage Derek in conversation, but had
⸺on realized keeping Derek's mind off Maleah's visit
⸺h Browning was an impossible task. Finally, the war-
⸺n had settled down to business as usual, made a cou-

ple of phone calls, went over various paperwork, a
drank three cups of coffee.

Derek decided he would give Maleah thirty mo
minutes and if she hadn't returned to the warden's
fice, he'd go get her. His gut told him that Browni
had been playing her—playing them—and today's
terview would be a burnt run. No matter what ha
pened, not even if Maleah retrieved some usable in
from Browning, she was not going to return to t
damn place for a repeat performance. This would
her final visit with the Carver. If he had to hogtie h
and guard her night and day, he would. She'd have
understand. A guy could take only so much waiting a
worrying.

When his phone rang, he paused mid-stride a
checked caller ID. A knot formed in his stomach. I
had already talked to Powell headquarters this mo
ing, via Barbara Jean, whom he affectionately called I
This call was from Sanders.

"Yeah, what's wrong?" Derek asked.

"There has been another copycat murder," Sand
said.

Derek's stomach knots tightened. "Who?"

"Saxon Chappelle's young niece, Poppy. She v
only sixteen."

"When? Where?" Derek cursed under his brea
"Hell, I don't suppose it matters, does it?"

"She was visiting Saxon's mother in Savannah for t
summer. Her grandmother found her in the backya
swimming pool this morning."

"This was kill number six and we're no closer to na
bing this guy than we were weeks ago."

"Is Maleah with you?"

"No, she's still in with Browning, doing her damn
est to get something out of him. Why?" Derek asked. "I

ou want us to leave here and head straight for Savannah?"

"No, we are sending Holt Keinan to Savannah today.
As we speak, Saxon Chappelle is over the Atlantic on
the Powell jet, accompanying Meredith Sinclair to London. On his return, he will be taken directly to Savannah and Holt will meet him. Griffin still wants you and
Maleah to return to Griffin's Rest as soon as possible."

"Can you tell me what's going on?"

"You and Maleah are the only two employees, other
than Luke Sentell, who are privy to all the information
we have accumulated on the Copycat Carver, a man
named Anthony Linden, and a mystery man who is calling himself Malcolm York. I believe Griffin wants the
two of you included in a strategic planning session."

"All right, then, as soon as Maleah finishes up here,
we'll go back through Vidalia, check out of our hotel,
and head your way."

"Very good. I will tell Griffin that we can expect you
this evening."

"Sanders?"

"Yes, sir?"

"How's Griff?"

Several seconds of contemplative silence followed.
And then Sanders replied, his voice a reflection of the
man's stoic personality, "You will be able to ask him
yourself when you see him tonight."

Without so much as a by-your-leave, Sanders ended
their conversation. Well, what had he expected? He
should have known better than to ask the man anything
personal regarding Griffin Powell. Sanders guarded
Griff's privacy as strongly as he guarded his own.

They were both men with secrets. Dark, deadly secrets.

What had really happened on Amara sixteen years

ago when Griff and his cohorts had killed Malcol[m]
York? Derek knew only the basic facts—Griff had bee[n]
kidnapped at twenty-two and held captive by a sadist[ic]
madman for four years before he, along with Sande[rs]
and Yvette, both also York's prisoners, had revolted an[d]
killed York. The details Griff had given him had bee[n,]
at best, sketchy, huge chunks of info not included. [If]
Nic knew more about the events that took place o[n]
Amara, she had not shared them with Maleah, wh[o]
seemed to know little more than he did.

"Has there been another copycat murder?" Claud[e]
Holland asked Derek.

He had forgotten that the warden was still in th[e]
room. "Yes, I'm afraid there has. This time, he's killed [a]
sixteen-year-old girl, the niece of one of our agents."

"I'm so sorry," the warden said. "Let's hope that M[s.]
Perdue has some success in getting Jerome Browning [to]
tell her everything he knows."

"I don't think Browning knows a goddamn thing[,"]
Derek said. "But Maleah just won't give up. She w[as]
damned and determined to give it one more try."

Warden Holland shook his head sadly. "I hate to s[ay]
it, but I agree with you, and I'm afraid Ms. Perdue [is]
going to come away from this latest interview with litt[le]
more than a few mental bruises."

He had been waiting for nearly six hours and was b[e]-
ginning to grow restless. When he had reported in aft[er]
he left Savannah before daylight this morning, his e[m]-
ployer had applauded him on a job well done, then i[n]-
structed him to check into a hotel in Atlanta an[d]
remain there until he got in touch with him again.

"I am finalizing my plans and should have further i[n]-
structions for you before noon Atlanta time."

During the past few months while he had been caring out the copycat murders, as soon as one kill had
een accomplished, he had been given the information
out the next victim. But not this time. Was the Copy-
t Carver's reign of terror over?

Stripped naked, down to his bare skin, the real man
vealed, he lay on the king-size bed in the four-star
otel and stared up at the ceiling. When on an assign-
ent, he always wore disguises and only in moments of
olitude such as this did he allow himself such indul-
nt freedom. Even with the expensive whores he
ught for a few hours of pleasure, he didn't remove
s wig or colored contacts or, if using them, the fake
ustache and beard. He kept his body in perfect con-
tion, lean, muscled, healthy. He kept his head and
est shaved and since he was not an excessively hairy
an, he had only a sprinkling of light brown hair on his
ms and legs.

When his phone finally rang, he didn't rush to an-
er it. *Let him wait.*

He picked up between the fifth and sixth rings.

"Yes?"

"I'm afraid you've been compromised. Or should I
y that Anthony Linden has been."

"How did that happen?"

"Not to worry, not to worry. The leak will be
ugged."

"Give me a name and I will take care of it myself."

"No, no, you're too valuable to me where you are.
meone else can resolve that problem. I need you
ere in America to handle something extremely deli-
te for me."

"Another kill?"

"Actually, no. I want you to pick up a guest for me
d bring her with you when you return to London.

There will be a private jet waiting for you in Nashvill
You and my guest will be the only passengers."

"Am I to bring her directly to you?"

"No, I have arranged for a lovely, private retre
where I want her guarded night and day."

"You're giving me a babysitting assignment?"

"I'm putting you in charge of a mission that w
allow me to continue with my attack against the Powe
Agency. Your job will be to deliver my guest safely
London. I wouldn't trust anyone else with such an ir
portant task. As soon as she is delivered, another pa
ment will be transferred to your bank account."

"Half now and the other half once I deliver her."

"If you prefer. I don't quibble over unimportant d
tails with people who have proven themselves to me th
way you have."

His employer gave him the necessary details, inclu
ing the name of his "guest" and her present location.

"I'll need twenty-four to forty-eight hours to put
plan into motion."

"Very well, but I need this done in no more tha
forty-eight hours. If you can pick her up and deliver h
by tomorrow morning, I'll add a bonus to your pa
ment."

Chapter 27

Even if the general description that Browning had given her of the copycat matched that of Anthony Linden, former MI6 agent, there was no way they could be certain the two were the same person. So far, the information Browning had given her was pretty much useless, just as Derek had warned her it would be. If he was right about how little Browning actually knew, then she would be wasting her time if she continued playing his game.

But what if he actually does know something that will help us? What if I give up now and walk away? If I do that, I'll never know for sure and I'll always wonder if I could have done more to stop the copycat killer.

She had to stay a while longer. She couldn't give up. Not yet. She had to keep trying. But at what cost?

Browning wanted to see her suffer. He wanted to stick the knife into her, figuratively speaking, and then twist it.

"Have you decided?" Browning asked. "Are you staying or going?"

His eyes all but sparkled with anticipation.

You son of a bitch!

"I'm staying," she told him.

"Ah, that's my girl. Just as I had hoped—a fighter
the bitter end."

"I want a show of goodwill," she told him. "I'll mal
a statement and all you have to do is reply yes or n
Agreed?"

Smiling as if she had just handed him a get-out-
jail-free card, he shrugged. "Maybe. If I agree and I gi
you this one thing, then you swear that you'll answer a
my questions, no matter what I ask?"

She hesitated, contemplating what he might ask he
But she knew she had to take the risk. "Yes, I'll answ
whatever you ask. But for every answer I give you, yo
give me one in return. Agreed?"

"Agreed. Now, the next move is yours, Maleah."

"The copycat chose the Carver's kills as the mod
for his murders because he wanted a connection b
tween the killer he mimicked and a Powell agen
Maleah said. "He chose you because you killed No
Laborde, who had been my college boyfriend."

Browning's smile widened. "Yes, of course. Any idi
could have figured that out. But you needed to hear n
confirm it, didn't you?"

Yes, of course she had known. And yes, she ha
needed to hear him confirm it. But his confirmation
that fact didn't necessarily confirm that Durham or Li
den or whoever the hell the copycat was had shared th
information with Browning. As he'd said, any idi
could have figured it out.

"Now, we get down to business." She met his eag
gaze, despising him, but determined to show no relu
tance. "You've already told me you don't know the co
cat's real name, and that you knew he wasn't the re
Albert Durham. Is that the truth?" When he opened h

outh to speak, she held up her hand in a Stop signal.
ou also implied that you know why the copycat is
lling people associated with the Powell Agency. I want
ou to tell me why. What's his reason?"

"That's really *the* question, isn't it? The one you'll
ay any price to know."

"You're such a smart man, I'll bet you already know
he answer to your own question."

"Do you trust me to tell you the truth?" he asked.

"No, of course I don't trust you."

Browning laughed. "You must have been a pretty lit-
e girl, all blond curls and pink cheeks. Did you smile a
t? Laugh a lot? Were you happy as a child?"

Those were not the questions she had expected him
ask, but she answered them all the same. "When my
ther was alive, I smiled and laughed a lot and I was
ry happy."

"And after your father died? He did die, didn't he?"

"Yes, he died when I was quite young." *But how did
u know?*

"Poor little Maleah."

She didn't flinch and never broke eye contact.

"Was your mother as beautiful as you are?" Browning
ked in a low, seductive tone.

"My mother was very beautiful."

"Was she a good mother? Was she a good role
odel? Did you want to grow up to be just like her?"

"She was the best mother she knew how to be,"
aleah said honestly. "Why do you want to know these
ings about my mother?"

Browning slowly twisted his neck around and
ound, as if trying to loosen aching muscles. Then
th his head down, his chin almost touching his chest,
rolled his eyes up and then lifted his head slowly.

In that moment, she realized she had said the wrong

thing, that her reaction to his questions about h
mother had triggered his curiosity. Unwittingly, she ha
played right into his hands.

"I want to know everything about you," he told he
"And where better to start than learning about th
woman who gave birth to you."

Maleah did not like where this conversation w
heading. Her gut instincts told her that someho
someway, Jerome Browning knew things about her th
he couldn't possibly know.

*Shake it off. All those doubts and fears and uncertaintie
Browning doesn't know anything about your personal li
He's guessing. He's smart. He picked up something in yo
reaction. The tone of your voice. A glint in your eye. An u
conscious gesture of some type. Don't give him any mo
ammunition to use against you.*

"I loved my mother," Maleah told him. "She was ge
tle and kind and sweet and—"

"And you swore you'd never be like her."

She simply stared at Browning without respondi
and then quickly realized that her reaction had spoke
for her. So far, in this stupid game, she was losing.

"Gentle, kind, sweet women tend to need a ma
around to take care of them," Browning said. "Did yo
have a stepfather?"

Don't go there. Please, don't go there.

There was no way he could know anything abo
Nolan Reeves, her mother's sadistic second husband.

"Yes, I had a stepfather."

"Was he a good man?"

"No."

"You disliked him?"

"Yes."

"Hated him?"

"Yes."

"Ah, Maleah, being worthy of your hatred must indeed be a sweet, sweet thing. I envy your stepfather. How wonderful it must have been having all that power over you when you were a helpless little girl."

Her heartbeat accelerated, the sound of her racing pulse drumming inside her head. *Don't give him one damn thing. Keep everything on an even keel. You can do this. You know you can.*

"Did he rape you?" Browning asked, excitement in his voice.

Perspiration dampened her forehead and hands. She swallowed hard. "No, he never raped me."

"Fondled you inappropriately?"

"No."

"Ah, nothing sexual. That means he must have beaten you. There are men like that, sadistic men who enjoy inflicting pain." Browning burst into laughter. "I'm going to tell you something that I've never told anyone else, not even Albert Durham, my so-called biographer. I didn't want his kills to be exactly like mine, so I failed to mention that before I killed, I waited for a few seconds before I plunged the scalpel into the jugular because I needed to see the fear and agony in their eyes. Just for a moment."

She sucked in a deep breath and released it slowly. "If I answer your last question, I'll expect you to give me more than your rambling memories that mean nothing to me. I'm not interested in your kills, only in why the copycat is killing Powell agents and members of their families."

"Then answer my question first. Did your stepfather beat you?"

"Yes."

"Often?" He was practically licking his lips over the prospect of hearing the gory details.

"Sorry to disappoint you, but he beat me only once

"Only once?" Disappointment in his voice, Brownin
frowned.

"Yes, only once, but it was a severe beating. I ha
bruises and welts on my back and legs and buttocks an
I could barely stand after he finished."

*There, you son of a bitch, are those details grueson
enough for you?*

"Why only once? Did you mother intervene?"

"No." Maleah stood her ground and stared the dev
down. "And if you want any more answers, then I'
need a few from you."

Browning studied her as if trying to decide whethe
or not the pleasure he derived from tormenting her wa
worth the price she was asking.

"Durham and I actually played our own game'
Browning admitted. "He came to understand that h
wasn't dealing with an ordinary person, that I was h
intellectual equal and therefore deserved his respec
Once I realized he was not the real Albert Durham,
demanded payment for my services."

"You asked for a new lawyer and a female visitor .
what else?"

"Information."

"And he was willing to tell you whatever you wante
to know? I can't believe—"

"No, of course not. But I didn't ask for very muc
We understood each other, so he was willing to give m
what I required. He knew that the information I r
quested would in no way harm him. I asked him why F
had chosen me. And he told me what I believed was th
truth. After all, who was I going to tell?"

"And he explained why—because of your conne
tion to Noah Laborde, who was the former boyfriend
a Powell agent."

"Not in those exact words."

Maleah glowered at Browning, her patience growing
[th]in.

Stay calm. Pace yourself. Let him have all the time he
[ne]eds.

"Explain," Maleah said. "Give me his exact words."

Browning ran his tongue over his teeth, licked his
[lip]s, and sighed dramatically. "I'm afraid that I don't re-
[cal]l his exact words."

"Then paraphrase."

"He told me that he admired my work. I thanked
[hi]m. I asked him why he had chosen me. He simply
[sai]d, 'You killed a man named Noah Laborde.' I said
[ye]s. And when I told him that I didn't understand the
[sig]nificance, he told me that I didn't need to under-
[sta]nd."

"Did he ever mention the Powell Agency or Griffin
[Po]well by name? Did he tell you or did you sense that
[he] was a professional?"

"That's two questions," Browning reminded her.
"[N]either of which you've paid for, my dear."

She nodded as dread spread through her like quick-
[sil]ver, fast and poisonous, because she knew what was
[co]ming next.

"Why did your stepfather beat you only once?"
[Br]owning asked, the glint of anticipation sparkling in
[hi]s eyes again.

Maleah knew she could lie to him, perhaps even con-
[vin]cingly, but she couldn't fake the emotion that went
[alo]ng with lying. And it was an emotional reaction that
[Br]owning wanted from her. *Blood, sweat, and tears.*

"Because my big brother made a bargain with our
[ste]pfather to take both his own beatings and mine."

Browning's eyes widened with exhilaration. "How
[no]ble and heroic of your brother. But you must have

felt terribly guilty allowing someone else to take yo
punishment while you got off scot-free."

Answer him, damn it. No, wait. Let him see how much
question affected you, how it brought back painful mem
ries.

"What's wrong, Maleah?"

"Nothing." *That slight tremor in your voice was a ni*
touch. Browning had to know it was real and not faked.

"Then answer me."

"I didn't know . . ." Maleah admitted. "Not until yea
later. All I knew was that my stepfather never beat r
again."

"But you were afraid of him, weren't you? Why w
that?"

"You already know the answer. I'd think it would
obvious to you."

"Ah, but I want to hear you say it . . . in your ov
words."

"Yes, I was afraid of him, deathly afraid. Afraid for n
mother and my brother and for myself. He was a cru
heartless bastard." With tears misting her eyes, s
looked right at Browning. "He never beat me again, b
he berated me every chance he got. Once a day a
twice on Sunday."

Browning chuckled. "It's good to see you're able
maintain a sense of humor about such a tragic chi
hood. That shows just how tough you are now, does
it, Maleah? And you pride yourself on being tough,
being strong and in control."

"Damn straight about that," she told him, not tryi
to conceal the anger in her voice. *He wants emotion—*
give it to him. She shot up out of her chair and look
down at him. "Did the copycat ever mention either t
Powell Agency or Griffin Powell by name?"

Browning didn't respond.

"Answer me, you goddamn, sadistic, lowlife son of a bitch. I paid for your answer and you're going to give it to me."

Angling his head sideways, he rolled his eyes upward and glanced at her. "What a delicious thing your anger and hatred is, my dear Maleah. I can't tell you how much pleasure you're giving me."

"Tit for tat, Jerome. I give to you. You give to me. If you try to change the rules of the game now, I'm out of here so fast that—"

"He never mentioned Griffin Powell by name," Browning said.

"What about the agency?"

"No. The name Powell never came up, not the man or his agency."

"Then the only name the copycat ever mentioned was Noah Laborde?"

"That's right."

Once again, Browning had given her information that was all but useless.

"Did you ever suspect or did the copycat ever imply that he was a professional, that he was working for someone else?"

"That's the sixty-four-thousand-dollar question, isn't it?" Browning stretched languidly, rotating his shoulders slowly and then twisting his head from side to side.

"What's the going exchange rate between sixty-four thousand and my tears?" she asked, knowing what he wanted.

"A few more insights into the real Maleah Perdue," he said. "And one small stipulation."

"What small stipulation?"

"I want to taste them."

"You want to taste what?" Dear God, he couldn't mean what she thought he did.

"Your tears. I want you to come close enough for me to wipe away your tears with my tongue."

No way in hell was this monster going to put his mouth on her!

"It's not going to happen," she told him.

He shrugged. "It's your choice. But I can answer your question with certainty. And maybe, just maybe, I can give you even more."

She didn't believe him about the even more part and wasn't sure she believed that he could or would answer her question. But she was close, so very close, to ending this. She couldn't stop when she had made it almost to the finish line.

"If I cry, then you tell me what I want to know first and if your answers are worth anything to me, you can use your fingertip to wipe my tears."

"Hmm . . . a compromise." He nodded. "Agreed."

"Agreed."

"Sit back down, Maleah. Let's get all comfy cozy."

She sat, crossed her ankles, and folded her hands together in her lap. She didn't try to hide her apprehension. Allowing her emotions free rein was the only way she could give Browning what he wanted. A large part of the pleasure he was seeking would come from knowing how difficult it would be for her to relinquish control over her emotions.

"Your stepfather, did he beat your mother?"

"Yes, I believe he did. I know he slapped her quite often whenever she did anything that displeased him."

"And what do you think it was like for her during sex? Did you ever think about how he must have brutalized her? I'll bet you could hear her crying, couldn't you?"

Memories that she had kept buried deep inside her

subconscious broke through the barrier of her iron control, memories that she didn't want to recall.

"Yes, I heard her crying, but . . . I was too young and innocent at the time to know why."

"But when you were older and you knew all about sex, about what goes on between a man and a woman—"

"I tried not to think about it."

"No, of course not. You wouldn't let yourself, would you? No man would ever hurt you. No man would ever dominate you, control you, beat you into submission." He paused, as if waiting to see if one of his accusatory arrows had hit their mark. "And yet here you are giving me something you've never given another man."

She clenched her teeth, hating Browning, hating herself.

Finish it. Give him everything he wants. Pay the price. And then get the hell away from him.

Maleah brought the memory up from the dark corners of her soul. Her naked mother running down the hall, her face bloody and bruised. Nolan catching her, shoving her down on the floor and—

Thirteen-year-old Maleah had heard her mother's screams, gotten out of bed and opened her door. Jack had been gone for only a few weeks. He had joined the army and left her all alone in the family's house of horrors.

Maleah hadn't realized she was crying, not until she heard Browning's deep intake of breath, so satisfied, so pleased with himself.

She looked at him through her tears.

"Did you ever try to help your mother?" Browning asked.

"No."

After all these years, she still felt guilty that she hadn'
done more to save her mother. But even as a teenager
she had been terrified of Nolan Reeves, of the threat
he had made to kill both her and her mother if she ever
interfered or told anyone "lies" about him.

"Your stepfather beat your mother, raped her repeat
edly, abused her terribly and you did nothing," Brown
ing said.

Tears threatened to choke Maleah. Emotions long
bottled up inside her rose to the surface. It took all of
her energy to hold them at bay.

Enough!

She had paid his price. She had given him her tears
Now, by God, he'd give her whatever information he
had or . . . Or what?

"Tell me," she managed to say, her voice a mere whis
per.

"Thank you, Maleah." Jerome Browning leaned bac
his head, closed his eyes, and released a heavy, orgasmi
sigh. "It's been a long time since a woman has given m
so much pleasure."

Every instinct she possessed urged her to attack, t
rip out the monster's heart and throw it to a pack of wil
dogs. At that very moment, she hated Jerome Brownin
almost as much as she had hated Nolan Reeves.

"Tell me, damn it," Maleah demanded.

"Of course, my dear. I am an honorable man who a
ways pays his debts. You give to me and I give to you."

"Then give, you sick son of a bitch."

"He referred to himself as a death technician and a
international contractor. I like those terms, don't you.
Browning's gaze sparkled with amusement, but he didn
smile when he said, "As a professional courtesy, on
skilled death technician to another, the man you refe
to as the Copycat Carver did not deny it when I aske

him if he was a professional hit man. As far as I'm concerned, his silence was a confirmation. He knew that as well as I did."

Maleah swiped the tears trickling down her cheeks.

"Save just a taste for me," Browning reminded her and then ran his tongue across his upper lip.

Ignoring his comment and gesture, she asked, "Do you know anything at all about who hired him and why?"

"Perhaps."

"I've paid you in full, so don't try to play me. Not now. It's too late in the game," she reminded him. "You still owe me."

Browning hesitated for a moment before replying. "Why would you think he would have shared that kind of information with anyone, even with me? He is no sloppy amateur. He kills people for a living. And he's quite good at it, isn't he?"

Instinct told her that Browning did know something else and she was determined he share that info with her, no matter how insignificant. "I want the rest of the information I paid for."

"Yes, of course. A deal is a deal." He couldn't take his gaze off the tears clinging to her lashes and seeping from the corners of her eyes. "Sometimes, during his visits, we talked philosophy, past experiences, things like that. We exchanged confidences the way people in the same profession do. It's not often that you meet someone who is your equal, perhaps even slightly superior. Of course, he didn't mention names, but . . ."

Maleah waited, allowing him this one final moment of victory.

He savored the moment, let it drag on and on, and he knew what he wanted.

"But what, Jerome?" She jumped up, leaned over

him and glanced at the guard out of the corner of her
eye, trying to nonverbally ask him to stay put. "You can't
tell me anything, can you? You've been stringing me
along all this time. You really are a son of a bitch, aren't
you? And I hate you." She balled her hands into fists
and held them in his face, letting him see how much
she wanted to pummel him. "I hate you, hate you, hate
you, hate you!" she shouted.

"My copycat is a very proud man and if he has one
flaw, it's that he's boastful." The words flowed out of
Browning like water from a dam that had just burst
wide open. "He liked to brag about how rich and powerful those who have employed him are. As I said before, he couldn't mention names, but he did tell me
that he has worked for political leaders and crime
bosses throughout the U.S., Europe, and around the
world. That makes him an international contractor. His
current employer is a billionaire who owns a private island retreat where he enjoys some of the perks of his
business."

A billionaire? A private island retreat.

"Exactly what are those perks?"

"Human trafficking," Browning said with such delight that it was all Maleah could do to stop herself from
actually striking him. "A smorgasbord of human delights. Whatever your pleasure. Male or female. Child,
teen or adult. Dark or fair. Experienced or virginal."

The description of a billionaire who made his fortune from human trafficking and who owned an island
retreat sounded all too familiar.

Malcolm York.

The real Malcolm York.

But that isn't possible.

The real York is dead, has been dead for sixteen years.

"A deal's a deal." Maleah leaned close enough for Browning to touch her.

Smiling, he lifted his cuffed hands, and then slowly and very tenderly wiped a tear from the corner of her eye. As she lifted her head, she watched as he placed his index finger on his tongue, licked his finger and then sucked it into his mouth.

Maleah turned and, without a backward glance, walked away.

When she reached the guard who had been assigned to escort her to and from the interview, he opened the door for her. At that precise moment, Browning called her name.

"Maleah?"

She paused, but didn't turn around or look back.

"It was good for me," he told her. "Was it good for you?"

The sound of his laughter followed her as she hurried away from him as fast as she could.

Chapter 28

The moment he saw Maleah, Derek sensed she was on the verge of collapse. Not that anyone else would even notice. She managed to hide her emotional stress remarkably well, especially considering what he suspected she had just endured at Browning's cunningly cruel hands. What Derek wanted to do and what he did were two entirely different things. He wanted to grab her, hold her, and tell her it was all right to fall apart because he'd be there to take care of her. What he actually did was walk over to her, give her a casual glance, and ask her if she was ready to leave.

"Yes, I'm ready," she told him, her voice deceptively calm.

They both shook hands with Warden Holland and thanked him.

"Will you be scheduling another interview?" the warden asked.

Derek wanted to shout "no way in hell."

"No. This was the final interview," Maleah said, absolute certainty in her voice.

As they walked together out into the parking area, he

waited for Maleah to speak first and was prepared to take his cue from her on how to proceed. If she wanted to talk, he'd talk. If she wanted to be quiet, he'd keep his mouth shut. If she needed time alone when they returned to Vidalia, then he would give her some time alone. But within a few hours, he would have to tell her about Saxon Chappelle's niece. Only sixteen. *Sweet sixteen and never been kissed.* He hoped the lyrics to that old song weren't true in Poppy's case. He hoped the girl had been kissed at least once by a young boy who had made her toes curl.

Sixteen was far too young to die.

As Derek and Maleah approached her Equinox, she pulled her keychain out of her pocket and tossed it to him. He caught the chain mid-air, keys jangling together when he grasped the large silver "M" to which the chain was fastened.

"You drive, okay?" Maleah did not make eye contact.

"Yeah, sure," Derek said.

For a woman who usually insisted on driving her own car and even the rental cars they had used in the past, a woman hell-bent on always being in control, handing over her keys and asking him to drive meant only one thing. Maleah didn't trust herself to drive. Outwardly she appeared to be completely fine, but it was obvious to Derek that she was far from all right.

This was the second time she had asked him to drive after a visit with Browning. The first time, her request had taken him by surprise. This time, he had known she would ask. He had expected her to come out of this final interview in bad shape. What he didn't know was just how bad it really was.

He unlocked the doors before they reached the SUV, and then he opened her door. But he stopped himself just short of actually touching her, despite wanting to hug her to him and then ease her gently into the passenger seat. By the time he rounded the hood and slid behind the wheel, Maleah had put on her seatbelt and sat there ramrod straight, her fisted hands crossed at the wrists and resting in her lap.

As soon as they were on the road, he asked, "Want some music?"

"Not especially."

"Want to stop for—"

"No, please, I don't want anything. Not right now. Nothing except peace and quiet. All right?" She leaned back her head and closed her eyes.

"Yeah, sure."

They spent the next twenty-one miles in complete silence. Derek kept his eyes on the road, not once glancing at Maleah. But she was all he could think about. If only she'd make a sound. A gasp or a sigh or even a hiccup or a sneeze. It was as if she had hit some sort of mute button inside her.

Less than thirty minutes after leaving the penitentiary, Derek turned in at the Vidalia Hampton Inn, parked the SUV and killed the engine. When Maleah didn't open her eyes or say anything, he came damn close to grabbing her and shaking her. But the minute he looked at her, really looked at her, his heart stopped. God in heaven!

"It's going to be okay, Blondie," he told her in the calmest, most reassuring tone he could muster. "It's going to be okay."

He undid his seatbelt, got out, pocketed the keys, and rushed around to her side of the SUV. When he opened the door, she sat there unmoving. He reached in, unhooked her belt, and very gently reached down and peeled back the clenched fingers of her right hand. She had clutched her hand so tightly that her short, neat nails had dug into her flesh so deeply that her palm was bleeding. He repeated the process with her left hand and found it to be in the same condition.

"Ah, Maleah, sweetheart . . ." He pulled a white monogrammed handkerchief from his inside jacket pocket, wiped the bright red droplets of blood from each palm and wrapped the handkerchief around her right hand. "Come on, let's get you out of here and into the hotel."

When he grasped her shoulders and turned her sideways, she opened her eyes and stared at him. After slipping his arm around her waist, he lifted her up, pulled her out of the SUV and straight into his arms. Then he eased her down onto her feet.

She looked up at him. "Thank you."

Keeping his right arm around her waist, he caressed her cheek with a gentle backward swipe of his left hand. "You're welcome. Come on. You need to lie down and rest for a while."

She nodded and then followed him into the hotel and down the corridor to the elevator. He kept his arm around her, supporting her, sensing that without him, she would spiral down to the floor and curl up in a ball. He didn't bother asking her for the key to her room; instead he walked her straight to his room. He unlocked the door and led her over to his freshly made bed. She didn't protest when he eased her down onto the edge of the bed. But when he moved away from her, intending to take off her shoes before getting a washcloth to clean her hands, she reached out and grabbed him. The bloody handkerchief wrapped loosely around her right hand slipped off just as she gripped his shoulders.

"Don't leave me, Derek. Stay, please. I—I . . ."

"I'm not going anywhere," he told her. "I just want to take off your shoes so you can lie back and relax. Then

I'm going to get a warm washcloth and wash your hands. Okay?"

"I won the game," she said. "Browning told me everything he knows."

Derek lifted a stray tendril of glossy blond hair that had escaped from the soft bun atop her head and wrapped it behind her ear. "I never doubted for a minute that you would beat him at his own game." *But at what price to you, Maleah?*

"I need to tell you what he said, everything about—"

Derek tapped his index finger over her lips, effectively silencing her. She gazed up at him with questioning eyes.

"You can tell me everything. Just not right now. You need to rest for a few minutes. You need to let me take care of you. Just this one time. All right?"

She nodded. "All right. Just this one time."

He smiled. "That's my girl." And in that moment, Derek Lawrence admitted an undeniable truth—he thought of Maleah as his. His girl. His woman. His to care for and protect.

Heaven help us both!

Derek knelt in front of her, removed her sensible pumps, set them under the bed, and then lifted her feet and legs. He turned back the covers at the head of the bed, stacked one pillow on top of the other and gently eased Maleah down until her head rested on the double pillows.

"I'll be right back," he told her.

A few minutes later, he returned with a warm, damp washcloth and his shaving kit. He sat on the edge of the bed and tenderly washed her hands. And then he took out a tube of salve from his kit and rubbed the soothing cream into the shallow nicks her nails had made in her palms.

She lifted her hands, one at a time, inspected them and said, "Thank you. I didn't realize what I was doing. I was just trying so damn hard not to fall apart."

He leaned down, kissed her forehead and said, "I know, Blondie. I know."

"I'm all right. Really. I'm just a little shell-shocked."

He set his shaving kit on the floor, dumped the washcloth on top of it, and then turned his attention back to Maleah. "Tell me what you want right now. Tell me what you need."

"What I want and what I need aren't the same," she told him. "I want to forget everything Browning said to me, every question he asked, every innuendo, all the memories he made me dredge up from my childhood. I want to pretend that I didn't let all those horrible memories make me feel the way I did when I was a child and a teenager. Helpless. Frustrated. Frightened." She grabbed Derek's hands and curled her fingers around them. "What I *need* is to exorcise whatever remains of those old demons. I thought I'd done that in my twenties during a few years of therapy sessions, but apparently, the roots of those memories were buried a little deeper than I realized."

"Then talk to me. Let's dig up those roots and burn them to ashes."

"If anyone had ever told me that I'd be asking you, of all people, to be my father confessor, I never would have believed it," she said, the corners of her mouth lifting in an almost smile.

He eased his hands from her death grip, tapped her playfully on the nose, and then sat down beside her. He focused on her eyes. "Anything you say will stay between the two of us for as long as we live. You already know my ugly secrets. You know that I despise my own mother, my money-grubbing, social climbing mother who drove my weak, spineless father to drink and eventually to suicide. And she's never felt guilty about it a day in her life. And you know that when I was young and stupid, I did some pretty awful things. You know that I've killed people."

He took her hands in his and held them so loosely that she could easily pull away. The last thing he wanted was for her to feel trapped by his superior male strength.

"Nothing you ever did could be half as bad as what I did." He lifted her right hand, kissed it, then lifted the left and kissed it.

She pulled her hands out of his and eased up into a sitting position, her back against the headboard. "When my father was alive, we were all so happy. Mama and Daddy and Jackson and me. Then my father died when I was just a little girl. And my mother, my weak, lonely, needy mother, married a monster."

"My mother was married three times, but both of my stepfathers were decent guys. I sort of felt sorry for them. If anyone was a monster in those marriages, it was my mother."

"Nolan Reeves was a sadist." Maleah clutched the sheet on either side of her hips. "He abused my mother every way a man can abuse a woman—physically, sexually, emotionally, mentally. And he beat Jack unmercifully for years, until Jack got big enough to stand up for himself. I think by the time Jack left home and joined the army, Nolan was halfway afraid of him. He wasn't as mean to Mama for a couple of years before Jack left. But then, later, when Jack was gone . . ."

Derek circled her wrists, moved his hands downward and opened her clenched fists. He held her hands. She closed her eyes and breathed deeply.

"When I was thirteen, I saw them," Maleah said. "I saw my mother running from Nolan. She was naked, her body and face were bloody and bruised and . . ."

She gulped several times. "He caught her and threw her on the floor and . . . and . . ."

Derek squeezed her hands tenderly.

"I didn't do anything. I just stood there in my bedroom door, frozen to the spot and scared out of my mind," Maleah told him. "I closed the door, got back in bed and covered my head with a pillow so I couldn't hear her crying while he raped her."

Tears trickled down Maleah's cheeks.

"You were a child, even at thirteen. There's nothing you could have done."

"I know that. As an adult, I know. But on an emotional level, that thirteen-year-old girl blames herself for not trying to stop him." Her gaze locked with Derek's. "He . . . he told me that if I ever interfered in what was a private matter between my mother and him or if I ever told anyone our family's private business, he would kill Mama and me."

Derek pulled her gently into his arms and held her. She wrapped her arms around him and laid her head on his shoulder. And while she cried, he tenderly stroked her back and whispered reassurances.

"That's it, honey. Let it all out. I'm here. I'll take care of you. No one can hurt you." More than anything, he wanted to take away her pain. If he could, he would suffer it for her.

During their flight from Knoxville to London on the Powell jet, Meredith had, thus far, kept to herself as much as possible. Her escort, Saxon Chappelle, had not pressed her to carry on a conversation, not even when they had eaten a meal together. She greatly appreciated how considerate he was. From the moment he had shaken her hand and said, "Please, call me Saxon," she had sensed that he was a good man. She instinctively trusted him and felt at ease around him, neither of which was true when it came to a great many people.

She suspected that he had been told enough about her so that he knew when she touched him she would be able to "read him" to a certain extent. And that's why he had immediately shaken hands with her, to reassure her, to let her know he was a decent human being.

Even when she couldn't see Saxon and wasn't touching him, she occasionally could pick up on his fleeting thoughts, flashes of memory, and even his feelings. And the same held true for the pilot and co-pilot. Saxon loved his mother and worried about her. A young girl named Poppy kept slipping in and out of his thoughts. She was his niece and he worried about her, too.

Meredith wasn't sure if it was the pilot or the co-pilot who kept thinking about women. Their breasts. Their legs. Their hips. Kissing them. Fondling them. She had deliberately shut out those sensual thoughts. They were far too personal and absolutely none of her business. It wasn't that she wanted to invade other people's privacy. She didn't. But she couldn't help it. For as long as she could remember, she'd had "the gift." Her Granny Sinclair had had the "second sight," too, and people in their small Louisiana town had called her a witch. Some people even accused her of practicing Voodoo. It had been Granny who had learned about Dr. Meng and made plans to send Meredith to the woman who was now her mentor. She'd been seventeen when Granny died and old lawyer Dupree had read Granny's will.

"She wants you to go to London," Mr. Dupree had told her. "To a doctor over there, some woman named Yvette Meng. She managed to set aside money for your plane ticket and enough for you to live on for at least a year, if you live frugally."

In the six years since she had become one of Dr.
Yvette Meng's protégés, Meredith had progressed from
a frightened, awkward, hostile and misunderstood girl
to a cautious, curious, often outspoken woman who was
still, on occasion, quite awkward, especially around the
opposite sex. Men were not attracted to her. She wasn't
pretty. She was short, plump, and plain. And covered in
freckles. Her hair was carrot red, wild and curly and un-
tamable. The best she could do with it was pull it back
into a ponytail. And even if a man could get past her
lack of beauty, he would certainly be put off by her ability to read his mind.

But she couldn't actually read minds.

She sensed thoughts.

And when she touched someone, she could feel what
they were feeling.

Yvette had told her that she had never known anyone whose "gifts" were as varied or as strong as Meredith's were.

"You are very special," Yvette had told her. "Once you
learn to harness and control your abilities, there is so
much good you can do."

And that was why she was on the Powell jet, heading
to London, straight into the arms of a man she feared.
From the moment she had met Luke Sentell, she had
known he was a killer.

As hard as she had tried not to think about Luke during the flight, he kept creeping into her mind. She had
read for a while, watched a movie, taken a nap, and
meditated. Without those quiet, still, soul-refreshing
moments of meditation, she didn't believe she could
survive.

And now they were over the Atlantic, on their way to
a city that held so many good memories for Meredith,
memories that included her first meeting with Yvette

and her introduction to other gifted people. When Yvette had moved her academy/sanctuary from London and resettled all of them in the U.S., at Griffin' Rest, Meredith had hated leaving London. But eventually she had become accustomed to her new home in the U.S. and oddly enough now dreaded returning to London. When they landed at Heathrow, Luke Sentell would be waiting for them. No doubt he would whisk her away, via a limousine, to some fancy London hotel where he would keep her a virtual prisoner while he watched her, pushed her to the brink of exhaustion and guarded her from the outside world. She would force herself to delve into the unknown mystical realm of her mind and use her psychic gifts because Yvette had asked her to help Griffin Powell. And if she failed to give Luke the results he wanted, he would move her to another city, to another country, to wherever he thought she might "pick up the scent" of their prey. He treated her as if she were nothing more than a hunting dog.

She had been sent to London on a mission and Saxon Chappelle would hand her over to Luke, a man she neither liked nor trusted, so that she could help him find a man named Malcolm York.

Chapter 29

Maleah awoke disoriented and confused. She was ng in bed, fully clothed, and cuddled against Derek wrence. The last thing she remembered was weeping his arms. Apparently, she had cried herself to sleep. hen she looked directly at him, he looked back at her d smiled. Her mind told her to disengage her body om his, to lift her head from where it lay nestled on s shoulder and to move her arm from around his ist. But she didn't change her position by more than fraction as she leaned back her head and tilted her in so that they wouldn't be practically nose-to-nose.

"How long have I been asleep?" she asked.

"Not long. A little over an hour."

"Have you been awake the entire time?"

He nodded.

"Why didn't you—?"

"I enjoyed watching you sleep," he told her. "And u were exhausted. You needed some rest."

She eyed him speculatively. "You enjoyed watching e sleep?"

His grin widened. "Yeah. Did you know you make

funny little noises in your sleep? You fell asleep in m
arms, the two of us sitting up, so I just eased us dow
onto the bed and when I did that, you whimpered an
cuddled up against me."

She lifted her head from his arm and scooted awa
from him, putting a couple of feet between them. '
need to tell you about my interview with Browning."

"Your final interview," he told her.

"Yes, my final interview." She sat up and leaned bac
against the headboard, determined to return her rel
tionship with Derek to business only. "Browning an
the copycat killer made a bargain. We already figure
out that the copycat agreed to provide Jerome with
new lawyer, a female visitor, and a new victim, one h
couldn't actually kill, only emotionally torment."

"And you were that victim." Derek grumbled uninte
ligibly, no doubt a few choice curse words. "I'd like
have five minutes alone with Browning."

Maleah laid her hand on Derek's shoulder. His ga
connected instantly with hers.

"I'll condense things for you," Maleah said. "It seen
Browning and the copycat formed a rather unique rel
tionship, one killer to another, during their phor
calls, letters, and visits. The copycat never told Jeron
his real name, but when Jerome asked if he was a pr
fessional, he didn't deny it."

"Which was as good as an admission, right?" Dere
sat up beside her.

"Right."

She noticed that several buttons in the center
Derek's shirt were open, leaving the material gappin
Had she done that—unbuttoned his shirt in her sleer

Concentrate on what you need to say and not on Derek

Keeping strictly to the facts and not elaboratin

Maleah told him about her conversation with Browning and the information he had given her.

"Browning said that the copycat is an international contractor, his word—contractor. And his current employer is a billionaire who owns a private island retreat, where he enjoys the perks of his business."

"And his business is human trafficking." Derek frowned. "The description sounds familiar, doesn't it, so familiar."

"Are you saying Browning was lying?"

"No, I'm saying that maybe the copycat was lying to Browning, knowing he would pass along false information."

"If you're right about that, then Browning actually gave me nothing. I paid for more useless information."

"I didn't say that. For all we know, everything Browning told you is the truth."

"But you said—"

"I said maybe the copycat was lying to Browning. Maybe he wasn't. But any way you look at it, you came away with one very important piece of information."

"Okay, maybe I'm slightly addled from my mini-emotional meltdown and mid-day nap, but you're going to have to enlighten me. My brain isn't—"

"The copycat, whoever he is, knows something about Malcolm York, either the original York or the pseudo York rumored to be in Europe somewhere at present."

"You're right," Maleah said, suddenly feeling more like her old self by the minute. "And this info adds more weight to Griff's theory that the copycat murders are connected to his past and to both Malcolm Yorks."

"I think we can safely assume that Griff's theory is correct. I have little doubt now that the copycat is, as we suspected, a hired assassin."

"An assassin hired by the fake York, right?" Maleah got up, brushed off her wrinkled slacks and searched for her shoes. "We should contact Griff right away and let him know." She found her shoes halfway under the bed, dragged them out, and slipped into them.

"First of all, yes, logically, we can assume that the man who calls himself Malcolm York hired the copycat, but we need more proof before we can be certain." Derek buttoned his shirt and got out of bed. "Secondly, there's no need to call Griff because we'll see him this evening. I got a call from Sanders while you were in with Browning this morning. It was bad news."

"And you're just now telling me about it?"

"I thought it could wait," Derek said. "All things considered."

"You mean considering the fact that I came away from the interview with Browning an emotional wreck."

"You just needed a little time to recover, honey. You should be proud of yourself. You held your own against a psychopathic monster."

"If you say so." *He's right, damn it. You might have come away with a few battle scars, but for all intents and purposes you won the game. And you survived.* "What's the bad news from Sanders?"

"The copycat struck again."

Oh God, no. "Who?"

"Saxon Chappelle's sixteen-year-old niece."

Maleah sucked in an agonized breath. How could anyone kill a young girl who was little more than a child?

"Poppy Chappelle was spending the summer with Saxon's mother. The grandmother found her this morning."

"They didn't let Saxon go to Savannah on his own, did they?"

"Saxon may not even know yet," Derek told her. "He
ft early this morning to escort Meredith Sinclair to
ondon. But once he hands her over to Luke, he'll re-
rn to the U.S. tonight. Griff sent Holt Keinan to Sa-
nnah."

"Griff wants us at Griffin's Rest by tonight because
's circling the wagons, isn't he?"

"Yeah, probably."

"Then let's get the show on the road. I need to go
ick to my room and grab my suitcase and then we can
ieck out."

"Take your time, Blondie. I'll check us out. You can
eet me in the lobby. But first, wash your face, put on
me lipstick, and comb your hair. You look like you
st got out of bed."

The Berkeley Knightsbridge, a five-star luxury hotel,
as located on Wilton Place, in the heart of residential
elgravia. From this location, they were only moments
om the hustle and bustle of Knightsbridge and not far
om Buckingham Palace, Hyde Park, and Belgrave
quare. During the years Meredith had spent in Lon-
on with Yvette and her fellow misfits, they had lived in
omfort, but not in splendor. She suspected that Griffin
well had arranged for the two-bedroom suite at this
xurious hotel just for her. He understood the type of
crifice she was making in order to help him find and
op a killer and no doubt wanted to compensate her
r the mental and emotional pain and anguish. Mered-
i was doing this out of a sense of loyalty to Yvette, but
so because she, too, did not want to see another inno-
nt person die.

"We can order room service for dinner," Luke Sen-
ll told her as he escorted her into the spacious living

room, which was both elegantly sophisticated and y
beautifully understated.

The moment she walked into the room, the image
a woman appeared in her mind. Blond and attractiv
Possibly the interior designer. Someone who liked
clean, lean and yet classic look.

"Thank you, but I'm not hungry," Meredith replied

"I've given you the master suite," Luke told her as I
walked across the living room and opened the bedroo
door. "I'll put your suitcase in here and if you'd like
rest for a while—"

"I'd like to call home and speak to Yvette. I'm co
cerned about Saxon Chappelle." Meredith glowered
Luke, whose stoic stare slightly unnerved her. "Yo
could have been a little less blunt when you told him h
niece was the Copycat Carver's latest victim."

As if ignoring her comment, Luke disappeared in
the bedroom for a couple of minutes. Once again,
she had done in the past, she tried to sense somethin
in Luke Sentell other than his steely determination
protect himself from her probing. On the outer edg
of his consciousness, she picked up on rigid control ar
single-mindedness, both aspects of his apathetic pe
sonality.

Deciding not to make an issue of his rudeness, sl
surveyed her surroundings. The cool taupes and gra
and beiges used with the dark, gleaming wood in th
room soothed Meredith. She preferred the gentleness
neutral colors, the peacefulness of muted tones.

"I assume you can unpack for yourself," Luke said
he emerged from her bedroom.

"Yes, certainly."

"I told Chappelle the facts. If I had put my ar
around him and shed a few tears, do you honestly thir
it would have helped him any?"

"No, but you were so cold and matter-of-fact."

Luke grunted. "Make your call to Yvette while I order ur dinner."

"I don't want anything," she told him.

"Well, I do." His scrutinizing gaze raked over her ith cold precision. "You need to eat something to uild up your strength before you start earning your eep."

"I'll be sure to eat a substantial breakfast."

"You'll eat a substantial dinner, too, because I intend or us to begin work tonight."

"Tonight?"

"Yes, tonight."

"But—"

"I realize that you're probably tired from your long ight and more than a little pissed about getting stuck ith me as your babysitter, but the sooner we locate Anony Linden, the sooner we will be able to stop him om killing anyone else. Do you understand?"

"Yes, I understand. I just didn't realize you had anying available here at the hotel for me to use to conect with Linden."

"I do."

"Then let me freshen up and unpack while you rder dinner. And as soon as I call Yvette, I'll be ready."

She didn't bother asking him what he had in his posssion that had at some time belonged to Anthony Linen. She would know soon enough. Even something as significant as a cigarette lighter or an unlaundered andkerchief could be used as a catalyst to connect her ith the person or persons who had used the specific bject. The fewer people who had handled the object, e more precise her revelations.

"Do you have any preferences about dinner?" he sked. "Protein of some type, right?"

"Yes, protein," she told him. "For strength and sta
mina."

"And if I remember correctly, no wine, no liquor o
any kind. Just water."

"That's correct."

Meredith found herself unable to break eye contac
with Luke, his steel-gray eyes holding her attention lik
metal to a magnet. A whirlwind of energy spun aroun
them, cocooning them together inside a kinetic forc
neither could control.

Trust me. I'll take care of you.

Luke hadn't spoken, but Meredith had heard hi
thoughts.

But that was the problem. She wasn't sure she coul
trust him. "If I go in too deep, you're the only one wh
can save me."

"Yes, I know." He turned, walked away and entere
the foyer that led to the entrance to the second bed
room that was attached to and yet separate from th
rest of the suite.

Prompted by the incentive of a bonus, he had waste
no time in making arrangements to pick up the specia
guest for his current employer. Locating her had no
been a problem, but removing the obstacles in his pat
would require quick, decisive action. Complicated b
the presence of a private security agent who mad
rounds outside the home every two hours, as precise a
clockwork, and disarming the home's security syster
had taken a while longer than he had anticipated. H
was pretty sure the guard wasn't a Powell agent. H
wore a uniform of some kind and Powell agents didn
wear uniforms. His guess was that the family had hire

im for protection in case the Copycat Carver targeted
ne of them.

Unlike the Chappelle home in Savannah, there was
o outside basement entrance, leaving him with only
ie windows and doors on the first and second levels of
ie house as a means of entry and exit. With a guard on
uty, probably stationed downstairs, his best bet was to
nd a way to enter through an upstairs widow. And
nce time was of the essence if he wanted that big bonus,
e needed to check out the house's interior quickly and
inpoint her bedroom. But with only three occupants,
:her than the bodyguard, it should be a relatively sim-
le matter. All he'd have to do was look into the bed-
ooms to find her. At this time of night, she would be
one. And her room would no doubt be distinctly dec-
:ated.

With a few twists, he locked the carbon steel talons of
ie compact grappling hook into position and sent the
ook sailing up and atop the sloping roof at the back of
ie house. Testing the connection and finding it se-
ire, he began his ascent up the lightweight nylon
ope. Once on top of the roof, he made his way care-
lly over to the nearby single window, one he assumed
ould take him into a bathroom. He removed the glass
itter from his pocket, along with a suction device, and
moved a section of the windowpane without breaking
. He reached through the opening, unlocked the win-
ow and raised it high enough to allow him enough
ace to slip inside the house.

As he had assumed beforehand, he now found him-
:lf inside a small bathroom, well lit with a decorative
ot pink glitter nightlight. How lucky for him that he
ad, no doubt, entered through her bathroom window.
ot having to search the entire upstairs to find her sim-

plified his job enormously. The bathroom door stoo
wide open. With practiced stealth movements, he er
tered the bedroom silently, not making a sound. Ar
other nightlight identical to the one in the bathroor
cast a pink glow across the carpeted floor and moonligh
streaming through the sheer striped curtains illum
nated the wicker bed in which she slept.

He reached into his pocket, removed a small via
and a linen handkerchief and then opened the vial an
soaked the linen with its contents as he crept closer an
closer to the bed. She lay there in all her beautifu
blond innocence, never knowing the part she woul
play in a madman's diabolical scheme. But this specifi
madman paid extremely well. And it wasn't his place t
judge the people who employed him to do their dirt
work.

He leaned down, placed the ether-soaked handke
chief over her nose and mouth and positioned hi
other hand in the center of her chest to hold her i
place if she woke. Her eyes flew open. She stared up a
him for a few moments and then closed her eyes as th
anesthetic took affect. He reached inside the inne
pocket of his snug-fitting jacket, removed an envelop
and laid it beside her pillow. Without hesitation, h
flung back the covers, lifted her up and into his arm
and retraced his steps through the bathroom. He ease
her through the window, placing her solidly on the roc
before he climbed out and joined her. The moonligh
struck the tiny pink sequins outlining the ruffles on th
hem of her gown.

After checking below on the ground, he hoisted he
up and positioned her beneath his arm, clamping he
securely between the inner curve of his elbow and h
ribcage. Mindful that one wrong move could result i
him dropping her to the ground, he grasped the nylo

ope and descended with careful precision. Once on
e ground, he lifted her up and across his shoulder,
ke a sack of potatoes, and then ran up the alley toward
e car he had parked there less than twenty minutes
go.

A private jet would be waiting for them in Nashville.
 two and a half hours, he and his employer's special
uest would board the jet and be ready for take off to
ondon by daybreak.

Chapter 30

Meredith glared at Luke across the breakfast table. Despite having kept her up until the wee hours of the morning, he had knocked on her bedroom door at precisely seven-thirty and informed her that room service had just delivered their breakfast.

"I ordered the full English fry-up," he had told her. "Eggs, bacon, sausages. Plenty of protein, along with baked beans, mushrooms, and fried bread. I expect you out here and ready to eat in ten minutes."

Knowing that if she didn't join him for breakfast within a reasonable time, he would come in and get her, she had grabbed a quick shower, washed her hair, and slipped into a pair of ratty sweat pants and a soft cotton T-shirt. Leaving the towel wrapped around her damp hair, she had arrived at the table less than ten minutes after he had summoned her.

"Eat hearty," he said. "We have a lot to do. Maybe after a good night's sleep, you'll be working on all cylinders this morning."

He had been referring to the fact that last night when he had placed what Luke had told her had been

t of cuff links owned by Anthony Linden in her
nds, she had drawn a blank. It was if no one had ever
ndled the cuff links, other than Luke. After more
an an hour of useless efforts to use the links as a con-
uit to previous wearers, Luke had told her to go to
d.

Now, as he sipped on his breakfast tea, she watched
m until he set down his cup and looked at her.
Vhat?" he asked.

"I've eaten all that I can. I'm fueled and ready to per-
rm, hopefully on all cylinders," she told him. "But if
you have for me to use is those cuff links, then forget
For some reason, all I picked up when I handled
em were some vague faces of various people. One I
lieve actually made the gold links and another was
e jewelry store salesman. And you. I saw you tossing
e cuffs back and forth in your hands."

Luke's lips twitched as if he were about to smile. He
dn't. "The cuff links never belonged to Anthony Lin-
n. I purchased them new yesterday."

She stared at him in disbelief. "Why would you—?
amn you! You were testing me. Was that your idea or
re you instructed to—?"

"Testing you with the cuff links was entirely my own
ea."

"Why?"

"Because although I've seen you in action a few
nes, I find it difficult to believe in what you and Dr.
eng and her other protégés do."

Without giving any thought to what she was doing,
eredith shoved back her chair, stood, picked up a
ece of the soft fried bread on her plate and flung it at
ike. It hit him mid-chest, the grease staining his navy
ue polo shirt.

"What the hell," he grumbled.

"Don't you ever do something like that to me agaii
She planted her hands on her hips.

"Go get dressed," he told her. "I'll change my sh
and then I'll bring you something that actually l
longed to Anthony Linden."

"Are we going out somewhere today?" she asked.

"Probably not."

"Then I'm dressed for the day," she informed hi
"I'll go dry my hair and be right back."

Luke shrugged. "Suit yourself."

After slamming her bedroom door, Meredith debat
whether or not to change clothes. She had broug
along a pair of jeans, dress slacks, and several ni
blouses. But fifteen minutes later, with her hair dry a
pulled back in a loose ponytail, she stormed back in
the living room wearing the same sweat pants and T-shi

The table had been cleared, with only a fresh pot
tea now in the middle of a tray that held two clean cu
Luke sat on the sofa in his khaki slacks and a navy a
red striped button-down shirt, the short sleeves reve
ing his muscular arms.

"Sit down here beside me," he ordered her.

She sat, obeying without question, although relu
tantly and with great reservation. He glanced at t
round coffee table in front of the sofa. There beside
clear glass vase filled with white lilies lay a rectangul
shaped box.

"Open it," Luke said.

She did. Inside, she found a handgun.

"What's this?" she asked.

"It's a SIG Sauer—"

"No, I don't care what make and model the weap
is," she told him. "I hate firearms of any kind. If this
another one of your tests—"

"It's not a test. That pistol is supposed to have l

longed to Anthony Linden and has never been owned
or used by anyone else."

When she simply stared at the gun for several minutes, Luke apparently grew aggravated with her. He removed the pistol from the box and held it out to her. "It
isn't loaded."

"I should hope not." She opened her palm and held
out her hand.

The very instant he placed the gun in her hand and
the cold metal touched her skin, she cried out.

"What's wrong?"

She heard Luke's question, but despite the fact that
he was sitting right beside her, he sounded as if he were
in another room. As people's faces flashed through her
mind like images from a television screen, moving at
top speed, she sensed that all those people were dead.
Three men, two women, and a child. When she closed
her eyes, she saw only black emptiness and felt an odd
rush of adrenaline soar through her body. And then the
rapid fire of a pistol echoed inside her head.

"Oh God," she whimpered. "He killed them. All of
them."

"You're getting something about Linden. What is it?"

"He's killed so many people with this gun. I saw
them, six of them. One was just a boy."

"We already know he's a killer, that he's a professional hit man. I need for you to move on from that and
try to tell me something we don't know. Try to focus on
finding the son of a bitch, not taking a gruesome walk
down memory lane."

"Don't . . . please . . ." *Leave me alone. You don't understand. I have very little control over what I see and what I
feel.*

She wrapped her fingers over the butt of the gun
and clutched it tightly.

"He has a good job and he likes it. He likes it a lot," Meredith said. "The money he earns affords him a lifestyle he enjoys. He tells himself that he kills for the money, but . . . he kills for the pleasure, too."

Although she felt Luke's hands on her shoulders, felt the non-too-gentle shake he gave her, only her body was in the room with him. She tried harder to concentrate on the man who had owned the gun, on his present location. Where was he right now?

The face that appeared to her kept changing. Dark hair, light hair, red hair, bald. Blue eyes, brown eyes, hazel eyes. Mustache, beard, clean shaven, sideburns. Glasses. No glasses. The image of his features wasn't clear. It kept changing too quickly for her to describe him.

"He wears disguises."

"Meredith, concentrate completely on where he is right now, this very minute," Luke told her as he ran his hands down her arms and then released her. "Any other information is useless to us."

Concentrate. Concentrate.

I'm trying. I'm trying.

Suddenly she felt weightless. She floated above the earth as if she had wings. Clouds surrounded her, white and fluffy. She loved the sensation of flying and had had visions, for as long as she could remember, of leaving her body and soaring into the heavens.

And then all of her feelings of joy disappeared and a dark, foreboding fear claimed her. The hum of an engine grew louder and louder, and louder still, until it drowned out every other sound, every thought, every feeling.

She gasped for air, trying to escape from the onslaught of the roaring engine, and fought her way back

o rejoin her mind with her body. Her head ached. Her
stomach lurched with nausea.

As she slowly opened her eyes, the gun she had been
clutching dropped from her weak hand and hit the
floor. "He's on an airplane."

"Right now?" Luke asked. "Is he on an airplane right
now?"

She stared at Luke. "Either now or very recently.
He's coming toward me."

"What do you mean by that?"

"He's coming toward me," she repeated half a second before she collapsed in a heap at Luke's feet.

When Maleah and Derek had arrived at Griffin's
Rest late yesterday, they had found a high level of anxi-
ty that spread from the very top and filtered its way
down through every employee. If they thought security
had been tight when they left there the last time, they
found out as they drove through the security gates just
how much tighter it could be. Barbara Jean had met
them at the front door, and Maleah had noticed Bren-
nan Richter hovering in the background.

"My God, you'd think we were being invaded,"
Maleah had said as she entered the foyer. "Is all of this
because of Saxon Chappelle's niece?"

"Partly," Barbara Jean had replied as she'd glanced
from Maleah to Derek. "Sanders is waiting for you in
the office. He needs to speak to you now." She had
looked up at Maleah. "Nicole wants to talk to you.
She's upstairs in her sitting room."

After that, Maleah hadn't seen Derek again last
night. How long he spent in the auxiliary Powell office
headquarters there at Griffin's Rest, she didn't know.

Nor did she have any idea where he'd slept or if he had slept. She had spent more than two hours with Nic after being allowed entrance into Nic's bedroom suite by her private guard dog, Shaughnessy Hood. One look at her best friend and she had realized just how bad things were with her and Griff. Nic had looked like death warmed over.

"If you think I look bad, you should see Griff," Nic had said. "He was in rough shape before Poppy Chapelle was killed, but now . . . Oh, Maleah, I'm worried sick about him. I haven't seen him all day. He hasn't ventured out of his den and my guess is that by now he's drunk himself into a stupor and passed out."

Unlike the other Powell agents who were assigned a bedroom in the house when they rotated shifts at Griffin's Rest, Maleah had her own room, a perk of being Nic's best friend. Since she spent almost as much time here as she did in her Knoxville apartment, she kept several changes of clothes in the closet and an assortment of toiletries in her private bathroom.

When she had finally gotten in bed well past midnight, she had tossed and turned for nearly an hour before dozing off to sleep. And she had awakened at a little after six, feeling a bit groggy and sleep-deprived. Her first thought had been about Derek. She had wondered if he was awake and if he was, had he already gone downstairs for breakfast. Odd that she should have had such an overwhelming desire to see him, talk to him, be with him.

Now less than an hour later, freshly showered, dressed for the day in tan twill slacks and a black, short-sleeved cotton sweater set, she found herself taking more time than usual to apply her makeup and fix her hair.

This is ridiculous. You're primping like a teenager getting ready for the prom.

She stared at herself in the vanity mirror, her long hair framing her face as it fell in layers down to her shoulders. She had even taken great pains to use a curling iron to style her hair.

All because you want Derek Lawrence to find you attractive. And don't you dare try to deny it.

She couldn't deny it. Not to herself and not to the reflection staring back at her from the mirror. "All right, so what's the big deal? Why shouldn't I want to look my best this morning?"

While in the midst of having an in-depth conversation with herself, Maleah heard a repetitive rapping at her bedroom door. It might be Nic, even though she hoped her friend was in bed with her husband, the two of them getting some much needed rest. But more than likely Griff was still in his study and Nic had lain awake half the night worrying herself sick about him.

When she opened the door, she halfway expected to see either Nic or Barbara Jean, but instead Derek stood there, a dead serious expression on his handsome face.

"Good morning," she said.

"How are you today?" he asked.

"I'm fine, all things considered. How about you?"

"I've been better," he admitted. "May I come in?"

"Sure." She moved back so that he could enter, and then she closed the door before asking, "What's wrong?"

"I was up until after one this morning," Derek said. "Helping Sanders with Griff. He . . . uh . . . he drank a little too much. We managed to walk him into the bathroom connected to his study, put him in the shower and finally got him into a clean pair of jeans and a T-shirt.

Sanders sent me on to bed around one-fifteen. I think
he sat up all night while Griff slept it off on the sofa."

"I was with Nic until well after midnight. She wasn't
drinking, but she wasn't in much better shape. She's
worried about Griff and she figured he was drinking."
She stared at Derek. "Tell me why a man who professes
to worship the ground his wife walks on shuts her out
the way Griff does Nic when he needs her the most. The
way he's acting is killing her."

"I've told you that big strong men don't like to appear weak in front of their women. No matter how mis-
guided his actions, Griff's intention is to protect Nic.
He didn't want her to see him the way he was last
night."

"Men! I don't understand any of you."

"That works both ways, Blondie. We men don't understand you women either." He looked her over and
smiled. "You sure do look pretty this morning."

She felt the warmth of a blush creep up her neck.
Turning away from him, she picked up a pair of small
pearl studs off her dresser. "Thank you for the compliment." She slipped one stud and then the other through
the holes in her ears before turning back around to
face Derek. "Have you been downstairs yet?"

"I went down for a cup of coffee about fifteen minutes ago. Sanders and Barbara Jean are in the kitchen
preparing pancakes and sausage. I spoke to Griff briefly
before he came upstairs to see Nic."

"Then they're together now?"

Derek nodded. "Griff has a meeting planned for ten
this morning in his office here at the house."

"Who's being invited to this meeting?"

"Only the people Griff and Nic trust with their
lives—Sanders, Barbara Jean, you, me, and Yvette."

She hadn't realized that her expression had altered in any way at the mention of Dr. Yvette Meng, not until Derek said, "Making a face like that is a dead giveaway, you know. It implies that you don't like Dr. Meng."

"It's not that I dislike Yvette. I don't. She seems like a very nice lady, but . . ."

"But what?"

"Her presence here at Griffin's Rest creates problems for Nic, for her marriage."

"It shouldn't," Derek said. "Yvette Meng isn't a threat to Nic's marriage. If ever a man was completely in love with his wife and totally dedicated to his marriage, that man is Griffin Powell."

"Is that your professional opinion?"

"That's my gut instinct. If there was anything more than friendship between Griff and Yvette, it's in the past, and Nic needs to believe that."

"So you do think there was something more than—?"

"Whoa there, Blondie. Don't put words in my mouth. I said *if* there was."

Maleah felt the need to defend Nic. "I think Nic has every right to feel the way she does. How would you like it if the woman you loved moved a dear old friend, who just happened to be male, into your home? And you knew with absolute certainty that she loved this man?"

"There's love and then there's love," Derek said. "I'm surprised that a woman such as Nicole Powell would be so insecure."

"Loving someone the way she loves Griff can make a woman vulnerable, even someone like Nic."

"Yeah, love can make us all vulnerable," Derek agreed. "And to answer your question—no, I wouldn't like it if the woman I loved brought an old friend whom she loved into our lives on a daily basis, had him practically

living at our back door, especially if I thought they had
once been lovers. But I'd deal with it somehow, if the
only alternative was giving up the woman I loved."

"That's what Nic is doing, what she's been doing ever
since Griff built the sanctuary for Yvette and her protégés here at Griffin's Rest."

"You disagree, don't you?" Derek asked. "What
would you do? How would you handle the situation differently?"

Maleah hesitated, uncertain just how honest she
should be with him. *To hell with it.* "If I were in Nic's
shoes, I'd tell Griff to choose. He could either have
Yvette living within a stone's throw of us, a constant
presence in our lives, or he could have me. If he didn't
move her out, then I'd leave."

"Why do you think Nic hasn't done that?"

"I think the answer to that would be obvious."

"Enlighten me."

"No." She had already said too much about her best
friend's personal life. Her only excuse was that it had
become so easy to talk to Derek.

"Nic's afraid that if she demands he make a choice
between Yvette and her, he might choose Yvette," Derek
said. "That's the reason."

Maleah didn't confirm his assessment of the situation, but she wasn't the least bit surprised that he had
zeroed in on the exact reason.

"I'm hungry," she said, deliberately changing the
subject. "Let's eat breakfast. I love Barbara Jean's pancakes."

Derek nodded, and then opened the door and offered her his arm. "Shall we?"

She slipped her arm through his. "Derek?"

"Hmm . . . ?"

"I don't think I ever thanked you properly."

"For what?"

"For looking out for me after that last interview with Browning." It had been on the tip of her tongue to say, thank you for taking such good care of me. For holding me, comforting me, letting me draw strength from you.

"Hey, no problem, Blondie. That's what partners do, right?"

"Yeah, right."

Why was it that she wished he'd said he had done it because he cared about her and not just because they were partners?

The phone rang at precisely at 7:30 A.M. that morning.

"Well, hello there. What a nice surprise to hear from you. How are y'all doing? How's—?"

"Listen very carefully," he said. "You are going to receive a phone call later today with instructions on what you have to do, and if you don't do exactly as he tells you to do, she's going to die."

"What are you talking about? Who's going to call me? Who's going to die?"

The caller explained about the kidnapping, that the person they both loved had been kidnapped, taken from her bed in the middle of the night, and a note had been left on her pillow. Someone had managed to break in through an upstairs bathroom window, go into her bedroom and abduct her without anyone being the wiser.

Whoever had taken her was not an amateur. He had to be a professional.

Had the Copycat Carver taken her? If so, why had he changed his MO? Why had he kidnapped her instead of killing her? It didn't make any sense.

"You understand, don't you?" the caller asked. "If you don't do what he tells you to do, we'll never see her alive again. Please, please tell me that you'll do whatever he asks you to do."

"Yes, of course I will."

"Swear to me."

"I swear."

The reality of the situation was difficult to grasp. This was a nightmare of monumental proportions. Life or death. But no matter what the instructions or how difficult the assignment, the orders would be carried out. There was only one choice—to do whatever was necessary to save her life.

Chapter 31

The private jet had landed safely at Heathrow. He and his employer's guest, both equipped with false IDs, including passports, zipped through customs without a problem. When she had awakened en route, frightened and confused, he had explained in simple terms what had happened, what was going on, and what he expected her to do. And quite amazingly, she had not screamed or cried. Undoubtedly, she was suffering from a mild form of shock, which actually worked in his favor.

As a general rule, he didn't hire out as a kidnapper. Too many things could go wrong. Murder for hire, on the other hand, was his forte. A quick, clean and simple kill. If the money had not proven to be irresistible, he would never have taken on the current assignment.

Until they had cleared customs, he didn't draw an easy breath. Anything might have happened. But he had warned her that he would kill her if she did not cooperate. He had learned long ago that fear was a great inducement in gaining obedience, especially from females.

After picking up a hired car, he placed her in the

backseat, forced a couple of sleeping pills down her throat and told her to lie down and keep quiet. She had choked on the pills and had coughed and cried. When he had wiped the tears from her cheeks, she had gazed at him with fear and wonder.

"Be a good girl and you'll come out of this alive. Understand?"

She had nodded, but said nothing.

Using the GPS system provided with the rental vehicle, he had no trouble navigating through the city and after less than an hour, he drove through the thousand-year-old town of Harpenden, located in Hertfordshire. Tourists as well as London residents no doubt flocked here because of the town's traditional English village atmosphere.

A few miles out of town, they arrived at their destination, a secluded house surrounded by trees and isolated from any prying neighbors. He parked the rental behind the house, opened the back door and lifted her into his arms. She would probably sleep for several more hours, possibly the rest of the day.

As he had been told, he found the back door unlocked and the key lying on the kitchen table. He carried her through the kitchen and down a narrow hall until he located a small bedroom with only one window. After laying her on the double bed, he covered her with a quilt. He checked the window and found that it was sealed shut with countless layers of paint that had been applied over the years. Leaving the door open behind him, he returned to the kitchen, pulled out a chair from the table and sat. Checking his mobile phone, he found there was decent coverage here in the country. He dialed the number that he had memorized and waited for his employer to answer.

"You've arrived safely with my guest?"

"We're at the house. I didn't encounter any prob-
ems."

"How is my guest?"

"Right now, she's sleeping."

"Then now is the perfect time for you to make an-
ther phone call. Memorize the instructions I will give
ou and repeat them word for word."

"Very well."

He listened as his employer told him in quite suc-
inct terms about his plan and the message he was to
elay, word for word.

"Now, repeat it back to me."

He did as he had been instructed.

"Yes, you have it precisely. As soon as we end our con-
ersation, make the phone call. Be sure it is understood
hat you will call again for an update and to give further
nstructions."

"I understand and I'll stress the importance of fol-
owing your instructions to the letter."

"Yes, yes. And in the meanwhile, take good care of
y guest. She's very important, at least for the time
eing."

"Yes, sir."

His employer never bothered with pleasantries nor
id he. Their association was strictly business.

He would enjoy a cup of tea, but first things first. He
alked down the hall, checked to make sure she was
ill sleeping soundly and then returned to the kitchen.
tanding by the windows overlooking the private gar-
en in back, he dialed another memorized number.

"Hello." Such a nervous, frightened voice.

"Listen very carefully," he said. "I will not repeat
nese instructions. You are to do exactly as I tell you. If
ou do not—"

"Don't hurt her. Please. I will do whatever you war me to do."

"Good. If you cooperate fully, then she has a goo chance of coming through this unharmed."

Luke Sentell had spent the day waiting for Meredit Sinclair to recover from whatever kind of spell she' had that morning. He didn't pretend to understan what made the woman tick, any more than he could be lieve without question the validity of her psychic abil ties. If he couldn't see it, smell it, hear it, taste it, or fee it, it didn't exist. Not in his world. Not for any norma logical human being. And yet he had seen Meredit work her hoodoo on several occasions and without fai her visions—or whatever the hell you wanted to ca them—had proven to be accurate.

He sorely wished that his path had never crosse with Meredith's, that Griffin Powell had not chosen hi to accompany them on his initial European manhur when rumors about Malcolm York had first begun ci culating. His boss had brought Meredith along, usin her as his bloodhound, hoping she could sniff out wh had started the rumors. Griff had assigned him Meredith's personal bodyguard. The job had quick become a combination of babysitter and nursemai Whenever Meredith had come out of one of her trance she would sleep for hours, as if whatever she had e perienced had zapped every ounce of her energy.

A really crazy thing had happened on that first par nership with Meredith, and every subsequent time th had been together. For some unknown reason, whe ever he was around, his presence seemed to fine tur her sixth sense. He had no idea why. Considering h was a skeptic, you'd think having him around would have an adverse effect. Instead the opposite was true. He had to accept the truth—it was what it was. And that's why he was here with her now, the two of them stuck with each other on another manhunt.

That morning, after she had fainted and fallen in a heap at his feet, he had lifted her and put her on the sofa. Trying to wake her had been pointless. He knew from past experience that the best thing to do was simply let her rest until she came out of it on her own. She had slept for hours and when she awoke, she had gone to her room after telling him that she needed to be alone for a while.

Here it was after three in the afternoon and she was just now emerging from her bedroom and gracing him with her presence. When he glanced up at her from the copy of the *Daily Telegraph* he'd been reading, he was surprised to see her looking so well. Her eyes were bright and clear, her cheeks had color, and her voice was quite strong when she said, "I'm ready now."

"Do you want something to eat?" He folded the newspaper and laid it on the coffee table. "It's nearly three-thirty and you skipped lunch."

"No, I'm fine, thank you. I just want to try again. I've spent time concentrating on what I saw and felt this morning, trying to make sense of it all."

"And did you?"

"Only partly," she admitted. "When I told you he was coming toward me, I wasn't sure what I meant, but now I know. This man who calls himself Anthony Linden was in flight, coming here."

"Here as in London or here as in this hotel?"

"Here as in London."

"Are you sure?"

"As sure as I can be," she told him. "I'm never a hu
dred percent sure of what I see and feel. All I can do
let it happen and afterward try to figure it out."

"So, you're guessing about Linden being in Lo
don."

"I suppose you could call it guessing."

"What would you call it?"

"Sensing."

"Humph."

"I'm well aware of the fact that you consider me
freak of nature, Mr. Sentell. And you think I'm mental
disturbed, that anyone who claims to be gifted is act
ally crazy."

"There you go again, putting words in my mouth."

She glared at him, her hazel green eyes sparkli
with anger. "We're wasting time with this conversatio
I'm ready to go to work. Where's the gun?"

Where's the gun? The first thought that went throug
his mind was that she wanted to shoot him. He bare
managed not to smile.

"The gun isn't going to help you," Luke told h
"You've been there, done that. You probably got ever
thing from handling the gun that you could. Right?"

"Possibly, but I need something to connect me to A
thony Linden if I'm going to find him."

"Then let's go where you think he's been. If he fl
into London, the odds are that he came through Heat
row." Luke glanced at her wrinkled sweats and T-shi
"Change clothes. We're going out."

"We're going to the airport?" she asked.

"Yep."

"That's a great idea."

"Yeah, I thought so."

*   *   *

When Maleah and Derek arrived together at Griff's office, a first-rate, state-of-the art complex housed within his home at Griffin's Rest, they passed by several agents who flanked the open door to the auxiliary headquarters for the Powell Agency. Brendan Richter nodded and spoke to them. He had been assigned to keep tabs on Barbara Jean and act as backup for Sanders. Shaughnessy Hood, a giant of a man and the only agent physically larger than Griffin Powell himself, threw up a hand as they walked past him. Griff had given him the task of guarding Nic twenty-four / seven. On the opposite side of the door, Cully Redmond watched them approach.

"Morning," Cully said.

"When were you called in off patrol?" Derek asked.

"About an hour ago," the big, robust redhead replied. "Sanders assigned me temporarily to Dr. Meng because Michelle came down with a stomach virus this morning."

"How's Michelle doing?" Maleah asked.

"I haven't seen her, but Sanders said it's probably just a twenty-four-hour bug and she'll be right as rain by tomorrow."

"That's good."

Derek cupped Maleah's elbow and escorted her into the office. Apparently they were the last to arrive. As soon as they entered, Sanders closed the door and took his usual place, standing directly behind Griff. Derek had decided quite some time ago that Griff and Sanders were closer than brothers, the bond between them stronger than any blood tie could ever be.

Seated at the head of the table, Griff presided over the small group. Not for the first time, Derek was struck by Griffin Powell's commanding presence. More than the fact that he was a large, tall man was the air of con-

fidence and the demeanor of authority that radiate
from him.

Having been fascinated by human nature all his lif
and with a natural aptitude for the subject, he found hin
self more often than not making mental mini-profile
of others, in both social and professional settings. Th
ability came to him so naturally that he often didn't r
alize what he was doing until his mind had alread
formed an opinion.

Nic sat on Griff's right. Usually, she sat at the oth
end of the conference table. Her having moved close
to her husband could mean nothing more than th
meeting would be comprised of a small group. Bu
Derek surmised that not only did Nic need to be nea
Griff, but that she wanted to send a strong message t
everyone in the room that she was Mrs. Griffin Powel
always at her husband's side.

BJ sat in her wheelchair on Nic's left. Barbara Jea
Hughes possessed an ageless beauty, which meant sł
would still be attractive at eighty. And despite her beir
a paraplegic, she exuded a *joie de vivre* he admired an
envied.

The exotically beautiful Dr. Meng, her head bowe
and her hands folded together in her lap, sat beside B
He sensed a deep sadness in Yvette. She wore th
melancholy like a thin shawl about her shoulders, an a
cessory to her soul, not the soul itself.

Maleah rushed ahead of him, went straight to Ni
and gave her friend's arm a reassuring squeeze befoı
sitting beside her.

Maleah Perdue was a special lady.

Blondie.

His Blondie.

Without realizing what was happening, Maleah ha
as the old saying goes, gotten under his skin. Although

ısn't something he wanted, he actually found the fact
at he cared about Maleah rather amusing.

Care about her?

It's more than just caring.

Admit it, Lawrence, you're in love with her.

He watched her hovering over Nic and sensed her
ısperate need to console her friend. Maleah might be
control freak, but God help her, she was a caretaker,
e two traits often related. Sister traits. And even if she
dn't know it—which he suspected she didn't—
aleah had the capacity to love deeply. He had seen
at manifested in her feelings for her brother Jackson,
s wife Cathy, and their son Seth, as well as in her love
r her best friend, Nic.

Would she, considering her deplorable childhood,
er trust any man enough to love him with that same
pth of emotion and loyalty?

Any man?

*Damn it, Lawrence, that's enough introspection for one
y. You've admitted that you're in love with Maleah. You
n't need to figure out anything else right now. Things like
ıether or not she loves you and if she does, do the two of
u have a future together. Considering you both have an
ersion to commitment, marriage is probably out of the
estion.*

So what's wrong with an affair?

Determined to refocus on business, Derek surveyed
e room's occupants again, quickly scanning everyone
fore he took the seat beside Maleah, which put him
rectly across from Yvette Meng.

Yvette lifted her head, a fragile smile on her full, red
ıs, and looked at him with large, luminous brown
es.

"How are you this morning?" he asked, simply being
ılite.

"I am well, Mr. Lawrence. And you?"

"Just fine, ma'am."

When Maleah pivoted around in her chair a[nd] glanced from Derek to Yvette, Yvette lowered her he[ad] again, as if sensing Maleah's disapproval.

No doubt Yvette Meng had endured men's lust a[nd] women's envy all of her life. Men saw her as a sex o[b]ject; women saw her as a rival. And yet if you look[ed] closely, you would realize that Yvette was heartbrea[k]ingly alone, separate and apart from all others, and [by] her own choice.

Obviously Griff hadn't called the meeting to ord[er] yet. He seemed preoccupied, his gaze unfocused as [if] he was deep in thought. Ever the stoic solider, Sande[rs] stood with his arms crossed over his chest. On the d[e]fensive. Always guarding Griff as if it was his sole pu[r]pose in life.

Knowing what little he did about the years Griffin ha[d] spent in captivity on the island of Amara with Sande[rs] and Yvette, Derek understood the bond comrades-i[n] arms shared. But the depth of their relationship we[nt] beyond the norm. Derek could only imagine und[er] what circumstances their three souls had joined.

Griff lifted his head, cleared his throat and looke[d] from one person to another, beginning and endi[ng] with Nic.

"We asked a great deal of Maleah," Griff said. "S[he] interviewed Jerome Browning, the original Carver." [He] looked directly at Maleah. "Nic told me about the info[r]mation you shared with her last night. Thank you f[or] what you did."

Maleah simply nodded.

Derek reached out and took her hand in his. S[he] gripped his hand tightly, but kept her gaze focused [on] Griff.

"I realize that we can't automatically take Browning's ord for anything," Griff said. "But I believe he was :lling the truth when he told Maleah that the Copycat arver is a professional assassin, just as we suspected. erek had come to this same conclusion while working p a profile of the killer."

All eyes on Griff, everyone remained silent, waiting or him to continue. Derek understood now why only ie ones present in the room had been included in this rivate meeting. Griff intended to keep the circle of itimate knowledge as small as possible. Across the At- .ntic, Luke Sentell and Meredith Sinclair were search- ig for the truth—and the whereabouts of two men who ere presumed dead. Maleah had confronted the copy- at killer's mentor and paid a high emotional price for iformation that confirmed the worst case scenario. he had every right to be here. Derek had been in- luded today because of his status as a profiler. Nic was ere because she was Griff's wife.

And then there were three.

The Amara Triad, as Nicole Powell referred to her usband, Sanders, and Yvette.

"Jerome Browning informed Maleah that the copy- at killer had bragged about his billionaire employer," riff said. "He did not mention the man by name, but e did tell Browning that the billionaire owned a Pacific land and enjoyed the perks of his profession—human afficking."

"It is not possible," Yvette said, a slight tremor in her oft voice. "He lied. Either the copycat lied to Browning r Browning lied to Maleah."

"I don't believe Browning lied," Griff said. "I believe iat the man the copycat killer works for is passing him- :lf off as Malcolm York."

"But who is he and why is he pretending to be York?"

Yvette asked. "And why would he want to avenge the real Malcolm York's murder?"

"That's what we have to find out," Griff told her. "The first step is to locate Linden, if he is the copycat and stop him before he kills again. Once he's eliminated, we'll have a brief window of opportunity to find this pseudo-York before he hires another assassin."

"Do you think he plans to continue killing people associated with the Powell Agency?" Maleah asked.

"I do," Griff replied. "I am his ultimate target . . ." Griff paused, glanced over his shoulder at Sanders and then at Yvette. "My guess is he wants to draw out the three of us. What his reasons are, I don't know. What his connection might have been to Malcolm York, I don't know. And why he's striking out now, after sixteen years, is a complete mystery."

"It would seem that we are at his mercy," Yvette said. "But I refuse to believe that we cannot stop him."

"We will stop him," Nic said, her gaze colliding with Yvette's.

Griff reached out and grabbed Nic's hand, bringing her attention away from Yvette and to him. "Less than half an hour ago, Luke Sentell contacted me with news, interesting news, if true. Meredith believes Anthony Linden is now in London."

"If Meredith senses Linden's presence, then you can be sure that he is there," Yvette said.

"Why would Linden, if he's the copycat killer, go to London?" Maleah asked. "Is it possible that he's chosen Luke or Meredith as his next victim?"

"I think that's highly unlikely," Griff replied. "Certainly not Meredith since they were en route to London less than a day apart. And I can't imagine anyone being able to find Luke Sentell unless he wanted to be found."

"Then why would the copycat go to London?" Derek
.ed. "Unless his employer recalled him."

"That would be my guess," Griff said. "The only prob-
m is that we have no idea why he would have recalled
n. If this fake York intends to continue killing people
nnected to the agency, why rein in his pit bull?"

When Luke had carried an obviously unconscious
:redith through the hotel lobby and to the elevator,
ople had stared at him as if he were a murderer.

"I'm afraid my wife can't hold her liquor," he had ex-
ained, smiling like an idiot.

They had spent half an hour at Heathrow before
:redith passed out from sheer exhaustion. She would
obably sleep soundly the rest of the evening.

He laid her across the foot of the bed and removed
r shoes. Then he turned down the covers and placed
: fully clothed Meredith beneath the sheet and light-
ight blanket. She looked about fifteen lying there, her
e void of makeup, her hair fiery red against the white
lowcase. He lifted her head enough to maneuver his
lex finger beneath the tight band holding her pony-
l in place, and with one quick snap freed her thick
ine of wild curls.

"Sleep tight, Orphan Annie," he said as he paused in
: doorway.

He closed her bedroom door and returned to the liv-
g room. After sitting down and pulling his thoughts
gether, he called Griffin Powell.

"Luke?"

"Yes. Are you free to talk?"

"I'm alone at the moment. Nic and I have been in a
:eting with Maleah and Derek. Sanders and Yvette,

too, of course, and Barbara Jean. I've filled them
about the possibility that Linden is in London."

"Linden's not in London."

"But I thought Meredith was sure he was there."

"She was and he was," Luke said. "I took her
Heathrow this afternoon and she picked up his scent
most immediately. She says he was there at the airpo
sometime recently, perhaps only hours before we a
rived, and he wasn't alone. But she doesn't know wh
was with him, only that his companion was female."

"If Linden is not in London any longer, then whe
is he?"

"Good question."

"Didn't Meredith pick up on anything else, get a
sense of which direction—?"

"Of course she did," Luke said. "North of Londo
possibly northwest."

"She couldn't be more specific?"

"She was trying . . . before she passed out."

"Is she all right?"

"Yeah, I think she's fine. You know what happens
her after she has one of her visions. She's sleeping n
and I expect she might sleep through the night."

"Do you think she can find Linden?" Griff asked.

"Maybe. Of course my brain is telling me no way
hell."

"Your gut, Sentell, what's your gut telling you?"

"That there is a fifty/fifty chance she'll lead r
straight to Linden."

Silence. Long and drawn out, only the sound
Griff's deep breathing.

"I'll take those odds," Griff said. "And Luke, wh
you find Linden, you know what to do."

"If he is the professional you believe him to be

won't be able to make him talk. He'll die before he'll break."

"No, he won't talk. He will never reveal any information about his employer."

"Then what you want is for me to simply eliminate him."

"Yes, when you find the bastard, kill him."

Chapter 32

After Griff ended the morning meeting, which ha[d] lasted about forty-five minutes, Maleah had taken [a] walk around the property, something she often did t[o] clear her head. Derek had insisted on going with he[r] and after Griff told her that no one left the hous[e] alone, she reluctantly agreed to let Derek tag alon[g]. Much to her surprise, he had not insisted on conversa[-] tion, which was the last thing she had wanted [or] needed. What she had needed was time alone, but ap[-] parently unless she secluded herself in her room, tha[t] wasn't an option anytime in the near future. And bein[g] a girl who loved the outdoors, the thought of spendin[g] the rest of the day cooped up inside would have mad[e] her agree to having Genghis Khan as her companion.

Her life had suddenly, in the past couple of week[s,] become extremely complicated. For most of her adu[lt] life, she had been able to enjoy a certain amount [of] peace and privacy in her personal life, which counte[r] balanced her exciting and often dangerous job as [a] Powell agent. But both her personal life and profe[s-] sional life were at risk. Until the Copycat Carver w[as]

:aught, no Powell agent or family member was com-
oletely safe. It wasn't enough that she had to worry
about her own life, but she lived in fear for her family.
Then to make the situation worse, teaming up with
Derek again had created an unexpected problem, one
she wasn't sure how to handle. Somehow, someway, the
impossible had happened.

She had fallen in love with Derek Lawrence.

Derek Lawrence, the rich, spoiled, pampered, wom-
anizing playboy she had disliked from the moment they
met.

But that was just it—the real Derek was a different
man entirely. Oh, he was rich, a millionaire many times
over, and he did have a reputation with the ladies that
he couldn't deny. But he was not spoiled or pampered
and his playboy image had been greatly exaggerated,
probably by Derek himself.

He had allowed her to see a side of him that she suspected not many even knew existed. Few people would
believe that the debonair, sophisticated Southern
charmer's youthful past included a nefarious secret.

By the end of her long walk—with Derek—she had
come to the conclusion that she could handle only one
major problem at a time. She'd just have to put her feelings for Derek on the back burner. Being in love was a
foreign concept to her. She had spent her entire life trying to avoid repeating the mistake she had made with
Noah—becoming involved in a committed relationship
that could lead to marriage.

After lunch, which she and Derek had shared with
Nic, Griff, Sanders, and Barbara Jean, she had returned
to the Powell Agency office there at Griffin's Rest. With
the bulk of the agency's employees working day and
night on the Copycat Carver case and with reports
pouring in from various legal and illegal contacts the

world over, the staff at their Knoxville headquarters was
suffering from information overload. Add to that the
fact that only a handful of agents were privy to the most
sensitive information and that meant piles of reports
were waiting to be read, studied, and digested. Every
one except Barbara Jean had worked all afternoon and
until well past seven. They had taken a long overdue
break only when Barbara Jean had summoned all of
them to the dining room for dinner. The group had
eaten in relative silence, their conversation limited to
their compliments to the chef, Barbara Jean, on the delicious meal. She had smiled, said thank you, and had
been gracious enough not to point out that no one had
eaten very much. Afterward, Sanders had helped with
cleanup and then he and Barbara Jean had bid everyone goodnight shortly after nine o'clock. Nic finally
persuaded Griff to call it a night around 10:00 P.M., and
Maleah had sensed from the way they'd been looking at
each other, they wouldn't be going to sleep anytime
soon.

Alone in the living room with Derek, she shifted the
file folders in her lap into a neat pile and laid them
aside on the sofa cushion beside her. She glanced at
Derek, who seemed absorbed in a crossword puzzle he
had ripped out of today's copy of the *Knoxville News
Sentinel.* As if he had sensed her staring at him, he
glanced up from the newspaper and smiled at her.

"Alone at last," he said jokingly.

"So it would seem." She returned his smile.

"I could fix us a drink," he suggested. "Or we could
raid the kitchen for another piece of BJ's pecan pie."

"I shouldn't have eaten the first piece." Maleah patted her hips. "I think they're an inch wider already."

Derek rose to his feet, dropped the folded newspaper
in the chair, and came straight toward her. Before she

ealized his intention, he leaned over her and placed
is open palms on either side of her hips.

"They're wider by a quarter of an inch at most," he
old her, barely managing not to laugh.

All the while faking a frown, she swatted at his hands
ntil he lifted them off the cushions and away from her
ips. He dropped down on the sofa beside her and
ested his head on the back cushion.

"You're tired, aren't you?" she said.

He glanced at her. "Yeah. You are, too. It's been a
ong day."

"We should probably go upstairs and try to get some
eep," Maleah said. "But I swear I'm so wired I can't
nagine being able to sleep right now."

"I know what you mean. It's been a pretty intense day,
arting with this morning's top secret meeting. Griff's
ound so tight, he's on the verge of snapping. His
rinking binge last night didn't solve anything for him
nd it sure didn't take the edge off."

"I'm worried about Nic. I've never seen her so
ared. I honestly think she's afraid she's going to lose
riff, that somehow their marriage is going to im-
ode."

"When a husband and wife keep secrets from each
her, it puts a major strain on their marriage."

"I agree," Maleah said. "And the not knowing causes
much damage, if not more, than sharing the secret
ould. In theory, of course. With what's happening
w, a killer targeting the Powell Agency, finding and
opping the killer has to take priority over everything
se in Nic and Griff's life."

Derek pivoted his head so that he faced her. "In your
e and mine, too."

She nodded. "Finding Anthony Linden has to be our
p priority."

"You know, I think I have Anthony Linden figure
out, at least as much as I can with the info I have and b
gauging his personality by other professional killers I'v
studied. They all have certain characteristics in com
mon. You'd be surprised at how much a hired assassi
has in common with a Special Forces soldier, althoug
society sees one as immoral and the other as a hero."

"Despite any similarities, there is a difference though
isn't there?"

"For some, yes," Derek said. "The fine line that sep
rates the two—villain and hero—is the reason he kill
That and the emotion or lack of emotion involve
Some men enjoy killing. Others hate it, even after it b
comes easy to kill."

"The way it did for you?"

"Yeah, the way it did for me." He reached out an
twined a tendril of her hair around his finger. "Did
ever tell you that I like blonds?"

"You like brunettes and redheads, too."

"You're right, I do, but I'm partial to one particula
blond."

She allowed him to pull her toward him by gent
tugging on her hair. When they were face to face, only
few inches separating them, she asked, "Is she anyone
know, this particular blond?"

"All you have to do is look in a mirror."

Her breath caught in her throat.

"Do you have any idea how much I want to kiss you
he asked.

"Yes." She knew because she wanted that kiss eve
bit as much as he did. Maybe more. After all, she was i
love with him, but she had no reason to believe that I
felt the same way. For Derek, this was probably a flirt
tion that he hoped would lead to sex.

Derek released her hair, leaned forward enough

that their mouths touched, and whispered against her lips, "I swear to God, I won't ever hurt you. I'd cut off my right arm first."

Excitement and anticipation ignited inside her and spread through her like a wildfire when he kissed her. Aggressive yet gentle, he took her mouth, but otherwise didn't touch her. She returned the kiss eagerly, wanting him and needing so much more.

The urge to touch him became overwhelming. She lifted her arms and draped them around his neck as she deepened the kiss. Taking his cue from her, Derek delved his tongue inside her mouth as he eased his hands beneath her and lifted her up and onto his lap. With their mouths fused together and their bodies straining for closer contact, she clung to him. He roamed his hands over her back and hips while she forked her fingers through the long, thick hair at the nape of his neck.

When they finally came up for air, both breathing hard, their gazes connecting, Derek smiled and then glanced at her throat and the expanse of flesh exposed by the V-shaped neckline of her blouse.

"We have on too many clothes for what I have in mind," he told her.

She nodded. "Your room or mine?"

He chuckled. "Whichever is the closest."

"Mine," she said.

He stood, taking her up with him, still holding her in his arms.

"We'll get there faster if you put me down and let me walk."

He eased her slowly to her feet, her body sliding along his, arousing them both even more. She grabbed his hand and yanked him along with her as she raced out of the living room, down the hall and up the stairs.

* * *

Shiloh Whitman often wondered why Dr. Meng had accepted her as a student and wondered if the others saw her as a wannabe psychic. After all, how valuable would she ever be as anything other than a sideshow amusement? She didn't possess the gift of clairvoyance or channeling or precognition or psychometry or telepathy. All she had was the ability to sense psychic energy and entities and to see the aura around a person.

When she was a child, her siblings and cousins had laughed at her when she told them they had different colored lights shining around them. And her parents had scolded her, telling her to stop lying or people would think she was crazy. She had always been a misfit, the one thing she did have in common with the others, especially with Meredith. A sympathetic friend in college had told her she should find someone to help her figure out what was wrong with her. And oddly enough less than a year later, Dr. Meng actually found her, quite by accident, in of all places a bookstore in New York City.

Looking back now, she realized that if Dr. Meng hadn't taken her back to London with her, she wouldn't have survived. She had been on the verge of suicide, her life meaningless.

Shiloh had never been happy and never expected to be. There was an emptiness inside her that couldn't be filled. But she lived a productive life by keeping busy, studying, practicing, and assisting Dr. Meng in any way possible.

Lately, she had begun to feel an inexplicable restlessness and deliberately stayed away from the other students, not wanting anyone to probe inside her mind.

Tonight the peculiar restlessness had grown worse, so much so that she felt as if she were on the verge of

climbing the walls in her room. Feeling trapped, smothered by the confinement, she knew she had to find a
way to go outside, to breathe the night air, to look up at
the stars, to escape from that overpowering sense of imprisonment.

But Dr. Meng had warned them not to go anywhere
outside the sanctuary alone, to go in pairs and always
with one of the guards.

If she slipped out the back way, who would see her?

*What if one of the others realizes you've gone outside
alone?*

That wouldn't happen. One of Dr. Meng's strictest
rules was that none of her students could use their gifts
to invade the privacy of another.

Hurriedly changing from her pajamas and house
slippers into a jogging suit and running shoes, Shiloh
prepared for her escape.

I can't kill her.
I won't do it.
But he's given you no choice.
You must take a life in order to save a life.
*Do what you must do. Do it quickly. She doesn't have to
suffer. Make it as painless as possible.*
*You mustn't let yourself hesitate at the last minute. Once
she sees your face, once she can identity you, you will have
no choice.*
*There she is. See her. She's all alone, as if she's waiting
for you.*

Slipping away had been much easier than Shiloh had
thought it would be. Perhaps because she had been
keeping to herself so much lately, no one really cared

where she was or what she was doing. And although the guards roamed the grounds day and night, she had been able to avoid them without a problem. And even the two agents staying at the sanctuary, Ms. Allen and Mr. Redmond, had no idea she wasn't sound asleep in her bed. After all, they assumed that all of Dr. Meng's protégés would request permission to leave and then be given an escort.

She promised herself that she wouldn't stay outside for very long, only long enough to clear her head and relieve the nagging restlessness keeping her on edge. Even with the bright moonlight, darkness filled the night, and only the security lights around the sanctuary kept the hovering black shadows at bay.

As she followed the clear path along the lake, one used by residents and guests alike for morning and evening jogs and leisurely walks, she paused occasionally to look out over the river. A feeling of calm began growing inside her and ever so gradually the restlessness that had forced her out into the night subsided, leaving her in peace.

She heard footsteps behind her. Had one of the guards seen her? Or had one of the others followed her?

Shiloh turned and stared into the darkness. "Hello. Is anyone there?"

Silence.

It must have been a nocturnal animal scurrying through the underbrush or perhaps it had been nothing more than the wind. She turned around, breathed in the fresh night air and looked at the moonlight dancing on the water.

Odd how bright the moonlight is. Shimmering. Intense. And very white.

Mesmerized by the unnatural radiance of light, she

moved closer to the water's edge. Fixated on the glow, she gasped as she realized what she saw was not moonlight, but the reflection of her own aura. Transcendent. Spiritual. Non-physical.

A white aura often signified a new undesignated energy in a person's aura. Or it was a harbinger of—

There it was again. The same noise she had heard earlier. Footsteps directly behind her.

She turned, sighed heavily, and said, "It's you. I thought I heard someone. Have you been following me?"

"Yes."

Even in the darkness, Shiloh saw the other person's aura, heavy swirls of gray and black smoke, dirty, muddy colors indicating dark thoughts and fear and negative energy. And in that moment, seconds before her life ended, Shiloh understood why her aura had been such an intensely bright white.

A glowing white aura was also a harbinger of death.

Chapter 33

Maleah and Derek barely made it to her room before tearing at each other's clothes. The moment Derek kicked the door shut behind them, his mouth and hands otherwise occupied, Maleah attacked the buttons on his shirt. When she ripped open his shirt, he slid his hands up under her blouse and paused to fondle her breasts through her bra.

"Lift your arms," he told her.

She did. He pulled her buttoned blouse over her head, yanking at the sleeves to free her arms. He threw the blouse on the floor. Repaying him in kind, she shoved his shirt off his shoulders and tossed it on the floor on top of her blouse.

Derek walked her backward toward her bed, all the while unbuttoning her slacks and lowering the zipper as she unbuckled his belt and unsnapped his jeans. When he toppled her over onto the bed, he rose up long enough to yank her slacks down her legs and then divest himself of his jeans.

She reached for him, wanting the feel of him against her, needing to touch him, kiss him, love him. He strad-

ed her, his long, hairy legs brushing her smooth legs
 he looked down at her, his gaze moving apprecia-
vely over her from face to thighs.

"If I tell you how absolutely gorgeous you are, will
ou slap me?" he asked, a playful grin curving the cor-
ers of his mouth.

"Not if you don't mind my telling you that you're
retty gorgeous yourself, Mr. Lawrence." She reached
 and caressed his chest, loving the feel of the curly
air covering the well-defined muscles.

"I don't mind at all. As a matter of fact, I insist you
ll me."

She laughed. "I'll bet you make all your women feed
our ego with flattery, don't you?"

Bracing on his elbows, he lowered himself until his
s reached hers. "As far as I'm concerned, there are
 other women, and there never have been. There's
ly you, Blondie, only you."

Emotion caught in her throat. Damn it, she should
ve known he would know the perfect thing to say.
fter all, he was a renowned charmer, wasn't he?

"How many women have believed that smooth line?"
e asked as she nuzzled his neck.

He kissed her ear.

She shivered.

"You're the first one I've used it on, honey. How do
ou like it?" He circled her ear with the tip of his
ngue, and then took her earlobe between his teeth
d nipped playfully.

"I like it just fine," she said. "And just for tonight, I'll
etend you mean it."

Gazing into her eyes, he reached under her to un-
ook her bra. With their gazes solidly melded, he eased
e bra down her shoulders, taking his time, letting the
ft material rake over her hard, sensitive nipples.

She gasped.

He smiled.

They didn't break eye contact until he laid the b
aside and looked down at her bare breasts.

"I meant what I said," he told her. "I mean it tonig
and I'll mean it tomorrow and—"

She placed her index finger over his lips, silencir
him. "No promises, no vows, no declarations."

"Is that what you want or is that what you think
want?"

"You have commitment issues, remember," she to
him.

"And you have control issues." He pressed his ere
tion against her. "But tonight we're going to share th
control. I'm going to show you that you can trust me
never make you do anything you don't want to do. Ar
you're going to willingly give yourself to me, no strin
attached, solely because you want me as much as I wa
you."

"I guess we both have something to prove, to ou
selves and to each other."

"I'm going to start right now by proving to you tha
want to make love to you more than I've ever want
anything in my entire life."

"I like the sound of that."

The moment his mouth covered her breast, her hi
bucked involuntarily, lifting her lower body ha
against his. He groaned deep and low as he slid l
hand inside her silky panties and cupped her moun
When he inched his fingers lower until he found h
clitoris, she rubbed his penis through the thin materi
of his briefs. He caressed her intimately, eliciting
throaty moan.

"I've got some condoms in my pants pocket," he to
her as he inserted two fingers inside her.

As her body gushed around his fingers, she writhed beneath him. "You came prepared? You must have been pretty sure of yourself. Or do you always carry around condoms in your pocket?"

"Blondie, I put those condoms in my pocket when I got up this morning because I knew that I couldn't go another day without staking my claim on you." He removed his fingers from inside her, slipped his hand out of her panties and hooked his thumbs beneath the elastic waistband. He kissed her and then lifted his head. "Before you open your pretty little mouth to protest, you should know that before tomorrow morning, I expect you will have laid claim to me, too, lock, stock and barrel."

"You can bet your life on it," she told him.

When he pulled her panties down and off, she cooperated fully. Once he removed his briefs, his penis sprung free. And then he grabbed his jeans off the floor and retrieved a condom from one of the pockets.

She expected him to take her then and there. A part of her wanted him now and she wouldn't have complained if he had rushed through the preliminaries.

But he didn't.

During the next hour, Derek loved her more thoroughly than she had ever been loved. He touched her all over, his mouth and hands familiarizing themselves with every inch of her body. He licked and sucked and caressed her breasts and teased her unmercifully until she ached with wanting. After bringing her to the brink again and again, only to draw back at the last minute each time and make her wait, he finally lifted her hips and thrust into her. Deep and hard.

She gasped for breath when he entered her, filling her completely.

They fucked in a frenzy of ravenous need and hot de-

sire. And when Maleah came, she felt as if she had ex
ploded into a thousand pieces.

Derek grunted and shivered as his orgasm hit.

She clung to him, kissing him, murmuring erotic
sweet nothings in his ear as he collapsed on top of her.

Derek woke her sometime between midnight and
dawn and they made slow, sweet love again. And then
she slept in his arms, her body wrapped around his
When he woke her again, the tender light of dawn
peeped through the plantation blinds on her bedroom
windows.

He slid his hand between her legs and parted her
thighs." Are you sore?" he asked.

"A little," she admitted.

He kissed her mouth, and then ran the tip of his
tongue between her breasts, over her belly and dipped
into her navel. "It had been a while for you, hadn't it?"

"Uh-huh. There haven't been that many men," she
told him honestly.

"God, Blondie, don't you dare tell me anything
about any of them." He reached out, jerked her up and
rolled her over on top of him. "The thought of another
man touching you makes me a little crazy."

She smiled. "I don't exactly like knowing you've had
sex with countless other women."

He laughed. "Hardly countless women." He stroked
his open palm over her buttocks. "Besides, they were
just rehearsals. You, Maleah Perdue, are the main act.

She spread her legs, straddled him, and took him in
sider her. Then she tossed back her head and shook her
hair. He grasped her hips.

She smiled down at him. "Just in case you don't a

ady know it, you, Derek Lawrence, are, as far as I'm
ncerned, the one and only main act."

This time around, she was in complete control, set-
g the pace, deciding how far to take him near the
ge before withdrawing and prolonging his agony
th the promise of ecstasy.

Finally, she put him out of his misery. She climaxed
st and half a second later, he grabbed her by the back
her head, tossed her over onto her back and jack-
mmered into her for a couple of heart-pounding
nutes before he came.

Later, damp with sexual perspiration and sleepy with
isfaction, they lay together spoon fashion, his arms
lding her securely against his body. He nuzzled her
r. She sighed with pleasure.

"I don't know if you want to hear this or if this is the
ht time to say it, but . . . I love you, Blondie."

She wrapped her arms around his arm that bound
r to him in a possessive gesture. "I love you, too . . . so
ry much."

"We need to—"

The thunderous pounding on her bedroom door
pped Derek mid-sentence.

"Maleah, wake up. Now," Barbara Jean called to her
ough the closed door. "Please, come downstairs as
ickly as possible. And if you know where Derek is, tell
n to do the same. Shiloh Whitman has been mur-
red."

Meredith had awakened Luke at 6:30 A.M.

"Get dressed immediately. We're leaving," she had
d him.

He had stared at her standing there in his bedroom

doorway as he roused from a deep, dreamless slee
"What's going on? Is something wrong?"

"Anthony Linden is definitely north of London.
keep seeing green fields. He's out in the country som
where. I'm pretty sure that wherever he is, he's not f
from here. And he isn't alone."

"He's probably still with the female companion yo
woo-woo senses picked up on at the airport last night

Meredith had frowned. "I couldn't sense anythi
about her last night, but this morning, I'm getting t
distinct impression that there isn't anything roman
between them."

"Romantic meaning sexual?"

She hadn't replied to his question, instead she h
said, "I'll call down and have them prepare somethi
for breakfast that we can take with us. In the meantim
get ready. I can't explain it, but I feel that we need
start our search immediately."

And that was exactly what they had done. They h
left in the midst of Thursday morning London traffic

Now, more than six hours later, Luke was beginni
to think of their trip as nothing more than a wild goo
chase. He realized that if Meredith could pinpoint e
actly where Linden was, she would do it. But as she ke
explaining, she had only limited control over her
sions. Knowing very little about psychically gifted pe
ple, Luke saw Meredith as a puzzle, one he needed
somehow figure out and then put together. Griff h
entrusted him with her care. Babysitting a woman th
Dr. Meng believed to have what she referred to as "e
ceptional abilities" wasn't easy for a guy like hi
Meredith needed someone patient and kind, someo
who accepted her psychic talents without questio
someone who didn't find himself occasionally wanti
to shake her until her teeth rattled.

Meredith was certain that Anthony Linden had
nded at Heathrow last night and had left London and
aveled north with a female companion.

Even if she was right about Linden, north of London
overed a lot of territory. He had contacted the head
an of Powell's London based headquarters, Thorn-
ike Mitchum, before they left the hotel, given him
Ieredith's info, and hoped like hell that it would help
Iitchum and his team of investigators.

Once out of London that morning, Luke and Mere-
ith had traveled sixteen miles due north to Waltham
bbey, the first stop on their psychic trek to locate Lin-
en.

"No, this isn't the place," Meredith had told him as
ley drove through the village. "I don't sense him any-
here nearby. Drive west."

And so they had taken M25 to Potters Bar in Hert-
ordshire.

"This isn't the right place either," she had said after
ley had fully explored the small town. "Maybe we need
o go farther north from here."

Leaving Potters Bar behind, they headed to Abbots
angley and then when that also proved to be the
rong town, they had driven even father north and
ere now a few miles outside of St. Albans.

Luke could tell that with each subsequent disap-
ointment, Meredith had grown weaker, as if some
orce she could not control was draining the energy
om her body and from her mind.

"When we arrive in St. Albans, we're staying for a
hile," he told her.

"What if it's not the right place either?"

"It doesn't matter. We need to eat and you need to
est." When she looked at him with gratitude in her

eyes, he quickly added, "You're no good to me if yo
pass out from exhaustion."

The tenderness in her eyes faded and her gaze hare
ened.

Damn it, Sentell, would it have killed you to be nice
her, to let her believe that you actually give a damn abot
her as a human being?

"You think I'm some sort of freak, don't you?" sh
said.

"I don't think you're a freak."

"You do. I can see it in your eyes every time you loo
at me."

"You're an enigma to me," he admitted. "I don't ur
derstand how you do what you do. When I'm aroun
you, half the time, I question my own sanity."

"Thank you for being honest with me." There was
hint of sadness in her voice.

"Look, Merry Berry, I'll make a deal with you," Luk
said. "I'll always be honest with you, even if it upsets yo
or hurts your feelings, if you promise you will trust m
to take care of you and you won't question me when
tell you to do something or not to do something."

"I'm a great deal of trouble, aren't I?"

"Yeah, you are. But most things worth a damn are
lot of trouble."

"Oh."

"So, do we have a deal?"

"Yes, I suppose we do."

She remained quiet for several minutes, and the
she asked, "Luke, why did you call me Merry Berry?"

"Huh?"

"You called me—"

"It's just something that popped into my head. You
name is Meredith, so the short version is Merry. An

u're covered in a million freckles that look like tiny
pper berries."

"Oh, I see. I've never had a nickname before. Hmm . . .
erry Berry." She smiled. "I think I like it."

Luke barely stifled a groan.

"The authorities have been notified," Griff ex-
ained. "Sheriff Fulton will handle this case personally,
a favor to me. And he'll deal with the TVAP. Fulton
s promised to keep his personnel to a minimum and
e promised that we will cooperate fully with his de-
rtment."

Everyone seated at the conference table remained
ent and attentive. Griff had called this meeting of
ghly trusted personnel to share information about
iloh Whitman's murder and how the crime would be
ndled by the Jefferson County Sheriff's Department,
e TVA police, and the Powell Agency. Griff issued or-
rs for the agents present to deal with their subordi-
tes.

"I expect Sheriff Fulton's team will arrive within the
ur," Griff said. "That gives us precious little time to
epare for their investigation and to secure Griffin's
st. At no time will any member of our staff interfere
th the sheriff's investigation. But that doesn't mean
r people can't ask to see everyone's ID, which I fully
pect them to do."

Derek watched and listened, his gaze moving from a
ggard Griff to his equally fatigued wife. To a person,
eryone in the room understood the significance of
iloh Whitman's death. Someone from the outside
ing able to break into Griffin's Rest would be the
uivalent of someone breaking into Fort Knox. The

possibility of that happening seemed highly improb
ble. How could the Copycat Carver have gotte
through security? How could a stranger have pen
trated the seemingly foolproof protection surroundir
the compound?

"I don't think I have to tell y'all how Nic and I fe
about Shiloh's death." Griff reached out to Nic, who ir
mediately stood up and took his hand. "And you've a
undoubtedly asked yourselves the same questions v
did, and no doubt came to the same conclusions."

"Since the copycat has murdered three Powe
Agency employees and three members of employee
families, it would be reasonable to assume the copyc
killed Shiloh," Nic told the group. "We are not rulir
out that possibility. However, there are two very goc
reasons to consider an alternate possibility—that th
copycat did not kill Shiloh."

As if they were a tag team supporting each oth
through this ordeal, Griff took over again from Ni
"One: It would have been virtually impossible for
stranger to have gotten inside Griffin's Rest. Two: Wh
ever killed Shiloh did not slit her throat nor did he m
tilate her body in any way."

"How was she killed?" Michelle Allen asked, h
voice quivering slightly.

"From what we can tell—and an autopsy will r
doubt reveal—Shiloh was attacked, subdued, and h
head held under the water at the edge of the lake un
she drowned. There is bruising on Shiloh's body ar
upper arms."

"So you can see that the killer's MO does not mat
that of the copycat," Nic explained. "But that does n
necessarily mean the copycat didn't kill her. If th
Copycat Carver is, as we believe he is, a professional a

ssin, it would have been easy enough for him to alter
s method."

"But if the odds of the copycat breaching Powell se-
rity are slim to none, then we have to broaden our
arch and accept the possibility that someone on the
owell staff killed Shiloh," Maleah said aloud what she
ew everyone there was thinking.

Luke drove down Chequers Street until he reached
. Peters at the southern end of the main street in St.
bans. Then he headed down Hollywell and turned
to Sopwell Lane.

"There it is," Meredith said. "The Goat Inn. It looks
e a nice place."

"There's no point in going back to London tonight,"
ke told her. "I'll see if they have a couple of rooms
re. If they do, you can rest for a while after we eat
nch and maybe even take a nap."

When she opened her mouth to argue, he held up
s hand in a Stop gesture. "Remember our deal. You're
ing to trust me to take care of you."

She nodded.

After parking the rental car, they got out and walked
to the Goat Inn in the old centre of St. Albans. The
rmer coaching inn was now a bed and breakfast that
so provided home-cooked meals.

When Luke tried to book two rooms, he was told that
nly one was available. "It's a nice sunny room," the
roprietor told him. "And it has two beds."

Luke booked the room, explained the situation to
eredith, and much to his surprise, she didn't com-
ain.

"I trust you," she told him.

After lunch—hot baguettes, with ale for him an
bottled water for her—they went upstairs to the ni
sunny room. As it turned out their room was small an
neat with white walls, blue curtains at the single wi
dow, and two beds with white and blue coverlets an
blue throw pillows. One bed was a double and the oth
a twin.

"Lie down and rest," Luke told her. "I'll run out an
see if I can pick up a few necessities like toothbrush
deodorant and—" he ran his fingers across his jaw "–
razor."

"You won't go far, will you?"

"No, I won't go far. Just lock the door when I lea
and don't let anyone in while I'm gone."

When Luke returned with a small bag of toiletri
that he had purchased at a local drugstore called Boo
on St. Peters Street, he had checked on Meredith. Aft
he found her sleeping soundly, he went back dow
stairs, drank a bottled lager beer and telephoned Grif

"Meredith thinks she can find Linden," Luke tol
Griff. "We've traveled north of London and have bee
eliminating village after village."

"Linden may not be in the UK after all," Griff said.

"What makes you think he might not be her
Meredith seems pretty certain that she is slowly b
surely zeroing in on him."

"Someone killed Shiloh Whitman last night," Gri
told him. "One of the guards patrolling the groune
found her body a little after daybreak this morning."

"And you think it was the Copycat Carver. Was h
throat slit?"

"No. She was attacked and held down in the lal
until she drowned."

"Then it may not have been the copycat."

"Yeah, my gut tells me it wasn't."

"I believe Linden is in England. Between Meredith's weird sixth sense and Mitchum's team of experts, it's only a matter of time until we find him."

"Even if Linden is in England and you can track him down and eliminate him, doing that will solve only one of our problems. If Linden didn't kill Shiloh that means someone inside Griffin's Rest killed her, possibly someone employed by York." Griff paused for a brief moment. "And then there's York himself. Until we find the man masquerading as Malcolm York, no one I care about, no one I employ and no member of their family will be safe."

Chapter 34

He would not depend on underlings to make this very important telephone call, as he had originally planned. No, he had decided that he wanted the pleasure of issuing this specific order himself. As he placed the call, he thought about Griffin Powell, a man he hated with every fiber of his being.

"I assume that Shiloh Whitman is dead, isn't she?" he asked the moment his puppet inside Griffin's Rest answered. "If you lie to me, I will know."

"Yes. I did what you told me to do and I expect you to keep your part of our bargain. Don't hurt her. Please. Let her go."

"No one has hurt her. She is alive and well. And as long as you continue to follow my instructions, no harm will come to her."

"I was told that if I killed—"

"Be very careful what you say. You do not want to be overheard, do you? It would be a shame if anyone found out what you had done, at least not before you are able to give me everything I want in exchange for what you want."

"I am not going to kill anyone else for you!"

"Yes, you are, if you ever want to see her alive again."

"Damn you!"

He laughed, gaining great pleasure from having ᴜsed so much anger and pain to someone Griffin well trusted. "I've chosen your next target. This time ᴉant you to strike a lethal blow a little closer to Griffin ɪ Nicole. I want this kill to be more personal than all others. It's time to up the ante before the Grand Fi- ʟe of Act I."

"Why do you hate Griffin Powell so much?"

"My motives are of no concern to you. Your only pur- ᵉ is to obey my orders."

"I swear to God if you hurt her, if—"

"You are in no position to make threats. But I have reason to kill her. She is nothing more than a means ᴀn end. As long as you do what you're told, she stays ᵉ. Tell me that you understand."

"Yes, I understand."

"Good," he said. "Now, while Griffin's Rest is in a ᵉ of turmoil today, when no one is expecting an- ᵉr strike so soon, I want you to kill Maleah Perdue as ɴ as possible. Take her by surprise."

"Maleah? You want me to kill Maleah? I can't. I ɪ't."

"Are you sure you are willing to trade one life for an- ᵉr? Does Maleah Perdue mean more to you than—?"

"How do you expect me to kill her in broad daylight ɪ Powell agents and guards and the sheriff's depart- ɴt covering every inch of Griffin's Rest? It will be im- ⸱ble to isolate her."

"Find a way. If Maleah Perdue isn't dead by morning, ᴀeone else who is very important to you will be."

"No! God, no . . . I—I'll do it. I'll find a way."

"Now, that's what I want to hear. By following my or-

ders, I will get what I want and you will get what y
want."

"What I want is for you to rot in hell, you son of
bitch."

Luke had begun to think Meredith would sleep
night. She had certainly slept the day away. But s
roused a little before seven and after freshening up, s
met him downstairs for a bite of supper. She order
tiger prawns for a starter, and then honey roasted ha
served with fried eggs, house fries, and baked bea
She ate like a ravenous wolf, as if she hadn't eaten
days. Luke had settled for the homemade lasagna, a
when Meredith had suggested dessert, they had bc
ordered the sticky toffee pudding.

Just as the waitress set their puddings in front
them, Luke's phone rang. "Excuse me." He remov
the phone from his jacket's inner pocket.

Meredith nodded. "Yes, of course." She picked
the dessert spoon.

"Sentell here," Luke said.

"We have a couple of possibilities," Mitchum to
him, skipping any preliminary pleasantries. "All part
who arrived by private plane in the specific twenty-fo
hour period have been accounted for except two. A g
named Horacio Vasquez Luna. He has a Venezue
passport and he was traveling with a female, suppose
his wife. No one by that name has checked into any
tels in or around London. He hasn't rented a condo
house or an apartment. And there is no record of a
service picking him up at the airport."

"Any physical description?"

"Late fifties, heavyset, beard and mustache."

"Our guy isn't that old, but then we have reason

elieve he's a master of disguise. Keep looking for
una," Luke said. "Who's the other possible?"

"A man named Zachary Fairweather. He had a
ritish passport. Our report said early forties, average
ze. No one at Heathrow remembered much about
im, but they all remembered his daughter."

"His daughter?"

"What?" Meredith dropped her spoon in her half-
mpty pudding dish, the metal clinking against the
hina.

"Hold on a minute," Luke told Mitchum. He asked
Ieredith, "Are you okay?"

"Whose daughter are you talking about?" she asked.

Glancing around the noisy pub, Luke realized that
o one was paying any attention to them and figured
hat, over the loud din, it was highly unlikely anyone
uld hear more than a word or two of their conversa-
on.

"A man who may be our guy got off a private plane at
Ieathrow last night, along with his daughter," Luke
old her. Before he could say more, her eyes widened
id she suddenly turned as white as a sheet. "Damn,
Ieredith, don't you pass out on me."

"Luke . . . Luke . . ." She gasped for air. "His female
ompanion. Not sex. Oh, God, oh God . . ."

"Pull yourself together." He reached across the table
id grabbed her hand. Then he said into the mobile
hone, "Call me back in five—"

"There's something else you need to know about
airweather's daughter," Mitchum said. "She's a child
: six or seven."

"Then Fairweather wouldn't be our guy, would he?"
uke squeezed Meredith's hand and then released it.
Ie would hardly be traveling with a kid."

"I don't know," Mitchum said. "Can you think of
better cover?"

"His female companion is a little girl," Meredith sai
in a strong voice. And when Luke nodded, she tol
him, "Don't hang up. Find out everything about th
man right now." She offered Luke a weak smile. "I'll b
all right."

"Anything else?" Luke asked Mitchum, all the whil
looking directly at Meredith.

"Zachary Fairweather hired a car," Mitchum said
"We've been able to trace the route the car traveled o
of London."

"And?" Luke prompted.

"Fairweather rented a black Mercedes C220 Euro
car." Mitchum recited the tag number. "He took M
north out of London."

Well, I'll be damned. North of London, just as Meredi
had said.

"Run a detailed check on Fairweather."

"I have people working on that as we speak."

"Contact me again when you have more informatic
on both Luna and Fairweather."

"Fairweather," Meredith whispered the name. "Fai
weather."

"What about him?" Luke asked.

"Forget about the man named Luna. Concentrate o
Fairweather."

"Are you sure?"

"Yes, I'm sure."

Luke relayed the message to Mitchum, ended th
conversation, and stared at Meredith. "You're pickir
up on something, aren't you? What happened? Wh
got your woo-woo mojo working again?"

"Tell me everything Mitchum told you and don
leave out even the most insignificant detail." She shove

back her chair and stood. "We need to leave now. We have to go farther north as soon as possible."

By late afternoon, the invasion of Griffin's Rest by what seemed to be half the law enforcement personnel in the state of Tennessee had begun to wane. Sheriff Fulmer was still with Griff, the two overseeing every aspect of the investigation, but only a CSI team and a few deputies remained on the property. Shiloh's body had already been taken to the lab in Knoxville for an autopsy. The detectives had questioned everyone there at the compound, beginning with the guard who had found Shiloh's body. And Sanders had followed up with interviews of his own.

Maleah had spent most of the day glued to Nic's side, the two women supporting each other. And Derek had been going over the personal files of everyone living and working there at Griffin's Rest, searching for anything that might alert him to a problem. Every guard employed by the Powell Agency who had undergone a thorough background check before being hired and, to a person, each man and woman now working at Griffin's Rest had been with the agency for years. There was not one single new employee working there at present.

As for the Powell agents on duty at Griffin's Rest . . .

Derek didn't want to consider the possibility that one of them could have killed Shiloh Whitman. He knew these men and women and was on a first name basis with most. In his opinion, both personally and as a professional profiler, they were all good people. Not one of them would kill without just cause.

Or unless they were under duress, forced to act against their will.

"Hey you." Instantly recognizing Maleah's voice,

Derek turned to glance at the open office door where she stood staring at him. "It's about time for a late afternoon break, isn't it?"

"Hi yourself." He closed the file folder in front of him, shoved back his chair and stood. "What do you have in mind?"

She came over to him, lifted her arms up and around his neck and kissed him. As she ended the kiss, she murmured against his lips, "I still love you."

He grinned as he cupped her butt. "I'm glad to hear it since it just so happens that I still love you, too."

Maleah eased her arms downward and spread her hands out across his chest. "I wish we could pretend that everything is all right, that none of these horrible things have happened. I wish we could concentrate on each other and forget everything and everyone else."

He reached up, took her hands in his hand, and held them between their bodies. "Want to get out of the house and leave all this behind for a while?"

"Is that possible? The grounds are crawling with law enforcement and—"

"I think we're down to a few essential crime scene investigators for the most part."

"I guess I'm behind on the latest. Nic and I have been holed up in Griff's study for the past few hours."

"How's Nic doing?"

"She's tough. She'll be okay. She's worried about Griff more than anything else," Maleah said. "He just came back up to the house and found us in the study. So, I thought I'd make myself scarce and give Nic time alone with her man while I went to look for my man."

"Your man, huh? I like the sound of that."

She pressed her cheek against his. "Don't remind me later on that I ever said this, but . . . I need you, Derek. I need for you to hold me and tell me that everything is going to be all right."

"In case you didn't already know it, Blondie, I need you just as much as you need me." He tugged on her hands. "Come on, let's go outside and sit on the patio. We can breathe in a little fresh air and soak up some sunshine while we're holding on to each other."

As they made their way through the house like two kids rushing away from school to play hooky for the day, they crossed paths with Sanders and Barbara Jean, who were walking toward the kitchen. Brendan Richter and Shaughnessy Hood were following them.

"We're all in need of a caffeine pick-me-up. I'm going to put on a couple of pots of coffee," Barbara Jean said. "There will be plenty in the kitchen if y'all want some."

"Thanks," Derek replied.

A few minutes later, Derek and Maleah found the patio deserted. There wasn't another person, not even a Powell Agency employee or a sheriff's deputy, anywhere in sight. Derek guided Maleah to the canopied swing at the edge of the huge brick and stone floored patio that overlooked the lake. He sat down and pulled her onto his lap. She wrapped her arms around his neck and laid her head on his shoulder.

"We should be talking about you and me and being in love and what we're going to do about how we feel," Derek said. "But instead of being able to focus on the two of us, we're embroiled in what would appear to be a never-ending nightmare."

"God, Derek, who could have killed Shiloh Whitman?"

He hugged her to him and nuzzled her cheek, his actions comforting. "I don't believe it's possible that anyone from the outside could have somehow gotten through security and into Griffin's Rest."

"I think you're right, so that means . . ." She paused, obviously reluctant to say aloud what they both knew to be true. "That means whoever killed Shiloh is either working here or lives here."

"I've spent most of the afternoon going over the personal files on every guard and every agent who is here at Griffin's Rest right now."

"I can't believe that it's one of the agents. It couldn't be." Maleah lifted her head and looked at Derek, her eyes wide and round. "What about one of Yvette Meng's protégés?"

"I seriously doubt that one of them killed Shiloh."

"No, I didn't mean I thought one of Shiloh's fellow students killed her. What I was thinking, wondering really, is why didn't Yvette or any of her other students sense that Shiloh was in danger? They're a group of psychics, aren't they? You'd think one of them would have seen it coming."

"I'm not sure I can explain it," Derek told her. "But as far as I know, neither Yvette nor any of her protégés claim to be able to see into the future and predict events that haven't happened."

"I don't understand all that psychic stuff."

"Psychic talents are like any other talents, no one person can do everything. Just as other people are sculptors or painters or writers or musicians, these people have specific gifts, too, and it all falls under one heading."

"I guess that makes sense."

"And it is my understanding that Yvette strictly forbids her students to intrude on the private thoughts of others. She's trained them to control any mind reading or empathic abilities."

Maleah laid her head back on Derek's shoulder. "Do you think the killer could be one of the guards?"

"Possibly."

"I refuse to believe that the killer could be one of the agents," she said adamantly.

"I think at this point, the only people we can rule out completely are you and me, Griff and Nic, and Yvette, Sanders, and BJ."

"It doesn't make sense. What possible reason would anyone have to kill Shiloh? Why her?"

Maleah burrowed closer into Derek, as if she could draw strength from his body. He stroked her silky hair and pressed his cheek against the top of her head.

"I've given it a great deal of thought," Derek told her. "And the only thing that makes sense is that Linden or York or whoever is running this horror show forced one of the guards or one of the agents to kill."

"How could he force them to kill against their will?"

"I'm not sure. He would need some type of leverage."

"A threat, maybe." She lifted her head. Her gaze locked with Derek's. "If he has threatened to harm someone they love, a member of their family, then that type of threat would be some mighty powerful leverage, wouldn't it?"

Luke had gone through three traffic circles and headed due north from St. Albans, straight toward the next village—Harpenden. And that's where they had been for the past few hours, driving up one street and down another.

Hunting.

Up High Street until it turned into Luton Road.

Then they had back-tracked toward town, taking side streets to investigate every psychic twitch Meredith had. Vaughn Road. Leyton Road. Bower's Parade. And all the while, they had both been on the lookout for a black Mercedes.

Searching.

"It's nearly midnight," Luke told her. "I say we call it a night, check into a hotel and get a fresh start in the morning."

"No, Luke, please. I know I'm not wrong about this. I know they're here somewhere. We can't give up."

"We're going around in circles now," he said. "I'm surprised the local police haven't stopped us to ask what the hell we're doing. I saw what looked like a really nice hotel right off High Street, someplace called Eagle Glenn Manor."

"Another thirty minutes," she pleaded. "Take one of the roads leading out of town. I think if they were in town anywhere, I'd have sensed it by now."

"Thirty more minutes isn't going to matter. I'm tired. You're exhausted. I don't think you'll last another thirty minutes."

Disregarding her pleas for them to continue tonight, Luke headed for the hotel. Just as he turned off High Street onto Townsend Lane, his phone rang. He pulled into the hotel car park and stopped.

Meredith stared at him, her eyes suddenly bright with speculation, as if she knew the call was important. Or maybe she just hoped it was.

"Yeah, Sentell here."

"We've got an address," Mitchum said, then gave Luke the information. "It's about a mile outside Harpenden. From the real estate photo, it's a small cottage situated in a wooded area that is fairly secluded."

"You're sure about this?"

"The house was rented by a Zachary Fairweather for
entire month."

"Son of a bitch."

Meredith tugged on Luke's arm. "He's here, isn't
? He's in Harpenden or somewhere close-by."

"Go ahead and put everything into play on your end.
ll take it from here," Luke told Mitchum. "And
anks." He turned to Meredith. "I'll check us into the
otel and get you settled before I leave."

"Damn it, Luke Sentell, you're crazy if you think
u're leaving me behind. I'm going with you."

"Like hell you are."

"Like hell I'm not."

"I have a job to do, and your coming along for the
de will only complicate matters. Do you understand?"

"There is a child involved. When you rescue her,
e's going to be very, very scared. It will make things
sier for her if I'm there, because I'm a woman and
e's more likely to trust me than you."

As much as he hated to admit it, her lopsided logic
ade a weird kind of sense. "No way. You can do your
rturing female thing when I bring the child back
re with me."

"No."

"What do you mean no?"

"I mean that I'm going with you and that's that."

"Meredith, I can't do my job and worry about some-
ing happening to you."

"I swear that I will stay in the car, with the doors
cked. I'll even lie down in the floorboard and hide if
u want me to."

"We're wasting time arguing." He held up his index
nger and wagged it in her face. "You will stay in the car
d out of my way, no matter what you hear or see."

"I swear I will."

"And when I bring the child out to the car, you will not ask me any questions about what happened."

"I won't. I swear." She looked him square in the eye. "You're going to kill him, aren't you?"

Luke didn't answer. He put their vehicle in reverse, drove out of the car park and back onto Townsend.

Chapter 35

Luke parked the Volvo sedan on the side of the road, but a hundred yards down from the driveway leading to the rental house. When he had driven by, he hadn't any sign of a vehicle. More than likely the black cedes was parked behind the cottage. He opened driver's door, got out, leaned over and looked back Meredith.

Stay put."

she nodded.

He rounded the side of the car, popped open the k, and retrieved his MK23 OWSH, a .45 caliber pis- a laser aiming module, and a sound and flash sup- sor.

Meredith opened the passenger door. Damn it, what of "stay put" hadn't she understood? He reached open door before she had a chance to move.

What do you think you're doing?" he demanded.

I'm not getting out," she told him. "I just want to you . . . to say . . . please be careful."

hit! Bringing her along had been a huge mistake, a lapse of judgment on his part. But in his own de-

fense, he had given in to her pleading to avoid hav
to knock her out and tie her up. He had known so
stubborn women in his life, but none as obstina
bullheaded as Meredith Sinclair.

"Close the door and lock it. And whatever you
don't leave the car while I'm gone."

"Where did you get the gun?" she asked.

"Good God, woman, what a question. I brough
with me. Now close the damn door."

He couldn't worry about Meredith and do his jol
she followed orders, she should be safe.

Creating a path through the wooded area to the
of the cottage, he made his way toward the backya
Just as he had thought, the black Mercedes was par
at the back of the house and couldn't be seen from
road. The cottage doors and windows would be lock
but with no security system, breaking and enter
would be a piece of cake. However, if Linden was
pecting him, he could easily be opening a door to
own death. There was a root cellar which could
booby trapped, just as the doors and windows might

With weapon drawn, Luke circled the cottage.
peered into the windows, one by one, and found ev
room as dark as pitch, except what appeared to b
bedroom at the back of the house. A dim light glo
softly on one wall, probably a nightlight plugged in
wall outlet.

Luke swallowed.

This would be the child's bedroom.

If he could get her out of the house first . . .

Not an option. Too risky.

Keeping the child safe was his number one priori

* * *

He woke with a start, his heart pounding and a rush
adrenaline pumping through his body at breakneck
eed. Sitting up in bed, the lightweight cover falling to
s hips, he listened for any sound that might have
used him to wake so suddenly.

Silence.

The only sound he heard was his own breathing.

He shoved back the covers, got up, slipped his bare
et into his Italian leather loafers, and reached for his
G on the bedside table. Not taking time to put on his
jama top, he walked quietly out of his bedroom and
oved carefully down the narrow hall to the child's
om. She lay curled in a fetal ball, the sheet and blan-
t kicked to the foot of the bed. He scanned the room,
om wall to wall and from floor to ceiling. The old
use had no closets and the wardrobe in that room
s too small to provide a hiding place for an adult.

The room was clear.

Vigilant to any sound or movement, he walked into
e room and over to the bed, and then reached down
d gently shook the child.

"Wake up," he whispered.

Her eyes flew open. She stared up at him. When she
ened her mouth, he knew she was going to scream.
clamped his hand over her face, covering her
outh and chin.

"Be quiet and I won't hurt you," he told her. "I'm
ing to take you out of bed now and carry you with
. Be good. Don't fight me. If you're not a good girl,
u will be very sorry."

He snatched her up and out of the bed. While keep-
g a tight grip on his pistol, he maneuvered her to his
t side and balanced her with one arm.

Pausing for a moment, he heard nothing, saw noth-

ing. And yet he knew someone was in the house. Yea
of training had honed his senses.

He couldn't understand how someone had manag
to find them. An alias had been used at Heathrow. Zac
ary Fairweather. His employer had rented the Merced
and the cottage under that name. How had someo
connected Anthony Linden to Zachary Fairweather?

It wasn't possible.

And yet someone had tracked him.

Someone had been sent to rescue the child.

Who was the only person who knew where the chi
was being held?

Malcolm York!

The son of a bitch had set him up. But why?

Regardless of his employer's reasons for betrayal,
had no intention of dying tonight. Survival first I
would use the child as a bargaining chip or if necessa
a shield. He'd take care of York later.

When he walked toward the open bedroom door,
tending to close it, he sensed danger all around hi
But he could not pinpoint the presence of another p
son other than the trembling child he held against I
body. He would wait there, in the bedroom, for his
tacker to strike. Depending on the other man's skil
he should have a fifty / fifty chance of survival. Just as
reached out to close the bedroom door, a bullet zipp
through the darkness and entered the front of his hea

The bullet had severed his brainstem, killing him i
mediately. Luke came out of the shadowy hallw
grabbed the screaming child as Linden slumped do
onto the floor. He hoisted the little girl up and onto I
hip.

"It's all right, honey. You're safe. Nobody is going to
rt you. I'm taking you home to your mommy and
ddy."

She stopped screaming and stared at Luke with a
ir of huge blue eyes.

He carried her out of the bedroom, down the hall
d straight through the front door. "There's a very
ce lady waiting in my car. I'll take you to her, okay?
e will look after you while I make a couple of phone
lls, and then you and I and the nice lady are going to
ave here and we'll take you home as soon as we can."

As if instinctively believing she could trust Luke, she
apped her little arm around his neck and held on
htly as he rushed across the front lawn and down the
ad to the Volvo. The minute Meredith saw him com-
g, she opened the car door and jumped out.

Damn it. What did I tell her? Stay in the car.

He and Meredith exchanged glances as she held out
r arms to the little girl. "Come here, sweetie."

The child went to Meredith somewhat reluctantly.

Luke turned and walked away several feet.

Before Meredith closed the car door, she spoke to
e child again. "I'm Meredith Sinclair. Who are you?"

Too far away to hear the child's whispered response,
ke immediately contacted Mitchum, who told him
 already had a cleanup crew en route and they would
ke care of everything there at the cottage. Luke's sec-
d phone call would be to Griff. He checked his
atch, an MTM Black Patriot, noted it was ten till one
d calculated the time difference.

Just as he started to make the call, Meredith opened
e car door and called his name. "Luke?"

"What?"

"Please come here. There's something you need to
ear."

Luke stomped over to the side of the Volvo. T[
child sitting in Meredith's lap looked up at him.

"It's okay, sweetie. Luke is one of the good guys. T[
him what you told me. Tell him your name."

"My name is Jaelyn," she said. "Jaelyn Allen."

The name reverberated inside Luke's head. *Alle*
Allen. Allen.

"Good God." Luke knelt down in front of Jaelyn ar
forced a fake smile. "Do you know someone name
Michelle Allen?"

The child's face lit up the moment he mentione
the trusted Powell agent's name. "That's my au[
Chelle."

Derek shared after-dinner drinks with Griff ar
Sanders in Griff's study. Dinner had been sandwich[
and chips served in the kitchen, which had given the
all a chance to wind down as much as possible after
grueling day. For the past half hour, ever since the me
had left the ladies in the kitchen, their conversatio
had been limited, as if they didn't know what else the[
was to say. Sanders had poured their drinks and a
though he had not told Griff that one drink should [
his limit tonight, he had given Griff a stern look as [
handed him a second glass of Scotch whisky. Derek ha
noticed that, like him and Sanders, Griff had leisure[
sipped on his first drink.

"Our not talking about the situation won't chang
it," Griff finally said, breaking the strained silence.

"No, of course not," Sanders agreed. "But perha[
any more discussion should be postponed until tomo
row. It has been a very long and trying day for all of us[

"Before we call it a night, I'd like to run a thought [
two by y'all," Derek said.

Griff eyed him, curiosity in his hard gaze. "A thought bout what?"

"About who may have killed Shiloh," Derek replied.

Sanders squinted his almond-shaped eyes and foused directly on Derek. "You think you know who the nurderer is?"

"No, I can't name the killer, but I believe there is nly one reason either a guard here at Griffin's Rest or ne of the Powell agents would kill Shiloh Whitman."

"I think we all agree that it had to be someone inside Griffin's Rest, someone we trusted." Griff heaved a eavy, labored groan. "I've tried to fight accepting the ruth, but that one thought has been in the back of my nind all day."

"Maleah and I discussed the possibility that the person who calls himself Malcolm York is the mastermind ehind all the murders. And this man found a way to orce a Powell guard or an agent to kill Shiloh. He's sing some type of blackmail to—"

Griff's cell phone rang. He let out a few choice curse vords.

"It's probably Sheriff Fulton." Griff got up and valked across the room to where his phone lay atop his lesk. He picked up the phone, glanced at it, and said, It's not Fulton." And then he answered the call. Luke?"

Derek watched as Griff listened, his face growing larker with each second and his body visibly tensing.

"Charter a jet," Griff said. "You and Meredith bring he child back to the U.S. as soon as possible. I'll call er parents in Paducah to let them know their child is afe. And we'll handle things here at Griffin's Rest."

Griff laid the phone on the desk. He looked at Derek nd then at Sanders. "Linden is dead." He paused for a noment. "Linden kidnapped Michelle Allen's niece.

He had the child with him when Luke arrived. She's safe."

"We have to find Michelle," Derek said. "She needs to know that her niece is all right."

"Yes, and after that, we will have to deal with what Michelle has done," Griff told them.

When Nic came out of the bathroom, the test stick in her hand, Maleah rose from where she sat on the edge of Nic's bed.

"Well, are you or aren't you?"

Nic hurried toward Maleah, tears in her eyes, and held out the stick to show her. "It's positive. I'm pregnant." She grabbed Maleah and hugged her. "I'm really pregnant. I had just about given up hope of our having a baby."

Maleah grasped Nic's trembling hands, took the test stick from her and laid it on the nightstand. "Have you been experiencing any symptoms? Didn't you suspect you might be pregnant?"

Nic shook her head. "I guess I've ignored the symptoms and chalked them up to nerves, which is understandable considering the stress we've been under for several months now. But when I missed my period again, I began to wonder."

"Good thing you already had a test kit."

"Yes, it was, wasn't it. Remember I bought several of them about six months ago when I thought I might be pregnant. But it turned out that I wasn't pregnant then."

"But you are now." Maleah grabbed Nic's hands again and squeezed. "You've got to tell Griff as soon as possible. He'll be thrilled."

"We both want a child so very much." Nic swiped the

rdrops from beneath her eyes. "But dear God, what
l timing."

Maleah hugged Nic again. "Maybe it was simply
ant to be. We could all use a little good news about
w."

'I feel as if I've been given a miracle."

When they pulled apart, Maleah said, "You should
e a nice, long bubble bath, put on your sexiest lin-
ie, and call downstairs to tell your husband that he's
ded upstairs immediately."

"I like your suggestion."

'I'll bet Griff will like it, too. And, Nic, just for
ight, forget about everything else and concentrate
you and Griff and your baby."

Maleah kissed Nic's cheek. "I think I'll go back to my
om, grab a shower, and see if I can find something
y to slip into before Derek stops by to say good-
ht."

Nic laughed. "Can you believe it? In the midst of all
s chaos, you fall in love and I find out I'm pregnant."

Maleah waved at Shaughnessy Hood, who stood
ard outside Nic's bedroom. The big bear of a man
led and nodded. She took her time meandering
ng to the other side of the house where the guest
oms were located. It seemed wrong somehow to be so
ppy. But Nic was pregnant. Her best friend, who had
en trying to get pregnant for several years, was at
g last going to have a baby. And Maleah having
len head over heels in love was as much of a miracle
Nic being pregnant.

She was in love with Derek Lawrence of all people.

Laughing softly to herself, savoring Nic's secret and
nking about the night ahead with Derek, Maleah

opened her bedroom door and flipped on the li
switch to turn on the bedside lamp. The low-watt b
gave off a dim radiance, creating a romantic glow si
lar to candlelight. She took off her jacket, tossed it or
a nearby chair, and then removed her holster and slipp
it into the right-side nightstand drawer. She kicked
her shoes and waltzed barefoot across the floor to
bathroom. After turning on the shower, she adjus
the water to a toasty warm. Then she stripped off
clothes, tossed them into the laundry hamper a
grabbed a washcloth from the stack on the vanity. Af
lathering her hair with the floral scented shampoo a
following with a silky conditioner, she shaved her l
and under her arms.

If only she had something really sexy to slip into af
her shower. Although she owned several nice sets
lacy panties and bras, she didn't have any sexy sle
wear. Considering the fact that her sex life had be
pretty much non-existent for a number of years, s
hadn't needed anything other than cotton sleep shi
for summer and wintertime flannel pajamas.

After she stepped out of the shower and wrappe
towel around her wet hair, she ran a second towel ov
her arms and legs.

Suddenly Maleah heard a noise outside in her b
room. "Derek?"

No response.

"Derek, is that you?"

Silence.

Odd, she could have sworn she heard somethi
that sounded like a door opening and closing.

"Cully says that Michelle has been staying in h
room a lot since her stomach virus, which we now kn

she faked," Griff told them. "Them" being Sanders, BJ, and Derek. "But she's not in her room now and when he checked, Cully found her window wide open."

"She's going to kill someone else tonight," BJ said. "But who? Her target could be any one of the other students or one of the agents or a guard or . . . or even one of us."

Sanders clamped his broad hand down on BJ's shoulder. She glanced up at him and they exchanged looks of care and concern.

"I've filled Cully in on the situation," Griff said. "Sanders, please contact the guards and tell them to be on the lookout for Michelle. Derek, you speak to Brendan and I'll let Shaughnessy know what's happened when I go upstairs to check on Nic. I'll alert Nic. You—" he looked at Derek "—let Maleah know what's going on and ask her to join us. I want an all-out manhunt underway immediately. We have to find Michelle before she kills again."

Maleah yanked her knee-length cotton robe off the hanger on the back of the bathroom door, slipped into it, and took a tentative step over the threshold, one foot in the bedroom and one still in the bathroom.

"Derek?"

Maleah heard only an eerie silence in the semidark bedroom.

She didn't like this one little bit. Her stomach churned with uneasiness. A sense of foreboding spread through her as she took another step into the bedroom. Something was wrong. She felt it in her bones.

Damn it, she had put her holstered pistol inside the nightstand drawer.

"Derek, if you're trying to surprise me, please don't.

I'm warning you that if you grab me, I'm going to clobber you. I'm pretty sure I can adequately kick your butt."

With her breath caught in her throat, Maleah took another step before halting and scanning the room. Her gaze paused on the sitting room, where she noticed a slender silhouette near the windows.

"Who's there?" Maleah asked.

Not Derek.

The silhouette moved out of the shadows and revealed herself.

"Michelle? What's wrong? Has something happened?"

For a few seconds, Maleah felt a huge sense of relief, thinking perhaps Griff had sent Michelle. But when Michelle didn't respond, only stood there staring at Maleah, her eyes wide and glazed as if she were in a trance, Maleah knew something wasn't right.

"What are you doing in my room? Did Griff send you?"

As Michelle walked toward Maleah, she brought the hand she held behind her back to her side. She lifted the gun she was tightly clutching. And then she pointed the 9mm at Maleah.

"I'm sorry, Maleah," Michelle said. "I'm so very sorry, but I have no other choice. I have to kill you."

Derek explained the situation to Brendan Richter and then headed upstairs only minutes behind Griff. He hated having to tell Maleah that Michelle Allen was the one who had killed Shiloh, that she had been forced to kill in order to save her seven-year-old niece's life. Apparently Anthony Linden had kidnapped Jaelyn Allen and held her hostage in order to force Michelle into killing for his employer. Derek didn't know all the

articulars of course, but he couldn't understand why
ichelle hadn't come to Griff and Nic and explained
nat had happened. He felt certain that Griff could
ave figured out a way to help her convince Linden that
e was following his instructions without her actually
aving had to kill anyone. But it was impossible to truly
ut himself in Michelle's shoes. No two people reacted
e same way to similar events. He and Michelle were
o very different people who had come from vastly dif-
rent backgrounds and had different life experiences.
ot that he thought a man would have handled the sit-
tion differently or better than a woman or that a priv-
ged background made him superior in any way. All
meant was that he knew he shouldn't judge another
rson's reasoning simply because they chose a differ-
t solution than he would have chosen.

As Derek approached Maleah's bedroom, he stopped
d thought about what he was going to say to her. Ma-
ah and Michelle weren't close friends, but they were
ends nevertheless. Michelle had been Maleah's mar-
l arts instructor and had been the one who had en-
uraged Maleah to work toward perfecting her skills.

He knew his Blondie. She presented a hard-as-nails
ade to the world, but inside, she had a marshmallow
nter. She would take the news about Michelle hard.

If only they could find Michelle quickly—before she
led again.

Maleah stared at Michelle—her friend Michelle—
o held a gun on her and obviously intended to kill
r.

"Why?" Maleah asked. "I don't understand."

"He has my niece, Jaelyn."

"Who has your niece?" Maleah took a hesitant step

toward Michelle. If she could get close enough, she ha
a reasonable chance of overpowering her.

"Stop right there. Don't come any closer."

Maleah stopped. "Michelle, we can work this ou
Whatever you need—"

"I need for you to shut up." Tears glistened i
Michelle's eyes.

Keep her talking. Find a way to move in closer.

"I knew I would have to shoot you," Michelle said.
knew I wouldn't be able to overpower and subdue yo
the way I did Shiloh."

"Please, talk to me. Let me help you. I know yo
don't want to do this."

"Can't you see that I don't have any other choice?
I don't kill you, he will kill Jaelyn."

As Derek reached for the doorknob, he heard voic
inside Maleah's room. Two female voices. Malea
and—?

He pressed his ear to the door and listened.

"I'll make it quick and painless, I promise," Michel
Allen said.

Derek's heart stopped.

Michelle was in Maleah's room.

His first instinct was to draw his gun and burst in
the room. He had been wearing his holster at Griffir
Rest since Shiloh's murder last night. But if he bur
into the room, he might spook Michelle and she mig
fire her weapon instantly. On the other hand, if he didr
act immediately, she would shoot Maleah anyway.

He reached under his jacket, flipped open the ho
ster, and removed his 45 Colt XSE. Praying with eve
breath he took, Derek turned the handle and eas
open the door, inch by inch. He stepped inside the be

oom, gun in hand, and as soon as he saw both women,
e aimed his weapon directly at Michelle.

"Drop your gun," he told Michelle in a deceptively
alm voice. He was anything but calm.

In that split second when Derek's command dis-
acted Michelle, Maleah made her move. Before either
erek or Michelle realized what was happening, Ma-
ah sent her arms and legs into deadly motion, ironi-
ally enough, using the skilled maneuvers Michelle had
ught her. The student against the teacher. Maleah's
ot struck Michelle's hand and sent the gun she held
ying. Realizing her weapon of choice was no longer an
ption, Michelle instinctively retaliated.

With his pistol aimed and ready to fire, Derek held
ack and watched while Maleah and Michelle engaged
a hand-to-hand combat. This was Maleah's fight. She
ouldn't appreciate him interfering unless it was to
ve her life.

Back and forth, Michelle attacked and Maleah coun-
rattacked. Both women were skilled warriors, pretty
uch evenly matched, every move each made a combi-
ation of reflex and training. Repeated force-against-
rce blocks took a toll on both of them. With each
ck, each painful blow, each woman weakened, but
either gave an inch. Maleah punched harder and
ster, using the front two knuckles of her fist to strike at
er opponent, and then successfully blocking each
ow Michelle aimed at her.

By the time Maleah pinned Michelle to the floor,
th women were bloody and breathless. Sweat glis-
ned on their skin.

"Oh, God, please," Michelle whimpered. "Jaelyn . . ."

Griff, Nic, and Shaughnessy rushed into the room
d halted abruptly behind Derek. They looked past
m to where Maleah straddled a defeated Michelle.

Derek holstered his weapon and with the others a
his back, he rushed over to Maleah, yanked down he
robe that had hiked up to the edge of her buttocks, and
then pulled her off Michelle and into his arms. Breath
ing heavily, she put one arm around him as she looked
down at her opponent.

Griff and Shaughnessy lifted a bruised and battered
Michelle to her feet. Shaughnessy quickly yanked he
arms behind her, shoved her in front of him and held
her securely.

"She kept saying that Linden had her niece and he
would kill her if she didn't do what he told her to do,
Maleah explained. "She admitted that she killed Shiloh.

"Luke called. He found Linden," Griff said. "Appar
ently Linden had been ordered to abduct Jaelyn Aller
and hold her captive as a way to control Michelle and
force her to kill for him."

"Jaelyn?" Michelle asked pleadingly. "Is she all right?

"Your niece is fine," Griff told her. "Luke and Mered
ith are bringing her back to the U.S. as soon as possible
They'll take her home to your brother and his wife."

Moments after hearing the good news about Jaelyn
Michelle fell apart emotionally, weeping, shaking he
head, and muttering incoherently. Shaughnessy gentl
led her from the room.

Nic grabbed Maleah out of Derek's arms an
hugged her. Then she stepped back and wiped the tear
from her cheeks. "Thank God you're all right."

Griff put his arm around Nic's shoulders.

Maleah looked at Derek. He reached out and swiped
away the smear of blood from her mouth. "Blondi
don't you ever scare me like that again. When I sa
Michelle holding a gun on you . . . Maleah Perdue,
anything had happened to you . . ."

She offered him a fragile smile. "You're my hero, you know."

"Who, me?" He pointed to his chest.

"Yes, you. If you hadn't startled Michelle, I might not have gotten the opportunity to catch her off guard the way I did." She lifted her arms and wrapped them around his neck. "And you're my hero because once you saw I could handle the situation without your help, you let me fight my own battle."

Chapter 36

Derek had held her in his arms all night Friday night and finally sometime over in the morning, she had fallen asleep.

Maleah awoke to a new day, yet she was haunted by yesterday's events. Physically, she ached like hell from the beating Michelle had given her. Emotionally, she was a wreck. Her thoughts and feelings were all over the place. She was shocked and angry and sad about Michelle's betrayal and equally sympathetic about the intolerable choice Michelle had been forced to make. Maleah wanted to believe that if she had been put in such a horrific position, she would have chosen a better solution. Poor Michelle, her life was all but destroyed.

What was going to happen now that Anthony Linden was dead? Would it be only a matter of time before the pseudo-York sent another gun-for-hire to terrorize Griff?

Most of Saturday passed in a blur. Sanders chauffeured them—Nic and Griff, Shaughnessy, Derek and Maleah—to the sheriff's department to give their statements concerning the attempt on Maleah's life. A distraught Michelle had confessed that she had killed Shiloh Whitman and had been ordered to kill Maleah. Griff had contacted Camden Hendrix, an old friend and head of a law firm the Powell Agency kept on retainer. Despite what Michelle had done, Griff had instructed Cam to provide her with the best legal representation possible. Griffin Powell believed that, no matter what, you took care of your own.

After their trip to the sheriff's office, Maleah and Derek spent most of the day with Nic and Griff and Griff didn't mention anything about Nic being pregnant. When Maleah and Nic were finally alone for a few minutes, Maleah asked Nic why she hadn't told her husband about their baby.

"I'm going to tell him. But not yet. Not for a few more days. Not until we all have a chance to come to terms with what Michelle did and sort of get our bearings."

And so that was what they did the rest of the day Saturday—tried to get their bearings in a sea of mixed emotions.

Saturday night Derek made love to her so slowly and tenderly that she cried. And being the man that he was, he understood that those tears of joy also released a myriad of pent-up emotions. A lifetime of emotions.

Odd that in the midst of all the chaos and upheaval in their lives, she could, on a very personal level, be so happy. Happier than she had ever been in her entire life. She loved Derek Lawrence and he loved her.

That morning, after they made love again, Derek propped up on his elbow, looked down at her, and said, "I think you're going to have to marry me."

Smiling like a lovesick fool, she stared up at him and asked, "Why would you think that?"

He grinned. "Maybe it's because I love you and you love me and I can't imagine spending the rest of my life without you." He swooped down and kissed her. Then he lifted his head and laughed. "I know it sounds corny, but I want your face to be the first thing I see every morning and the last thing I see every night."

When she socked him in the chest, he fell over on his back and laid his hand over his heart.

"You're right. That did sound corny." She leaned down and nuzzled his nose with hers. "But since I happen to feel the same way, I think you're right. You are going to have to marry me."

Griffin Powell stared at the letter in his hand, the letter that had arrived special delivery this morning via an international courier. The return address was a hotel in London, Berkeley Knightsbridge, where Luke and Meredith had stayed.

If that was someone's idea of a joke, that person had a truly warped sense of humor.

Griff had read and reread the letter before he called Yvette.

Once she arrived, Sanders joined them in Griff's private study. Sanders closed and locked the door before Griff gave the letter to Yvette.

After she read the letter, she stared at Griff, a combination of doubt and hope in her eyes. "Could this possibly be true?"

"I don't know."

Yvette handed the letter to Sanders.

He read it quickly.

With concern in his black eyes, he looked from

vette to Griff and said, "You cannot believe what this
etter says, not without proof."

"I'm well aware of that," Griff replied.

"I want to go to England, to Benenden and see her
or myself," Yvette told them. "If there is the slightest
hance that she really is . . ." Yvette closed her eyes.

Griff could not bear to see her in such pain. "I don't
ant you to get your hopes up. This letter proves noth-
g except that someone wants to hurt us, someone
ho knows about what happened on Amara."

"Whoever sent the letter signed it Malcolm York and
hat signature looks authentic," Sanders pointed out to
hem. "But we know that it is not possible for him to be
he real York. This man, whoever he is, is a fraud. And
his girl mentioned in the letter, even if such a girl ex-
sts, may well be a fraud, also."

"But what if she does exist? What if she's not a
raud?" Yvette opened her tear-misted eyes and looked
leadingly at Griff. "If I can see her . . . touch her . . . I
ould know. Even without a DNA test."

"It would take a DNA test to convince me," Sanders
aid. "This man who calls himself Malcolm York has sim-
ly found a new means of tormenting us. Apparently
illing Powell employees and members of their families
as not enough for him."

Griff nodded agreement. "You're right, Sanders, but
his letter is not something we can ignore." He walked
ver, caressed Yvette's damp cheek and said, "I'll make
rrangements for us to take the Powell jet to London
omorrow. But before I finalize my plans, I have to show
ic the letter and I have to tell her everything."

"Do you think that is wise?" Sanders asked.

"No, Griffin is right," Yvette said. "He has to tell his
vife. She has every right to know." Yvette glanced at
anders. "Perhaps you should tell Barbara Jean."

"No," Sanders replied. "Not now. Not until we know
for sure."

Nic kept rehearsing how she would tell Griff that he
was going to be a father. Should she say, "We're pregnant?" Or maybe she should hold his hand over her still
flat belly and ask, "Which would you prefer, a son or a
daughter?" Then again, she could just put her arms
around him, look up into his gorgeous gray eyes and
say, "We're going to have a baby."

In the end, it probably didn't matter how she said it.
Griff would be thrilled. No, the timing wasn't perfect
and Griff, who worried about her way too much as it
was, would hover over her night and day. And she had
every intention of letting him smother her with attention. After all, why not give him the pleasure of pampering her for the next seven months?

When she arrived outside Griff's study, she found the
door open and Griff waiting there alone.

She could tell him about their baby this morning.
She could walk right into his study and deliver the good
news that he was going to be a father.

But when he looked at her, the expression on his
face stopped her cold. Something was wrong. Horribly
wrong. What had happened now?

She rushed over to him. "Griff, what is it? What's—?"

He grasped her shoulders. "I love you. If you never
believe anything else, believe that."

"You're frightening me. Please, tell me what's
wrong."

"First, tell me that you know I love you more than
anyone or anything on this earth."

"Yes, I know you love me. And I love you."

He released his tenacious grip on her shoulders. "

:ceived a special delivery letter from London a little
ver two hours ago. The signature on the letter was a
ecent forgery of Malcolm York's signature."

"Then it was a letter from *him*, this man you refer to
; the pseudo-York."

"I want you to read the letter." Griff reached behind
im and lifted the envelope from the desk. "After you
ead it, I want you to sit down and let me tell you about
hat happened on Amara. It's something I should have
lready told you."

Nic felt sick at her stomach. It could be nothing
ore than morning sickness, but she suspected it was
erves. Fear-induced nerves.

Griff removed the letter from the envelope and
anded the single page to Nic. She took the letter in
er unsteady hand. When she first glanced at it, her vi-
on blurred for a few seconds and then instantly
leared.

Dear Griffin,

*I hope this letter finds you and your wife well. Give
Mrs. Powell my sincerest regards. And please give my regards to our beautiful, delectable Yvette. I think of her so
often, of the two of you and dear Sanders, too. Ah, what
wonderful times we shared on Amara. How I wish we
could all be together again, as we were then.*

*I have been fortunate not to have spent all these years
alone, to have been able to keep a part of Yvette with me.
She is almost seventeen now. I gave her a little red
Porsche for her sixteenth birthday. She calls me Papa
and adores me as I adore her.*

*I believe I've been selfish far too long by keeping her
all to myself. Being a generous man, I have decided to
share her with her mother. If Yvette would like to meet her
daughter, tell her that she can find Suzette at the Benen-*

den School in Kent. As you can imagine, I've spared no expense on her education. You will find her to be as beautiful and brilliant as her mother and as strong of heart as her father.

> *Sincerely,*
> *Malcolm York*

The letter slipped from Nic's hand and sailed slowl onto the floor. She lifted her gaze and stared at Griff.

"Yvette has a daughter?"

"She gave birth to the child nearly seventeen year ago when we were on Amara."

"I don't understand. Where has the girl been a these years? And how would this pseudo-York know about her? If what he says is true, this girl thinks of hin as her father. But if the real Malcolm York was her fa ther—?"

"York wasn't her father."

"But Yvette was York's wife."

"In name only."

"What are you saying?" When Griff didn't immedi ately respond, she demanded, "Exactly what are you try ing to tell me?"

"Come over here and sit down." When Griff reache for her, she jerked away from him.

"I don't want to sit down," she told him. "I want you to explain. Tell me what happened on Amara. Tell me about this girl, about Suzette."

"You have to understand what it was like for us, fo me and Sanders and for Yvette, who was as much a pris oner as we were. She was forced to do things she didn' want to do, just as Sanders was. Just as I was."

"I know that he used you and the other men he cap tured as prey in his savage hunts, that you were treate like an animal, that you were forced to kill in order t

alive. I know that eventually, you and Sanders and
tte killed York and . . . But there's more to what hap-
ed on Amara, isn't there, a lot more?"

'Yes." Griff watched her closely, a look of agony and
plication in his eyes. "And I will tell you everything.
vear I will. But for now, I have to explain about
tte's child."

Nic instinctively knew she did not want to hear what
 husband was about to tell her. But she had to know
 truth. She needed to know.

'Tell me."

'York was involved in numerous illegal activities.
at's how he made his billions," Griff said. "His two
st lucrative business ventures were drug trafficking
 human trafficking."

'Human trafficking?"

'All the captives on Amara were not there just to be
d as prey to hunt and kill. Some were there to amuse
k and his closest allies . . . his business associates."

'You're talking about selling human beings into slav-
 Children and women and—"

'York was a sick son of a bitch. He didn't get any
asure from sex with his wife or any other woman. He
ferred to watch rather than perform."

Bile rose from Nic's stomach, the taste bitter in her
uth.

'Are you all right?" Griff asked.

She swallowed. "Go on. Tell me the rest of it."

'York found Yvette the perfect tool to give him united pleasure. He forced her to use her gifts as an
path to connect with the men's minds, the men he
ated and killed. Everything he could learn about
v they thought, how they felt, how they might react
iny given situation, gave him an edge over even the
st resourceful prey."

Nic felt dizzy. *Don't faint, damn it, don't faint.*

"Are you sure you're all right? You look so pa
Once again when Griff tried to touch Nic, she avoi
him.

"Please, don't touch me." She couldn't bring her
to look directly at him. "Don't stop until you've told
how all of this connects to Yvette's child."

Griff took in and released a deep breath. "Y
forced Yvette to have sex with any of his business asso
ates who wanted her. He used her to find out their
crets. When he realized that by her having sex wit'
man, Yvette was able to connect with his thoughts a
feelings more intensely than simply by touching the
he began bringing whatever man he intended to h
the next day into his home and forcing him to have .
with Yvette . . . while he watched them."

Nic swayed. She backed up and braced her h
against Griff's desk.

"When Yvette became pregnant, York threatened
abort the child, but being the evil son of a bitch that
was, he decided to allow her to have the baby. And th
when the infant was only a few hours old, he too!
away from Yvette."

Nic couldn't imagine the agony Yvette must have
perienced. "And all these years, what did she think h
pened to her child?"

"She didn't know," Griff said. "After we left Am
and managed to claim some of York's fortune
Yvette, we started searching for the child. We've be
looking for nearly sixteen years."

"What about the child's father?"

"Yvette doesn't know who fathered her child.
could have been one of several men she was forced
have sex with during the specific time in which she
came pregnant."

And then Nic asked the only question that really mat-
ed to her. "Were you one of those men?"

"Yes."

That single word upended Nicole's entire world,
rything she believed in, every emotion, every
ught, sending her into a tailspin of confusion and
e.

"Damn you, Griffin Powell. You swore to me that you
d Yvette were never lovers!"

"We weren't lovers. Not ever." He grabbed Nic's
ulders and shook her gently. "What Yvette and I did
s not making love. God, Nic, it wasn't even having
, not really. We were forced to perform in front of
rk."

Nic jerked away from Griff, rushed behind his desk,
ubled over and threw up in his wastebasket.

When Griff reached her, she stood up straight and
cked away from him. "Please, don't touch me. Not
w. I—I can't think straight. You have to give me time
think, time to sort through what I'm feeling . . .
out you and me and about Yvette. And . . . and about
r child." She looked Griff square in the eye. "She . . .
zette could be your daughter."

"Yes."

Nic walked across the study, opened the door and
chout turning back to look at Griff, said, "I'm going
stairs to pack a suitcase and then I'm going to Gatlin-
rg to our . . . to my cabin." Knowing how she loved
e mountains, Griff had given her the cabin as a Christ-
is present.

Stay strong. You can do this without crying, without
eaming, without hysterics, without falling apart.

"I don't want you to follow me or contact me in any
y," she told him. "When I've had time to think about

everything, I'll come home. I'll come back to Griffin
Rest and—"

"You can't go off by yourself," Griff told her, his voi
pleading. "It's too dangerous for you to be alone. If y
have to do this, then I'll send Shaughnessy or one
the other agents with you."

"I want to be alone, Griff. I have to be alone. Try
understand."

I need to think. And cry and scream and rant and r
and go slowly out of my mind.

"How about a compromise?" he asked. "Ask Male
to go with you."

"I won't do that. She and Derek . . ." Nic swallow
her tears. "No, not Maleah. Not now. If you insist on
not going alone, then send someone to follow me
the drive to Gatlinburg. And you can post guards at t
cabin twenty-four / seven. But I want to drive there
myself and I do not want a bodyguard in the house wi
me."

"I don't want you to leave, Nic. Stay here. I'll give y
all the time and space you need. Just don't leave me."

"You don't understand. I can't bear to look at y
right now." She walked out of the study, her head he
high, her shoulders straight, and her heart breaki
into a million pieces.

Maleah didn't know all the details, only that Nic h
left Griffin's Rest after Griff told her that Yvette hac
child, a nearly seventeen-year-old daughter that s
hadn't seen since the day of her birth.

"Griff may be the girl's father," Nic had explained.
can't stay here at Griffin's Rest. I need to get away
don't want to look at Griff and see the pain in his ey
every time he looks at me."

"I'll go with you," Maleah had told Nic.

"No, no. You and Derek, you two need to be together
ow. I want you to enjoy being in love. Those first few
ys and weeks are so incredible. I don't want you to
iss them."

When Nic made up her mind, there was no arguing
th her.

Maleah stood in the open doorway and watched Nic
ive away from Griffin's Rest. When her Escalade was
rely out of sight, Griff motioned to the man behind
e wheel of the black Hummer. He pulled out and fol-
wed Nic.

At that precise moment, Maleah knew what she had
do. She turned to Derek, who stood beside her, his
m draped around her waist, and said, "She shouldn't
alone. Will you understand if I—?"

Derek clasped her hand. "Come on, Blondie, I'll
lp you pack a bag. But not until after I give you a
oper send-off."

"I'm going to miss you terribly."

"Call me every hour on the hour," he teased.

"I'll call you every morning and every night and
ink about you every hour in between. How's that?"

He pulled her into his arms as they reached the top
the stairs. "When this crisis with Nic and Griff is over,
ou and I, Ms. Perdue, have a future to plan. A future
at includes a wedding and a honeymoon."

"Yes, we do." Maleah stood on tiptoe and kissed him.

Loving and being loved gave her the strength to be-
eve in the possibility of a happily-ever-after.

Epilogue

From time to time, Nic caught a glimpse, in her rear view mirror, of the black Hummer that had followe her from Griffin's Rest. When she stopped at a gas st tion just outside Pigeon Forge, Cully Redmond pulle into the parking area and waited for her.

Now, for the past few miles on her drive up th mountain to the beautiful, secluded cabin Griff ha given her as a Christmas gift, she hadn't seen Cully Hummer. Apparently, he had dropped back out of sigh to allow her time to arrive at the cabin and get settled before he parked outside to keep watch over her. N doubt, Griff would send another agent to relieve him the morning and the two would change shifts ever eight hours.

She parked the Escalade in the circular drive, g out, grabbed her suitcase from the back, and walked u to the front door. She drew in a deep breath of cris fresh mountain air. She unlocked the door and walke into the foyer. The cabin was so quiet, so peaceful, u like the daily chaotic noise that had plagued Griffin Rest recently.

After shoving her suitcase into the master bedroom closet, Nic walked through the living room and opened the door leading out onto the back deck. She went over to the edge of the wooden deck, clasped the top of the carved guardrail, and looked out at the breathtaking view below, the lush green hills and valleys.

Griff lied to me about his relationship with Yvette. He did have sex with her.

But they were never lovers. Griff said that what happened between them wasn't really even sex.

Maybe it wasn't, but I know one thing for sure—Griff loves Yvette.

He loves her because of the hell they shared, because of the torture they endured together.

He loves her because he may be the father of her child.

Nic laid her hand protectively over her belly.

She heard the sound of a car door slamming. Cully Redmond must have arrived. He probably needed to stretch his legs.

With her hand still resting over the tiny life just beginning to grow inside her, Nic jerked around when she heard a noise. Sound echoed in the empty stillness of her mountain retreat, so she wasn't surprised that she could hear footsteps on the front porch.

Damn it, she had told Griff specifically that she wanted to be left alone.

Don't bite Cully's head off. Just tell him you're fine and for him to report to Griff that you arrived here safely.

Nic went back into the cabin and made it halfway across the living room when the front door opened. Great! Cully would be sure to tell Griff that she'd left the door unlocked. How could she have been so careless?

With "get out and leave me alone" on the tip of her tongue, Nic stopped dead still when a man she didn't

know walked into her cabin. This was definitely no
Cully Redmond. And he wasn't another Powell agent.

"Who are you? What do you want?"

When he simply stared at her, Nic stood her ground
Show no fear.

"I'm expecting someone any minute now," she tol
him. "I didn't travel alone."

"If you're expecting the man driving the black Hum
mer, then you're going to be disappointed. I'm afraid
he's been delayed. Permanently delayed."

Fear clutched Nic's gut. Had this man killed Cully?

"I don't know what you want, Mr.—?"

"Where are my manners," the man said, a bone
chilling smile curving his lips. "Let me introduce my
self, Mrs. Powell. I'm Anthony Linden."

"That's not possible. Anthony Linden is dead."

"Yes, I know. And so is Malcolm York. And yet here
am, in the flesh, come to take you to see another dea
man. Mr. York is eager to meet you."

r Reader,

d by Morning was the second book in my *Dead by* tril-
 and leads directly into the third and final novel,
d by Nightfall, set for a December 2011 release. The
hanger ending I presented in the epilogue of *Dead*
Morning prepares you for what is to come in the next
 k, which begins where this book leaves off—with
 ole Baxter Powell in grave danger. When Griffin
 vell discovers that his wife is missing and soon there-
 r learns that she is in the hands of a "ghost" from his
 t, he moves heaven and earth to rescue her. Griff,
 ders and Yvette, the Amara triad, who suffered un-
 rable torture during their years as Malcolm York's
 tives, must come to terms with their past lives. Sets long buried in the depths of their tortured souls
 rface and are revealed in the cold, hard light of
 ir present realities. You will learn more about the
 sive and deadly Raphael Byrne, another of York's vic-
 s.

 those of you who love the Powell Agency books, you
 be pleased to know that I hope to write more novels
 turing Powell agents and others associated with the
 ncy. If while reading *Dead by Morning* you found
 ke Sentell and Rafe Byrne interesting alpha males,
 n you will probably agree that both of these hard-
 ged, dangerous men deserve books of their own.

 er I complete *Dead by Nightfall*, I'll be writing the se-
 el to my September 2010 novel *Don't Cry*, bringing
 ck TBI agent J.D. Cass and mental health therapist
 drey Sherrod. You'll be seeing more of several sec-

ondary characters, including J.D.'s daughter Zoe, drey's best friend Tamara and Tamara's parents, as w as J.D.'s sister Julia. Many of you contacted me askin Tamara and Marcus will reunite and if J.D. and Aud will get married, and wondering if J.D. and Zoe wil nally bond as father and daughter. I'll give you all answers in *Don't Say a Word*, set for release in 2012.

I always love hearing from readers. You may contact through my Web site at www.beverlybarton.com or writing to me in care of Kensington Publishing. Wh visiting my Web site, you can enter contests, sign up my e-mail newsletter, and check out a list of all books. You can also find information about my upco ing book signings, speaking engagements, and conf ences. And be sure to take a look at the videos about and my books. Also, go to Facebook and sign up a friend on my Beverly Barton Official Fan pa http://www.facebook.com/beverlybartonfanpage.

Warmest regar
Beverly Barton

WHEN to ENGAGE
an EARL

Also by Sally MacKenzie

WHEN to ENGAGE an EARL

SALLY MacKenzie

ZEBRA BOOKS
KENSINGTON PUBLISHING CORP.

http://www.kensingtonbooks.com

ZEBRA BOOKS are published by

Kensington Publishing Corp.
119 West 40th Street
New York, NY 10018

All Kensington titles, imprints, and distributed lines are available at special quantity discounts for bulk purchases for sales promotion, premiums, fund-raising, educational, or institutional use.

Special book excerpts or customized printings can also be created to fit specific needs. For details, write or phone the office of the Kensington Sales Manager: Attn.: Sales Department. Kensington Publishing Corp., 119 West 40th Street, New York, NY 10018. Phone: 1-800-221-2647.

Zebra and the Z logo Reg. U.S. Pat. & TM Off.

First Printing: June 2017
ISBN-13: 978-1-4201-3716-3
ISBN-10: 1-4201-3716-6

eISBN-13: 978-1-4201-3717-0
eISBN-10: 1-4201-3717-4

10 9 8 7 6 5 4 3 2 1

Printed in the United States of America

For my wonderful editor,
Esi Sogah,
who shone the light that
showed me the way through the weeds.
I shall inscribe her immortal words
above my computer:
"Easy fixes are the best fixes."

Chapter One

Evans Hall, August 1817

Alex, Earl of Evans, rode slowly up the drive to his country estate. He'd left the little village of Loves Bridge shortly after the weddings of his friends Marcus, Duke of Hart, and Nate, Marquess of Haywood, and had spent the last two months wandering the Lake District with only the hills and water and sheep for company.

No, that wasn't quite true. He'd had one constant, unpleasant companion: envy.

Marcus and Nate had found wives without even trying. Trying? Ha! They'd been trying to *avoid* marriage, believing Marcus was under the shadow of an ancient family curse. *He* was the one who'd been looking for a wife.

I'd be married now if Lady Charlotte hadn't jilted me.

He scowled at his horse's ears. Charlotte was in his past. In the days he'd spent scrambling up and down the fells, he'd vowed to leave the past with all its pain behind. There were plenty more fish in the sea, after all. He knew what he wanted: a quiet, restful sort of female, one who wouldn't constantly busy herself about his or other people's affairs, dragging confusion and hubbub into his life like his mother and sister still did on occasion.

The *ton* was littered with women who would suit. He just needed to put his mind to wooing one. He'd shop the Marriage Mart, attend the balls and house parties, and talk to every eligible lady. He was an earl, after all, albeit a jilted one. How difficult could it be? By this time next year, he'd have joined his friends in married bliss.

He stretched his neck, loosening the tension that had gathered there, and looked around at the familiar landscape. "It's good to be home, isn't it, Horatio?"

His horse shook his head in apparent agreement, making the bridle jingle.

"Uncle Alex!"

He reined Horatio to a stop. That sounded like Rachel, his sister's eight-year-old. Lord! Was Diana at the Hall?

Tension came rushing back, unease prickling the back of his neck and shivering down his spine. He loved his sister, but she would be certain to notice his blue-devils and hound him until she discovered their cause. If he let on that he was considering marriage again . . .

He shuddered in earnest. Diana was five years older than he and had always had a finger—or both her hands— in his affairs. She would tell Mama and the two of them would assemble a queue of eager matrimonial candidates before he could say Jack Robinson.

They might have his best interests at heart, but he didn't want them meddling in this.

I'll just have to paste a smile on my face for as long as it takes to get rid of Diana.

Rachel *could* have come with her father, Roger, Viscount Chanton.

He breathed a sigh of relief. Ah, yes, that was likely it. O'Reilly, his head groom, must have encountered an issue in the stables and Roger, thinking Alex still in the Lake District, had ridden over with *his* groom to offer his opinion. Rachel was horse mad and would have teased her father to bring her along.

If Roger noticed Alex's low spirits—highly unlikely— he'd have the good sense to ignore them.

"Where are you, Rachel?" he called, looking around.

He heard giggling. Was it coming from the tree on his right? He turned Horatio in that direction.

Rachel was the fifth of Diana's eight girls. *Eight!* With luck the baby Diana was carrying now was a boy so Roger could stop trying for an heir.

He snorted. The needs of the viscountcy had nothing to do with the matter. Diana and Roger had been nauseatingly in love since they were children, and while Roger must prefer a son of his own inherit rather than his cousin Albert, he'd never shown the slightest disappointment when Diana presented him with yet another daughter.

Where *was* his niece? "Rachel!"

More giggling, definitely from that tree. He rode closer and looked up.

Rachel grinned down at him from a branch about ten feet above his head. She had a streak of dirt across her forehead, an assortment of leaves in her hair, and her skirts—

Of course Rachel wasn't wearing skirts.

"Where did you get those breeches?"

Her grin widened. "Papa had them made for me after I borrowed Jeremy's and put a hole in the knee."

All Diana's girls were spirited, but Rachel was a complete tomboy. He didn't envy his sister the task of introducing her to Society when the time came, though one could hope Rachel would learn a little decorum before then.

"And who might this Jeremy be?"

Rachel's grin turned to a frown. "You know. *Jeremy*. The vicar's son, the one who's almost my age."

The vicar had a lot of sons. Alex had never bothered sorting them out. "The one with the red hair?"

Rachel rolled her eyes. "No! That's James. He's ten, the same as Esther. Jeremy has curly hair."

"Ah." He'd take her word for it.

Horatio shifted, reminding him that he was keeping the horse standing.

"Horatio's eager for the stables. Do you want to ride down with me?"

He wasn't surprised to see Rachel's face light up. She scrambled down the tree like a monkey and skipped over, extending her arms. As soon as he swung her up to sit before him, she leaned forward to pet Horatio's neck.

"What a handsome fellow you are, Horatio. Mr. O'Reilly thinks you'd make lovely babies with our Ophelia. What do you say? Would you like to be a papa?"

"Rachel! O'Reilly never discussed, er, *that* with you." He hoped. His head groom had a few rough edges, but Alex was almost certain the man wouldn't talk about horse breeding with a young girl, even one as horse mad as Rachel.

She giggled again. "Course not. He was talking to Lionel. I was in Primrose's stall, so they didn't see me."

Alex might not know the vicar's children, but he knew his employees. Lionel was one of his stable boys.

"You should have let them know you were there," he said. "It's not polite to eavesdrop."

"Oh, pooh. I'd never hear anything interesting if I didn't eavesdrop."

He bit back a laugh, suddenly reminded of Miss Jane Wilkinson, the new Spinster House spinster in Loves Bridge. She wouldn't let a small thing like social proprieties keep her from her goals either.

He smiled. The woman was a good friend of Marcus's and Nate's brides, but she was also an extremely outspoken, independent female. At twenty-eight years old, she was firmly on the shelf—precisely where she wished to be. And now that she'd installed herself in the Spinster House, she'd never have to look for a husband.

In fact, he was quite certain she'd had a hand in turning her friends, the previous Spinster House spinsters, into wives. He'd been standing next to her when Nate and Miss Anne Davenport had announced that they, too, were leaping into parson's mousetrap and for one brief moment, he'd thought Miss Wilkinson was going to hug him, she was so delighted.

He'd admit he'd been disappointed when she hadn't.

Rachel looked over her shoulder at him. "*Are* you going to breed Horatio with Ophelia, Uncle Alex?"

Right—breeding.

Horse breeding.

He was not going to discuss that topic with Rachel, either. "I'll have a word with your papa about it."

"When?"

"When we see him. Isn't he at the stables?"

"No. He's at Briarly."

His stomach plummeted to his boots. Briarly was one of Roger's other estates.

But wait. Roger didn't like being away from his family. He always loaded them into his carriage—and Alex's, since there were so many of them—and took them with him when he journeyed anywhere. Anyone encountering them lumbering along the road would think they were a traveling circus.

With that many children, they *were* a traveling circus.

"Why didn't you go with your papa?"

"Because Mama can't sit in a carriage that long anymore."

"Ah." Alex gave the house a nervous look as they passed it on the way to the stables. How pregnant was Diana? She'd spent the last twenty years in some stage of childbearing, so he'd stopped keeping track. "When is the baby due?"

"Any day now. Mama hopes it will wait until Papa gets back." Rachel shrugged. "But babies come when they want to."

Sweat blossomed in his armpits. "I would have thought your mama would wish to stay at home if she is so near her time."

"Oh, no. She can manage the short trip to the Hall, and she and Grandmamma wanted to be certain they'd have uninterrupted time to discuss Bea's come-out."

His heart stuttered.

Lord, Mama is here too?

He'd thought she was in London. Sweat trickled down his sides now, and his collar was suddenly too tight. Diana was bad enough, but Mama? She would not give up until she'd ferreted out every last one of his secrets.

The only way to handle the situation was to take the coward's way and run. But where? Mama might well follow him to Town.

Loves Bridge isn't far.

And the village fair should be almost underway. He could use that as an excuse.

"Beatrice is old enough for a Season?" he asked while he considered his escape. He could see the stables now.

"She'll be seventeen in October."

He was momentarily diverted trying to imagine his bookish, opinionated, and dangerously outspoken eldest niece at Almack's. Odds were Bea would dump a glass of punch over some Society popinjay's head inside of her first hour in those hallowed halls. Hmm. He'd better keep an eye on her when she came to London. Roger and Diana hadn't attended a Season in years. They might not be aware of all the traps awaiting a girl making her debut.

"Bea doesn't want a Season," Rachel was saying. "She is quite wild about it. She says that she will *not* be put on the Marriage Mart like a broodmare at auction."

Good Lord! "It is not as bad as that."

"How would you know, Uncle Alex? You're a man."

"Yes, but, unlike Bea, I have been in London for the Season." And would be looking for a wife this year, though not for a girl as young as Bea. That thought was more than a little revolting. "And even if it were true that some parents treat their daughters that way, your parents would not. You know that."

Rachel shrugged. "Perhaps, but I think she's right not to want to go. Jeremy's brother Jacob was in London last Season and he told Jeremy that the girls are all extremely silly and the *ton* parties dreadfully dull. The real fun happens elsewhere."

"Where no respectable young lady ventures." He could imagine exactly what mischief a young cub, even a vicar's son—no, *especially* a vicar's son—could get up to in Town. He'd got up to many of the same things in his youth.

"I *know* that, Uncle Alex. I just want to go to Tatt's and see the horses."

Tattersall's was not a place for ladies, either, but there was no point in telling Rachel that.

They finally reached the stables. Alex had never been so happy to see O'Reilly's craggy face.

"Milord, it's good to have ye home. And I see ye've found yer niece. Let me help ye down, Miss Rachel."

"I don't need any help."

That was foolishness. Rachel might be a respectable rider, but Horatio was far taller than her pony. "Perhaps you don't need help, Rachel, but you shall let O'Reilly assist you anyway."

She frowned, but since he had no intention of letting go of her until she agreed, she finally let out a short, annoyed breath. "Oh, very well."

Alex stayed in the saddle.

"Milord?" O'Reilly looked up at him questioningly.

"Do get down, Uncle Alex. Mama and Grandmamma will want to see you."

Of course they will. And they will ask me questions and give me advice and start thinking of eligible young ladies for me to marry and it will be hellish.

He'd probably sweated through his coat by now.

Horatio pawed the ground and shook his head. He was very well-behaved, but he was getting impatient.

"Shall I take Horatio to his stall, milord, so ye can go up to the house straightaway?"

He made his decision. He couldn't run fast enough. "As it turns out I'm not staying, O'Reilly."

His groom, not surprisingly, looked at him as if he was mad.

Rachel put her hands on her hips and frowned. "But you've just arrived, Uncle Alex."

"Well, yes. But I've suddenly remembered somewhere else I need to be."

"Where? Mama will want to know."

He felt the cowardly impulse to ask Rachel and

O'Reilly not to mention they'd seen him, but he discarded that notion at once. Several stable boys had walked past while they'd been standing here. There was no keeping his visit secret.

"I'm off to Loves Bridge for the village fair."

Loves Bridge

Miss Jane Wilkinson put her hands on her hips and glared at the slimy little man. "You said you had a kangaroo."

She and Mr. Waldo W. Wertigger, proprietor of Waldo's Wondrous Traveling Zoo, were standing on the Loves Bridge village green. It was the afternoon before the day the village fair was supposed to begin.

"I do have a kangaroo."

"A dead one."

The object under discussion was propped against the side of what had clearly once been a simple farmer's cart. Someone—likely the rogue standing in front of her—had added a canvas arch proclaiming the business's name, or what would have been the name had someone with any skill or literacy been in charge: Waldo's Wundrus Travling Zu. The concluding *u* was a muddled drawing of a snake— or perhaps a large worm.

She returned her attention to the only snake—or worm— at hand.

Mr. Wertigger tugged on his collar. "A *stuffed* one. It was alive once."

"That's beside the point. It's dead now." Her fingers itched to shake the fellow.

She felt partly to blame for this disaster. The Loves Bridge fair committee had been going to engage last year's organ-grinder and trained monkey when the Boltwood sisters suggested that a traveling zoo would be something special and, as the Duke of Hart was back at the castle, married, and soon to be a father, they should make this fair special.

What they hadn't said but everyone thought was that this might be the duke's last fair if the duchess was carrying a boy. For two hundred years, thanks to an angry spinster by the name of Isabelle Dorring, no Duke of Hart had lived to see his heir born.

A thread of worry twisted in her chest. The duke's new duchess was Catherine "Cat" Hutting, one of Jane's two close friends. If the duke died . . .

She took a calming breath. Everything would be fine. Only superstitious cabbageheads believed in curses, but even if there was a curse, legend had it that it would be broken when a duke married for love, which this duke most certainly had. It was rather nauseating watching him and Cat together, they were so besotted.

In fact, love, like a miasma, had settled over the village. Just days after that wedding, Jane's other close friend Anne Davenport tied the knot with the duke's cousin, the Marquess of Haywood.

An odd, hollow sensation formed in Jane's stomach. It wasn't envy, was it?

Nonsense! She was merely hungry. She had got exactly what she'd wanted from those weddings: the Spinster House. For the first time in her twenty-eight years, she was living all by herself.

Well, if you didn't count Poppy, the Spinster House tricolored cat, but at least Poppy was a fellow female. She didn't leave cravats festooning chair arms or crumb-filled plates on every horizontal surface like Jane's brother Randolph did.

She turned her attention back to Mr. Waldo W. Wertigger. She had wanted to see a kangaroo—a *live* kangaroo—so she had supported the Boltwoods' suggestion that they bring this . . . this charlatan to Loves Bridge.

If curses were real, she'd curse this humbug.

"Your advertisement claimed your kangaroo could jump over several grown men standing on one another's shoulders."

"And my kangaroo could"—he cleared his throat—"when it was alive."

Jane took another deep, calming breath and tried not to shout.

She did not succeed.

"We wanted a *live*, *jumping kangaroo*, you despicable mountebank."

The Worm tugged on his waistcoat. "Now, now. There's no need to call names. My poor kangaroo, sadly, may no longer be able to jump—"

"Or breathe!"

Mr. Worm Wertigger ignored her. "But I have other attractions. See my rare onager?" He pointed to a creature tethered to the back of his cart, contentedly grazing on the grass.

"That's an ass." *As are you.*

"An *Asiatic* ass."

Jane snorted derisively.

"And I have Romeo, the talking parrot." He wrestled a cage draped with a blanket out of his wagon and removed the covering with a flourish.

A gray parrot with a dark reddish tail cocked his head at Jane and gave a loud, rude whistle. "Hey, sweetheart—"

The Worm quickly dropped the blanket back over the cage.

"Sir! That parrot is *not* appropriate for a village fair."

The miscreant shrugged a shoulder. "Well, he did come cheap. I got him from a brothel that was closing."

"A brothel?!"

She was shouting again. Fortunately, Poppy appeared at that moment to rub against her ankle, calming her—

"May I be of assistance?"

A jolt of some unidentifiable emotion shot through her at the sound of that male voice. It couldn't be the Earl of Evans, could it?

Of course it can't. Lord Evans left Loves Bridge almost two months ago.

She glanced over her shoulder.

Lud! It *was* the earl. He looked . . . rough. Not quite civilized. His dark blond hair edged over his collar, and his face was weathered, making his eyes appear even bluer.

That's right. He'd gone off to walk the Lake District.

"What are *you* doing here?" She flushed. She was afraid that had sounded rather unwelcoming. She hadn't meant it to. She liked the earl and was actually happy to see him. She just hoped he didn't think to swoop in and save her from Mr. Wertigger. She could handle the Worm all by herself.

Lord Evans's right brow arched up and his firm lips twitched into a brief smile. "I'm delighted to see you, too, Miss Wilkinson."

"Pardon me." She gestured toward the Worm. "I'm afraid I'm rather busy at the moment."

"So I see. What seems to be the difficulty?"

The Worm's expression brightened at the sight of a fellow male. "The lady is being most unreasonable, sir."

"Unreasonable?!" She'd show him unreasonable.

"And emotional." The Worm leaned toward the earl as if sharing a male confidence. "But that's the way women are, isn't it? A rational, calm, male head is needed to do business properly."

Jane hissed—or maybe that was Poppy.

The Earl of Evans laughed. "You'd best look to *your* head, sir. I believe Miss Wilkinson would like to sever it from your neck and kick it all the way to London."

Mr. Wertigger glanced nervously at Jane and then back to the earl. "Since you know the lady, perhaps you can explain matters to her."

"I do know the lady and have found her understanding to be superior." Lord Evans turned to Jane. "Can *you* explain matters to *me*, Miss Wilkinson?"

She *did* like Lord Evans. He was one of the few reasonable men of her acquaintance.

"This, Lord Evans, is Mr. Waldo Wertigger. The fair committee thought his traveling zoo would be a splendid addition this year because of its exotic animals"—she narrowed her eyes and was gratified to see the Worm tug at his collar—"specifically its kangaroo"—she pointed to the sad, stuffed creature propped against the wagon—"which Mr. Wertigger advertised as able to jump thirty feet in the air."

Lord Evans pulled out a quizzing glass—she'd never seen him use one before, but he wielded it with great effect—and examined the kangaroo. "Jump, you say?"

"It did, milord." The Worm tugged at his collar again. "Until it met its untimely end. Apparently the English climate did not agree with it."

Jane suspected the Worm had not taken proper care of the animal, but since she had no proof of that—and it was beside the point anyway—she didn't dispute his theory. "He says that sad-looking donkey is an onager."

"It is," the Worm insisted.

She couldn't disprove that either, so she moved on. "And his parrot learned its conversation in a brothel. It's completely unsuitable to be exhibited at an event with young children and sensitive ladies. People would be shocked and distressed."

"Were *you* shocked and distressed, Miss Wilkinson?" Lord Evans asked, his eyes glinting with what might be suppressed laughter.

"Yes." Though not so much by what the parrot had said as by the realization that the entertainment she and the fair committee had arranged—and which she herself had so looked forward to—was a complete and utter disaster. And the fair was tomorrow! What were they—what was *she*—going to do?

There was no question—the Worm and his menagerie would have to go. She looked the man directly in the eye and said firmly, so he could not misunderstand, "We shall not have need of your services, sir. Please leave at once." She wouldn't put it past the fellow to lurk about and cause trouble.

Mr. Wertigger frowned. "I'll leave after I've been paid."

"*Paid?!* What do you mean, paid? You won't be paid a single farthing, sirrah!" The gall of the fellow.

His jaw hardened. "I *will* be paid. You can't drag Waldo W. Wertigger out to this sorry excuse of a village without paying him for his trouble. I've come quite a distance at considerable expense."

"And under false pretenses!"

He looked at Lord Evans. "Milord, you are a man of experience. Explain to this woman, if you will, that she cannot contract for services and then decide at the last minute that she does not want them." He paused to scowl at Jane. "We had an agreement."

Jane could not believe what she was hearing. "Yes. That you would provide a *live* kangaroo and a zoo that was suitable for a village fair—a fair that would be frequented by families, not by light skirts and libertines and . . . and other people of ill repute. You did not do that." She crossed her arms. "Thus you shall not be paid."

The Worm took a threatening step toward her.

"See here!" Lord Evans started to reach for him, but Poppy was faster. She jumped in front of Jane, arched her back, and hissed.

The Worm paused. "Madam, control your cat."

"Poppy is not my cat, sir, but even if she were, she has a mind of her own. I would caution you to stay back if you don't want your boots—and your flesh—slashed." She said that last part with great relish.

The Worm looked at Lord Evans. "Milord, please."

"I'm afraid Miss Wilkinson is correct, Wertigger. Poppy can be quite dangerous. She attacked the Marquess of Haywood's boots on several occasions, and I'm sure she would not hesitate to do the same to yours." He smiled. "Her teeth look very sharp as well, don't they?"

Poppy hissed again to underline Lord Evans's observation.

The Worm stepped back. "Very well, I'll complain to the authorities then."

"You can complain to anyone you want," Jane said. "You are still not getting any money from me."

"I'll get it from someone."

Her hands flew to her hips. "I shall be happy to watch you try."

His hands curled into fists. "I *will* be paid, madam."

"No, you won't."

Lord Evans sighed and reached into his pocket.

"Enough. I find you a complete bore, Wertigger. Oblige me by taking yourself off."

"You can't pay him," Jane said, but it was too late. The earl had already tossed the man a coin.

The Worm snatched the money out of the air and looked at it. "It's only a quid."

"And far more than you deserve," Jane said, and then glared at the earl. "I can't believe you gave that dastard anything."

"I want him to go away, Miss Wilkinson, and this seemed the fastest way to accomplish that goal." He looked back at the Worm. "I advise you to cut your losses, sir, and leave at once. My friend, the Duke of Hart, whose principal seat is here, and his wife—Miss Wilkinson's good friend and another member of the fair committee— are unlikely to be sympathetic to your position."

The Worm scowled, and for a moment Jane thought he'd take issue with Lord Evans, but then he let out a long breath and his shoulders drooped. "Very well. But don't expect Waldo W. Wertigger to ever come back here." His jaw hardened. "And I'll tell my friends to avoid the place too."

Jane very much doubted the scoundrel had any friends, but if he did, she certainly didn't wish to meet them. She opened her mouth to tell him exactly that, but the earl laid his hand on her arm to stop her.

"You must do as you think best," Lord Evans said, and then he turned his back on the miscreant, smiling down at Jane. "Shall we repair to Cupid's Inn for a bracing cup of tea, Miss Wilkinson?"

She glanced over at the Worm to be sure he was indeed leaving.

He was, but he treated her to a very nasty look.

She might be independent, but she wasn't stupid. Now that the fury of the moment had passed, she was happy to have the large, obviously fit earl at her side. Men could sometimes be dangerous. It was extremely annoying that women were at such a physical disadvantage.

"Merrow."

Well, yes, Poppy had helped rout the fellow too.

She turned her attention back to the earl. If he wanted to put his nose in her business, he could help her solve her problem. The fair was tomorrow and the main act was departing.

If we go to the inn, we'll get interrupted constantly. Everyone will want to know what he's doing in Loves Bridge.

What is *he doing?*

Likely visiting the duke. His travels were none of her concern. The fair, however . . .

"Let's go to the Spinster House instead. You can help me come up with a replacement for Mr. Wertigger."

Chapter Two

Jane shut the Spinster House door after the earl and Poppy entered, closing out the bright August afternoon and the drone of village life: the birdsong, the buzz of insects, the distant murmur of voices—

Suddenly, everything was dark and quiet and . . . intimate. It was a little hard to breathe.

Ridiculous! Lord Evans hadn't grown nor the house shrunk. The man wasn't even standing next to her. She should not be feeling crowded and, well, a bit over-whelmed.

Or, worse, expectant. Still and heavy like a summer day before a storm.

She leaned against the reassuringly solid door for a moment to steady herself and glanced at Poppy.

The cat looked oddly pleased before blinking and turning her attention to cleaning her paws.

Poppy never looks pleased unless I'm obeying her rare demand for petting or offering her some tasty tidbit from my dinner.

Truth be told, Poppy made her a little nervous. There

was something vaguely supernatural about her, as if she'd once been a witch's familiar or something—not that Jane believed in witches or any other supernatural foolishness, curses included.

Lord Evans had moved farther into the sitting room and was examining a large, faded square on the wall. "Didn't care for the picture that hung here, I see."

She took a deep breath and shook off her peculiar feelings. "I did not." She started toward him, but stopped a few feet away. She didn't want to get too near—

Oh, for goodness' sake, the man isn't going to bite!

She forced herself to close the gap between them. "It was hideous. Haven't you seen it?"

"No, this is my first time in the Spinster House." He lifted a brow. "What was it of? Some very un-spinsterish bacchanal?"

He was teasing her again. She'd missed that. No one else—especially no other man—was as much fun to match wits with.

"It was a painting of a hunting dog with a dead bird in its mouth. Quite, quite bloodthirsty—and ugly. I don't know what Isabelle Dorring was thinking when she hung it there."

He frowned. "Oh, I don't know. I'd say Miss Dorring was a bit bloodthirsty herself to have cursed the Duke of Hart's line as she did. She caused centuries of anguish"—his frown turned to a scowl—"and is still cutting up the current duke's peace."

"And Cat's peace, too." Cat's baby was due in just over six months' time. If it was a boy—

No! Curses aren't real. They're as make-believe as witches and fairies—she glanced at Poppy who had moved on to grooming her private parts—*and supernatural cats.*

"The third duke *was* a scoundrel to get poor Isabelle with child and then marry another woman," she said.

She'd always thought that duke a terrible villain—all the village girls had—but in a fairy-tale sort of way. She'd never considered how Isabelle's curse would affect a real person until she'd met the current titleholder.

Lord Evans's scowl deepened. "I'll grant you that wasn't honorable of him, but he didn't force Miss Dorring, did he?"

"No." Rape had never been part of the story.

"And Miss Dorring wasn't some naïve young miss. The stone in the graveyard says she was twenty-four. Surely *you* knew how children were created when you were twenty-four?"

She flushed. "Of course." She'd never had a man mention procreation to her. It was . . .

Freeing. Lord Evans was speaking to her as if she was an intelligent equal, not some fluffy-headed virgin who needed to be shielded from the world.

"And if I have the story right, her father was a wealthy merchant who left her this house and his fortune. She chose to invite the third duke into her bed. I'd say she bears some responsibility for the outcome."

"Well, yes, but—"

Both brows went up. "What? Is independent Miss Wilkinson going to tell me that poor Isabelle was a meek, spineless creature who couldn't make her own decisions?"

"No, of course not." To be honest, she'd never understood why Isabelle had been so reckless. She'd had her freedom. Why had she squandered it? "Perhaps she was overcome by love."

Gaah! Had she really just said that? But it was true. From her observations, love all too often disabled a woman's good sense.

Lord Evans snorted. "Or perhaps she was overcome with a desire to be a duchess."

That surprised her. The earl had a sharp wit, but he wasn't normally caustic. "So cynical!"

"Sadly, Miss Wilkinson, it is not cynicism. I have observed such machinations firsthand."

Of course he had. He was handsome, intelligent, amusing—*and* an earl. The London ladies must trip over one another to catch his attention.

She felt an odd mix of sympathy for him, anger at the ladies, and . . . jealousy?

No. Surely not.

"Do they hound you unmercifully, then?"

"Me?" His brows shot up in surprise. "What do you— oh. No. You misunderstood. I was referring to Marcus— the duke. Society women dragged him into the shrubbery on many occasions in the hope they could force him into marriage." He smiled. "Though I'll admit his last trip to the vegetation ended well."

"You aren't suggesting Cat was angling to be a duchess, are you?" Jane felt insulted on her friend's behalf. "Cat went through with the Spinster House lottery just the day after she visited the trysting bushes with the duke, if you'll remember."

"Yes, I know, Miss Wilkinson. I'm not lumping her in with the Society misses." He grinned. "I know Loves Bridge women are not at all like them."

She would take that as a compliment. "I'm quite certain Cat loves the duke. And more to the point, the duke loves her."

If the Duke of Hart *hadn't* married for love, then the curse wasn't broken.

If there *was* a curse.

Lord Evans nodded. "I agree." He looked back at the

empty square on the wall. "I suppose we'll know for certain soon enough."

Worry twisted in her chest again. "You don't believe in the curse, do you?"

"No."

Ah, thank God.

But her relief was cut short by his next words.

"But Marcus does, at least on some level." He frowned. "And there *are* those five dukes before him."

"Yes." Lud! If only they knew.

He put a hand on her shoulder. "Don't worry."

The weight and warmth of his touch were surprisingly comforting. She let out a shaky laugh. "How did you know I was worrying?"

That made *him* laugh. "Let's just say it would be best if you not take up games of chance."

No one had ever said her expression was easy to read. In fact, she prided herself on how well she hid her emotions. It was . . . unsettling to learn that the earl could see through her.

No. What was she thinking? Everyone in the village was worried about the duke. It didn't take any great perception to know she was, too.

"Yes. Well. Let's hope for the best. Now, I have a far more pressing concern. The fair is tomorrow, and I've just sent away the main attraction. What am I going to do?"

He grinned. "Shall I offer to put myself on exhibit? Though I'm afraid I'm not as interesting as a kangaroo, even a dead one."

She laughed. "You are here in Loves Bridge. You are already on exhibit—you know how the village is. I'm surprised the Boltwood sisters aren't peering in my window right now to see what you're up to."

They aren't, are they?

She glanced over. Whew! No faces pushed against the glass.

"Now come along. I'll make us a cup of tea and then we can put our heads together and come up with a plan."

"I think I'll need something stronger than tea," he said as he followed her into the kitchen.

He might be right. "I'll get the brandy."

"Miss Wilkinson! You have brandy? I would never have thought the Spinster House spinster would be partial to spirits"—he glanced down at Poppy, who was sprawled on the floor in a patch of sunlight—"at least of the alcoholic sort."

Did Lord Evans think there was something odd about Poppy too?

"I'm not responsible for bringing the brandy into the house—it was here when I arrived." She put it on the table along with two teacups.

"Teacups, Miss Wilkinson?"

"The house did not come with brandy glasses, Lord Evans."

He grinned as he reached for the bottle. "I see. I suppose it *will* look better if you are caught with a teacup rather than a brandy glass. May I pour?"

"No one is going to 'catch me,' Lord Evans. That is the beauty of the Spinster House. I live here quite alone"—she tilted her head toward the cat sprawled in the sun—"except for Poppy."

She held out her cup for him to splash some of the amber liquid into it. He had a very nice smile. It wasn't stiff or merely polite—it creased his entire face and lit his eyes.

"Right." He raised his cup. "To spinsterhood."

"Hear, hear." She tapped her cup against his and took a

sip. The liquid burned a path down her throat as she watched Lord Evans glance around the kitchen.

"This place looks as lost in the early 1600s as Loves Castle. Didn't any of the spinsters feel the need to redecorate?"

"Apparently not. But I will." She took another sip. Warmth curled through her stomach. She exhaled, feeling the tension start to drain from her shoulders and neck. She could finally relax—

No, I can't! The fair is tomorrow and the Worm has just left with his stuffed kangaroo and profane parrot.

A vise clamped around her neck and tightened. She took another, larger swallow of brandy.

Mistake. She gagged and coughed.

"Careful!"

Through blurry eyes, she saw Lord Evans jump up and pour a glass of water from the pitcher. In a moment he was offering it to her, his steadying hand on her shoulder again.

Odd. She'd never been much for having people touch her, but she didn't mind the earl doing so.

"Here. Only a sip. I don't want you inhaling it." He smiled. "Don't drink brandy much, do you?"

She scowled at him. "Of course I don't drink brandy much, but that's not what caused me to choke. Must I remind you that I have less than twenty-four hours to come up with a replacement for the much-anticipated kangaroo?" She moaned and dropped her head into her hands. "This is a disaster."

"Oh, it's not that bad. I've been to my share of village fairs, and unless the inhabitants of Loves Bridge are a very different sort, you'll be fine as long as there's plenty of food and drink. The adults just want to gossip and the children to run around outside."

The annoying man was likely right.

"But we wanted this fair to be special because—" She raised her head and looked at him. "Because of the duke."

He frowned, his right brow arching up. "Because he'll be in attendance for the first time?"

"Well, er, yes." Before May, the duke had only been to the village once. Twenty years ago, when he was a boy, he'd come to choose the Spinster House spinster—the one before Cat. "But more because if there *is* a curse, this might be his last time."

The earl nodded, digesting that. "Let's hope it's not, but even if it is—" He smiled. "The duke has seen a kangaroo before, Miss Wilkinson."

"Oh. Yes. Of course." How silly of her. There were menageries in London, and a wealthy duke had wealthy friends who likely had their own private collections of exotic animals.

"But even if he hadn't—even if you'd managed to assemble ten kangaroos riding on elephants, attended by giraffes, Marcus wouldn't care. He's still newly in love. All he can see is his duchess."

That was rather sweet—nauseating, but sweet. And true, now that she considered the matter.

Did Lord Evans have experience with love? Cat had said something about him being jilted almost at the altar . . .

How could a woman do that? If *she* were going to wed— Which she was not!

She must be letting Cat corrupt her thinking. Now that Cat was married, she believed every woman should be a wife. She was like a missionary, trying to convert all she saw—particularly Jane—to her religion.

Well, Jane was not going to be converted! She'd spent too many years waiting on her brother to wish to take on another male. And, as she'd come to realize as she got older, early exposure to her father's temper had turned her against ever giving herself into a man's keeping. Papa had never hit anyone—at least he'd never hit her—but his shouting had felt like a blow.

Still, Lord Evans wasn't Papa. He'd yet to raise his voice or show any temper in her presence. She was here alone with him—except for Poppy—and she didn't feel any of the expectant dread she'd always felt around Papa.

Well, she did feel oddly expectant. . . .

Her stomach twisted again. She really should eat something, especially now that she was drinking brandy. "Would you like some seedcake? It's rather good."

The earl's expression turned guarded. "Did you make it?"

That made her laugh. "No. My culinary skills are quite limited, as I see you've guessed. Mrs. Chester up at Loves Castle baked it and Cat brought it by."

He grinned. "Oh, well, then, I'll definitely take a slice or two. Mrs. Chester is an excellent cook."

She sliced her last loaf, put it on a plate—and watched in dismay as Lord Evans inhaled three slices before she'd finished her first.

He *was* her guest.

She took a sip of water—no more brandy for her—and focused on business.

"Now, about the fair. I'm sure you're correct that the duke won't care what entertainment we provide, but that really doesn't solve my problem. We've been promising people for weeks they'll see a live kangaroo. I need to offer them something in its place."

The evil man took yet another slice of cake.

She'd best act at once if she wanted any more. She reached for the last slice—and saw him eyeing her fingers.

"You've had more than your share, you know."

The miscreant had the temerity to grin. "Yes. The seed-cake *is* quite good, but I'll be a gentleman and let you have that last bit."

If he thought that act would win him the prize, he was very much mistaken. Jane liked seedcake too. She plopped it on her plate.

The earl brushed some crumbs off his waistcoat. "You aren't going to find a kangaroo in the Loves Bridge bushes."

"I *know* that," Jane said, rather impolitely, her mouth still being full of seedcake.

"So we'll have to come up with something else."

She was surprised at the warmth she felt at his use of *we*. It was nice not to have to face this impending disaster alone.

"How about pig races?" Lord Evans said. "I enjoyed those when I was a lad."

"We already have pig races." She took a swallow of water to wash down the last bit of cake.

"A pet show, then?" Lord Evans looked down at Poppy. "I imagine Poppy would win most inscrutable."

Poppy yawned and sat up to clean her tail.

"We have a pet show. People dress their animals in the most outlandish outfits they can think of."

Lord Evans laughed. "I cannot imagine Poppy consenting to *that*."

Neither could Jane.

They both looked at Poppy, who sneezed, stretched, and walked slowly to the door. She stopped on the threshold and stared at them.

"I think she wants us to follow her, Miss Wilkinson."

"Don't be silly." Though it did appear Poppy thought—

No. Poppy is a cat. *She doesn't think.*

"Merrow!"

And she certainly couldn't read minds. . . .

Could she?

Jane had lived with Poppy for two months now, and she'd admit, if only to herself, that, while the cat couldn't really be supernatural, there was definitely something very odd about her.

"Don't you wonder where Poppy wants to take us?"

She had no time for curiosity. "We're supposed to be discussing the fair."

"We can discuss the fair while we follow Poppy. There's nothing keeping us in the kitchen." He gave the empty seedcake plate a regretful look and stood, extending his hand to her.

She regarded his broad palm and strong fingers for a moment, her own palm itching to feel his skin against hers.

Good Lord. It's a hand. *Everyone—or almost everyone—has two. There's nothing special about Lord Evans's.*

"Oh, very well." She stood—without his assistance—and started toward the door, ignoring what sounded suspiciously like a chuckle from the man behind her.

Miss Jane Wilkinson was so prickly. It was quite amusing.

Alex swallowed his mirth as he followed the woman out of the kitchen. They made quite the parade: the cat strolling in the lead, tail high, tip curled as if in a question mark; Miss Wilkinson next, her back as straight as a fireplace poker, radiating annoyance; and him.

He'd made an excellent decision in coming to Loves Bridge. Sparring with this sharp-tongued spinster was exactly what he needed. It made him feel alive and energized again.

The cat led their little parade up the stairs.

He'd help Miss Wilkinson with the fair, and then he'd go off wife-hunting. Perhaps by this time next year, he'd not only be married, but on the verge of joining Marcus in fatherhood.

If Marcus is still alive, that is.

His heart stuttered, and he took a deep breath. Of *course* Marcus would still be alive—but Alex would be very happy once March came and he saw Marcus holding his heir in his arms.

The parade arrived on the next level where there were three doors to choose from—two on the right and one on the left. Poppy darted through one of the right-hand choices.

"Your room, Miss Wilkinson?"

He had a sudden odd desire to see her bedchamber.

And her bed.

Does she lie there stiffly on her back every night, bed-clothes pulled up to her chin, a long-sleeved, high-necked virginal—spinsterish—white gown covering every inch of her body?

A completely inappropriate part of his anatomy grew quite stiff at the thought.

What was the matter with him? Miss Wilkinson was amusing, and, yes, attractive, but she was a dedicated spinster—and most certainly not the restful sort of female he was looking for. He'd almost had heart failure this afternoon when he'd looked across the village green to see her brangling with that Wertigger fellow. She'd been all alone with him and clearly unwilling to give an inch.

Good Lord! The man was only about her height, but he was several stone heavier. If he'd turned violent, she would have been in serious danger.

She seemed not to have realized that. She certainly

hadn't looked relieved when he'd come up to them. Oh, no. He could tell she hadn't welcomed his interference at all.

He frowned. He admired her independence and courage, but she could do with a little fear to keep her bravado in check. Caution was a virtue she appeared not to have.

"No, my room is the one on the left. It's the largest."

"Ah. So I assume it was Isabelle's?" He stepped over to peer inside. It was rude of him to invade her privacy that way, but he couldn't help himself. It was almost as if an invisible string pulled him to the doorway.

The room was rather dark, especially for a lady, with oak paneling and a large, red-curtained four-poster bed—a bed too large for one lonely spinster.

He'd like to—

Good God! He could not entertain lascivious thoughts about Miss Wilkinson. They weren't married, and they weren't going to be. She had no interest in that institution and he . . .

He scowled at the bed. He wanted a *restful* sort of woman remember, someone like Charlotte, someone who would let him protect her and not be *annoyed* by his efforts to keep her safe.

Zeus, Miss Wilkinson would probably try to protect *him* if they were ever in danger.

That sounds rather stimulating—

No, it doesn't.

He'd felt strong and larger than life when he'd had Charlotte on his arm.

And a little bored—

No. He hadn't been bored. He'd—

Oh, what did it matter? Miss Wilkinson had no interest in marriage. And he certainly didn't wish to be rejected again. Once had been painful enough.

"Cat told me a full-length painting of Isabelle hung

there when she moved in." Miss Wilkinson pointed to a conspicuously empty portion of the wall.

"Are you going to replace it with something?"

"Of course. I just haven't had time to—"

"Merrow!"

He looked over. Poppy was sitting in the doorway of the room she'd first disappeared into, tail twitching. She did not look happy.

"I think the cat has lost patience with us."

Miss Wilkinson sighed. "Yes. We'd best do what she wants. I assure you, she'll not give us any peace until we do." She started toward the other room.

"Do you mind living with such a, er, managing cat?" he asked, following her. It was rather amusing how the strong-willed Miss Wilkinson danced to Poppy's tune.

She laughed. "Poppy isn't managing, precisely." She suddenly frowned, as if annoyed with herself. "She's not managing at all. She's a cat, Lord Evans. An animal. She doesn't think."

Poppy hissed.

He put too much value in his skin and the leather of his boots to argue with Poppy and her sharp claws. "She does appear to get the humans in her life to do what she wishes, however."

Miss Wilkinson grimaced. "I suppose she does."

They stepped over the threshold into what once must have been a study or a sitting room, but was now jammed with household castoffs.

"I've been meaning to ask the duke to send someone to help me clear all this out," Miss Wilkinson said.

"Hmm." Alex's attention was caught by a large painting propped against a worn upholstered chair. It was of a girl dressed in clothes that looked to be from the early 1600s. "Is that Isabelle?"

"Yes. Can you imagine going to bed each night with her staring down at you?"

I can imagine going to bed each night with you—

He jerked his unruly imagination away from naked, sweaty, intimately entwined bodies back to the painting. "She doesn't look like the evil, angry woman I'd thought her to be." The girl was pretty, but not beautiful. More to the point, she looked young and happy—and vaguely familiar. He frowned. "She looks like the new duchess."

"Yes, I suppose so. They're related, you know—some sort of cousins."

"Ah." He hadn't known that. "It's hard to imagine this girl cursing the duke's line and then drowning herself and her unborn child in Loves Water."

"*If* she did those things. Cat told me she and the duke found a letter in there"—she pointed to a large cabinet—"which made them wonder if any of the story is true." Miss Wilkinson shook her head. "But if the story isn't true, where did Isabelle go?"

Marcus had mentioned something about a letter, but there hadn't been time to discuss it before the wedding—and then Nate had got married and Alex had left for the Lakes.

"Perhaps she didn't go anywhere. Perhaps she really is buried in the graveyard." It would be a huge relief to prove now that there was no curse, rather than having to wait six long months. Not that he was about to exhume Miss Dorring.

Miss Wilkinson looked unconvinced. "But what about her baby?"

"He—or she—could have died in infancy. Many children didn't live past their first birthday back then."

Poppy sneezed, but whether the cat agreed with their theory or not, Alex couldn't say.

"Oh, bother." Miss Wilkinson's voice suddenly held more than a touch of impatience. "This isn't getting me any closer to a plan for tomorrow's fair. Much as I might want to, I can't take Isabelle's painting out to the village green and invite people to throw things at it."

Poppy hissed.

"I *said* I couldn't do it."

Was Miss Wilkinson going to get into an argument with the cat? That would be unwise. Her nails were no match for Poppy's claws.

"Perhaps Poppy will show us why she was so insistent we follow her." He looked down at the cat. Was *he* going to talk to it?

He was.

"*Do* you have a suggestion, Poppy? As you can see, Miss Wilkinson is getting anxious."

Poppy blinked at him and then turned her back rather pointedly and disappeared into the clutter behind the chair.

Miss Wilkinson emitted a short, annoyed breath. "Wonderful. What a wild goose—or a wild cat—chase this has been. I've less than *twenty-four* hours to come up with a substitute for Mr. Wertigger's traveling zoo, Lord Evans, and I'm no closer than I was when we were in the kitchen. What in God's name am I going to—"

"*Merrow!*"

Poppy had returned and was staring up at them from under the chair. Clearly, she wanted him to follow her—but he was not a cat.

He sighed and struggled out of his coat.

"Lord Evans, *what* are you doing?"

"Preparing to dig through this pile of things, Miss Wilkinson. Would you be so kind as to hold this?" He handed her his coat.

Her brows slammed down into a scowl as she took it.

"We do not have time to waste looking for . . ." She waved her hand at the jumble and then glanced back at him. "What *are* you looking for?"

"I have no idea. Pardon me."

Miss Wilkinson stepped back, his coat clutched absently in her hands, as he moved Isabelle over to lean against the cabinet.

"Have you lost your mind?"

"I don't believe so, but I might be mistaken." He eyed the chair. He couldn't see anything leaning up against it now, but he didn't want to move it and send the whole pile crashing down on Poppy.

But then cats had nine lives, didn't they? And he'd wager Poppy had more lives than most. He was confident she'd find a way to avoid getting crushed.

"You might want to wait outside, Miss Wilkinson. This could get messy." He sneezed. And dusty. Likely there were two centuries' worth of dirt behind that chair.

Of course the woman ignored him.

Well, there was nothing for it. He grasped the chair's arms. Lord, they knew how to make furniture two hundred years ago. The thing was incredibly heavy.

He wrestled it out of the way.

"Lord Evans, we really do not have time for this. You said we'd discuss the fair. I'm counting on you to help me come up with a plan."

"I think that is what I am doing."

He might have heard her grind her teeth.

He surveyed the clutter he'd uncovered. There was a small table with water stains marring its surface; a chipped pitcher and several chipped bowls; a broken mirror; and a cushion that looked like it might be hosting a family of mice.

Or had been hosting. One hoped Poppy, being a cat, had

encouraged the rodents to move along, if she hadn't made them her supper.

"Lord Evans, please. The clock is ticking."

And the cat was growling. Where *was* she?

Ah, he saw the tip of her tail sticking out from behind a stack of boards someone had propped against the outside wall. He moved the table and other things aside—fortunately, no mice fled the cushion—and carefully picked his way across the room.

He squatted down to peer into the shadowy space between the boards and the wall. Poppy looked back at him—as did a pair of lifeless eyes.

He must have made some sound, because suddenly Miss Wilkinson dropped his poor coat on the floor and rushed toward him.

"Lord Evans! What's amiss? Are you all right?"

He shot up to his full height. "Careful! You'll trip."

Which is exactly what she did, of course. He'd only a split second to brace himself before he took her full weight.

"Oof!"

He wasn't completely certain which of them had made that sound. Her momentum had propelled him backward so he'd collided forcefully with the wall—fortunately or they would have ended up sprawled on the ground, he on the bottom, likely impaled by a splintered table or discarded candlestick, and she on top.

His brainless cock ignored the impalement part of that story, focusing instead on the notion of Miss Wilkinson's feminine curves pressing against it. It started to swell with excitement.

He took a calming breath—and breathed in Miss Wilkinson's scent. Blast.

His unruly cock grew larger.

"Oh." Miss Wilkinson gaped up at him, clearly stunned by her sudden change in position and—fortunately—unaware of his body's reaction. If she'd noticed, he felt quite certain he'd be gasping in pain now, her knee having taught his cock proper behavior.

If I lean forward just an inch or perhaps two, our lips will—

Zeus! Was he losing his mind? He grasped her elbows to move her away just as she planted her hands on his chest to do the same. She stepped back—and stumbled again.

He reached for her, but she was able to recover without his help.

"What did you see? You made a noise, as if you were . . . startled. Was it something"—she swallowed—"alive?"

Not anymore.

No. If the thing had been alive and was now dead, it would stink.

"I *was* startled—and I'm not certain what I saw. I'll have another look, shall I?"

He started to squat, but Miss Wilkinson put a hand on his arm, stopping him.

"Are you certain it's safe?" She glanced down nervously.

Poppy, sitting by the opening, interrupted her grooming long enough to look up at them.

He laughed. "Poppy apparently thinks so."

Miss Wilkinson did not let go. "Poppy is a cat. She may not realize the danger."

What did she think might be lurking in that shadowy space? If it was indeed dangerous, it would have already . . . what? Darted out and nipped their toes? "Are you afraid, Miss Wilkinson?"

She bristled. "Of course not." Her jaw hardened. "I'll look myself."

"No, you won't." He certainly wasn't about to let her take any risk, if there was one. That would not be at all chivalrous.

She squared her shoulders. "This is my house, Lord Evans. It's my responsibility to see that it's kept up properly."

Oh, Lord, he'd only meant to tease her. "But consider my mortification, Miss Wilkinson, should word get out that the Earl of Evans had a female, ah—"

That was the wrong thing to say. Miss Wilkinson's eyes snapped and she opened her mouth to blister his ears. Time to change course.

"And the floor's very dusty. My clothes are already covered in dirt. No point in getting your dress soiled as well."

That stopped her. "Oh." She frowned. "Yes. Well, I suppose, when you put it that way, you have a point."

Of course he did, but he didn't waste any more time arguing. He squatted down again and peered into the shadows. The thing was still there.

Poppy butted her head against his arm to encourage him.

Very well. It was time to show some courage. He reached gingerly into the space—

And laughed.

"What is it?" Miss Wilkinson asked anxiously. "What have you found?"

Chapter Three

"A puppet!"

"A puppet? What's a puppet doing here?" That came out sharper than Jane had intended.

At least she was feeling more herself. She'd been off balance there for a bit—literally, of course, but also emotionally.

Silly. Being pressed against Lord Evans's chest, having his arms around her, should not have affected her. She'd stumbled; he'd caught her. His actions hadn't been amorous. They'd been reflexive. He'd have reacted the same way were anything thrown at him.

And yet, after the shock of tripping had abated, she'd felt . . .

The closest she could come to describing the emotion was *home*. She'd felt as if she was finally where she was meant to be.

Which was the stupidest notion. The Spinster House was her home. When the tenancy had opened up in May with the sudden, surprising marriage of Miss Franklin to the now-Duke of Benton, she'd known immediately that she wanted to be the next Spinster House spinster. The vacancy had been the answer to a prayer she hadn't had the audacity to utter. When she'd lost the Spinster House lottery, she'd schemed to get Cat and then Anne wed—to men they loved, of course—and out of the house. And now she was here.

She'd never been happier. She had no one—except for Poppy—to answer to.

She loved her brother, but she loved him even more now that she wasn't living with him.

Lord Evans held the puppet out to her. "Take this, will you? I want to see if there's anything else of interest back here."

She examined the puppet as the earl resumed his rummaging. The gold-and-red-striped outfit, floppy legs, little arms, and wooden head with its big hook nose and red, conical hat were all very familiar.

"It's Mr. Punch!"

"Yes." Lord Evans stood, a puppet in each hand and a large smut on his cheek. "And here's his wife, Joan, and the baby."

His dishevelment was oddly appealing.

What is *the matter with me?*

Yes, she'd admit Lord Evans was far more attractive than any of the men in Loves Bridge. He was even more attractive, in her opinion, than her friends' husbands, the duke and Lord Haywood.

And it wasn't just his physical appearance that was so pleasing. It was his smile, the way his eyes lit with mischief when he teased her, the way—

No. She was beginning to sound infatuated. She was not. Lord Evans was merely a friend—at least she hoped he was a friend since their paths were certain to cross frequently over the years.

"You've dirt on your face."

He laughed and pulled out his handkerchief. "I said the floor was dusty. See what I saved you from?"

She bit back a smile. "Thank you. And the spot's on the other side."

She might not be interested in a husband—not that Lord Evans had shown any sign of wanting her as a wife—but she was still a living, breathing female. There was nothing wrong with admiring a handsome man. She'd admire a handsome horse as well.

"And you have a large piece of fluff in your hair." She reached up without thinking and brushed it away, her fingers tangling briefly in the silky strands.

That might have been a mistake. His eyes narrowed slightly, his gaze sharpening.

She flushed and looked down at Punch.

"Thank you, Miss Wilkinson."

His voice sounded deeper, oddly intimate.

"Y-you're"—she swallowed—"welcome."

She was behaving like a complete widgeon. How many times had she laughed to herself when other girls turned into simpering cabbageheads around an eligible male?

"It looks as if one of the Spinster House spinsters was a devotee of Punch." Lord Evans's words broke the odd tension that had sprung up between them.

"No, not a spinster," she said, giving herself a mental shake. "A tailor—Mr. Denton. We used to have a puppet show at all the fairs when I was a child. My father said Mr. Denton made everything himself—the puppets, their clothing, even the stage and scenery."

Papa had thought the puppet shows very funny, especially Mr. Punch's antics, but Mama had not been at all certain they were appropriate for children. They'd argued, and Papa had won—as always—leaving Mama to stand next to him and Randolph and Jane, wringing her hands—and laughing, too, from time to time.

"We haven't had a show since Mr. Denton died years ago. I'd forgotten all about them. I wonder what the puppets are doing here."

"Likely someone concluded this was the perfect place to store them. The Spinster House *is* right on the green and has only one occupant." He put the puppets down. "I'm going to investigate those boards. Unless I miss my guess, we've found what Poppy dragged us up here for."

Poppy must have agreed that her work was done, because she darted out the door and disappeared down the stairs.

"But what are three puppets going to do for us?"

"Three puppets and a stage, Miss Wilkinson." He grinned. "You can replace Mr. Wertigger and his sad excuse for a traveling zoo with a puppet show."

Was the man daft? "Lord Evans, you are missing the point. We might have the puppets. We might have the stage. But we do not have Mr. Denton, unless you or Poppy can conjure him from the grave. Who is going to put on the show?"

The impudent man bowed. "I am, Miss Wilkinson."

Jane stood on the green early the next morning and watched Lord Evans set up the puppet stage. She'd hardly slept a wink the night before.

She liked to be in control of things, and she was not in control now.

"Are you certain you know what you're doing?"

He paused long enough to give her an annoyed look.

Perhaps she *had* asked that question one—or several—times too many.

"It's just that I feel responsible." She wished she could put on the show herself, but she knew that would be a disaster.

"I don't know why." He tested the stage, pushing on the sides to be certain it was stable.

"Because I was the one who dismissed Mr. Wertigger."

His brow arched up. "Do you think the other members of the fair committee would have wished him to stay?"

"N-no. But I didn't ask their opinion."

"Of course you didn't. You were the one confronted with the issue. You didn't have time to assemble the committee."

"True." She wanted to believe him. She *did* believe him—and appreciated his support. But she couldn't stop worrying. "Perhaps the children would have liked to see a kangaroo, even a stuffed one."

"Perhaps." He stepped back to survey his handiwork. "But remember the parrot. I can't imagine their mothers would wish them to hear the parrot."

Lord Evans was correct about that. She should stop fretting and believe what he said. But still . . .

"You're certain you know what you're doing?"

The earl came as close to rolling his eyes as she'd ever seen a man come. "Miss Wilkinson, how many times must I—"

"If it isn't Lord Evans!"

They both turned to see Randolph coming toward them.

Perhaps it was the angle of the sun or because she wasn't sharing a house with him any longer, but Jane was surprised to see how thin her brother's hair had got and how thick his middle. He'd just turned thirty-three this year.

"I heard you were here when I stopped by Cupid's Inn for my breakfast, Evans." Randolph looked at Jane. "Now that my sister has moved into the Spinster House, I need to take my meals out."

"You could pay Mrs. Dorn more," Jane said. Mrs. Dorn was Randolph's unpleasant maid-of-all-work. "Then she would make you your breakfast."

Randolph pulled a face. "You know Mrs. Dorn's food is barely edible."

That was very true. And every meal came with a grumble and a dark look. Quite disturbed one's digestion.

"Well, *you* could learn to cook."

Randolph's eyes widened in shock—and then he laughed. "Oh, no. Cooking is women's work"—he looked at the earl—"isn't that right, Evans?"

She expected the earl to agree, but he didn't.

"The Prince Regent is quite happy with his male French chef, Wilkinson," the earl said, smiling. "In fact, French chefs are quite the thing among the *ton* these days."

Randolph made a dismissive gesture. "The French! They are a different breed, are they not?" He looked back at Jane. "But where's the kangaroo, Jane? I thought you said there'd be a kangaroo this year. I came over early to have a look at the beast."

Oh, dear. This was exactly what she'd feared. People would be so disappointed. "It turned out to be stuffed, Randolph. You can be sure I sent the zoo proprietor away with a flea in his ear."

Randolph looked crestfallen. "That's too bad. A kangaroo would have been splendid. What are you going to do instead?"

One would think Randolph might have taken note of the tall wooden structure literally at his elbow, but he'd always been one to focus only on things right under his nose, and then only when he had on his reading spectacles.

"We found Mr. Denton's puppets and stage. They were

stored in the Spinster House." She smiled in what she hoped was a confident fashion and said brightly, "Lord Evans is going to put on a performance."

"Oh." Randolph frowned and then stepped round to examine the stage more closely. "By Jove, that *is* Denton's. I remember it well." He looked at the earl. "Do you know what you're doing, Evans?"

The earl did not strangle Randolph—he laughed instead. "Your sister has been asking me that very question, Wilkinson. Several times in fact."

Randolph nodded. "I should think so. She *is* on the fair committee and apparently sent the prime attraction packing."

Anger and anxiety battled in Jane's stomach.

"It's not as if I had a choice, Randolph." She took a deep breath and struggled to speak more calmly. "Besides the stuffed kangaroo, the man had a very rude parrot."

Randolph's eyebrows shot up. "He did, did he?"

"Yes. He'd got it from a brothel."

Randolph pressed his lips together as if he was struggling not to laugh. "Yes, I suppose I can see why that might not be suitable."

"*Might* not!? Randolph, the bird, er,"—she hoped she wasn't blushing—"flirted with me."

Randolph snickered, but recovered quickly. "Pardon me. The image of a randy parrot . . ." He shook his head. "I do wish I could have seen your face."

"It was *not* amusing."

"Jane, you could do with a sense of humor."

"I have a perfectly good sense of humor. This wasn't funny."

Randolph opened his mouth to retort, but fortunately the earl interrupted.

"It looks like a crowd's gathering. I think now would be a good time to start the performance."

"*Do* you know what you're doing, Evans?" Randolph asked.

"Actually, I do. I took an interest in puppetry when I was at university and had some lessons with a professional performer."

"You'll remember there are children present?" Jane asked. Puppet shows could be as ribald as the Worm's parrot, especially if one were used to a university audience of young, rowdy males.

"Of course, Miss Wilkinson. Don't worry. I've entertained youngsters. My nieces are very fond of puppet shows and cajole me into performing whenever they can."

Jane blinked. She'd never thought about Lord Evans's family. "You have nieces?"

"Yes, eight of them." He shrugged. "Or perhaps nine by now. My sister is due to deliver at any moment. Now if you'll ring the bell to gather a crowd, I'll get to work."

"I remember that bell," Randolph said. "Let me do it."

Jane happily handed the bell to her brother while Lord Evans disappeared behind the stage. In no time, a sizable crowd had gathered.

Punch appeared on stage with his wife and baby.

"Look, Mr. Punch," the wife said. "Look at all the people who have come to see us."

Mr. Punch answered in a high, almost incomprehensible squeaky voice, and the audience roared with approval.

"Evans has got Punch's voice down," Randolph said. "I think he's as good as Denton was."

"You hold the baby while I go get some tea," Mr. Punch's wife was saying. "Should I have Mr. Punch hold the baby while I have tea, boys and girls?"

The children, most of whom likely had never seen a puppet show, hesitated, but their parents didn't.

"No! Don't leave the baby with Mr. Punch," they shouted, and the children soon joined in.

Randolph was grinning like a child himself. "By Jove, Jane, I think Evans is better than a kangaroo, even a live one."

"I'll tell him that," Jane said, amused, but relieved as well. "I'm certain he'll be quite flattered."

"As he should be. I—" Randolph glanced to his right and stiffened. "Lord, here come the Boltwood sisters. I'm off." He handed Jane the bell before dodging round to the other side of the crowd.

"Is that Billy Denton's stage and puppets?" Miss Cordelia, the shorter of the two sisters, asked, a note of awe in her voice. "Wherever did you find it?"

Her sister, Miss Gertrude, put what looked like a comforting hand on Miss Cordelia's shoulder.

"It was dismantled and stored in the Spinster House," Jane said, "shoved in a small room behind a lot of other things."

"I thought we were going to have a kangaroo," Miss Gertrude said as Miss Cordelia watched the performance.

"Yes, but when Mr. Wertigger, the zoo owner, arrived, I discovered the kangaroo was stuffed. The man was a complete charlatan. You may be sure I sent him on his way at once."

"This is far better than any kangaroo." Miss Cordelia sighed, her lips turning up in a wistful smile. "Remember when Billy used to do the shows, Gertrude?"

"Yes." Miss Gertrude patted her sister's shoulder.

Miss Cordelia sniffed and dabbed at her eyes. "I still miss him, you know."

"I know."

Good heavens, had Miss Cordelia had *romantic* feelings for Mr. Denton? Jane remembered him as an old man, but then she'd probably been only six or seven when he'd died. Every adult had seemed old then.

But, no, he must have been past forty when he departed this earth, unless Miss Cordelia had taken up with a man much younger than she. The Boltwoods had at least sixty if not seventy years in their dish now.

Miss Gertrude raised her voice so she could be heard over the cheers of the crowd. Mr. Punch's wife was beating him with her big stick for throwing the baby out with the bathwater. "Who's working the puppets?"

"Lord Evans."

That got both ladies' complete attention.

"Lord Evans?" Miss Gertrude looked at her sister. "Well, well, well. Clearly we should not have spent all yesterday inside working on our tarts."

The Boltwood sisters always entered—and always won—the village baking contests.

"Yes, indeed." Miss Cordelia put aside her melancholy to waggle her brows. "I thought Lord Evans went off to walk the lakes."

"He did." The sisters weren't trying to imply the earl had a romantic interest in her, were they?

Of course not. She was the Spinster House spinster— and oddly flustered at the moment. She hoped she wasn't blushing. . . .

Lud! She had to keep her wits about her. One false step and the Boltwoods would concoct some ridiculous rumor about her and Lord Evans and send it flying through the village before the puppet show was over.

"But he came back," Miss Cordelia said, her tone heavy with meaning.

The sisters looked at her expectantly. What did they want her to say?

"Er, yes."

"Why do you think he did that?" Miss Gertrude's brows were waggling too.

"I imagine he wanted to visit the duke."

"Is he staying at the castle, then? I didn't see him arrive with His Grace." Miss Gertrude smiled slyly. "But then I suppose Lord Evans came in early to take charge of the puppets. You did say they were kept at the Spinster House, didn't you? Did you have to . . . help him?"

Once the sisters discovered the earl was putting up at the inn, they'd likely add more towers to the air-castle they were building.

"If you want to know the earl's plans, you'll have to ask him."

Jane started to walk away, but Miss Cordelia caught her arm. "Miss Wilkinson, please let me give you some advice based on my own sad experience." She spoke urgently and, Jane thought, sincerely. "I promise you you'll regret it every day of your life if you let the earl slip through your fingers."

Jane stared at her, unable to form a reply. She felt genuine compassion for the woman—how sad to spend your life with such regrets—but she also knew that trying to explain to Miss Cordelia that she'd completely misconstrued Jane's situation would be futile.

Her speechlessness had *nothing* to do with the confusing feeling of loneliness and need that suddenly knifed through her at the thought of Lord Evans.

"Thank you, Miss Cordelia," she finally managed, "I'll remember that."

* * *

Alex put down the puppets and stretched his hands and then his back. He'd done three shows. He was tired, but the crowd was still cheering. Miss Wilkinson should be happy.

"Come take a bow, Alex."

He looked over to see Nate, the Marquess of Haywood, grinning at him.

"Nate, what are you doing here?" He grasped his friend's hand.

"My wife was part of the fair committee, remember? She insisted we come back so she could see how all their plans turned out." He frowned. "More to the point, what are *you* doing here—and why aren't you staying at the castle?"

"I didn't want to intrude."

Nate snorted. "The castle is very large, as you well know, and Anne and I were already intruding."

"Well, I didn't know you were there, did I? And in any event, you're Marcus's cousin."

"And you're his friend." Nate sounded exasperated, but thankfully didn't pursue the topic. "Now come acknowledge your adoring public before they knock the stage down."

"All right, but what I really want is some ale. Playing Mr. Punch wears out the voice."

"I imagine it does. I'll have a large mug waiting for you." Nate gestured toward a big oak. "We're sitting over there." He grinned. "The ladies tire easily, given their delicate condition, so we found a comfortable spot in the shade."

"Yes, I expect—" Alex paused. Wait a minute . . . "*Ladies?*"

Nate's grin couldn't get any wider. "Yes. Anne is increasing as well."

"Ah." So Nate hadn't wasted any time starting his

nursery. Alex clapped him on the back and shook his hand again. "Congratulations. That's wonderful news."

He was delighted for Nate—but he felt a sharp pang of envy as he took his bows and watched his friend go off to join his wife.

No. No envy. I'm done with that useless emotion. In the morning, I'll go to London and look for a bride.

Again.

The thought was quite depressing. Perhaps he wasn't completely over Charlotte yet.

Well, the best way to recover was to dive back into the social pool and start swimming.

"You are very talented, Lord Evans."

Oh, Lord, that was one of the Boltwood sisters. Thank God she'd approached from behind. He schooled his features and turned. It was the shorter sister—Miss Cordelia, if he recalled correctly.

"Thank you."

"You were almost as good as Billy—" The woman flushed. "That is, Mr. Denton." She cleared her throat. "I was rather attached to Mr. Denton, you understand."

"Ah." He didn't want to think about that.

"He would have been very proud to have his puppets and stage used to such good effect."

That made him smile. "If Mr. Denton was as good a performer as he was a craftsman, that's high praise, madam. The puppets, the stage, the scenery and props— everything was made with careful attention to detail."

Miss Cordelia beamed at him. "Billy was passionate about everything he did." She blushed again.

Lord, please don't let her tell me any more about Denton's passion.

For once, the Almighty granted a sinner's prayer. Miss Cordelia limited herself to a fleeting smile.

"I hope you will perform at every fair," she said.

Every fair? "Well, as to that, I was merely helping Miss Wilkinson out this time. She found herself in a bit of a pickle when the traveling zoo proved to be unsuitable."

Miss Cordelia dismissed that with a wave of her hand. "Yes, but now that we know your skills, we can put you on the regular program, just as we did Billy."

The woman knew he wasn't a villager or a professional performer. Why would she think he'd wish to be part of the fair again?

Perhaps she was still caught up in the memories of this Mr. Denton. No need to be rude.

"If I'm visiting the duke at that time, I would be happy to help out, of course."

Miss Cordelia's brows rose—an ominous sign.

"Was it the duke you came to visit this time?"

"Er . . ." He'd best tread carefully. He couldn't tell the woman his main goal had been to escape his mother and sister. "Yes. And to attend the fair. I'd heard so much about it."

Her brows tilted at a skeptical angle. "If you came to visit the duke, why didn't you go directly to the castle?"

Perhaps there *was* a need to be rude. "I had not sent word ahead that I'd be coming. Now, if you'll excuse me?"

She put a hand on his arm. "But what about Miss Wilkinson?"

Confusion and alarm scrambled in his brainbox— followed quickly by wariness. "The Spinster House spinster?"

"Yes, of course. Didn't you *really* come to see her?" Her expression was as hopeful as it was suggestive.

Oh, Lord, he knew where this was headed. Best nip it in the bud—if he could. "No."

Miss Cordelia was not deterred. "But you did spend time with her . . . alone . . . in the Spinster House."

He supposed Poppy didn't count as a chaperone.

"And you're in need of a wife."

That, unfortunately, was true, but Miss Wilkinson was not in need of—or even desirous of—a husband.

He felt an odd pang of . . . disappointment? Ridiculous! He might enjoy sparring with the woman, but she was definitely not the restful sort of female he wished to marry.

Or thought he wished to marry . . .

He dismissed that momentary doubt. He couldn't appear anything but certain under Miss Cordelia's sharp eyes. And to tell the truth what he did or didn't want made no difference in this case. Miss Wilkinson was not interested in the position of Countess of Evans. There were no two ways about it. She already had her heart's desire— her independence.

He'd never considered the matter before, but now that he did, he thought it a terrible shame that most women had only two futures to choose from: living with a relative as a glorified servant or marrying and submitting to a husband.

"Miss Cordelia, even if I wanted to wed Miss Wilkinson"— he would indulge her fantasy that far—"Miss Wilkinson does not want to wed me."

"Oh, I think she does."

"What?!" He leaned slightly closer and sniffed. The woman didn't smell as if she'd been sampling the ale too freely.

"I saw how she looked at you the last time you were here. My sister remarked upon it as well. I'm certain Miss Wilkinson would give up the Spinster House in a twinkling if you offered for her."

He laughed. "Miss Cordelia, you know Miss Wilkinson has wanted the Spinster House from the moment the new Duchess of Benton vacated it. I suspect—and I imagine you do, too—that she had a hand in matching her friends to the duke and marquess so as to open the position for herself."

Miss Cordelia was looking a bit mulish. "Ask her. You'll see."

For one insane moment he was tempted—

Insane, indeed. Miss Wilkinson would either fall over laughing or snap his nose off.

"Yes. Well. Thank you for your opinion. Now I'm sorry, but you must excuse me." He bowed and tried to stroll, rather than run, to join Marcus and Nate and their wives. He needed that large glass of ale even more now.

"Hallo, Marcus. Good afternoon, Your Grace. Lady Haywood."

"Oh, please, Lord Evans, call us Cat and Anne," the duchess said, and then gestured to the tall mug waiting for him. "Sit down. You must be worn to a thread."

"I am, rather." He hadn't realized how tired he was. He lowered himself into the chair and took a long drink.

"Enjoy your chat with Miss Cordelia?" Marcus asked.

Alex choked. Ale threatened to come out his nose.

"Sorry." Marcus grinned as Alex mopped his face with his handkerchief.

"Does anyone but her sister enjoy talking to Miss Cordelia?" Alex asked once he could speak.

"No." Nate grinned as well, the dastard. "I will admit that the Boltwoods are one—or I suppose two—reasons I'm happy my estates aren't near Loves Bridge."

"But what did she want to discuss?" The duchess leaned toward him. "Jane thought she might be telling you about Mr. Denton."

"She did mention the fellow, but didn't go into any detail." *Thank God.* "She mostly talked about Miss Wilkinson." Where *was* Jane? Alex looked around—oh, there she was, having a word with her brother. "Can you believe the woman thinks I came here to see the Spinster House spinster?"

He laughed—but neither Nate nor Marcus nor their wives looked shocked by the idea. Perhaps they didn't understand.

"She thought I had a *matrimonial* interest in Miss Wilkinson."

Still no shock.

"Which is ridiculous," he said, a bit sharply.

"Of course it's ridiculous."

That was Miss Wilkinson's voice. He turned to discover her behind him.

"You can be sure I disabused her of the notion." He stood politely. For some odd reason—perhaps because he'd just been talking to the very short Miss Cordelia—he was struck by Miss Wilkinson's height. Most women didn't reach his shoulder, but her head came up to his chin.

It was pleasant not to have to look down so far to converse.

"Good."

She sounded annoyed.

He must be imagining it. She should be happy he'd set the busybody straight.

"Did you think the puppet show was as successful as a live kangaroo would have been, Miss Wilkinson?" he asked, pulling a chair out for her.

"Oh, yes. You were quite a hit, Lord Evans."

Definitely annoyed, but why? "I warn you I think Miss Cordelia would like to add me to the regular fair offerings."

"How nice to know you have a trade to fall back on should you lose your fortune."

He frowned, unsure how to reply without stirring her ire more.

She must have had a disagreement with her brother. That was why she was so tetchy.

"How long are you staying, Alex?" Nate asked, distracting him.

"I'm leaving for London in the morning." Which could not come soon enough. He held up his glass to his friends. "You and Nate have inspired me to go shopping on the Marriage Mart."

The duchess and Lady Haywood were positively scowling at him now.

"I wish you happy hunting, Lord Evans," Miss Wilkinson said.

At least there was one sensible female at the table. "Thank you, Miss—"

"Lord Evans?"

He looked to his right and saw a man dressed in his brother-in-law's livery. That could only mean one thing— Diana had had her baby. He hoped Roger had got back in time.

"Do I have a new niece, then?"

"No, milord."

His gut clenched, and ice flooded his veins. Women did sometimes die in childbirth, even women who'd had many successful deliveries.

"My sister." He cleared his throat, took a breath, tried to speak calmly. Through the dark fog suddenly pressing round him, he thought he felt Miss Wilkinson's hand on his arm. "She's well?"

"Oh, yes, milord. Very well." The man grinned, clearly oblivious to Alex's panic. "But it's not a new niece, ye have. It's a nephew."

Chapter Four

Loves Bridge, October 6

Jane was straightening the papers on her desk, getting ready to leave for the day, when her brother came back to the office. He was looking down at a sheet of paper, a slight smile on his lips.

"Did you get things sorted out between Mr. Linden and Mr. Barker, then?" she asked. One of Mr. Linden's pigs had paid a visit to Mr. Barker's mother's flower bed. Mrs. Barker, not the easiest of women, had demanded bacon for breakfast.

Randolph looked up and blinked as if it was taking him a moment to understand her question.

"Oh, yes. Once I brought Linden and Barker together without Mrs. Barker present, they readily agreed it was likely one of the Hutting boys who had let the pig out. Linden's going to have a word with the vicar, and I suspect Henry or Walter or both of them will be planting some new flowers for Mrs. Barker."

"I doubt that will satisfy the woman." Jane gave her

desk one last inspection and stood. She was eager to get back to the Spinster House.

Though it is *a bit lonely . . .*

Nonsense. It was merely that the initial excitement of living on her own had worn off.

"You are likely right." Randolph sighed and shook his head. "It's a pity Barker is cursed with such an unpleasant mother. He wants to wed, you know. I've told him he'll have to change his living arrangements to accomplish that goal. I can't see any woman being willing to move in with that harridan."

Jane snorted. "His mother is not the only impediment to his marriage." Mr. Barker had been courting Cat for months before the duke entered the scene, so Jane and Cat and Anne had discussed his strengths and weaknesses in detail.

Well, his weaknesses. They hadn't identified any strengths. "He smells of manure and has no conversation, unless you're interested in sheep and farming."

Randolph scowled at her. "He's not a bad sort, Jane. He's a hard-working, steady, reliable fellow."

"*I* wouldn't want him."

He raised a brow. "That doesn't have much to say to the matter, does it? You don't want any man."

Except Lord Evans—

No! Where in the world had *that* thought come from?

"Very true," she said, a bit more sharply than she'd intended. "Now if you'll excuse me, I'm off—"

"Just a moment." Randolph flourished the paper he'd been reading. "I wish to discuss this with you." He sounded oddly excited.

"What is it?"

"An invitation to a house party celebrating the birth of Lord Chanton's heir."

Lord Evans's nephew.

Her heart lurched and then began to hammer alarmingly in her chest. Fortunately, the desk was near at hand. She leaned against it. "Why are you invited?" She would know if Randolph had done business with the viscount, wouldn't she? She wrote all his correspondence, since his handwriting was illegible.

"Not me, us. We are *both* invited."

Lud! Her heart went from hammering to wild pounding. She leaned more heavily against the desk.

This was foolishness.

She swallowed and tried to sound dispassionate. "Very well, but my question remains. Why?"

Randolph regarded her expectantly. "Is there something between you and Lord Evans, Jane? He's sure to be at the party, you know."

She shook her head—she didn't trust her voice.

But it's true. There is *nothing between us.*

She'd heard him herself at the fair—he was going wifeshopping in London. Which was perfectly fine. He was an earl. He needed an heir.

Perhaps he'd already found a suitable female to marry.

Lud! She felt as if someone had thrust a knife into her belly.

"He came to Loves Bridge in August," Randolph said. "For the fair."

Randolph laughed. "You don't really think the Earl of Evans would make a special trip to Loves Bridge to attend a common village fair, do you, Jane? The man spends a good bit of his time in London. I assure you there are many more interesting entertainments available there."

True. She didn't know why the earl had come—she'd been so intent on finding a replacement for Worm Wertigger's zoo, she hadn't asked him—but it clearly had not been to see her, if that was what Randolph was getting at. If it had been, the earl would have said something, wouldn't he?

Or he would have *done* something. They had been alone in the Spinster House. He'd even had his arms around her when she'd tripped and fallen into him. And then there'd been that odd moment when she'd brushed the fluff out of his hair.

Though, to be fair, she hadn't encouraged him.

Oh, bother. She'd admit she knew very little about such matters. She'd always thought the flirting women did to attract male interest was silly. More to the point, there'd never been a male in Loves Bridge whose interest she'd wanted to attract.

Do I want to attract Lord Evans's interest?

Of course not. I'm the Spinster House spinster.

And yet . . .

It was true he made her feel more alive. She enjoyed bantering with him. She'd even admit she found him very handsome. What woman wouldn't?

But was any of that worth giving up her independence? No.

What a silly question! Lord Evans wasn't interested in her that way. He'd left Loves Bridge over a month ago. If he'd felt any sort of a tendre for her, he would have come back to see her. It would have been so simple. He could have paid the duke a visit and then stopped by the Spinster House when he was in the village.

The duke—that was it!

"You forget the Duke of Hart is Lord Evans's good friend, Randolph. He came to visit him."

Randolph gave her a long look.

"I suppose it's possible the invitation is for me and you

were included out of politeness." Again, there was that odd excitement in his voice.

That didn't make much sense either. Randolph hadn't been away from Loves Bridge in a long time. "Have you been corresponding with the viscount, then?" She supposed it was possible that someone other than she could decipher Randolph's handwriting.

"No." He looked back down at the sheet of vellum. "I, er, knew Chanton's cousin years ago." He was definitely biting back a smile now.

He'd never mentioned knowing a cousin of Lord Chanton—and why would he suddenly seem eager to meet the man?

"Are you going to accept?" It certainly sounded as if that was what he was planning to do. "I can't imagine you wish to be in a household with a new baby, Randolph." Her brother was very set in his ways.

Randolph hesitated, but only for a moment. "The viscount must have an army of nursemaids to attend to the baby."

"He certainly has an army of daughters. You did know he has eight, didn't you?"

Her brother paled a little at that. Eight girls plus a new baby equaled a lot of commotion.

"Chanton's estate must be large enough to keep his guests from tripping over his children. And the girls will likely be busy with their governess most of the time." Her brother's jaw hardened, a sure sign he'd made a decision. "We'll go."

"*We'll* go?" Perhaps she was a little set in her ways too. The thought of staying in a strange house with people she didn't know—and likely Lord Evans as well—made her very uncomfortable. "You go. I'll stay here."

He frowned at her. "How am I to explain your absence?"

"Tell them I'm busy."

"With what? Redecorating the Spinster House?" He snorted. "At the rate you're going with that, you can use that excuse forever."

It was true she'd been dithering over every decision. It was very unlike her. "I've got the lending library to see to as well."

"No one ever goes there. Even when the current Duchess of Benton was the Spinster House spinster and ran the library daily, it was deserted."

Sadly, that was very true.

"You've never been to a house party, Jane. You should go."

"I've never wanted to go to a house party." She didn't see the point of parties of any sort. She had a few good friends—

Well, she had *two* good friends, Cat and Anne, who now seemed far more interested in their husbands and growing families than they were in her. But that still didn't mean she wanted to spend several days trapped in a strange house with people she didn't know.

Randolph had never been eager to rub elbows with strangers either.

"Why do you want to go, Randolph?"

Randolph looked away—and then looked back, meeting her gaze directly. "Now that you have your own place, I'm thinking of marrying."

Jane felt her jaw drop.

The cynic in her wanted to say something caustic about looking for a free cook or to ask if his Wednesday evening visits to the Widow Conklin no longer satisfied, but the loneliness she saw in his eyes stopped her.

Randolph had upended his life for her when she was fourteen and their parents were killed in a carriage accident. He'd come home from London to be father and mother to her. Yes, it had been understood that he would join the family business eventually, becoming yet another Wilkinson in Wilkinson, Wilkinson, and Wilkinson, but he'd planned to spend several years in Town first. She remembered him and Papa shouting over it on occasion.

And then their parents' carriage had collided with a big oak tree. No one had ever known exactly what had happened, but the horse Papa was driving was new and a bit skittish. A rabbit or a fox or some other animal had likely darted across the road, causing the horse to bolt. It was just bad luck it had happened at a curve with a tree.

She'd been young and self-centered and devastated by loss, so she'd taken Randolph's sacrifice for granted. He was five years older than she. She'd thought him grown, and he'd seemed very mature, but looking back now, she realized he'd been only nineteen. A man, yes, but hardly ready to be chained by so much responsibility.

And then there was the rumor that he'd been in love but the woman had refused to marry him, not wanting to be stuck in a small village with a fourteen-year-old sister-in-law to raise.

Randolph had never mentioned a lost love, and Jane had never asked. Perhaps she should have, but feelings were not something they discussed.

And after fourteen years of silence, how was she to find the words?

"You never said anything about wanting to marry."

He shrugged. "All men want to marry, Jane." He frowned at her. "As do most women."

For once she didn't rise to the bait.

"And you think you'll find a suitable candidate at this party?"

He shrugged and his eyes slipped away from hers. "I

don't know. Perhaps. At least it's an opportunity to meet people other than the Loves Bridge villagers."

That was true. And perhaps it would be good for her, too. Seeing Lord Evans again might cure her of her odd blue-devils.

"Very well. If you want to go to this party, I'll go with you."

He grinned and handed her the invitation. "Splendid. Could you pen our acceptance?"

Chanton Manor, October 27

Alex smelled a rat.

When he'd arrived at his brother-in-law's estate a few minutes ago, Charles, one of Roger's grooms, had given him a pitying look before taking his curricle off to the stables. And now Jennings, the butler, informed him Lord Chanton had suddenly remembered urgent estate business and gone out. The way Jennings refused to meet his eye as he said "out" made it painfully clear Roger had fled the moment he'd seen Alex approach. Why?

Jennings ushered him into the red drawing room, where he found his sister nursing her son.

"What's going on, Diana?"

"Don't growl at me like that, Alex. You'll upset poor Christopher's digestion."

The only parts of the Honorable Christopher Alexander David Philip Livingston-Smythe that were visible were his feet. When Diana had been a first-time mother, she'd nursed in private, but now she just covered herself and her baby with a large shawl and carried on.

By the ninth child, privacy must be only a faint memory.

"And do sit down. You are making me queasy as well."

Alex sat on the edge of the nearest chair. "Diana—"

"Tell me how things go on in Town," she said quickly. "I'm dying to hear the latest gossip."

He took a deep breath. His sister was an old hand at turning the conversation when she wished to avoid a particular topic. He was not going to let her get away with that this time.

"I'll be happy to talk about London after you tell me what the hel—" He cleared his throat. This was his sister he was speaking to after all. "What is going on."

She frowned and deftly switched the baby to her other breast. "I don't know what you mean."

He snorted. "Oh, you know exactly what I mean." He ticked off the evidence of Diana's meddling on his fingers. "One, Roger has fled the house. Two, both Charles and Jennings looked at me as though I was a lamb going off to slaughter. And three, your eye is twitching like it always does when you are up to something."

Diana put her free hand to her face. "My eye isn't twitching."

What plot could Diana be hatching at her son's christening? It wasn't a celebration that lent itself to machinations. . . .

Perhaps it had something to do with the guest list. "This is just a family gathering, isn't it?"

"Mmm." She looked down at Christopher—or the lump in the shawl that was Christopher—instead of meeting his gaze.

Blast it, that was the answer. "Whom else have you invited?"

"Er, just one or two extra people." She stroked her son's foot.

He would not shout. For one thing, it would likely make the baby cry. "Diana, I mean it. Tell me whom you've invited."

Fortunately for her an interruption appeared in the form of their mother.

"Oh, Alex! Jennings told me you'd arrived," Mama said, hurrying into the room.

Likely Jennings, sensing trouble, had run to find Mama. Alex stood to greet her—and noticed the speaking look she exchanged with his sister.

He forced himself to smile. "Diana was just about to tell me whom she's invited to this party."

"Oh." Mama looked at him and then back at Diana. "I do think we should let him know, dear. It would be rather dreadful to have him caught unaware."

Zeus! His fingers flexed. *I cannot strangle my female relatives.*

A pity.

Diana sighed. "I suppose you are right." She looked up at him as Mama took the chair next to her. "You see—oh, do stop looming over us."

He frowned, but lowered himself back onto the edge of his seat.

Diana had finished nursing. She held the baby against her shoulder, patting him on the back. "I didn't precisely invite Lady Charlotte—"

"What?!" Alex shot to his feet again.

The Honorable Christopher Alexander David Philip Livingston-Smythe emitted an impressively loud belch.

"Well done, Stinky!" Diana grinned at the baby as if he'd just taken a first in oratory.

"Stinky?" Alex was momentarily distracted.

"Martha can't say 'Christopher,' and even Judith gets

lost in all those syllables," Diana said, referring to her two youngest daughters, "so Judith gave him the nickname." Diana held her son's face close to hers and spoke in the high voice people so often used with babies. "And you are stinky sometimes, aren't you, my brilliant widdle boy?"

Christopher's tiny face lit with a wide, toothless grin and a bit of milk drooled out.

Alex felt a pang of . . . longing. He'd not paid much attention when Diana had had her first babies—he'd been only a young lad when Bea was born—but now that he was thinking of marriage, infants seemed to affect him rather strongly.

He forced his thoughts back to the matter at hand—the guest list. Surely he had misunderstood Diana. His sister would never invite the woman who'd jilted him to her home. She'd been beyond furious on his behalf when the wedding had been called off. "Whom did you say was coming?"

Diana grimaced as she settled Christopher in the crook of one arm. "You heard me. Lady Charlotte."

He looked to his mother for confirmation.

Mama nodded.

He sank back down to his seat.

I'm going to see Charlotte again.

He was too shocked to feel dread or delight—or simple distaste.

"I didn't set out to invite her, Alex," Diana said. "I invited Roger's cousin Imogen, Lady Eldon. Eldon's been gone almost a year now, so Imogen's coming to the end of her mourning. We thought this would be a pleasant way for her to start to reenter Society."

"I see." He vaguely remembered Lady Eldon. He'd met her over a decade ago when she'd married the much older Lord Eldon. "But how does that get us to Lady Charlotte?"

"Lady Charlotte is Imogen's companion."

"Oh." He'd wondered what had become of Charlotte, but he hadn't bothered inquiring. He'd been too relieved not to encounter her at any *ton* events.

"Of course Imogen couldn't travel alone," his mother said. "So if Imogen was to come, Charlotte had to come as well."

"But what is Charlotte doing as a companion? She's an earl's daughter."

Mama's brows angled down into a deep scowl. "You must know Buford was very angry when she jilted you, Alex."

"Yes." The earl had brought him the unpleasant news himself. He'd given Alex the distinct impression that he would have dragged Charlotte into the church and up the aisle if he thought he could have forced her to say her vows.

He'd tried to calm Buford by assuring him that Charlotte had done exactly the right thing in calling off the wedding. If she found she couldn't like the match, then there was no more to be said.

Which was, of course, true.

He'd told himself as he'd walked mile after solitary mile in the Lake District this summer that he'd just have to go wife shopping again. Inconvenient, but not a disaster.

But over the last weeks in London, he'd come to realize that Charlotte's decision to call off their wedding hadn't just embarrassed and disappointed him. It had completely shaken his confidence with women.

He'd dived back into the social pool only to sink like a rock.

Bloody hell!

He prided himself on his ability to read people, and yet with Charlotte . . .

How had he been so fooled? He'd thought she loved him. Clearly she hadn't.

Now every time he considered paying court to a woman, doubt whispered in his ear: *Will you be fooled again?*

"There was quite a scandal, of course. Buford needed to send Charlotte away, so it was lucky—" Mama stopped, and then shrugged. "Well, you can't call a man's death lucky, precisely, but Eldon wasn't well and his departure from this realm couldn't have come at a better time. Imogen needed a companion at the exact moment Charlotte needed to leave London."

"I see."

Oh, blast. Diana's brow was wrinkled with a look of concern.

"You *are* over her, aren't you, Alex?"

"Of course," he said quickly. He'd never spoken about his feelings, and he certainly wasn't going to start now. "It was nothing. An unfortunate situation, but it's in the past."

"It *was* something," Diana said rather fiercely. "She *hurt* you. Mama and I both saw it, much as you tried to hide it."

"Ah. Well." He shifted on his chair. He did wish his female relatives wouldn't so busy themselves in his affairs. "As you can see, I'm fine now."

Diana and Mama exchanged one of their "poor Alex" glances. He rushed to speak before they could pursue the topic further.

"I do hope Charlotte can return to Society. Would it help if I had a word with Buford?"

Mama shook her head. "No. Don't worry about Charlotte. I think things will work out for her."

"That's good, then." He started to rise, eager to escape. "If you'll excuse—"

"It's you we're worried about," Diana said. She looked at Mama again.

He made the mistake of turning his eyes in his mother's direction as well.

Oh, Lord.

He sank back down onto his chair. Part of him wanted to run, but he knew that would be futile. There was no running from Mama.

"Alex," Mama said, "we know you want to marry."

He'd swear the back of his neck suddenly flushed from the hot breath of the horde of eligible young women Mama and Diana must be assembling. "All peers need to marry to get an heir, but I'm only thirty. There's no hurry."

Mama ignored him, of course. "My particular friend, the Duchess of Greycliffe—or, as the wags call her, the Duchess of Love—wrote me a few weeks ago to say you'd been attending every party in Town and begging introductions to all the unmarried girls."

Diana nodded. "My friends told me the same."

Zeus, how he hated that London was full of spies.

"So I invited someone you might be interested in," Diana said.

His stomach knotted even as a certain spinster's face popped into his thoughts.

Why the hell am I thinking of Miss Wilkinson?

"Diana, Mama, I know you both mean well, but I would *greatly* appreciate it if you would stop meddling in my life."

Diana was as good at ignoring him as Mama. "You don't have to worry. We didn't let on that you might be considering her for the position of countess." She grinned. "We were very clever. I'm quite certain she has no inkling of it."

Dear God, save him from clever women.

"Please. I can manage this matter by myself." He wanted to say—and think—no more about it, but he couldn't keep one question from slithering snakelike through his mind: *Who?*

He hadn't met any woman in London who appealed to him.

Yet. Surely he would eventually. Someone who would be open and honest and let him trust his instincts again.

"Well, you haven't been doing such a wonderful job of that so far, have you?" Mama said, though in a gentle rather than hurtful sort of way.

Diana nodded. "We invited her brother as well, you see. He knew Imogen years ago and has been in touch with her."

"Oh?" Something in Diana's tone made his stomach shiver with unease. And Mama was smirking . . .

What the hell have I got myself into?

Diana looked damnably pleased with herself. "I wondered why you ran off to Loves Bridge back in August. It was very odd of you."

Unease turned to horror. Surely Diana hadn't invited—

The door opened. Jennings stood there, a man and a woman behind him.

"Milady, Mr. and Miss Wilkinson have arrived."

Chapter Five

Jane scowled at her reflection. She was quite sure the neckline hadn't been so low the last time she'd worn this dress. Had Poppy somehow altered it?

Ridiculous. The cat might be . . . unusual, but Poppy couldn't sew.

She fastened her mother's pearls around her neck, but they didn't begin to cover the vast expanse of exposed flesh. She tugged on the fabric, but of course that didn't help, either.

What she needed was a fichu. She would have sworn she'd packed one, but she hadn't been able to find it in her luggage just now. Hmm. Now *that* was something Poppy could have had a hand—or a paw—in. She wouldn't put it past the cat to have snatched it out of her portmanteau when her back was turned.

She blew out a long breath. She should have known better than to bring this dress. She'd worn it only once, to attend a ball the first Lady Davenport had held before Anne went up to London for her debut Season. That was . . . lud! She counted the years in her head and then recounted them.

The dress was almost *ten* years old. Not only was it immodest, it was dreadfully out-of-date.

She squeezed her eyes shut. *I'm going to look a complete fool. I should change.*

But she was so tired of her only other choice: a serviceable white frock she trotted out for every Loves Bridge party.

She'd wanted to look special for this gathering.

She grimaced. She certainly looked special—like unfashionable, skimpily clad mutton dressed as lamb.

Oh, why was she worrying about how she looked? No one would pay her any attention.

Her shoulders slumped. Right. To be honest, she'd thought the silly dress would give her courage. She'd wanted to look beautiful, composed, and confident.

She'd wanted to impress Lord Evans. More, she'd wanted him to admire her.

Apparently, she'd let Randolph's suggestion that the earl had had a hand in this invitation take root and grow like a weed one didn't know was there until it suddenly poked up from among the flowers.

How mortifying.

Admiration was not what she'd seen in his eyes when the butler had presented her and Randolph earlier. The earl had hidden his reaction quickly, but not quickly enough.

He'd been shocked and, she thought, dismayed.

"I'm *such* an idiot," she said out loud as if actually hearing the words would cause her stupid heart to let some sense into its murky center.

She looked around the elegant bedroom, at the mahogany washstand, the rich yellow bed hangings and matching window curtains, the bright paintings in their elaborate, gilt frames. It was a good thing the earl wasn't interested in her. She didn't belong here. She belonged in Loves Bridge, in the old, comfortable Spinster House.

Well, it wasn't *that* comfortable.

She'd never admit it out loud, but after years of wanting to live on her own, free of the need to consider Randolph's preferences and tidy up after him, she'd expected to be wildly happy every single moment she spent in the Spinster House.

She was not.

Some days she wanted more companionship than an independent, inscrutable cat could provide.

She stared back at herself, lifting her chin and squaring her shoulders. Ridiculous! The problem was simply a matter of adjustment. Her friends had moved on in their lives. Anne had physically moved to her husband's estate, and Cat was consumed with all her new duties as duchess.

She'd only been in the Spinster House for a few months. Things would improve. For now, she—

Someone knocked. It must be Randolph, the person responsible for dragging her into this uncomfortable situation.

She opened the door—and stepped back. *She* might not have kept up with the latest fashions, but apparently Randolph had.

Well, she couldn't actually say whether his waistcoat was fashionable or not. She squinted.

"Are those peacocks?"

"Yes." He tugged on it, stretching it tight over his thickening middle and making the peacocks' tails spread wider. "Do you like it?"

"Er." It *was* pretty in a gaudy sort of way. "I suppose so. Did you get it in the village?" Though she couldn't imagine Mr. Wilcox, the Loves Bridge tailor, working on such a flashy garment.

"No, London."

Randolph had gone up to Town? London wasn't far from Loves Bridge, but Randolph didn't make a practice of going there, particularly to waste time and money shopping.

Hmm. There *had* been a few days when he'd left the office early and hadn't got back before she went home to the Spinster House, but she'd just assumed he'd had business elsewhere in the village.

He cleared his throat and tugged on the peacocks again. "Well, I've come to take you downstairs," he said. "Are you ready?"

Something in the way he'd said "downstairs" made her focus on him rather than the peacocks. There was an odd tension about him as if he were both anxious and excited.

Perhaps he was off balance as well.

"I should change."

He frowned and looked her over. "Why? You've got a dress on."

Clearly, her brother hadn't *really* looked at her. "It's not suitable."

"It's fine."

"Randolph, the neck is too low."

He glanced at that portion of the dress. "It looks all right to me, but if it bothers you, take a shawl."

She consulted the mantel clock. "It's only just the hour now. We don't want to be the first ones in the drawing room."

"We won't be." Randolph took a half step down the corridor. "Do come along."

Why is he in such a hurry?

He took another half step.

He won't go down without me, will he?

She didn't want to find out.

And there was no point in delaying. She couldn't magically conjure a new dress from thin air—or from the window curtains—and she truly didn't want to wear her white gown every single night. A shawl would have to do. Likely the other guests would be too transfixed by Randolph's peacocks to notice her.

"Very well." She grabbed her shawl, wrapped it around her shoulders, and stepped into the corridor. When she put her hand on her brother's arm, she felt how tense he was.

Clearly, she wasn't the only one dealing with a fit of nerves. "Why are you so eager to go down to the drawing room, Randolph?"

She felt him flinch ever so slightly.

Perhaps that had sounded a bit harsh, especially as she could think of only one reason for his tension. She tried to soften her tone.

"I know you said you'd like to find someone to marry, but I'm very much afraid you won't have any luck here. From what Lady Chanton said when we arrived, this is a small, family gathering."

Which raised the question again—why had they been invited?

Randolph shrugged and didn't meet her gaze. She waited for him to say something.

He didn't, which was unlike him.

Alarm bells went off. Something was indeed up.

She was not about to face a roomful—or even a handful—of strangers without knowing if there were hidden traps to stumble into.

"Randolph, what aren't you telling me?"

More silence.

Good God, there *was* something.

"You *have* to tell me." She stopped, grabbing his forearm with both hands and squeezing. "I can't go in there not knowing."

He hesitated—and she squeezed harder.

"Very well, though it's nothing that affects you. I told you I've been corresponding with Lord Chanton's cousin."

"Yes. And you expect him to be here." Randolph could not be this nervous over seeing an old friend.

He smiled. "*Her*, Jane. I expect *her* to be here."

"Oh." He'd been corresponding with a *woman*. So that was why he'd been so keen on fetching the post recently.

The notion threw her a bit off balance. They might not discuss their lives with each other, but she'd never have guessed Randolph had secrets. Certainly he'd never hidden his weekly visits to Mrs. Conklin.

"Jane, I'm not sure if you're aware—I don't believe we've ever talked about it—but before Mama and Papa died, I was . . ."

His voice trailed off. Normally, she would push him to continue, but this time she didn't. She was a little afraid of what he would say.

"When I was nineteen, I fancied myself in love."

"Ah." So the rumor had been true.

A muscle jumped in Randolph's jaw. "Papa was furious."

Papa was often furious. "Was the woman unsuitable?"

"No. He thought I was too young."

Nineteen *was* too young.

"He came up to London to have it out with me, but I refused to give in. He left in a complete fury. I'd never seen him so angry."

Randolph wasn't one to exaggerate. She didn't remember Papa being angry that day, but then she'd tried to escape Papa's tirades, either by going for a walk or losing herself in a book. And, to be honest, her memories of that horrible time were very hazy.

"The next day he drove his carriage into a tree, killing himself and Mama." His voice was clipped, his expression, bleak as though he—

Jane inhaled sharply. "Randolph! You don't blame yourself for their deaths, do you?"

She saw in his eyes that he did.

Lud! Her brother had carried this guilt for over a decade, and she never knew. Never even suspected. "It was an *accident*. A simple, unfortunate accident."

"Papa was an excellent whip."

"Yes, but even excellent whips have accidents. And Papa was driving a new horse, remember. I distinctly recall hearing him say when he first bought the animal that it was hard to handle."

Randolph looked off down the corridor. "Perhaps. But, Jane, I'd truly never seen Papa so angry as he was during our, er, discussion in London. I think he and Mama must have been arguing about me, and that's why he lost control at that curve."

That *was* possible.

But it was just as possible something else had caused the crash.

Jane shook Randolph's arm. "Stop! You can't know that. A bee might have stung the horse or a rabbit startled it and it bolted at just the wrong moment."

He shrugged, clearly not willing to accept her explanation.

"I wager Papa regretted arguing with you as soon as he got back to Loves Bridge, if not sooner."

Her brother snorted.

Well, yes, she doubted it too.

"In any event, if Papa's anger *did* cause the crash—

which we have no evidence is the case. You know he was often very angry and yet he'd never crashed his curricle before. But if he *was* so angry that he lost control of his horses, then that was his fault, not yours."

Randolph's jaw was set—he was not buying her argument. Very well then.

"Even if you *were* to blame, you've more than paid your penance. You had to give up all your plans to come home to take care of me." She'd never told him how much she appreciated that. She shook his arm in an appreciative way this time. "Thank you. I *am* sorry you had to make such a sacrifice."

He frowned. "It wasn't a sacrifice. I'd always intended to come home and take my place in the firm. The accident just made that happen sooner."

"But I'm the reason you didn't marry." She forced a smile. "It's really not surprising the woman didn't want to take on mothering a girl only a few years younger than herself." She should be completely honest. "An opinionated, stubborn, unhappy girl. I realize I could not have been an easy charge."

Randolph's frown deepened. "That wasn't it at all. Oh, I don't doubt Imogen's parents used you as an argument against our marriage, but they had never favored the match. They didn't want their daughter to waste herself on a mere solicitor."

"Oh!" She would like to find these people and give them a piece of her mind.

"And a penniless one at that."

"It wasn't as bad as that." Though it was true Papa had not left them in a good way. Things had been very difficult those first few years.

"It *was* that bad, Jane." Randolph shrugged. "In any event, Imogen married Eldon. When I read of his passing,

I wrote her a note of condolence and she replied. And when the invitation for this celebration arrived, I hoped she might be attending."

He grinned, barely contained elation in his voice. "And she *is* here. Can you wonder I'm anxious to go down and see her?" He tugged on his waistcoat, bringing the peacocks to attention. "It's been years and nothing may come of it." He looked endearingly hopeful. "But something might."

Jane managed to smile back at him. She was suddenly swamped with love for him—and worry. What if this Lady Eldon hurt him?

But what if she didn't? What if Randolph married the woman?

Oh, God. First Cat and then Anne and now perhaps Randolph. Everyone she cared about was pairing up two by two like the animals going into Noah's ark.

She was the one left behind, standing out in the rain as the floodwaters rose around her—

Ridiculous! There was no rain or ark or any such nonsense. She didn't need a partner to be complete—she was complete by herself. She was the Spinster House spinster.

Though she did wish Lord Evans had wanted her to attend this gathering.

Alex strode into the drawing room where everyone was to gather before dinner. He'd come down early to find the room empty and had taken a turn or two or three around the terrace, trying to get his feelings under control.

It had not worked.

But now Roger and Diana were here. Excellent. It was time to get a few things settled.

"Alex." Roger slapped him on the back. "Sorry I missed you earlier. Had a tenant issue I needed to address."

"Oh? How convenient that the problem came up just the moment I arrived."

Roger grinned, not at all repentant. "Yes. Funny how that happened."

There was nothing funny about it. Roger had long practice in avoiding the worst of Diana's machinations.

Alex turned to his sister and spoke quietly—but emphatically—keeping one eye on the door. "I cannot believe you invited Miss Wilkinson to this *family* gathering."

He'd wanted to corner her and Mama after Mr. and Miss Wilkinson had gone up to their rooms, but his wily relatives had accompanied their guests, ostensibly to be certain they were comfortable. He'd waited and waited in the drawing room for Mama and Diana to reappear and had finally gone in search of them, looking in Roger's study, the music room, the library, and finally the nursery, where he found his three youngest nieces.

He smiled inwardly. The girls had been delighted to see him. Their words had stumbled all over one another's telling him about "Stinky." They'd showed him their dolls and got him to read several stories, Martha, the youngest, in his lap and Judith and Rebecca leaning against him on each side. Their sweet childish excitement, their innocence, their easy laughter filled him with happiness and with longing for children of his own.

When he could finally break free, it was time to get ready to come down here.

"I thought you'd thank me," Diana said. "You *are* looking for a wife, aren't you?"

"Diana, I don't need your help."

Her right eyebrow arched up. "Oh, really?"

Roger cleared his throat. "Perhaps we should change the subject."

Alex and Diana ignored him.

"Miss Wilkinson is the Spinster House spinster, Diana."

"Precisely. That means she's available."

"No, that means she has no interest in matrimony."

Diana snorted. "Pshaw! Every woman has an interest in matrimony."

"Not Miss Wilkinson."

"Even Miss Wilkinson. She just hasn't met the right man"—his sister grinned—"until now."

He would not strangle Diana, much as he would like to. "But she *has* met me. Several times. You know that."

Diana's smile turned rather sly. "Yes, I do. Just as I know that when you got back from the Lake District, you rushed off to Loves Bridge without stopping overnight at the Hall or even coming inside."

"That was to avoid you and Mama."

"Oh? So why didn't you go to London or one of your other estates?"

"I, er . . ." He cleared his throat. He had a good reason. "Horatio was tired and Loves Bridge was relatively close. And I'd heard about the fair when I was there in the spring. I wanted to see how it turned out." He would *not* run his finger under his collar. "And my good friend, the Duke of Hart, is now at Loves Castle, you know."

"Ah. And I suppose you went straight to the castle when you arrived?"

She wouldn't say that unless she knew he hadn't, blast it. Diana and Mama had spies everywhere.

"Since I hadn't sent word I'd be coming, I went to the inn, of course. To show up on the duke's doorstep unannounced would be rude." Not that Marcus would agree.

What else could he say to throw Diana off the scent?

There was no scent to be thrown off of. Diana was completely misconstruing his minor connection to Miss Wilkinson. He merely enjoyed teasing the woman.

"And since the fair was the next day, it was more con-venient to stroll over to the village green from the inn than to ride in from the castle."

Even Roger choked on that one.

"Ah, yes. Of course." His sister's voice was dripping with sarcasm. "You are such a devotee of village fairs, you seek them out wherever you can."

"Diana . . ." He looked at Roger to rein in his wife.

Roger smiled and shrugged—and fled to the sherry decanter.

He felt Diana's hand on his arm. "I saw how she looked at you this afternoon."

"How—" No, he would not ask Diana what she meant. If she thought Miss Wilkinson had looked at him with any-thing other than disdain, she was mistaken. The woman had been quite chilly—glacial wouldn't be an exaggeration—toward him when she'd arrived and had clearly been eager to leave him for the sanctuary of the room Diana had as-signed her.

Diana shook his arm slightly. "I only want you to be happy, Alex."

He sighed. He knew that. "You can make me happy by not meddling in my concerns."

Diana continued as if she hadn't heard him. "And I wasn't thinking only of you when I invited the Wilkinsons."

"Oh?" What new trick was this?

This time Diana was the one who dropped her voice and watched the door. "I told you Imogen had been in touch with Miss Wilkinson's brother." She smiled. "She has a tendre for him."

"For Randolph?"

"Shh! Do you want them to hear you?"

"They aren't here to hear me."

Diana smiled far too knowingly. "I suspect they'll be down at any moment."

"Ah." He should *not* feel a jolt of anticipation at the thought of Miss Wilkinson's imminent arrival.

He would consider Randolph instead. Unlike Diana, he didn't waste time wondering about a man's marital intentions, but now that he had, he was surprised to realize that Randolph was only a few years older than he.

"I'm hoping they will make a match of it," Diana said.

This could actually be a good thing. If Diana was busy poking her nose into Randolph's business, she'd have less time to meddle in his.

He heard voices in the corridor then—and his heart jumped. Diana was right—the Wilkinsons had come down early. He turned to see them enter the room. Randolph glanced around eagerly as if he were looking for someone—and then only partly hid his disappointment when he didn't find . . . Imogen?

Perhaps Diana wouldn't have to expend much energy on that match.

Miss Wilkinson hung back. If Alex didn't know her better, he'd think she was trying to hide behind her brother.

"Mr. Wilkinson, Miss Wilkinson," Diana said, dragging Alex along with her to greet them, "you are the first to arrive downstairs." She smiled at Randolph. "I believe my husband wishes to have a word with you, sir."

Alex would wager Roger was going to be quite surprised to hear that.

Wilkinson looked puzzled, too, but nodded and walked over to Roger, exposing his sister to Alex's interested eyes.

"I'll leave you in my brother's capable hands, if I may, Miss Wilkinson. I'm afraid there's something I must check on."

Diana went off on her imaginary errand. Probably just as well. Miss Wilkinson looked uncomfortable, though that could be because her shoulders and chest were swathed in a heavy wool shawl.

"Cold?" he asked. It *was* October, but the weather was quite mild.

She raised her chin and glared at him as if something—the temperature?—was his fault. "Yes."

She was so warm, her cheeks were flushed. Why in the world was she wearing that shawl?

He could just ask, but what fun would that be? "Then please step over to the fire."

She hesitated.

He mentally rubbed his hands together with glee. "I assure you it is much warmer there."

Now would she admit she was too hot? Not Miss Wilkinson.

"Er, thank you."

He walked with her to the blazing grate. "I hope you found your room to your liking?"

"Yes, it is very nice." She stopped several feet from the hearth, but Alex went closer so she had to come with him or betray herself.

Of course, the problem with this game was that *he* might melt. "I believe my sister put you in the yellow bedroom?"

"Yes."

Sweat beaded on her forehead. . . .

"I hope your trip from Loves Bridge was uneventful?"

"It was."

. . . and above her upper lip. She had nice lips—thin, but well shaped. At the moment they were parted, and she was panting slightly.

"If there is time, perhaps I can take you—and your brother, of course—over to see my estate. My lands march with Chanton's."

Two beads of sweat joined together and ran down her nose to dangle on its tip.

"That would be pleasant." She flicked the sweat away—and tried to fan herself with her hand at the same time.

This was ridiculous. "Miss Wilkinson, surely you would be more comfortable without that shawl."

She gripped it as if she feared he would tear it from her. "No. Thank you. I'm fine."

She did not look fine.

"Well, perhaps you would like to use a corner of it to dry your face." He probably should not have said that, but he was worried she would make herself ill. He felt quite heated himself. "Good Lord, one would think you were naked under that thing."

He *definitely* should not have said that.

Zeus! Did Miss Wilkinson turn even redder? He eyed the offending drapery. *Was* she naked?

His cock reacted in predictable fashion.

Idiot! Of course she's not naked.

A pity.

Fortunately, before he could act on any of the insane thoughts ricocheting around his brain, he was distracted by a voice coming from the corridor.

Lord, is that . . . ?

He turned to see two more guests enter the room. His eyes slid over the dark-haired woman in the lead to focus on the demure, blond girl behind her.

Charlotte.

His heart stopped. This was the first time he'd seen her since before her father had brought him word their wedding was off.

Good Lord, had she always looked this young?

His heart started beating again. He felt . . . well, embarrassed to think he'd ever thought himself in love with her.

He was suddenly *very* happy Lord Buford had paid him that visit.

Chapter Six

Jane carefully speared a pea with her fork and put it in her mouth. Surely this meal must almost be over. As soon as the women left the men to their port, she'd flee to her room. It might be cowardly, but . . .

Don't be silly.

Right. She wasn't afraid of anyone. She merely felt, er, slightly overwhelmed at the moment. It was to be expected. She never left Loves Bridge—and very few people ever came to the village—so she wasn't used to conversing with people who hadn't known her since she was in leading strings. Of *course* it would be wearing to find herself in a roomful of strangers.

She speared another pea with rather more force than necessary.

Strangers with ulterior motives.

Lady Chanton was clearly set on matchmaking, but Jane had hoped Lord Evans's sister was trying to match only Randolph and Lady Eldon. Now she was beginning to fear the woman—and Lord Evans's mother—thought *she* might be an appropriate wife for the earl.

Lady Chanton had told everyone not to stand on ceremony, to sit where they wished . . . and then somehow Jane had got stuck next to her. They'd no sooner taken their seats than she'd started in questioning Jane about Loves Bridge, her friends, her brother, her parents, and the Spinster House. She'd been cordial, but by the time she turned to address her daughter Bea on her other side, Jane had felt like she'd been knocked down and run over by several carriages.

She frowned at the next pea to feel the wrath of her fork. And now she felt as if someone was watching her. She glanced up—

Lud! Someone *was* watching her—the dowager countess, seated on the other side and the other end of the table. And instead of averting her gaze as any normal person would when caught staring, the woman smiled at Jane before turning to speak to Mr. John Grant, the widower of Lord Chanton's older sister and father of eight sons, two of whom were also at the table.

She was definitely fleeing to her room as soon as she could.

"May I serve you some more roast pheasant, Miss Wilkinson?"

Lud! Her heart jolted at the sound of Lord Evans's voice—as did her hand. Fortunately, none of the red wine in her glass made it onto the tablecloth.

The earl had been so busy conversing with the young, beautiful, *insipid* Lady Charlotte on his right, he'd likely just remembered Jane was here.

That's not very kind.

Perhaps not, but it was true. The girl was small and blond—like a china doll—and spoke in a breathy little whisper. Every time she smiled, she ducked her head, and she never once, as far as Jane could tell, looked anyone in the eye.

What can he find to talk about with that noddy?

It's none of my concern.

She kept her eyes on her wineglass. "No, thank you."

The pheasant dish didn't move away.

This time she looked up at him so he would be certain to hear her. "My lord, thank you, but I do not care for more pheasant."

He frowned at her plate. "You've hardly eaten a thing."

That was quite bold of him. "Oh? Are you my nanny now?"

He grinned. "Thank God. I thought the fairies had stolen away the real Miss Wilkinson and left a meek changeling in her place."

Oh? You seem to like meek women.

Fortunately, she managed not to say that out loud. What did she care about his preferences in women?

"Are you certain you won't take some more?" He dropped his voice. "You'll need your strength to withstand my sister." His eyes gleamed with amusement. "I heard her interrogating you."

So he *hadn't* been so entranced by Lady Charlotte that he'd forgotten she was here.

"You could have come to my aid, you know."

He grinned. "And risk having you bite my head off? No, thank you. I learned my lesson with Mr. Wertigger."

She felt herself flush. "I do apologize if I seemed ungrateful then. I was rather, er, annoyed with the man when you came up."

He snorted. "*Rather* annoyed? I thought you were going to eviscerate him with your bare hands right there on the village green."

She'd admit that she'd wanted to do exactly that. "He lied to me—to the committee."

"Who lied to you?"

Jane jumped at hearing Lady Chanton's voice and turned toward her, knocking against the platter of pheasant and sending her wineglass teetering.

She lunged for the glass as Lord Evans juggled the pheasant.

"Oh, I am sorry for startling you." Lady Chanton smiled with far too much satisfaction. Jane half expected her to waggle her brows the way the Boltwood sisters did when they thought they were observing a bit of romance. "You did seem quite, er, *engrossed* in your conversation."

Jane waited for Lord Evans to rein in his sister.

And waited.

She looked at the man. He was looking at . . .

Lud! In the confusion with the wine and the pheasant, her shawl had slipped off her shoulders. She tugged it back into place and turned to Lady Chanton.

"A person by the name of Waldo Wertigger lied to me, Lady Chanton."

"Oh, do call me Diana, Miss Wilkinson—and I hope you will give me leave to call you Jane. This is an informal, family gathering, after all."

"Ah." *Except I'm not part of this family.*

Yet. She might have a connection soon. Randolph and Lady Eldon had fallen into close conversation the moment they'd first seen each other and were now sitting together at the table.

"Of course you may call me Jane."

Lord Evans—surely Lady Chanton was not going to suggest Jane call the earl by his Christian name—leaned across her to address his sister. "The fellow advertised a live kangaroo, Diana, but when he arrived in Loves Bridge, it turned out the creature was stuffed. Miss Wilkinson was the one who had to deal with the charlatan."

The earl's face was just inches from hers. She couldn't breathe without inhaling his scent, a mix of soap and linen and . . . him. Her eyes traced his profile—the sweep of his long lashes, the faint shadow of his beard, the strong angle of his jaw—and then wandered back to his mouth. There was a small scar at the corner of his lower lip. How had he—

"Isn't that right, Miss Wilkinson—or may I call you Jane, since, as Diana says, this is a family gathering?"

He'd turned his head to address her, bringing his mouth even closer. If she leaned forward just the slightest bit—

She jerked back to put more space between them.

What were they talking about? Good Lord, she had completely lost track of the conversation. "Pardon me?"

"I asked if I might call you Jane"—he grinned, his eyes teasing her—"and you must call me Alex, of course."

She could never call the Earl of Evans Alex. That was far, far too intimate.

And terrifying.

Why?

Because it would open a door she could never again shut. Something important would change, though precisely what that was she wasn't completely certain.

"You must do as you please."

Fortunately—or unfortunately, perhaps—Bea chose that moment to say, quite heatedly, to Octavius Grant, her university-aged cousin, "Balderdash! Women are indeed capable of managing their own lives. Look at Miss Wilkinson."

That, of course, caused everyone to look at Jane—everyone but Lady Chanton, who sighed and addressed her daughter.

"Bea, it is not polite to voice such strong opinions in company."

"Octavius isn't company!"

"No, but you are getting ready for your come-out, remember, so you should pretend that he is."

Octavius made the mistake of snickering—and Bea's fingers tightened on her wineglass. Jane caught her breath, expecting to see wine stream down Octavius's face at any moment.

She'd never attended the London Season, but she expected Bea would make quite an, er, *splash*, though perhaps not in the way her mother would wish.

"And you certainly should not single out Miss Wilkinson."

Bea let go of her glass—Jane thought she heard Lord Evans sigh with relief at that—and raised her chin. "I believe in speaking my mind, Mama, and not allowing *men*"—she looked at Octavius—"to rule me. Surely you must agree, Miss Wilkinson?"

Jane hesitated, thereby giving Randolph a chance to jump into the fray.

"Oh, now, you can't let my sister's opinion on the matter influence you, Miss Livingston-Smythe. She's never been to London and she's more than ten years your senior." He chuckled. "And I must tell you that all the men in Loves Bridge go in fear of her temper."

A rather uncomfortable—appalled?—silence settled over the table.

Randolph cleared his throat. "Not that I mean to be critical, of course."

"Please do not murder your brother at my sister's table," Lord Evans murmured.

Jane swallowed her first impulse, which indeed had been to blast Randolph back to Loves Bridge, and forced herself to smile. "My brother is likely correct, Miss

Livingston-Smythe, that country manners are different from what would be acceptable in Town, but I must believe that any *intelligent* man"—she leaned over to direct a speaking look up the table at Randolph—"in either Town or country must value a woman's good sense. We are not children, so we no longer need an adult's constant guidance and supervision."

"Very true." Lady Chanton stood. "And with that, I think this is an excellent time to leave the men to their port."

"Yes, indeed." Lord Evans's mother also rose. "Don't linger too long, gentlemen."

"Well done," Lord Evans said quietly to Jane as he stood politely with the rest of the men. "Thank you."

She contented herself with a nod and then followed the other ladies out. Heavens, did he really think she'd brangle with Randolph in front of his relatives? She had more control than that. When she got Randolph alone, however . . .

That *discussion* would have to wait until morning. Now she was going up to her room. She should tell Lady Chanton, but the viscountess had gone on ahead and—

"Oh, Miss Wilkinson, may I join you?"

Apparently, not all the women had preceded her to the drawing room. Jane opened her mouth to explain to Miss Livingston-Smythe that she was retiring early, but the girl didn't give her the opportunity.

"When Mama told me you and your brother were coming, I was so delighted. I've been dying to speak to you."

"Oh. Well." What was she to say to that? "I don't know that I'm that interesting, Miss Livingston-Smythe." She cast a longing look at the stairs.

Miss Livingston-Smythe didn't appear to notice—or if she did, she didn't take the hint. "Please call me Bea. May

I call you Jane? Uncle Alex says you live by yourself in a place called the Spinster House. I so envy you."

She still could say she was tired and excuse herself, but she hadn't the heart to do something this eager young girl—Lady Chanton had mentioned her daughter had just turned seventeen last week—might take as a snub. Jane could remember being seventeen, though it did seem like a very long time ago.

So she repressed a sigh and went with Bea into the drawing room. The rest of the ladies had arranged themselves around the tea tray, but Bea headed for two chairs set off by themselves.

Jane pulled her shawl closer and followed.

"I will tell you," Bea said once they'd taken their seats, "that I am dreading going up to Town. I'm not certain I wish to marry at all, but I definitely don't want to be trotted around London to be"—she pulled a face—"examined like a horse for sale."

Put that way, a Season *did* sound unpleasant. "I have no personal experience, Miss"—the girl frowned and opened her mouth as if to protest Jane's formality—"er, *Bea*, but my one friend who had a Season thoroughly enjoyed all the parties and balls."

Anne's stories had been exciting, but they hadn't made Jane long for the social whirl.

Bea looked skeptical. "How could she have enjoyed it? Didn't her parents try to push her into parson's mousetrap?"

Anne's father *had* been anxious for Anne to wed, but that had been just recently when he'd wished to remarry. "No. Do you think your parents would pressure you to accept an offer you could not like? Pardon me, but I find that hard to imagine."

Bea sighed. "No, you are right. I'm sure they wouldn't.

But I still believe it's terribly unfair. Men have it so much easier than women, don't you think?"

Jane opened her mouth to agree—and remembered Randolph's sad tale of his dashed matrimonial hopes. "I'm not certain they do. It takes two people"—if one ignored the possibility of meddling relatives—"to make a marriage. Sometimes men face disappointment."

Bea looked oddly pleased by Jane's answer. "Yes, I suppose you are right. Uncle Alex was certainly disappointed."

Jane's attention sharpened.

I should not encourage Bea to gossip.

Nonsense. It is only sensible to be informed when the man's sister and mother have matrimonial schemes that might involve me.

Bea glanced over at the other women and then leaned close to whisper. "I had it out with Mama when she told me Lady Charlotte would be here."

"Oh?" How had Lady Charlotte entered the conversation?

Jane would admit to not immediately liking Charlotte— all right, she'd taken an immediate *dislike* to her—but she'd also admit, much as it pained her to do so, that her negative feelings were largely due to jealousy. Lady Charlotte was the epitome of English beauty with her blond hair, blue eyes, and flawless complexion.

The fact that Lord Evans had spent a significant part of dinner talking to the girl was beside the point.

"Yes. Mama said there was nothing to be done— Charlotte *is* Cousin Imogen's companion. But I'm afraid I'll have a hard time being civil to her."

"Ah." Jane repressed the urge to ask what made Lady Charlotte so dreadful.

She didn't need to inquire.

Bea's eyes had widened at her noncommittal reply. "You don't know, do you?"

"Er, know what?"

"That Lady Charlotte is the woman who jilted Uncle Alex at the altar." Bea shrugged. "Or almost at the altar."

Oh! Poor Lord Evans.

No, not "poor Lord Evans." Hadn't the earl already begun combing London ballrooms for a replacement bride? Clearly, his heart hadn't been injured.

Randolph hid his broken heart so well, I never had an inkling he was wounded.

The situations were not at all comparable. Of course she hadn't noticed Randolph's pain. She'd been only fourteen and overwhelmed by their parents' deaths when his romance had ended.

"He came home to the Hall to lick his wounds and hide from everyone," Bea said.

"I can't imagine your uncle hiding, Bea." She should be more charitable. Perhaps the earl's return to Society's ballrooms was merely a case of getting back on the horse that threw him. Earls needed heirs, after all. She—

She should not be encouraging Bea to gossip. "This is really none of my affair, you know. I'm certain your uncle would not wish you to discuss him with me this way."

Bea continued as if Jane hadn't spoken. "Charlotte should never have agreed to marry Uncle Alex. She loves Septimus—has loved him forever."

Jane blinked. "Septimus as in Septimus Grant, your cousin?" Septimus was older than Octavius, but he still seemed quite young to be thinking of marriage.

Bea nodded. "Charlotte—"

"Bea," Lady Chanton called from the group by the tea tray, "the men will be here soon."

"Yes, Mama." Bea turned back to Jane. "I can't say any more now. Meet me by the fountain later and I'll tell you the whole. I need your help."

"What?" Jane's mouth fell open. She must look like a beached fish. "Help?"

Bea nodded. "Alex needs a wife, and Mama said you are an accomplished matchmaker."

"Not really." She'd only made two matches and her goal with both had been to free the Spinster House for herself, though of course she wanted her friends to be happy.

"Bea!" This time Lady Chanton raised her brows significantly and gestured with her head at the door.

"Yes, Mama." Bea looked back at Jane. "Please? Meet me in the garden by the fountain later."

"I don't know. . . ."

They heard the deep sound of male voices. Bea jumped to her feet, so Jane stood as well.

"By the fountain," Bea murmured as her father and Lord Evans entered the room. "Promise?"

"Oh, very well."

Alex took a sip of tea. He'd much rather be drinking brandy.

During dinner he and Charlotte had spoken about the weather and the condition of the roads and other inconsequential topics. Well, he had spoken. She'd mostly nodded. The bulk of her attention had been directed at Septimus Grant on the other side of the table.

And now he was sitting with her in the drawing room, slightly apart from the others. He didn't have to be. He could have chosen a different seat, but he'd seen her alone and had thought it kinder to join her.

Earlier this year, he would have been delighted with the

situation. But now? He wished someone would rescue him. Miss Wilkinson, perhaps.

He smiled inwardly. He knew why she was so attached to that shawl. He'd much enjoyed the glimpse he'd got of her creamy skin when it had slipped off her shoulders at dinner.

"Do you think it will rain tomorrow, my lord?" Charlotte's voice trembled slightly and her eyes flitted from his face to a point on his right before returning to her teacup.

He forced himself to focus on her. "I don't know. Rain is always a possibility in England, isn't it?" Surely she wasn't afraid of him? "And do call me Alex, Charlotte. We were almost married, after all."

Her eyes came up to his again—and again slid off to his right before returning to her cup. "Yes, my lord."

Blast, he was gritting his teeth. He relaxed his jaw, took a breath, and idly glanced over to see what so interested Charlotte.

Miss Wilkinson was talking to Septimus Grant. Odd.

Well, perhaps not so odd. Everyone else was occupied. Randolph and Imogen were in close conversation in the far corner; Bea and Octavius were arguing; Roger and John Grant were likely discussing horses; and Mama and Diana had their heads together.

Oh, Lord. They're probably plotting something I won't like. Thank God this house party is to last only a few days.

He turned back to Charlotte and regarded her bowed head. He'd once thought her shyness appealing. Now he thought it annoying.

Well, this would be a perfect time to clear the air. "I wish to apologize, Charlotte."

That caused her to look up. "You do?" The smallest frown appeared between her brows. "Why?"

Wasn't it obvious? "I should have stayed in London and supported you after the news got round that you . . . er, that *we* had called off the marriage."

"Oh." The line between her brows deepened.

Was that all she was going to say? Miss Wilkinson would have—

This had nothing to do with Miss Wilkinson.

"I knew your father was very angry. I hope he did not, ah, take his displeasure out on you?"

She shrugged one shoulder. "Papa shouted. He always shouts." Her gaze slid back to Miss Wilkinson and Septimus. "And he sent me away to be Cousin Imogen's companion."

"I'm sorry. Do you miss London?"

"Not really."

Had it always been this difficult to converse with Charlotte?

"I imagine your father will relent. I'm surprised he hasn't already."

"He and Mama are busy with Felicity now—that's my next younger sister. He's forgotten about me," Charlotte said matter-of-factly.

"You must be mistaken." He'd never liked Buford much, but no man would ignore his own children.

"Oh, no. Papa was only ever interested in how much I could bring him on the Marriage Mart. It's the same with all of us." Her lips curved into the slightest of smiles. "He wanted sons, you see. He's quite bitter that he has only daughters. He'd keep trying for a boy, but Mama can't have more children." She shrugged. "Lord Chanton is very fortunate that he finally managed to get an heir."

"Er, yes." An heir was important, but Alex felt confident

Roger would have welcomed another girl had that been the new baby's gender.

Charlotte glanced over at Septimus and Miss Wilkinson again and something that might have been excitement lit her eyes. . . .

No, he must have been mistaken. The expression was gone almost immediately and when Charlotte spoke, it was in her usual soft, even tone.

"If you'll excuse me, my lord, I believe I'll go upstairs now to make certain all is ready for Imogen when she retires."

From the look of things, Imogen would not be retiring anytime soon—she was still talking to Randolph—but Alex grabbed at the words like a jailed man grabbing an open door. Freedom was at hand!

"Of course."

He stood and watched her leave. She was small and delicate and beautiful.

And dreadfully boring. How could he ever have thought himself in love with her?

Clearly, he had no business looking for a wife if his judgment of women, and more importantly, of his own feelings, was so faulty.

He took their teacups over to the tea tray. Apparently, others had decided to retire early as well, as the only people left—besides Randolph and Imogen in the corner—were Mama, Roger, and John Grant.

But where was his sister? "Has Diana deserted you?"

"No," Diana said, coming back into the room. "I was just checking on something. Would you like more tea?"

"No, thank you."

Roger grinned and pulled a bottle out from behind a potted plant. "How about some brandy?"

Brandy would have made his conversation with Charlotte much less painful.

But perhaps less enlightening.

"Is that what you've been drinking?"

Roger's grin widened. "Of course." He held the bottle out to Alex.

"No, thank you." He had brandy in his room, and the faster he retreated there, the less chance his mother and sister would quiz him about his conversation with Charlotte. "I believe I'll go up to bed."

"It's a nice night," Diana said. "You could go for a stroll in the garden first."

Mama nodded. "It might help you sleep, Alex. You seem a trifle out of sorts."

"I am *not* out of sorts."

He glared at Roger who, after one explosive guffaw—loud enough to momentarily capture Randolph's and Imogen's attention—was struggling to swallow the rest of his laughter. Grant, wisely, kept his eyes on his brandy cup.

All right, yes. He *was* a trifle out of sorts.

"I believe I saw Miss Wilkinson go out there alone. You should see that she doesn't get lost." Diana smiled blandly— it must be quite a struggle for her to appear disinterested. "I imagine she'd like to have a look at the fountain. It's so lovely and mysterious under a full moon."

There were times he truly detested his sister. "I'm certain Miss Wilkinson can find her own way. The garden is not that complicated."

"Not for you. You've walked through it many times. This is Miss Wilkinson's first visit, and the moon casts many confusing—and, er, *interesting*—shadows."

Zeus, no matter what Diana did, she always managed to make him want to brangle with her.

He would not give in to that base urge. He had more control—and he also knew he wouldn't win. He never did.

"Yes. Miss Wilkinson, however, is very resourceful. I'm not worried about her." He let his gaze touch on all of them—except for Randolph and Imogen. An earthquake could shake the walls and they'd not notice. "Good night then. I will see you in the morning."

"Alex," Diana said before he turned away, "will you visit the girls in the morning? The ones who weren't in the nursery when you stopped in today were very sad to have missed you."

He grinned. It would be a relief to spend some time with uncomplicated females who said exactly what they meant. "I'll look in on them after my morning ride, if that suits?"

"That would be splendid." Diana gave him one of her broad, sunny smiles.

She was a perfectly fine sister when she wasn't trying to run his life.

He left the drawing room and headed for the staircase— and paused with his foot on the first step.

Oh, hell. Miss Wilkinson truly was quite competent, but now Diana had got him worried. The garden *could* be confusing at night.

And he wasn't tired—there was no chance he'd be able to fall asleep anytime soon. He didn't feel like reading. Perhaps Mama was right and a walk in the garden, breathing the cool night air, would be calming.

He headed for the door.

Chapter Seven

I should never have told Bea I'd meet her out here.

Jane pulled her shawl more tightly round her shoulders as she hurried down yet another path. She'd seen the fountain from her room when she'd arrived earlier and had thought it a simple matter to reach it.

Ha! What had looked simple in daylight was impossible at night, even with a full moon. Whoever designed this garden had an evil sense of humor. The walks were a maze of wrong turns, dead ends, and endless loops, and the surrounding vegetation was planted so she got only occasional glimpses of the blasted fountain—and it was never where she expected.

If she *did* believe in curses and supernatural cats, she might think there was some evil magic at work here.

And then the moon went behind a cloud, turning the garden dark as ink. Something damp and feathery tickled her face, caught her shawl . . .

She squeaked, jumped, hit out—and discovered when the cloud moved on that her attacker was an errant evergreen branch.

She grimaced as her heart slowed. Perhaps she was a *little* on edge.

I hope there weren't any spiders on that branch . . . and now on me!

She frantically brushed her hands through her hair.

"Shh!"

She froze. That was a male voice, coming from off to her right.

"Someone's nearby."

"Silly. It's just an animal." That was a woman. Bea?

Jane debated what to do. If it *was* Bea, she should probably join her at once, though it was hard to see how Miss Livingston-Smythe could be in any danger of scandal here. All the men but Randolph were related to her.

"Kiss me again." The woman's voice was breathy and urgent.

Oh. It couldn't be Bea.

She should leave the couple to their privacy . . . except she had no idea how to find her way back to the house.

She scowled at the bushes. What to do?

She would approach them. It would be awkward but she didn't wish to wander the garden forever, especially when there were people nearby who could rescue her. And Bea should be here soon, so they would be interrupted anyway. Better that she, a mature woman, handle the matter than a young girl like Bea.

She turned a corner and finally found the fountain—and the couple, just as the woman pushed the man against a pillar near the fountain's edge and reached for his pantaloons.

Jane stepped back quickly. Had that been Septimus Grant and Lady Charlotte?

It *couldn't* be mousy little Lady Charlotte.

She peered through the leaves. No, it was indeed Lady Charlotte. It was difficult to see precisely what she was doing in the moonlight, but whatever it was involved Septimus's. . . .

Oh! Jane got a glimpse of something long and pale before Charlotte's fingers closed over it, stroking. . . .

She scrambled backward so the heat of her face wouldn't set the bushes on fire.

She knew that a man's male organ resided behind his fall. She'd felt one of those organs hard against her stomach when drunken Lord Dennis had got her alone in the Davenport Hall library during the party before Anne's first Season.

Her eyes narrowed. That had been more than ten years ago and the memory *still* made her angry. The oaf had trapped her against the back of a wingchair—she'd shoved on his chest, but it had been like trying to move a stone wall—and had stuck his tongue down her throat. She'd almost gagged.

She should have bitten him.

She'd never felt so helpless. That was what she'd hated most about the disgusting encounter. Thank God another couple had come into the library at that moment, causing Lord Dennis to release her.

And *then* the bloody blackguard had had the gall to chuckle and whisper that they could get back to their "play" later. Ha! Over her dead body.

Or, better, *his* dead body. She'd left the library and taken care to keep the length of the ballroom between her and the blackguard for the rest of the evening.

Septimus was making gasping, almost mewling noises. It was very embarrassing. She started to put her fingers in her ears—

"Imogen's going to marry Wilkinson," Charlotte said.

What?!

Jane forgot about embarrassment. Randolph had decided to marry? That was very sudden. Yes, he'd loved Lady Eldon—many years ago. People changed.

"And you know what that means," Charlotte said.

"Y-yes. Let's talk about this la"—Septimus's voice suddenly pitched higher—"ter."

"No, now. It means I'll have to go back to Papa, Septimus. And Papa might try again to marry me off to old Lord Evans."

Old?! Lord Evans isn't old.

"No. Can't. Evans won't have you af-after you j-jilted him." Some heavy panting. "Zeus!" More panting. "Finish me. Now. P-please!"

Charlotte was not going to be hurried.

"You saw how he singled me out tonight. He apologized for not staying in London to support me! Can you imagine? I didn't know where to look."

No, Jane could *not* imagine. Charlotte should have been the one apologizing.

"If he can be brought up to scratch, Papa will push me and push me to have him."

Charlotte must finally have done what Septimus had begged her to do, because the man drew in a sharp breath and then made a shuddering sound.

"You can't marry him." His voice was stronger now. Determined. "You love me."

"Yes, but you don't know Papa. I told him I loved you when I refused to marry the earl last time—and he locked me in my room and fed me only bread and water until I agreed to the wedding."

"The dastard!"

Jane nodded. She felt some sympathy for Charlotte. It was too bad every woman didn't have a Spinster House to fall back on when faced with a pigheaded, overbearing male relative.

"So you see, we have to run for Scotland."

"Elope?" Septimus sounded deeply shocked. "But think of the scandal! Your reputation is already a bit sullied from your breaking things off with Evans."

"I don't care. I love you."

"And I love you, too much to let you do anything so rash."

Jane scowled at an innocent leaf. *Typical male, thinking he knows best.*

"It's *not* rash."

That's right, Charlotte!

"What if I—or my father—talk to your father?" Septimus asked. "Perhaps we can make him see reason."

"You can't. Papa will *never* give his consent. You don't have a title, and he is *obsessed* with titles."

Just like Lady Eldon's father. Think of all the pain that dolt caused Randolph.

Jane was tempted to burst into the clearing shouting "Elope!"

"And I refuse to wait two more years until I'm twenty-one and can wed without Papa's permission."

"Two years! By God, you're right. We can't wait two years," Septimus said. "We'll have to—"

"Shh!" This time it was Charlotte shushing Septimus. "Someone's coming!"

Jane frowned. *Charlotte can't have heard me. I'm not movin—*

And then she heard it, too—the sound of someone walking purposefully along the garden path.

"We have to leave," Charlotte whispered urgently.

"Which way should we go?" Septimus whispered back.

Not this way! Jane looked wildly around, but there was

no place to hide. Her only option was to jump into the bushes—where there were likely spiders.

She did *not* like spiders.

And it was too late to hide, anyway. Lord Evans had just come round the curve in the path.

Oh, why couldn't a cloud cover the moon now?

Alex saw Miss Wilkinson up ahead—minus her concealing shawl. His eyes went at once to her lovely, long neck, and then slid slowly down over her creamy skin to stop, sadly, at the fabric skimming her small, delicate breasts. His lips and fingers begged to follow the same path and then dip below—

She inhaled, causing her bodice—as well as his heartbeat and, er, something else—to rise. Then she smiled in a rather forced manner and came over to him.

"This is a beautiful garden, Lord Evans," she said, rather more loudly than necessary.

Alarm bells rang in his head. There was some sort of meddling afoot. "Yes, it is. My brother-in-law and sister are quite proud of it."

"As they should be." She took a step in the direction from which he'd come. "But I'm afraid I've got a bit lost. Can you show me the way back to the house?"

What is she trying to keep me from discovering?

"It's only a few steps to the fountain. You must see it, Miss Wilkinson. It is most impressive, especially in the moonlight." For some reason his voice dropped on the last word, sounding seductive to his own ears.

She frowned—and then leaned close to whisper, "Did you come out here to find Lady Charlotte?"

"Hmm?" She smelled of lemons. Her skin looked so

soft. Was there some way he could touch her shoulder and make it look like an accident?

She shook his arm. "Lady Charlotte—are you looking for her?" Either the moonlight was playing tricks or worry clouded her eyes.

"No. Why are we whispering?"

"Because Charlotte is here—with Septimus Grant." She paused, biting her lip in what looked like embarrassment.

If the sun rather than the moon were out, he'd wager he'd see her lovely skin flush bright red.

He was more interested in her lovely mouth . . .

"And they aren't just admiring the fountain."

"Ah." He finally heard what Jane was saying.

Charlotte is here with another man.

If he had any lingering doubts about his feelings for his former betrothed, they were put to rest now. He wasn't even mildly pained to learn about her assignation.

Though he was very much afraid his sangfroid was due to Miss Wilkinson's presence.

Don't be a fool. The Spinster House spinster has no interest in marriage.

True. And hadn't he just concluded he shouldn't have any interest, either? Not now. Not until he sorted through his feelings and sharpened his ability to read himself and others.

She put a comforting hand on his chest. "I hope it's not too large a blow. Bea told me the girl . . . er, that you and Lady Charlotte had been betrothed."

"Yes. Charlotte jilted me. It's quite all right to say it." He almost relished the pain hearing the words brought him— though this time he felt only a dull ache. "Believe me, every last member of the *ton* knows of it."

Miss Wilkinson frowned. "I can see that would be rather"—she paused as if searching for the correct word—

"*uncomfortable*, but it was a very good thing she broke it off."

He felt like he'd taken a flush hit to his breadbasket. "Am I so bad then?" he asked, struggling to keep his tone light.

Miss Wilkinson's brows shot up—and then she scowled at him. "Of course not. This has nothing to do with you."

He snorted. How could a broken betrothal have nothing to do with him? Clearly, he hadn't been able to hold Charlotte's attention, let alone inspire any warmer feelings in her.

Miss Wilkinson dropped her voice even more so that he had to lean closer to hear her. "Lady Charlotte has loved Septimus all along. Her father forced her into the betrothal with you."

Zeus! This just got worse and worse. Had he really been that blind? "And how do you know this?"

"I overheard her tell Septimus just now."

He closed his eyes, mortification and self-loathing churning in his gut. *What a bloody fool I've been. Did everyone but me see the truth?*

But truth was truth, and no amount of wishing things were different would change that. Clearly, he needed to do some serious thinking about himself, women, and marriage before he tried again to find a wife.

"I'm sorry. I thought you should know."

"Yes." He didn't want Miss Wilkinson's pity. And he certainly didn't want to pursue the subject any further. A distraction was needed. "Do let me show you the fountain," he said at his normal volume. "Diana is especially proud of it."

"Shh," Miss Wilkinson hissed. "Charlotte and Septimus might hear you!"

"Miss Wilkinson, if they've not made their presence

known by now, they are long gone. We might have kept our voices low enough that they couldn't make out our words, but unless they are deaf they were very aware we were close by."

Miss Wilkinson looked for a moment like she would argue, but then she sighed. "I suppose you are right."

"Of course I'm right. Now do come along. Once Diana knows you've been in the garden, she's sure to ask you your opinion of the fountain."

Miss Wilkinson let him lead her into the clearing—and smiled broadly, as if she couldn't stop herself.

"Oh, how beautiful."

"Yes." The fountain wasn't elaborate, but something about its simplicity along with the water and moonlight gave the clearing a magical feeling.

Or perhaps the real magic was being here with this particular woman—

No. No magic. No thinking or planning or feeling anything with regard to this or any woman for a good long while.

They stopped close to the fountain's edge.

"Why were you strolling the garden alone, Miss Wilkinson?" he asked. That *was* odd. "I got the impression at dinner that you planned to run off to your room at the first opportunity."

Her chin went up at his words, and he swallowed a smile. She was far too easy to tease.

"I was indeed planning to go up to my room, but . . ." She hesitated.

"You thought that would look too cowardly?"

She frowned at him. "No. I, er . . ." She cleared her throat. "If you must know, Bea wanted me to meet her here." She looked back at the water. "Since she hasn't yet arrived, I assume she, ah, changed her mind."

"Yes, she must have. She left the drawing room before I did." He frowned. "Did she say why she wished to speak to you?"

"She . . ." Miss Wilkinson shook her head.

What was this? "Bea is only seventeen, Miss Wilkinson," he said sternly. "She should not have secrets from her parents—or her uncle."

"Oh, I suspect her mother knows precisely what Bea is about." She raised an eyebrow. "How did you happen to come out into the garden tonight, my lord?"

That surprised a laugh from him. "Diana suggested I follow you in case you got lost." So Bea was helping Diana do a little matchmaking? Foolish.

Miss Wilkinson laughed too. "Your sister was right—I *did* get lost."

A breeze fluttered through the clearing, creating small ripples on the water and causing a few strands of Jane's hair to fly in front of her face. Without thinking, he reached out and pushed the errant strands back. He'd do the same for Bea or any of his nieces.

The hair was soft and silky and smooth. It caressed his fingers . . .

He did not feel the least bit avuncular now.

Don't be an arse. She's the Spinster House spinster. She's happy with her independence. And you've sworn off romance for the foreseeable future.

But the quiet, the moonlight, the privacy of the clearing wove together to draw him to this woman. He stepped closer.

Has Isabelle Dorring's curse taken hold of me? Because I certainly feel bewitched.

He took a deep breath to steady himself and inhaled Jane's scent. It went straight to his head like a glass of brandy on an empty stomach. He felt slightly drunk. And reckless.

And totally uninterested in abiding by his new rule against romance.

They'd decided at dinner to use Christian names, hadn't they? Diana had said this was an informal, family gathering.

Miss Wilkinson is not your family.

He ignored the faint voice of reason. It had no place here in the magical moonlight.

"*May* I call you Jane?"

He watched her swallow, saw the tip of her tongue dart out to moisten her lips.

"Yes." She was back to whispering.

"And you must call me Alex." He was whispering too.

"A-Alex." Her expression softened as her fingers brushed his cheek. The touch was fleeting, but it shot through him to lodge in his heart—and his less noble organ. "Were you very hurt when it happened?"

He knew what she was asking, but he said the words anyway. "When Charlotte jilted me?"

She nodded.

He'd never admitted it to anyone, not even Marcus or Nate, but here in the moonlight, in the quiet privacy of the garden, somehow he could. "Yes."

"I'm sorry."

"It doesn't matter." It was true. He no longer ached for Charlotte and soon—he hoped—he'd get over this feeling that he'd been played for a fool.

Well, he *did* ache, but in a different location and for a much different reason.

No romance, remember?

That was reason talking again. His head. His heart and lower organ had a much different opinion.

Just one kiss. I haven't kissed a woman in so long. Just

one. What could be the harm in that? I'll stop at once if she doesn't like it.

Reason wavered, and in that instant his heart—or that lower organ—snatched control. He closed the small space between them to touch Jane's mouth with his.

She made a small, startled noise, so he drew back a fraction and waited for her to treat him to a thorough scold.

She didn't. Instead, she gave a little sigh and put her hands shyly on his shoulders.

An invitation—tentative, sweet.

He touched his lips to hers again, brushing lightly back and forth—and won a moan for his efforts. He moved from her mouth to her cheek and then to her jaw.

But she stood so stiffly, almost like a frightened horse, ready to bolt at his first wrong move. Why? She was twenty-eight. Surely she'd been kissed before.

He nuzzled the sensitive spot just below her ear, and won another moan. Yet still she didn't let her body relax against his.

Perhaps that was just as well. She might find the size of his cock more than slightly alarming. He was a bit alarmed himself—it felt as if it might explode. He moved his hips back an inch or two as a precaution.

"You aren't afraid, are you?" he murmured.

That had been exactly the wrong thing to say.

Or perhaps it was exactly the right thing. It was time for reason—and sanity—to return.

She shoved on his chest. "Of course not. I'm not afraid of anything."

He stepped back, beyond arm's length this time, and struggled to recover his equilibrium.

Miss Wilkinson was not the sort of quiet, restful woman he wished to marry. . . .

Oh, hell, I don't know what sort of woman I want—and until I do, I have no business kissing anyone.

He bowed slightly. "I apologize for my behavior."

She steadied herself against the fountain. "As well you should." She shivered—though not, he suspected, from cold—and wrapped her arms around herself. "Where's my shawl?"

"I don't know. Did you have it when you left the house?"

"Yes. I must have dropped it on the path earlier." She strode off, and he followed meekly behind her.

No, not meekly. Carefully.

"Here it is." She stopped by a shadowy heap on the edge of the path.

He waited for her to pick it up, but she didn't. Very well, he'd be a gentleman. He scooped the shawl off the ground and stepped forward to put it on her shoulders.

She dodged away. "Ah, could you shake it out, please?"

His brows rose, but he did as she asked.

"Harder?"

He opened the shawl completely and snapped it several times. "Will that suffice?"

"Yes, thank you." She took it from him and wrapped herself in it, hiding her lovely skin from his view.

A pity.

"What are you afraid—I mean concerned about?"

"Spiders." She cleared her throat. "I'm not fond of spiders."

He chuckled—and she glared at him.

"You know, Nate, Lord Haywood, is afraid of spiders too."

She raised a skeptical brow.

"Well, he was when he was a boy. I made the mistake

of dropping one in his bed at school and it was not well received."

That was putting it mildly. Nate had screamed like a girl—he looked at Miss Wilkinson and decided she would not approve of that description—and leapt out of bed. And then he'd chased Alex down the corridor, cursing and promising to beat him to a bloody pulp.

"I should think not." She gave him a reproachful look.

"Yes, well, I did apologize profusely." He offered her his arm. "Allow me to escort you to the relatively spider-free house."

They walked back in uneasy silence.

Chapter Eight

Jane walked down the sloping lawn toward a line of trees. She was feeling a little fragile.

She'd tossed and turned all night. Every time she'd closed her eyes, she'd relived the scene by the fountain. The moonlight. The quiet intimacy. The touch of Alex's— Lord Evans's—hand smoothing back her hair. The slight friction of his mouth on hers.

And the intense need that had surged through her, that was still beating inside her, even now, hours later, in the bright morning sunlight.

She stopped and touched her lips, swollen and sensitive with the memory.

The kiss had been completely unlike the one Lord Dennis had forced on her years ago at Davenport Hall. Then all she'd wanted was to escape. Last night, it had taken all her control not to press herself closer, wrap her arms around Alex's neck, and welcome him in deeper.

And it wasn't just the unsettling physical sensations that haunted her. She was twenty-eight. She had some inkling

about physical lust, not that she'd felt it often. This was
more than physical.

I care about his feelings.

Sometime during the endless night she'd conceded that
it had hurt her far too much to tell him what she'd overheard Charlotte say. Why?

She believed in speaking the unvarnished truth without
roundaboutation . . . well, except perhaps when she'd been
plotting to win the Spinster House. But nothing was ever
gained by living a fairy tale. It would have been a tragedy
for both of them if Lord Evans had married Charlotte.

Both of them meaning Lord Evans and Charlotte, of
course.

Except . . .

Lud! She squeezed her eyes shut. At the darkest part of
the night, she'd thought it would have been tragedy for *her*,
too. Which was ridiculous. Whom Lord Evans did or
didn't marry had nothing to do with her except insofar as
she would likely encounter the woman at any celebrations
Cat or Anne might have. Lord Evans was a close friend of
her friends' husbands, after all.

What if I were the next countess?

Good Lord, where had that thought come from? She
was the Spinster House spinster, happily and *permanently*
independent. She was not looking for a husband.

Clearly, she was far too tired to think rationally.

She'd decided when she'd finally given up on sleep and
got out of bed that a nice brisk walk would help settle her
chaotic emotions. From the house, she'd seen what looked
like a glint of sun on water, and, when she'd asked Lady
Chanton about it, the woman had confirmed there was a
pleasant woods with a lake and a lovely walking path at

the bottom of the hill. She'd encouraged Jane to go for a stroll—in fact, she'd almost pushed her out the door.

So she should start strolling again and stop thinking. But where was the path? She scanned the line of trees—ah, there it was. She adjusted her course, angling off to the right, and soon stepped into the cool, peaceful woods.

She felt better immediately. She took a deep breath, drawing in the scent of the forest, and listened to the rustling of small animals moving through the leaves, the call of birds above her, the splash of—

Splash?

It must be a duck landing on the pond. Several ducks. An entire flock.

The sound was far too loud and regular for that.

She cautiously followed the path down to the lake, the carpet of fallen pine needles muffling her steps, and looked out to see—

Lud! There's a naked man in the water!

She jumped behind the nearest tree.

No, I must be mistaken.

She peered around the tree trunk. Fortunately, her dress was a shade of green that would blend into her surroundings.

She hoped.

Yes, that was definitely a naked man. He was swimming away from her, so she could admire his broad shoulders and muscled back without being seen. Who was it? Not Randolph. Lord Chanton? No, the viscount's hair was darker and surely his shoulders weren't this broad. . . .

The man turned slightly—oh! She ducked back behind the tree. It was Lord Evans.

All the upsetting feelings of the night before came roaring back.

I should not be spying on him . . . though I do seem to be making a habit of spying these days.

She peeked again just as the earl chose to dive underwater, giving her an excellent view of his arse.

Mmm. That was very nice.

What was she thinking? She should be shocked. Embarrassed. Alarmed. Having a fit of the vapors. Instead she felt hot and breathless and her most private part was, well, *throbbing* and *damp*. She wanted to tear off her own clothes and dive into that nice, cold, *occupied* water.

He surfaced, swam a few more strokes toward shore, and stood. Water streamed down his muscled arms, broad back, and narrow waist and hips.

Oh. Oh, my.

He shook his head, sending drops flying, and ran his hands over his body to remove more water.

I'd like to help with that. . . .

She flushed even as her palms itched to feel those hard muscles and warm flesh—

What a shocking notion. She would not—

He turned to face her, and what little rational thought still remained in her poor brain was swamped by a raging tide of lust. Her gaze examined—far too avidly—the light-colored hair that dusted his chest and then traveled in a narrow line over his flat belly to a nest of curls where his male bit rested.

That was rather larger than any she'd seen depicted in art.

She squeezed her eyes shut and pressed her forehead into the rough tree bark. *Jane Margaret Wilkinson, you are not to be looking at the Earl of Evans's male bit!*

Yes, but . . . just one more peek?

She saw to her disappointment—no, to her *relief*—that he had turned away again and was reaching for his shirt.

Here's my opportunity to escape.

If she stayed where she was, she'd be discovered—and die of embarrassment. The path back to the house was only a foot from her current hiding place. The only way he'd *not* see her was if he were struck blind.

She would have to dart away when his shirt was over his head. If she made it to the bend in the path, she might be safe.

She lifted her skirt so she wouldn't trip and waited. As soon as Lord Evans's eyes were covered, she took off running—as quietly as she could—and didn't stop until she came to the end of the path. Once she saw the broad lawn in front of her, she dropped her skirt, took a deep breath, and stepped sedately out of the concealing trees. If anyone was watching from the house, they would assume she was calmly returning from a leisurely stroll around the lake and think no more of it.

Fortunately, they would not be able to see her legs trembling nor hear her breath coming in short gasps.

She lengthened her stride, heading for the back of the house and the garden door. She needed to put as much distance between herself and the woods as she could. Lord Evans would be emerging shortly and she did not want him to suspect she'd seen him.

Good God, she was turning into a wanton! Who but a light skirt would hide behind a tree to spy on a naked man? A respectable spinster should have turned her back and hurried away at once.

Mmm. I would never have guessed those chiseled arms and muscled, flat—

Do not *think about the earl's naked body!*

She fanned her heated face with her hand.

This was all Bea's fault. Bea was the one who'd persuaded her to meet at the fountain and then hadn't shown up. If not for that, she'd have gone straight to her room and

122   Sally MacKenzie

been safely reading while Lady Charlotte and Septimus and the earl prowled the garden. Her life would still be calm and orderly and . . . spinsterish. She—

She sighed. No, it wasn't all Bea's fault. She had to be honest. She bore a good deal of the responsibility. She should have insisted Lord Evans take her back to the house the moment she'd seen him and been firm about not wanting to see the fountain. She should definitely not have said one word about Lady Charlotte. The girl was none of her concern.

Perhaps not, but I hate to see Alex hurt . . .

Lord Evans was none of her concern either. Really, she'd been fortunate he'd behaved himself, at least for the most part. After that distasteful experience with Lord Dennis, she'd been very careful never to be alone with a man.

You were alone with Lord Evans in the Spinster House.

That was different. She was older and wiser now and Poppy had been present. One might not consider a cat an effective chaperone, but she had no doubt that if the earl had tried anything questionable under Poppy's sharp eyes, he would have found Poppy's claws buried deep in his lovely, muscled arse.

Do not *think about Lord Evans's hindquarters!*

She waved her hand in front of her face again. If anyone saw her and asked what she was doing, she'd tell them she was swatting bugs.

The truth was last night had been nothing like that dreadful time in Lord Davenport's library. With Lord Dennis she'd felt mauled. He hadn't cared who she was. He'd just wanted a female. Any female would have suited his purposes. But Lord Evans had invited *her*—Miss Jane Wilkinson—to join him in some wonderful adventure. An invitation she'd felt completely free to decline—but hadn't wanted to.

Lud! She'd wanted to abandon all reason and restraint and propriety and go wherever he led. It had taken all her willpower to keep from throwing her arms around him and pulling him full against her body, from breasts to . . .

She felt a hot blush flood her face. She'd even wanted to do whatever it was Charlotte had been doing with Septimus.

Lord Evans's virtue had been far more at risk than her own.

He is *looking for a wife. . . .*

She stopped by the garden wall and blinked at the ivy.

He hadn't mentioned marriage last night.

Of course he hadn't. They'd been talking about Charlotte and his broken betrothal. He clearly was still very much affected by that.

And yet he kissed me.

As had Lord Dennis, and he most certainly had not had marriage in mind.

Men were just very odd creatures when it came to such matters. Look at Randolph. He'd had a weekly appointment with Mrs. Conklin, the village's woman of accommodating morals, for years. It was simply a fact of life that men were able to separate physical actions from emotional attachments.

She went through the gate and followed the path toward the house.

And she had to admit, she wasn't an expert on the subject of physical love, even though she was twenty-eight. Besides that one dreadful encounter with Lord Dennis—and the lovely interlude with Lord Evans last night—she'd never been kissed.

She'd been too embarrassed to ask Cat and Anne any

questions. It had felt an invasion of their—and their husbands'—privacy. And she had no older sisters—no sisters at all—to turn to. Her mother had died before Jane's courses had even started.

She certainly wasn't about to ask Randolph—

She chuckled. Lord, poor Randolph had had to assure her she wasn't dying the first time her menses came—and then he'd hurried her over to the vicarage and asked Cat's mother to explain things. But of course Mrs. Hutting wasn't going to discuss marital duties to a fourteen-year-old girl.

She would guess, given how her feminine parts had reacted, that the business involved the male organ, nakedness, touching, and kissing.

Should *I see if I can make a match for myself?*

No! I'm not going to follow in Isabelle Dorring's footsteps and squander my independence for some man, no matter how attractive.

She turned a corner and saw a couple in an alcove, locked in a passionate embrace. She stepped back quickly. Lud! That had looked like Randolph and Lady Eldon.

She peered around the corner to check.

Yes, that's who it was. They really must be intending to wed and, from the look of it, soon. Well, why wait? Neither of them was getting any younger. And now that Jane had moved into the Spinster House, Randolph needed a woman to keep house for him.

She frowned. No, that was unkind of her. And unfair. She believed Randolph truly loved Lady Eldon.

She shifted from foot to foot. She didn't want to interrupt them and, well, she wasn't ready to hear her brother's good news. Not right now when she still felt off balance.

She retraced her steps—and then remembered she might encounter Lord Evans if she continued in that direction.

The image of his naked shoulders and chest and male bit leapt into her mind and she flushed again.

Where should she go?

She heard children's voices. Perfect. Children wouldn't notice her embarrassment, and their antics should distract her from a certain earl.

That swim had been just what he'd needed, Alex thought as he pulled on his breeches. He'd intended to ride as was his habit, perhaps going over to Evans Hall to check on things there, but he'd felt far too tense and out of sorts to inflict himself on poor Horatio.

Swimming had been a far better choice. The cold water and exercise had cleared the cobwebs from his brain and restored his equilibrium. Now he was ready to stop by the nursery to see the girls and then face Diana and her guests.

And Miss Wilkinson.

Lust slammed into his gut—and another, far more prominent organ. He shoved the misbehaving body part into his breeches, tucked in his shirt, and buttoned his fall so his, er, *thoughts* weren't so obvious. Not that he expected company. It was early. Everyone else—except for his sister whom he'd met on his way out—was still abed. The birds or squirrels or spiders wouldn't care that he was aroused.

Spiders. He smiled. So Miss Wilkinson was afraid of spiders. She should have left her shawl where it had fallen and let the spiders set up housekeeping. Why had she hidden herself under its over-warm folds? She was brave and independent about everything else—she should be equally confident about her lovely body.

His unruly body swelled with eagerness again, but the sturdy fabric of his breeches kept it under control.

He could have used some control last night he thought as he pulled on his stockings and shoes. He'd tossed and turned through a succession of heated dreams, all featuring a certain prickly spinster.

He picked up his waistcoat. Zeus, he was not a youth, new to romantic urges. He was a grown man with a normal history of sexual encounters. The thought that two brief kisses—

Well, it had been more than the kisses. It had been the light, tentative touch of Jane's hands, the softness of her mouth and cheek and neck under his lips, her sweet scent of lemon and woman, her air of brave innocence—they had all combined to condemn him to this sensual purgatory. Still, the fact that such small things could so affect him that he'd be standing here in the middle of the woods the next morning, no female in sight, with a throbbing erection was ludicrous.

And yet, here he was. Too bad he didn't have time for another dip in the cold lake.

He wrapped his cravat around his neck and made short work of tying it.

It made no sense. Miss Wilkinson was attractive, but she was not anything out of the ordinary. On the contrary, she was a little too tall, a little too thin, and much too opinionated. *And* she was twenty-eight years old—firmly on the shelf.

That was the most important point—Miss Wilkinson had gone to a fair amount of trouble to claim her spot on that shelf. She was very happy there. She would not welcome his—or any man's—attempts to dislodge her.

And he shouldn't try. He wasn't in a position to court any female, no matter how much Diana and Bea and likely Mama tried to meddle. Bloody hell, he'd thought himself in love with Charlotte, and he'd either been wrong or he knew nothing about the emotion. Just as bad, he'd thought she'd loved him, when clearly she had not.

It was very lowering to realize he was so blind.

He shrugged on his coat and started along the path up through the woods to the house.

Blind? Ha! He could see one thing clearly. He should not be feeling anything for Miss Wilkinson. She was nothing like the sort of wife he'd determined he required. Quiet and restful? Hardly. She'd already dragged confusion and hubbub into his life—into his soul, really.

There was only one thing for it: As he'd decided yesterday, he would put off looking for a wife until he felt certain he could trust his instincts on the matter.

He kicked a pinecone out of his path with more force than the small bit of vegetation warranted.

Likely a good part of his problem arose from the fact he'd been celibate too long. Once he was back in London, he'd visit that new brothel everyone was talking about.

The thought was frighteningly unappealing.

He stopped at the end of the trees, closing his eyes as the thought he'd been avoiding wormed its way to the surface.

Why in God's name did I admit Charlotte's actions had wounded me?

Blech! What a mawkish, namby-pamby sort of fellow Miss Wilkinson must think him. It was quite embarrassing. He would pretend that part of the evening had never happened. Undoubtedly, Miss Wilkinson would prefer to pretend that as well.

He started walking briskly up the lawn to the house, but changed direction when he heard the sound of children's voices. The girls must be out on the broad, level field beyond the garden.

Indeed, they were. The middle girls—Ruth, Esther, Rachel, and Rebecca—were playing a spirited game of tag. Bea and her next younger sister, fourteen-year-old Caroline, sat on a blanket, reading. Four-year-old Judith and two-year-old Martha stood with their nurse, Miss Conover, watching the game.

And Diana sat in a chair with Christopher—and next to her sat a suddenly red-faced Miss Wilkinson.

Why had she flushed so violently when she'd seen him? Was she as embarrassed about last night as he was? Or was there another, more immediate issue?

He glanced down to ascertain that the buttons of his fall hadn't somehow worked their way loose.

And then Martha caught sight of him and her chubby little face lit with a huge smile. "Unca Alwic!" she squealed, leaving Miss Conover to run toward him with her awkward, two-year-old gait.

Her sister Judith easily outdistanced her. "We have a new baby, Uncle Alex," she said excitedly, clapping her hands and giving a little hop. "A boy baby!"

"So I heard."

Martha arrived then and raised her hands to be picked up, so he lifted her small, sturdy body. She smiled and rested her head against his, patting his cheek with a pudgy, slightly sticky hand as he settled her into the crook of one arm.

Longing pierced his heart.

God, I wish I had children of my own.

He would someday. He was only thirty. He'd take some time to recover from his experience with Charlotte and then he'd try again.

Judith captured his free hand and pulled him over to

where Diana sat with her son—and a still very flushed Miss Wilkinson, who would not look up at him.

Diana, however, had no such problem. She caught his eye and smiled knowingly.

It was a good thing he didn't have a free hand, because his cravat was suddenly feeling quite tight. If he'd tried to loosen it, his sister's blasted smile would broaden so she'd look like a bloody Cheshire cat. Quite clearly, she thought her matchmaking efforts were succeeding.

But she was wrong—her meddling was not going to end with a wedding.

Judith tugged on his hand to regain his attention. "Stinky has a tiny, little doodle, Uncle Alex. I saw Nurse wash him. He piddled and hit her in the face. It was funny. Show Uncle Alex Stinky's doodle, Mama."

Diana, experienced mother that she was, didn't blush, but Alex felt his color deepen.

He didn't have the courage to look at Miss Wilkinson.

"Judith, remember how we talked about how some things are private?"

"But Stinky's a *baby*, Mama."

"Nevertheless, it's not polite to talk about him that way."

Judith frowned and then shrugged and looked up at Alex. "I suppose you have a big doodle like Daddy's, so you don't care about seeing Stinky's."

How was he to reply to that? He could see, from the corner of his eye, that Diana was trying valiantly not to laugh.

"Judith,"—she managed to sound stern—"you are not to talk about doodles at all."

"But, Mama—"

"Now go play with your doll and let Uncle Alex sit for a while with me and Miss Wilkinson."

That was the last thing he wanted. "I don't think—"

Miss Wilkinson looked up and spoke at the same time. "Oh, I should go back to—"

"Nonsense." Diana gestured to Miss Conover, who came and took Martha from him and led Judith away. "It is too nice a morning to spend inside." She smiled—rather slyly in Alex's opinion—and then feigned dismay. "Oh, dear! I've just remembered something I meant to discuss with Miss Conover. Will you hold Stinky for a moment, Miss Wilkinson?"

Alex wasn't so blind that he couldn't see an obvious ruse right under his nose.

Miss Wilkinson looked horrified. "I've never held a baby. I don't know what to do."

"Oh, don't worry. Stinky's almost two months old and quite sturdy." Diana plopped the baby onto Miss Wilkinson's lap and got up. "Just keep your hands on him and you'll be fine."

Christopher honored Miss Wilkinson with a toothless smile.

"Ohh." Miss Wilkinson smiled back. And then looked up at him, the beginnings of panic in her eyes. "I really never have held a baby."

He took the seat his sister had vacated. "No?" He thought all women had experience tending infants, but he sensed saying that would not help Miss Wilkinson feel more confident.

"No. Cat has lots of younger siblings, but I only had Randolph and he's five years older." She looked at him. "How much older than you is your sister?"

"Five years also." He pulled a face. "I got stuck playing tea party and other such girlish games quite a bit when I was still in leading strings."

Miss Wilkinson laughed. "Having an older brother was much different. Randolph ignored me when he could and tolerated me—barely—when he couldn't." She looked over at Bea. "You must have been . . . what? Thirteen when Bea was born?"

"Yes. And since, as you can see, Diana and Roger have been quite prolific, I've been surrounded by children of various ages for years." And soon he'd be playing honorary uncle to Marcus's and Nate's children.

I'd like to have my own children. My own family.
Right. But not yet. Not until I've sorted things out.
Christopher started fussing.

"Oh, what should I do?" The panic was now in Miss Wilkinson's voice. "Perhaps you should take him."

He could, but for some reason he was enjoying watching her manage the baby. "Try holding him up to your shoulder and patting him on the back."

She gave him a doubtful look, but did what he suggested. Christopher settled down nicely.

Miss Wilkinson giggled. "He's sucking on my neck. It feels so funny."

He had a very inappropriate urge to do the same thing.

It was going to get very uncomfortable—for him, if no one else—if he couldn't cure himself of these feelings for Miss Wilkinson. Even if he could indulge in a pleasant flirtation with her—which he was quite certain the Spinster House spinster would not welcome—he couldn't risk creating bad blood between them. How awkward that would be. Her closest friends were married to his closest friends. They were going to cross paths for years.

"Oh, dear. What's he doing now?" Miss Wilkinson looked at Alex in alarm. "What's wrong?"

Alex looked at Christopher. The baby's face was red and he was grunting.

He tried not to laugh. "I think Stinky may have just illustrated how he got his nickname."

She frowned at him—and then sniffed. "Oh." She

wrinkled her nose and looked back at the baby. "What do I do now?"

"Call in reinforcements. Diana!"

Diana looked over from where she was chatting with Miss Conover. "What is it?"

"Stinky is . . . stinky."

"Oh, he *did* just eat."

Miss Conover collected young Christopher, taking him off to be cleaned up elsewhere, while Diana got the younger girls settled with Bea and Caroline and came back to join them.

"Stinky didn't dirty your dress, did he, Jane?" Diana asked.

"N-no." Miss Wilkinson stood to inspect her skirt. "I don't think so."

"Well, if you find any, er, spots, you must let me know and we'll get everything set to rights."

Miss Wilkinson nodded.

"Where's everyone else?" Alex asked, hitting on the first topic that occurred to him which didn't involve Stinky's bowels.

"Here and there," Diana said. "Mama went into the village with Mr. Grant. You know they're going to make a match of it, don't you?"

"What?!"

Bea and Caroline looked over and even the game of tag paused.

"It's nothing," Diana called to her daughters and then looked back at Alex. "*Didn't* you know?"

"I never thought about it." Another example of his failure to understand the people around him. Now that he did consider the matter, he *had* seen Grant with Mama a lot recently. But . . . "Aren't they a little old for such things?" Mama had more than fifty years in her dish.

Diana laughed. "Clearly not. And it took me a while to get used to the idea, too, but I think they will be very happy together."

"If you say so." Likely they just wanted some companionship—some *platonic* companionship—in their twilight years.

Miss Wilkinson reclaimed their attention. "If you'll excuse me, I believe I'll go in now."

"Very well." Diana smiled—and Alex's inner alarms went off again. That particular smile always meant trouble. "I forgot to ask—how did you enjoy your walk this morning?"

"It was f-fine." Jane turned a truly remarkable shade of crimson.

Diana was grinning now. "The lake is very pretty in the early morning. I enjoy walking there myself—or I did before I had Stinky getting me up at all hours." She laughed. "But he'll sleep through the night eventually. They all do, thank God."

Alex knew Diana was talking, but her words were just a meaningless drone after the word *lake*.

He stared at Jane. "You were at the lake this morning?"

She stared back at him, swallowed—and then managed the smallest nod. "Y-your sister s-suggested I w-walk there."

He turned his gaze on his sister. He'd told her he was going for a swim. *"Diana."*

"What?" Diana pretended to look horrified, but her eyes were laughing. "Oh, dear. You didn't run into each other down there, did you?"

"No." He looked at Jane. Her face had gone from bright red to white.

"I really must go," she said, and fled toward the house.

Chapter Nine

Jane stood off in a corner of the drawing room, near where she and Bea had had their chat the night before, and tried to become invisible.

It was not a trick she'd practiced much.

She stole a glance at Lord Evans to be certain he was still safely on the other side of the room with the baby and two of his nieces—and the all too vivid memory of his broad, naked back, hard with muscle, flashed into her thoughts.

She flushed and looked away. She had to think about something, *anything* else.

She'd managed to avoid the earl since the disastrous morning. It hadn't been difficult—and likely he'd been helping, wanting to avoid her as much as she wanted to avoid him. There'd been the christening—Lord Evans had sat with his family and she'd been in a separate pew with Randolph and Lady Eldon—and then the large party Lord and Lady Chanton had hosted for their tenants, servants, and the local gentry. Fortunately, Lord Chanton had suggested an impromptu game of cricket early on, so that had kept the earl and the rest of the men busy. Even Randolph had joined in.

She'd say—quite without bias—that Lord Evans had been the strongest player.

And now she was lurking in the shadows while noise and activity went on around her. In celebration of their brother's christening that afternoon, all the Livingston-Smythe girls had been invited to join the adults after supper, and the drawing room was as close to complete bedlam as she could imagine. Eight girls *was* quite a lot, especially when not a one of them was either meek or retiring. When she'd seen them outside this morning, they hadn't been so overwhelming, but inside . . . they were very loud. And shrill, with all their high young female voices. And they had a tendency to jump and twirl and giggle and poke at one another.

But at least they were keeping Lord Evans busy and so away from her.

This was the last gathering she had to get through. In the morning she and Randolph—and Lady Eldon—would leave.

Lady Eldon was coming with them to Loves Bridge.

Randolph had found Jane soon after she returned to the house this morning—he'd likely been on the lookout for her—to tell her he was marrying Lady Eldon as soon as he could procure a license. She'd congratulated him and then they'd found Lady Eldon so Jane could welcome her into their family.

I must learn to call her Imogen, since she will be my sister.

She frowned. She knew she should be happy for Randolph—she *was* happy—but she was also . . .

She wasn't certain what she was. As she'd told Lord Evans, Randolph had mostly ignored her when she was a girl. However, she hadn't ignored him. Five years was just enough of an age gap that he'd been much larger and more accomplished than she. She'd looked up to him. Hero-worshipped him, really.

And then when she was fourteen and Mama and Papa had died, Randolph had come home to take charge. He'd given up his chance for love and happiness to be mother and father to her.

He'd said that wasn't the case, that Lady Eld—*Imogen's* parents had been so against the match they would never have agreed to it, but Jane wasn't certain of that. And if he hadn't had to drop everything to take care of her, he might have found the backbone to elope.

In any event, it was only fair he get this second chance now. As much as she complained about him, as much as he annoyed her, she loved him. He was her only family.

But having someone else join their little circle would take some getting used to.

She glanced at the earl again. Now he was laughing at something one niece said, the baby asleep on his shoulder.

He had such an easy confidence with children.

She'd never been one to coo over babies. To be honest, they frightened her a little. They were so small and unpredictable. But she'd been enchanted holding Christopher's sturdy little body this morning.

Cat, Anne, Randolph—their lives were all expanding to include a spouse and children, while she—

I've got Poppy.

Not the same.

"If I may have your attention," Lord Chanton said, shouting over the hubbub, "I have two announcements to make."

She could guess what one of them was. Randolph and Imogen were standing next to the viscount.

A footman appeared at her elbow, and she took a glass from him. Champagne.

"Do you mind that Cousin Imogen is marrying your brother?"

She startled, almost spilling her drink down her front— her well covered front in her high-necked, worn, *sensible* gown that no cat, no matter how supernatural, could render immodest.

"No, er . . ." Was this Rachel or Rebecca or Ruth? Really, parents should not use the same initial consonant for more than one child. When *she* had children—

She was the Spinster House spinster. She was never having children.

For the first time, that made her a little sad.

Nonsense. My feelings are merely disordered because I'm out of my element. I'll feel more myself once I'm back in Loves Bridge.

"I'm Rachel," the girl said, ascertaining her difficulty. She grinned. "There *are* a lot of us to keep track of."

Jane smiled. "Yes, there are. And, no, I don't mind that Randolph is marrying Imogen. I'm happy for them. It's not a sudden attraction. They knew each other years ago, before Imogen married Lord Eldon."

Rachel clearly knew the whole story. "Imogen should have stood up to her father. I'll give Charlotte that, at least." She scowled. "Though it would have been better if Charlotte had found her backbone *before* she accepted Uncle Alex's offer."

"Yes." Jane firmly agreed with that.

Rachel pulled a face. "I know I'm supposed to be polite to her, but I think she's silly and not very nice. *And* she hurt Uncle Alex when she jilted him. That was *mean*."

"Yes, it was." Very, very mean. Unconscionable. Lord

Evans would not welcome Jane's pity she well knew, but she did feel very bad for him.

Lord Chanton had announced Randolph and Imogen's betrothal and was now calling for a toast. Jane took a sip of champagne—

"I like you much better than Lady Charlotte," Rachel said.

The champagne went up Jane's nose.

Rachel helpfully slapped her several times on the back before Jane was able to step out of reach.

"I don't . . . that is . . ."

"And Uncle Alex likes you, too."

"Rachel, you don't . . . you mustn't . . ." This was all so ridiculous. "If you think your uncle has some special regard for me, you are much mistaken."

"No, I'm not. I've seen how he looks at you when he thinks you aren't watching."

She couldn't help herself. She glanced over at Lord Evans—

Lud! He *was* looking at her.

It's only a coincidence.

She turned her attention quickly to Lord Chanton, who was now announcing his mother-in-law's match with Mr. Grant.

That sent her eyes back to the earl. He didn't look surprised, so his mother must have had a word with him earlier.

"Everyone's getting betrothed, aren't they?" Bea said as she came over to join them. "Poor Uncle Alex is the last unattached male." She gave Jane a pointed look.

She was *very* happy she was leaving in the morning. "Don't forget Octavius." She supposed Septimus didn't count since he seemed to be privately betrothed to Charlotte.

Bea waved that away. "Octavius is too young."

"He's older than you are," Jane said.

"Yes, but boys are still idiots at twenty." Bea smiled at her. "Mama thinks you'd make Uncle Alex an excellent wife."

Oh, dear Lord. "Why in the world does she think that? She just met me."

"Oh, she knows more about you than you think," Bea said.

Rachel nodded. "Once she found out Uncle Alex had gone to Loves Bridge in August, she started looking into things. She has spies everywhere."

This was quite alarming. "Your mother can't know people in Loves Bridge. It's a small village."

Rachel shook her head. "No place is so small that Mama—or Grandmamma—doesn't know someone there— or they know someone who knows someone."

"And you're forgetting Cousin Imogen," Bea added. "She and your brother have been corresponding since shortly after Eldon died almost a year ago. It wasn't hard for Mama to put two and two together." She grinned. "Or in this case one and one—you and Uncle Alex."

"*Are* you going to marry Uncle Alex?" Rachel asked.

"No!" Jane was beginning to feel cornered. "I'm a dedicated spinster. I have no plans to marry anyone."

"But Uncle Alex isn't anyone," Bea said. "He's special."

"He needs a wife," Rachel said. "Mama says he's especially lonely now that his friends the Duke of Hart and Lord Haywood are married. If you don't take him, he might marry someone truly dreadful."

Jane understood the girls were concerned for their uncle, but he was not her responsibility, not to mention she felt quite certain he'd be horrified if he thought anyone considered him a charity case.

"What are you ladies discussing so seriously?"

Jane almost jumped out of her slippers at the sound of Lord Evans's voice—and his two nieces looked just as guilty.

"Pardon me. Am I interrupting a private conversation?"

He'd passed the baby off to someone else, but his cravat showed signs of having been clutched in tiny fingers and the shoulder of his coat had a wet patch from the baby's drool.

"Not at all," Bea said a bit too brightly. "We were just going, weren't we, Rachel?"

"Yes." Rachel smiled. If she thought she looked innocent, she was sadly mistaken. "Maybe you two should go for a stroll in the garden so you can have a private conversation."

"Come *on*, Rachel," Bea said, a note of warning in her voice. "Mama needs us."

Since their mother was happily chatting with her husband, Jane doubted she had any need of her daughters, but perhaps Lord Evans wouldn't notice that.

A vain hope. The man wasn't blind—or deaf. Rachel hadn't been at all subtle.

He raised a brow as the girls went off. "What was that all about?"

Jane sighed. "Have you ever considered your relatives are a bit *managing*?"

For some reason that surprised Lord Evans into an explosive laugh—which predictably drew all attention their way. Jane forced herself to look back at the staring eyes without flinching.

"Perhaps we *should* go outside," Lord Evans said.

Which would convince the meddlers that they'd been successful and that something was indeed developing between them.

Suddenly, she didn't care. She was feeling warm, and

the cool night air would be refreshing. It wasn't as if she were some naïve young miss. She was twenty-eight.

Lud, that sounded ancient.

"It *is* rather stuffy in here. A walk would be pleasant." She took one last swallow of champagne—because she *liked* champagne, not because she needed any liquid courage—and put her hand on Lord Evans's arm.

And immediately, *vividly* remembered how muscled it was. She glanced up and instead of cravat and coat, she saw the strong column of his throat, his broad shoulders and chest, the dusting of hair that trailed down to—

She felt her face flame as they stepped out onto the terrace.

"*Would* you like to stroll in the garden for a while?" he asked.

Last night in the garden, he'd kissed her.

Perhaps he would do it again.

She felt a frisson of equal parts excitement and alarm. It would be inappropriate, even dishonorable, to allow such intimacies when she had no intention of marrying the man.

Did she have no intention?

She wasn't entirely certain, and, well, she felt a little reckless. She wanted a small adventure before she went home and took up residence with Poppy again.

Not trusting her voice, she nodded. She walked with him across the terrace, down the steps, and along the primrose path—not that there were any primroses in evidence now, of course.

Her countenance must still be far too red to go back inside. Bea and Rachel—and likely Lady Chanton and everyone else—would leap to embarrassing conclusions if they saw her so flushed. It *was* better to walk for a while in the shrubbery.

And if something happened . . .

Nothing was going to happen besides, perhaps, a small kiss. She was in control of herself. She would enjoy the light breeze and the moonlight and then she'd say good night and good-bye. She'd quite likely be gone before the earl came downstairs in the morning so she'd not see him for several months, not until he came for the christening of Cat and the duke's baby. And then they might not have time to exchange more than a pleasantry or two. Assuming the duke was still alive—which is what she was going to assume—the christening would be a grand party, celebrating the breaking of the curse as well as the baby's birth. It would be crowded and chaotic.

She wanted these last quiet moments alone with him. She might not intend to take him as a husband, but she still liked him very much as a friend.

"I hope Bea and Rachel weren't annoying you," Lord Evans said, bringing her back to her surroundings.

"Oh, no. Of course not."

She did like his voice. It was deep, though not exceptionally so, and full of humor and intelligence. And kindness. Even as she sparred with him verbally—and, she'd admit the sparring was rather exciting—she knew she was safe. He'd never say or do anything to hurt her.

If she were going to marry, she'd want it to be a man like the earl.

But I am not *going to marry, am I? I have all I want.*

She didn't feel the satisfying sense of certainty she usually did when she contemplated her spinsterhood. Why?

Likely because as Bea had said, everyone around her was getting married—Randolph, Cat, Anne. As when an illness came through the village, she'd caught a touch of the wedding ague. That was all it was. She'd recover shortly.

"I believe your brother mentioned that you are returning to Loves Bridge in the morning?"

"Yes." She glanced at him. "Lady Eldon—Imogen—is coming with us. She is to stay with me in the Spinster House until the wedding." She smiled. "I do hope Poppy will not object."

His brow arched up. "And what of Lady Charlotte? She's Imogen's companion. I would have thought she'd come, too. Then they could stay at the inn and not inconvenience you"—he smiled—"and Poppy."

That would have been preferable. She truly did not like sharing her space, especially with a woman she barely knew.

"Apparently Lady Charlotte is staying here." Randolph had been too excited about his impending nuptials to have given Charlotte any thought, and Jane hadn't felt comfortable asking Imogen herself. "Perhaps your sister has decided Charlotte can help get Bea ready for her Season."

Lord Evans snorted. "Somehow, I can't see that working."

Neither could Jane, given how little Bea thought of the other girl. "Or perhaps they've hit upon a way for Charlotte and Septimus to marry."

The earl shook his head. "I don't see how they'll ever bring Buford around. If you think Imogen's father was bad, Charlotte's is ten times worse. He'll never accept an untitled, younger son for his daughter."

"Perhaps he won't be asked for his permission."

Their steps had taken them to the clearing with the fountain. Jane let go of Lord Evans's arm to go over to look into the water.

Lord Evans followed her. "What do you mean? Charlotte is only nineteen. She can't marry without her father's permission."

"Unless she elopes."

He laughed. "Shy, well-behaved Charlotte? She'd never do that."

If only he could have seen "shy, well-behaved" Charlotte with her hand on Septimus's—

Best not think about that.

"I heard the two of them discussing it here last night."

The earl's brows shot up. "And you didn't say anything to Imogen or Grant?"

"No." It had never occurred to her to tattle. Perhaps it should have—Charlotte *was* only nineteen. But she was also a complete stranger—*and* she'd seemed perfectly confident about what she wanted.

Lord Evans looked incredulous. "Meddling Miss Wilkinson, the woman who managed things so that my two closest friends are now married, didn't think to try to keep a man from running off with a young girl?"

"I'm not meddling." And she wasn't, except when the Spinster House was involved. It might not be flattering to admit it, but she'd been motivated by self-interest there.

And self-interest here, too.

Lud! Perhaps she *had* been a little interested in having Charlotte married to someone other than the earl. How dog in the manger-ish of her, since she had no thought to marry the man herself.

She again felt a small whisper of uncertainty.

She ignored it.

"And it wasn't a question of Septimus running off with Charlotte. The scheme was hers, not his. She had to work to convince him."

Lord Evans crossed his arms and grunted, but whether that meant he saw her point or not, she couldn't say.

"I'm sorry if it upsets you, but it is probably for the best if they do marry. It will force you to put Charlotte behind you and move on."

He grinned suddenly. "Is that an invitation?"

"What do you—oh!" He thought she was encouraging him? "No, of course it's not an invitation. I'm the Spinster House spinster, remember?"

"How can I forget?"

She wasn't quite sure what to make of his tone, so she said nothing.

He sighed and leaned against the fountain. "I did think I loved Charlotte, but now, to be honest, I doubt that I ever did. At least my feelings are nothing like your brother's. I don't plan to stay single in the hopes that I'll have another chance with her."

She'd admit to being surprised and, well, puzzled about Randolph's romance. He must care deeply for Imogen, but he'd never shown any sign of lovesickness that she had seen—and there had been those weekly visits to Mrs. Conklin.

Clearly, she had no understanding of romantic love from the male point of view.

"I need to marry," Lord Evans said. "I need an heir, and I want a family"—he grinned—"though perhaps not as large as my sister's."

She nodded. An earl would definitely need a son to continue his line and inherit his estates. And, after watching Lord Evans with the baby and his nieces, she thought he'd make an excellent father.

"I suppose I just convinced myself Charlotte would do."

But perhaps not the best husband. "Well, I'm certain you'll find a suitable replacement soon enough." He, unlike Randolph or Septimus, had a title, after all.

His brows rose, indicating he'd heard the waspishness in her voice, but he didn't comment on it. "I hope you are correct. My requirements aren't so unusual." Did his voice have a note of teasing in it now? "I just want a nice, quiet, restful sort of female."

She took the bait. "That sounds dreadfully dull."

He grinned. "I would call it heaven. You may have noticed my sister and nieces are not quiet or restful. I would prefer a bit less confusion and hubbub in my own home."

Jane had been around Cat's large family—there were ten Hutting offspring—so she had observed confusion and hubbub firsthand. "I don't see how you can completely escape those things with children."

That surprised a laugh from him. "All right, I'll grant you that." He frowned. "But I would also like a woman who isn't constantly meddling in my concerns. Diana and Mama have had their fingers in my affairs my entire life, and now even my nieces are getting into the act."

That was the beauty of the Spinster House, wasn't it? The only meddling creature in her orbit was Poppy.

However, these were Lord Evans's relatives. "Don't you think they meddle because they love you and want the best for you?" She sighed. "I sometimes wish I had . . . well, not someone to meddle obviously, but someone who cared about me so intensely." No, that wasn't fair. "Not that Randolph doesn't care. He does." And she cared about him—they just never talked about it. "But a brother's concern—or perhaps just the way he expresses it—is not the same as a mother's or, I would imagine, a sister's."

Lord Evans's expression suddenly turned sympathetic. "Right. How old were you when your parents died?"

"Fourteen."

"Caroline's age."

"Yes." Lord Evans's niece had looked so young, reading on the blanket this morning.

Jane had been reading when Cat's mother came to tell her about the carriage accident.

Lord Evans stepped closer, putting a hand on her well-covered shoulder. His touch was comforting.

"Had you no family to go to?"

"No. Not really." Papa and Mama had both been only children. There might have been a distant cousin who would have taken Jane in, but she hadn't wanted to leave Loves Bridge and grow up among strangers. And she couldn't desert Randolph—he'd needed her. His future was in the village with the family business. He'd never have been able to manage things by himself.

"We did very well. I do feel quite badly for Randolph, though." She shook her head. "I should have been more meddling. I've heard rumors over the years that he'd had to give up his love when he came home, but I never asked him about it."

Her eyes were suddenly wet. She sniffed. How could she have been so oblivious? She'd thought of no one but herself. "I should have meddled right away. Perhaps I would have saved Randolph years of loneliness."

Lord Evans put a finger under her chin to tilt her face up to his. "You were only fourteen. And Imogen's parents would never have allowed the match, Jane."

"But if I hadn't been an anchor around Randolph's neck, he and Imogen might have run for the border and married in Scotland."

Somehow her hands had found their way to Lord Evans's chest.

"You didn't stop him. Randolph could have taken Imogen to Gretna Green if he'd had the courage to," Lord Evans said. "Once they were wed, there would have been little Imogen's father could have done. And then Randolph could have brought her home to the village."

"And poor Imogen would have been stuck living with me. I'm only three years younger than she, Lord Evans, and, I will admit, not always the easiest person to get along with."

That made him smile. "Really? I never would have guessed."

She laughed and pushed away from him. "Don't tease."

He captured her hands, drawing her back. "You can't change the past, Jane, so don't fret about it."

That was true. As hard as it was, sometimes you just had to accept things as they were.

A breeze caused the branches around them to sway then, and a few strands of her hair fluttered over her face. Lord Evans—*Alex*—brushed them away as he had last night, but this time his fingers lingered on her temple and then slid down to cup her jaw. His eyes focused on her mouth.

The air felt charged. She moistened her lips—and saw his gaze sharpen.

I should move. This isn't the past. This I can change.

She didn't want to change it. She wanted him to kiss her again. She wanted to see if it had been as wonderful as she'd remembered.

An owl hooted in the distance. Her heart—and lower organs—pounded, making it difficult to breathe—

And then his mouth touched hers and she no longer cared about anything as mundane as air.

His lips were firm and dry. They brushed over hers as they had last night, the slight friction shooting straight to her breasts and the place between her legs.

This time she let herself relax into him.

Let herself? She melted—it was the only way she could describe it. Hot and boneless, she would have puddled at his feet if he wasn't holding her.

Mmm. His body was hard, warm. She remembered what it had look like naked. She wished his clothes would vanish—his clothes and hers—so she could feel his skin—

His tongue touched her bottom lip and, as if a spark had been set to tinder, need flashed through her. She opened her mouth, letting his tongue slip in as she pressed against him, her hands grabbing his arse—

Dear God! What is the matter with me? I've never felt this way before.

She shoved against Lord Evans's chest.

He let her go at once. Concern filled his voice and darkened his eyes. "Jane, what's amiss?"

"I . . ." He must think her mad. Likely no other grown woman reacted this way to a simple kiss.

She felt so out of control, her emotions a confusing, churning mess. She didn't like it. It . . . it frightened her.

"Nothing. I just wish to return to the house." Her voice shook slightly. "At once."

Chapter Ten

"Someone slept in," Roger said.

Alex observed his smiling, nauseatingly cheerful brother-in-law through bleary eyes. "Go bugger yourself."

Roger grinned. "Got up on the wrong side of the bed, did we?"

Did the man know how close he was to having Alex's fist shoved down his bloody throat?

"Why are you still in the breakfast room?" Though if he had to have company, Roger was far better than Mama or Diana or even one of the girls.

He walked over to examine the buffet. All that was left was part of a loaf of bread. Good. His stomach might be able to tolerate bread and butter. He cut himself a slice.

Roger ignored his question. "You can have that toasted."

"No need."

"The tea's fresh. Or I can call for coffee if you prefer."

"Tea's fine." Alex sat down. "Alone is fine too. I'm sure you must have something important you need to do."

Roger was still smiling, but his damn eyes held concern.

Alex braced himself.

"I'm afraid you're my important task at the moment." Roger poured himself and Alex some tea and handed Alex his cup. "Diana's worried about you."

Blasted meddling sisters.

He might be able to see Jane's point—well, he knew Diana loved him and her meddling was motivated from sincere concern—but that didn't mean he welcomed his sister sticking her long nose in his business. *He* wasn't one of her children. He was a grown man.

Though clearly you could use some help with women.

Had he been too passionate with Jane last night? He hadn't thought so. And she'd gone from pliant to panicked in the blink of an eye.

"I'm fine."

Even he would admit that sounded like a snarl.

Roger's brow rose skeptically. "You're lucky," he said. "Your sister wanted me to invade your room earlier to see that you were still breathing. I appeased her by promising to wait here instead—and to go in after you if you hadn't shown up in two hours." He checked his watch. "You could have stayed abed fifteen more minutes before I came bursting in." He snapped the watch shut and dropped it back into his pocket.

"Good God, Diana is being ridiculous."

"Hmm." Roger took a sip of tea, keeping his eyes on Alex.

Perhaps if he ignored his brother-in-law, he would get bored and go away.

He took a bit of buttered bread. Gah. He'd thought the Manor's cook quite good, but this tasted like sawdust. It likely didn't help that he'd consumed far too much brandy last night, but without the brandy, he wouldn't have slept at all.

Zeus! He'd thought he and Jane had shared something in the garden, something deeper than just physical attraction. He'd felt a connection akin to what he felt for his family but more intense, charged as it was with desire. He'd felt concern and need and protectiveness and—

Oh, why the hell was he torturing himself with this? Miss Wilkinson clearly had not felt any of the same things.

He must have totally misconstrued their conversation and misread the signs that had made him think she'd welcome his touch. Surely the kiss itself hadn't alarmed her—it had been quite tame.

Well, yes, his tongue and hands had got involved, but compared to what could have happened . . .

He was just thankful he'd kept himself on a short leash. If he'd let his urges run, Miss Wilkinson would have had an apoplexy.

Or murdered him. He couldn't rule out that possibility.

And she wouldn't talk to him on the brisk walk from the fountain to the house—though he'd admit he hadn't said anything either. He hadn't been capable of rational conversation.

He would just have to put the woman from his mind—and other organs—and mark the experience as one more sign that he should step back from the Marriage Mart until he'd sorted things out and could trust himself again. He would stay in the country, make improvements on his estates, and in a year or two see how he felt. He was only thirty. There was plenty of time to think of marriage and children.

"She's worried about you," Roger said.

Alex snorted—eloquently, he hoped.

Roger smiled, but kept on. "She feels the need to look out for you."

"Roger, I'm not in short-coats any longer. I do not need my sister managing my life."

Roger laughed. "Yes, but I think in Diana's mind you'll always be her little brother, even when you're eighty." He grinned. "I had an older sister, too, if you'll remember, so I do understand."

Alex grunted. Roger's sister had been more than ten years his elder and had married when Roger was still a young boy. More to the point, she'd moved out of the neighborhood—Grant's house was more than a day's ride away. He doubted that the situations were at all similar.

Roger sat back in his chair, thankfully abandoning that line of conversation. "Since you slept the morning away," he said, "you might be relieved to know that our other guests have all departed."

"Ah." He'd hoped to avoid Miss Wilkinson. Perhaps that was cowardly of him, but he'd prefer to describe it as chivalrous. She could not wish to see him, either.

"Miss Wilkinson and her brother took Imogen with them."

"Yes, I believe Miss Wilkinson mentioned that was their plan."

Roger gave him a long look but let that go unremarked upon. "The departure you might not be aware of is Lady Charlotte's. Apparently, she and Septimus eloped."

"Ah." So Miss Wilkinson had been right about that.

"You don't seem surprised"—Roger's brow winged up—"or at all distressed."

He probably shouldn't mention Jane had told him she thought an elopement was in the offing. "Roger, Charlotte and I parted ways almost a year ago. What she chooses to do is none of my concern."

His brother-in-law looked skeptical, but didn't argue. "That's good to hear."

"Has Grant gone off to try to stop the couple? Though if they left last night, it must be too late."

"No." Roger shrugged. "He seemed resigned to the situation, though I think he'd been hoping they could persuade Buford to countenance the match and so tie the knot in a less scandalous manner."

"Not much chance of that." If he was ever fortunate enough to have a daughter, he hoped he'd not make Buford's mistake and try to force her to wed a peer over a man she loved.

Jane would probably tell me to let the girl decide for herself—and she'd likely be right. Any daughter of Jane's would—

Would be none of his concern. And Jane wasn't going to have daughters. She was the Spinster House spinster.

"Precisely," Roger said. "So Grant and your mother and Octavius have gone back to Grant's estate to be there when the newlyweds return. Buford will be furious when he finds out, but there will be nothing he can do then except cut Charlotte off, and she and Septimus seem quite happy to risk that."

Clearly, he hadn't known Charlotte at all. He'd never have guessed she'd defy her father like this. "Well, then, I see I'm the last guest to depart."

"Don't feel you need to hurry off. Care for some more tea?" Roger held up the pot.

"No, thank you. I should get back to the Hall. If you'll excuse me, I'll go gather my things." The relative solitude of his estate would be heaven. "You can enjoy the peace of a guest-free house." Though Miss Wilkinson had been right about that: *Peace* was a relative term in a house so filled with children.

He started to rise.

"Don't go." Roger filled Alex's cup. "Have some more tea. I have something to discuss with you."

Alex could still leave, but there was no point in putting off the inevitable. If Roger let him escape now, Diana would just hunt him down later.

He sat back down. Perhaps the tea would help settle his nerves. He took a sip.

"About Miss Wilkinson—"

And spat it back out. "I do not wish to discuss Miss Wilkinson."

Roger acted as if he hadn't heard him. "When you came back from the Lake District in August and then immediately rushed off to Loves Bridge without even stopping in the house, you got Diana—and your mother—worried that something was seriously amiss."

Remain calm. "Yes, something was amiss. Mama and Diana were lying in wait for me. Of course I ran." He forced a smile. "I had no desire to face a very pregnant woman."

Roger's eyes didn't waver from Alex's. "Something tells me there is more to the story."

Alex looked down at his plate, pushing his leftover bread crust from one side to the other and resisting the urge to fill the silence. There wasn't any more to say. He *had* fled Evans Hall to avoid his female relatives, though Diana's advanced pregnancy hadn't been the main factor in his decision. He'd wanted to avoid them quizzing him when he was so . . . *confused* might be the best way to describe his state of mind then—and he'd chosen Loves Bridge simply because it was relatively close and the village fair had been about to begin. He'd not thought of Miss Wilkinson.

At least not consciously.

Roger gave up waiting for Alex to elaborate. "Well,

your bolting caused Diana and your mother to ask some questions."

His stomach cramped. Right. Diana gave birth, had a new baby in the house, and still managed to find the time and energy to meddle in his life.

Perhaps Miss Wilkinson was correct and Diana's interest was motivated by love and concern, but it was still annoying. Terrifying, too. Was there any place on Earth where he could escape Diana's and Mama's reach?

"She remembered that Imogen's lost love was a solicitor in that village. Letters were exchanged, and Imogen discovered that Randolph thought his sister might have a tendre for you."

He felt a jolt of surprised pleasure—quickly followed by discouragement. Randolph had been wrong, of course. That had been proved by Jane's reaction in the garden last night. And—

God's blood! Diana had spied *on Jane.*

How *dare* she? If his sister was in the room—

"Put down the knife, Alex," he heard Roger say.

He looked to see the butter knife clenched in his fist.

"Though you'll likely do more damage with your fork," Roger said helpfully, "if you wish to eviscerate me. The butter knife's too blunt to be efficient. Fork at least is pointy." He looked over at the buffet. "There *is* the bread knife. That would work rather well. Cut my finger with it once. Quite sharp."

"I am not going to attack you."

Roger grinned. "That's a relief."

"But I make no promises about Diana if she appears." He took a calming breath. He'd not touch his sister, of course, but he might blister her ears. "How could she pry into my life and Ja—Miss Wilkinson's to such a degree? Asking Wilkinson about his sister's sentiments—"

Words failed him.

Roger had the grace to look a trifle sheepish. "She loves you. She worries about you."

"All right. But there are lines she shouldn't cross, Roger. Boundaries." And speaking of lines crossed: "Did you know Diana sent Miss Wilkinson down to the lake yesterday morning when I was swimming?"

Roger looked guilty briefly, but then managed to produce a leer. "And did Miss Wilkinson like what she saw?"

"Bloody hell, Roger!"

Out of the corner of his eye, Alex saw a footman start to enter the room and then pivot to beat a hasty retreat.

"Sorry." Now Roger's look was merely hopeful. "But did she?"

"I hope she didn't see me." Likely a vain hope, but one he would cling to. "*Did* you know about it?"

Roger examined his fork. "After the fact. Diana said it was a spur of the moment thing. She just took advantage of an opportunity to, er, help foster the connection between you two."

"There is no connection."

"Oh?"

Damn Roger. "You said the bread knife was sharp?"

Roger grinned. "Very sharp." His expression grew serious. "You do look like hell, though. I wager I could take you out long before you reached the knife."

Roger might have the right of it.

"We will not put it to the test, because I'm going to leave." This time Alex did stand.

Roger stood, too, his eyes worried. "Diana will want to talk to you."

"Please dissuade her from doing so. I've said all I'm going to say on the subject—which is far more than I wanted to. She will have to be satisfied with your report."

He didn't get off scot-free, of course. He had just swung himself up into his curricle, ready to trot off to freedom when Rachel came running up.

"Uncle Alex! Wait!"

For a brief moment he considered pretending he hadn't heard her, but he knew if he didn't talk to her now, she'd hound Roger—or, worse, Diana—until they brought her over to the Hall.

"What is it, Rachel? I'm just on the verge of leaving, as you can see."

Rachel took a great gulp of air—she must have run all the way from the house to the stables—before blurting out, "What happened with Miss Wilkinson? Bea and I thought everything was going to work out when you took her into the garden last night, but this morning she looked so sad."

Jane had looked sad?

"You didn't hurt her, did you?"

Good Lord. "Of course I didn't." He should have had one of the grooms bring his curricle up to the front of the house instead of going down to the stables himself. There were far too many interested ears in the vicinity.

He looked pointedly at one man who'd stopped abruptly at the stable door.

The fellow flushed and continued about his business.

Alex did not want anyone hearing whatever other outrageous things Rachel was going to say. He quickly reached a hand down to her. "Come. I'll take you for a short drive." With any luck, the thrill of riding in the curricle would distract her.

Though . . . Jane had looked sad?

He wasn't certain what to make of that. She should have been happy, relieved that she was finally getting free of him and his meddling female relatives.

Rachel let him pull her up. She bounced slightly and then settled herself on the seat. "This is a bang-up curricle."

"I'm not sure you should be using such slang, Rachel," he said automatically.

She ignored him, as usual. "Papa's isn't half so fine."

Roger would agree with her, but then given his large family, his brother-in-law had little use for a vehicle that accommodated only two people comfortably.

"I'll take you down the drive and back, shall I?"

Rachel nodded enthusiastically, and he sighed—internally, so she wouldn't notice—with relief as he gave his horses their office to start. This should work. She'd be so distracted by his vehicle, she'd drop any talk of Miss Wilkinson.

His relief was short-lived. His cattle hadn't gone more than a handful of strides before Rachel started in again.

"If you didn't hurt her, why did Miss Wilkinson look sad?"

Why, indeed? A tiny scrap of hope fluttered in his breast. He squashed it. "I have no idea. You probably misinterpreted things."

"No, she definitely looked sad."

How could an eight-year-old read an adult's expression? "Perhaps she just wasn't looking forward to her journey. Many people don't enjoy coach travel. The roads between here and Loves Bridge are rather rough." Yes, that must have been it.

Rachel was quiet for a moment, but before he could congratulate himself on a narrow escape, she shook her head. "No, Bea agreed she looked sad. Not that Miss Wilkinson ever really looked happy while she was here, but this morning was different. She was very pale and the one time she managed to smile even a little bit, her eyes didn't."

Oh, Lord. He hadn't wanted to cut up Jane's peace. "Perhaps she had a headache."

Rachel considered that briefly. "Maybe. But you don't look happy, either."

He forced himself to grin. "Oh, now, I wouldn't say that."

Rachel rolled her eyes. "Of course you wouldn't say it." She frowned at him. "So what we want to know—"

"Who's we?" Not that he couldn't guess.

"Me and Bea, though I'm sure Mama and Grandmamma and everyone else wants to know, too. Why haven't you announced your betrothal to Miss Wilkinson?"

Lord, protect me from meddling women! "Because I'm not betrothed. Why in the world would you think I was?"

Rachel gave him a look only an eight-year-old girl could that said more clearly than words he was the greatest noddy in all of Britain. "Because you love Miss Wilkinson, of course!"

His hands jerked, causing his horses to toss their heads.

"That was cow-handed of you."

And now the eight-year-old was critiquing his driving. "Oh? And I suppose you could manage my cattle better?"

"I couldn't do any worse." Rachel reached for the reins. "Let me try."

Aha! A new way to avoid this uncomfortable conversation. "I'll let you handle the ribbons on two conditions."

Rachel's face glowed with excitement—and then her expression turned wary. One couldn't be the fifth child of eight—now nine—without learning that sometimes one needed to look a gift horse in the mouth in case it proved to be from Troy. "What are the conditions?"

"First, that you let me keep my hands on the reins. Driving a pair is harder than riding."

Rachel didn't hesitate—she was a smart, sensible girl. "All right. And the second?"

"That you promise to say no more concerning Miss Wilkinson."

"Oh." Rachel's shoulders slumped and she shook her head sadly. "I can't do that. I promised Bea if I got to you first, I'd have it out with you." Then she straightened and her jaw hardened as it did whenever she was determined not to be put off.

Oh Lord, here it comes.

She looked him in the eye. "We think you should offer for her."

He would *try* to put her off. It might be rude, but that couldn't be helped. He used his most earlish voice. "I don't believe I asked your opinion."

"Of course you didn't. I'm giving it to you, though."

Blast it, he would turn the curricle around and bring this conversation to a close that way.

If only that would work, but he knew from sad experience that unless he found a way to satisfy Rachel, she—and Bea and the rest of them—would keep after him.

"Did you consider that Miss Wilkinson might not wish to marry me? Perhaps I asked and was turned down."

Rachel made an astoundingly rude, dismissive noise.

That surprised a laugh out of him. "Thank you, but not everyone finds me irresistible."

"Don't be silly. You're a handsome, rich earl."

"I don't believe Miss Wilkinson is especially impressed with the peerage. And she's the Spinster House spinster, remember. If she'd wanted to marry she wouldn't have pursued that position."

He should have saved his breath—Rachel paid his reasonable speech no attention.

"You just need to ask her the right way."

What was it with today's youth? According to Nate, the new Lady Davenport's young sons had also tried to instruct him on the proper way to propose to his wife.

"You must tell her you love her."

He jerked the reins again—his horses gave him an annoyed look.

Do *I love Jane?*

He certainly felt something for her, but it had become painfully clear to him that he could no longer trust his instincts—which was why he was going to retreat to his estate and eschew any thought of marriage for a while.

That didn't keep him from asking, "Why do you think I love Miss Wilkinson?"

Rachel rolled her eyes again and hit the heel of her hand against her forehead.

"*Must* you be so dramatic?" he asked.

"Must *you* be so cabbageheaded?"

Diana—and Roger—really needed to exert more control over their daughters. "I'm an adult and your uncle. Please show a bit of respect."

"Respect won't get you Miss Wilkinson. You *have* to tell her you love her, Uncle Alex. Women like to know they are loved. Then she'll marry you."

His heart gave a most inappropriate leap.

No. This would never do. He *had* to nip this particular line of speculation in the bud if he didn't want his life to become unbearable.

"Perhaps I don't love Miss Wilkinson." He couldn't bring himself to lie and insist he had no feelings at all for her.

"Oh, puh-*lease*!" Another exaggerated eye roll.

He was getting rather tired of Rachel looking at him as if he were a knock in the cradle.

"You should see how you look at her when you think no one's watching. Your mouth goes all soft and silly like it wants to grin, but you won't let it. And your eyes go soft, too, and dreamy—when they aren't staring"—she grinned—"sort of like the way Stinky looks when he's starving and Mama opens her dress."

Good Lord! He stared at his horses' arses and willed himself not to turn a hundred shades of red. Surely Rachel was mistaken.

"And she looks at you the same way."

His head snapped back toward his niece, blast it. "She does?"

Rachel nodded. "Oh, yes, except she looks more confused because she doesn't understand what she's feeling, not having any marital experience."

His heart wasn't the only organ to lurch at Rachel's words. To think Jane—

Wait. *Rachel's* words? "Rachel!" Diana and Roger did let the girls run a bit wild, but Rachel was only eight. "What do you know of 'marital experience'?"

"Nothing," Rachel said cheerfully. "I just heard Mama tell Papa that."

"In front of you?"

"Of course not, silly. In back of me. I was reading, curled up in one of the library's wing chairs, so they didn't know I was there."

"And you didn't let them know?"

"Why would I do that?"

Right. Rachel had already told him she was a skilled eavesdropper.

"But I do know that marital experience leads to babies,"

she said, smiling brightly. "And you want babies, don't you?"

Lord, yes.

It was difficult being around Diana's family now that he'd started to consider marriage. The girls stirred such a jumbled stew of emotions in him—amusement, pride, annoyance, awe, love, worry, happiness. And holding Stinky—that is, Christopher—had made him ache, literally ache deep in his soul to feel the small, warm body of his own son or daughter in his arms. He wanted an heir, of course, to continue his line, but more, he wanted children to love and protect and guide into adulthood.

He cleared his throat. "This is a completely inappropriate conversation, Rachel."

"Why?"

"You're a child." Not that he'd want to have a conversation about babies with anyone except a wife.

Jane?

No. Jane wasn't interested in him, no matter what Rachel said. If she was, she wouldn't have shoved him away last night.

Rachel sniffed. "Children are very smart, you know. Smarter than *some*"—she gave him a pointed look—"adults."

Clearly, he needed a distraction. "It's time to head back to the house. Would you like to try handling the ribbons now that you've discharged your promise to Bea?"

"Yes!"

Thank God. He spent the next few minutes concentrating on keeping Rachel from ending them in a ditch.

Chapter Eleven

Loves Bridge, Mid-February 1818

Jane stood in the Spinster House study, books to her left, old harpsichord to her right, and looked out on the bleak landscape. The garden that had been so green and wild in the late spring and summer was shriveled and dead in the chill, gray February light.

She felt a bit shriveled and gray and dead, too.

Poppy jumped up on the window seat in front of her and leaned over to butt her head against Jane's limp hand.

"Oh, Poppy." She started stroking the cat. As her fingers moved rhythmically over the soft fur, the knot in her chest began to loosen.

She knew part of what was causing her low spirits. She wasn't lonely, precisely, but she definitely missed her friends. Anne had moved away entirely, and Cat might just as well have, being so busy at the castle.

No, that wasn't quite it, either. Jane had been avoiding Cat, because, well, she didn't want to talk about babies. Even Randolph and Imogen were infant-mad.

She liked her independent, orderly existence. She was in complete control of her days. She arrived at Randolph's office precisely at the same time every morning and left at the same time in the evening. She set her schedule at the lending library. She ate what she wished when she wished. If she wanted to go to bed early, she did—or she could stay up most of the night reading. No one would comment or complain or offer any sort of an opinion on her choices.

Well, no one but Poppy.

But if she had a husband, she'd have to consider his wishes. Even worse, husbands led to babies—she had plenty of evidence of that around her, didn't she? And then her precious independence would fly out the window. Babies ruled a mother's life completely.

"Being independent needn't mean being lonely, Poppy."

"Merrow."

Of course Poppy would agree. Cats were at heart solitary creatures. Jane just needed to find new friends, people she could discuss books and current events and other non-baby topics with. But who was there? Loves Bridge was a small village. Every woman her age was married, and she certainly couldn't join a group of men.

And that made her think of Lord Evans. She'd thought of him rather too often since she'd come home from Chanton Manor.

Of course she had. He was an intelligent, articulate man. It was a pleasure to converse with him.

And he made her feel oddly alive.

What would have happened if I hadn't stopped his kiss in the garden?

An unpleasant mixture of regret, desire, and nerves twisted in her chest.

She made a dismissive sound and looked away from the

window. The reason for her blue-devils was clear—and it had nothing to do with the earl. A dark sadness permeated the entire country. They'd only just put aside formal mourning for Princess Charlotte, who had died three months earlier after giving birth to a stillborn son. The succession was in shambles. The three royal dukes who were free to marry were scrambling to find a wife and produce a child.

And beyond that, everyone in Loves Bridge was on edge because of the curse. Cat's baby was due at the end of the month. The village was holding its collective breath, waiting to see if the duke would live to see his heir. Poor Cat was shredded with worry, afraid she and her baby would die like the princess and little prince or her precious Marcus would.

Cat *could* be carrying a girl.

"Merrow."

Jane sat down next to Poppy. "You're right. It would be better to learn now that the curse is broken." She looked carefully at Poppy. "The duke *will* live, won't he?"

"Mer-row." Poppy appeared to nod.

Jane released the breath she hadn't realized she'd been holding. "Good. That's what I was hoping you'd—"

Good *Lord*, had she completely lost her mind? It was bad enough talking to a cat—she'd been doing a lot of that recently, now that her friends and her brother were married—but to think that the animal was actually replying . . .

She got up and walked into the sitting room. She still intended to redecorate, but the only change she'd made so far was to replace the hideous picture of a hunting dog with a painting she'd found in the cluttered room where the puppet stage had been.

She studied the new picture. A tricolored cat—which

looked remarkably like Poppy—watched a brown bird intently.

Poppy passed between her and the painting, heading for the front door.

"So you want to be let out now, do you? All right, I'll—" Jane jumped in surprise as someone knocked. Who could that be?

Poppy looked at her as if to say "What are you waiting for?" and then sat down and proceeded to clean her paws.

I swear that animal is supernatural.

She threw open the door to find an extremely pregnant Duchess of Hart on her doorstep.

"Cat!" Jane looked behind Cat and then right and left. "Where's the duke?"

"Visiting Baron Davenport. I drove in with Mary."

Mary, one of Cat's younger sisters, was married to Theodore Dunly, the duke's assistant steward, and was expecting her first child at about the same time as Cat.

"Not in the pony cart, I hope?" Jane could not think it wise for two very pregnant ladies to be rattling around in such a conveyance.

Cat laughed. "Yes, in the pony cart. If we'd been rash enough to try any of Marcus's carriages, we'd surely have ended in a ditch."

"You could have had John Coachman drive you in."

"Oh, pooh! Why bother him?"

Everyone said Cat was carrying well, but she looked enormous to Jane. She stood back—way back—to let Cat waddle past her. "But the baby—well, the babies"—she shouldn't forget Mary—"are due so soon."

"Not for another week or two. Everyone says first babies are late." Cat was panting slightly, her hand on her belly. "And it's not like I traveled a great distance."

Any distance was too great, in Jane's opinion. "If you'd sent word, I would have come to the castle."

Cat lowered herself carefully onto the settee. "Oh, I didn't come in to see you—I came to see Mama. But then I saw the Spinster House and decided to stop here while Mary went on ahead to the vicarage." She smiled. "We haven't had a comfortable coze for the longest time. I don't know why."

Perhaps because I've been trying very hard to avoid one.

Jane sat in the armchair across from the settee—she didn't want to risk bouncing Cat and somehow hastening the emergence of the large melon in Cat's belly—and watched Cat look around the room.

"I thought you were going to redecorate."

"I'm still deciding what I want." There was no rush. She had the rest of her life here.

Her gray feeling grew a little darker.

"You know you can choose what you want and send the bills to Marcus."

"Yes." She did know that. She just couldn't find the energy to care much about her surroundings.

Cat's eyes focused on the new painting. "I see you at least got rid of that horrible hunting picture." She grinned. "Though I think perhaps this animal has hunting on its mind as well." She squinted and tilted her head. "Is it my imagination or does that cat look very much like Poppy?"

They both looked at Poppy.

Poppy raised her leg and started licking her nether regions.

They averted their gazes.

"I've made a lot of changes at the castle," Cat continued. "You must come out and see the place. Maybe you'll get some ideas for improvements here."

"Um. Yes. That would be nice."

Cat shifted on the settee as if she wasn't quite comfortable and tried again to find something they could discuss. "Did you hear Miss Franklin—I mean, the Duchess of Benton—had a healthy boy last month?"

"No."

Cat frowned. "I'm sure it was in all the papers."

Jane had stopped reading the papers. The news was too depressing, and her feelings were low enough. And, to be brutally honest, she didn't want to risk stumbling across mention of a certain earl linked to any Society woman. "I must have missed it."

Cat nodded doubtfully, and then changed the topic again, this time disastrously. "You've never really told me how your visit to Chanton Manor went."

Lud! Jane felt her face flush. She looked down quickly to hide her expression. She didn't wish to discuss that subject.

She cleared her throat. "It was fine."

Cat waited. Jane kept her lips firmly closed.

"How romantic that Randolph met Imogen again. And they didn't waste any time, did they?" Cat rubbed her belly. "To think Randolph will have a child six months younger than mine and Mary's—and Lady Davenport's. Lady Davenport's baby should arrive any day now."

Everyone is having babies.

Which was fine, of course. That's what married couples did. She was the Spinster House spinster. She wanted nothing to do with babies, though she would try her best to admire any that were presented for her inspection.

Poppy, having finally groomed herself to her momentary satisfaction, came over and jumped up into Jane's lap. She settled down, warm, heavy, and available for petting. Gratefully, Jane buried her fingers in the cat's fur.

There was something very calming about stroking a cat, even one with vaguely supernatural qualities.

"I wonder if Randolph and Imogen's baby will be a boy or a girl?"

This really was getting tedious. Jane understood babies were on Cat's mind and—Jane's eyes dropped again to Cat's enormous belly—other organs, but one would hope she might be a little more sensitive to Jane's position. Not that her baby-less future dismayed her. Not at all. She just found the topic deadly dull.

"It will be one or the other." Jane forced herself to smile. "Would you like some tea?"

Cat's face froze—and then fell into a polite, if hurt, expression. "No, thank you."

Lud! Cat had been one of her closest friends, and now it felt as if they were mere acquaintances.

It wasn't Cat's fault. Yes, her life had moved on in ways Jane's hadn't, but if Jane had been completely happy as the Spinster House spinster, it wouldn't have mattered. She would have been able to roll her eyes—figuratively speaking—and listen to Cat drone on about babies while she thought about something else.

There was a wall between them, a wall Jane had built.

"I'm sorry," Cat was saying. "You were busy. I shouldn't have arrived unannounced."

"I wasn't busy."

Cat ignored her. "I'll just be going." She put her hands on either side of her and tried to push off the settee.

Nothing happened.

"Oh, blast. I should have known better than to sit here. I'm like a beached whale. You'll have to haul me up if you want me to leave, Jane."

"I don't want you to leave." Oddly, she wasn't just being polite. While a moment ago she would have cheered Cat's departure, now she wanted her to stay. Clearly, she was becoming unhinged.

Poppy jumped off Jane's lap and eyed the place where Cat's lap used to be.

"I'm afraid, you'll have to sit here, Poppy." Cat patted the spot next to her on the settee.

Poppy decided that was acceptable and leapt up.

Cat looked at Poppy, but spoke to Jane. "Well, you probably will send me packing when I tell you Marcus and I had hoped something romantic might happen for you, too, at Chanton Manor."

Something romantic *had* happened, if one considered her two awkward fumblings in the vegetation romantic.

No. They had been far more than fumblings.

Jane forced herself to laugh—and then had to fight not to grimace at the weak sound that emerged. "Something romantic at *that* gathering? The male attendees—besides my brother—were all married, betrothed, or barely out of leading strings."

Cat's eyes held hers. "There was Alex."

Her treasonous body hummed at the sound of his name. It remembered in exquisite detail every touch, every brush of his lips.

No. He was an interesting companion, but that was all. She could not let her animal instincts rule her. If she did, she might end up giving everything to the earl. She would marry, and that would be far worse than living with Randolph. She wouldn't have to tidy up after Lord Evans—there would be servants to do that—but he would invade her life in far more intimate ways. Even her body wouldn't be hers any longer.

She eyed Cat's belly.

The thought of losing all control like that was terrifying.

"Lord Evans?" she said while pretending to pick a bit of lint off her skirt. "Yes, he was there, as was Lady Charlotte."

Cat scowled. "Who eloped with Septimus Grant. How did Alex take that?"

It was safer to look at Poppy than Cat. "I have no idea. I left with Randolph and Imogen in the morning while the earl was still in bed." *Oh, Lord. Don't think about the earl and beds.* "Don't you know? I thought Lord Evans corresponded with the duke."

"He does, but they never discuss anything *interesting*." Cat gave her a searching look, but then, thankfully, moved on. "Speaking of correspondence, Anne has been asking after you. She said she wrote you months ago and has not heard back."

Anne had written before Jane went to Chanton Manor. She'd started a reply too many times to count, but she always balled the letter up and threw it out.

"I suppose I'm just not much of a correspondent." She sighed and said a bit wistfully, "It was so much easier when we all lived in Love's Bridge and saw one another regularly. How does Anne go on?"

"She's well, but Nate, of course, worries about her and the baby." Cat smiled. "Nate worries about everything."

He did. He must be frantic now, concerned not only about his wife and child, but also about his cousin. Very soon they would know if Isabelle Dorring's curse was broken.

Unless Cat gave birth to a daughter.

"Does Anne plan to visit?"

"Not until after her baby's born. The physician Nate engaged says travel is too risky, and, well, after poor Princess Charlotte, Nate—and Anne—don't want to take any chances." Cat rubbed her belly. "None of us do. Oh!" She grimaced.

"What's wrong?" Jane leapt up and came over to her. "Are you all right?"

Cat smiled, a bit wanly to Jane's eye. "I'm fine. It was just a little pain."

Jane lowered herself cautiously next to Poppy, being very careful not to jostle the seat and disturb Cat. "Are you supposed to have a little pain?" She looked at Cat's belly and squeaked in alarm. A small tent had suddenly appeared in Cat's dress as if something was poking out of her. "What's that?!"

"What's what?" Cat looked down and laughed. "Oh, that's just the baby—likely a foot or an elbow. Here."

She took Jane's hand and placed it over the protuberance. "Feel it?"

"Y-yes." The bulge got larger, moved, and then disappeared. It was the oddest sensation—though it must have been even odder for Cat, experiencing it from the inside.

Jane put her hand safely in her own lap.

"Oh, Jane." Cat leaned forward—or as forward as she could lean with her enormous belly. "I do hope you'll find a husband someday and have a family."

"Merrow." Poppy butted against Jane's thigh in apparent agreement.

"We had such hopes for you and Alex."

Longing twisted through her. *A family with Alex . . .*

And no control.

Familiar panic gripped her by the throat. It was bad enough to consider her life with a husband, but with a baby as well . . .

Look at Cat. If she'd managed to preserve a thread of independence after marrying the duke, it was gone now.

Jane had observed enough mothers to know that even once their babies were born, they weren't free. Their minds and even their souls were tied forever to their offspring. She wasn't ready for that. She doubted she'd ever be ready.

"I'm the Spinster House spinster, remember?" She forced a smile. "I worked and plotted too long to give it up now that I finally have it."

"But—" Cat sucked in her breath and put her hand on her belly again.

Lud! "Was that another pain?"

Cat nodded. "A little bit stronger than the last one."

Jane knew nothing about childbirth, but this did not sound good to her. "Should I get your mother?"

"No, I'm fine."

Jane eyed Cat's belly nervously and then looked at Poppy.

Poppy yawned.

"Jane, Marcus and I—and Nate and Anne as well—saw how it was with Alex at the village fair."

"How what was with Lord Evans?"

Cat smiled. "He was quite taken with you."

Jane felt a sudden spurt of pleasure—which she repressed immediately. "Gammon! Lord Evans, if you'll remember, talked about going up to London to look for a wife." *She* certainly remembered. "*And* he explicitly denied having a matrimonial interest in me. I believe his exact description of the notion was 'ridiculous.'"

Cat frowned. "I don't think he meant that."

"I find it is best to take people at their word."

Cat sighed and her shoulders drooped a bit. "I was certain you two would make a match of it, but I suppose it's not to be."

"Merrow." Poppy put what looked like a comforting paw on Cat's belly, and Cat stroked the animal.

"Why do you care?" Jane asked. "It's not as if my marriage affects you." *She* had been very eager for Cat and Anne to wed so she could move into the Spinster House, but there was nothing Cat would gain from Jane's wedding Lord Evans or anyone, for that matter.

Both the cat and Cat looked at her.

"Oh, perhaps I'm just being selfish," Cat said. "If you married Alex, I'd see more of you, since he and Marcus and Nate are so close."

That *would* be lovely, but it was no reason to chain herself to the earl. "I hope you—and Anne when she's in Loves Bridge—will visit me here." She tried to inject a teasing note into her words. "You aren't planning to give me the cut direct, are you?" Though she could see it would not be the same. Once Lord Evans acquired a wife, that woman would become part of their social circle—Cat and Anne's social circle, that is. Jane would be very much in the way. On the outside. Alone.

Which was fine. She was the Spinster House spinster. She didn't need anyone else.

"Of course we aren't going to c-cut you." Cat flinched again.

Jane looked at Poppy.

Poppy groomed her tail.

Am I mad? Why do I think Poppy knows what's going on with Cat and her baby?

Poppy paused her ablutions long enough to send Jane a look.

All right, then.

"Is it the thought of the marriage bed that troubles you, Jane?" Cat asked.

"W-what?!" Jane's attention snapped back to Cat—and then she jumped to her feet. She did *not* want to talk about beds or marriage. "You know, I've just remembered an appointment. I hate to rush you, but I'm afraid I must go—"

"Would it help if I told you what happens between a man and his wife?"

"No." She might not be clear on the specifics, but she felt quite certain Alex could explain it all to her in detail—exquisite detail.

But she was not going to get married, so she didn't need the information.

"I know your mother died when you were fourteen," Cat was saying. "I imagine she didn't—oh." She sucked in her breath and rubbed her belly again.

"Are you *certain* I shouldn't get your mother?"

"Yes, yes. I'm f-fine."

Jane glanced at Poppy—and frowned. The cat was now standing and looking very alert. *Is she staring at Cat's belly?*

"But I suppose I should go. You did say you had an appointment."

"Er . . ." They both knew there was no appointment.

"And Mama must be wondering where I am." Cat smiled. "Though I think Mary has probably enjoyed having her all to herself for a while." She extended a hand. "Can you haul this poor whale upright, Jane?"

"Of course, though perhaps you'd best give me both your hands."

Jane pulled Cat to stand, and—

"Oh!" Cat turned bright red. A puddle had appeared at her feet.

"Er, should I get you the chamber pot?"

Cat shook her head. "I don't think that's the problem."

"*Merrow!*" Poppy ran toward the stairs, and then stopped at the bottom to look back at them.

"I-I think"—Cat sucked in a sharp breath and squeezed Jane's hands hard.

"Is it the baby?" *Oh, dear Lord!*

Cat nodded. "I—" She swallowed. "I-I think so."

Jane knew nothing about babies. What should she—

"Mer*row!*"

She looked at Poppy. Poppy looked at her, climbed two steps, stopped—and growled.

Her message was unmistakable.

Perhaps Poppy had had kittens. In any event, it would be impossible to know less about giving birth than Jane did. She would take the cat's advice.

If she didn't, Poppy would likely claw her ankles.

"Do you think you can climb the stairs? I'll get you settled in bed and then run fetch your mother." The vicarage was just across the street, and Mrs. Hutting had given birth to ten children. She would know what to do.

Cat nodded. "And get Marcus. Please."

"Yes. Of course." She guided Cat over to the stairs.

Cat paused with her foot on the first step and dug her fingers into Jane's arm so hard she'd probably leave bruises. "But don't tell him the baby's coming. I don't—" Cat caught her breath and her face twisted with pain.

Jane waited, helplessly patting Cat's arm.

"Sorry," Cat finally said. "The pain comes in waves, and I can't talk during the worst of it. Don't tell Marcus about the baby. I don't want him to . . ." Cat tried again. "I don't want him to do anything foolish and hurt himself."

Or kill himself.

Jane knew that's what they both were thinking.

"Don't worry. You concentrate on yourself and the baby. I'll take care of the rest."

Somehow.

She got Cat up the stairs. Once they reached the upper floor, Poppy ran into Jane's bedroom, so that's where she started to guide Cat.

"The other room will be f-fine," Cat said, leaning against the wall and panting until another wave of pain passed.

"Merrow!" Poppy poked her head out of Jane's room as if to hurry them along.

"I'm not about to argue with Poppy. You know that never ends well."

Cat laughed. "True."

It didn't take long to help Cat out of her dress and stays and settle her on the bed.

"Will you be all right alone? I'll be as quick as I can."

Poppy jumped on the bed and curled up next to Cat.

Cat laughed and stroked Poppy's head. "Poppy will watch me."

"All right." Jane didn't like leaving Cat alone, but she didn't have much choice. She looked at Poppy.

Poppy twitched her tail and bared her teeth briefly as if to say stop dithering and get on with it.

Jane nodded and took off, using the banister to help her swing round the turn in the stairs. She pelted across the drawing room, flung open the door—

And ran smack into a hard male chest.

Chapter Twelve

"Jane!" Alex grasped Jane's arms to steady her after she collided with him.

Lord, it was so good to see her, to feel her body against his. He'd tried to scrub the memory of their time together at Chanton Manor, especially their two brief encounters in the garden, from his thoughts, but now every detail came roaring back—

Even the one where Jane shoved on his chest to get free of him, which was exactly what she was doing now.

He let her go. What a bloody fool he'd been to think she'd welcome him. He'd come to see Marcus. He should have gone directly to the castle. He—

"Lord Evans, thank God you're here!"

His brows shot up and he grinned. Ah. This was better . . .

No, Jane's face was flushed, her bosom heaving. There was panic in her eyes.

His heart leapt into his throat. "Zeus, is there an intruder in the house? Where is he? Tell me. I'll take care of him." He stepped past her, putting his body between her and any danger. "Show yourself immediately, sirrah!"

Miss Wilkinson tugged on his arm. "No, there's no intruder." She frowned, apparently just now realizing he wasn't where he was supposed to be. "Why are you here?"

"I'm checking on Marcus. Nate wrote asking me to come since he couldn't leave his wife to come himself."

Fortunately, she let that go. It was true, but it didn't answer the question of why he was *here* in the Spinster House and not at Loves Castle where he'd be a lot more likely to find Marcus.

She'd probably berate me if I told her I've missed her.

She kept showing up in his dreams—and not just the salacious ones. And she drifted into his waking thoughts as well. He'd be working on household accounts and would picture her putting on her glasses to examine the ledger. Or he'd be riding over his estate and catch himself wondering what she would say about a certain view.

"Well, it's good that you're here now. You must go get Mrs. Hutting immediately."

"Why?" For the life of him, he could not think of a single reason anyone would need to make an emergency dash to the vicar's wife.

"Because Cat is going to have her baby, that's why!"

"How do you know?" Surely the duchess was at Loves Castle. She was very pregnant. She wouldn't be wandering the countryside . . . would she?

"Because she's upstairs. How else would I know? Now hurry."

"Upstairs?" He glanced nervously at the staircase. "Who's with her?"

"Poppy."

"*Poppy?!* You left a *cat* to keep watch over a woman in labor?"

"What else was I supposed to do? Send Poppy to get Mrs. Hutting?"

"No, of course not." He stepped back outside. "You go keep the duchess company. I'll fetch Mrs. Hutting straightaway."

Jane put her hand on his arm. "And after you send Cat's mother over, could you find the duke?" She frowned and said, a bit anxiously, "But don't tell him why he's needed. Cat doesn't want to, er, cause him to take any risks."

"Right." The mind was a powerful thing. If Marcus knew the duchess was in labor, he might feel the curse breathing down his neck and do something foolish.

Sometimes the difference between life and death was one single misstep.

"Where is he? I assume he brought Cat into the village?"

Miss Wilkinson shook her head. "No. Cat came in with her sister Mary while the duke was off at Lord Davenport's. He probably has no notion Cat is here."

Likely not. Alex couldn't see Marcus being happy about his duchess traveling anywhere without him so close to her time.

"Very well. Leave the duke to me. You go up and sit with the duchess."

Miss Wilkinson suddenly turned a bit green. "Do get Mrs. Hutting to hurry. I don't know the first thing about babies."

He put a bracing hand on her shoulder. "That's all right. You don't need to know anything. Just keep Cat company for the few minutes it will take for her mother to get there."

They heard a loud moan coming from upstairs.

"Go on."

Miss Wilkinson nodded. "Tell Mrs. Hutting to come

straight up," she said, and then headed for the stairs, quickening her pace when they heard another moan.

Brave woman. He felt a surge of pride—

No, pride implied a connection they didn't yet have— and might never have. Admiration. That's what he felt.

He ran across the road to the vicarage. The duchess's youngest brothers, four-year-old twins, opened the door when Alex knocked. Identical faces grinned up at him— and then looked behind him. When they saw he was alone, their faces fell.

"Where's dook?" one boy asked.

"I don't know," Alex said. "I'm going to find him after I speak to your mother. May I come in?"

"Course." The door swung open. "She's in Papa's study with Papa and Mary."

"What's going on, boys?" The vicar poked his head out of a nearby room. "Oh, Lord Evans." He smiled. "Do come in." He stood aside for Alex to enter. "You know my wife and daughter Mary, of course."

Alex executed a short bow. "Ladies." Mary looked very pregnant herself—she was due at roughly the same time as the duchess. He did hope she would wait her turn.

"What brings you to the vicarage, Lord Evans?" Mrs. Hutting asked. "Can I offer you some tea?" She gestured to the pot at her elbow.

"Or would you rather have brandy?" the vicar asked.

"Neither, I'm afraid." He turned to Mrs. Hutting. "I've been sent by Miss Wilkinson to ask you to come without delay to the Spinster House, madam."

Mrs. Hutting rose quickly to her feet. "Cat stopped there to visit." Her voice was tense. "Is she all right?"

"She seems to be in labor, madam."

Mary gasped, but Mrs. Hutting nodded in what seemed a competent fashion.

"Very well. I'll come at once."

"Is Cat having her baby, Mama?" one of the twins asked.

"Yes, she is, Tom."

"She's early." Mary sounded nervous. "She's not *too* early, is she, Mama?"

"Oh, no. I don't think so." Mrs. Hutting was now all business. She turned to her husband. "We'll need Mrs. Danford"—she looked at Alex—"that's the midwife." She frowned. "I believe she's visiting her sister over in Little Darrow."

Blast! "Is that far?" Alex tried to sound calm, but he could just imagine how Jane would feel if she heard this news.

"It's just the next village over. Too far to walk, but not far on horseback," the vicar said. "I'll send Henry on my horse to fetch her. He and Walter should be in their room, working on their translations." He left, taking the twins with him.

Mrs. Hutting frowned. "I do hope Mrs. Danford is still at her sister's and not out attending someone else. Well, I suppose in a pinch there's the London doctor Lord Davenport engaged for Lady Davenport—unless she's gone into labor, too." She smiled. "Is someone fetching the duke, Lord Evans?"

"No, madam. Finding the duke is next on the list of duties Miss Wilkinson assigned me."

Mrs. Hutting laughed. "She's probably frantic."

"I do believe she would welcome your prompt appearance." An understatement. Jane was very likely on her knees, if only figuratively, pleading with the Almighty to hurry Mrs. Hutting along.

"What can I do, Mama?" Mary asked.

"Nothing, dear. Just stay here and rest. I don't want poor Mrs. Danford to have to deliver two babies today."

"N-no." Mary looked a bit nervous at that thought.

"Now, don't worry," Mrs. Hutting said. "You should be fine, but if you do have need of me, send Walter or Pru or Sybbie—they are probably in the schoolroom. Or even the twins. I'll only be cross the street."

"What about Papa?"

"I think—oh, there you are."

The vicar came into the study as a gangling youth of sixteen or seventeen darted out the front door behind him.

"Yes, here I am and ready for my next instructions."

"I assume you'll help Lord Evans find the duke." Mrs. Hutting *finally* started for the door. She paused—and Alex had to struggle with himself to keep from pushing her on her way. "Though perhaps you shouldn't tell him Cat is in labor." She frowned. "The curse, you know."

Her husband nodded. "Yes. Right. Don't want to cause His Grace any anxiety about that, though I suppose it's always at the back of the poor boy's mind."

"And the back of Cat's," Mary said.

The Huttings stood there, apparently considering the matter of the curse.

Alex cleared his throat. "Mrs. Hutting? Miss Wilkinson and the duchess eagerly await your presence."

"Oh, yes. Of course. I'm off."

This time he didn't believe the woman was actually on her way until she stepped out the door, and even then he considered following her to be certain she didn't get detained in conversation with one of the villagers.

"Now, Lord Evans," the vicar said, "what's your plan with regard to the duke?"

Alex hadn't formulated one yet. "Miss Wilkinson told

me the duke had gone to visit Lord Davenport. Is that correct, Mrs. Dunly?"

The vicar and Mary stared at him blankly for a moment.

"Oh!" Mary said. "You mean me." She laughed. "I'm still getting used to that name. Please call me Mary." She nodded. "Yes, Theodore and the duke went together to visit the baron. After they left, Cat and I decided to come see Mama." Mary chewed her lip, looking rather pale again. "Do you suppose it was riding in the pony cart that caused Cat to go into labor early?"

"I doubt it," the vicar said.

Alex had no idea, but having Mary work herself into a lather worrying wouldn't help anyone. "Your mother did say she didn't think the baby was that early." He smiled. "My oldest niece came three weeks before she was expected and all was well."

"Oh, that's good to hear," Mary said, seeming to relax.

The vicar gave him a grateful look. "Now, my lord, I believe we should see if we can find my son-in-law. Do you know if Theodore and the duke planned a long visit with Lord Davenport, Mary?"

"They said they might be gone an hour or two. The duke wanted to get some matters settled before Lady Davenport has her baby." Mary smiled, putting a hand on her rather sizable belly. "And before Cat and I have ours."

According to Diana, Imogen was also increasing.

Zeus, Loves Bridge was experiencing a veritable population explosion. How did Jane feel, surrounded by so much fecundity?

The most relevant of his organs would like to—

He should *not* be having such thoughts in a vicar's study. And to be honest, he wouldn't be surprised if Jane swore off childbearing after today. He did hope Mrs. Hutting had arrived to rescue her.

Idiot! Miss Wilkinson had already sworn off childbearing. As she'd pointed out to him several times, she was the Spinster House *spinster*.

Well, there *was* Isabelle Dorring's example. . . .

Nonsense. Jane was far too wise to follow in Isabelle's footsteps.

Yet Cat, he was quite certain, had also conceived while still in the Spinster House.

If Jane—

Blast it all, he *had* to stop thinking about Jane this way. If she was indeed a dedicated spinster, he needed to respect that. And he'd promised himself not to consider changing his own unmarried state until he felt confident that he could trust his instincts. If he was lusting after a woman who had quite clearly expressed her complete lack of desire for marriage in general and him in particular, his instincts were still sadly unreliable.

And yet the first place he'd ridden was not the castle, but the Spinster House.

Instinct, good or bad, told him he and Jane had some unfinished business between them. At a minimum, they needed to discuss what had happened in Roger and Diana's garden.

Or at least he needed to discuss it.

And Rachel thinks Jane loves me. . . .

What the hell did an eight-year-old girl know about such matters?

He forced his attention back to the issue at hand. "How long have you been here, Mrs.—I mean, Mary?"

Mary looked at the clock. "About an hour."

"I see. So the duke and your husband could still be at Davenport Hall."

"Or they might be on their way back to the castle. We'll have to account for both possibilities." The vicar looked at Mary. "You'll be all right while we're gone? I can get Walter or Pru to sit with you."

Mary laughed. "Having one of them staring at me wouldn't help anything. I'll be fine on my own."

The vicar nodded. "We'll send Theodore to fetch you when we find him and the duke. Since Henry has taken my horse, I'll have to take your cart."

Alex and the vicar left the vicarage and walked briskly toward Cupid's Inn, where the pony cart and Alex's horse were stabled. As they passed the Spinster House, Alex glanced over to see Poppy on the front step, cleaning her side. She paused and looked up as they walked by.

He had the silliest urge to ask the animal if all was well. *I've not only lost my instincts, I've lost my mind.*

At least Mrs. Hutting was there now and, with luck, the midwife would be there soon. Jane didn't have to deal with things by herself any longer. And then once the baby was born and they got Marcus safely to meet him, the Spinster House curse would officially be broken.

"Do you give any credence to the curse, sir?" he asked the vicar.

To his surprise, Cat's father didn't immediately scoff at the notion.

"I'm a man of the cloth, Lord Evans. My life is spent contemplating things we cannot see or hear, taste or touch, things that can't be proven by any scientific method."

"But, sir! A *curse*?"

The vicar smiled. "Well, yes. I don't believe in witches and magic. But I do believe men can create their own burdens—or curses, if you will."

"I'm afraid you've lost me there, sir."

"Think about it, Lord Evans. Two hundred years ago, a desperate woman lashed out at the man who got her with child, and then she vanished. Everyone said she drowned herself. How could the man ever atone for what he'd done?"

"He couldn't."

The vicar nodded. "And how would you feel if you were that man?"

Alex could say how he felt right now—outraged at the mere thought of such a thing. "I would never behave in such a way!"

"Perhaps not, but indulge me for a moment and imagine you had. How would you feel?"

The notion was revolting. "If I had a shred of honor, I'd feel guilty, of course."

The vicar nodded. "I expect you would. Crushing guilt, guilt you could never absolve yourself of." He looked at Alex. "You'd feel cursed, wouldn't you?"

Alex blinked. "Yes, I suppose I would."

"You might feel that since the woman and child had died, you didn't deserve to live, either. Certainly you didn't deserve to be happy."

"Y-yes, I think you're right."

"Oh, dear," the vicar muttered suddenly, "here come the Boltwoods. Just smile and bow and, whatever you do, keep moving."

Alex snapped his head around—he'd been directing all his attention at the vicar—and saw the two white-haired ladies leave the village shop and scurry across the green toward them. Their mouths were opening—

The vicar held up his hand, never breaking stride. "Truly sorry. No time to stop."

They left the women, jaws dangling, behind and crossed the road to the inn.

"One thing I do know," the vicar said as they entered the inn-yard, "in the great poet Virgil's words, '*omnia vincit amor*'—'Love conquers all.' I feel certain the duke and my daughter love each other very much, so I'm not worried that they'll come to harm." He clapped Alex on the shoulder. "Now let's go find him, shall we?"

They waited while the ostler got Alex's horse and the pony cart ready and then headed out. Alex, following behind the vicar, watched the man bounce around whenever the convenience hit a rut. He knew nothing about the care of pregnant females, but he couldn't think it a good thing for a woman so close to her time to be jostled about like that. Perhaps they were lucky Mary's baby wasn't trying to put in an appearance as well.

The vicar stopped when the road divided, and Alex came up beside him.

"Here's where our paths diverge, Lord Evans. I'll take the left fork toward Davenport Hall, and you can take the right to the castle. Will that suit?"

Alex nodded. "And what will you tell Marcus if you find him, sir? He's sure to think of your daughter and the baby when he sees you."

"Yes. We don't want the poor fellow rushing to Cat's side and breaking his neck on the way, do we? Hmm." The vicar rubbed his chin. "I have it. We've been discussing various structural problems with the church. I'll tell him something new has developed that requires his immediate attention." He grinned. "I'm sure Our Lord will forgive me a little white lie in this instance. And what will you tell him?"

"That Lord Haywood asked me to stop by and see how he goes on."

The vicar's brows rose. "And that's your only reason for coming to Loves Bridge?"

"Er, yes." No point in mentioning Miss Wilkinson when his hopes—or whatever he had—might be dashed.

"I see." The vicar smiled a little too knowingly. "I believe the Lord will forgive you your white lie as well."

"Nate really did write me."

"I'm sure he did." The vicar nodded and then set the pony into motion.

Alex watched the cart rumble off. Why the hell did *everyone* wish to busy themselves in his business? At least Marcus wouldn't bother him about Miss Wilkinson.

"Come on, Horatio. Let's go find the duke."

Horatio didn't need to be asked twice—he'd been chafing at the bit, forced to walk at a snail's pace behind the pony cart. He surged into a gallop, and for a moment Alex felt the exhilaration he always did when astride his horse, flying over the countryside.

But there was no way to outrun his thoughts.

To be honest, he'd been fighting with himself ever since the christening party.

Every time he visited Chanton Manor, his sister mentioned Miss Wilkinson. She corresponded with Imogen, so she often had news of Jane. Which was fine. Good. He wanted to hear how Miss Wilkinson went on. The problem was, Diana wouldn't leave it at that. She always found a way to work in the question of his interest in the spinster. Even Bea and Rachel and the other girls had taken to asking him when he was going to try his luck with her again.

At least Roger had held his tongue on the subject.

Should he try his luck again? Was Rachel right that Jane loved him?

But then why had she ended their kiss so abruptly that night in the garden?

He'd planned to write her and beg her forgiveness if he'd insulted her, but he hadn't been able to find the words. The few kisses they'd exchanged had been quite chaste, hardly more than the peck on the cheek you'd give an elderly aunt.

But they had felt like so much more, at least to him.

In any event, even if he could have puzzled out what to say, sending Jane a letter would likely have started the village buzzing and caused her more problems. There were no secrets in Loves Bridge.

So when he'd got Nate's letter asking him to visit the castle he was all too happy to oblige. He could see how things went on with Marcus and then visit the Spinster House and make any needed apologies.

Only he'd gone to the Spinster House first. Fortunately, as it turned out. If he hadn't, Miss Wilkinson would have had to leave the duchess alone with Poppy while she fetched Mrs. Hutting.

Poppy seemed a very competent—almost supernatural— cat, but she *was* a cat.

He glanced around. There was still no sign of Marcus.

His thoughts went back to the Spinster House. Zeus, when Jane had crashed into him, he'd wanted to throw his arms around her, bury his face in her hair, and never let her go. When he'd thought her in danger, he'd been ready to tear the intruder's throat out with his bare hands.

And just the short, straightforward conversation they'd had had made him far too happy.

His gut told him Rachel was correct in at least one of

her observations—he loved Jane. But then, he'd thought he'd loved Charlotte.

Lord, the indecision—and the longing—were driving him mad.

Horatio suddenly picked up his pace. Why? Oh! Marcus was riding toward them, along with Theodore Dunly. Horatio knew George, Marcus's horse, from their frequent rides together.

Blast, Marcus looked worried.

"Marcus! I was just on my way to see you," he said as he reached them. Now that he thought of it, this was the direction he'd be traveling if he were coming from Evans Hall. No need to even let on he'd stopped in the village first. He smiled at Mary's husband. "Good day to you, Mr. Dunly."

"We can't stop, Alex," Marcus said. "Ride with us."

"Of course. Is something amiss?" Surely the curse didn't have a way of alerting the duke when his wife went into labor?

"My wife and the duchess took our pony cart into the village while the duke and I were at Davenport Hall," Mr. Dunly said rather tensely.

Marcus scowled. "They had no business rattling over the countryside in that vehicle."

Alex knew Marcus well. He sounded angry, but he was actually frantic with worry.

"It's not a long journey, is it?" Alex tried to sound soothing.

Both men glared at him.

"The women are nine months pregnant, Alex." Marcus bit off each word. "And the cart has no springs."

Alex nodded. Holding his tongue was clearly his best course of action here.

When they rode into the inn-yard and dismounted, the polite yet taciturn ostler Alex had encountered earlier gave a shout and came running over, a wide grin on his face. He threw his arms around Marcus and lifted him off the ground in a bear hug.

Alex saw Marcus's shocked face over the man's shoulder.

The ostler had seemed perfectly harmless earlier. Had he gone mad all of a sudden?

Alex started forward to intervene, but the man had already returned Marcus to earth and stepped back.

"His Grace is here!" he shouted. "He's here!" Then he turned back to Marcus and grabbed one of Marcus's hands in both of his. "Oh, Yer Grace, I'm so happy. And to think old Billy Binden lived to see it."

And then the man dropped Marcus's hand, covered his face, and started sobbing.

"My dear fellow," Marcus said, patting the ostler awkwardly on the back. "I'm afraid I don't understand."

That stopped the waterworks.

"Ye don't know? Of course ye don't know." The ostler turned to the crowd—many of whom were also sobbing—that had assembled in the inn-yard. "He doesn't know."

"*What* don't I know?" Marcus was moving beyond shocked surprise to annoyed impatience. He clearly didn't want to offend these people, but he desperately wanted to find his wife.

Oh! Now Alex understood.

"Tweedon, can you tell me what's going on here?" Marcus asked of a tall, thin man with a nose that strongly resembled a parrot's beak who was wending his way from the back of the crowd.

"Yes, Your Grace. We just got word from the Misses Boltwood that the duchess has delivered a healthy son."

Thank God! Alex felt weak with relief. *But how the hell did those two busybodies find out?*

"So we all assumed you were d-d—" Tweedon took a deep breath. "No longer with us." And then *he* started sobbing.

"And the duchess?" Marcus gripped the man's shoulder. "Is she well?"

"Oh, y-yes. Yes."

"Where is she?"

Alex finally found his voice. "At the Spinster House."

Chapter Thirteen

Jane stood by the chest of drawers in her bedroom, holding Cat's son and staying out of the way while Mrs. Hutting and Mrs. Danford, the midwife, finished up with Cat.

She averted her gaze from their activities—childbirth was quite messy—to look down at the baby. He was so tiny, though the older women had proclaimed him a good size for a newborn. And helpless. He couldn't even hold his own head up.

He was very different from Christopher, the only other baby she'd ever held.

One of his hands escaped his swaddling—Mrs. Danford had used Jane's spare chemise for that—and waved about. He was going to hit himself in the face. She caught his small fist, stroked his palm—and his tiny, perfect fingers wrapped around hers.

Oh. She felt his grasp in her heart—and her womb.

How much more would I feel it if he were my son—mine and Alex's?

She didn't want children, remember? Or a husband. She'd just got free of Randolph—

A husband isn't the same as a brother.

Well, no, of course that was true. A husband was *worse* than a brother. She could go to her room and shut the door on Randolph. With a husband, there'd be no escape.

Not to mention Lord Evans hadn't suggested marriage. *He's here in Loves Bridge.*

Her body thrummed, vividly remembering the feel of his hard length against hers when she'd collided with him earlier. Her brain had been too panicked to register much more than here was someone she could send for help, but her body had been taking detailed notes. It would like—

No, she had exactly what she wanted now: the Spinster House and her independence. She was perfectly happy.

The baby had opened his eyes and was staring up at her. She smiled, leaning closer, though she couldn't tell if he could actually see her or not.

She'd liked the sense of connection she'd felt during the birth, helping Cat, working with Mrs. Hutting and Mrs. Danford as part of a female activity as old as time. She liked the feelings holding Cat's baby churned up in her. They were confusing and unsettling, but they made her feel more alive than she had in a long time.

"Merrow." Poppy, having fled the room earlier, leapt up on the chest of drawers behind Jane and leaned forward to sniff at the new arrival.

Jane's first instinct was to snatch the baby out of the animal's reach, but before she could act, Poppy sat back and started grooming her tail.

Apparently, Cat's—and the duke's—son met with Poppy's approval.

"There we go," Mrs. Danford said, wiping her hands on Jane's spare towel. "Everything's been set to rights down here. Now we need to have the baby suckle. It helps the milk come in and the mother's body recover."

Jane's hold tightened—she didn't want to part with the infant—but then she came to her senses and carefully deposited him in Cat's arms. Mrs. Hutting helped Cat arrange things so the baby could latch onto her breast.

Lud! Cat looked so tired and worn from the exertion of bringing this little bit of humanity into the world, but she also looked gloriously happy.

Perhaps there was a balance to be struck between independence and dependence.

The baby lost hold of the nipple and started crying. The shrill sound ripped through Jane's head like a knife and set her heart pounding. How much worse it must be for Cat.

"He's a hungry little mite, isn't he?" Mrs. Danford said calmly, helping to get the baby settled again. "Handsome and healthy. The duke will be proud."

And then she frowned, likely thinking what Jane, what they all must be thinking: If the curse wasn't broken, the duke wasn't alive to feel anything.

Mrs. Danford shook off her dark thoughts, smiling once more. "You'll have to stay here for a few days, Your Grace. We don't want to take any added risks by moving a new mother and infant, even in a ducal carriage." She started packing up. "And this way you'll be close to your own mother so she can look in on you. You're an old hand at having babies, aren't you, Cecilia?"

Cat's mother laughed. "Yes, indeed. You can be sure I'll keep a close eye on Cat and the baby."

"I know you will." Mrs. Danford looked back at Cat. "When the wee bairn sleeps, you sleep, too. Being a new mother is hard work—don't overtax yourself."

"Yes, Mrs. Danford."

That made the midwife laugh. "You don't believe me. Very few new mothers do. But you'll learn—and I know your mother will rein you in if you try to do too much."

She put the last item in her bag. "I'm off now. Shall I stop to have a look at Mary, Cecilia?"

"Oh, yes, please do," Mrs. Hutting said. "I'll be over in a few minutes and will make you a nice cup of tea."

Cat sighed after Mrs. Danford left and said a little anxiously, "I guess I shouldn't have come into the village, but I truly didn't think riding in the pony cart would bring on labor."

"We don't know that it did." Jane jumped to reassure Cat, even though she knew nothing at all about the matter. "Mary's baby hasn't tried to make an appearance, and she rode in the cart too."

"Exactly." Mrs. Hutting touched her new grandson's fuzzy little head. "The important thing is that you and the baby are both fine."

Cat smiled. "He's beautiful, isn't he?"

Most people wouldn't describe the scrawny, reddish, squished-faced, awkward infant as beautiful. Likely nature made mothers see newborns that way so they didn't abandon their offspring.

Cat glanced up. "I'm so sorry to have taken over your room, Jane."

"It's nothing." Jane smiled. "And there's something satisfying about the curse being broken in the place where it all started."

Worry clouded Cat's eyes again. "*Is* the curse broken?"

They wouldn't know for certain until they saw the duke. But it *had* to be broken. Surely life—God—could not be so cruel as to take the man now, just as his son was born.

"Of course that silly curse is broken," Cat's mother said in a no-nonsense tone. "I'm sure Marcus will be here any minute now. Papa and Lord Evans went to find him right after I left the vicarage."

Cat smiled, but she didn't look completely convinced.

Then she turned back to Jane. "I'm afraid I'm going to have to take over more than your room, Jane. Marcus will stay here with me, but the baby's nurse will need the spare bed, and I'm sure you don't want to be disturbed by all the commotion a new baby causes, with people up and down all night."

Jane hadn't thought of that, but she'd already concluded she couldn't stay in the Spinster House. "That's all right. I'll just take my things"—though with Cat in her spare nightgown and the baby wrapped in her one extra chemise, she had fewer things to take—"and go stay with Randolph and Imogen."

Cat shook her head. "Oh, no, there's no need for that. You'll be stumbling over one another. I insist you live at the castle for as long as we're here."

At the castle? She wasn't certain she wanted to stay in that huge, echoing pile alone. "Oh, I'm sure Imogen—"

"Don't be silly. Your brother and Imogen are still almost newlyweds, and their house is very small. I expect you'd be very much in the way."

Almost newlyweds? But Imogen was increasing. Surely nothing of an almost newlywed nature would be occurring, would it?

Jane felt a little queasy at the thought of surprising her brother and his wife in flagrante delicto.

"The castle is enormous," Cat was saying. "You could sleep in a different room every night for a month if you wanted to"—she grinned—"though I'll admit some of them aren't quite habitable yet."

There it was again—the castle's size. It was larger than Chanton Manor, which had felt overwhelming enough and that was with other people around.

Though she did know many of the people who worked at the castle. Perhaps it wouldn't be too bad. And surely

Cat and the baby would be able to travel in a few days, giving her back the Spinster House.

"Very well. I just hope I don't get lost."

Cat's grin turned sly. "You'll have Alex to rescue you if you do."

Lord Evans! Oh. Of course he'd be staying at the castle—unless he took a room at the inn, but with the castle so large . . .

But it wouldn't be proper for them to sleep under the same roof, no matter how large the roof was, without a chaperone.

And with her confusing emotions.

Jane looked at Mrs. Hutting, expecting her to object.

"That sounds like a perfect solution," the vicar's wife said.

Where were the arbiters of social behavior when you needed them?

The baby had now fallen asleep and dropped off Cat's breast, so Mrs. Hutting took him and carefully put him in the temporary bed they'd made out of a drawer and one of Jane's bedsheets.

"I'm off to see how Mary's doing and fix Esther that cup of tea I promised her," Mrs. Hutting said. "I'll be back later to check on you, but in the meantime I leave you in Jane's capable hands." She smiled at Jane before she left the room.

Jane did not feel at all capable, but the baby was asleep and Cat was in bed, so she didn't think anything dreadful could happen.

"Mrs. Danford said you should sleep when the baby sleeps, Cat."

"I can't sleep. I'm still too excited by what just happened." Her fingers picked at the bedclothes. "And worried.

When do you think Marcus will get here?" Her voice dropped to a strained whisper. "If he gets here."

Jane could tell Cat not to worry, but they both knew those would be empty words.

Fortunately, they heard footsteps pounding up the stairs just then. Cat's face brightened and she looked at the doorway just as the duke burst into the room.

"Catherine!"

Cat's smile lit her face, dispelling all signs of strain and tiredness. "Marcus!"

And then the duke was across the room and his arms were around Cat. "Catherine, thank God you're all right." He buried his face in her neck.

Jane bit her lip. *What would it be like to have a man care so intensely for me?*

To have Alex *care?*

It might be suffocating.

Or it might not.

Cat rubbed her husband's back. "Marcus, aren't you going to look at our son?"

He raised his head—his eyes were suspiciously damp. "Son?"

"Yes. That's what I was doing here, you know. I worked very hard, even though Mrs. Danford said I had a relatively easy labor."

Cat pointed to the drawer-turned–baby bed, and the duke peered in, looking equal parts horrified and fascinated. "He's so small."

Cat laughed. "I assure you he seemed huge when he was being born. I'm very thankful he's not larger." And then she sighed happily. "Isn't he wonderful?"

Jane began to feel as if she was intruding on a private moment. Poppy must have agreed, because she jumped down from her perch and ran out of the room—past Lord Evans.

"Oh!" Jane's heart seized and then began to execute a reel all around her chest. She swallowed and sent her frolicking organ a stern reprimand. "I didn't see you there, Lord Evans."

He smiled—he had lovely eyes when he smiled. "I came up with Marcus." He gestured with his head that they should follow Poppy. "Shall we?"

Jane nodded. "I'll be downstairs if you need me, Cat," she said.

Cat didn't reply. She'd likely not even heard.

Lord Evans stood aside to let her pass and then followed her down the stairs.

"Would you like a cup of tea?" she asked when they reached the sitting room. She had a sudden, rather desperate craving for a nice, calming cup.

"I think we need more than tea," the earl said. "Do you still have that brandy?"

Perhaps he was correct. "I certainly didn't finish the bottle myself."

She led him into the kitchen—and almost tripped over Poppy, sprawled on the floor.

"Careful." Lord Evans's hand shot out to steady her.

Lud! His touch was far from steadying. Yes, it kept her from measuring her length on the floor, but it had a disastrous effect on her knees, causing them to wobble alarmingly.

Only because she'd just been through such a draining and yet exhilarating experience, of course. She told her knees to behave themselves and grabbed the brandy bottle from the cupboard.

"Would you be so g-good—" She cleared throat. "Could you get the cups for me, Lord Evans?"

He grinned—and her knees threatened to go out again.

"What? Still no brandy glasses?" He got the cups and put them on the table as she collapsed as discreetly as possible onto one of the chairs.

"As you know, I do not make a habit of imbibing spirits, nor did I expect to have to entertain you again." Lud! Even she would admit she sounded unbecomingly petulant. It was her ridiculous nerves speaking. She was happy he was here—happy but nervous and unsettled. Not in control. *That* was what she disliked. "I beg your pardon."

The earl gave her a probing look as he joined her at the small table, but let her comment pass unremarked upon.

"I think I'm still"—she groped for the right word—"overwhelmed by the birth."

"Did you stay then? I'd thought you'd be sent downstairs once Mrs. Hutting arrived. You are an unmarried lady, after all."

"Did you think I would have a fit of the vapors?" To be honest, she was surprised that she hadn't.

He raised an eyebrow as he poured a little brandy in her cup and rather more in his. "I would never think that, Miss Wilkinson. I have complete faith in your ability to weather any storm with aplomb."

She scrutinized his expression, but when she found no sarcasm there, she let the initial pleasure she'd felt at his compliment grow. But she wished to be honest—she shouldn't let him entertain false notions of her strength. She leaned closer to admit, "I think I only kept my composure because I had to. I was terrified—as you might have noticed when I ran into you."

He grinned. "Literally."

He had such a nice smile. It made her feel warm and relaxed—and as if they were on the same side, and he was welcoming her into some private mischief.

Lord, she hadn't even taken a sip of brandy yet.

"I did try to get Mrs. Hutting to hurry over to you," he said. "But she didn't appear to feel the same sense of urgency you and I did."

That was another thing she liked about him—she knew she could depend on him. He understood immediately what was needed and set about to accomplish it. Look at the way he'd solved the last problem they'd discussed at this table—the Waldo W. Wertigger disaster. He'd found the puppet theater—with Poppy's help—and put on an excellent show.

"I'm sure you did try to hurry her." She smiled and shook her head. "I'll admit I was never so happy to see anyone in my life as I was when I saw Mrs. Hutting." She'd tried to remain calm, but until Cat's mother arrived, it had been very much a case of the blind leading the blind. "Mrs. Hutting knew just what to do—and it wasn't very much longer until Mrs. Danford joined us."

She took a sip of her brandy—she'd learned last time the danger of taking anything larger than a sip—and contemplated what had just happened upstairs. It was hard to think of anything else, the experience had been so vivid with so many sights, sounds, and—she wrinkled her nose—smells.

"Have you ever attended a birth?" she asked the earl.

Lord Evans's brows shot up. "No, thank heavens. I will leave that to you women. You are the stronger sex, after all."

She examined him closely—he was teasing her.

It was amazing how much the male of the species didn't know about some basic facts of life—though she'd just learned this particular lesson today, so she supposed she shouldn't hold it against him.

"We *are* the stronger sex, Lord Evans. We have to carry

a growing person inside us for nine months and then struggle to push him out."

Lord Evans, looking uneasy for once, held up his hand. "Please, Miss Wilkinson. If you are thinking of sharing the gory details, spare me, if you will. You may have nerves of steel, but mine are far more gelatinous. I would like to go to my grave unenlightened on such matters."

Well! She'd expect someone like Randolph or the detestable Mr. Barker to hold such a ridiculous opinion, but she was disappointed to hear the earl voice it.

"Why should that be? The father helps make the baby, doesn't he? If he's to be involved at the beginning, I don't see why he's allowed to be absent at the end. That's the hardest part."

Lord Evans's face had got rather flushed. Was he embarrassed? She *had* been unusually frank, perhaps.

There was no perhaps about it. She'd leapt far beyond the normal boundaries of polite discourse. She should apologize—

Except it isn't embarrassment in his eyes. It's something far hotter.

She took another swallow of brandy.

"Miss Wilkinson, I shall tell you a secret that I now realize doesn't reflect very well on me," he said. "When I came to Loves Bridge in August, I was fleeing my very pregnant sister. She and my mother were visiting my estate when I returned from the Lake District and instead of going inside to speak to them, I ran like the great coward I am."

So that's why he came to the fair.

She felt a bit deflated. She'd known it hadn't been to see her, but the notion kept poking into her thoughts like thistle that was impossible to uproot. She'd pull it out in one place only to have it appear someplace else later.

"You were afraid your sister would have her baby in your house?"

He looked down at his brandy cup. "Yes."

She sensed there was something more that he wasn't saying, but she let it go.

"Has Lord Chanton never kept your sister company during a birth?"

"Not that I know of."

That was rather sad. "If you ever have a child, Lord Evans, you should try to find the courage to support your wife during the birth. It is an intense experience and not always comfortable"—she gave him a speaking look—"especially for the laboring woman, but it is . . ." How to describe it? "Quite remarkable."

He was watching her intently. Likely he was shocked at her outspokenness. Well, she was not about to beg his forgiveness for that. If he did not care for it, he could leave.

Except it sounded like they'd be staying at the castle together.

Not a problem. As Cat had pointed out, the castle was enormous.

"You are not the only one who found this day momentous, Miss Wilkinson. The entire village is celebrating. Poor Marcus has had at least two gentlemen cry all over him in addition to any number of ladies." He laughed. "A passerby might be forgiven for concluding that the birth's outcome was exactly the opposite of what it was."

"I suppose someone must have spoken to Mrs. Danford when she left a little while ago."

He nodded. "That someone—or someones—being the Boltwood sisters, I suspect." He grinned. "And we should celebrate as well, don't you think? A toast." He raised his cup. "To the breaking of the Spinster House curse."

She clinked her cup against his. "But I thought you didn't believe in the curse."

"I'm not certain what I believe, but it doesn't matter any longer, does it? If there ever was a curse, there isn't one now. The Duke of Hart has lived to see his heir born."

"Yes. That *is* wonderful." She let her thoughts roam over the day as she sipped her brandy. Hmm. "You know, I never asked how you came to be here."

Did Lord Evans look a little uncomfortable? No, it must be her imagination because now he was smiling.

"Nate—Lord Haywood—wrote and asked me to stop by. He was worried about Marcus, but didn't feel he could come himself, not wanting to have his wife travel or to leave her at home."

That made sense—sort of. "But why did you come *here*, to the Spinster House? Had you tried the castle first?" She frowned. "But then surely someone would have told you the duke and Theo had gone to visit Lord Davenport." She smiled. "Not that I wasn't delighted to see you, of course. You could not have appeared at a better time."

"Er . . ." The earl straightened, inhaled, and—

Poppy jumped onto the table, almost upsetting Jane's teacup.

"Where are your manners, Poppy?" Jane asked, grabbing her teetering cup. "You almost put a paw in my brandy."

She thought about pushing the cat back to the floor, but quickly decided that would be a bootless effort. Poppy always did exactly what Poppy wanted.

The cat gave her a speaking look and then turned her back to face Lord Evans.

The earl chuckled and scratched Poppy's ears. "I guess you know what she thinks about your reprimand."

Jane glared at Poppy's back. "Yes. Poppy can be quite articulate when she wishes to be."

Poppy waved her tail in Jane's face.

Jane pushed it aside and looked at Lord Evans. "I think you were about to tell me why you stopped by the Spinster House."

"Yes. I—"

"There you are!"

"Eep!" Jane almost knocked over her teacup herself as Mrs. Hutting stuck her head into the kitchen.

"Oh, sorry," Cat's mother said. "I banged on the front door, but no one answered so I let myself in." She smiled. "I see you're having a nice cup of tea."

"Er, yes." Jane looked at Lord Evans—the evil man was smirking. They'd both stood to greet Mrs. Hutting, so Jane couldn't administer a swift kick to the earl's shins.

"I assume the duke is upstairs?"

"Yes, madam," Lord Evans said.

Mrs. Hutting smiled. "It *is* wonderful that that dreadful curse is no longer hanging over his head—and Cat's head as well. I'll go up and see how they're doing. If you'll excuse me?"

Poppy jumped down and went over to rub against Mrs. Hutting's ankles.

"Are you coming, too, Poppy? You'll be careful around the baby, I hope."

"Merrow."

Mrs. Hutting must have taken that for assent—not that she could easily keep Poppy from following her in any event—because she and Poppy left together in apparent harmony.

They listened to Mrs. Hutting's feet climb the stairs, and

then Lord Evans looked at Jane. "Might I have some more *tea*, Miss Wilkinson? It really is quite extraordinary."

"Very funny." She poured more brandy into his cup and then, somewhat recklessly, added more to hers.

"If you'll remember, I told you your teacup subterfuge would work to your advantage." He shook his head in mock dismay. "And you scoffed at me."

"It's not a subterfuge. And if Mrs. Hutting hadn't been distracted, she'd likely have noticed the brandy bottle and put two and two together. Now, about your—"

"Alex! Jane!" The duke bounded into the room, grinning so widely Jane blinked. His joy was almost tangible.

She'd never thought he looked older than his age, but now that the burden of the curse had fallen from him, he looked much, much younger.

He gripped Lord Evans's hand and they pounded each other on the back, proper British restraint thrown out the window. Lord Evans was facing away from her, but she could see the duke's expression.

The emotion it revealed made her own eyes sting and a lump form in her throat.

Then the men separated and the duke turned to her.

"Miss Wilkinson—Jane—thank you for all you did for Catherine today." He was still smiling broadly and looked as if he might be thinking of hugging *her*, so she stepped back out of reach. "I can never repay you for taking care of my wife until her mother arrived."

"Oh, well, as to that, Your Grace, I wish I could say I'd done anything to merit your thanks, but I really only just stood around taking up space. Poppy did as much as I did."

Poppy trotted into the room and jumped back onto the table. She looked quite proud of herself . . . but then she was a cat. She always looked proud of herself.

"Please, call me Marcus. You are one of Catherine's closest friends, after all."

"Very well, Your G—Marcus." Using the duke's Christian name felt too familiar—and she'd rather keep her distance at the moment. There was far too much emotion in the room for her comfort.

"I'm surprised to see you downstairs, Marcus," Lord Evans said. "I didn't think anything would separate you from your wife and son." The earl grinned. "Care for a spot of tea?"

"Tea? No tha—"

The earl held up the brandy bottle. "It's a very special sort."

"Oh, well, in that case, yes, I'll take some."

Jane fetched another teacup and gave it to Lord Evans to fill with brandy.

"As to why I am here," the duke said, "Mrs. Hutting shooed me out of the room so she could attend to Catherine's and William's, er"—he cleared his throat and flushed slightly—"needs."

"William?" Jane realized she'd never asked Cat what they planned to name their son.

The duke nodded. "For Catherine's father." And then he grinned at Lord Evans. "William Nathaniel Alexander."

That provoked another round of emotional backslapping.

"Here's to a long and happy life for young William Nathaniel Alexander," Lord Evans said once he and the duke were done. And then he added with a rather salacious grin, "May he have many brothers and sisters."

The duke laughed as they clinked teacups. "I think it will take a while for Catherine to agree to that." He raised his cup to Jane. "If I ever doubted it, I do no longer: The female is definitely the stronger sex. From Catherine's account, I would never wish to go through childbirth myself."

Jane couldn't help it. She gave Lord Evans an "I told you so" look.

"But I'm here not only because I was banished from Catherine's room," the duke continued. "I need to have a word with you both. Alex, Mrs. Hutting tells me the vicar has returned with the pony cart. Could I impose on you to take it to the castle? Theo will pick it up later from the stables."

"Of course I'll take it"—Lord Evans pulled a face—"though I can't say I'm looking forward to handling *those* ribbons."

The duke grinned. "I'm sure your reputation will survive the experience."

"It's not my reputation I'm concerned about—it's my bones and teeth. I observed that, er, equipage in motion when the vicar drove it off in search of you. 'Rattletrap' doesn't begin to describe it. I suspect I'll feel like I've traversed all of England when I finally reach the castle."

The duke nodded in acknowledgment of that truth. "You can see why Theo and I were so concerned when we discovered our very pregnant wives had gone off with it." He turned to Jane.

Lud! Here it comes.

"Jane, Catherine tells me you've graciously agreed to turn the Spinster House over to us for the time being and move to the castle, so it seems exceptionally rude of me to subject you to the pony cart. If you prefer, Alex can send my coachman back to get you in a far more comfortable vehicle."

"That's not necessary, Your—"

The duke's eyebrow rose.

"M-Marcus. I'm not made of glass." *Nor am I pregnant. Oh Lord, I didn't need that thought. Please don't let me blush.*

She could almost hear the Almighty laughing at her.

"I'll go in the cart."

With Alex.

Her skin turned a deeper shade of red.

Chapter Fourteen

Alex poured himself another glass of brandy while he waited in the study for Jane to join him. Poppy lounged on one of the settees. The cat had jumped into the pony cart right before he'd driven out of the inn-yard and had planted her furry little arse on the bench between him and Jane.

Not that Poppy's wall-like presence had made any difference. He couldn't very well apologize or have any sort of intelligent conversation when he felt like his brains were being shaken from his skull.

He frowned at his brandy. He would broach the subject as soon as Jane put in an appearance. There was no one else at the castle but the servants, and they were off somewhere celebrating the end of the curse. He and Jane would not be interrupted—he glanced at the cat—unless Poppy did the interrupting.

On the other hand, speaking of things now could lead to a certain awkwardness. They *were* alone and would be stuck here together until Miss Wilkinson could return to the Spinster House. Perhaps he should put the discussion off. . . .

No, if things got awkward, he could decamp to the inn. Or, well, the castle *was* very large. They could probably live in it for the short time they'd be here together without crossing paths.

Oh, who the hell am I trying to fool? Things already are *awkward.*

It would be best to try to clear the air now. And then, maybe, once he apologized and understood what had happened in the garden, perhaps then he would find out if Rachel was right, if Jane cared for him.

I hope Rachel is right.

He looked over at Poppy. "Couldn't take young William's crying, eh?" He sighed. "I don't fault you. For such a tiny creature, he has an excellent pair of lungs." And the quality of the sound itself was more effective than fingernails on slate for setting one's teeth on edge and getting one's heart—and head—pounding. He'd been very happy he hadn't had to linger within earshot.

The cat ignored him. She was too interested in sniffing the settee's arm.

"Do you approve?"

Poppy spared him a look.

"Hey, you're lucky you weren't here before Marcus married. I assure you, the duchess has done wonders. Got rid of all the uncomfortable, ugly, ancient furniture and replaced it with pieces that aren't instruments of torture."

But she'd kept the portrait of the third duke—the first Cursed Duke.

He walked over to examine the fellow in the old-fashioned garb. "Do you suppose he knows the curse is broken?"

Poppy did not venture an opinion. If she had, Alex would know without a shadow of a doubt that he had drunk far more brandy than was good for him.

He checked his watch. Where was Jane?

The news of the baby's birth had definitely set the castle at sixes and sevens. When Alex told Mr. Emmett, Marcus's steward, the old man had thrown his arms around him and sobbed into his shoulder, quite soaking his coat, while Alex had patted him awkwardly on the back.

And then the story had flown through the castle and likely the entire estate. Everyone had wanted to hear the details and have Alex confirm that, yes, he had indeed seen the baby and the duke in the same room at the same time, both breathing. One of the maids had worried that the duke's real son had died and someone had substituted another child, so Jane had been compelled to admit she'd seen the baby, ah, emerge.

She'd turned a very interesting shade of red at that.

"I don't believe there was a dry eye in the castle, Poppy." He frowned. "Or that there's now a sober head." Because once the tears passed, the celebration began.

He looked at his watch again. He'd assumed at least one footman would wait to imbibe long enough to lead Jane to the study, but perhaps that was a false assumption. "Do you think I should go in search of her?"

Apparently, Poppy did. She jumped down and led the way, tail high, through a series of rooms and up the main staircase. The animal appeared to know exactly where she was going.

"Are you part canine?"

Poppy paused long enough to look back at him and sneeze with apparent disdain.

"I meant that as a compliment. You seem to have re-markable tracking skills." *And I'm talking to a cat.*

Alex stopped, one foot on the next step. Good Lord! He was indeed losing his mind. There was little question of it now. He should just go back to the study, pour himself another glass of brandy, and wait. Miss Wilkinson would show up eventually.

Or perhaps she's hit upon a way to avoid me.

His stomach suddenly felt filled with lead.

Of course. Likely the woman had managed to get the attention of one of the servants and had had them bring up her supper so she could hide in her room. And here he'd been cooling his heels in the study for—

"Mer*row*!"

Poppy reclaimed his attention. She'd come back to him and was now eyeing his boots with malice. As she'd decorated Nate's with her claw marks, he took note. He did not wish his footwear to suffer the same fate.

"All right. I'm coming."

Poppy snapped her tail several times and hissed briefly, a clear warning that any further loitering would be dealt with severely, and then started back up the stairs.

The oldest part of the castle had been built long before William the Conqueror set foot on English soil. The building was enlarged over the centuries—well, until Isabelle Dorring's curse, when the Duke of Hart stopped visiting—with new sections added higgledy-piggledy. Now it resembled a very elaborate stone maze with a roof. It had taken Marcus, Nate, and Alex a few days to get their bearings.

Poppy turned down a corridor Alex was certain he'd never seen before.

"Surely Emmett didn't assign Miss Wilkinson a room this far from civilization?"

The cat did not venture an opinion on the matter.

Several turns later, when Alex was wishing he'd had the forethought to mark his path so he could retrace it, they came to an intersection.

"Which way now?"

Poppy raised her face as if sniffing the air.

Alex knew better than to say what he was thinking—he hoped her tracking skills were indeed as good as any hound's.

And then they heard a woman's voice coming from the left.

"Help!"

He and Poppy exchanged a look. "That's Jane."

They both broke into a run, pounding—well, Alex was pounding—down the corridor, around another corner—

And there was Jane, standing next to a narrow window, looking pale and anxious—until she saw them. Then relief washed over her features and she smiled—and looked down at Poppy.

"Oh, Poppy. I'm so happy to see you." She knelt and buried her face in the cat's fur.

Aren't you happy to see me?

Alex realized rather painfully that he would much rather Jane bury her face in his chest than Poppy's back.

"What are you doing here?" All right, then. That had come out harsher than he'd intended.

Miss Wilkinson looked up at him, and then gave Poppy one last stroke before standing. "I, er, thought I'd explore a little."

To put off meeting me in the study.

The lead in his stomach got heavier.

"I've not been to the castle before."

Did she expect him to believe that? "I thought the duchess was your good friend."

"She is. But she's been busy, er"—Jane flushed—"being married."

Perhaps it was due to Jane's heightened color, but an extremely inappropriate, deliciously graphic image of what "busy being married" entailed sprang full-blown into his thoughts. It involved this annoying, managing woman, a soft bed, and hopelessly twisted sheets.

His unruly cock swelled with anticipation.

He blinked and realized she was looking at him as if she expected some response. Apparently she'd been talking while he'd been lusting.

"I'm afraid I was woolgathering." Ha! If only he'd been engaged in something so boring. "I missed what you said."

And I hope to God I'm not blushing.

He must be, because Miss Wilkinson gave him a wary look before repeating herself.

"I've been busy, too, with my work at Randolph's office and with the lending library." She cleared her throat and looked down at Poppy. "I've started cataloging its books."

Poppy yawned.

"It's true the collection isn't extensive," she told Poppy, "but no one has ever sorted it out before. I found several very old copies of a treatise on rodent control."

Poppy stared at her. Alex sniggered.

Miss Wilkinson lifted her chin. "Rodents can be a very serious problem."

"Which I'm sure Poppy can deal with quite well without recourse to a dusty tome on the subject."

"Well, of course. She's a cat. And I expect having a few cats about is mentioned in the treatise."

"You expect? You haven't perused this exciting find?"

Miss Wilkinson scowled at him. "I didn't say it was exciting. *I'm* not interested in rodent control. As you just pointed out, Poppy does an excellent job of keeping the Spinster House free of vermin. Isn't that right, Poppy?"

They both looked down to see if the cat concurred, but the cat was nowhere to be seen.

"Well," he said, "that's a problem."

Miss Wilkinson's head snapped up and she stared at

him. "What do you mean 'that's a problem'? What's a problem?"

"I was hoping Poppy would show us the way back."

She sucked in her breath. "You don't know the way back?"

"I've only been in the castle twice before, Miss Wilkinson, and I didn't go wandering about either time."

She frowned, looking a bit offended. "I'm not one of the Boltwood sisters. I wasn't trying to stick my nose into cabinets, if that's what you mean to infer."

"I don't mean to infer anything. I know why you were wandering around up here—you wanted to avoid me."

The stricken look on her face told him he was correct.

"Come along. Let's see if we can find our way without Poppy's help."

Clearly, if Miss Wilkinson had resorted to exploring the castle corridors to avoid him, Rachel was wrong. The interesting discussion he'd hoped to have concerning their future was not going to happen. They had no future. His instincts—and that of his female relatives—had failed him again.

He'd find Miss Wilkinson's room for her, apologize for taking liberties—*mild* liberties—with her in Diana's garden, and wish her a happy life in the Spinster House. He didn't see how he could avoid her completely unless he gave up his friendships with Marcus and Nate, but the discomfort and awkwardness would fade with time. His stomach wouldn't always feel as if he'd swallowed a cannonball.

Of *course* things would improve. In just a little over a month he'd be back among the *ton* and attending any number of balls and parties. He wished to go to support Bea on her come-out, but perhaps he'd find a woman to marry. Not to love. He was done with that nonsense. But to wed. A marriage of convenience.

A debutante like Bea?

The iron ball in his stomach heaved.

No, he wouldn't look at the young girls—that had been one of his many mistakes with Charlotte. He'd look for an older, more mature woman. There were always a few of that sort who either hadn't taken or had delayed their come-outs for one reason or another. Or he might consider an impoverished companion. Or a young widow. Davenport had married a widow and that seemed to be working out very well. There was no rush. He would take his time.

At the moment it felt as if any woman would do if he couldn't have the prickly Spinster House spinster. He had to marry someone. He needed an heir. Many *ton* marriages were just such practical arrangements. The man got a son or two, the woman a home.

Miss Wilkinson already had a home, so she had no need of a husband to clutter it up.

He'd been walking as his unhappy thoughts rolled through him like noxious clouds, taking them round a number of corners and turns, hoping his sense of direction would get them back to the main part of the castle, but at the next intersection, he came to a complete stop. Nothing looked remotely familiar.

He must have made an annoyed sound, because Miss Wilkinson, who'd been uncharacteristically silent, spoke.

"I'm sorry for being such trouble," she said in a rather small voice.

She actually sounded abashed. He looked down at her. He couldn't help it. His right eyebrow rose skeptically.

"What?" Now there was the familiar edge of annoyance in her voice.

He grinned. "Thank heavens. For a moment there I was afraid the real Miss Wilkinson had been spirited away."

She smiled a bit sheepishly. "You were right, you know. I *was* avoiding you."

Was it time for a discussion, then? Though not the one he'd hoped to have.

"Why?"

"Er . . ." Oh, lud, why had she said that?

The proverb was wrong—honesty was *not* always the best policy. It certainly wasn't in this case.

Lord Evans was frowning. "You aren't afraid of me, are you?"

"Of course not. What a ridiculous suggestion." She wasn't afraid of him—she was afraid of herself.

Her head knew what she wanted—a controlled, even-keeled independent life—but her foolish heart kept insisting that no, what she *really* wanted was this man.

The sooner the Earl of Evans left Loves Bridge, the better for her sanity.

But first they had to find their way out of this maze. How—

The earl suddenly started sniffing the air.

Oh, dear. Is there an odor about me? I bathed yesterday.

She tried to execute a few discreet sniffs herself. . . . "Do I smell shepherd's pie?"

He grinned, and her silly heart fluttered.

He should not be allowed to smile. When he smiled, his slightly aloof, stiff, earlish air vanished to be replaced by a warm, almost boyish appeal. Smiling made him far too endearing.

And it scrambled her emotions.

"I believe so. Let's see if we can follow our noses to the kitchen. From there we can get directions to a more familiar part of the castle—after having sampled the pie, if it's ready."

The scent led them down a corridor and around a corner to a very narrow, circular stone stairway.

"The smell is definitely coming from somewhere below us," Jane said, eyeing the stairs with trepidation.

"Yes." Lord Evans looked at her dress and his brow furrowed. "The footing appears quite treacherous here. Perhaps you should stay—"

"Oh, no. I'm coming with you." She'd spent enough time alone in this maze.

His lips turned up into a faint smile, but his eyes were still worried. "I won't abandon you, you know. I'll come back as soon as I discover how to get here from the main part of the castle."

Waiting might be the wiser course, but she wasn't going to take it. "I'll manage."

"But your skirt . . ."

"The female servants must use these stairs in skirts *and* with their hands full."

"*And* having had years of practice."

"Yes, but I will have my hands free. I only have to make it down once."

The man sighed, apparently realizing further argument was futile. "At least let me go first to break your fall if you trip."

"I won't trip."

He let that pass. "Keep your feet to the outside where the step is wider and brace yourself against the wall."

"Lord Evans, I *have* navigated circular stairs before." Though never any this dark and narrow.

The earl showed exceptional restraint—he bit his tongue and started down the stairs.

Jane quickly discovered the footing was even worse

than it looked. The stairs descended in an extremely tight spiral, the inner portion of each step being a mere sliver of stone. Even the outer edge was narrower than she'd like, since she wasn't blessed to have dainty little feet. And while she'd hoped to put a hand on the inner as well as the outer wall, she immediately discovered that wasn't possible—she needed her left hand to hold her skirt out of the way.

Just go slow. One step at a time. Keep your eyes on your feet.

"I've reached the bottom," she heard Lord Evans say.

She looked up and realized he was out of sight. He sounded close, though. She must be almost done with these blasted stairs.

And then she felt an odd tickling sensation on the hand that was resting against the wall. . . .

She glanced over to see a fat, hairy spider ambling over her fingers.

"Eek!" She snatched her hand back, shook it violently to dislodge the hideous creature—and lost her balance. *"Ahh!"*

She tried to catch herself, but her feet got all tangled up in her skirt. She was going to pitch headfirst down the stairs—

"Oof!"

She pitched into a hard, male chest instead.

This was becoming a far too frequent occurrence.

She wrapped her arms around Lord Evans, pressing her cheek against the rough wool of his coat as she struggled to get her breathing and heartbeat under control.

Was his heart beating rather wildly, too? Did his lips brush her hair?

No, it must be her imagination.

"Are you all right?" he asked. His arms were around her

as well, holding her securely. It was very comforting. Calming.

But she couldn't stay here all night.

"Y-yes." She took one last, shuddering breath, inhaling the by now all-too-familiar mix of wool and linen and soap that was Alex, and disentangled herself.

He kept hold of her shoulders. "What happened?"

"Spider." She cleared her throat. "There was a spider—"

Dear God, she *had* shaken it off, hadn't she?

She started to brush wildly at her arms and then jumped about the corridor, shaking her dress.

Lord Evans made an odd, choking noise. "Is this some new dance? Pardon me, but I doubt it will catch on among the *ton*. It's a trifle too, er, energetic."

She could tell he was struggling to keep from laughing.

"I told you I don't like spiders."

"Yes, I remember that." He pointed to something on the ground. "Is that your villain, Miss Wilkinson?"

She inspected—from a safe distance—the eight-legged monster now making its way up the steps.

"M-maybe. Though I think the spider that attacked me was much larger." She shook her arms and jumped again. Did she feel something else crawling on her?

He grinned. "Would you like me to examine you to be certain you are spider-free?"

She eyed him warily.

He held up his hands, palms toward her. "I promise not to touch—unless it's to brush off a trespasser."

"Very well." She stood still, arms a bit away from her sides, and let Lord Evans walk round her. It was awkward and a bit embarrassing, but it helped that he acted very matter-of-fact about it.

He came back to face her. "There you go. I pronounce

you spider-free. Now shall we continue? Unless my nose lies, I think we are very close to our goal."

Lord Evans was right. Now that she wasn't obsessed by the fear of eight-legged creatures, she noticed that the stone corridor was filled with the scent of shepherd's pie and other gustatory delights. And as they made their way down the corridor, they heard further evidence they were approaching the kitchens—clanging pans, chopping knives, people talking and laughing.

The talking and laughing were rather louder and more exuberant than Jane would have expected, not that she had any experience with servants and large kitchens. And then—

"Is that a fiddle?"

"It certainly sounds like one." Lord Evans smiled, as one eyebrow winged up. "I'd say the servants are celebrating the heir's birth."

And indeed, turning one last corner, they came to a large kitchen filled with people eating, drinking, and dancing.

"And there's Poppy." The earl pointed to a small table where the cat crouched, delicately consuming a piece of fish.

One of the castle maids caught sight of them. Her hand flew up to cover her mouth, her eyes widened in apparent horror, and then she ran to grab the arm of an elderly gentleman energetically dancing a jig.

It was Mr. Emmett! Jane had never seen the steward so, er, relaxed.

"He's quite spry for a man of eighty," Lord Evans said. They watched the steward weave toward them. "And drunk, I suspect," he murmured by her ear.

A buzz passed through the crowd. The dancing and music stopped, and all the servants turned to stare nervously at them.

Mr. Emmett was too deep in his cups to be alarmed. "Oh, L-lord Evans. And Miss Wil-Wilkinson. Have ye heard? The curse is broken."

He turned to repeat that announcement to the room. Everyone raised their mugs and cheered—and took another drink of ale.

"Yes, we've heard," the earl said, rather loudly to recapture the steward's attention. "We're the ones who told you, Mr. Emmett."

Mr. Emmett's head bobbed in inebriated agreement. "Right. Isn't it wonderful? The curse is broken."

More cheers. More drinking.

"I say, did George bring you your supper?" Mr. Emmett asked as if the thought had just occurred to him.

Jane saw the maid who'd first noticed them talking animatedly to a thin, young footman whose face suddenly turned as white as his cravat.

"Er, no, I'm afraid he didn't," Lord Evans said.

"Oh." Mr. Emmett looked concerned, but then he washed away any uneasiness with another swallow of ale. "Suppose he forgot. The excitement, you know. I say, have you heard? The curse is broken."

He raised his mug yet again. This time the crowd's cheer was a little louder. Likely they'd decided Lord Evans wasn't going to cut up stiff over one missed meal.

He wasn't going to go hungry, either.

"Yes. So do you suppose we might trouble you for a bit of that shepherd's pie and some wine?" the earl asked.

"Oh, yes, yes. Help yourself. Or, Dolly, help the earl, will you? And you, too, George. Did you know you forgot to feed Lord Evans and Miss Wilkinson?"

"I'm sorry, milord, Miss Wilkinson," George said, having hurried over. He sounded wretched.

"It's all right," Lord Evans said. "Just get us a tray, will you?"

George got a tray and Dolly filled it with far more food than Jane, at least, could eat.

"I'll take it to the dining room, shall I, milord? And wait on ye there." George couldn't keep from throwing a forlorn look at the kitchen and all the fun he'd be missing.

"Nonsense," Lord Evans said. "I'm more than capable of carrying a tray. You go back to the party. We'll do very well on our own, if you'll just point us the way."

"Of course, milord. This way, milord." George led them across the room to another doorway. "Just through here and up the stairs, milord. Ye'll come out right by the dining room."

"Excellent. Thank you, George. Now go and enjoy the party."

"If yer certain, milord?" George looked hopeful, but still willing to do his duty.

"Of course I'm certain."

George grinned. "Thank ye, milord. Miss." He bowed—and took off before the earl could change his mind.

"You don't object, do you, Miss Wilkinson?" the earl asked as they stepped through the first doorway. "Though of course I should have asked that before our friend George departed. I will, if you wish, call him back, but I imagine he will be very unhappy."

Unhappy? Poor George would be despondent. "Of course I don't object. I did not grow up with servants, Lord Evans. I am very much used to managing for myself."

They started up a far more suitable flight of stairs—broad, straight, and—as far as she could see—spider-free.

"You pride yourself on your independent ways, don't you, Miss Wilkinson?"

"Yes, I do." She'd had to be independent. She'd had no choice.

Lord Evans likely wouldn't understand.

It hadn't just been losing her parents in one fell swoop

that had made her grow up so quickly and resolve to rely only on herself. It had been discovering that Papa had lied to her.

Well, not to her directly and not in words. But she'd thought him an intelligent, principled man, if also all too often an angry one. And then she'd discovered her secure, comfortable life was all a sham.

She still got a sinking feeling in her stomach when she thought about that bleak afternoon that Randolph had sat her down in Papa's study and told her the truth.

"I suppose I've always been a bit strong-willed, but when my parents died, Randolph discovered our father had not managed his finances well." Ha! That was a major understatement. "We'd been living on credit for years."

"Ah."

"Randolph moved to address the problem at once, of course." Which meant they'd gone from a comfortable to an almost hand-to-mouth existence. "He worried we'd lose everything, that he'd have to sell the house and the business."

Why am I telling him all this? I've never talked to anyone about it before, though everyone must have guessed.

There were no secrets in Loves Bridge.

That bothered her too. Lord Davenport, the Huttings—surely the Boltwoods—they all must have known or had an inkling of how things stood, but no one ever said a word to her.

Well, she'd been only fourteen. But Randolph had been taken by surprise as well.

"If I'd been three years older, I might have looked to marry." Thank *God* that hadn't been an option. A marriage made in desperation could not have brought anyone happiness. For her, it would have been . . .

No, the thought was too horrible to contemplate.

"Randolph could have married."

"Yes, but Imogen's father wouldn't give his consent, remember." She might not understand romantic love, but she couldn't wish Randolph to wed someone when he'd given his heart to another.

"Imogen married Eldon."

"Not until the following year and by then we'd got things under control so Randolph didn't need to sacrifice himself on any matrimonial altar. We weren't completely out of the woods, but at least we'd beaten the wolf back from the door." She smiled. She was very proud of what she and Randolph had accomplished on their own.

"Now we're on very good footing. I see that the bills are paid on time and that we, in turn, are paid by our clients. I remind Randolph of deadlines, rescue important files from under piles of books and newspapers, and, in general, keep the office organized and running smoothly." She smiled. "I used to have to do much the same at home, but now that part of Randolph's life is Imogen's problem, thank heavens."

That's right. It was a great relief not to have to take charge of—or at least consider—someone else twenty-four hours a day.

Except it's also lonely.

This wasn't loneliness she was feeling—had been feeling—since Lord Evans's arrival in Loves Bridge. It wasn't loneliness that had sent her into the castle corridors instead of going downstairs to find the earl.

It was something far more unsettling.

Did she want the sort of connection she'd seen between the duke and Cat? Did she want Lord Evans to love her that way?

"Right. You have only Poppy to look after."

She laughed, trying to push aside her confused feelings.

"Oh, I wouldn't say I look after Poppy. I think she is even more independent than I am. I do, however, have to deal with a significant quantity of cat hair, so I *am* still cleaning up after my housemate."

They'd reached the large—*very* large—formal dining room with its long polished table and massive chandelier.

"Oh." Jane stopped on the threshold. "It's rather grand, isn't it?"

"Yes. There's a smaller family dining room, as well, which I think I can find now that we're back in the main part of the castle, but I wonder if we wouldn't be more comfortable in the study."

She didn't want to look at one more echoing room. She just wanted to sit down with a slice of that shepherd's pie and a glass of wine and relax.

Or as much as she could relax with Lord Evans there. "The study sounds lovely."

The study *was* lovely. The dark wood paneling and heavy curtains gave the room an intimate feeling, and the desk, though it was much larger and finer than hers, made her think of the comforting familiarity of Randolph's office.

Well, perhaps not. She'd never experienced this odd churning of excitement and anticipation when at her desk.

Being alone with Lord Evans in a private room was not a good idea. She'd been wise to avoid it earlier, even though she'd got terribly lost in the castle corridors.

There was no avoiding it now.

What do I want?

She walked over to examine a hideous suit of armor and put more space between herself and the earl.

I don't know.

She wasn't used to this feeling of confused indecision.

She'd always known exactly what she wanted—until she'd met Lord Evans.

She turned her attention to the globe next to the armor, spinning it while the earl set the tray on a table and poured them each some wine.

She'd never traveled much. Her journey to Chanton Manor in October might have been the farthest she'd ever been from the village. She'd certainly never been to London, though she read the London papers, of course—or had read them before she'd worried about seeing the earl's name linked to a Society woman's in the gossip columns.

Cat was the one who'd chafed at the boundaries she thought Loves Bridge drew round her. Anne, as the daughter of a baron, had had a London Season and had visited many grand estates for house parties. But Jane . . .

She'd been content to do her traveling through books. Actually going to new places, meeting new people—no. It wasn't something that had ever appealed to her.

Have I grown a little too set in my ways? A little too cautious?

Cat and Anne had many new adventures ahead of them. Jane had . . . nothing. Just the same work at Randolph's office, the same shabby house—she'd admit that after just a few months, the Spinster House didn't cause her heart to beat any faster—and the same village she'd known her entire life.

And a supernatural cat. She mustn't forget Poppy.

Oh, and the lending library. After she finished with the books on rodent control, she could explore the collection's other treasures—the four or five books on the most common diseases of sheep, for example, or the illustrated guide to local beetles.

Is that all I want my life to be?

She was here with Lord Evans. They were quite alone. The castle staff was in no condition to disturb them.

Was it time to be a little less cautious?

Perhaps a kiss or two will cure me of this odd disquiet. Perhaps then I'll know what I want.

At the moment she was afraid she wanted Lord Evans. It was almost like she had a fever. She felt her forehead. No, that wasn't where the heat was.

The earl brought her a glass of wine. "Studying the blackguard who started the curse?"

"What? Oh."

She'd been staring at—but not seeing—a full-length portrait of a man in early seventeenth-century garb. A young man, trying to look older and wiser than he was, she thought. If there was malice in the fellow, the painter had hidden it well.

"He doesn't look evil, does he?" She took a large drink. The wine warmed her, settled her.

"No, he doesn't." The earl examined the painting. "Marcus said he found a letter this duke wrote to Isabelle, telling her he was coming to Loves Bridge to marry her. Unfortunately, she never read it. She had already, er, left."

"Oh." Could two hundred years of heartache have been avoided if a letter had arrived just a little earlier? But then the current duke would never have been born. Cat would not have met him, and the beautiful baby Jane had watched come into the world earlier wouldn't exist. "It doesn't matter any longer, does it, A-Alex?"

"No, I suppose it doesn't." He smiled—and then his expression grew serious. "Jane, I tried to say this at the Spinster House, but we kept getting interrupted. I told you I came to Loves Bridge because Nate asked me to check on Marcus, but I also came to see you."

Her silly heart leapt with delight. She took another sip of wine to steady it. "Oh?"

"Yes. To apologize."

"Oh." That sounded bad. She took another sip. "You don't need to apologize for anything."

"I think I do. I think I frightened you when I kissed you in the garden that night—well, both nights, I suppose—at Chanton Manor."

Ah, so here we are.

She took another drink. Warmth spread through her, relaxing her, blunting her worries, making her head buzz just a little, and waking other parts of her that she'd kept under strict control most of her life. She wasn't drunk—not that she knew precisely what drunk felt like. She just felt braver, more daring, as if many of the rules that confined her—rules she'd put in place and rules Society had placed on her—had loosened. Become negotiable or irrelevant.

She was going to throw caution to the wind.

Chapter Fifteen

"You didn't frighten me, Alex." Jane smiled a bit too brightly. "It was only a kiss."

He liked hearing her say his name. He liked it far too much.

Hmm. Her glass was empty already. She'd probably drunk her wine too quickly. And when was the last time she'd eaten? They'd had brandy, but no food, when they'd been in the Spinster House kitchen.

"I'm glad." He took her arm to urge her toward the table. "We should eat before the food gets any colder."

She leaned into him—she'd definitely had too much wine.

"I'm not used to being kissed, you see. I was just st-startled."

He sat her down, gave her a sizeable slice of shepherd's pie, and then took his own seat and cut a piece for himself.

"I liked it, though. I'd like to do it again."

He almost dumped his pie onto the table.

"Ah." How was he to respond to that?

"It made me feel quite . . ." She put a forkful of pie in

her mouth and appeared to savor it. "Tingly. It made me feel tingly in all sorts of odd places."

Good Lord! He immediately started thinking of all the places she must mean. "The pie is very good, isn't it?"

She nodded and reached for her wineglass—and seemed surprised it was empty. "More, please."

"Er, don't you think you've had enough?"

She scowled at him. "I am not a child. I think I know if I wish more wine or not."

Right. That was the problem here. She wouldn't be drinking wine at all if she were a child—and he wouldn't be having salacious thoughts about her.

She lifted her chin. "I shall have more wine, if you please, Lord Evans. Or if you'll pass the decanter, I can pour it myself."

So, I'm back to Lord Evans.

He shrugged off his disappointment and reached for the decanter. As she said, she was an adult.

It might be that she was just now reacting to having witnessed Cat give birth. It must have been a stressful, intense time. She'd clearly been on edge when they'd arrived at the castle.

Perhaps that was also why she'd taken to the corridors to avoid him.

He poured her a moderate amount of wine—and then filled her glass when she gave him a stern look. Then he poured the rest of the decanter—it was almost empty—into his own glass to save her from herself.

He might be a bit bosky soon.

He took a mouthful of pie.

"I imagine you've done a lot of kissing," Jane said.

He was in the middle of swallowing. Part of the shepherd's pie went where it was supposed to, part returned to his mouth, and a rogue bit decided to explore his nose.

He tried to sort matters out with a large swallow of wine.

"And other things," she added. "Haven't you?"

How to answer that? He certainly didn't want to ask what she meant by "other things."

"I'm a man, Jane. I have some experience, yes, but I don't believe I have any more than most men."

She frowned. "Randolph visits the Widow Conklin weekly, you know—or did before he married."

He grunted, hoping—weakly, but optimistically—that this was just a bizarre non sequitur and the widow ran a book club or some such thing.

Jane leaned forward to clarify. "Mrs. Conklin—well, we're rather sure there was never a Mr. Conklin. In any event, Mrs. Conklin is a perfectly pleasant, ordinary-looking woman in her middle age who earns her living by welcoming the village men into her bed."

Blast it, the woman was exactly what he'd thought she was.

"She's very particular, though, that if the man's married, his wife give permission for the visit. She doesn't want to offend any other women. The wives are her neighbors after all, and Loves Bridge is a small village."

He drank more wine and nodded. He knew that very well.

She frowned down at her shepherd's pie—or what was left of it. Fortunately, she'd eaten quite a bit.

"I suppose I understand why *she* does it—it's her trade, just as Mrs. Greeley is a dressmaker and Mrs. Bates runs a shop. But"—she looked back at him as if he were an exotic beast, not unlike Mr. Wertigger's kangaroo, before its demise—"why do men do it?"

He took another swallow of wine, hoping that was a rhetorical question.

It wasn't.

"Why would you visit a, well, light skirt, Lord Evans?"

"Er, well . . ." It wasn't a subject he cared to explain to a well-bred, strong-minded, inquisitive virgin. "I don't believe we were speaking of me."

Miss Wilkinson dismissed his observation with a wave of her hand. "Do you have a Mrs. Conklin?"

"No." He wasn't a virgin, but he'd also never wanted a mistress or even to single out a particular woman at any of the brothels. That seemed too much like a marriage without the love or commitment.

"But you've"—she finally seemed to realize she was deep in inappropriate territory, but she pressed on anyway, face flushed—"done it before."

At least Jane's wineglass was almost empty.

Perhaps it was safest to divert the conversation into slightly less personal territory. "Jane, do you know what 'it' is?" She should. Yes, her mother had died when she was young, but she had two close friends who were now married—and increasing—so they clearly understood the mechanics of the deed.

But one could never be certain of anything with Miss Wilkinson.

She looked away. "Not really." And then she smiled, drank the last of her wine, and said the most shocking of all the things she had said yet. "Why don't you tell me?" Her gaze dropped to the table. "Why don't you *show* me?" And then she popped the last bite of pie in her mouth.

Alex picked his jaw up off the table and sent his cock a stern warning to behave.

He would pretend she hadn't said anything. That was the only way to deal with the situation. And in a way, she hadn't said it—it had been the wine talking. She'd be grateful for his discretion in the morning.

He drew breath to tell her it was time they went up to bed—to their separate beds in their separate bedchambers—but the words that came out were, "You've got a crumb on your mouth."

The tip of Jane's tongue ventured out in search of the errant bit of pastry, and his temperature shot up about ten degrees.

"It's on the right."

So of course her tongue moved to the left.

"Your other right. Here." He should have handed her a napkin, of course. Instead he reached over and used his finger to push the crumb over so her tongue could capture it.

Her tongue captured his finger as well. The sensation of the warm, wet stroke shot directly to his eager cock with predictable results.

He finished his wine in one large gulp—it went straight to his head. He felt very . . . happy and quite, er, eager.

Surely he could keep his impulses under control until he deposited Jane—Miss Wilkinson—safely in her—

Good God, her hand was going to her neckline. She loosed a few buttons. "Is it hot in here?"

It is now. "No, I don't think so. Perhaps you should go up to your room."

She frowned at him. "Alone?"

"Yes." *Be strong.*

She looked very disappointed. "So you aren't going to explain things to me?"

Very strong. "No."

"But how will I ever find out?"

"I'm sure you can discuss the matter with your friends."

"But they're women."

Has any man in the world ever had to endure this sort of trial?

"Miss Wilkinson, surely you see how inappropriate this conversation is."

"I thought we were friends."

Oh, Lord. "We are friends, but—" No, it was impossible to explain. They were both too bosky—particularly Jane. If she were sober, they'd be discussing literature or something else unexceptional.

She nodded, looking crestfallen. He wanted to wrap his arms around—

No. That would be a mistake. A *big* mistake. Bigger even than his cock in its current swollen condition.

"Very well. If you'll excuse me?" She stood—and started to list to one side.

He was on his feet at once, his arm going round her waist to support her.

She had a lovely, small waist.

Judgment! Where is my judgment?

Slipping under waves of alcohol and desire.

"Oh." She blinked up at him. Her lips were so close to his. "I seem to be a bit unsteady on my feet."

He exerted Herculean control and straightened, putting more space between his mouth and hers. "I think you've had a little too much wine."

She nodded—and wrapped *her* arm around *his* waist. At least it was on top of his coat.

"I'm sorry, but I think I'll need your help getting to my room, Lo-lor"—she let out a small growl of annoyance that she couldn't seem to manage his title—"Alex."

His foolish cock was singing. And he had no choice. She was leaning heavily against him. If he let go of her, she'd fall flat on her face.

"Come along." Perhaps he could pretend she was his sister or his niece or, or some poor stranger he'd come upon.

He took a step and she stumbled against him, giggling.

Jane was not one to giggle.

"Do I need to carry you?" Though that would not be the best idea. He thought he was steady enough to manage the stairs with her, but he wasn't entirely certain. It would be wiser not to put it to the test.

She shook her head—and snaked her arm *under* his coat. "No. I'm f-fine."

She wasn't fine, but she did appear to be ambulatory.

They made their way out of the study, up the stairs, and down the corridor to Jane's bedchamber without seeing another living soul. Er, another living *person*. They found Poppy sitting outside Jane's door, tail twitching as if they'd kept her waiting.

"Oh, P-Poppy," Jane said, "did you have f-fun in the kitchen?"

Poppy blinked at Jane and then turned to give Alex a look of disgust.

Well, he was surprised at Jane's overly sweet tone too.

Jane opened the door and Poppy dashed inside.

"Do you think you can manage on your own now?" Alex asked. If he stepped over the threshold, he was very much afraid he would lose his struggle with his baser instincts.

They both looked at the vast distance from the door to her bed. Zeus, Emmett must have put her in the largest guest bedroom in the entire castle.

"I—I can try," she said doubtfully, but her arm tightened around his waist.

He sighed inwardly. She had about as much chance of

safely navigating the path to that bed as Poppy did of flying
to the moon.

Actually, he'd put his money on Poppy over Jane at the
moment. He would just have to find some heretofore un-
explored reserves of self-control. "I'd better help you."

He got her through the door and then closed it carefully
behind them. Given the celebrations belowstairs, it was
highly unlikely anyone would come this way, but there
was no point in tempting fate. Then he guided her over to
the bed.

"There you go," he said with false heartiness.

Her hold on him tightened.

"Could you." She cleared her throat, staring at the bed
instead of him. "That is, I doubt I can manage the buttons
down the back of this dress at the moment. Could you
undo them for me?"

That shouldn't be so difficult. A woman's back was relatively safe territory. Even if her dress drooped once he'd
got it unbuttoned, there would still be her stays and shift
between his fingers and her soft skin.

Don't think about skin.

Women's buttons were designed by the devil. They were
so blasted small, and his fingers felt unnaturally fat and
clumsy—and yes, the alcohol he'd consumed didn't help.
It took what seemed like forever, but he finally managed
to wrestle all the buttons out of their buttonholes.

"There you go," he said, stepping back and forcing his
hands to clasp behind him. Perhaps that would keep them
out of trouble. "I'll just be . . ."

Jane pulled her dress down and stepped out of it, leaving her in just her shift and stays.

Correction—just her shift. Her stays quickly followed
her dress to the floor.

"Ah, that's better."

Zeus! The sigh of pleasure she gave with those words went straight to his cock. It was pleading with him to touch her.

His fingers tightened their clasp behind his back.

No. No touching.

And then she turned toward him, and he could see the shadow of her nipples through her shift.

His blasted cock started shouting. It was hard to remember, over its desperate exhortations, that he was an honorable gentleman and Jane—Miss Wilkinson—was a gently bred virgin. Honorable gentlemen did not tup gently bred virgins.

Unfortunately.

She raised her arms to pluck the pins from her hair. The thin fabric of her shift drew tight across her chest. Not only could he see her nipples clearly now, but he could also admire the soft, full shape of her breasts.

He forced his eyes up to her face, a face that was much, much too close to his. He wouldn't have to take a single step to reach her—he could just lean forward slightly and put his mouth on hers.

A mouth that was now smiling.

Dear God, he was in trouble. Her lovely, feminine body called to his cock, but the warmth and intimacy of her smile melted his heart.

He could not let it melt his resolve. His honor. He knew what he should do, much as he didn't want to do it. He needed to move his feet right now and walk out of this bedroom.

"Thank you, Alex. I—"

And then disaster by the name of Poppy struck. The cat ran toward them, chasing a mouse—though Alex wouldn't put it past the animal to be intentionally herding the rodent their way—and Jane screamed, leaping the inch that separated them and throwing her arms around him. Her soft, unbound breasts flattened against his damned waistcoat and her lower parts rubbed against his eager cock as she twisted to avoid the scurrying little creature and the larger furry she-devil in pursuit.

And of course he'd put his arms around her to catch her when she'd jumped toward him. His traitorous hands, recognizing a prize, wasted no time. One pulled her closer, while the other set off to explore the lovely curve of her back, the firm roundness of her buttocks.

I should leave. If I don't leave now I'll end up in bed with Jane. I'll end up in Jane.

Honor tried vainly to break through the alcohol-fueled lust surging through him, but it was like throwing up a sheet of paper to stop a raging river.

He buried his face in her lovely, silky hair.

It's not just lust. Surely this time what I'm feeling is love.

No matter. He couldn't take advantage of Jane. Neither of them were precisely sober.

He might still have been able to save her virginity and his soul, but just at that moment Poppy and the mouse ran by again.

"Oh! Eek!" Jane scrambled to get her feet off the floor by wrapping her legs around his waist, thus bringing his cock's favorite feminine body part hard up against it.

Hard. Yes. Hard. Very hard. Achingly hard.

He tried valiantly to stay upright and hold her without thrusting his hips against her soft, wiggling, warm, inviting self.

He won the thrusting battle, but lost the one with gravity. The cat and rodent came by again, and Jane tried to scramble higher as if he were a tree she was climbing. Over they went onto the bed.

At least he'd landed on the bottom so he wasn't crushing her. However, if he didn't stop her desperate thrashing to get completely off the floor—he would not point out that mice could climb if that truth had not yet presented itself to her—his cock was going to get a very painful introduction to her knee.

He held her hips tightly against him. "Careful, Jane. Please."

That got her to stop. She raised her chest so she could look at him, causing her lovely breasts to dangle, barely covered, just inches from his mouth. The silky length of her hair slid down to curtain him.

He was lost.

"What?" Jane blinked. Oh, how embarrassing. She wasn't a skittish person except when things that darted or crawled were involved. Spiders and mice—and, well, she wasn't hugely fond of snakes, either. She should apologize. Poor Alex. Here she was on top of him in bed. . . .

And he was staring at her breasts. Rather hungrily, she'd say. His palms were flat on her bottom—she could feel the pressure and heat of them through the thin fabric of her shift—holding her against a hard bulge that felt as if it was getting larger and larger.

She pressed her hips a little toward him and was rewarded by his sharp intake of breath and the small, moaning exhale that followed it.

So. It was time to decide. *Was* she going to throw caution to the wind?

She felt certain a proper English virgin would swoon or cry or demand in no uncertain terms to be released. Her conscience told her she should do exactly that, though she knew just a polite request would get the job done.

On the other hand, a slightly inebriated spinster bent on seduction would take full advantage of the situation.

She pressed against the bulge again. This was what she wanted. *He* was what she wanted.

Alex closed his eyes and pressed back. Now he was panting a little.

She felt quite powerful. And . . . tingly. His male bit wasn't the only body part in the room that was swelling.

But her conscience wasn't giving up yet. *What about your virginity?*

That was easy. Virginity was for young maidens in search of a husband. She was neither young nor husband-hunting.

And she trusted Alex. She might even love him. She certainly felt things for him that she'd never felt for another man. He was kind and strong and responsible and gentle. If virginity was a gift and not just a mark of inexperience, then she wanted to give hers to him.

She rubbed gently against him and felt need shoot to her breasts, causing her nipples to tighten.

But what about pregnancy?

That thought did give her pause. She didn't want to follow in Isabelle Dorring's footsteps.

But not every marital act results in a child. She'd been around female conversation enough to have learned that.

No, she wasn't about to let the fear of something that *might* happen keep her from her one chance to satisfy this need growing in her. She wanted to discover what it was like between a man and a woman.

That's what a brave, independent spinster would do.

As well as one who was slightly tipsy and very, very aroused.

One of Alex's hands left her bottom to touch her hair. "It's so silky."

She'd always thought her hair was one of her best features, but having Alex's fingers combing through it made her want to purr just like Poppy.

She did purr when his hand moved from her hair to her breast. Or maybe she moaned.

"You should stop me, Jane," he whispered as his finger touched her nipple.

"N-no." She pressed her hips against his again.

A small frown formed between his brows. "I shouldn't—"

"You *should*." She also wasn't going to let his male honor keep her from this. She bent her head to kiss him. His cheek, his mouth. She remembered how she'd felt when his tongue had touched hers in the garden, so she traced the seam of his lips—

He made an odd little sound, something like a growl, and rolled them over so he was now on top. Then his tongue plunged into her, touching, stroking, exploring.

Oh! She welcomed it. She welcomed it all—the invasion of his tongue, the weight of his body pushing her into the mattress, his scent, his heat. Somewhat to her surprise, she didn't feel at all subjugated or powerless. On the contrary, she felt quite powerful.

No, she felt desperate. She wanted—needed—more. She needed to feel his skin against hers and his hands—his lips—everywhere.

His mouth finally left hers to trail kisses over her cheek and down her jaw to a spot under her ear.

"Alex."

"Hmm?"

"Aren't you hot?"

He lifted his head. "Hot?"

"Yes." He didn't seem to be getting her point. "You have too many clothes on."

"Oh. Yes. You're right." He gave her a slightly lopsided grin and lifted himself off her, making short work of shedding his clothes. By the time she'd removed her shift, shoes, and stockings, he'd got out of his coat and waistcoat and was unwinding his cravat.

Mmm. She wanted to help—

No! Help him get dressed. That's what you should do. Push him out the door and lock it behind him!

That was her conscience again, reduced to a tiny shocked voice leaping about deep in the back of her mind.

Well, she knew it must be shocked, but the wine had nicely muffled the priggish old biddy so the words came more as an annoying whine, easily swatted away.

She was fearless, independent, a spinster with very demanding needs.

She put her hands on his, stopping him before he could pull off his shirt. "Let me."

He smiled, heat flaring in his eyes. "Just don't take too long, Jane. I can't wait."

She couldn't wait, either. Perhaps now she understood Randolph's visits to Mrs. Conklin.

It's not the same at all, her conscience shouted, trying to be heard through the lovely wine-glow and hot desire befogging her brain. *You're risking something Randolph never did.*

She'd already looked at the odds of pregnancy and decided to roll the dice.

That's not all. You're risking your reputation.

She didn't care about her reputation.

And perhaps your heart.

That made her pause, but for only a moment before need silenced her annoying conscience for good.

It was too late to turn back. Her fingers had pulled Alex's shirttail from his pantaloons. All she could hear now was his sharp intake of breath—or perhaps that was hers—as she slid her hands up over his hard, muscled belly.

"I saw you at the lake, you know." She'd wanted to touch him then.

"D-did you?" His hands gripped her hips as if he needed to hold on to something or he'd collapse.

She smiled, loving the surge of desire and power she felt. She leaned forward to plant a kiss on his chest.

He growled and jerked his shirt from her, pulling it over his head and tossing it off to the side.

Perhaps quick *was* better.

Lud, he was beautiful. She wrapped her arms around him, hugging him, pressing her naked breasts against his naked chest and her naked hips against his—pantaloons.

That would never do.

His hands had slid down her back to her bottom. It felt so good not to have her annoying shift in the way.

She should return the favor. She leaned back to reach his fall's buttons. Ah. His male bit was making quite a bulge in the fabric. It must be very eager to be freed. She cupped her hand over it—and felt it twitch into her palm.

Alex shuddered. "Jane, you're killing me."

She giggled. "Oh, I don't want to do that. I'm expecting you to show me any manner of carnal delights, my lord."

"I'll do my best, my lady." He kissed her again, his tongue stroking hers while his hands slid up her sides to her breasts, turning her nipples—and another nub lower on her person—into hard, aching points. She was quite breathless when his mouth moved on to explore her jaw. She wanted to melt into him and have him melt into her.

Which brought her back to his pantaloons. She dodged his kisses to free his buttons and—

"Oh." His male bit sprang out to greet her.

She'd thought it had looked sizeable when she'd seen it

at the lake, but then it had been dangly and relaxed. Now it was hard and straight, eager to be about its business.

She giggled.

Alex sounded slightly offended. "Why are you giggl—oh!"

He moaned as she wrapped her hands around the warm, thick, ungainly organ. Poor thing. It was rather ugly. But apparently very sensitive. She stroked it, and Alex moaned again, gripping her waist and then pushing her away so she had to let go of him.

"Bed," he panted. "We have to go to bed now, or I'm going to pick you up and have you against the bedpost."

That sounded surprisingly appealing, but probably not a good idea for a first time.

He scooped her up and deposited her on the mattress. She sprawled there, quite naked and feeling very wanton as she watched him pull off the rest of his clothing.

He *was* beautiful. She'd seen his body at the lake, but that had been at a distance. Up close . . . He was so different from her—all hard planes and muscles—

And enormous male bit.

A proper virgin might be alarmed, but this tipsy spinster was entranced. Eager. Her feminine bit ached— *throbbed*—to welcome him inside.

"Should you snuff the candles?" she asked, pulling back the coverlet as he joined her on the bed.

He stretched out beside her and leaned up on one elbow. "No. I want to see you, Jane, every lovely inch of you. I want to watch your skin flush, watch you open for me, hear you moan and beg me to come into you."

"Ha! I don't beg." *And I'm already flushed and damp and needy.*

His grin was extremely cocky. "We shall see, won't

we?" And then he grazed her lips with his before turning his attention elsewhere.

He stroked the side of one breast. "Remember when you tried to hide under that ridiculous shawl at Chanton Manor?"

"Um." Remember? She couldn't think of anything but the exquisite sensations his fingers were evoking. Her nipples tightened even more, and, as if connected by an invisible string, the nub between her legs throbbed. She wanted him *there*. Her feminine bit was wet, almost crying for him to visit, to slide deep—

"I've dreamed of you in that dress. And every time I do, I wake up hot and hard. It's very uncomfortable, Jane."

"Uh." *She* was uncomfortable. She arched up to encourage him to use his mouth and tongue for something other than talking. "Please, Alex."

He chuckled—and she felt the small stir of air on her aching nipple. "Are you begging already, then?"

She suddenly had no interest in making this a struggle for dominance. "Yes, I'm begging. I need you, Alex. Now."

His gaze sharpened and his face suddenly looked very stark and hungry. "I need you, too, Jane."

And then his mouth moved back to her breast, but this time close to her nipple. His tongue traced a wet circle round it.

"Alex!"

"Trust me."

She did trust him, but she still laced her fingers through his hair and tried to tug him—

Oh! The tip of his tongue flicked over one hard nub while his fingers tweaked the other.

Her hips lurched up off the bed. "Oh, Alex. Oh, Alex." It was a moan.

Or a prayer.

"Shh." His clever mouth played first with one nipple and then the other as his hand slid down over her belly, down to rest on the thatch of hair above her legs. The pressure was a relief, grounding her, keeping her from flying apart—

And then one long finger slipped down to lie, warm and still, above the aching, *throbbing* nub hidden in her folds.

So close—but not close enough.

If he wouldn't come to her, she'd come to him.

She tried to tilt her hips, but his hand kept her still.

She was panting and, well, mewling. "Alex."

"So demanding." He laughed, but the sound was short and breathless, so she forgave him. "Impatient."

"Alex!"

"If you insist." His finger brushed the sensitive nub, starting a promise of intense pleasure vibrating, and then slipped just inside her. "Zeus, Jane." He was panting too. "You are so wet. So ready."

Yes, she was ready. She was wildly, desperately, completely ready.

His finger stroked lightly over her, teasing little brushes that drew her tighter and tighter and tighter until she felt she would break.

And then she did break. She moaned and whimpered as waves of exquisite pleasure rolled through her.

But she needed something else, something to anchor her—

Alex lifted himself over her, supporting his body on his arms so he only touched her at one point—her entrance. If she hadn't still been so drugged by her release, she might have tilted her hips to take him in.

She was glad she hadn't. He finally moved, causing new ripples of delight as he slowly pushed into her. She closed her eyes to concentrate on the sensation of being stretched, filled—

"Oh!" She tensed, feeling a dull pain as something deep inside her gave way.

He stopped and waited until she relaxed. Then he slid farther in, closer to her womb. A second wave of pleasure built as he moved in and out and in, but this was different from the first. It was calmer. Deeper.

I love him.

He pushed all the way to her heart and held there, his body heavy on hers as he spilled his seed in her.

Stunned, she wrapped her arms around him, burying her face in his shoulder.

Oh God, I love him.

Chapter Sixteen

Jane woke, disoriented. The room was beginning to lighten, but full dawn was still an hour or so away. This wasn't her room in the Spinster House, and—

Lud, I'm naked! And sore between my—

The events of the last few hours came rushing back.

Alex had loved her twice during the night.

Mmm. She closed her eyes, remembering that second time. It had been almost leisurely. She'd been asleep, deep in some very, er, *exciting* dream of Alex and had come gradually awake to the sensation of a hand on her breast. When he'd seen her eyes open, he'd kissed her, slowly, thoroughly while his hand stroked down her body and the tip of one finger slipped inside her.

And found she was already wet.

He'd smiled at that, and then had shifted, raising her leg and coming into her in one smooth, deliberate, unhurried motion.

The moment his body had been fully sheathed in hers, they had climaxed, together.

God, Jane, I love you, he'd whispered, and then he'd slipped out and fallen back asleep, his arm round her waist.

And I love you, she'd answered, but she didn't know if he'd heard her.

She stared up at the ceiling, still lost in shadows. The first time she might have been able to blame on the wine, but not the second.

Oh, God, she *did* love Alex.

She turned her head to gaze at him. He looked so young and approachable in sleep, his long lashes fanning out on his cheeks, his mouth soft. A lock of hair had fallen over his forehead. She wanted to reach over and push it back off his face, but she didn't.

He'll ask me to marry him.

When he woke, he would ask—or perhaps he assumed by her actions that she'd already answered yes.

He wanted to marry; he'd been shopping for a wife. He needed an heir. And an honorable man did not consort with a virgin—nor did a well-bred virgin go to bed with a man—without marriage being understood. It was simply not done. Even Isabelle Dorring, if the story was to be believed, thought she'd be marrying her duke.

And he loves me.

She looked back at the ceiling.

And I love him, but is that enough to give up my independence?

She'd wanted for years to be on her own and had schemed and plotted to win the Spinster House tenancy once it became available. She couldn't throw it all away after two splendid tuppings.

She frowned. No, she wouldn't belittle what they'd done. Perhaps men could brush off sexual encounters— Randolph *had* visited Mrs. Conklin regularly for years—

but she couldn't. What she'd done with Alex had been far more than sport.

Lud, what if I'm carrying his child?

She blinked up at the ceiling, a confusing broth of terror and anticipation bubbling in her gut.

If she was increasing, she'd have to marry him. She couldn't bring a bastard into the world. That would be too cruel to the child, even more so if it was a boy and Alex's heir. . . .

Oh, God, Alex is an earl! If I marry him, I'll be a countess.

She felt as if an elephant had suddenly plopped its hindquarters on her chest.

If she married Alex, she'd have to leave everything behind—the village, her office, the lending library, the people she'd known all her life, Randolph. She'd have to move to his house—well, houses, she presumed. She'd have to take charge of his households. She'd have to get to know his staff, his tenants. She'd have to go to London and mingle with the *ton*.

And he lived next door to his sister. Jane would be swept up into his sister's busy—and busybodying—life. She—

She pushed the elephant firmly off her chest. She was getting ahead of herself, likely still too affected by what had happened in this bed to think clearly. It had been quite a shock to her system. Well, it wouldn't be surprising if the female body was designed to crave marriage once it engaged in procreative activities . . . unless, like Mrs. Conklin, one had chosen or been compelled to earn one's bread on one's back. The natural scientists would probably have some explanation for the phenomenon based on physiology.

She took a deep breath and tried to get her emotions and her thoughts under control. She might not have conceived.

There was no need to make any life-altering decision right now. In a month at the most, she'd know if there were any permanent consequences.

"Good morning."

She turned to see Alex leaning up on his elbow, smiling at her, his expression open and happy. Dear God, how she loved him. If he were just a man, just a Loves Bridge villager, she would—well, she might—throw away her independence and marry him. But he wasn't just a villager.

"Oh, Alex." She reached for him somewhat desperately. She needed to feel him moving in her once more, needed his weight covering her one more time before she said good-bye.

He gave her exactly what she needed, hard and fast. No kissing. No sweet words. Just seconds after she touched him, he buried himself deep inside her, his body covering hers as she came apart. She breathed him in, her arms wrapped tight around him, and wished she could keep him there forever.

"That's a lovely way to say good morning," he murmured by her ear, half panting, half laughing. And then he kissed her, as slow and carefully as he'd been fast and hard before.

I love you, she thought as he lifted himself off her.

"I'd better get dressed and go to my own room," he said, climbing out of bed. "It's possible that a few servants have recovered from yesterday's celebrations and are up and about." He grinned at her. "No need to give the Boltwoods more to gossip about."

"No." Though a large enough scandal might force her to overcome her fears.

She watched him move around the room, collecting his discarded clothing. He was smart and funny and kind, but he also had a lovely arse and wonderful shoulders and chest and . . .

And a large—and growing larger—male bit.

Her female bit clenched with the memory of its most recent visit.

Alex glanced back at her and paused, clothing in one hand, gaze sharpening. "Jane, if you keep looking at me like that, I'm going to climb back in that bed and have you again."

She shivered in anticipation. "That sounds lovely."

He snorted. "You are insatiable, Miss Wilkinson, but I will not let you tempt me into further misbehavior." He pulled on his pantaloons and buttoned his fall. "You cannot have your wicked way with me again until you are my wife." He dropped his shirt over his head so his words were a bit muffled. "I'll leave for London today, get a marriage license, and—"

His head popped out, and he looked at her. His face stilled. "What is it?"

How was she going to tell him? "I love you, Alex."

His face grew even more guarded. "Why do I hear a 'but' after that? You love me but . . . ?"

She shook her head and looked away, her throat suddenly too clogged with unshed tears to speak.

"But you can't marry me?"

She nodded.

"Why the hell not?"

He was angry. She tried to stoke an answering anger in herself, but she couldn't find any fire for it. Instead, she felt the sick, churning distress she used to feel when her father would start shouting. Then she'd slip off to her room—it was usually Mama or Randolph whom Papa was berating rather than her—and escape into a book.

She hadn't felt this way since her parents died. That was

another benefit of her spinsterhood: Her life was tranquil, undisturbed by any intense emotion.

"I don't want to be a countess." It was more than not wanting it—the thought made her heart seize.

"Bloody hell! Then you shouldn't have gone to bed with an earl."

"I know." She could blame the wine, but she didn't want to lie. The wine had only given her the courage to do what she'd wanted to do.

He looked like he would say something else, but instead he started storming around the room. "Where the hell are my boots?"

"Are they under the bed?"

He got down on his hands and knees to look. "Yes. And here's the bloody cat, as well. She'd better not have scratched the bloody leather."

Poppy shot out from under the bed, but instead of jumping up next to Jane to give her some moral support, she stalked across the floor and leapt up on a chest of drawers by the door—and then she arched her back and hissed!

Alex finished dressing and strode toward the door as well, still clearly very angry. He put his hand on the latch—and then turned back to sneer at Jane.

"You must make Isabelle Dorring proud, Miss Wilkinson. You, too, are a witch, luring a randy, idiotic man to your bed."

He didn't shout, but his cold, precise tone was almost worse.

He paused as if he expected her to brangle with him, but what could she say? He was entitled to his fury. To his pain. She should never have let her body rule her mind.

Perhaps that was what had happened to poor Isabelle. For the first time, she felt true sympathy for the woman.

Her lack of response only seemed to enrage Alex more.

"Since you've refused my offer of marriage, madam, I must assume you had a different reason to bed me." He pulled a coin from his purse and slammed it onto the chest next to Poppy.

That surprised her. "Wh-what?"

He glared at her. "I always pay for my pleasure, madam." He sniffed, sounding like she'd once imagined a haughty peer would sound. "I believe you'll find I've been quite generous, but then you did, after all, give me your virginity."

His eyes narrowed, and he said, still in that hateful, demeaning voice, "A word of advice, madam. In future, you would be better served to negotiate a sum prior to any transaction. A man can be quite stupid when his cock is doing his thinking."

She sucked in her breath.

Oh, Lord. The distress on Jane's face slammed into his gut, replacing anger with remorse.

"Jane, I'm sorry. I didn't mean that." He took a step toward her and then stopped. She was on the verge of tears.

Well, of course she was. What he'd said was cruel. And unfair. He was the one with experience. He should have kept his bloody fall buttoned.

She's the one who unbuttoned it.

That was his cock talking. He could have—*should* have—stopped her.

But she'd been so eager yesterday.

Hell, *yesterday*? She'd been eager just a few minutes ago. She'd initiated that encounter.

Zeus, as confused and upset as he was, his cock still hardened at the memory of their joining.

Well, the memory and the fact that Jane was still naked, her lovely brown hair loose about her shoulders.

Oh, God. I want her so much I ache—and not just my cock and ballocks.

His heart ached, too. He wanted her *love*.

But she didn't want him.

So why had she gone to bed with him? She'd been a virgin. He'd thought she'd meant marriage. It wasn't as if she hadn't known he was an earl.

Zeus, he'd never had a woman hold his rank *against* him, but then, Jane was not like other women. "Why don't you want to be a countess?"

She looked down at the sheets. That wasn't like Jane, either. She was usually direct to the point of bluntness.

"I don't want to leave Loves Bridge. It's my home. My work's here. My brother's here—and soon my nephew or niece."

He'd thought Jane was more annoyed by Randolph than attached to him. Was she really going to sacrifice her own life to stay near her brother?

She raised her chin. "And I don't want to give up my independence."

Ah. That rang truer. Spinsterhood was what she wasn't willing to sacrifice.

But she said she loved me.

Perhaps she does love me, but she loves her precious independence more.

She might not have a choice. "What if you've conceived?"

"I'll marry you then," she said quickly. "I won't have our child born a bastard."

Thank God he didn't have to fight *that* battle.

"And you'll write me when you know?" It was going to be a long month, waiting for word. And he did need to hear something—he wouldn't trust silence. "One way or the other?"

"Yes. I promise I'll write."

"Thank you." He cleared his throat. "One other thing." Since she was new to carnal relations, she might not have considered all aspects of the issue. "I, er, I don't mean to be insulting. It's a compliment, really, but as you were a virgin, you might not . . . that is . . . not that I'm an expert, but . . ." How to say it?

"But what, Alex?"

Best to be blunt. "You have a lusty nature, I believe, Jane. Now that you've awakened it, I suspect you will need a lot of vigorous tupping to keep you content. You may well find spinsterhood no longer satisfies you."

Jane turned bright red—even her lovely breasts were flushed.

Don't look at—don't even think about—Jane's breasts.

"It may be difficult." He cleared his throat again and admonished his cock to stop suggesting he let it remind her now exactly how lusty a nature she had. "You know we'll see each other from time to time. We'll likely both be invited to events at the castle, but we won't be able to do this"—he gestured toward the bed and rumpled bedclothes—and her naked breasts—"again."

She pulled the bedclothes up to cover herself. "I know."

"If you haven't conceived, I'll have to marry eventually." At the moment the thought of having conjugal relations with anyone but Jane was revolting, but he did have a title to pass down. He *was* an earl.

"I know."

She looked as bleak as he felt.

He would just have to hope that, if she wasn't enceinte, a few weeks of celibacy would persuade her their marriage was worth any sacrifice.

"Well, then, if you find you've changed your mind—for any reason—write me. My offer is on the table until you are completely certain you prefer spinsterhood."

"Oh. Yes. Er, thank you."

He nodded. There was no point in belaboring things. "I'm off. I think it best if I leave the castle—and the village—straightaway. I'll tell Emmett I have business at my estate that can't be put off. No one should suspect my departure has anything to do with you, but if you hear any gossip that makes you uncomfortable, let me know."

She nodded.

"Very good." He glanced at Poppy.

The cat gave him a look of feline disdain and then extended one paw to push the coin he'd slapped on the chest over the side. He watched it hit the floor, bounce, and roll under the bed. He heard it spin in smaller and smaller circles until it finally stopped.

He looked at Jane one last time and left.

Chapter Seventeen

Loves Bridge, May 1818

Jane stood in the Spinster House study and looked out on the garden. Spring had come. What had been gray and barren in February was now lush and green. The bushes were thick with concealing leaves. The ivy was running amok.

But her heart—her soul—was still in winter.

She turned away from the view and went into the sitting room where the painting of the tricolored cat that looked so much like Poppy hung. She would like a little furry companionship, but Poppy had deserted her. When Jane had come back from the castle after her short stay in February, Poppy had not.

It was probably just as well. Poppy would not have approved of all the commotion in the house recently. Once Jane had discovered she wasn't increasing, she'd decided it was time to take positive steps to move her life forward and make the Spinster House truly hers. She'd finally thrown herself into redecorating. Every spare moment had been taken up with choosing colors and fabrics. The work had not been completed until yesterday.

She smiled. One unexpected benefit had been discovering Imogen not only had quite an eye for decorating but also actually enjoyed it. She'd been happy to help, and, through working together, they'd started building a friendship.

One that would likely be completely changed when Imogen's baby came in a few months.

Jane looked around. The place did look much better. The walls were freshly painted, most of the furniture had been replaced or recovered, and new curtains hung on every window. The house was clean and modern. Perfect.

And perfectly depressing.

Redecorating had not helped her mood.

She wandered into the kitchen. Perhaps a cup of tea would lift her spirits.

She'd written to Alex—no, *Lord Evans*. She had written to Lord Evans in March, telling him their ill-advised activities had not borne fruit and releasing him from his marriage offer. It had felt wrong to hold him to it when there was no child to consider. And truthfully, she'd thought once all the renovations were done, she'd be her old self.

Apparently not.

Lud! She squeezed her eyes shut and leaned against the counter, resting her head on the cabinet. When would she stop feeling this dull ache in her heart?

At least it wasn't a throbbing pain any longer. She'd get over it eventually. She was just lucky she hadn't conceived.

She didn't feel lucky. She hadn't even felt lucky when her courses had started. She'd felt relieved, yes, but disappointed too. Bereft, really, at losing something she'd never had.

She'd cried so hard she'd made herself sick.

How ridiculous.

I'm crying now.

She swiped at her tears. She never used to be such a watering pot. She didn't know herself anymore.

Perhaps intimate relations changed a body's humors in some fundamental way.

She got down a teacup, realized it was one of the ones she'd drunk brandy from with Alex—and cried harder.

And then heard a knock at the door. Who could that be?

She wouldn't answer.

The knocking got louder.

She sighed, took out her handkerchief, and blew her nose. She'd better see who it was. Perhaps the unthinkable had occurred and someone actually wished to get a book from the lending library.

She opened the door to find Cat and baby William. "Oh!"

Cat hadn't stopped by the Spinster House with William since his birth, and Jane hadn't had time to go to the castle.

Well, Jane hadn't *made* time. There were too many unpleasant memories there.

No. Most of the memories were pleasant. Very pleasant. It was just the ending that was painful.

She smiled at William. He was nothing like the spindly creature she'd held right after his birth. "He's got so big!"

Cat laughed. "He's growing like a weed. And he should be. He eats constantly."

William gave Jane a big, toothless smile, and her heart turned over.

"Jane, it looks like you've been crying." Cat frowned at her, worry now in her eyes and her voice. "Are you all right?"

"Oh, er, yes, I'm fine. I must have got something in

my eye. It wouldn't be surprising. All sorts of ancient dust has been stirred up here the last few weeks."

Cat smiled, though she still looked suspicious. "I'm dying to see all the changes you've made."

"Then come in." Jane looked behind Cat as Cat and William stepped by her. "Where's Betty?" Betty was the village girl Cat had hired to help out with William, not that Cat needed much help. When one had grown up with nine younger siblings, one became a bit of an expert in childcare.

"At the castle."

"Oh." Unease twisted in Jane's stomach. Cat was quite alone—not counting William, of course—and there was only one reason Jane could think of for that. Cat wished to have something out with you. "Who drove you?"

"Marcus. He's at the vicarage."

Oh, Lord. If the duke had been sent off to visit his in-laws without the baby, something was definitely up, and young William was going to play a role in it. She looked at him again.

He cooed at her. He was *so* precious.

The voice that had been whispering in the back of her mind since the return of her courses whispered again.

If you marry Alex, you might have a child of your own one day.

She didn't even like babies. They were smelly, messy, demanding little animals that made her feel awkward and inexperienced. She hated feeling that way.

And, to be honest, the thought of having such responsibility for another life was quite, quite terrifying.

Anne had delivered a boy as well. She and Lord Haywood were bringing him to Loves Bridge next week for baby William's christening. Cat—and Jane, too, of course—

were surprised and delighted that Lord Haywood had overcome his natural cautiousness to attempt the journey.

"Will you take me on a tour?"

"Of course. We'll start upstairs, shall we?" Jane led the way. "Imogen was very helpful, you know."

"I'm glad. It must have been difficult for her when she came here, knowing no one but Randolph, but she seems to have settled in quite well, don't you think?"

"Yes." It was true. Imogen had made many friends in Loves Bridge.

Just as you would make friends if you married Alex and moved to his estate.

Perhaps. But there was also his meddling sister to consider.

You're Randolph's sister.

I don't meddle. She looked at Cat and William as they surveyed her refurbished bedroom. *Much.*

"Do you remember being born here, Wills?" Cat asked her son.

The baby laughed. Of course he didn't remember.

But Jane did.

They moved on to the other rooms.

Diana just wants her brother to be happy.

True.

"Oh, you've cleared out the storage room!"

"Yes." The room that had been cluttered with odds and ends—and the puppet stage—had returned to what likely had been its original purpose—a sitting room. It was very nice, but Jane couldn't bear to spend any time here. For her, it was haunted with too many memories of Alex.

She'd thought in the back of her mind that redecorating would banish Alex's ghost, but it hadn't. He was everywhere she turned—here, the kitchen, the sitting room. She couldn't escape him.

She led Cat back downstairs to show her the kitchen and the music room/study.

Imogen corresponded with Diana and had gossiped a bit about Lord Evans when she and Jane weren't comparing shades of yellow or discussing window treatments. She'd said Diana was worried about him, that he'd been morose about something since February. She'd given Jane a very speaking look at that, but Jane had just smiled and expressed sympathy—and tried to convince herself it was worry he might have to marry her that disturbed his peace.

Though since Imogen had told her this in April, when Alex should have been leaping and capering about with joy that he was a free man, Jane had not been very successful in persuading herself.

And then just last week Imogen told her Lord Evans had shocked his family by not going up to London for Bea's come-out, which Jane agreed did seem very odd, Lord Evans being so close to his niece and so supportive. One would think he'd make a point to be on hand to smooth Bea's way if he could.

"You've done a wonderful job with the place," Cat said as they finished the tour and returned to the sitting room.

Jane laughed. "It was a lot of work, but I do think everything turned out well."

"Will you hold William?" Cat asked before Jane sat down. She gestured to a bag she'd brought. "I want to spread his quilt on the floor."

"I can spread the—"

Too late. William was already heading Jane's way.

"Aren't you afraid I'll drop him?" she asked, as her arms closed round him. She held him close and watched Cat smooth out the brightly-colored cloth.

"No. Holding babies isn't hard once they can manage

their own heads." Cat smiled at Jane. "You held him when he was first born and did fine."

"Yes." His little body was so soft and yet sturdy, too. And he smelled so sweet—at least for the moment.

She looked at him a bit warily. He stared back at her and grinned—another big, toothless smile—and then began to suck on her dress. She was going to have a large wet spot, not that it mattered. None of her dresses were fragile and no one but Cat and William would see her.

Apparently her dress didn't satisfy him. He moved on to her neck, just as Diana's baby Christopher had at Chanton Manor when she'd been sitting by the field with Alex. She'd been so nervous then—but Alex had calmed her fears. He was so good with children.

Cat straightened and laughed. "It looks like Wills is hungry." She checked her watch. "Right on schedule. The little devil eats every two hours, but at least he's sleeping more at night." She sat down and opened her dress very matter-of-factly. "There we go. Give him to me."

Jane handed her the baby, and watched as, with a sound of apparent glee, he lunged for Cat's nipple and latched on. One small hand, its tiny fingers spread out, rested on Cat's breast, patting it from time to time while he fed.

Oh! Longing hit her so hard she could barely breathe. Suddenly she remembered—*vividly*—the exquisite sensation of Alex moving deep within her, the contentment—the love—of being so close to him.

"So you aren't swaddling him?" She didn't know the first thing about infants, but the ones she'd observed were usually wrapped tight.

Cat laughed. "No. He howls if he can't get to his hands. He likes to suck on them."

Wills must have felt Jane's regard, because he stopped

nursing for a moment and grinned at her, milk dribbling from his mouth, before resuming his meal.

If only we'd made a child together.

No! Remember how uncomfortable Cat was when she was pregnant! Remember the mess and confusion of the birth! Think of how Cat's life is ruled by this tiny tyrant, how she can't be away from him for long because she's his source of food.

None of that mattered now, looking at this perfect, beautiful baby.

Likely there was some scientific explanation for the silly infatuation she felt. If one focused on the discomfort, the pain, the inconvenience, and the mess of childbearing, no sane woman would consent to subject herself to it. The species would die out.

Well, all right. Likely the sensual attractions of marital relations would overcome even the most sensible woman's reservations.

Wills let go of Cat's nipple, and Cat lifted him to her shoulder, patting his back as she looked around the room. "It's odd not to see Poppy here."

"I guess she decided she prefers the castle."

Cat frowned. "That's odd, too. She's come and gone as she pleased since she first showed up at the Spinster House almost a year ago. Why move to the castle now?"

Perhaps Poppy disapproves of sharing quarters with a fallen woman.

No, that couldn't be it. Given the timing of Cat's wedding and pregnancy, Jane was almost certain she wasn't the first Spinster House spinster to fall into bed with a man she wasn't married to.

The first Spinster House spinster besides Isabelle Dorring, that was.

"Perhaps now that the curse is broken, she doesn't feel the need to stay," Jane said.

"But why come to the castle?"

"Because that's where the Duke of Hart lives?" Jane laughed at the absurdity of the exercise. "Why are we trying to comprehend Poppy's thoughts? She's a cat. She has no thoughts beyond those dealing with feeding and grooming."

"True." Cat didn't sound completely convinced of that, however. Clearly, Jane wasn't the only one who thought Poppy had a touch of the supernatural about her.

"I can't see her living in the stables," Jane said. "Where has she installed herself?"

"That's the oddest thing of all. She insists on staying in the room you had while I was here with Marcus and William. And even odder, the housemaids tell me she sniffs around on the coverlet and always settles in the exact same spot." Cat shook her head. "The housekeeper insists the bedding has been washed many times since your visit."

"Ah." *Please, God, don't let me turn bright red.*

Fortunately, little Wills emitted an impressive belch at that precise moment.

Cat focused completely on her baby. "Oh, what a good boy you are, Willsy-poo," she said in the high, singsong voice adults often use when they address infants. "That was a *big* one."

The baby grinned as if he, too, was very proud of his achievement.

Cat offered him her other breast and then rubbed his fuzz-covered head with a completely fatuous expression.

Jane heaved a cautious—and silent—sigh of relief. It looked as if she'd worried needlessly. Cat had come by only to see the refurbishments. Of course the duke had skipped the visit. He wouldn't be interested in such things. She could relax—

"I love seeing what you've done to the Spinster House, Jane, but I stopped by with another purpose in mind."

Every one of Jane's muscles tensed while her stomach dropped to keep her feet company.

She cleared the panic from her throat and tried to sound calm, even slightly bored. "Oh?"

Cat examined her rather too closely. "Yes. Well, I suppose I have *two* other purposes."

Worse and worse.

"Really?" *Don't react. Don't anticipate. It might be nothing.*

"Yes." Cat smiled at her. "The first is to ask you to be William's godmother."

"Oh!" She hadn't expected that. "Yes, of course, I will. I'm very flattered, but I thought you'd ask Anne."

"Anne will be busy with her own baby. And you were there when Wills was born. I can never thank you enough for everything you did for me—for us."

Jane felt herself flush with embarrassed pleasure. "Oh, I don't think I did a thing but pray for your mother and Mrs. Danford to come as quickly as possible. We were just fortunate Lord Evans arrived when he did and could go for help."

Jane smiled, remembering with stark clarity the relief—and happiness—she'd felt that day when she'd realized whose hard male body she'd run into.

"Yes," Cat said. "Which brings me to my second purpose for visiting."

Jane's smile froze as anxiety danced a reel up and down her spine. *Oh, no. Here it comes.*

She'd gladly face an attack of mouse-mounted spiders rather than Cat right now.

"Did something happen between you and Alex at the castle?"

Yes, something happened.

She was not about to tell Cat that. What she'd done was shocking, shameful—except shame wasn't what she felt. She had absolutely no regrets about any of the wonderful things she'd done with the earl.

Well, she did have one regret—that she wouldn't be able to do them all again.

Why not?

She ignored that shocking whisper. She'd decided. She did not want to be a countess and leave Loves Bridge.

And that's making you so happy, isn't it?

It was rather sad when one's internal voice turned to sarcasm.

"Lord Evans was all that was honorable."

"Oh." Cat looked extremely disappointed. "I was hoping he'd seduced you." She grinned. "Or you'd seduced him."

"Cat!" Dear Lord! She was beset on all sides.

For good reason. You're being an idiot.

Cat frowned. "So then what's amiss? I've never seen you so blue-deviled."

"I'm not blue-deviled." *Deny everything.*

"And I suppose you'll insist you weren't crying when I arrived?"

"I told you I-I'd got something in my eye."

Cat made a scoffing sound. "Jane, everyone knows you're in the dismals. You've been walking around quite Friday-faced since February."

Now it was her turn to make a scoffing sound—even as anxiety took to jigging in her stomach. If people were indeed speculating about her and Lord Evans . . .

Absurd. "This is the first I've heard of it."

Cat didn't look surprised. "Everyone else is afraid to mention it to you, you glower so when someone tries to approach you."

Jane snorted. "The Boltwood sisters aren't afraid of anyone or anything if they suspect there's a tasty bit of gossip to be had."

"Not in this case."

"Oh, please!"

"I mean it, Jane, though I'll grant you it does sound ludicrous." Cat frowned. "Miss Cordelia, in particular, is very worried about you."

Jane felt her jaw drop. Her eyes couldn't widen any more. Cordelia Boltwood was worried about her? It was beyond ludicrous. It was . . . it was . . .

There was no adjective to describe how unbelievable it was. She examined Cat. "You haven't been drinking, have you?"

"Of course not."

William made a little squeaking noise and they both looked down at him. He'd dropped off Cat's breast and was now fast asleep. As Jane watched, his eyes seemed to roll back under his eyelids and his half-opened little mouth wavered in and out of a smile. It looked rather alarming.

"Is he all right?"

Cat smiled and smoothed his fuzzy head again. "Oh, yes. He does this often. We think he's dreaming, though what a little baby could have to dream about, I don't know." She looked at Jane again. "But to get back to Miss Cordelia."

Oh, blast. She'd hoped they'd *not* get back to Miss Cordelia.

"She took a special interest in you and Alex when he used Mr. Denton's stage and puppets at the fair. Apparently, she'd been in love with Mr. Denton, but declined his offer of marriage because she hadn't wanted to leave her sister alone. He died a year or two later, and she's regretted her decision ever since. It's rather tragic, really." Cat sighed—and then caught and held Jane's gaze, speaking very deliberately. "She made a special trip to the castle to tell me the story. She wants to save you from the same mistake."

Jane tried to laugh, but she was only partially successful. "She probably just wanted a tour of the castle."

Cat frowned.

Yes, that hadn't been a kind—or a fair—thing to say. Miss Cordelia *had* come up after the puppet show to give her vague, unsolicited advice.

Well, the woman's story was sad, but sadder still was the fact that she had allowed herself to wallow in regret. She'd made her decision. She should have embraced it and moved on.

As you're doing?

Of course.

"I don't see how Miss Cordelia's situation has anything to do with me."

Cat's right brow arched up skeptically. "Don't you?"

"No," Jane lied.

It's only been three months. I'll get over my . . . my infatuation soon.

Mr. Denton's been dead at least twenty years, and Miss Cordelia hasn't got over him yet.

"Imogen's mentioned your low spirits too," Cat said.

"Oh?" She was surrounded by spies. "She never said anything to me about it."

But had she said something to Diana and had Diana told Alex? If so, he hadn't taken that information as a reason to come see her. It wasn't as if he didn't know where she lived.

Yes. And you told him in no uncertain terms you wouldn't marry him. Why would he come?

"She was afraid to push too much," Cat said, "since she's so new to your family, but she was concerned enough to seek me out."

Jane emitted a short, sharp breath. She *had* to nip this meddling in the bud at once.

"Cat, listen. I appreciate everyone's concern, but I can take care of myself. There's no need for anyone to worry about me."

Cat ignored her. "Alex is in very low spirits, as well," she said as she carefully transferred sleeping William from her arms to the quilt. William startled briefly at the change in location, his arms going over his head, his tiny perfect fingers splaying wide, but he settled down again almost immediately. His long lashes fanned out over his chubby cheeks, his perfect little mouth moving from time to time as if he were still suckling at Cat's breast.

"Imogen did mention Lord Evans seemed a bit out of sorts," Jane said. "Not that it is any of my concern."

"A bit out of sorts?!" Cat snorted—and caused William to startle again. "He didn't go up to London for his niece's come-out."

"Yes, so she said. I was sorry to hear it, but I don't see what it has to do with me."

Cat rolled her eyes. "It has everything to do with you, Jane. The man is in love with you—and I think you're in love with him."

Jane pressed her lips together. Blast it, her heart had leapt at Cat's words—or at least the words about Alex. She struggled to speak dispassionately. "Has Lord Evans confessed his feelings to you or the duke?"

Cat frowned. "Of course not. Men don't talk about their feelings."

"I see." Jane's stomach sank. Fool! Clearly she needed to face facts. She thought she'd been doing that, but this sinking feeling just proved that what she'd really been doing was building air castles. "Has it occurred to you that Lord Evans may be distressed—if he is indeed distressed— over something completely unrelated to me?"

"No."

"He might have had a financial reversal."

"Marcus says Alex is like Midas—everything he touches turns to gold."

"Perhaps he . . . he had a falling out with his m-mistress." It hurt to say that, but she couldn't be naïve. Yes, Lord Evans had said he didn't have a Mrs. Conklin, but he was a member of the *ton*, a peer. She'd read enough gossip columns to know mistresses were common among that set.

"He doesn't have a mistress."

"You can't know that."

"Marcus knows."

"Then perhaps . . ." Jane tried to think of another possible excuse.

"Nor does Alex have a dog that died or a ruined pair of boots or any other ridiculous thing you can come up with." Cat leaned forward, her eyes catching and holding Jane's. "Alex didn't even stay to see the baby, Jane. Marcus was surprised and a bit hurt by that. Instead he left directly from the castle the morning after William was born—after you and he had spent the night there quite unchaperoned."

"Oh."

She could use a distraction. She looked down at William, but he was, unfortunately, still sleeping peacefully. Didn't that baby ever cry?

Cat touched her hand. "I want you—and Alex—to be happy, Jane. And neither of you is happy now."

"But—"

Cat raised her brows, clearly waiting to refute Jane's next argument—and suddenly Jane was tired of arguing. The truth was she *wasn't* happy and she was growing more and more afraid that she'd never be happy again.

"And there's more, Jane."

"More?" What more could there be?

Fortunately, William finally started to fuss. Well, and Jane suspected the duke and Mr. and Mrs. Hutting might be starting to fuss, as well. Cat had been here quite a while.

Cat scooped up the baby, flipped him over, and sniffed his bottom. "I think I can wait to change him until I get to the vicarage."

Some good news for once!

"I'll help you pack up." Jane stuffed the quilt into Cat's bag and then they headed for the door.

"Marcus wrote to Alex a few weeks ago," Cat said, "asking him to be William's godfather."

Jane's heart started thudding painfully. *Alex will be here next week.*

"We got his reply this morning."

She swallowed and tried to sound calm. "Oh?" *What am I going to do? I can't miss the christening, especially now that I've agreed to be William's godmother.*

Alex will be an adult about it. We'll both ignore each other. That will work.

That would be a little hard to do in such an intimate setting.

"Jane, did you hear me?" Cat looked very serious. Even William was frowning at her.

"Oh. No. I'm sorry. I'm afraid I was woolgathering."

Cat shook her head. "No. You were panicking because you thought you'd see Alex again."

She forced herself to shrug nonchalantly. "Why would I care if I saw Lord Evans?"

"That's the question, isn't it?" Cat's brows were raised again—and then she looked down at William. "Well, you don't have to worry. Alex declined."

Jane stared at Cat. She must have misheard. "Declined? Declined what?"

"He said he was very sorry, but he couldn't be William's godfather."

"Oh." Perhaps Alex thought Lord Haywood, as the duke's cousin, should have that honor.

"Because he's not coming to the christening."

"What?!" Jane knew she was gaping, but what Cat had just said was shocking. Alex and the duke were very close friends. Alex loved children. Only some very serious issue would keep him away from the christening.

A different sort of panic grabbed her by the throat. "His family . . . they're all right, aren't they?" Though surely Imogen would have told her if there was a problem.

"His family is fine."

"And the earl? You aren't hiding something from me, are you? Oh, God, he's ill, isn't he?" Anxiety made her voice shrill.

Cat put a steadying hand on her shoulder. "If he's ill, it's with lovesickness. Imogen said Diana and the girls think he's pining for you—and I'd say you're pining for him."

"No—"

Cat held her hand up to stop her. "Jane, you are my friend, and Alex is Marcus's friend. We want to see you both happy." Her brow wrinkled with concern. "I know it's none of my affair, but can you at least write to him?"

"Ah . . ." Write to Alex? What would she say?

"Clearly, you can't marry him if you don't wish to, but it would be nice if you and he could find a way that you could both be at William's christening." Cat made a face. "Does that sound selfish? But I'm thinking of more than just that one occasion. Marcus and I want you both in our lives. It would be so much more comfortable if you could work out your differences now."

That was true. "Very well. I'll write him today."

Cat grinned. "Excellent. I'll stop by on our way home from the vicarage. If the letter is ready, Marcus will send it by messenger immediately."

"All right." A deadline would force her to attend to the matter at once. There was no point in putting it off. It would just hang over her, or she'd revise and rewrite and rewrite again until the day of the christening arrived.

But what am I going to say?

Should I tell him the truth? Tell him everything? But if I do that . . .

Oh, I don't know what I want.

But she knew she hated the thought she might be the cause of Alex's unhappiness. And the fact was, much as she'd denied it, she wasn't happy either.

Perhaps I don't want my independence more than I want Alex. Perhaps my love for him is stronger than my fear of change.

She watched Cat make her way down the walk and across the street, and then she closed the door, leaning her forehead against it briefly.

Courage. Twenty years from now I don't want to have Cordelia Boltwood's regrets.

She straightened and headed to the study for a pen and paper.

Chapter Eighteen

Evans Hall

Alex rode up to the stables as the sun sank low in the sky. His tenants might be wondering why the lord of the manor kept showing up to help rebuild stone fences and mend thatched roofs, but he needed the physical exercise. He hoped he'd worn himself out enough to sleep tonight without the aid of half a bottle of brandy.

"Milord, I've been on the watch for ye," his head groom said, coming up to him the moment Horatio put a hoof in the stable yard. "I was about to send someone to find ye."

Anxiety cramped Alex's gut. "What's amiss, O'Reilly?" he asked as he swung out of the saddle.

O'Reilly shrugged and handed him a letter. "Maybe nothing, but a man in the Duke of Hart's livery delivered this about half an hour ago. They sent him down from the house with it so I could give it to ye straightaway."

"Ah." Anxiety moved from his gut to his chest. Why was Marcus writing to him? Had something happened to the baby?

He took a deep breath. Likely he only wished to urge him to reconsider his decision about the christening.

He'd been very sorry to decline the invitation, especially the honor of being William's godfather, but much as he wished otherwise, he found he just couldn't bear to see Jane. Perhaps someday he'd be able to meet her and act as if she were merely a friend of his friend's wife, but not yet. The wound was still too raw.

Raw? Hell, three months after the fact, it was still a gaping, jagged gash. He had to force himself to get out of bed in the morning.

She said she loved me. She—

No. He slammed the door shut on those thoughts as he did every time they tried to force their way in. He wished he could lock and bolt that door forever, but no matter how many hours he rode poor Horatio, how hard he worked his body, or how many glasses of brandy he downed, the memories still teased and taunted him.

The fact was she didn't love him enough.

He turned the letter over in his hands. As he'd expected, the direction was written in Marcus's bold scrawl.

Why had Marcus sent this by messenger?

The christening was still almost a week away. There was no urgency. Nate was going to be there, so they didn't need Alex as godfather. Regular post would have worked perfectly well.

Horatio nudged his shoulder, understandably annoyed at being ignored. And O'Reilly was still standing in front of him, patiently waiting for him to come out of his reverie.

"Thank you, O'Reilly. Will you take charge of Horatio for me?"

"Of course, milord." O'Reilly's brow furrowed as he

took Horatio's bridle. "Ye've been riding him hard again." He couldn't quite keep a note of criticism out of his voice.

O'Reilly would take issue with the Prince Regent himself if he thought he wasn't treating a horse properly.

"But not too hard, I think," Alex said.

O'Reilly's brow arched up. Clearly, he didn't agree. Then he glanced at the letter in Alex's hands. "If ye'll be wanting a horse again today, milord, it will have to be Primrose. Horatio needs his rest."

Alex nodded. He'd learned long ago not to argue with O'Reilly about such things, but this time the man's stubbornness wasn't a problem. "It's almost night. I'm not planning on going anywhere."

O'Reilly looked at the letter again. "Best read that afore ye make up yer mind. The fellow who brought it thought it so important, he was going to try to hunt ye down himself." He snorted. "As if he could find ye in all these fields. He'd only take himself off when I swore on my mother's grave that I'd keep a watch out and hand it to ye the moment I saw ye."

With one last dark look at the letter, O'Reilly took Horatio off to the stables.

Alex watched him until he disappeared into the stable's shadows and then looked back at the paper in his hand. *I'm delaying.*

Yes, he was. He was afraid to discover what was inside. *Best get it over with.*

He walked over to a more private location under a nearby oak and broke the seal. Another sheet fluttered to the ground. Hmm. He picked up the errant paper as he scanned the cover letter. *I don't know what this says,* Marcus had written, *but whatever it is, I'm sure you need to read it.*

His heart attempted to leap into his throat and strangle him. Dear Lord!

That might have been a prayer.

No. He crumpled the paper in his fist. Reading this would be like rubbing salt in his wound.

I should throw the bloody thing on the fire. I—

I'm not a coward, am I?

It had been three months since he'd left Loves Castle and he *still* felt as if someone had cut his heart out with a blunt knife. Whatever the letter said could not make things worse.

He smoothed out the paper. As he expected, it was from Jane.

Dear Lord Evans it began—but then she'd crossed out "Lord Evans" and scribbled "Alex" over it. *Cat tells me you are not coming to William's christening. I hope you will reconsider. I—*There was a blot and several more cross-outs. Was that "wish" Jane had written? He couldn't be certain. *I regret what I said at the castle. I—we—*More crossing out. *I can't write it in a letter. Perhaps we can talk if you come, though I understand if you don't want to see me.*

There was another blot here as if Jane had been startled and shaken her quill.

Cat's at the door to get this. Please excuse its sloppiness. It's my tenth attempt.

Yr Obedient Servant,

Miss Jane Wilkinson

Ha! Jane was no one's obedient anything, but especially not servant.

He sighed and looked out over the lawn. What was the point of talking? She didn't want to be a countess and he was an earl. No matter how much he loved her, he couldn't cast away his title and run off to live in Loves Bridge. He had responsibilities to his people and his land. Not to mention that Waldo, his distant cousin and heir, would be furious. An unmarried Oxford don in his sixties, he would not be at all happy to leave his books, and he certainly would not wish to have anything to do with getting an heir of his own.

No, there was no point in talking, but Jane was right. He shouldn't stay away from the christening. That *was* cowardly of him. And selfish. He would write Marcus tonight, before he changed his mind.

He glanced at the letter one more time before stuffing it in his pocket—and saw he'd overlooked some words at the very bottom of the page. They were blurred as if she'd written them in haste and folded the paper before the ink was dry. What did they say?

He squinted, trying to make them out—

I miss you.

Zeus!

Had he read that correctly?

The light was beginning to fail. He held the sheet closer, turned so he got the last of the sun.

Yes. He'd read it correctly.

He closed his eyes as the words sunk in. *She misses me. Jane misses me.*

She regretted something, something she couldn't put in a letter. Their union, perhaps? She *should* regret it—it was not the sort of thing a well-bred spinster should have done.

No, she'd written she regretted something she'd *said*.

She wanted to talk. The christening was not for another week.

What did she want to say that she couldn't put in a letter?

He needed to know the answer now, not in a week.

He turned and strode toward the stables. "O'Reilly," he called, "I'll be needing Primrose after all."

Later, just outside Loves Bridge

Alex reined Primrose in when they reached a fork in the road near Loves Bridge. She was a good horse, but she wasn't Horatio. It had taken far longer than he'd planned to make the relatively short journey from Evans Hall. The sun had set and even twilight was fading.

At least there was a full moon.

Blast it, he should have waited until morning to set off. What had he been thinking?

He hadn't been thinking. He'd had a vague notion of stopping at the Spinster House, talking to Jane, and then . . . what?

Well, yes, he'd hoped their discussion would end in a marriage offer accepted and a romp in Jane's bed.

Idiot.

Even if he'd ridden Horatio, it would have been hard to make it to Loves Bridge and back in the same day, and yet he hadn't taken time to pack a bag. And if things didn't go well with Jane, he couldn't stay at the inn without everyone in the village knowing he was there. How was he going to explain that without sullying Jane's reputation?

Perhaps he could sneak off to the castle. He could pretend he'd had a sudden urge to talk to Marcus about . . . nothing.

Right.

He frowned at the road that ran off to the left and would take him past the inn and by the village green. He hadn't given this harebrained dash any thought at all. Someone was bound to see him—he'd swear the Boltwoods had spyglasses trained on all the public areas—and then word would spread. Everyone would start speculating—if they weren't already—about the nature of his connection to Jane.

Primrose, an extremely, er, *cautious* horse, shied then, bringing his attention back to her. Something had moved in the shadows.

"Shh, Primrose," he said soothingly, patting her neck. "It was only a rabbit or a fox or—"

A tricolored cat.

"Merrow." Poppy walked calmly into the moonlight, twitching her tail impatiently as if she'd been waiting for him.

"Good evening, Poppy. What are you doing out and about?"

And what am I doing talking to a cat again?

She gave him a very direct look and then headed down the right side of the fork.

"Lovely to see you, too. Have a good evening," he called after her, as he urged Primrose forward, along the road to the left. He *should* turn back, but he couldn't come this far without seeing Jane.

Perhaps he'd be lucky and no one would notice him. Or they wouldn't recognize him in the dim light.

Right. They wouldn't wonder at all at a man riding up to the Spinster House at night. Of course—

"Mer*row*!"

Poppy darted in front of them, almost under Primrose's hoofs, setting the horse to dancing.

Even a placid, plodding steed could be hard to handle when spooked. It took Alex some effort to get Primrose back under control.

"What were you thinking?" he yelled at Poppy.

She's a cat. She doesn't think.

But Poppy looked as if she had a definite plan. She walked back toward the road he hadn't taken.

Alex tested his theory by having Primrose take a few steps farther along his current path.

Poppy's ears went back and she hissed, making Primrose shy again.

Clearly, the cat wanted him to take the other road. Hmm. It might connect to the lane that ran past Randolph's office. Then he could take the path through the woods to reach the Spinster House. It would be better than riding through the center of Loves Bridge—if Poppy would even let him choose that route.

"Very well, Poppy. Since you insist." He started Primrose down the cat's preferred path, noticing as he did so that Poppy stationed herself behind him in case he changed his mind.

He was a bit concerned a short time later when he turned off the lane and up the narrow, rocky path through the woods, but Primrose, while slow, was surefooted, and there was enough moonlight filtering through the trees that they could see where they were going. When they reached the gate to the churchyard, he dismounted and looked around. There was no one in sight, thank God. He led the horse out of the woods and along the walk between the headstones.

He'd never been one to worry much about the supernatural, but if any of the "guests" here objected to his presence, he—and perhaps more importantly, Primrose—didn't feel it. At least the dead weren't going to gossip about him. It felt quite peaceful, actually, the moon lighting his way, the sky so clear he thought he could see every star God created.

He passed Isabelle Dorring's headstone. Was her soul finally at rest now that her curse was over?

If there had ever been a curse, that is.

He led Primrose down the hill and across the road toward the Spinster House—and his spirits fell. The place was completely dark. Was Jane not there?

"Merrow."

But Poppy was. The cat stepped out of the shadows by an old lean-to near the garden gate, causing Primrose and—yes, he'd admit it—Alex to jump.

"Take a shortcut, did you?"

Poppy stared at him, and then headed for the garden.

Alex took a moment to look inside the shabby lean-to. There was a single stall, but the place was dark and cramped and Primrose didn't appear eager to stay there. He'd do better to let her roam the garden. He'd just—

Good God! Poppy had suddenly started caterwauling, the noise loud enough to wake the dead. Was she trying to get Isabelle to return? She'd more likely have the vicar running over to see if someone was being murdered.

Perhaps that's her plan—to have Mr. Hutting discover me here.

He'd admit he wasn't totally opposed to that outcome.

He sighed and urged Primrose out of the building and through the garden gate. He didn't want Jane to be forced into marriage. That would be painful for both of them.

I'll have to try to muzzle the cat.

But Poppy had sharp claws—he'd seen the evidence of that on Nate's boots. He'd rather not have his blood splattered over the plants. He'd need something to throw over her. . . .

He wrestled out of his coat as he hurried toward the Spinster House's back door where Poppy was performing.

Full night had fallen only fifteen or twenty minutes earlier, but Jane had donned her nightgown, brushed and braided her hair, and climbed into bed long before the light faded.

She lay stiff as a board under the coverlet, her eyes wide open. She was afraid it was going to be a long night with little sleep.

She'd tried reading, but she couldn't focus on the words. She couldn't focus on anything.

Has Alex got my letter yet? Has he read it?

He probably won't read it at all.

But what if he does? What will he think? Will I hear from him? Maybe I won't. Maybe he'll just write to the duke. Maybe—

"Meerrooooww!"

She bolted out of bed. What the hell was that? It sounded as if someone was being murdered in the garden.

She tried to open the window, but it was stuck fast. She pressed her nose against the glass, craning this way and that—there! Poppy was sitting by the back door.

As she watched, the cat let out another bloodcurdling yowl.

"All right, all right. I'll let you in," she muttered as she lit a candle in the fire and hurried downstairs. Poppy was going to wake the vicar if she kept this up—or more likely the Boltwood sisters, who seemed able to hear a pin drop anywhere in the village at any time of day or night.

She'd admit, though, that she was happy Poppy was back. The Spinster House had felt very lonely without her.

It's not Poppy's *absence that's made me feel lonely.*

Sadly, that was very true. She missed Alex. She missed the intellectual stimulation and excitement of bantering with him. She missed his humor, his kindness, his male way of thinking. His voice. His . . .

Oh *God*, she missed his body.

She'd thought—on the rare occasions she'd thought about it at all—that losing your virginity was just that—a loss. It was the beginning of years of subjugation, the price women were forced to pay to avoid a lifetime lived in the shadows as a poor relation.

When she'd taken Alex to her bed, she hadn't lost a thing—except her heart.

Poppy yowled again.

Lud! She needed to attend to that crazed cat before she had the village on her doorstep.

She almost ran the last few steps.

"Poppy," she said, as she opened the door, "I—*eek!*"

A man was there, too, in his shirtsleeves, his coat raised in both hands—

Oh. It was Alex.

"I'm sorry, Jane." He lowered his arms as Poppy darted past her feet. "I didn't mean to startle you."

Her heart had stopped when she'd seen him. Now it started up again with slow, painful, breath-stealing thuds.

The letter just went out this afternoon. He couldn't have got it and come so quickly, could he?

He's here.

"Ah." She swallowed. Tried again. "What are you doing here?"

"Trying to stop your cat from waking the neighborhood." He sounded a little breathless, too. "And not get clawed in the process."

"She's not my cat." Blast, did she sound annoyed? She wasn't, of course. She was . . . nervous. But she saw Alex flinch slightly, his mouth twisting briefly into what looked like a grimace.

"I mean what are you doing *here*?" She gestured to encompass the house and the garden.

Wait—was that a horse wandering in the foliage?

"I got your letter."

"Oh. But . . . it only went out this afternoon." His gaze sharpened. "*Did* you miss me?"

"Ahh."

"What couldn't you put in writing?"

"Ahh." She had to tell him she'd changed her mind and would marry him. But she'd thrown his offer back at him when she'd told him she hadn't conceived. Perhaps he was done with her.

Cat and Imogen said he'd been in low spirits. And he was here. He'd come at once.

"I see I've made a mistake," Alex was saying. "My apologies for disturbing you." He started to turn away.

Oh, God! He was leaving. "Wait!" She lunged forward to grab his arm. She could feel his muscles under the fine lawn of his shirt. "Don't go. You're right. We need to talk. I need to tell you—"

The enormity of the situation struck her again and her throat closed. If she let him in now, she would go to bed with him. She knew it with the same degree of certainty that she knew the sun would rise in the morning. And if she went to bed with him again, she'd marry him and leave Loves Bridge to become a countess with all the frightening, *public* responsibilities that entailed.

Am I entirely certain I want that?

He'd raised an eyebrow, waiting for her to finish her sentence.

"Things." She swatted at some flying insect. Her candle was beginning to attract a crowd. "I need to tell you things."

He nodded as he picked a sizable moth off her nightgown, his hand brushing against her breast.

The accidental touch shot through her, and a predictable part of her trembled.

"I suggest we close the door then," he said, removing yet another moth from her hair.

"Yes. Do come in." She backed up and he stepped over the threshold, shutting the door behind him.

And somehow sucking all the air out of the room.

He smiled. "I take it you don't mind moths?"

"Ahh, no. Just spiders. And mice." *Think. Breathe. Tell him you love him. That you'll marry him.*

What if he's changed his mind and doesn't want to marry me?

Why would he have ridden all the way from Evans Hall if he'd changed his mind?

"Y-you got my letter?" she asked as she lit the candle in the wall sconce and then blew hers out. She was shaking too much to be trusted with fire.

Of course he'd got her letter. He'd just said so. He would think she'd lost her wits completely.

He nodded. "Yes. Do you want me to put my coat back on?"

His coat? Oh, right. It was rather scandalous that he was here in his shirtsleeves, but then she was here in her nightgown.

And I've already seen everything his clothes hide.

Her heart—and other parts—throbbed.

"No."

She wanted him to drop the blasted coat and bring her up against him. To kiss her and make love to her so she didn't have to say anything.

He stayed with his back to the door, coat clutched in his hands almost like a shield.

Poppy came back, perhaps to see what was keeping them, and found a moth that had flown in before the door shut. She pounced on it and then batted it around on the floor.

"What couldn't you put in the letter, Jane?"

She tore her eyes away from Poppy's antics to look back at Alex. His face was guarded.

This is ridiculous. Where is my courage? I've never been a cowering, pigeon-hearted female before.

She raised her chin. "I've changed my mind. I'll marry you"—her voice faltered—"that is, if you still want to marry me."

His smile was blinding but sadly, brief. "I thought you didn't want to be a countess."

"Right. I would rather not, but I realize there's no way around it if I'm going to marry you." She frowned. "It would be so much easier if you weren't an earl, you know."

He raised a brow. "Would you rather I be a penniless itinerant, like Mr. Wertigger, perhaps?"

She wrinkled her nose. "No. But maybe a nice, solid farmer."

"Like Mr. Barker."

She laughed. "No, not like Mr. Barker."

Alex smiled in an encouraging fashion. "In a way, I *am* a farmer. Much of my wealth and my attention is on my lands and crops."

"You are *not* a farmer."

He shrugged, clearly deciding not to brangle with her further on that head. "And I'm afraid you will have to leave the village and come live with me." He leered at her. "It will not be at all convenient for me to have my wife so far away." He grinned. "And I believe once we exchange our vows, you will be ineligible to continue on here."

She frowned. "I do not like change, you know."

"No? Excellent. I certainly don't wish to worry that you'll be thinking of changing husbands."

She glared at him. "And don't think to be taking mistresses. I will not stand for that sort of behavior."

He waggled his brows. "Good. If our night at Loves

Castle is any indication, I'll have no time or energy for a mistress—I'll be worn to a thread keeping you satisfied."

She flushed, remembering all too well what they'd done at the castle—which she'd like to do again. But not yet.

"I have no experience with servants, you know, or with running any household larger than Randolph's."

"Jane, you're intelligent and capable—you've run Randolph's business since you were fourteen, correct?"

"Yes."

"And really, Mrs. Frampton, my housekeeper, is very good at what she does. She'll likely be just as happy if you don't meddle too much with her system." His grin turned a bit lascivious. "I'm not out to hire a steward or estate manager, Jane. I want a wife."

Alex had grown up in the peerage. He had no idea what a change this would be for her. "I can't spend my entire life in your bed, you know."

His smile turned positively lecherous. "That's a pity." He stepped closer. "My estates have run well enough without a countess, Jane. Don't worry. If you find something you enjoy doing, then do it. Otherwise"—if it was possible to look even *more* lecherous, he did—"you can help me secure the succession."

"But what about your London town house and other obligations?" She stepped back. "I've never even been to London."

"Then I'll enjoy showing you the sights."

"I don't know the first thing about being a countess. All your friends will laugh at me."

"They will not. My closest friends are Marcus and Nate, and they will be delighted." He smiled. "As will their wives."

"I'm twenty-eight. Firmly—happily"—*until now*—"on the shelf. Are you certain you wish to marry me?"

"Yes." He cupped her face. "Jane, I'll confess I thought I was in love with Charlotte earlier this year. Having her jilt me, realizing she'd never loved me . . . well, it shook my confidence. But what I feel for you . . ." He smiled. "What I felt for Charlotte is nothing at all like what I feel for you. I know now that when I offered for her it was the idea of marriage and family that I loved, not, I'm embarrassed to say, Charlotte." He sighed. "I never really knew her. The woman I thought she was was a figment of my imagination."

"Why do you think you know me?"

"Don't I?" He swept an errant tear away with his thumb—she hadn't realized she was crying. "Aren't you a fiercely independent, intelligent woman who cares deeply for the few"—he smiled—"the *very* few people you let get close to you?"

She flushed. "You flatter me."

He grinned. "Then let me rephrase that. You're a stubborn, infuriating, maddening female who gives no quarter in an argument"—his smile turned heated—"or in bed. And I wouldn't want you any other way."

"Nonsense. I'm nothing of the sort."

That surprised a snort of laughter from him. "Right. My mistake. You're a meek, quiet Miss. Everyone says so."

She had to laugh at that.

He smiled, but then his expression turned serious. "Marry me, Jane. We'll face the challenges that come together."

She looked at him, caught in the moment of decision. She could hold to the past and the comfort habit and familiarity brought or she could take his hand and jump into the unknown.

She would be brave.

She closed the last distance between them, putting her hands on his chest. "Yes, Alex. Yes, I'll marry you."

"Jane!" His voice held joy and relief and passion. His arms went round her, crushing her to him with a need she shared, and then his mouth came down on hers.

Ahh. This was what she wanted. She parted her lips and welcomed him in, pressing up against him, pulling his shirt from his pantaloons, running her hands up his hard, muscled back. This was what she'd missed.

His lips had moved to her neck, so her mouth was free. "Come upstairs, Alex. Come to bed."

"Can't." His hand cupped her breast through the thin fabric of her nightgown. "I left Primrose loose in your garden, still saddled and bridled."

"Primrose?" Her hands had dived down to cup his arse and pull him closer.

"Horse." He was panting. "Been riding Horatio into the ground." He paused to grin at her. "Horatio and O'Reilly, my head groom, will be so happy I can"—his lips turned up into a slight leer—"ride something—*someone*—else now."

She took advantage while he spoke to slip the first buttons on his fall free.

He frowned. "Remember. Primrose."

"Primrose can wait." She rubbed against the prominent bulge straining against his fall. "But *I* can't. I need you now. Part of me is literally crying for you. It's wet and—"

And he covered his ears with his hands. "Primrose. In your garden."

She took the opportunity to pull off her nightgown so she stood naked in front of him. Then she lifted her arms and started to loosen her braid. "It won't take long. I think I'll come apart the moment you touch me."

His face was tense with need. "I'm trying to be noble."

"You *are* noble. You're an earl." She came back to free his fall's straining buttons before they popped.

He didn't try to stop her. Instead his hands went to stroke her naked arse. "I—I doubt P-Poppy will approve."

He didn't try to stop her. Instead his hands went to stroke her naked arse. "I-I doubt P-Poppy will approve."

"I think she will. She didn't object at the castle. In fact, I suspect she instigated our union." There was one more button left. Jane paused to address the cat. "What do you say, Poppy?"

They both looked down to see Poppy licking her paws. There was no sign of the moth. Had she eaten it?

Ugh. Best not think about that.

Poppy paused long enough to blink at them and yawn—and then she returned to her toilet.

"I'd say she approves." Jane worked the last button free and Alex's lovely, long, thick male bit sprang out into her hands. "Or at least she doesn't object."

Alex made a sound that was a cross between a grunt and a groan. Then he scooped her up and carried her to the sitting room settee.

"I'll never make it upstairs to your bed," he said as he deposited her on the less-than-comfortable piece of furniture.

Comfort didn't matter.

"Neither will I." Jane jerked his pantaloons down to his thighs.

"Let me get my boots off first."

"No time for that, either."

Their joining wasn't polished or elegant or graceful. It also wasn't long. On his first thrust, the now-familiar waves of pleasure spread through her. On his second, his warm seed flooded her. This time she welcomed it, hoped it would take root and would give them a child.

But if it didn't, she looked forward to trying again.

And again.

"Lord, Jane, you are going to be the end of me," Alex said, lifting himself off her. "You *are* a witch."

She grinned. "That's been said of the Spinster House spinster before."

"I've said it to you before, if you'll remember." He fastened his pantaloons—she stayed sprawled naked on the settee, enjoying the way his eyes studied her.

"I believe you also told me I have a lusty nature and will require a lot of 'vigorous tupping' to keep me content." She grinned. "I hope you are prepared to perform your marital duties, my lord."

"God save me, I shall attempt to, er, rise to the occasion." He scooped up her nightgown and tossed it at her. "And now, Primrose awaits—patiently, I hope."

Lud, she wished Alex didn't have to leave. "You aren't going to ride all the way back to Evans Hall tonight, are you?"

"No." He tugged on his jacket. "I'm going to stop at the castle and see if they'll let me stay the night."

Jane brightened. "You can stay here."

He frowned at her, even though he looked tempted. "No, I cannot. Remember Primrose."

"There's a stable of sorts outside."

"*Of sorts* being the point. We—Primrose and I—looked at it and found it wanting."

Well, yes, likely it was on the verge of collapse. None of the spinsters she knew had kept a horse.

"And by stopping at the castle I can tell Marcus and Cat our good news and discover if they object to us marrying here the day of the christening. That is, if the plan suits you, of course. I favor it because Nate and Anne would be able to attend, but if you prefer, we can choose a different day." He grinned. "But not too far off, if you please. We must consider your lusty nature."

Her lusty nature wanted to drag him up to her bedroom and never let him leave.

"The day of the christening is fine if Cat and the duke agree." Jane would be happy to marry Alex here in the drawing room with only two witnesses, just as the Duke and Duchess of Benton had, but the christening was next week. She could wait that long. And she didn't want their marriage to appear a completely harum-scarum affair.

"Excellent. I'll talk to the vicar in the morning."

"And then stop here?" Perhaps she could lure him upstairs. . . .

"No." He laughed. "I know what that look in your eyes means. You are not going to have me again until we say our vows before God and man."

"That sounds like a challenge." She stood, dropping her nightgown on the floor.

He picked it up and handed it to her.

She reached for him instead, but he evaded her grasp— and then Poppy planted herself between them.

"Excuse me, Poppy," she said, moving to step around the cat.

"*Merrow!*" Poppy swiped at her naked foot, missing it by an inch—perhaps on purpose.

"I believe that was a warning," Alex said. "Poppy agrees it's time for me to go." He headed for the door.

"I don't know why." Jane grudgingly put on the nightgown. "She didn't complain before."

"Perhaps she's in communication with Primrose," he

said, and then laughed when Jane gave him an incredulous look. "You must agree nothing about Poppy is normal."

"True." *And Poppy looks rather smug about that.*

"After I talk to the vicar, I'll ride for London to get the marriage license and break the news of our wedding to my mother and sister." He frowned. "They will want to come, of course. I'd better mention that to Marcus in case it affects his feelings on having a joint celebration. This might turn out to be a rather large party, since Diana will wish to bring all the children."

Jane's stomach fluttered with something other than desire. Imogen's father hadn't wanted Imogen to waste herself on a solicitor's son. Alex's family might feel the same about him marrying a solicitor's sister.

"Will they approve of me? I'm not much of a catch for an earl."

He laughed. "You must be kidding. They'll be delighted. Didn't you see how they were trying to push us together at Chanton Manor?"

She'd suspected Diana, at least, had ulterior motives when she'd sent her down to the lake where Alex was swimming.

"Don't worry," he said, giving her a quick—a far too quick—kiss. "They'll be happy because I'm happy. And I am happy—very, very happy."

He grinned at her and then he left.

"He did look happy, didn't he, Poppy?"

Poppy yawned—which in this case Jane would take for agreement—and then headed upstairs.

"I suppose it *is* time for bed," Jane said, following behind. She wished her companion was Alex, but in less than a week, she'd be married. Which raised another question.

"What's going to become of you and the Spinster House, Poppy? I don't think any new Spinster House candidates have come to Loves Bridge since the lottery last year."

Poppy paused to look back at her and give her an inscrutable smile before running up the rest of the steps.

Epilogue

Loves Bridge, a week later

"What a difference a year makes," Alex said. He was standing with Marcus and Nate on the edge of the village green, enjoying a few moments of calm while the party celebrating his marriage and the christening of Marcus's son went on nearby.

The entire village was there laughing and talking and toasting, well, everything. And it wasn't just the village. His mother and John Grant had come, along with Diana and Roger and their brood. Rachel and some of the other girls were playing with the Hutting children. Caroline, Diana's fourteen-year-old, might even be flirting a bit with the vicar's sons.

Marcus's mother, Mrs. Cullen, and her second husband had traveled all the way from Ireland—they were speaking to Emmett at the moment—and even the Duke and Duchess of Benton and their son were in attendance.

"Yes." Marcus tugged his cravat out of William's grasping fingers. "This time last year I was still under the bloody curse and now?" He laughed as the baby managed to get a handful of the white cloth in his mouth. "My linen will never be the same."

"At least you're not sporting baby spit-up," Nate said, his son asleep on his shoulder, a wet patch of drool and, yes, baby curds decorating his coat.

Marcus grinned. "Not yet, but I likely will be after William's next feeding." He looked at Alex. "Are you certain you wish to follow us into fatherhood?"

"Yes." With luck and hard work—he grew hard at the thought of the, er, *work* involved—he and Jane would have a son or daughter next May.

Alex's eyes found Jane again, not that they'd ever strayed very far from her. She was laughing, talking to Cat and Anne. She looked as happy as he felt—and he felt very, very happy.

"Are you still determined to take your bride back to Evans Hall tonight?" Marcus asked. "You're more than welcome to stay over at the castle, you know."

"Yes, Alex," Nate said. "Do stay. Anne and I will be there. It's been too long since we've had a chance to sit and share a glass of brandy."

Clearly, fatherhood had muddled his friends' thinking.

"Much as I enjoy your company, I do not intend to spend my wedding night drinking brandy—or anything else—with you two."

Marcus laughed. "Oh, right. I suppose you have other plans."

"Yes." *Many very detailed, very carnal other plans.* He consulted his watch. How soon could he and Jane politely be on their way?

"You should probably wait another hour," Marcus said, laughing, "if you don't want people's thoughts going immediately to what you'll be"—he grinned—"*up* to tonight."

Nate snorted, causing his son to startle. "From the look in Alex's eyes, I don't believe he's waiting for nightfall."

It was time to change the subject.

"What are you going to do about the Spinster House now that the curse is broken and all the interested Loves Bridge spinsters have been turned into wives, Marcus?" Alex asked.

Marcus frowned. "I'm not sure. I suppose I should ask Randolph—or Jane."

"Ask Jane what?" Jane said, coming up with Cat and Anne.

"What is to become of the Spinster House now that the last spinster is married?"

"Ah. I actually spent some time this week"—Jane smiled at Alex and put her hand on his arm—"while Alex was away, rereading the documents. All I could find was a paragraph indicating the house should go to Isabelle's direct descendants. But since Isabelle had no direct descendants, that's not very helpful."

Marcus frowned. "True."

"I'm actually more concerned about Poppy," Jane said.

"Poppy?" Marcus laughed. "Somehow I think Poppy will land on her feet."

"Apparently so." Alex gestured down the green. Poppy was approaching with a tall, thin man whose thatch of thick hair was almost the same shade as the reddish-orange of Poppy's fur.

The newcomer bowed when he reached them. "Guid day." The man spoke with a definite Scottish burr. "My apologies for arriving in the middle of a celebration." He smiled, glancing between Alex and Marcus. "I'm Angus MacLeod in search of the Duke of Hart. I was told he was holding his son, but I see there are two gentlemen with bairns in their arms."

"I'm the duke," Marcus said, before introducing Alex and the others.

MacLeod's smile widened. "Ah, Your Grace, I've heard so much about ye, it's guid to finally meet ye." He laughed. "Not that I believed most of my granny's tales about my noble—and cursed—cousin."

"Cousin?" Marcus asked, clearly bewildered.

"Aye. That's how my granny, at least, thought of ye."

"Oh?" Marcus's brows rose before he introduced the man to everyone else and then asked. "And what have you heard about me, Mr. MacLeod?"

"Weel, I've an ancestor from here, ye ken." MacLeod shrugged. "I've meant to stop by many a time on my way home to Edinburgh, but when I heard in Town that your son was born, Your Grace—" He grinned. "I niver really believed the tale my granny told about the duke's curse, but I was that glad to hear it wasna true."

Alex looked at Jane. Surely MacLeod's relative couldn't be . . .

Jane didn't hesitate. "What is your ancestor's name, if you don't mind me asking, Mr. MacLeod?"

"Isabelle Dorring." MacLeod stooped to pet Poppy, who'd been rubbing against his ankles during the conversation, so he didn't see all their jaws drop. "Ye're a wee bonnie lass, aren't ye," MacLeod told Poppy as he scratched her chin. Poppy bumped against his hand in feline bliss. "What might your name be?"

Alex wouldn't have been surprised if Poppy herself had answered.

"Poppy," Jane said. It came out as a bit of a croak.

"Mr. MacLeod, the story here is that Isabelle Dorring drowned herself and her unborn baby in Loves Water."

MacLeod laughed and straightened. "Oh, she dinna drown herself, o' course. A tinker found her at the edge o' the water and persuaded her to throw her lot in with his. They wed and he adopted her bairn, making him a MacLeod. When they had no bairns between them, Isabelle's child took over the business. Turned out he was better at making a living"—he grinned again—"and making bairns than his step-da."

"I see." Marcus frowned. "But if Isabelle didn't drown herself . . ."

Cat put her hand on Marcus's arm. "It doesn't matter anymore."

"But Mr. MacLeod's arrival is quite fortuitous," Jane said, enthusiastically. "He can take ownership of the Spinster House."

MacLeod looked a bit alarmed. "Spinster House? As in a house full of spinsters?" He laughed, though the sound had a definite nervous edge to it. "I've not had the courage to take on even one spinster, Lady Evans. I'm a bachelor— a *happy* bachelor."

Jane shook her head. "It's just a house, Mr. MacLeod, empty now, which is why it's yours. If you'll just come—"

Alex grabbed her arm. "Randolph can handle that, Jane. It's his problem now, remember?"

"Oh. Right."

"Lady Evans's brother is the village solicitor," Marcus told MacLeod. "Lady Evans has been his assistant for many years, but she just married Lord Evans this morning and is on the verge of departing."

MacLeod bowed again. "My felicitations."

"Thank you." Jane was clearly back in work mode. "I reviewed the documents this week, Mr. MacLeod, and it's my understanding that when there are no more Loves Bridge spinsters seeking to live in the Spinster House, the house is to go to Isabelle's descendants. I was the last spinster. It's quite remarkable that you should appear now."

"Remarkable?" MacLeod looked rather bemused. "Aye. A wee bit odd, isn't it?"

"Merrow." Poppy butted against MacLeod's leg.

"Poppy seems to come with the house," Jane said.

MacLeod's brows rose again. "Does she now?"

"And she seems to have taken a liking to you," Anne added.

Cat nodded. "And she doesn't usually like men."

MacLeod looked rather alarmed.

"Come, I'll introduce you to Randolph," Marcus said. "We can discuss the Spinster House with him."

Marcus and Cat moved off with MacLeod, Poppy at his heels.

Alex took another look at his watch. "I believe it's time for us to leave, Jane."

"Oh, can't you stay a little longer?" Anne asked.

Nate grinned knowingly at Alex.

"Well . . ." Jane began.

"No, we cannot." Alex had waited long enough. He was eager to begin the journey back to Evans Hall. More to the point, he was eager to shut the coach door and have Jane to himself. "We need to leave now to reach Evans Hall in good time." He stroked Jane's palm with his thumb when she opened her mouth to protest.

"Ah. Er, yes. Of course." She smiled at Anne. "We'll see you soon. We'll come to visit the baby."

"You'd better."

"We have to say good-bye to Randolph and Imogen and your family," Jane said as they walked away.

Oh, Lord, she was right. "But no long conversations, if you please."

"Why are you in such a hurry?"

He bent his head so he could whisper the words. "Because I haven't made love to you in a week. I am dying to strip you naked and come into your hot, wet body in one quick stroke and hear you scream my name."

"Oh."

He watched her beautiful neck as she swallowed and her eyes grew a bit needy.

"And then I'm going to love you again, but slowly until you beg me to finish."

Her tongue peeked out to moisten her lips. Her bodice rose and fell faster. And then her chin went up. "And I'm going to love you until *you* beg *me* to let you in."

He grinned. Zeus, he loved his prickly, passionate, independent countess.

"I look forward to it. So . . . shall we say good-bye to our families now?"

Jane nodded.

It was likely the fastest leave-taking on record.

And then he and the last Spinster House spinster left Loves Bridge to begin their lifelong adventure together.

Love the Spinster House stories?
Don't miss the rest of the series:

WHAT TO DO WITH A DUKE
HOW TO MANAGE A MARQUESS
and the novella
IN THE SPINSTER'S BED

Available now
everywhere print and eBooks are sold!

Books by Bestselling Author
Fern Michaels

___The Jury	0-8217-7878-1	$6.99US/$9.99CAN
___Sweet Revenge	0-8217-7879-X	$6.99US/$9.99CAN
___Lethal Justice	0-8217-7880-3	$6.99US/$9.99CAN
___Free Fall	0-8217-7881-1	$6.99US/$9.99CAN
___Fool Me Once	0-8217-8071-9	$7.99US/$10.99CAN
___Vegas Rich	0-8217-8112-X	$7.99US/$10.99CAN
___Hide and Seek	1-4201-0184-6	$6.99US/$9.99CAN
___Hokus Pokus	1-4201-0185-4	$6.99US/$9.99CAN
___Fast Track	1-4201-0186-2	$6.99US/$9.99CAN
___Collateral Damage	1-4201-0187-0	$6.99US/$9.99CAN
___Final Justice	1-4201-0188-9	$6.99US/$9.99CAN
___Up Close and Personal	0-8217-7956-7	$7.99US/$9.99CAN
___Under the Radar	1-4201-0683-X	$6.99US/$9.99CAN
___Razor Sharp	1-4201-0684-8	$7.99US/$10.99CAN
___Yesterday	1-4201-1494-8	$5.99US/$6.99CAN
___Vanishing Act	1-4201-0685-6	$7.99US/$10.99CAN
___Sara's Song	1-4201-1493-X	$5.99US/$6.99CAN
___Deadly Deals	1-4201-0686-4	$7.99US/$10.99CAN
___Game Over	1-4201-0687-2	$7.99US/$10.99CAN
___Sins of Omission	1-4201-1153-1	$7.99US/$10.99CAN
___Sins of the Flesh	1-4201-1154-X	$7.99US/$10.99CAN
___Cross Roads	1-4201-1192-2	$7.99US/$10.99CAN

Available Wherever Books Are Sold!
Check out our website at **www.kensingtonbooks.com**

Romantic Suspense from
Lisa Jackson

Absolute Fear	0-8217-7936-2	$7.99US/$9.99CAN
Afraid to Die	1-4201-1850-1	$7.99US/$9.99CAN
Almost Dead	0-8217-7579-0	$7.99US/$10.99CAN
Born to Die	1-4201-0278-8	$7.99US/$9.99CAN
Chosen to Die	1-4201-0277-X	$7.99US/$10.99CAN
Cold Blooded	1-4201-2581-8	$7.99US/$8.99CAN
Deep Freeze	0-8217-7296-1	$7.99US/$10.99CAN
Devious	1-4201-0275-3	$7.99US/$9.99CAN
Fatal Burn	0-8217-7577-4	$7.99US/$10.99CAN
Final Scream	0-8217-7712-2	$7.99US/$10.99CAN
Hot Blooded	1-4201-0678-3	$7.99US/$9.49CAN
If She Only Knew	1-4201-3241-5	$7.99US/$9.99CAN
Left to Die	1-4201-0276-1	$7.99US/$10.99CAN
Lost Souls	0-8217-7938-9	$7.99US/$10.99CAN
Malice	0-8217-7940-0	$7.99US/$10.99CAN
The Morning After	1-4201-3370-5	$7.99US/$9.99CAN
The Night Before	1-4201-3371-3	$7.99US/$9.99CAN
Ready to Die	1-4201-1851-X	$7.99US/$9.99CAN
Running Scared	1-4201-0182-X	$7.99US/$10.99CAN
See How She Dies	1-4201-2584-2	$7.99US/$8.99CAN
Shiver	0-8217-7578-2	$7.99US/$10.99CAN
Tell Me	1-4201-1854-4	$7.99US/$9.99CAN
Twice Kissed	0-8217-7944-3	$7.99US/$9.99CAN
Unspoken	1-4201-0093-9	$7.99US/$9.99CAN
Whispers	1-4201-5158-4	$7.99US/$9.99CAN
Wicked Game	1-4201-0338-5	$7.99US/$9.99CAN
Wicked Lies	1-4201-0339-3	$7.99US/$9.99CAN
Without Mercy	1-4201-0274-5	$7.99US/$10.99CAN
You Don't Want to Know	1-4201-1853-6	$7.99US/$9.99CAN

Available Wherever Books Are Sold!
Visit our website at **www.kensingtonbooks.com**